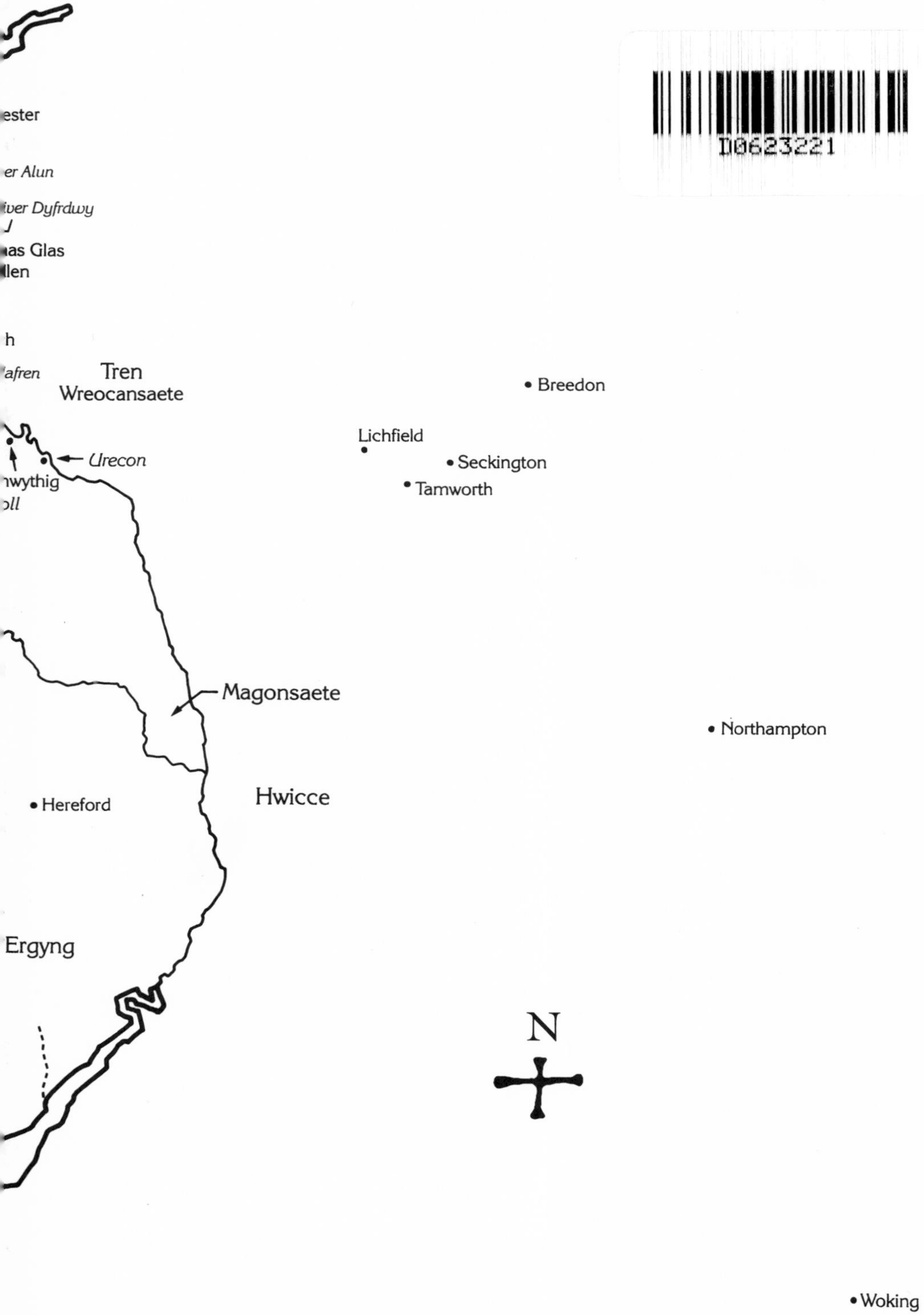
Tren
Wreocansaete
Urecon
Breedon
Lichfield
Seckington
Tamworth
Magonsaete
Northampton
Hereford
Hwicce
Ergyng
N
Woking

AWEN

Also by Susan Mayse

Merlin's Web
(Runner-up for first novel prize from the Crime Writers of Canada)

Ginger: The Life and Death of Albert Goodwin
(Edna Staebler Prize for Creative Non-Fiction
Arthur Ellis Award from the Crime Writers of Canada)

AWEN

by Susan Mayse

EWU
P·R·E·S·S
Eastern Washington University Press
Cheney, Washington 1997

Printed in the United States of America.

Library of Congress Cataloging-in-Publication Data
Mayse, Susan.
Awen / by Susan Mayse.
p. cm.
ISBN: 0-910055-37-8 (cloth)
I. Wales — History — To 1063 — Fiction.
II. Civilization, Medieval — Fiction.
PR9199.3.M4234 A97 1997
813/.54 21 97-028782
CIP

I'r beirdd.
For the poets.

Acknowledgements

Awen would have been impossible without the generosity of many people. For information and help in research I am grateful to John and Honor Bickford, Donald Blackley, the late Joanna Bond, Patrick Ford, Paul Hannah, David Hill, William Jones, D.P. Kirby, the late Frank Noble, Ifor Owen, Llywela and Huw Pritchard, Brinley Rees, Samuel Rees, Jenny Rowland, Chris Schoen, Peter Tudor, Alex Woolf, and Margaret Worthington.

For advice and encouragement I thank Charles Barnitz, Martina Boone, Priscilla Ewbank, the late Arthur Mayse, Heledd Mayse, Dianne Meili, Karen Muntean, John Pearce, Gillian Ranson, Marsha Skrypuch, the late Rosemary Sutcliff and Jonathan Williams.

CONTENTS

People Recorded in History

Powys
Brochfael Powys - *king of Powys*
Anghenell - *Brochfael's sister, considered a saint*
Cadell - *Brochfael's son*
Cyngen - *Cadell's son*
Nest - *Cadell's daughter*
Cynfarch - *historian, poet or priest; served Powys "at the command of my king Cyngen"*
Brochfael Meirionydd - *lord of cantref Meirionydd, a terhitory in Powys*

Gwynedd
Caradog Rhos - *king of Gwynedd*
Elfoddw - *bishop, reunited British church and Roman orthodoxy, died 809 AD*

Isle of Man
Gwriad Manaw - *king of Man*
Merfyn - *Gwriad's son*

Ceredigion
Arthen Ceredigion - *king of Ceredigion*

Mercia
Offa - *king of Mercia, king of all the English south of River Humber*
Egfrith - *coruler of Mercia, Offa's son*
Brorda - *Mercian nobleman*
Cenwulf - *Mercian nobleman, Offa's distant kinsman*
Ceolwulf, Cuthred - *Cenwulf's brothers*

Wessex
Eadburh - *queen of Wessex, Offa's daughter*
Bertric - *king of Wessex, Eadburh's husband*
Egbert - *exiled heir of Wessex*

Northumbria

Alffled - *queen of Northumbria, Offa's daughter*
Alcuin - *Northumbrian monk, Charlemagne's teacher and scholar*
Athelred - *king of Northumbria*

East Anglia

Athelbert - *king of East Anglia*

Frankia

Charles (Charlemagne) - *king of Frankia*
Berta - *Charles's daughter*
Angilbert - *abbot, poet, scholar, Berta's lover*

People Not Recorded in History

Powys

Brys - *poet, Brochfael's grown foster son*
Maen Pedr - *priest and healer*
Rhydion - *Brochfael's pencerdd or court poet*
Adwen - *queen of Powys, Brochfael's wife*
Bened - *Brochfael's priest and confessor*
Gellan - *Brochfael's war commander*
Pol, Rhirid, Gwyddien - *Brochfael's bodyguard captains*
Cian, Elgan, Addonwy, Marc - *some of Brochfael's bodyguard men*
Tegwy - *Brochfael's cup-bearer and foster son*
Garmon Penllyn - *lord of cantref Penllyn in Powys*
Geraint - *Garmon's son*
Eli Elfael - *lord of cantref Elfael in Powys*
Bleddri - *Eli's poet*
Owain Tegeingl - *lord of cantref Tegeingl in Powys*
Cadwr - *farmer, Brys's brother*
Angharad - *weaver, Cadwr's wife*
Alban - *huntsman and farmer*
Bethan - *weaver, Alban's wife*
Digain - *landowner*
Meirwen - *goldsmith*
Heilyn - *goldsmith*
Rendil - *landowner*

Gwynedd

Gwydron - *Caradog's pencerdd*
Padrig - *goldsmith*
Anna - *goldsmith*

Manaw [Isle of Man]

Neithon - *trader, Gwriad's messenger*
Edern - *Gwriad's envoy to Frankia*

Bro Waroc (Annorica, Brittany)
Macliau - *king of Bro Waroch*

Mercia
Leoba - *tavern keeper*
Ordric - *landowner*
Wulfric - *Ordric's son*

Frankia
Gereon - *nobleman*

people recorded in history before 793 AD

Arthur - *war leader and king, fifth-sixth century*
Bede - *Northumbrian monk and historian, early eighth century*
Bedwyr - *Arthur's captain and possibly harper, fifth-sixth century*
Cynddylan - *king in eastern and southern Powys, Penda's ally, seventh century*
Eiludd - *king in northern Powys, Penda's ally, seventh century*
Elisedd Powys - *king of Powys, early eighth century*
Heledd or Elen - *Cynddylan's sister, later a homeless exile, seventh century*
Llywarch mab Elidir - *a lord of Rheged, later of Powys; Owain's uncle, sixth century*
Llemenig mab Mawan - *nobleman in Powys, seventh century*
Meigant - *possibly Cynddylan's poet, seventh century*
Owain mab Urien mab Cynfarch - *king of Rheged, sixth century*
Penda - *king of Mercia, seventh century*
Taliesin - *poet in Powys and Rheged, sixth century*
Talhaearn, Aneurin, Afan - *poets, sixth century*

Cyngen . . . erected this stone to his great-grandfather Elisedd.
Elisedd annexed the inheritance of Powys . . . from the power of the English,
making it a region of sword and fire. Cyngen with his hand
[returned territory] to his own kingdom of Powys.... Cynfarch
drew this writing at the command of his king Cyngen.

Elise's Pillar

White town in the breast of the wood,
This forever is its custom:
blood on the face of the grass.

The Heledd Poetry

PICTLAND
YSTRAD
CLUD
Lindisfarne
ULSTER
RHEGED
Carlisle
MANAW
NORTHUMBRIA
York
Ireland
Elfed
Elmesaete
gwynedd
MUNSTER
MERCIA
powys
EAST ANGLIA
dyfed
gwent
London
Canterbury
WESSEX
Southwark
Rochester
KENT
Winchester
SUSSEX
CERNYW

PART I

Anno Domini 793 to 794

Ny elwir coet o vn prenn.

One tree is not called a forest.

The Heledd Poetry

High above the old borderland, the sun traveled its long road from the eastern plain to the western hills. Noon seemed endless; time lingered on this neutral ground.

His hands were cold in the noon heat. A symptom of shock, his training silently warned, but he pushed that knowledge under. Rawhide strips cut hard into his crossed wrists, and he flexed his fingers on the rampart timber to keep life in them. All he could think of, all he could see, were his own hands. Riding down to the border this morning, he had seen nothing but his hands tied on the saddle bow.

A west wind drove broken clouds across the scarred landscape below the fortress catwalk. The eastern lowlands were dull with cloud shadow while sun shafts brilliantly lit the forested western highlands. Soon the light would shift. Below this gorse-studded hill, the land dropped gently eastward through a wasteland of wild barley and burdock that had been farm fields until nine years ago. Farther east the oakwood stood black and lifeless where it had burned standing. The last time he had stood on this border looking eastward, cold to the bone, it had been overcast night. Three years ago, with Meirwen. *I'll race you down there,* she said after she lifted his horse, half-convinced of her own daring.

His hands might have been a stranger's. Square palms seamed with dried blood. Long fingers. Calluses on the fingertips. Evenly trimmed nails. One was torn past the quick. Last night he hadn't noticed. Although he was a prisoner, his guard nearby on the timber catwalk was not an enemy. He stared at his hands until his vision blurred, and the morning sunlight twisted down to the narrow end of a black tunnel. His guard leaned closer, asking something. He made himself breathe again. It was too easy to escape that way, out of the bright day and into darkness. One breath. Another breath. Breath is understanding. Breath is the center. He forced himself to breathe, and breathing brought back sight, and sight brought back thought. He began to remember. *Moonlight on a tall stone overgrown in thorns. Meirwen's dark hair unbound. A gleam of iron.* Better not to think. Not yet.

Brys — his friends called him that — watched sunlight and shadow wheel across the lost territory below. From up here the alien land looked flat, exposed, unwelcoming, but it was wealthy in cattle and corn. Farm and forest stretched as far as he could see eastward; a few abrupt hills stood up from the plain. He felt no need to look west. Home. Breath is the center. He stood in his point of balance, in stillness, in the hub. An old memory surfaced: he lay in long grass between his brothers, watching a horse cart enter Hirnant ford. Spokes slowly revolved as wheels rolled down into the glittering water, axles squealed for grease, the green world flickered between hub and rim. Light and shadow spinning into a silver blur. He blinked grainily, half asleep where he stood.

The guard moved restlessly, but there was still no sign of the English king. Brys looked back down into the sunny courtyard of Dinas Glas. The English garrison guards clustered near their east gate into Mercia, watching the British guards at their west gate into Powys. Other days they collected tariffs and watched for cattle raiders.

Now the king stood below, giving his captain quiet orders. The captain took the stairs two at a time; when he reached the catwalk his knife was in his hand. *Not like this.* Brys lost his breath at the naked iron, but the commander only motioned for him to lift his hands. The cool knife point slid between his wrists and jerked up through the rawhide.

"Wait here, Cynfarch." The captain dismissed the guard and stood a moment looking hard at Brys. His colorless eyes gave him a falcon stare, intense and shifting. He dropped his hand onto Brys's shoulder, briefly enough to be accident with the king watching.

Brys let his hands fall to his sides, though he badly wanted to rub at the sting of returning circulation. So he was not to be a prisoner under English eyes. It was going to be a family matter instead. And once the English were gone? He paced a few steps slowly, afraid his knees would fold and send him headlong. He ached from head to foot as though a horse had rolled on him.

Brochfael Powys climbed to the catwalk. Somehow between last night's bloody wreckage and this morning he had found time to change his clothing. The king's white linen was as plain as a servant's. All that glittered about him was the heavy-linked gold chain of kingship around his neck. He was tall and rawboned, grey-eyed like all his family. Lately the greyness had seeped into the creases of his immobile face. Today he looked greyer than usual and pale around the mouth from controlling his anger.

"Cynfarch mab Cadeyrn," the captain announced formally.

"Lord king." Brys dropped one knee to the splintered timber in front of his foster father.

"You may speak in your own defence," Brochfael said coldly.

Brys knew the law. "Is this a murder trial?"

Brochfael turned to his commander. "Make the guard ready."

The captain hesitated but went down. The king's bodyguard had been ready for an hour.

"Judgment is not possible without an allowable witness or a surety or a confession," the king said. "As you know."

Brys knew. In a trial he would speak and when he spoke he would be called a liar. Why bother to speak?

Brochfael turned abruptly to lean on the railing. "Why did you kill Digain?"

"Digain can tell you that, lord, if the dead can tell anything," Brys said.

Brochfael straightened, looked at him with distaste as though a slave had spoken uninvited, turned and went down the stair.

Haste had given Brys his nickname. But whatever his teachers said — the priest, the pœt, the captain, the king — he did think before speaking. Then he carefully whetted his words. A youngest son, let alone an unwelcome foster son, learns to be quick with fists or words. Wit was a weapon; discretion was a dull tool. Neither skill was much good to him now.

Brys stayed on his knee a moment longer, tempted to lie down right there and sleep. Or drop outside the gate. But Dinas Glas was full of the king's bodyguard, waiting further along the catwalk or down in the courtyard. And there was also the dishonor. He got up stiffly and scrubbed his hands over his face, alone at last after many hours. Even without the rawhide he was in no hurry to rejoin his friends. He knew what they were thinking. *Penllyn, with its curse of blood. First the father, now the son.* Maybe they were right.

The sky had dulled to grey. Rain from the west soon. He leaned on the timber railing again. Still nothing moved against the charred forest. A long time ago, before all the wars, the plain was the eastern region of the British kingdom of Powys. Now it was the western borderland of Mercia; all of the survivors spoke English. In the distance a red earth track emerged from living wildwood, snaked westward past another ruined farm and climbed toward this grassy spur, a rare outlying fist of Powys highlands rammed into Mercia's lowlands. Nine years ago Brochfael had lost another eleven hundred acres in his border negotiations. A small country negotiates; its powerful neighbor commands. Offa's border ditch and dyke abutted the fortress earthworks and stretched as far as the eye could see north and south, grassed over in this section. There were a few controlled gates like this old hillfort at Dinas Glas. This was the ninth year of an unlikely peace. People were starting to believe it could last: a dangerous faith.

A sullen gleam of metal moved deep among the blackened trees below. The sun momentarily rode clear of cloud and lit spear blades and mail shirts, emerald and crimson and saffron cloaks, a few flashes of gold. The road flooded with riders. An English war horn boomed out; from the rampart one of the Powys guard answered on a sharper note.

A handful of nobles and about twenty of King Offa's household warriors, not quite a war band, rode with spears slanted down in peace. The wind tossed the riders' cloaks and the kings' banner; on its yellow silk the black Mercian eagle flew with wings spread and talons clutching air. At some unheard command the Mercian English broke into a canter and surged up the hillside in a brilliant tide. The spear points rose level. Offa of Mercia understood how to create an effect or a threat, if he distinguished between the two.

An English voice called orders, and the timber gates squealed open on their socket stones. The garrison guards grounded spears thunderously on the rampart catwalk. Brys turned with his back against the warm timber to watch the two Mercian kings, rulers of all the southern English, ride into the fortress. Both were slight, light-eyed and light-haired, though the father's hair had faded to a sallow white and the son's was like spring butter. Offa stared rigidly forward; his son Egfrith looked around him with interest. Behind them nobles, priests, bodyguard and servants rode in and dismounted.

Brys went down to join Brochfael's guard; his friends made way for him uneasily. Outside the stronghold's small sleeping hall, at the doorkeeper's post, the Mercian kings' guard added their swords and long *seax* knives and leaf-bladed English spears to the British weapons. Inside, the central hearths were banked for the day, and the shutters were latched open. Cool air stirred the floor rushes.

Offa stalked to the trestle tables pushed together in the middle of the hall. He looked years older than at last summer's meeting; his color was bad, his hair was thinner and tendons stood out at his neck and wrists. His stare was still fierce as he exchanged the kiss of peace with Brochfael Powys. When he sat, his servants rushed to arrange the stiff layers of gold-bordered crimson silk around him in the chair. Egfrith sat without ceremony. The household warriors found space on the sleeping shelves or stood.

Brochfael took his place, and his counselor Idris sat at his right hand. Brochfael's badger, some called him behind his back, for his dark hair striped with white; but unlike a badger he was mild-natured and slow to speak. He was lord of Meirionydd, perhaps the most powerful of Brochfael's lords now that Penllyn was at heel.

The priests intoned their blessings. Scarcely waiting for the amen, Offa poured out a flood of English for translation.

Brys found a place under the loft overhang among Brochfael's bodyguard. They were taking the measure of Offa's household warriors, also sons of powerful families, also wearing gold bracelets and mail shirts; a few had artfully curled hair and shirts laced with bright ribbons, the fashion in Tamworth and London this year.

Near his shoulder the hall harp hung in its place. On its peg it became a projection of a wall painting, a whimsy of the artist who painted the hunting scene on the planed boards. Long ago, by its smoky gloss. A hunter with his face turned away wore the harp on his back. He could be Brys, a black-haired and stocky young man with his spear braced lefthanded. As if anyone, even a pœt, would carry his harp to the hunt. But artist's truth was not always historian's fact. Brys touched a few notes softly from the braided horsehair strings on the hanging harp. It was in tune.

Somewhere outside a woman called out to a child. Brys studied the crudely carved interlace on a loft pillar, the handiwork of some bored garrison guard, and wondered if he could raise gold or cattle to pay his fines. Impossible. *Exile if I'm lucky, if* Brochfael *dœsn't turn me over to Digain's kinsmen — but Meirwen. Where is she now?*

Brys, who had been half following the English and Latin, straightened suddenly. Brochfael's captain twitched toward a weapon that wasn't there. A long silence.

Brochfael's priest Bened flushed to the rusty fringe of his tonsure. "Offa and Egfrith, kings of the Mercians and of all the English, regret there can be no further negotiation concerning the position of the north border," he translated and clamped his mouth shut.

What now? One of Offa's tricks, but which one?

"So be it," Brochfael answered through the priest and folded his arms.

Offa seemed untroubled to have his bluff called. "Cenwulf?"

The Mercian noble spoke softly to a gaunt priest standing at his elbow. A raid two days ago farther south near Long Mountain, on one of the noble's Wreocansæte estates, the priest translated. Cenwulf listened with an aggrieved frown as the priest listed missing slaves, livestock and possessions. Offa watched Cenwulf with his blandest expression, the one he saved for either amusement or anger.

Why would he be angry at Cenwulf? A typical English border noble, arrogant, vain, aspiring to piety. Some of his estates in Magonsæte and Wreocansæte were once Powys estates. He wore red silk braided into his ashen fair hair and his shirt was the rare, costly blue of lapis lazuli. But surely Offa had him well in hand, or he would have gone missing like all the others. Offa must be angry about the raid, then. Or amused. Incomprehensible English politics. They were a grasping, restless people, always eyeing the main chance; in truth not so different from the British.

Offa clasped his hands on his belly like a smug merchant. Offa traded in lives; to others he left the business of souls. Cenwulf finished. His priest said, "People are dead."

"What people?" Brochfael didn't wait for Father Bened's translation. "Let us see bodies."

One of the Powys guard laughed in his hand.

Egfrith flushed — he had the thin skin of a pale-haired man — and glanced at his father. Egfrith spoke a few words before Brys realized he was attempting a strangely accented British. "When we prove the raid came from Powys, you will pay compensation."

Offa leaned forward quickly, tossing instructions to his priest before Egfrith could become too accommodating. "Until then you give us surety."

"We have never —" Brochfael began, but Idris Meirionydd delayed him with a racking cough and one quiet word. The king of Powys said, "Into your safe-keeping I give my kinsman Cynfarch mab Cadeyrn."

Brys stepped forward and kneeled in the floor rushes beside Brochfael's chair. Fear hit him while he was still on his knees. The English killed hostages. Or worse. Brochfael never yielded them until now. It settled all questions about his future — under death sentence he had none. *But let no one fault my manners.* Brys got to his feet at Brochfael's word. Offa nodded in satisfaction, but Egfrith looked surprised. Cenwulf examined his hands and decided not to speak. The Powys bodyguard men were muttering. Brys avoided their eyes, not wanting their sympathy.

"Maybe," Offa said mildly, "we should proceed with the north border. Consider the silver-lead mines, the farms and the river trade. . ."

Brys watched Offa manœuvre, as no doubt he had planned all the way from his court at Tamworth, and also saw the slight narrowing of Brochfael's eyes that meant he was enjoying this.

Outside on the rampart at mid-afternoon, Brochfael and Offa leaned together. Their interpreters were below, out of earshot with the rest. From the far end of the catwalk Brys heard talk in three fractured languages and Offa's occasional barking laughter.

Brys pulled off his arm ring and asked Cian, "Remember my brother? Give him this."

Cian took the silver arm ring without comment. It was two fingers wide, unjewelled, engraved with ravens in a net of interlaced vines. Its pattern was worn almost smooth. Eight years ago the new lord of Penllyn had relinquished it, shrugging it off as personal property. His own insignia was a leaping hound. Brochfael's loyal dog, Brys had said angrily. It had been just before the king of Powys took him south as foster son or prisoner, whatever he chose to call it. His brother had turned away, saying, All that's behind us now, it's finished. Now the same ruthless man had again made Brys a hostage. *Nothing is finished.*

Cian turned the arm ring around once and dropped it in his belt pouch. "What did Offa really want?"

Brys shrugged. "We've kept the peace since he rammed this marked border down our throats. Why would he accuse us of breaking it now?"

"Maybe someone did." Cian smiled ferally. His dog teeth looked filed. Half a head shorter than Brys, he had black hair and slanted blue eyes in a tawny face. Some people, with cautious irony and fullblown superstition about the small people of the hills, called his older race the fair family.

"No one's fool enough to provoke Brochfael. The peace is too fragile, too finely balanced."

"Mercia is more powerful," Cian agreed. "But Powys is more dangerous."

"Let's hope we all keep thinking so."

Cian leaned on the timbers, staring east into Mercia. "Where was the old court?"

"Pengwern?" Brys thought about it. "Farther south, I think. Probably one of the old hillforts."

"You don't know, pœt?"

"No one from Powys has seen much of cantref Tren lately," Brys said, surprised by the anger in his own voice.

"I've seen it. Cynddylan's country."

"What was it like?" Brys looked at him with interest. Cian's kindred, who came and went much as they pleased, found borders a strangely ornamental idea. Time, also, apparently. Cynddylan Powys had been dead for a hundred and thirty years.

"Not worth dying for." Cian found this amusing. "What is?"

"Home," Brys said. "I had two brothers once. One died nine years ago at Mæs Derwen. He sleeps in an unmarked grave." Nourishing the rich soil in cantref Tren, down there in Mercia.

"Yes," Cian said. *Meaning, I agree? Or we don't have to agree? Or who cares now?* Cian was hard to read even when his words were clear.

Brys looked southwest reluctantly. Soon he would be in that landscape, a black speck diminishing among its alien fields and woodlands. Swallowed by it. Better not to think that. Better not to think. But he still kept searching the lowlands for something too far away to see. A hillfort with charred timbers fallen under thistles and thorns, maybe, or a town of whitewashed houses and orchards sloping down to the ford that Cynddylan died defending.

Not worth dying for? What is? Do we ever have a choice? Death is the center of a long life, his wisest teacher said, the hub of life's many-spoked wheel, forever turning and changing. It carries us forward out of death toward life, out of darkness toward light, out of destruction toward the good — if we make it so. *Whatever the good might be. One thing in Mercia, another thing in Powys? Or is it the same everywhere? A roof, enough to eat, a song, family and friends, peace?*

A man shouted orders in English down below, something about horses. Cian had departed unnoticed. Brys took a deep breath and climbed down into the noisy courtyard. The wind was out of the west, warm and scented from the green folded hills of Powys. In summer Powys was the heartland of west Britain, a fruitful garden.

An hour later the wind and the country were at his back.

5 May 793 + Llanfair

"Come outside, girls, and look." It was the round-faced cook, not one of the nuns, and she was excited.

Gwladus left the yellow striped kitten attacking the toy, a scrap of wood with a tail of red yarn, and went out. Something happening at last? Something besides singing plainchant and weaving and listening to the abbess drone on through the gospel book? The shy novice with bad skin came out, too, still mouthing her prayers.

Dark outside, and cold for early May. In the monastery orchard, nuns and monks and a few servants stared up. Above the thatched roofs and the dark wall of wooded hills, many-colored lights rippled in the northern sky like a curtain in the wind. The lights were so intense they briefly formed shapes, gone with the next ripple.

"I saw this in the far north. It's just a light in the sky, like the sun or the moon," said one of the herdsmen, but he had a slave voice, so the others paid no attention.

"A dragon of fire," said the youngest monk, a black-haired boy with fine blue eyes.

"It's the old palace burning, down at Pengwern," said another as the light rippled like flame, and crossed himself.

"Idle superstition," said mother abbess. "They're all long dead, and no loss to Christendom."

Gwladus said nothing but made a face in the dark. It was Gwladus's ancestors that mother abbess slighted as vainglorious, heretical and worse; the nasty old prune never missed an opportunity.

"It's the face of God," said the novice with bad skin.

Mother abbess agreed. "The face of God."

An hour later, when her father rode in from the south road, Gwladus was playing with the kitten again. She was supposed to be embroidering an altar cloth, but it was a boring pattern and she was tired of it.

The sister with the mole on her nose came to fetch her, giving a tug at her skirt and another tug at one tawny braid hanging below her veil. That was spite, not tidiness.

"Act like a young woman, not a foundling child," the nun hissed.

Twelve last week. Had her father come to take her away? No, he'd say, your mother's dead and my wife's not going to take in my love-child. When Gwladus was little she thought that just meant he loved her. On his last two visits he had been nervous, wanting to say something to her. Maybe he wanted forgiveness for locking her away here until she was too old to foster. Now she was old enough to marry. Would he have brought her another gift? Silver hair-combs? A cloak with plumes around the hood? Now that she was a woman. The sisters would never let her keep it. *Too fine, too frivolous.*

In the guest house at the far end of the orchard, her father waited. Beeswax candles, lit only for special occasions, instead of smoking tallow candles, burned fragrantly in the table sconces. He had another man with him, a handsome man with light hair and a neatly clipped beard. He wore fine linen just the color of his deepset eyes, a smoky blue, and a large cross of gold on a silver chain around his neck. Father wore a new gold collar with boar heads at the opening; he looked tired and distracted. Gwladus kissed his cheek. She knew without mother abbess telling her that he was not the great man he believed himself to be. But he was still her father and, apart from dimly remembered cousins and rumored half-sisters, everything that she had in the world.

"I have brought someone to see you." Father motioned her abruptly to one of the chairs near the hearth. Since it had been a warm day the fire was still banked low in slabs of peat with only a few coals glowing. The stranger took the other chair.

"Didn't you bring me a gift? You always do." Gwladus sat.

"I —" He started to say something and changed his mind. She often thought of that later. Whatever was he going to say? "You're a grown woman now. Remember the good manners the sisters taught you. And ask your Savior in heaven to forgive your sins."

And that was all. Nothing about a gift. Father walked out of the guest house, closing the door behind him. Gwladus sat for a long time, waiting for him to come back. She smiled at the blond man. He looked at her intently, his eyes traveling all over her face and homespun robe, as though he couldn't see her properly. No, as though she were blind and couldn't see him. Gwladus folded her hands in her lap, wishing her father would come back. Not knowing what to do or say, she suddenly felt like a clumsy child again, caught spilling her porridge or skinning her knees. She supposed she could expect this, now that she was twelve. He would want her to marry, and men would come and look at her. But this one was out of the question, staring as though she were a cow at auction. A woman of good family, bastard or not, could do better.

"Have you made a long journey?" Gwladus asked politely. No answer, only the smoke-blue stare. "Do you live nearby? Where is your home?"

The blond man frowned and said something she didn't understand. A strange language. Now Gwladus stared in her turn. A foreigner. He looked like anyone else, apart from this ill-bred staring. Where was her father? In the church she heard the first strains of plainchant for the nocturne, then the swelling of many voices as monks and nuns joined in singing the office. The blond man got to his feet, and she sighed. Good.

But instead of leaving he walked across and pulled the veil from her hair. Gwladus caught her breath in surprise more than pain as the bronze pins pulled free. She stood and reached for her veil, and he smiled and held it out of her reach. Silly insulting tricks. He could keep it. She hated wearing it anyway. And this was quite enough. Her father had started talking to someone and forgotten her. Gwladus turned to the door, and the man was suddenly close behind her. He seized one elbow and twisted so that she gasped. And then he let her go, smiling with his mouth but not with his eyes.

A hideous game began. If Gwladus went near the door, the man hurt her. When she screamed, he smiled. No one came. In the church, the chant and singing would fill their ears. A distant scream would sound as small as her kitten's mewling. He stalked her around the guest house for a long time, as though he had to gather his courage. She had heard enough talk from the kitchen girls to understand what he wanted. But soon she saw it was different. Mostly he wanted her to be afraid.

When finally he twisted her arm and forced her down on the sleeping shelf, Gwladus lay quite still and watched him untie his breeches under his shirt and pull up her homespun robe. She watched his seething rage when he could do nothing to her, certainly not what he wanted. Instead he hit her, first in slaps that were more noise than pain, then hard so she felt her bones were breaking and twisting in their sockets. Gwladus cried out at last in a whimpering fear. Mother abbess. Someone. At that he threw himself down, pulling handfuls of her hair, and shoved part of himself deep inside her, tearing painfully. It was over quickly. Then it hurt more than her pulled hair and her bruises. The man got up smiling to himself, straightened his clothes and went out.

Gwladus went to the door as soon as he was outside, trying to smooth her hair and dress with shaking hands. The door was locked. She was bleeding inside. Could she bleed to death? She sat down with her hands pressed between her knees, rocking herself as someone had rocked her when she was little, she thought, and waited until nocturne was over. Then she shouted and shouted for hours. No one came. She cried for her Mama, whom she wanted to believe she could remember, and she cried for her father, though she understood that he had sold her, that he cared nothing for her at all.

In the morning the door opened quickly when Gwladus was half asleep, and the sister with the mole on her nose threw all of Gwladus's possessions into the room. They landed randomly, a blue silk dress, an ivory hair brush, a book of prayers with her initial G worked in gold on the cover.

"Let me out. Please, sister." Gwladus crawled out of the linen she'd thrown on the sleeping bench. "Please."

"Whore," the sister said over her shoulder and slammed the door.

Food arrived through a window, dropped onto the floor by the same nun. She had always been the one who shook her head at the silk dress and said, So you think you're beautiful. Pray to be scoured clean of your sinful pride and your family's wickedness. Beautiful? Gwladus had never seen a mirror. The food the nun brought was penitential food, water in a leather bottle and black bread.

No one came. Gwladus was already forgotten, a marginal note in someone else's life. She cried that day and the next, then she was silent. She found a far safe place to go in her spirit and decided not to return. Still no one came.

The sixth night, very late, the sister pulled her from her bed and slapped her awake. There were new clothes trimmed with gold and fur and soft feathers. Gwladus dressed in a daze and went outside to find an old man waiting with two horses. One was her white mare. In the torchlight by the guest house door she saw the new saddle and harness of red leather chiming with silver bells.

A gift.

6 May 793 + Tamworth

Rain swept eastward into Mercia with King Offa's company for two days, through dense forest and occasional farm clearings, only lifting when they could see the ramparts of Tamworth.

Brys felt naked and unshielded in this level landscape. Near Tamworth it was cleared bald for plowland, teeming with people, prosperous, impossible to defend, utterly alien. He heard no language but broad Mercian-accented English. They began to overtake carts screeching on their axles under loads of grain, dressed carcasses and lumber, all bound for Offa's main court. Men and women carried food baskets on yokes, and one solitary leper made her way alone in the reedy ditch.

Evening was settling in. The west gates stood open, but sentries prowled above on the rampart. The fire-hardened stakes embedded in the earthwork bristled like a thorn thicket in the ruddy sunset. Tamworth looked immensely strong, though much of the town sprawled beyond the wall. Once this fortress swallowed him . . . but in reality a hostage's life ends at his own border. Would he ever come back out through those gates? No one had spoken to him, nor had he spoken, in two days. No one had shown him hostility or, for that matter, interest. How long would he survive? Clearly it mattered to no one but him.

When they rode under the gate, the guards blared a welcome on their raucous war-horns. The muddy streets were narrow and stank of gutter sewage. Some houses had two or three storeys and stood so close there was barely room for a cat to slide between, but even the tallest houses were overshadowed by King Offa's great thatched timber palace on its mound. Beyond the palace at an open grassy space, the riders halted and were engulfed by court servants. The curious spilled from street stalls and houses and taverns to see the returned kings; they paid no attention to a solitary hostage. Tamworth already had too many *Wealas.*

Offa's second-best guest house smelled of emptiness and mold. Fewer visitors came from the continent, no doubt, since the Frankish king's shocking insult to Egfrith several years ago. The doorkeeper, an old man with a sword scar across his face and a flattened nose, brought Brys's meals. No one else came.

On the second morning a book from Offa's great library waited on a table just inside the door. It was a Latin translation of Aristotle's *Rhetoric,* which Brys devoured word by word for several days. Who had brought it? Not the old doorkeeper, an unlettered man who wheezed about the dangers of too much reading. On the parchment inside the embossed leather cover, a few words of Latin were scribbled in charcoal: *Tell him Egbert is returned to Britain.*

It must have been years ago that someone wrote it. Wasn't it four years since Offa drove Egbert from his patrimony of Wessex? Uneasy all the same, Brys smeared the charcoal with his thumb.

He found he was free to go where he pleased, though without coin he stayed away from the market stalls and taverns. A guard appeared from nowhere to trail him by a few paces whenever he stepped outside but offered no interference, merely shrugging at both Brys's British speech and his attempts at English. Brys heard the guard following silently when he went one evening to Offa's hall.

Offa's great chair occupied the highest step of the dais, in front of a brilliant wall-hanging showing the Mercians as Isrælites arriving from the east in the promised land, never mind that it already belonged to others. He was flanked by Egfrith, his advisor Brorda, Cenwulf with his brothers Cuthred and Ceolwulf, other nobles Brys didn't know. A quartet of monks stood behind him in uneasy compromise with worldly ways. Officials and ministers were in attendance, as were a display of guests — or hostages — from Mercia's subject kingdoms. Brorda talked with them and pulled the ears of a black dog which rested its grey muzzle on his knee. Offa's pœt, a wiry little man, drew idle notes from the small English harp on his knee and talked over his string arm to Egfrith.

After a while he sang. Like many of their songs this one was about Powys, or at least about the Mercian king who killed Cynddylan Powys long ago. It said nothing of Mercian treachery and betrayal.

Brys strained for the words; even in broad English they had kinship with his own end-rhyme and in-rhyme, a sensuality of sound. He drank the clover-honey mead a servant brought him, sweet and bland compared to heather mead. Strange to think Powys and Mercia were allies once, until Mercia broke the treaties. Or so they sang it in Powys.

He looked into the drinking horn, remembering the lament of Cynddylan's pœt Meigant for his king, which no Mercian would ever sing: *A cyn ethwyf i yno i'm bro fy hun, nid œs un car, neud adar yw warafun.* And though I went there to my own country, not one friend remained; carrion birds detained them.

Brys drained his mead. With his sullen shadow at his heels he went out between the torches, past the guards and into the rain, and walked between the dark buildings of the palace compound through smells of forge charcoal and dung and physic herbs. Somewhere monks were chanting. He passed a man and woman standing wedged in the barred shadow of a weedy courtyard, coupling. Rain dripped from the thatch to hiss on the packed earth. He felt far, far from home.

A silent week passed. By the end of it, Brys began to doubt his own existence. No one came or went except the doorkeeper. He valued solitude, all the more because he found it rarely at Brochfael's court; but the relative meaning of the idea now shifted. This was slow torment, an excommunication from words and humanity. If ever he felt tempted to monastic life, he would avoid all vows of silence.

How long would Offa keep him? Eventually, perhaps, he could slip away from this dubious hospitality and head for London, then Frankia or Armorica or Ireland, wherever he could get passage.

Nothing drew him home. Not Brochfael, who had sent him here among murderous English. Not Powys. What happened in Powys was no affair of his now, and even if Brochfael spared him exile, he couldn't pay his fines. Not Penllyn, God knew. If he could do some good there, bring some healing, he would go. But he could do nothing. Not Meirwen, though if he could only find her —

Anger had pushed him forward every day for eight years, and he missed it now.

He felt desolate without the anger. Fear — of loss, of disgrace, but mostly of sudden silent death — was no substitute.

One night he woke in a cold sweat from a nightmare of exile without end, exile for life. He saw his brother's hill farm overgrown in weeds and willow scrub, the house door hanging open. The curse on his house. Superstition. There was no curse, only bad luck and bad judgment — yet here he was with blood on his hands like his father. For the first time in years he wanted to see his brother, desperately, never mind the old quarrels. He reached into his *awen*, the pœt's gift, but no sound or sight or sign came to him, nothing to absolve him or lighten his sick dread. He wanted to run until he fell exhausted in the night rain, but from here there was nowhere to run, and what he feared most he couldn't run from. It had already pursued him, brought him down and torn the words from his throat.

For the rest of the night he sat crosslegged on the floor near the open window, silently reciting memory work from his training. It was hours before he could slow his heartbeat and regain his balance at dawn.

14 May 793 + Tamworth

Offa, king of Mercia and all the southern English, turned his freshly minted silver penny between his fingers. It portrayed him as a beardless man with short curly hair, a long straight nose and an expression of elegant disdain. An Italian had designed the coin. Offa had an abrupt nose and clipped beard, his remaining hair was lank and he was in a slow rage.

Guards paced slowly outside the door of this locked room in a palace wing; no doubt they were as weary as the three men inside. They'd been in session since dusk and now it was past midnight. Offa cared little for anyone's comfort, least of all his own. A lifetime of this had brought him to coughing blood and railing at the need for even a few hours' sleep; he said his Mercia was only half built, he needed another life. This one was wearing thin.

Brorda watched the elder king turn his penny a few more times and caught the eye of the younger king. Egfrith nodded and rubbed his face wearily. For a moment he looked so much like Offa in his youth that *wyrd* lifted the hair on Brorda's neck. Father and son were both quick-moving and wiry, with the same pale coloring, but forty years separated them. Offa hunched at the table like an old bird of prey. He wore a red silk shirt with ornate needlework borders in gold thread; he had laid his slender circlet of gold beside his son's on a sheaf of parchment. Two crowns to bind first Mercia, then all of the warlike English kingdoms, into one island nation; that was Offa's ambition. Egfrith would inherit a Mercian England. Egfrith shared his father's vision though he lacked his passion. The silver cross he wore on a chain was Alcuin's gift for his crowning six years ago. Few nobles, let alone kings, could live a Christian life in complex times. Egfrith tried, with frequent avuncular reminders from the Northumbrian Alcuin, teacher and scholar to Charles of Frankia. Speaking rationally, Brorda would say he liked Egfrith better than Offa, but reluctantly, sometimes angrily, he loved Offa. He was bound by years of loyalty, years of shared hardship and loss and victory, to his lord king. The old devil. God help him. God help them all.

Egfrith laid down his tax rolls and moved the oil lamp toward the center of the table in his own silent and exact way. "You shut your eyes to Eadburh's wrongdoing, father. She has seized estates before but this time she has also committed murder. She's heavy-handed, bloody-handed. Curb her now or we'll have civil war among the West Saxons."

Few people could bluntly tell Offa his mistakes without fear of retribution. One was Egfrith; another was his oldest friend Brorda.

"She's your sister," Offa snapped. "Bloody-handed, what dœs that mean? Another king's blood spilled forty years ago. If it hadn't been, there would be no Mercia for you to pray over. All power is bought in blood."

Blood that had splashed wider than Offa, Brorda remembered too clearly. The tyrant Athelbald had been plowing a nun's furrow — both of them drunk witless at the king's estate of Seckington near Tamworth — when the royal bodyguard killed him. Offa and his captain Brorda had embraced the naive idea that the old king's death would end the bloodshed. But it had no end.

"The estate," Egfrith persisted.

"Queen Eadburh of Wessex has no title to this holding," Brorda said warily. Bloody Eadburh was the king's darling, his favorite. It was not difficult to guess why; under her mother's sleek looks Eadburh had her father's savage nature. "She is clearly interfering with a legal inheritance."

"If we let unlawful detention and torture go unchecked —" Egfrith began.

"Evidence?"

"Scant." Brorda privately thought Eadburh belonged under lock and key like a mad bitch, but they had no time for a family quarrel. "Remember, also, she has enemies who would accuse her of any crime."

"Brorda, write and tell her to yield the estate. Deplore the violence."

"Very well." It was more than Brorda had hoped.

"Censure is not enough." Egfrith said, ignoring his father's angry protest. It never paid to yield any weakness or hesitation to Offa. "She is accused of sleeping with every man, free or slave, in Winchester, riding out with her husband's household guard to raid her own tenants, and murder. The West Saxons hate her. Because of her they hate Mercia and hate her husband though he's a West Saxon himself. She might as well openly invite Egbert's attack. He's been in exile long enough to gather an army and now he's back in Britain."

"What?" Offa spat the single word.

Egfrith, his father's son, said nothing and let silence do his work.

When Offa turned furiously, Brorda shrugged. "Unconfirmed."

The elder king chewed on that, flashing his coin between his fingers like a horse trader, and dismissed it. "Egbert's no threat. He has no army and no fortress. And he thinks too much to act."

Brorda frowned at this uncharacteristic nonchalance, but the king eased his mind by adding, "Of course, we'll assume he's here to raise a rebellion and regain

Wessex. Where is he?"

"A wine trader brought him into London last week, I believe," said Brorda.

"Heading for one of the Saxon kingdoms, which will foster Egbert's ambitions for its own ends. Watch him," said Offa, and visibly put the dispossessed West Saxon heir out of mind. "Do we have charters to approve?"

Brorda lit a sconce of tallow candles from the guttering oil lamp and pulled forward the top sheet of parchment. He read, "An estate in Wreocansæte, deeded to Saint Peter's at Lichfield by Cenwulf."

"Why?"

"For his soul's sake."

"Maybe," said Offa. "Or maybe he wants something from the church. Find out."

Suspicious as always, even of his own family. No more, Brorda thought. Sweet Savior, no more blood. The tyrant's death was going to be the last but it turned out to be only the first. Long ago Brorda forced himself to accept that the Offa who built laws, borders, coinage, diplomacy, trade — everything that transformed waste land into civilization — was also the Offa who hacked down the powerful Mercian families to reduce the threat to his own rule and Egfrith's succession. Maybe the king could loosen his grip now that he'd found a suitable bride for his only son after Charles's humiliating refusal to give up his daughter. Maybe.

Brorda had grown old striving for ways to disengage from the bloodshed, to create an equilibrium, to have peace within Mercia as well as with old enemies like Powys. But it seemed there was no balance. One either moved forward or fell back, most likely with one's throat cut. Did peace exist anywhere under heaven? Not in Frankia, or Rome, or Constantinople. Maybe, though he doubted it, in the land of silk.

"I have too many clever kinsmen," Offa said pensively into the night silence, "who remember their royal blood."

True, but that thought led to more bloodshed. Brorda knew how to redirect the king's suspicion. "One of the northern British kings went hunting with Brochfael the week before the border parley."

"Who? What did he want?" Offa's light eyes sharpened.

"Information is always incomplete from the west," Brorda hedged. "It was Gwriad of Man, the islander. He wanted trade agreements with Powys, maybe other British kingdoms. He went home angry."

"Brochfael refused him, then. Good. Will he try others?"

"Powys is the cornerstone of any such plan," said Egfrith. "Other kingdoms are mired in civil war, courting the Irish or committed to our trade and tariffs. But Brochfael holds North and South Powys together by sheer force of will. A British agreement would be nothing without Powys."

Egfrith took pains to understand the *Wealas.* Offa distrusted and feared them, not that he would ever admit to fear of anything. For thirty years, until the last nine years of peace, he had fought them for Mercia's survival. Egfrith hadn't, and would never be permitted to forget it.

"We can't allow them to build power," said Offa. "Keep a watch on Gwriad —"

A knock at the door cut him short. Brorda opened and saw a guard waiting uneasily in the dark corridor. Offa was known for reacting violently to bad news. The man kneeled. "Lord kings, the raid last week on the Powys border. The lord Cenwulf has recovered his cattle and slaves. Alive."

"Where?"

"North of Long Mountain, lord king."

Where they had been all along? Brorda wondered. The guard got up and backed out quickly at Brorda's nod. Offa stared at the closed door for a long time, thoughtfully silent. In Offa that was more unnerving than anger.

15 may 793 ✝ tamworth

It was late afternoon when the doorkeeper hastened into the room motioning Brys to kneel and speaking urgent English, something about a great lord. Brys closed the *Rhetoric* carefully and stood. His house did not kneel to Mercian nobles. A big man came in, stooping under the lintel: Brorda, Offa's right hand. The doorkeeper shook his head in disgust as he closed the door.

Brorda crossed to the open windows and looked out. The sky was grey; it would rain again today. A band of armed men executed some manœuvre in the grassy square outside, following a captain's shouted orders. The air was heavy with woodsmoke. Brorda turned, and Brys found himself under close assessment.

"You enjoyed the *Rhetoric*?"

"Yes." Brys looked at him with more interest. So it was Brorda who'd sent the book. He knew Offa's old counselor as an administrator, not a scholar. "Thank you."

"I thought you might," said Brorda, "as a pœt."

What dœs that mean? Speaking English was difficult enough without having to plumb Brorda's subtleties. He waited.

A smile touched Brorda's face. Brys realized he'd hooked his thumbs in his belt and was rocking on his feet like a tavern fighter, a habit that annoyed his teachers. Brorda would probably share their view; he had an old-fashioned look. He wore a shirt of good white wool, narrowly bordered in white-thread embroidery, over loose cross-gartered breeches. His only jewelry was a massive gold thumb-ring that looked like a seal. Last traces of brown threaded his hair and beard; he was younger than Offa by a few years and looked in better health. His eyes were a startling and direct summer-sky blue.

"You have been Brochfael's bodyguard soldier for six years?"

"Four years." Turning sixteen had been a great day, after two years of chafing at the bit since legal adulthood at fourteen. Brochfael said he didn't send children to war. He had once.

"And soon you will be Brochfael's pœt." Brorda had a way of making a statement into a question.

Scarcely. It seemed a strange idea now that everything had changed. What did Brorda really want to know? Not the plans of Brochfael's castoff kinsman. Brys let a change of orders on the distant training ground claim his attention for an instant. Brorda's light eyes sharpened. There was no throwing this man off so easily.

"Brochfael has a *pencerdd*," Bryn said. His graduation as a pœt would be put aside now, perhaps forever. He'd had a week to think about his downfall: he had committed murder any way he looked at it, and Brochfael himself had stepped in too late to end the bloodshed. "Rhydion is in good health and good voice."

"But he needs to read Aristotle, judging by what I heard last year," said Brorda, glancing at the book on the table. "Offa's pœt is the same. They sing in stilted language no one has ever understood or will ever understand."

Brys found himself smiling as he gestured Brorda to a chair and reached for the *Rhetoric.* He liked Brorda; like Egfrith, he tempered Offa's ferocity at the parleys. Perhaps they agreed beforehand to sing in different modes; Brys thought not. He turned a few pages and read, "'What we write should be easy to read and easy to speak, which comes to the same thing.'"

Brorda sat awkwardly as though he were fighting stiffness. "That's too simple, I suppose. Pœts must warrant their upkeep."

"Pœtry must be straight and clear if we want people to listen. No audience, no song. If no one in the hall understands me, I might as well sing to oxen before the plow. Do you keep a pœt, Brorda?"

"Not for many years. Nor shall I," Brorda said dryly, "if you think to find a place."

Brys flashed a smile. "Our best songs are about Mercia, it's true . . " He waited long enough for Brorda to sharpen. " . . but they translate badly."

Brorda laughed abruptly, a good solid laugh from deep under his ribs. He understood: songs about the Powys host cutting down Mercians in battle, for example. He looked at Brys piercingly for a long moment and nodded.

"I hope to hear you sing someday, Cynfarch."

"Someday you will." It was bravado, all Brys had now, and it sounded thin even to him.

"I brought something else." Brorda laid a flat rectangular wooden chest on the table, inlaid with light and dark squares separated by silver wire.

Pulling it closer, Brys found the latch. Inside, nested carefully in niches, were sixteen light warriors, eight dark princes and the dark king. The small chest would fold out flat to make a board of a hundred and twenty-one squares. It was a lovely set. "*Gwyddbwyll,* wood-wisdom. A game."

"How do you play it?"

Brys glanced up quickly. Brorda had spoken in British with an archaic northern accent. Of course, some of his lands were in northern Mercia. The language of the conquered survived in the mouth of the conqueror. *Why ask me how the game's played?* he thought. *You've been playing it for half an hour. What royal enemy are you pursuing to sanctuary?* But in courtesy Brys answered in his mother tongue, as slowly as Brorda had spoken English, "You speak well."

"My grandfather's falconer taught me." Brorda picked up the king and turned him around slowly. The small figure wore a British king's gold chain, not a crown. "He always said he was of the old royal house of Elfed. He seemed happy enough as a falconer."

"Then he was not of any royal house."

Brorda looked up, and Brys met a long pale blue gaze. "Some endure dispossession better than others, Cynfarch mab Cadeyrn Penllyn."

That name had ceased to exist with his father's disgrace and death. To hear it from a Mercian . . . Brys took a deep breath. Refusing to show Brorda he'd drawn blood, he said coolly, "Alternating turns. The defending player has a king and eight princes. The other has sixteen men and must attack the king on every side." *And at the turn of the wind, attacker may become defender, as in life, as in battle.*

Brorda asked more of the game's strategy. Brys told him, wondering. A man who spoke good British must know the game, but who could say? For all the blood on his hands, Mercian blood and Powys blood and all the rest, he had guileless eyes.

After a while Brorda said, "Another time let us play. Not now. This border breaking is settled. Compensation is paid." He went on, explaining about prisoners recovered alive in a Powys border settlement.

A tale cobbled together to save Mercian face, Brys thought. At least he didn't claim they lost their way in a ground mist. Not quite.

"What dœs this mean?"

"You're free to go home tomorrow."

"Where?" Brys asked stupidly, his thoughts veering away from Powys and Penllyn.

Brorda was amused. "Long Mountain ford is the closest border gate to South Powys. Brochfael is expecting you in Mathrafal."

A GIRL WITH BROWN BRAIDS tied in yellow ribbons came to pour mead after the meal. She spoke good British with Brorda's accent and said she was indeed from the north.

Brys thought briefly that she might be Brorda's daughter or niece but soon he learned otherwise. The Mercians had a well-earned name for decadence; she was highly skilled. But all he could think of was Meirwen's tarnished bronze hair — coarser, more alive to the touch — and her breasts as soft as dœskin. He would never know either again, moonlight silver or sunlight bronze . . . If only she had told him, told someone. Justice could do nothing for one who kept silent about wrongdoing. A servant too proud to speak, who could help her? His conscience answered uninvited. A friend could help her, if he were anything but a blind fool . . . Where was she now? But this train of thought led nowhere he wanted to follow. He forced his thoughts aside and gave himself to the pleasures of the hour.

Later the girl wanted to talk about Elfed, then about the other kingdoms. She would like to go there, she said. Had he seen Gwynedd? The Isle of Man? Brorda had left the game on the table. She won twice, both attacking and defending, before Brys sent her off doing her best not to yawn.

In the morning, accompanied by his silent guard, he rode west.

15 May 793 + Tregeiriog

As it turned out, leaving Tregeiriog was easy. Meirwen packed her tools, her comb and her other dress into her satchel. While people in the township ran about wringing their hands over Digain's death, she walked away. If she'd known it was this easy, she could have left a month ago. If she'd left a month ago . . . But this idea bore only thorns, and she dropped it in her tracks as she walked west.

Anyone who bothered to wonder would suppose she had headed north to her married sister. Instead she walked upstream by talkative River Ceiriog, west toward the high moors and wild Edeirnion.

Silver chimed at her ears with every step. Meirwen worked silver often and gold occasionally, but all her wealth was the three silver hoops in each ear. They made a small music which helped her keep to a rhythm walking over the rough ground, some of it still spongy with water from the high country's spring melting snow.

For the first hour Meirwen walked and ran. Above the confluence of small Teirw stream with River Ceiriog, she slowed her pace and relaxed into her habit of looking for medicinal herbs as she went. It was too early for some. She skirted an expanse of bog where last year's cotton grass hung crestfallen and soiled on fragile stalks. Beyond was a clump of bog asphodel, but it wouldn't produce its yellow dye flowers until July. Ahead, to the west, she could see for many miles across the tilting moorland to the distant snow mountains.

At sunset, on a grassy hillside marked with old hut rings, Meirwen crouched to drink at a spring. It tasted of peat and iron. She paused over her reflection. The woman who looked back up at her was too tall, too thin, dressed in homespun. Her dark hair was straying from its braid over one shoulder. In the fading light the reflection erased her freckles for once; she could still see them all too well on her wrists and hands, though every day she faithfully applied her lotion of vervain and rose. Her eyes also were in shadow. Like her sister's they were brown, lightening to deep amber when the sun caught them. Daydreaming. Meirwen got to her feet and walked on. She'd brought no food; she wasn't hungry anyway. She felt watched and remembered there were earth houses up here. But the fair family wouldn't bother her or even make themselves visible.

Among the stream sources there was little shelter. The wind was cold and full of voices. Meirwen had flint and tinder but wanted no fire. Or food. Or light. Sitting on her heels and looking west into the wind, over the folding moorland to the mountains, she knew what she wanted was some tangible shape to her grief. Illogical. It should be anger. A pair of curlews passed overhead, a tawny blur against broken overcast, leaving her with only their bubbling cry. Without noticing, she slowed down to the land's own respiration. When she blinked it was night. Meirwen rolled in her russet cloak among the rusted stalks of bracken and dreamed of foxes.

At dawn she woke cold and wet, raging at the stupidity that had brought her here. It was a moment before she remembered she'd had no choice. Her life in Tregeiriog had ended. Unbearable for months, now it would have been unlivable. Good. That meant there was no going back. She had a roaring hunger now. Hunger she could manage. She drank as much water as she could stomach, then stood shivering in the warm west wind blowing from the heart of cantref Penllyn.

Damn him to a frozen hell. Cynfarch and his kind could do anything they pleased. He could even kill a man, then buy his way out and resume his pleasant life at court. But Meirwen was landless and kinless except for her distant sister. By fleeing she was now breaking her year's service pledged at last summer's hiring fair. Give evidence at the trial, the king had told her, you're not to blame. But Cynfarch could fend for himself; he didn't need her help. Justice protected the powerful. A woman with no one of rank to speak for her, on the other hand, would surely be found guilty of something. All she had was the illegal skill her father had taught her while he lived, the tools in her satchel, her wits and her waking nightmares. Now Digain was dead, mercifully. But not because anyone cared about Meirwen. She meant nothing to these gold-laden men who ruled kingdoms without a thought for the people who made up those kingdoms. Digain was dead not because he mistreated a servant but because he threatened the northern king's intrigues.

One foot in front of the other, Meirwen walked until the slow swell of the land captured her. She had a wax tablet in her satchel. At noon she sat and drew hill folding into hill, turned it into a sensual pattern of interlace that came to her as music came to some . . . she smoothed the wax again with a finger. Looking around she realized it was mid-afternoon and she was still in sight of last night's stopping place. It was only two days and a night since she ate, yet she was lightheaded. She dug lily bulbs with her knife and broke her fast as the sun went down. The bulbs were bitter but they were food.

She slept that night curled among scrub willows, listening to the sea-susurration of their leaves, and woke suddenly and fully at first light to the sound of a dog whining and snuffing very near. A tracker? Digain's kin wouldn't bother with that except to have her killed. She lay very still and moved her right hand slowly, slowly to her knife hilt. Between a lacework of narrow willow leaves she saw a sinewy dark-bearded man with a spear on his shoulder, frowning around as though he'd mislaid something. She didn't know him. The hound growled low in its throat. The man cuffed it and went on. The dog stared at her thicket one last time and trotted after the hunter. In a while Meirwen got up to walk west. Her shœs were parting at the sole seam and she took them off.

A bracken slope soon swallowed her. Some stalks stood as high as a house in an eerie rust-corroded corridor; others were lodged flat to the stony hillside. She left blood on the stones as she picked her way down and found a cairn at the bottom. The cairn stirred and sent forth a chattering bundle of skins and rags. A hermit, living in a cell of piled stone. He scuffed close to her, peering. One of his eyelids gaped over a crusted cavity. The other blinked feverishly below his matted grey hair. He stank.

"Welcome the wanderer." His voice scratched like the wind on his ridge. "Wild sister, mad as a hawk."

He showed broken black teeth in a grin and lurched into his cell. He was out again in a moment with honeycomb dripping from a slab of bark in one filthy hand. Meirwen shook her head. He closed his one eye to pray, though the other festering socket held her with a sinister vacancy.

"Enough for each day are its own troubles." His voice mimicked, or perhaps recovered, the sonorous tone of a priest offering mass. "Blessed the wanderer who takes no thought for tomorrow."

Benediction she accepted. She found tears burning silently into her eyes and scalding down her cheeks. The hermit also began to weep. He reached to touch her face and licked his scabbed finger.

"Good, good. Salt in the wilderness. A pillar of salt. Never look back." His voice cracked and wavered in madness. He seized her hand and shoved the bark into it. Honey oozed down her thumb and between her fingers. Meirwen licked it and then ate hungrily around wax and bee larvæ until the bark was clean. The anchorite laughed and retreated to crouch in the mouth of his cell.

Downhill she heard running water. When she reached the reedy bank she looked back up and saw the hermit skylined on his ridge. The stream was only her arm's length wide. It led her down through hummocks of sedge and moss, over rocky shallows and between quiet stretches of bog. She walked sometimes in it, sometimes beside it. At last it carried her to a poor exposed farm. Meirwen stood ankle-deep in icy water, her satchel over one shoulder and her tangled braid over the other, and saw that she was over the backbone of Powys into Edeirnion. When she reached Gwynedd, all the streams would run to the sea, and the sea ran to Ireland. There, travelers said, lived the world's great goldsmiths.

At the farm, faded blue eyes watched her from a worn face. The old woman gave her a wooden bowl of goat's milk to drink, and then a second.

"Smith, are you? My cauldron's lost a plate and it's too heavy to carry down to the lake. The tools are here, my man used to do his own work." Between a storage chest and a stack of uncured hides in the dim hut, the cauldron was a blacker globe of shadow.

"We need bronze scrap," said Meirwen.

Mice had claimed and abandoned the forge, wind-sheltered between two sheds and an apple tree. Meirwen swept out their nests and made her fire of hazel branches. It built heat quickly. The old woman took the bellows, which hissed more air onto her hands than onto the coals. Two women turning their hands to smithcraft; the king of Powys and the lord of Penllyn were too far from this poor farm to enforce their laws about what women might and might not do. Most people didn't care anyway, as long as the shovel got mended or the knife blade tempered. Fowl pecked around her feet as she worked, and the goat watched insolently.

Meirwen shaped rivets on the pitted anvil and lined up the cauldron plates. Heating, fitting, tapping rivets through, flattening their inner flanges, the work enclosed and created her, and she became her skill.

16 May 793 + Tamworth

Brorda sat in the guest house chair, under the same open window as yesterday, with a fine mist of rain blowing onto his face. He had returned to collect the *Rhetoric;* now he sat as though waiting to collect something else also, something displaced from reflection or memory.

Brochfael's kinsman — by fostering only — was gone. What had Brorda learned? Not much. Cynfarch had a pœt's showmanship and a quick mind, and he loved his wood-wisdom game. He also spoke English, albeit like something caught in his teeth. Cynfarch was going to be a problem, now or later. Had he and Offa been so sure of themselves at his age, forty years ago? No doubt. Offa was only a few years older when he took the throne, and his captain Brorda was even younger. In Mercia today, such an ambitious young man would be dead. Maybe not. Cenwulf was alive, and his brothers. There were ways to make oneself indispensable to Offa.

Leoba's British girl also extracted nothing from him about Gwriad, another of Cynfarch's putative kinsmen. That many-times-cursed northern kindred cropped up like burdock in the barley no matter how often they were safely turned under. Hunting the raven lords out of old Rheged two centuries ago had only scattered their seed wider. The spinners twist some threads stronger than others, thought Brorda, and it made him shiver. *Wyrd.* Offa didn't believe in fate or anything else, for all that he played the part of a Christian king. Brorda believed enough in *wyrd* to listen to its wind-whisper now.

Some change was taking shape in Powys, and the only cause he could see was Gwriad. Cenwulf's border raid, if there was one, had to be coincidence. An hour's word games yesterday with Cynfarch gave him nothing. He needed something. I need to know, Offa said often, and I trust only one man to find out. At least Brorda was spared the role of torturer and executioner; Cenwulf did that job with enthusiasm, a student of Offa's brutality as Brorda was a student of his justice and his shrewdness. But information from Powys? It was always difficult, always unreliable.

Powys, and a new threat of alliance among the British kings. There had been alliances before, none of them beneficial to Mercian interests. Offa's frontier was only an idea translated into earth and timber, impossible to garrison except at a few gates. If the British ever joined forces as a war host, they could flood over the border earthwork like a spring tide and drown Offa's vision of one England.

Brorda picked up the *Rhetoric.* Inside the cover was a smudge of charcoal. Maybe he should have given him the book in the interests of diplomacy. But knowing Cynfarch's kind, he'd probably committed the whole volume to memory already.

17 May 793 + Western Mercia

Riding west for two days, Brys considered ways to evade Offa's surly guard. Soon they would turn southwest to the River Hafren and the Powys border — home. But in Powys he faced fines he couldn't pay, and worse, he faced Brochfael's wrath. Instead he would head south alone for one of the Gwent seaports and trade the horse he rode for ship's passage.

In a flea-ridden village inn by a small lowland river, Brys sounded out the guard as they ate. "This was punishment, to ride west with me?"

The guard kept on chewing his bread and cheese.

"You have better things to do," Brys tried again. "So have I. You can leave me here. No need to go another twenty miles."

That drew the first word the guard had spoken in two days. "Why?"

Brys hesitated. The whole truth was too complicated. He said, "A girl."

The guard returned silently to his meal.

Outside, Brys watched the inn stableboy brush down their horses. It was early evening. If the guard went back to Tamworth, Brys could reach Gwent in a few days. Then a message to let Brochfael know Offa didn't keep him or kill him; that much he owed the king of Powys. Another message to Meirwen — but he couldn't think where to find her. Not in Tregeiriog, surely. Maybe some day, if he returned to Powys. Past that point he couldn't see. At the far end of the inn porch, now that Brys was impatient to travel on, the guard was deep in conversation with the innkeeper.

Two riders came in on the south road as he waited. A grey-haired servant led in a rich man's courtesan dressed in plumes and finery on a fine white mare; silver bells chimed on her red leather harness. The servant dismounted and went into the inn. The girl waited. Brys saw that she was only a child, a beautiful child, with a yellowing bruise on the left side of her face. He was reminded of someone . . . Then she looked up, at him or through him, and leaned forward reaching out one hand. Her eyes were the same dark gold as her hair but as expressionless as the eyes of the dead. Brys took an involuntary step backward into the inn wall.

"Don't mind her, she's touched," said a broad English whisper at his shoulder. The servant walked out to her and handed up a crockery bowl. "Here, lass. Take a sup."

She poured the milk slowly onto the ground where it pooled for an instant like semen. Then it soaked in, and she dropped the bowl. All the while she stared at Brys gravely as though he might shift shape to become some bird or beast, and he wondered in confusion which his face showed more clearly, his grief or his terror. The servant sighed and stooped to pick up the pieces of the bowl and handed them to the stableboy. Then he took the reins to lead her mare away.

The girl turned in the pretty saddle and said to Brys in his own language, "I know thee."

"No." His throat squeezed the word to a husk.

She looked down at her hands on the chiming reins.

The skin was walking on Brys's back. He asked in a bare whisper, "Who are you?"

"My name is salt. I am a place of salt," she said. Her lips were cracked, perhaps split.

"What say?" the old servant asked him.

Brys gave a start, unaware that he had spoken. The child looked at him again from shadowed eyes and nodded. *Consent. To what?*

Brys watched them take the Tamworth road eastward, down past a hawthorn flowering on a cairn, down past the tumbled stones tangled in briars, down toward the shallow ford. This was the straight old Roman road from the western hills to the lowlands, part of Powys long ago. Where else would two travelers cross paths? She wasn't the first fair child sold into a great man's bed — but he had one desperate thought of riding after her, seizing the reins and taking her west where she belonged. They wouldn't get far. What was the Mercian penalty for stealing a slave? Some sickening mutilation, probably amputation. It was a foreign land, even if half the faces were British. In any case, his last attempt to aid a wronged woman had done more harm than good.

Slowly the girl and the old servant rode eastward, deeper into Mercia, out of sight. But a chill had gathered at the back of Brys's neck like the touch of a cold hand. Though he crossed himself, the chill deepened. Now he knew this place.

Y Drefwen was its name once, the white town near River Tren in lost cantref Tren. He'd always pictured it as a town of whitewashed houses in hillside apple orchards. Maybe it was, once. Not any more. A hundred and thirty years ago Cynddylan tried to hold this ford, this gentle eastward slope of riverbank, this old heartland of his kingdom in Powys. He died here with his brothers when Mercia swept down upon them like the wild hunt. His sister's bitter words, refusing the Mercian marriage, destroyed them all. What had been her name, Elen? Helena in Latin, probably, all those years ago.

Even now she walked Powys, the story said, as a proud girl in her finery or as a ragged crone, from the ruins of Y Drefwen west to Edeirnion in Penllyn. It was an old story, half-remembered, of a broken peace and a broken country. Cantref Tren, once lowland Powys, was part of Mercia now; they called it Wreocansæte after the hill called Urecon.

Elen. Helena. Nothing so simple as a ghost, Brys thought, fairly rational for one trembling with cold on a hot afternoon. *A ghost would not have a bruised face.*

A burst of laughter ended the guard's conversation with the innkeeper, who handed over clinking silver coins. Maybe the guard had won a bet. Brys didn't care. This place pulled at his memory, compelling him to stay. Suddenly he wanted only to be gone from here, far away from unlucky cantref Tren.

At the next crossroads, without a word, the guard reined his horse around and took the righthand road. God speed him, the brute. That road went to Amwythig, which the English called Shrewsbury, perhaps past the ruins of Cynddylan's court at Pengwern. Brys wanted the south road. He heeled the dun mare on westward, and a few minutes later turned south at the next lefthand fork.

Soon the sun rolled down beyond the shoulder of Cær Digoll, which the English called Long Mountain. The road was more obviously Roman here, straight as a spear and surfaced with broken stone. At twilight Brys watered the mare at a brook, taking in the hill scents of heather and new bracken. The May evening was heavy with rain and stitched with swallows. Offa's second-best hospitality hadn't detained him long, against all expectation, and he was ready to enjoy his freedom. He breathed deeply and smiled. Even the air smelled unfettered. In a few days everything could be all right. He rode on.

Dark soon. He needed a place to sleep, but so far he'd seen only farms reclaimed by wilderness. Farther south would be better —

Two hunters sat their horses in the road ahead. The spears laid across their thighs caught the twilight. No dogs, no kill. Only one kind of hunter waits for his quarry to ride into range. Brys looked back and saw a third man clear the alders behind him. He was trapped.

The mare was weary. Brys heeled her into a canter, then a lurching gallop straight at the two riders ahead. As they raised their weapons he turned off the track through a tangle of nettles. It gave him a lead, and they crashed into the waste after him at a disadvantage. The mare held her own until the scrub opened to old plowland, and they pounded closer and closer. He pulled out his knife. The mare's stride faltered, and foam sprayed back onto his face. A spear hissed past his elbow. Wide, but in range.

Two riders flanked him. The mare understood the hunt. Stretching her legs, she flew with all her remaining strength. Not enough. One of them cut across her path and reined his grey horse rearing sideways. He held a long-bladed *seax* knife. The English fight on foot. Brys gambled that their horses were untrained for war and drove straight at the man ahead. The dun mare crashed solidly into the off shoulder of the grey, and the man dropped his guard as he struggled for balance. Brys stabbed in over the *seax,* but before he could try again, the second man was on him.

"Now!" someone shouted behind, and he was wedged between them.

The lathered horses sidled uneasily. The mare hung her head and heaved for air. She could run no farther. The third rider came up behind, and Brys felt a spear point prod between his shoulderblades.

"Knife," one of them demanded.

Struggle was wasted now. He handed over the knife and tried not to flinch when the spear probed. His breath was a storm roar in his ears and his heart flung itself against the bars of his ribs.

"This shit cut me." The spear jabbed, and he felt the tickling warmth of blood on his back.

Brys twisted against the blade, driving it fractionally further. He said in English, "I have safe passage from King Offa."

"He forgot to tell us." The others laughed at this wit.

At least they had more to say than his guard . . . Brys thought about silver changing hands at the inn. Maybe no one had won a bet after all. Whose silver? Not Offa's. Now they were arguing about killing him. Speaking too quickly. Something about proof. Two of them were flaxen-fair and the third had red hair. Their voices and their gear marked them as landed men, not common thieves.

"Silver if you ride me to the border gate," he lied, trying it out. "If you kill me you get nothing but the horse."

"Wrong," one of the blond men said. "Gold either way, dead or alive."

The oldest told him to shut his mouth and nearly toppled Brys from the saddle with a ringing blow on the side of the head. They bound his wrists with a thong which burned into the skin, un unwelcome reminder of recent captivity, and turned for the road. The redhead took the mare's reins and led her stumbling back the way Brys had come. He slowed his breathing and heartbeat, and exhaustion returned with the ebb of immediate danger. The hedgerows gave off an evening exhalation of honeysuckle.

Brys felt no surprise when they stopped in Y Drefwen. The place of salt tears and blood had claimed him after all. They passed the shabby inn, raucous now with its tavern overflowing, and rode upstream to a farm with a large hall. They halted in the apple garth. Somewhere among the outbuildings a woman was keening; the sound made his scalp prickle. Once Cynddylan's sister keened here for her lost brothers. Brys knew that no one here would mourn him now or ever.

One of the blond men went into the hall. The redhead came to seize the thong binding Brys's wrists, meaning to pull him headlong onto the ground. Brys kicked the man hard under the ribs and sent him stumbling back crowing for breath. Again, the spear probed.

"Down."

A grey-haired man, tall and narrow in the shoulders, came out of the hall with the blond man. The resemblance was strong; father and son. Brys dismounted stiffly. The man behind pushed him forward with the spear, the butt end this time, but after a single involuntary step he braced his feet and stood his ground.

"I have safe passage from Offa."

"I know nothing of that," said the older man easily. He had a nasal, brassy voice. "You're an intruder on my lands."

"On the king's road." The landowner's backhand caught Brys across the mouth. Truth unrewarded. One of these days he would try discretion, just for the novelty. He spat blood. "You need instruction in receiving your king's guests."

Next time it was a fist. Brys felt his nose splinter like stone splitting inside his head. Another fist. It seemed to go on and on. He found he was watching from the ground as boots and spear butts descended. People stood around in watchful knots, not interfering. He tried to roll but nothing responded. One of his captors kicked him in the groin, another in the head. The twilight went red and black, and dissolved.

"THIS IS THE ONE." The man's voice was dark, deep, almost gentle; a voice he knew. A sound of silver coins. Or silver bells. "You can finish him. Dump him on the west bank."

Brys drifted in and out of blackness. Something was sticking stiffly to his face, maybe straw. He sprawled on it. A light overhead. Lantern.

"I want some use out of him first." A second voice, a brassy voice, defying authority. The landowner, and he was speaking to . . . Who was it?

"What use is that? Or do I want to know?" The first voice, the dark voice. Cloying, insinuating words. The voice made Brys's stomach turn and his head spin. Everything did.

The landowner snorted. "This isn't Tamworth. Hard labor is the only use I have for this offal. I send ten men on a construction crew tomorrow. If I send him I can keep one man to plow. I can barely manage —"

"Complain to Offa." The dark voice; its owner enjoyed the other man's fear. It contained a depth of cruelty. "You know what I think of this border."

"I do, lord." By the constriction of his voice, the landowner bowed as he spoke.

Lord? Not Brorda. Who? I read voices, faces, not minds . . . Brys let it all drift away.

"LIE STILL, GAMECOCK, you're all there." An old man's voice: British, from somewhere in the south.

Faint light. He let himself drift to the surface and break into consciousness. The bloodshot blackness stayed. Night. He lay on his back on straw, with a hide pulled up under his chin, where it chafed. His feet were cold. Breathing hurt. Bruised ribs, not painful enough to be broken. Face full of broken crockery. Loose teeth, none missing. Someone's hands began to take assessment of his smashed nose.

"It has to be set —" *Or I'll be singing through it? That's one thing I won't have to worry about.* He was waking up, more's the pity. "Who are you?"

"Hush," the man said. "The one who heals the beasts is who I am. You'll want to keep still, gamecock."

It made a kind of sense. Beaten like an animal, healed like an animal. Brys started to laugh and sensed his own hysteria. A hand clamped his mouth. The animal healer laid thumb and forefinger either side of his nose and gave an agonizing wrench. He gasped. The hand lifted from his mouth.

"Where —"

"Ordric's tun. You're slave, same as us."

"Rack of Cerne I am," Brys said.

The southerner crossed himself at this and reached to shift an unfamiliar weight on Brys's bare ankle. An iron fetter. A heavy chain linked it to the old man's. When he dragged on it, someone a few feet away swore in English. Chained slaves. Brys sat up, dizzy, and something ground on his collarbones. Stiff riveted rawhide. A collar. At least they hadn't driven the awl through his ear. Yet.

"You won't go far," said the old man morosely.

"Watch me," Brys said.

He fell into a fragmented sleep, dreaming of black riders with silver-eyed black dogs in pursuit of a red stag. But he saw that the hunters were warriors and the stag was a king at bay. All of them flattened and fell like pieces on a ruined gameboard, then blackened like a flower under flame.

He was barely conscious of walking west from dawn to dusk the next day. Someone supported him most of the way, cursing him steadily in an unknown language, and later he thought he rode on a cart for a while. The morning after that he woke in an open-sided shed. By daylight he saw it was a cowshed on a ruined farm. By dawn they were hauling red earth and stones out of the deep westward ditch of Offa's border dyke.

17 May 793 + Tamworth

Inlay, enamel, filigree, interlace, wax casting, forging. Any ornament, tool or weapon made to order. After ten years of feeding the forge hearth, melting metal scrap, collecting payments and pouring ale, Heilyn was a better jeweler than the old Mercian who trained him. And now what was changed? Nothing. Only a new set of worries, a new earring and a raw naked place around the neck.

Heilyn crossed the plankway into Offa's wonder, the water-driven corn mill. The timber building shook with the thundering millstones and the hidden river below. A slave with a sack of wheat on his shoulder staggered to the hopper swinging from a roof beam. Heilyn watched with interest; he hadn't been inside the mill before. The slave poured grain in a steady pale golden flow. Flour sprayed out into the pan, and dust rose to coat the beams overhead. In a few minutes the millstone ground as much as an hour's labor with a hand quern, but only for the rich. The monstrous machine was built with Mercian tax gold, but what good was it to the slaves and the poor of Tamworth? Sod it.

The foreman shouted something at Heilyn, who shook his head. He could wait. Soon the millstones pounded out the last of the flour. The miller signalled to another slave squatting on a beam overhead, who shifted a tiller. The diabolical rhythm stopped. Heilyn now heard as well as felt the captive river's unrelenting attack on the foundations of the millhouse.

"You the smithy slave?" the foreman shouted, deaf from the mill racket.

"No." It gave Heilyn pleasure to say so, despite everything. "I'm the smithy freeman."

"Forgive me, your lordship." The miller spat neatly into a corner. "Would your lordship kindly get his arse upstairs? We're too slow for the palace. They want their flour."

Two hours later, around time for the midday meal by his belly's reckoning, Heilyn climbed down the stair with his tool satchel clanking at his back. Replacing the worn pulley and chain was a four-hour job. He should have worked at his ease, made it seem more difficult, and hoisted his fee accordingly, but once he began to study it out he thought of nothing else. Fixing things, that was best. He would squint by candlelight all evening to restitch a pair of shœs, even now that he could buy new ones. Freemen threw away broken things. Slaves put them to rights or did without. Also, though he would never have confessed to the old smith, work well done gave him a shining satisfaction. God loves the good craftsman, one of his owners used to say, the priest. "The laborer is worthy of his hire, my child." Maybe God should pay the hire, then, since no one else will if the laborer's a slave; for suggesting this Heilyn had tasted the old priest's lash.

He waited at the foot of the ladder for the miller, who came out of an inner room with his mouth full of bread and garlic. Phew, the stench.

"One penny," Heilyn said. "Half for the iron I brought, half for labor."

"I'll tell the reeve's man the fee. You can go around to the palace tomorrow."

"I'll have it now."

"Sorry, your lordship." Another gob in the corner, this one garlic-scented.

"I want it now. One penny." Heilyn stood his ground, refusing to lower his eyes or let the slave whine creep into his voice. If he didn't conquer it now he never would. He waited. Blood pounded into his face.

"I don't have coins here. Go to the reeve tomorrow," the mill foreman said reasonably. He loosened the top of his shirt and revealed the same welted mark, half callus and half scar, that the rawhide slave collar had left on Heilyn's neck.

Heilyn shrugged and turned away. The man was just another creature to be bought and sold, as powerless as himself. Nothing changed, not really.

"Wait!" The shout caught him at the door. "Want to eat?"

Heilyn stopped, thought about garlic which he disliked, and nodded sullenly.

"When were you freed?" the miller asked, pulling another bench into the inner room.

"Last week." Heilyn remembered that the miller talked to the reeve, who talked to Offa's administrative clerks. Around a mouthful he said, "I want to find a place at the palace smithy, or maybe the abbey. I'm a goldsmith."

I want. I shall. They still sounded impossibly strange. For the first time in his life he could decide — had to decide — and after years of work to buy his freedom, suddenly that necessity made slavery look more comfortable. On his way out, he nodded at the mill slave overhead. The slave looked balefully down, a white-masked demon crouching in the rafters, and coughed into his hand.

It was raining outside. The court smiths lived under Offa's roofs, ate meat every day and got annual payment in silver pennies. If one of them were to slip on the river path one dark night . . . but they would choose another damned Mercian, somebody's nephew who didn't know the working end of a bellows. He hadn't a chance. He picked at this scab yet again, exposing raw nerves from a lifetime of contempt and self-contempt.

Heilyn found his way homeward across Tamworth on the boardwalk. At every step it squealed and oozed stinking sewer muck. Rain dwindled as he passed the palace compound, then fell as heavy as guilt. His hair dripped over his eyes in brown tails. His cloak was wet through. A dun man in a drab cloak going his solitary way in a dull afternoon. Invisible. People could see right through him; wherever he happened to stand they saw nothing. Some thought he had the devil's squint, but it was only an old scar beside one eye that had pulled tight in healing. He'd been caught stealing ale from a storeroom.

It was better to think about the hanging bowl for Saint Peter's at Breedon. He'd raised the silver body but needed a motif for the hanging plaques. Amber, perhaps, captured in a complex net of engraving? He'd been trying to work out the British style of interlace. Maybe another slave could help him. Maybe a slave — no longer fellow slaves. Then, instead of stultified English worms, he could shape wise and witty British serpents twining around their sun stones. As if anyone here knew the difference. He wondered what time tomorrow he could pick up the penny.

Lichfield abbey was not his first choice, but he hadn't yet summoned the nerve to approach Offa's head smith. Maybe soon. Maybe never.

As he waited outside the sacristy the next morning, Heilyn's valise weighed heavier on his knees by the minute. It contained superb work, the best in Tamworth. He could set any jewel, forge any shape, make any mold and cast a perfect piece from it. He had a rare eye and hand for cell enamel. Many smiths of his skill became landholders or traders. The abbey would be lucky to have him even briefly.

Two hours later Heilyn stood with arms impatiently folded, watching the steward's assistant line up his metal pieces like draftsmen on the edge of a table.

"I've heard of you. In Tamworth." The monk sat back with his hands folded on his belly. Every so often he tossed his head so the oiled curls at his temples danced; on a young boy this might be fetching, but on a stout stubble-chinned man of fifty it was ludicrous. He would avoid this one in dark corridors.

"My last commission was this bowl." In fact the commission went to the old Mercian smith, but for years he'd been sliding further into the lees of Burgundian red; Heilyn had handled every part of this job from talking design with the prior to kneeling through the endless dedication mass. Worthwhile, all of it. It was a beautiful piece. It lifted the brothers' eyes and it lifted his heart. "Perhaps that's what you heard."

"No." The monk smirked over his linked fingers. "Not that."

Heilyn decided not to believe his ears and eyes. This creature wasn't really suggesting, not when half the church . . . It had to be a test. "You must use a goldsmith for your altar pieces."

"We have a blacksmith who forges our farm tools. He turns his hand to gold and silver when need be."

"I also temper iron to strength and resilience and work bronze of my own alloy," Heilyn persisted. "My work is the best between York and Canterbury."

"Work? Ah, you mean this." He pinged a silver chalice with a forefinger. Heilyn watched anxiously. He'd wheedled it back from the chapel for a day and couldn't return it damaged. "You're how old, my child?"

Heilyn frowned to cover panic. Should he add or subtract years? The truth was always so vulnerable. "Eighteen."

"A little old," the monk said. He lowered his eyes and smiled sweetly to show how regretful he was that Heilyn wasn't a boy of ten, prinked out in ribbons and bells. *And whose catamite were you, as a novice among Mercian churchmen whose depravity scandalized even licentious Rome?*

Now it was all predictable. Cell enamelling: solder the walls, pour the molten glass, let the enamel cool in its confinement. He should have foreseen this. Heilyn began to gather his silver candlesticks and gold brooches, his bracelets and necklaces, his jeweled gospel book cover. Without a word he wrapped them carefully in sheepskin and settled them in the valise, though he was sorely tempted to caper before this vile old hypocrite and threaten acts of blasphemy. Instead he bowed obsequiously with downcast eyes and edged out of the sacristy. The door closed firmly at his back.

A mile down the Tamworth road Heilyn turned to stare back at Lichfield abbey's bell tower and the steep roof above the surrounding treetops. The British burned it once, someone had told him. Twice was overdue.

It was an afternoon of high cloud driven across a cornflower sky. Shadows were sharp underfoot on the dusty track; dandelions beamed under the hedges. A perfect day throbbing with blind mindless life, promising sensual and unattainable delights. Heilyn stood motionless in the rutted northwest road with his colorless hair spiking out over his ears and his drab cloak hanging limp. Daydreaming.

"Lost, friend?" asked a barefoot monk leading a calf toward the abbey. Or addled, his kindly face suggested. Who could be lost on six miles of traveled road from Lichfield to Tamworth?

"*Ar goll,*" Heilyn agreed, and the brother's doubtful look warned him he'd slipped into his mother tongue. "Lost, yes."

"In nomine Domini," The brother began a prayer. Heilyn stood with his head bowed and watched a waterman swim the ditch water. "Amen."

Heilyn had devised a handful of barbed answers to the steward's assistant by the time he reached Leoba's tavern near Tamworth's west gate. In his favorite corner he drowned them all ceremoniously in her dark ale. The old sod barely even looked at the workmanship, the fine chasing and engraving. Fool.

"So sad, lovey?" Leoba stopped at his bench on her way to the door. She wore her blue veil bordered in gold thread, so she was bound for the palace. Rumor persisted that she delivered personal services to one of Offa's henchman. Heilyn knew her brother cooked in the palace kitchens, but he'd never bothered to spoil a good story for others. An unimaginable number of years ago she'd been Offa's mistress, they said. The paint on her face was as thick as enamel and her hair flamed henna red. At ten paces she still looked a great beauty. "Go up and see the girls. No payment."

It was a longstanding joke, battle of wills, insult . . . Heilyn wasn't sure which, but she bore him no malice. He asked no more than that of anyone.

"Next time."

"Anytime." Leoba gave him a slow and sultry wink and twitched her corseted haunches off toward Offa's great hall. Heilyn hoisted another and left when a noisy knot of Offa's bodyguard came in slumming.

Now what? He supposed he'd go pick a fight with the old smith, once his owner and now his employer, and see if he could get himself thrown back into the gutter.

22 May 793 + Offa's Dyke

By the ninth day it was ritual; Brys had never done anything else. A bowl of barley and onions in the dawn murk, then a guard unlocked the chain in a long rattle of links through the ten fetters. Five of them were English, either born slave or sold into bondage, three were British and one was Irish. One was a dark-skinned man who spoke no word of any language the others understood.

Every day a slave foreman counted ten slave laborers out of the shed and two guards, one fair and one redhaired, goaded them through sodden fields to the border earthwork. As long as the daylight lasted they scraped earth from the trench and carried it up to heighten the wall. Their hands blistered and bled from Ordric's crude tools.

For the first few days Brys squandered his anger on the humiliation of slavery. He felt powerless and shamed, as he supposed Meirwen had felt that night at Tregeiriog. Then shame evaporated like standing water after rain, leaving a useful residue of hate. Most of his mind was numb. Only the hating part worked. In Tamworth he had regretted his missing anger; now it had returned to comfort him.

As he dug Brys looked south at Offa's border. The border ditch and dyke crossed a gentle height on its westward slope, carefully sited to give a vantage westward into the hill country that by nature looked mainly eastward into the plains of western Mercia. Most of the earthwork was already made, all but a few gaps like this one and the still disputed northern section. He had ridden patrols along the agreed border the last four summers, north and south, while Mercian patrols paced them east of the frontier. Both Brochfael and Offa punished border raids with hanging — when they could capture the raiders. In Mercia some resented the border as a curb to expansion. In Mathrafal there was talk of its threat to the integrity of Powys; it was new, it was unsanctioned by tradition and it prevented further settling of old disputes. And that, exactly, was its purpose.

One day five years ago he and Cian had lain unseen in Powys bracken to watch the Mercian surveyors sighting with staves from hilltop to hilltop — a year earlier they had ringed and burned trees that obscured their sightlines — signalling others to mark the line with cord and pegs. Then came work levies from all over Mercian territory, a few men from each estate, free laborers or slaves wearing rawhide collars, working in crews. As he was now.

Every day Brys made a ritual with the blond man. His name was Wulfric Ordricson, the old southerner said. He was easily made angry.

"Sais." Mercians, of the Anglian tribe, hated to be called Saxons in any language.

Wulfric scowled.

"You have three things of mine."

The first time the Mercian was curious, counting only the knife and boots he'd stolen. The redhead had taken his cloak.

"I have nothing of yours. Slaves own nothing."

"You have my iron, my leather and my life. I will have them all."

The first day Wulfric laughed and turned away. The second day the spear butt whipped the side of Brys's head. The third day, lasting silence. Brys worked on it like a new song, shaping it this way and that, calling on the patient red earth and the bleak overcast and the bubbling stream only a spear-cast west in a Powys meadow. Most of all, he called on his anger.

Every day when they stopped at midday to eat where they worked, Brys gave food scraps to the ravens that hovered near the border's raw earth. He talked loving nonsense to them in the Penllyn dialect of his childhood, calling them little brothers. The old man who healed the beasts began to cross himself whenever a raven darkened the sky.

The cycle was rain, heat, dust, barley mush fouled with rat dung, sleep shattered by every night movement of every man fettered to the chain. Patience had never been his strength. Now Brys courted it, laid his snares, and talked with the stooped old southerner who showed him a tolerant kindness.

"Ordric's lord," he asked. "Who is he?"

"How would I know that, gamecock?" the old slave asked. But late that night he crouched clanking to whisper, "Cenwulf."

This is the one. Dump him on the west bank. You know what I think of this border. All the times he had listened to that slow dark voice at the border parleys. Brys had known, he realized, for days. Offa's kinsman Cenwulf. Brys shivered.

"Why do you say that?" the old man asked uneasily.

"What?"

"Something about a *torc*. An offering." The old man patted his shoulder comfortingly with an expression reserved for the mad.

Brys nodded. He was mad, mad with rage and a need to escape. *The salmon is mad, wisest old creature, when she makes her river run.*

"You have my iron, my leather and my life." The ninth day his voice was rain blown oblique through a wall of mist. "Give them to me or die."

Wulfric stared. Brys held perfectly still with his bleeding left hand stretched to the sky. Nine slaves took it as benediction and leaned on their tools to rest. They were getting used to the ritual. The old southerner forgot to cross himself. *I can do this every day, forever, however long it takes.*

But this day Wulfric licked his lips, unable to look away. In the noon of a hot windless day, the brook murmured louder as though a mountain stream had leapt to strengthen it. The silence stretched, until his raven came.

"Brân!" he greeted it.

The raven coiled down with sun-fire striking blue from its black wings, counter-sunwise out of an enamelled sky. It settled with a bare caress of claws on his torn left hand. When he flexed his fingers and flung it aloft like a falcon, it lifted effortlessly to the top branch of a lightning-shattered oak that cast a crazed shadow over the raw red earth. Waiting.

Wotan's raven in Thor's tree, said Wulfric's expression of deep shock. Brys laughed aloud. The raven stirred and settled. Wulfric dropped his gaze and, by his look, saw a bloody-handed madman with hair as black as the raven's wing. *Good.*

Before anyone could gather his wits, Brys flung himself on Wulfric and knocked him flat on his back. His own knife was in Wulfric's belt, old iron honed as narrow as a razor by his grandfather and father, with the grip shaped for the left hand. He claimed it and got up.

"Give him yours," Brys told the redhaired man without looking.

Angry strength flared in him, sweeping away nine days of hunger and exhaustion. When Wulfric had the knife, Brys flung himself in before the Mercian was ready. Something sliced air beside his left shoulder, and he parted the shirt over Wulfric's belly. They circled. Brys stabbed low but found the man holding back, unwilling to close, though he was taller and lighter, as smooth on his feet as a dancer.

The raven creaked and lifted its wings on the blasted tree. *Soon time will run out.* Brys feinted low, spun away and counted on Wulfric's stunned fear for a chance. He seized him by the wrist and flung his arm up. A sudden twist sent the knife flying in a bright curve toward Powys. A knee in the groin sprawled him on the red earth. Brys flung himself down to kneel on the Mercian's straining arms and set the knife point under his fine flaxen beard.

"Why did he do it, your father?" No answer. He pressed harder, just below the knob in Wulfric's throat. "Why did he take silver?"

Wulfric shook his head. White showed around his eyes.

Brys broke the skin, mindful of unhealed scars on his own back. "Why?"

"Some Powys noble."

Impossible. "Why?"

"Hates Brochfael." He shaped the words without sound.

Brys saw the trickle of blood, itched to drive the knife home, and made himself lift it instead. "So for a few pieces of silver you kill a man you never before saw."

"You look alive," Wulfric said sullenly.

Brys showed his teeth. "So are you. For now." He called over his shoulder, "Bring the horse and a spear. Then stand back."

Movement behind him, a horse's hoofsteps. The animal healer said, "Here, lord."

Brys risked a glance and saw the slaves had closed around the foreman and the redheaded guard with mattocks and shovels held two-handed. *Let them be caught into my madness one minute longer. And the raven. Stay.* It cronked once on its branch.

"Live or die, Wulfric? Lie still and you live." He lifted the knife blade a little, and Wulfric nodded stiffly. Tears of rage swam in the corners of his hot blue eyes. Brys knew how that felt.

Brys got up slowly, took the spear and shoved the knife in his belt. The horse was Wulfric's tall sorrel gelding, left unsaddled until dusk. Someone took one step forward. *Out of time.* Brys took the reins in his spear hand, slapped the horse forward and risked a spear vault onto its back. He nearly went over the far side, but righted himself with a handful of mane. He took off with a rearing start westward, clinging like a burr as they plunged down into the new ditch and up on the Powys side. He couldn't look back. He might see Cerne leading his wild hunt through the raven dark, neither alive nor dead, riders and hounds with silver eyes.

Three spear casts west of Offa's border Brys reined and risked turning. Wulfric had risen to his feet, but otherwise it was the same. The raven was a scab of darkness on silvered oak branches against deep summer sky; it ruled a territory of raw trenched earth, grass flattened by a west wind, men frozen in a haze of bronze dust. *Impossible. How did I do that? I should have asked for my boots.* He heeled the sorrel horse headlong into Powys.

29 May 793 + Mathrafal

It was long past midnight when he reached the sanctuary west of Mathrafal. As Brys tied the horse near the standing cross, a wind stirred the offerings hanging from the oak branches. An owl glided over, feathered moonlight, and the sorrel sidestepped. Brys walked carefully into the candlelight pooling at the open oratory door. Mæn Pedr knelt inside with his arms outstretched, praying. A single candle on the altar threw a tall shadow cross onto the plaster wall. He heard cool disembodied Latin, and the horse shifting among the grave markers.

"So be it," said Mæn, and dropped his arms.

"So be it," Brys echœd from the door. He stepped in unsteadily, dropped to his knees beside the priest and leaned his forehead on the front of the altar. "I claim sanctuary."

"Given." Mæn turned. Shock. Arms around him as he began to lose his grip on the carved oak. "Fair God."

Outside, he crouched naked beside the sanctuary spring while Mæn combed vermin out of his wet hair, washed him, wrapped him in a blanket. Sometime later he drank ale and ate bannock smeared with honey. A moon splinter rocked gently across the face of the dark water.

The morning drone of bees in the sanctuary fruit trees was the sound Brys heard on waking. He lay on the sleeping shelf in one of the guest cells, blinking up at roof beams and thatch. The rawhide slave collar was gone. Mæn's honey salve soothed the raw place on his neck and, it felt, everywhere else on his body. Brys turned his head, and saw Mæn sitting crosslegged on a floor mat, turning the iron ankle fetter in his square hands. He vaguely remembered the priest cold-chiselling the flange that held it closed.

Mæn Pedr squinted into the morning sun at the east-facing door. The small mark between his brows stood out plainly, a pale old burn scar. His hair was white, though he was only a few years older than Brys, and he wore it untonsured. Working outdoors had browned his skin and hardened his hands, yet they were a healer's hands, gentle and ruthless.

"Brochfael will be here soon from the court in Mathrafal." The rough speech of a herdsman's son still underlay Mæn's calm voice, smoothed by long apprenticeship in Ireland and his novitiate at Meifod abbey.

"Why?" Brys asked. He ached all over, and when he looked at his hands he regretted it. He levered himself onto one elbow.

Mæn smiled. "You still talk in your sleep. All night you've been telling him something about the border."

Brochfael dismounted alone outside the thorn hedge an hour later, and crossed himself as he walked in past the great oak hung with gold and silver and carved wooden objects. He didn't like this place, but although he could order it destroyed and consecrated to the church, instead he chose to regard it as an anchorite's retreat. When the king came in sight, Brys rested his scythe against a plum tree and waited. Brochfael nodded curtly and started toward the oratory.

"Pedr," Brochfael said. Mæn Pedr came from the hives with a freight of bees on one homespun sleeve. "Tell me the injuries."

Brys pulled the borrowed robe over his head at Brochfael's order. Mæn told him, all the while lifting stumbling bees from his arm and sending them on homeward. Brochfael listened, and looked, with a muscle dancing in his cheek. Brys felt like a horse up for sale at summer fair, a broken-down nag.

"Drop your drawers," Brochfael said curtly. Brys pulled the drawstring and stepped out of the linen, borrowed like Mæn's robe. "Good. You wouldn't be the first man they castrated."

Brys fought the impulse to cover his genitals. He'd tried not to dwell on that possibility. Brochfael turned toward the cell. Brys dressed himself, awkwardly because his hands were stiff, and followed the king. Mæn shook his head and went back to his bees.

"Why are you here, Cynfarch?" demanded Brochfael, not looking up. He had found the leg iron and was opening and closing it with great interest.

"Digain's kin," Brys said, not yet ready to raise the greater reason. "If they were at court —"

"Your fine is paid," Brochfael cut him short. "I couldn't risk a blood feud. Why are you in Powys? I heard you were bound for the continent in some kind of self-imposed exile. God knows you have the arrogance to try and sentence yourself without judge or witness. Then I heard you were dead on the border."

And that would have made your life easier by far. Brys occupied himself with tying the belt of the robe. Brochfael made an impatient sound and tied it for him. Then he turned away.

"I was planning to seek passage," Brys admitted to Brochfael's back, where the thick links of the *hual,* the chain of kingship, glittered between his iron hair and plain linen shirt. No Powys king, North or South, for generations had worn a golden collar in the ancient way. Cynddylan had worn a boar-headed torc, the stories said, but it had been looted from his body at Tren. It was probably still in the treasury at Tamworth unless the Mercians had broken it into a crucible to pay for another mile of frontier against Powys. Brys sat down on the edge of the sleeping shelf, suddenly very tired. "But there was something you had to know first."

Brochfael came and sat beside him, resting his big-boned wrists on his knees, while Brys told him. Afterwards there was a long silence.

"You don't believe it," Brys frowned at his torn hands; at least no fingers were broken. *Is it because I tell you that you won't believe it? Would you believe it from another?*

Brochfael sat motionless. "Why would a Powys noble and a Mercian noble both want trouble on the border? Are you suggesting a conspiracy? What's to gain?"

"Power. Wealth. Revenge. And you know there are factions on both sides that hate this border." *Including half of your guard in Mathrafal.* A honeybee flew in the open window and circled in frustration before she landed on the back of Brochfael's hand. Brys watched her crawl one way and another unnoticed. "'Borders are drawn in blood.' How often have you heard that?"

"Never," the king said coldly, "to my face."

"Brorda came to ask me questions in Tamworth."

"About?" Brochfael's voice closed up.

"Pœtry. The rules of wood-wisdom. Nothing in particular. That night a girl came, a well-trained courtesan, saying she had heard Gwriad of Man was a great king." Brys paused. "I regretted I'd met him only briefly."

"A spy. Not surprising." Brochfael almost smiled. "I learn most about what's happening in Tamworth by the back door."

Brys remembered something else. "I found a note in a book Brorda loaned me. *Tell him Egbert is returned to Britain.*"

Brochfael didn't move, but the bee now decided to stab the back of his wrist. Gently he picked her up and dropped her to the floor, then brushed out the sting. "Egbert? It's a common name."

You know which Egbert. Why the evasion? "Egbert of Wessex has been in exile in Frankia for how long?"

"Three or four years." Brochfael let the silence grow.

"I hear he's been serving Charles of Frankia as a mercenary captain." Brys watched the bee crawl toward the door, then find her wings. She would die soon without her small weapon.

"He's not the first."

"If he had returned," Brys pressed, "what would it mean?"

"A West Saxon rebellion to give Egbert his rightful crown, probably. Death or exile for Offa's daughter Eadburh and her husband. Given time and strength, he might try to bring down Offa."

"How would it affect Powys?"

Brochfael studied his face. "You're Egbert, newly returned to Britain. What will you do?"

Many times over the years they'd talked this way; much of Brys's education consisted of these questions. *You're Arthur. The Saxons have just broken the Thanet treaty. What will you do? You're Alexander. . .* He answered, "Make headquarters far from Offa's eyes, get Mercia into a war with East Anglia, and while his back's turned, seize power in Winchester."

"No," Brochfael said. "East Anglia's too weak. Offa would lay it waste and be over the West Saxon border in five weeks. Something more difficult. Something that takes time."

"Then," Brys thought hard. "I'd get Mercia to attack a powerful and warlike country, maybe one with difficult terrain . . ." *Powys.* He turned to Brochfael, who was looking at the welt on the back of his wrist.

Brochfael got to his feet. "It's all imagination, in any case. Brorda's son Egbert went on pilgrimage to Rome. It's a perilous journey. Offa was pleased he returned safely this spring. No doubt that was the meaning of the message in the book." He stopped at the open door. He looked out into the sunny glade within its grove of noble trees. Ash, birch, hawthorn, apple, rowan, oak. Brys had grafted the youngest apple last year, but it had yet to bear fruit.

"Do you trust this man Pedr?" Brochfael could not bring himself to say priest.

"Yes, lord."

"Then stay until you're healed. Do what he tells you. You have your father's anger. Keep it sheathed until you need to draw blood."

Brys opened his mouth to argue, but that would only prove the point. They walked together to the thorn hedge. He remembered, "There were two fines, not one."

"I paid the murder price only, not insult price, since the servant left Tregeiriog. She has family in Iâl."

"She's alive?" Everything had happened too quickly that night.

"We questioned her afterward. I thought you knew." Brochfael glanced at Brys in surprise and visibly decided not to ask. "She wouldn't tell us much. And she had no kinsman to charge Digain with rape, so we dropped it as she asked. He was dead anyway."

Meirwen — Is she all right? When did she leave? Are you sure she's in Iâl? Where in

Iâl? Questions Brochfael couldn't answer even if Brys could ask. Brochfael would only warn him against consorting with a servant; it was exploitation, not unlike Digain's own wrongdoing. So the king would see it, whatever the truth. That was one reason he couldn't ask. Brys looked at the gifts slowly turning among the oak branches. Silver and bronze, shimmering. He saw nothing else. "I won't have you paying my fines."

"God my judge, Cynfarch, you will have it. Swallow your pride before it brings you down like —" He stopped himself. "Never fear, I'll wring ten times as much compensation from Offa for the brutal treatment of a hostage in his care."

Two mentions in one day of my father, rarely mentioned in a year? Brys veered from questioning it too closely. If he thought too hard about anything, now that he was safe . . . But now he was indebted to Brochfael, the last man on earth to whom he wanted to owe anything. With a curt nod to his foster son in the sanctuary priest's homespun robe, Brochfael went to his horse and rode away without another word.

Brochfael had few words, no warmth, no color, no charm, a hand of tempered iron on Powys — and Powys loved brilliance, eloquence and heart. His father Elisedd had been a grasping, bloodthirsty warlord; Powys still held him dear. Brochfael needed a new *pencerdd*, as Brorda had suggested, someone to remind him that a king must give his land more than justice. Brys watched him out of sight between the great oaks, more regretful than angry.

Afternoon. The honeybees drowsed between the blooming plants and their basket hives on the far side of Mæn Pedr's garden. Sunlight had crept across the grass of the sanctuary clearing, and now Brys sat in dappled shadow; only the plastered wall of the cell at his back still held the sun's warmth. He had written three pages today. A lefthanded copyist, after the hard lesson of rescraping a few smeared parchments, dœs slow and careful work. Anyway, he had only a few sections to write down: metaphor, wit, other fragments from memory. It was a small fraction of the *Rhetoric*, but some was better than none.

The garden was weeded, clods were hœd between the rows of kale and carrots and onions, bindweed was pruned away from the spring, grave markers were cleared and mended. He'd helped with the bees for years, but now they wouldn't tolerate him. His anger made the hives angry. Yesterday Mæn had him start working with the gentle-voiced harp strung with horsehair. It was an old harp, its belly well raised by the string pull of arm and pillar.

Cian had come and gone a few times, telling him Mathrafal's court gossip, once bringing the silver arm ring and another time a wolf cub his cousin had tamed. Mathrafal was two miles east; it might be two hundred. In the warm evenings Mæn asked Brys for mountain airs and laments, but the anger trapped in his hands demanded the bloody war songs of old Powys. When he thought Brys didn't notice, Mæn watched him from unhurried brown eyes. If there were peace anywhere, it would be in this sanctuary.

Brys slept in a guest cell, worked, ate with Mæn at sundown and didn't count the days. His cell was spare and clean: whitewashed rough plaster walls, roof beams showing the adze marks, scoured floor planks, unbleached linen and quilts folded on the sleeping shelf, uncarved and unpainted storage chests. These buildings dated from Arthur's time. Mæn said the site was much older; he could recite the names of men and women who had served here, healing through medicine and dreams and prayer.

Most nights Brys woke sweating with his own words hanging in the air. Mæn, unwilling to trouble the traveling spirit by waking him, would be sitting silent in the dark.

After a while he asked Mæn for a healing dream. Mæn thought about it for days before he agreed. One sunset the priest brought a jug of icy water from the sanctuary spring to Brys's cell and prayed with him. Then he touched the four points on his forehead, chest and shoulders, and went out quietly. Christ's cross of sacrifice or the radiant sun wheel of fair-handed Lleu, it made no difference. Each point burned like a blow. Brys drank the water and recited the triads. He kneeled a while looking at the last dusk glow through the stretched parchment window. When he lay down sleep came, then a dream.

I dream and I know that I am dreaming. I consent.

But this was no healing dream, it was a nightmare. He dreamed he was back at the place he could not bear to see even in memory, the king's hunting lodge near Tregeiriog. Everything seemed more sharply defined this time, as though a cold fire burned inside each object and face.

Gwriad is speaking: wiry, quick, a red beard parted in the middle, costly clothes. After a week he is still trying to sell Brochfael his idea. The idea is simple enough under its elaborate robes of diplomacy: a trade alliance as an instrument of peace. And what might this alliance become if peace fails? No one will say. Brochfael stares into the fire as Gwriad talks, then gœs down to the stream with Idris to argue. He returns saying he will answer in the morning. Gwriad pins his saffron cloak and gœs out smiling.

Time passes. I walk the path downstream toward Tregeiriog.

Meirwen waits at the grey stone tangled in hawthorn and briar. As the moon sails between cloud fortresses, the light picks out her silver earrings and the shine of her eyes. The dream light shows her trout freckles and the copper gleam in her dark hair. A stubborn girl with a mouthful of thorns. Friends for years, lovers now, at least when I'm north on border patrols or Brochfael's hunts. Seventeen, all her friends have married. Meirwen is different: a woman who openly practises the smith's art, a landless woman who speaks and reads fair Latin. She knows there are girls in Mathrafal. Maybe there's a man here. I don't ask. Her mouth is cool to the touch, the rest of her is warm. Even at this point the dream is cool and chaste, as though someone tells a story of what happened long ago. After we love, we lie wrapped in both cloaks and listen to the wind combing the hillside. Faintly we hear springwater flowing from a hidden source. Stars gleam between the bare oak branches over our heads.

The safe darkness explodes into lantern light. Digain comes forward and stands blackly outlined in its yellow globe, a big-shouldered man with sandy hair.

"You have assaulted a woman in my protection," the landowner says. His voice is angry, yet there's an undercurrent of entreaty. What dœs he want?

I get to my feet blinking in the sudden glare, naked and unarmed. My first mistake: being unarmed.

"But I'll give you a chance." Digain sounds nervous now. "Brochfael means to sell Powys out to this foreigner. We think you can prevent that. Convince him otherwise."

"We?" So this is entrapment. I measure the distance to my clothes. My knife is among them.

"Men loyal to Powys."

"What do you suggest? Sing a little satire on Gwriad? Forge one of Offa's threatening letters?" My second mistake: mocking him. Seeing this I shift weight and fall back a step towards my knife. And another step. "Anyway, I like Gwriad's alliance. Persuade him yourself." My third mistake: refusing outright. I should have delayed.

"I charge you with the rape of my servant."

Meirwen's on her feet, wrapped in one of the cloaks. Digain takes a step forward and grabs her bare arm. The cloak falls away to her waist, and lantern light flickers on the bruises. Many bruises, blue, purple, fading yellow. The worst covers one breast, bone-deep bruises from five fingers of one hand. She never told me.

"Who did it?" I ask her. Sick, I know the answer. If I'd asked before, if I'd known . . . I could have found her a place at court, a place somewhere. Digain's hand on his knife hilt. A long silence. I ask her again. I need to hear her say it.

"Digain. Since my father died last year."

Shame in her voice, to my dismay, not anger. I tell her, be angry — And then blue iron hisses past my cheek. Somehow I evade that blade long enough, stumbling barefoot among the thorns, for Meirwen to put my knife into my hand. Darkness rushes back; the man with the lantern is gone. Even the dream light cannot illuminate the time that follows, until I see Digain kneeling with both hands on the knife hilt that stands out from his chest. Strong hands drag me to my knees, someone shouts my name. Brochfael. Digain's steward is back with the lantern, out of breath. Questions in the trampled grass under the oaks. The steward's accusation. Questions in the king's hunting hall. Meirwen, where is she? No one knows . . .

When I ride east to the border the next morning my hands are still bloody under the tight rawhide. I can see nothing but my hands. . .

Brys woke at dawn in a cold sweat. Not a healing dream.

But among the bean rows at noon that day he remembered Gwriad's angry departure when Brochfael put him aside; now at least he could bear to think of that ill-fated night. It was something.

Now, sitting with his back to the sun-warmed plaster wall, he tuned the harp, set it to his left shoulder and sang, I will mourn until I lie in silent oak, Cynddylan slain with his war host. Over the curved string arm Brys saw Mæn coming towards him with a bundle and broke off the old lament.

"Fair weather tomorrow."

Brys waited. Anything Mæn said had its reason.

"You've done violence of body and spirit."

"A penitence?"

"Will you take one?" Mæn often answered question with question.

"Yes." Brys didn't much care what it was. Assisting the surgeon at Meifod abbey for a month was a favorite; it also served to appease the prior. Mæn's penitences were never idle but intended to lessen the spiritual debt next time around. *Death is the center of a long life, the hub of a wheel with many spokes and an endless rim.* "I consent."

"You go tomorrow. A month outside this region, working for your keep."

Brys laid the harp carefully on its back beside him. Its slight weight bruised a warm breath of summer from the dry grass. This he hadn't expected. "I want to stay. I've done my time digging Offa's border. I thought I was digging my grave."

"You can't stay. Not here. You're full of hate," Mæn said abruptly and dropped the bundle on the grass. Clothing. "We all dig our own graves."

Brys didn't watch him leave. The oratory door slammed. He leaned his forehead on bent knees and wept for the loss of his sanctuary as Adam must have wept outside the east gate of Eden. After a while he wiped his face on the homespun sleeve. Had Mæn planned all this? He picked up the harp and fumbled his way into a gentle air of his own hills. The music caused him more pain than Cynddylan's bitter elegy, but he persevered.

An hour later, having done some penitence of his own for rare anger, Mæn returned and said, "Take nothing with you."

"Easily done," Brys agreed. "I have nothing."

Mæn laughed.

At first light, Mæn Pedr slapped him lightly on each cheek to separate past from future, embraced him and went to hœ his onions.

June 793 + North Powys

Summer traveled the hills. Lush grass sprang in the high pastures, green apples swelled under leaves, iridescent dragonflies hovered the moors. Between the wooded breasts of the upland, shearing and first haying reached the folded farms.

Brys journeyed with the season. At first he worked silent and frowning, took his day's payment in food and kept to himself. In field and cattle shed he met other wanderers, landless or dispossessed as he was — more accurately, dispossessed as his father had been — poor men and women drifting unremarked from one valley to the next. No one asked questions. Imperceptibly, he dropped the dead weight of his anger and shared wayfaring food and leather scraps to mend his shœs. He wore Mæn's gift of a homespun long-sleeved shirt; no breeches, since he was not riding. Unshaven for weeks anyway, he let his beard grow in. If he kept quiet, guarding his trained voice and polished accent, he was any black-browed laborer. In tawny dusk at one farm Brys drove the cows home. At the next he built walls of drystone slate in patterns as exact as a triad. South was Mathrafal, east was Mercia, west was Penllyn. He worked his way north.

By midsummer his palms were as callused as his leathery fingertips, and he was burned brown to the waist from long days in the fields. Thatching, mending nets, harvesting fish from weirs, he worked dawn to dark for a full belly and a dry bed. Mostly he was too tired to think by sundown.

Midsummer fires he kept at a hill farm where the people were small and dark with slanted eyes. The priest danced in the terrifying guise of Cerne, with antlers spreading from his brow and a stag's hide tied over his shoulders. Brys joined in their wild spinning dance and spun off from it with a small woman twice his age, who contributed to his education in ways that would bemuse Mæn Pedr. *Midsummer*, he thought, sliding toward sleep: *that was when I would have graduated in song*. It was a different life, when he cared about the pœt's craft and Powys and Gwriad's better world.

At dawn he woke in the cool earth house with a sudden terror that three hundred years had fled while he slept, his friends were long dead and he would crumble to dust in the daylight. Driving the pigs from their shed for mucking out, he yawned and forgot it. The reek of pig manure was real.

At peaceful Llandegla yn Iâl, in the gentle embrace of green hills, he spent a week hœing fields and chanting offices with the monks. The old surgeon had a burn scar between his brows like Mæn; like Mæn he healed with dreams as well as his infusions and poultices. He had been dedicated here as a boy to the fair-handed lord of light — Tegla was one of Lleu's many names — but an Egyptian monk pausing on his way to Ulster last year had told the abbot the name honored an eastern Saint Tegla instead. Brys liked the place's tacit duality, the female saint and the male god sharing in name and worship. At Llandegla, having wisdom in common and no quarrel, old way and new kept the peace.

Brys took the holy waters of Ffynnon Degla, known to ease the falling sickness, and received the benediction of dreamless sleep. Throughout one quiet afternoon and evening he kneeled beside the sacred spring in the dappled grove guarded by ancient stone heads, the gift of a forgotten priest or patient. He could stay here, serve the old healer, perhaps take vows. But in the morning he accepted traveler's bread from the hosteller and walked on north.

One afternoon, half by chance, he stood outside a cowshed in northern Iâl. The dairywoman had a baby on her hip and a small boy clinging to her skirt. She was taller than him, and her freckles and stubborn mouth made him smile for no good reason, except that she was Meirwen's sister.

"For all I know she's in Armorica or Frankia or Constantinople. Her head's full of dreams about foreign goldsmiths." She fetched him cool buttermilk from the river shed and watched him drink. "Tell Meirwen we want her here, when you find her."

"In Constantinople?" he asked her over the dipper. "Not me."

She smiled and touched his cheek, then turned away to her milking.

Mæn's month of penitence was paid out on a clear July day, but he was too restless to settle back into music, arms training, the constant activity of the court. Why would he bother turning south?

North of Rhuddlan township in Tegeingl, where River Clwyd broadens into its marshy estuary on the Irish Sea, he found work carrying ale kegs and stacking bales of trade goods for a riverside tavern. Tegeingl had always been disputed territory between Powys and Gwynedd to the west. Gwynedd was weak under Caradog, so these days Tegeingl leaned to Powys.

Deep-sea trade curraghs and wooden-hulled lapstrake ships came here to trade and recaulk. Their crews were Irishmen, tattoœd Picts, black Danes and fair Frisians, brown-skinned Moors, British of every nation, Saxons out of London and Anglians out of Chester. Though the merchants and crewmen were civil enough, he found himself watching the English with cold and deadly care.

Every night Brys drank in his tavern or the other tavern farther down the river quay, and in both he left word that he wanted to work ship's passage to Armorica.

"Brys?" A trader greeted him one afternoon by the only name he used now.

"That's me. You need a crewman?" Brys sat clasping an ale cup, swinging his bare feet over the pier and watching a heron stalk the reeds of the red riverbank.

The trader was a quick little Manxman with a red moustache and gold earrings; he wore a hooded Irish tunic chequered in garish purple and green. He'd been in the tavern earlier, driving a hard bargain with the innkeeper over the new Falernian red. Neithon was his name. He had a foxy smile and a feral instinct for the kill, like any good trader.

"I may take one anyway, if you can tell me what I need to know. I hear you're from Mathrafal."

"I've spent time there." Brys took a mouthful.

"Know many people at court?"

"Every living soul." *Especially if information means passage.*

"Come down to the ship. We'll talk business."

They walked a few spear casts downstream from the quays. A beamy offshore curragh with watchful eyes painted either side of her prow lay keel-up on the riverbank. Nearby was an ill-kept hut half dug into the grassy slope. At a glance from their captain the two crewmen sauntered off toward the taverns. They left a pitch-pot beside a dying fire and an awl dangling by its greased cord from the gunwale. Neithon handed Brys a pitch dauber and settled on the trampled grass to watch him work.

"You lost someone?" Brys said as he traced warm pitch over the laced seams of the oxhides. He would stop at giving information that could harm Brochfael; he remembered Brorda's prying in Tamworth a lifetime ago.

"Cynfarch mab Cadeyrn Penllyn is the name."

Brys looked down to dip his stick in the pot. The pitch was getting sluggish and needed reheating. *A huge temptation to laugh myself sick or walk away. But I'm curious.* "Where I come from, a dispossessed man is without family, an outcast, and so are his sons. It's unlucky to name the house."

"Some houses and some men," Neithon shrugged, "make their own laws. And I heard things had smoothed over."

"Did you?"

"Where might I find him?" Neithon said patiently. "He left Mathrafal in May as Brochfael Powys's envoy to Offa."

"Hostage," Brys corrected. "What happened, did someone die and leave an inheritance?" *Fair God, that would mean my brother . . .*

"His kinsman wants him."

"Which one?"

"Gwriad Manaw."

Cousin Gwriad? Brys managed not to laugh outright. *Cousin, certainly, but many times removed.* "And you're the king's messenger?"

Neithon stood up, still smiling under his moustache. "That's his business. And on second thought, I'm over-crewed now. Take my advice, Powys, if you want to pull an oar, mend your manners first. You can leave that," he nodded at the pitch pot.

Brys squatted on his heels and shoved the stick into the cooling pitch. "Maybe you wouldn't know him if you found him."

"He wears the Penllyn arm ring, God alone knows why. The new lord of Penllyn — Garmon, isn't it? — must be soft-headed."

"Far from it, I promise you. What use could a younger son make of it?" *Is this really a good idea?* Brys pushed up his long sleeve and slid the arm ring over his left elbow. He had the satisfaction of seeing Neithon's smile slip its moorings and become a cold appraising stare. He had guessed; he had not been certain.

Neithon was shrewd. He took Brys's hands, treble and bass, and felt the fingertip calluses. Then he examined the arm ring inside and out, rubbed its dents and scratches with a thumb, asked why Penllyn used ravens and grilled him through genealogies and ancient history for an hour. As he talked, Brys relit the fire with flint and tinder from his belt pouch, heated the pitch pots and went back to work on the hull. It gave him something to do with his hands. He wanted harp strings between them, for the first time in many weeks, to gather his thoughts. Finally Neithon handed back the old silver and gave him a fold of parchment written in Gwriad's round hand. Brys barely glanced at it, something about Neithon as Gwriad's trusted messenger. The interrogation was better proof.

"What dœs cousin Gwriad want?" he asked straightfaced.

Neithon pulled his moustache. "Come inside."

22 July 793 † Rhuddlan

Trade goods overflowed the hut in an exotic tumble. They drank fragrant mead from fine Italian glassware, swirled in green and blue like waves of the sea, and sat on chests that spilled other goods: watershedding British cloak lengths, a Moorish steel sword inlaid with charms in silver, glass vials of Persian scent, vellum books destined for Neithon's winter port in Armorica, more outlandish Irish tunics like the one he wore, a brindled hound puppy the size of most grown dogs. All lay in no apparent order. In a warm wash of light from the open window, the puppy sprawled across Brys's bare feet chasing dream hares.

"No," Brys said again. "Not me."

Neithon realized this was more than hard bargaining and dropped his tally stick to the parcel of silks on his knee. "Gwriad needs you."

"No."

"He said you talked late one night about his idea of alliance."

"We did." That night in Tregeiriog, after Brochfael went to argue it out with Idris and left Brys to occupy Gwriad. Before he went to meet Meirwen. . . To deflect the trader's next question he said, "I liked his idea of alliance among the British, but even the best idea fails in a bad time. Warlike Powys, people still say, but do they realize how close to the bone Offa cut? We can't take the risk."

"Is that your view or Brochfael's?"

Brochfael's, mostly, but he may be right. And either way it's not your business. Brys stared into his drinking cup of Ravenna glass and tried to clarify his own thoughts. "What would this alliance cost us? Nothing in tax or tribute, you say. But we trade cattle to Mercia, wool to Munster and hunting dogs to Armorica, among other things. If we were bound in trade to Manaw and Gwynedd —"

"You won't be bound to anything. But trade within the alliance will be free of tariffs and port fees, prices will drop, trade will increase and we'll all prosper."

"You know Brochfael thinks this is a Rheged plot, the narrow edge of Gwriad's play for power. He's an ambitious man, you won't deny that, and he has ambitious sons."

Neithon was startled. "Rheged hasn't existed for two hundred years."

"Not in Carlisle."

"Ah." The trader understood. "The Cynferchin, the royal house in exile."

"Do you think we're going back to defend the Roman wall against the Picts? To defend York against the Anglians?" Brys had argued this with Brochfael, student with teacher. "Let them have it all. We're here to stay."

Neithon pursed his mouth in a silent whistle and carved a notch on his tally. "Do you talk to Brochfael in those terms? No wonder he's watching his back. Elfæl and Penllyn —" He shrugged.

Brochfael's fears were not allayed by shutting them in the dark, and God knew it was hard work dragging them into the light. *But that's not for you to know. And if you mention Penllyn once more —*

What about the southern kingdoms? Dyfed and Gwent and Cernyw?" Brys asked.

"Gwriad will approach them once we have an agreement in the north. But remember, Dyfed's royal house is half Irish and most of its trade is with Munster. Gwent trades and marries with Hwicce and the West Saxons and has its own treaties. With Magonsæte and Ergyng between it and Mercia, Gwent is not overly concerned about Tamworth. And Cernyw is effectively under West Saxon influence."

"Still, they're British kingdoms. An alliance could benefit from their inclusion."

Neithon nodded. "I'll take it to Gwriad. Perhaps he'll approach them later."

"Another thing. Trade alliance will look the same as military alliance to Offa, just as it did to Brochfael. If he sees a threat he'll be over the Powys border with the whole English fighting force."

Neithon picked up his knife and tally stick, counted out ten folds of bright silk and carved a notch. "And how would you prevent Offa from seeing a threat?"

Interesting problem. Brys combed a hand through his hair, which he now realized needed cutting. He saw the trader smiling at his woven rainbow, an estate's worth of silk, thinking no doubt how easily he could lead Brys into political speculation. Politics, overt or covert, were daily fare in Mathrafal. Trade was only another face of politics. "I'd offer Mercia an advantage — lower prices in exchange for dropping the port duty at Chester. Brochfael controls enough of the trade to do that."

"What would the Mercians do?" Neithon dropped his tally, unnoticed.

"Dœs it matter? If they accept, you gain a market. If they refuse, they've had a fair chance and they know what you're about."

"Maybe," Neithon said and gave him a sideways look. "Tell me why you won't help Gwriad."

"I'd be barred from graduating in song, and Brochfael would expel me from his guard. I'm a landless man, Neithon. The guard is all I have to return to, some day." A trader understands economic reasons better than any talk of bright *awen*, rising like a stream source between hand and harp string. "Gwriad can find someone else."

"You're the one he wants."

"Why?"

Neithon also loved his art. Brys saw the gleam in his eye at the prospect of close trading. He held up a hand and began to count on his fingers, yet another tally. "You're kin to Brochfael by fostering. You're kin to Gwriad —"

"That's all past. Now I have no kin."

"Cynfarch, everyone knows . . . " Neithon saw something in his expression and changed tack. "You're also dyed in the weave of Powys, and Powys is embattled, it dœsn't matter whether by war or peace. You're trained in law, genealogy, history, music and rhetoric."

"So I'm told. But not in the art of the envoy."

Neithon hesitated. "Gwriad wanted two of you to go together. An envoy and a pœt to talk to the kings."

"His envoy can go alone."

"His envoy is no longer available."

"Dead?" Brys asked, liking this less by the minute.

"Alive and flourishing in Aachen. Where he's needed." Neithon saw that he needed to say more. "Charles and Offa have been quarreling for three years. Charles talked of invading Mercia, he petitioned the Pope — you know all of that. As long as they're at odds, he may be more kindly disposed to hear British envoys. Gwriad may throw away years of work if he pulls out his man now."

"There are others. What about his sons?"

Neithon leaned forward. "Gwriad heard you sing. He said your *awen* speaks with its own voice."

More interesting. "And?"

"You'll need it. For the good of Powys."

And is the good of Powys now my overriding concern? But the less Neithon and his master knew of Powys problems, the better. " My head would be served on a platter to Brochfael in Mathrafal hall." Brochfael had been angry with him since Tregeiriog anyway. Could anyone blame him?

Neithon laughed and crossed to one of the chests. "Will you at least help me with this? I have something else to do." Then he went out silently.

Brys nodded, entwined in his thoughts, and reached for a square package bound in oiled hide. Trade goods to sort, maybe books. Brys drained the glass and held it against the window light to examine its rare beauty. He poured it full, with water this time, from a silver pitcher studded with rock crystal. Once long ago he had taken such treasures for granted in his father's court. *What in the name of radiant Lleu am I going to do now? For the good of Powys? What about Penllyn? I'm in enough trouble now — an ungraduated pœt, a homeless wanderer — but will a chance like this ever come again?*

Gofyn i mi, mi a'e gwn. Ask me, I know it. Words surfaced like a bubble of laughter, the invitation of the hall pœt to his audience.

Thoughtfully he sat crosslegged on one of the folded cloak lengths and held the brimming glass between him and the window. He could see his fingers through it and on its surface a distorted reflection of an apple bough outside the window. He shut out everything but his own steady heartbeat, watched the rippling surface and waited.

Awen. Invocation and welcome. His thoughts stilled. All else fell away as the small disturbance smoothed out and a hundred colours rose from its quietude.

Awen is wiser than will. Nine parts labor and one part elation, the river's voice rose between his hands. It had been silent for a long time. *Listen.*

Wind in the apple boughs. A fragment of song and laughter from the tavern. Below all, the rush of River Clwyd to the sea. Peaceful, bountiful, full of life.

Yes, murmured the light on the water. Knowledge rose into his awareness. As naturally as a key fitting its home lock, part of his being returned to him. *Awen.* That was all: no dragons in the sky, no shooting stars. *Yes. I consent.*

Brys found himself lying sprawled back against the oilskin bundle, the chalice of water spilled near his hand. Mercifully it hadn't broken or splashed the precious goods. Outside, the river talked its way slowly between reedy banks.

Dusk had fallen when he got up stiffly to look out the window. Neithon stood on the riverbank talking with a ruffian who might be one of his crew. He had an oar on his shoulder and his finger hooked in the gill cover of a silver-scaled fish. The puppy romped at his heel.

Brys turned back inside to Neithon's books. He poured more water, drank it and set aside the lovely goblet. A stroke of his knife parted the thongs binding the oiled hide. Inside another wrapping of cured leather lay a wooden crate which held objects padded with lamb's wool. They were all the wrong size and shape for books. Puzzled, he freed the largest piece from clouds of wool and revealed a thick wooden block tapering to one end.

A harp's sound box lay between his hands, a single block of willow carved with endless interlace. Serpents, demons, beasts, human heads emerged from the pattern, then shuttled again into a woven rhythm of artistry. It was an illuminator's skill brilliantly translated through a woodworker's hands. A carved head crowned the narrow end: a snarling mythical sea-cat with ears laid flat to her skull, eyes of amber set in silver, lapped scales instead of fur. Smiling, he found the sweetly curved string arm and muscular bowed pillar, so precisely formed in oak that he had to rock them into their sockets. String tension would hold them in place. Brys turned the harp around, admiring its solidity and grace, like a bird about to fly, substantial and delicate at the same time.

Strings. He found three sets coiled in a dœskin pouch and laughed. A harp from Ireland, strung with bronze and silver instead of gut. He threaded the wires through the sound board spine and stretched them to their pegs, painstaking with their fragility. The bass strings were of thick silver and the trebles of steadily finer bronze. The tuning key was a sleeping bird with her head tucked back against her wing. The harp maker, enjoying his joke, had carved a gentle wren to tune Palug's fighting cat to song.

Brys rough-tuned, then tuned the central sister strings by ear and worked his way up and down until he was satisfied. He settled the sea-cat's head to his left shoulder, meaning to start with training pieces to ease the harp's newness and his own long silence. His hands, captured by the shining wire, decided otherwise. Song leaped in the strings like sun-fire: a tumult of triumph, melody threading the thunder with sweet elation, mellow peace in the last bronze echo. The sound was splendid, like nothing he had heard before, and if the wire shredded his fingers it would only be fair payment. Brys strayed on through airs and improvisations until he heard a discreet cough in the doorway.

Neithon stood framed against the last twilight. Brys let the strings between his hands hold a fading memory of song. The trader eyed his guest with new interest.

"I wondered how she would sing."

"She's worth your weight in silver." Brys drew out a freshet of clear notes and saw Neithon smile at the tuning key pushed through his belt from habit.

"I paid nearly that for it." He eased in and sat on a chest. The brindled puppy trotted past him and flopped again on Brys's feet. "When I rode into Tara, the old man was finishing it for the king of Meath's harper. I couldn't buy it at any price. The belly wasn't lifted, the tuning wasn't settled, it belonged to another man." The Manxman spoke lightly but watched closely from the tail of his eye. "I told him it would sing high praise on the island of Britain. He changed his mind."

The Meathman could wait for another harp. Brys found ogham notches carved inside the oaken pillar, but his fingers couldn't read the Irish words in the wood alphabet. The small Latin lettering he could read by turning the harp over. *Tange canere, clamere percute.* Touch me to sing, to shout strike me.

"It's a good thing I decided beforehand," Brys said over the string arm. "I'd rather choose than be seduced."

"You'll do it." Neithon's dark eyes showed no surprise.

"I will."

Gwriad's request was simple. As Neithon recited it word for word, Brys recognized a trained memory. He was more than a trader, but so were many who had reason to travel by sea or land. He repeated names and places, whom to trust and where. The timing was good, a week before the Lammas feast and summer cattle fair.

Near midnight their talk ran dry. Brys settled the harp in its otterskin bag and turned to the door. He tossed Neithon's pouch of gold pieces and silver bars in one hand and dropped it down the front of his shirt. At a farm on the far bank of River Clwyd someone was out in the garth with a lantern. It bobbed and traveled among the fruit branches like a captive star. A boy was singing in English; some English farmed here and paid their tax not to Offa but to Brochfael.

Brys hesitated, then gave Neithon a message, should he encounter a freckled dark-haired girl chiming with silver: her sister worried about her daydreaming her way to Constantinople. He headed back through the dark to the tavern. The innkeeper, a kind soul, would fret until he returned. Then he would roar at him to stack another hundred or two gargantuan ale kegs in the cellar.

24 July 793 + The Waste Land

In the empty land east of Chester, a vixen lost her territory after a snarling scuffle with the strongest of her daughters. She limped toward sunrise through the heather, stopping now and again to whine and lick her torn shoulder. The hurt slowed her hunting. When a carrion scent reached her nostrils, she was hungry enough to brave the man reek clinging all around. Ravens lifted complaining from their feast in the bracken, already stinking and ripped open for her. She fed well for days, keeping badgers and most of the birds from her prize; the wolves were busy elsewhere in their run. Slowly she regained strength.

Playful as a cub one morning, she worried a scrap of crisp skin from a pouch at the dead man's belt. It lacked food taste and had bitter marks on one side, so she returned to tearing at easier meat and snarling at the bracken. A stealthy fierce shadow, she padded homeward one evening to redefine her boundaries.

In the wind from the old borderland, the folded parchment stirred and shivered. Bracken fronds screened it; two rains lashed the hillside before water smeared past reading the long-tailed English script.

25 July 793 + Tamworth

Leoba admired the new ring on her forefinger. So she might, thought Heilyn. It was a clean job, well cast and enamelled in Heilyn's best blue, yellow and red. While she turned her hand to catch the light and told him he was a rare jewel, he checked his payment carefully. She was quite capable of shorting anyone and thinking it a wonderful joke. So was Heilyn.

A scratch at her chamber door, and one of her girls slid in. She had some ungodly mess smeared on her face, and her unwashed blonde hair was showing brown at the roots. From Leoba's chambers Heilyn caught unwelcome glimpses behind the illusion of beauty.

"You're wanted at the palace," the whore announced. Leoba's brother in the kitchens must have gambled too much again. Heilyn kept counting over his silver pennies, but the girl walked up brazenly to prod him in the arm. "You deaf, foreigner? Get moving. He's waiting in the king's council room."

"Me?"

The girl rolled her eyes at Leoba — stupid *Wealh,* the look said — and sauntered away.

Heilyn forced himself to walk calmly, though his hopes lifted like thistledown, out through the half-empty tavern and through the grey afternoon to the palace compound. Someone had praised his skill, it seemed, someone appreciated fine work even in this viper's nest. A royal smith! He would have the best equipment, regular payment, living quarters among the court buildings. And a special request gave him leverage to bargain for the best of everything.

The doorkeeper passed him into the compound and pointed out the small building behind the great hall. Another doorkeeper, and he was in an antechamber. Maybe he should have brought samples of work? In the inner room, he froze with his hand still on the latch. The man who sat at the polished table was no clerk but the noble Brorda.

"You are Helm?"

"I am, yes, lord. That's me." *Babbling. Fool.*

"You have recently bought your freedom."

"My work is superb, lord. Strength in tools, edge in weapons, beauty in jewels —"

"No doubt," said Brorda, raising a hand. "I'm not interested in your metal work."

Heilyn stared in stunned disbelief. He gathered his wits and took a step back toward the door, but it had closed quietly behind him. "In that case, lord, there's some misunderstanding."

"No." The noble leaned on his chair arm and gazed out the window.

What in heaven's realm? Nothing he could remember. An occasional mutter about gilded English farts who thought they owned creation, but that wouldn't bring him before Offa's chief henchman.

"Have you been in Powys, Heilyn?"

"Never, lord, not in eighteen years. I have fifty witnesses who'll tell you I haven't left Tamworth in all that time." Heilyn started to sweat.

Brorda traced a finger along the oiled grain of the table. It was some black foreign wood. "So you've never been back to your family."

There was a bench. Heilyn sat down on it and clenched his hands between his knees. The pause was enough for him to realize that he wasn't accused of anything yet, and that Brorda had spoken, as he had unthinkingly answered, in his mother tongue. Brorda's accent was a strange mixture of constricted northern British and broad northern English — his great estates were in Elmesæte, they said — and he used old-fashioned words.

Heilyn cast through a number of plausible lies and regretfully settled on the truth. "My mother was taken in the wars with Gwent. I was born a year later. I wouldn't even know how to find them. Her people." Or bother trying. He would be as welcome as plague, a half-English manifestation of their kinswoman's defilement.

"Is she alive?"

"I don't know. I was sold away from her at seven." He had selfishly hated her with a child's helpless hatred: for not protecting her small frightened son, for being a weeping slave spreadeagled by every drunken freeman, for not being English. Since then he had learned too well the helplessness of one person alone against brutality. And he had learned that he had hated her much less than he had loved her, also helplessly.

Brorda only nodded. The questions went on. Heilyn, desperate to get out of this room past two doorkeepers and armed guards, answered. He talked about the old priest who taught him letters, he talked about the forge in Tamworth. Anything.

At last Offa's minister fell silent and considered him with a weary look that suggested neither of them enjoyed this performance. Heilyn measured the distance to the door and stared at his clenched hands; they slipped sweatily in each others' grasp. Hell swallow the palace smithy, the gold and jewels. He would never see them. Hope was fool's fare. He had deluded himself to think he could prosper here. Heilyn imagined a booming English belly-laugh at the boneless creature he was, and bile stung his throat. Bile, not salt.

"A smith can travel anywhere freely," Brorda said, returning to English. "I want you to go west. You'll have to listen carefully and make reports."

Each word fell like a lash as the noble talked on. So they didn't trust *Wealas* and couldn't slide a Mercian over the border. Anger mixed with terror brought color to Heilyn's sallow face. Offa's upright old noble thought he could buy half a man, no doubt at half the price. Was it the *Wealh* half he wanted to buy or the English half? *Simmer in hell,* he wished silently. *Why should I care if Wealas plot to overthrow Mercia? But why should I refuse the task? Or the gold? Not in deference to British dung lords with their high contempt for tainted blood.*

Brorda knew when to make music. Coins chimed as the noble spilled two pouches across the table. Silver for traveling. Gold on his return. Heilyn counted quickly. Enough to build a smithy and buy the finest gear, maybe a bellows slave. He heard his own stammered astonishment and hated himself and Brorda equally.

"I'm going to tell you about this man," said Brorda, moving gold pieces with one finger as though they were draftsmen.

His words squeezed a boil of resentment in Heilyn, making all of this fractionally easier. He managed a flicker of sarcasm when the noble finished. "And shall I deliver him back to you in silver chains?"

Brorda pursed his mouth. "Information will do."

"And if I —" He couldn't say refuse. " — would rather not do this?"

"What do you think?" Brorda looked at him balefully. Heilyn's imagination seethed. *Torture. Death by night.*

"Of course, great lord, it will be my very dearest pleasure." His only remaining defiance was to overplay his servile scraping.

Brorda fixed him with bleak blue eyes and got to his feet behind the table. He seemed about to speak again, then shook his head and stepped out into the room. Heilyn winced away from his outstretched hand as from a blow until he saw it held the smaller pouch. The gold's mellow radiance still flooded the polished surface. Its after-image lit the dim anteroom as Heilyn went out with the pouch held to his breast.

Brorda sat, head in hands, long after the outer door closed. He could have said, "I heard of your splendid work. We need another smith." In sheer despair he had nearly done it. He almost smiled in contemplation of the head smith's outrage. But he saw no humor in the thought of finding someone else to send west.

Leoba's girl from the north was clever. He trusted her more than a southerner, but her voice and face could betray her. This smith was unknown there, if he spoke one word of truth. Sweet Savior, a mixed-blood freed slave, alternately insolent and obsequious, and of bad character. Yet, merciful God, if his own children had been born slave, what would they be? Slaves were by nature slow-witted and coarse, folk said, but in Brorda's experience people were made dull by servility and want. Thank God the brightest and best men could buy freedom. Socrates had debated philosophy with a boy who plied an unspeakable trade in the public baths; Brorda could hire whom he pleased to spy. But he prayed for a clear road. Neither Helm nor Heilyn would stand up well to trouble.

Trouble reminded Brorda of the messenger from the Isle of Man, now overdue by a fortnight. How wide had Gwriad cast his net? Offa needed to know.

29 July 793 + Mathrafal

West in Mathrafal's broad valley, Heilyn shifted his heavy pack as he walked. The second hay crop was knee-high, and corn stood green or golden in square open fields. Farmsteads parcelled the valley, some solitary and some in scattered groups, unlike the strip fields and clustered houses of Mercian farms. Above, the wooded hills opened in places to wood-pasture where stock grazed.

They thatched their buildings with heather or bracken as well as wheaten straw, whitewashed their walls, planted fruit trees around the least hovel and called their hogs to slops the same as anyone else: so far this was the sum of Heilyn's knowledge about warlike Powys.

This morning he'd sweated for hours, it seemed, at Long Mountain gate. First the Mercian border guards muttered over Brorda's safe-passage parchment. A few paces west, the Powys border guards took cold interest in his English flattening of British speech. From a border town with Mercian allegiance, he lied, which made him one among thousands. Finally he walked into Powys with his belly roiling and his back crawling.

Now the main track had brought him to the south bank of a broad stream. He squinted into the low sun at the stronghold on the other bank. He saw timber and turf ramparts, men moving back and forth on some kind of catwalk, heavy gates, an overflow of houses and buildings outside the walls. All day he had wondered, where are all the people? The countryside seemed almost uninhabited except for the farmsteads clustered in broad fields, more pasture than cropland. Brorda had spoken of plague a hundred years ago and the endless wars. Still the land seemed empty compared with Mercia, and Mercia in turn seemed empty to traders he'd met from London and Quentavic. But finally he had come to something resembling a town to English eyes.

Another traveler told him it was Brochfael's main court of Mathrafal. He was disappointed, briefly, thinking that murderous Powys should have a capital bristling with warriors and defences. But when he passed into Mathrafal among a knot of countrymen, his worst fears sprang to life. A guard captain in a mail shirt and a gold bracelet leaned near the door of the gatekeeper's cubby. Yawning, he dropped a square-headed spear to bar Heilyn's way.

"What's in the pack?"

"Smith's tools." Heilyn looked at him sideways. "I can make any weapon you can imagine and make it better."

The captain motioned him to open it. By the time he'd spread all his samples and tools on the dusty cobblestones, seven or eight of them had crowded around to look. The king's guard, there could be no doubt. Their cloaks and shirts were brilliant colors, their ornament was gold and silver, their weapons were good, but most of all they shared the casual arrogance of Offa's bodyguard in Leoba's tavern. When they drifted off, he had a knife hilt to rivet and a sword to straighten. And he was still alive. Curiosity. It was just curiosity.

Next morning he shook dew out of his cloak in the chapel garth, wondering if the mound were a grave. Dead monks were unlikely to pilfer a smith's pack. At worst they made peaceful ghosts; Heilyn feared the dead less than the living.

Inside the west gate he made a small hearth, brought out his traveling anvil and set to work. He took a bucket rim to reshape, then a necklace with a broken clasp. The others — women with weaving, a salt merchant, a potter with rough grey cookware, a brother and sister with leather bottles, buyers, idlers in the gate's shadow — told him he would do better in a smaller place after Lammas fair in two days. Heilyn listened well, but most of their talk was dross. The information he needed wouldn't fall into his crucible. He would have to seek it out.

In the late afternoon, as he gathered his gear, an old woman creaked up with an ancient kettle. When he told her it was too rusted for any repair, she cursed him as Saxon scum. He packed and fled, a victory she announced loudly on all sides. Out the gate and down to the river, shaking like a poplar leaf. Stupid. He had forgotten that *Sais* was an all-purpose insult for every English nation and a throng of miscellaneous evils. Heilyn found a rock slab beside the river and stayed there hunched until he pulled himself together.

Banwy, this river was called. The low bank was churned where horses had been watered, now grazing again in the stable pasture upstream. Heilyn watched the brown water shelving over long rock grooves that looked as though they were shaped by giant claws. On the other bank two girls called their cows home. The air smelled of high summer — dust, tired vegetation, horses, food, offal — but a breeze dropped lightly down from the hills to wash it with the scent of forested heights and ripening crops. Peaceful. Strange. Did Brorda grasp that knowing the language was no promise of understanding *Wealas?*

Sais in Mathrafal. *Wealh* in Tamworth. Once he had dropped an ale jar on the old smith's clay floor. It had shattered into two neat halves as though to unmold the ale and not spill it, yet as carefully as he scoured the corners, a few pieces had flown beyond retrieval. Two halves never made a whole, neither in broken crockery nor in people.

First report from the west, never to be committed to parchment or messenger: *Brorda: To get information, first know your informer. But it's your gold. Soon mine.* This whole idea was unspeakably stupid, and only threats had brought him to it. The sooner he got this over, the sooner he could set up his own forge. A hanging bowl first, perhaps. Better still, a chalice. He could see it shining on the altar, a small gift. Awestruck admiration. Orders, more than he could fill . . .

Always supposing he found this sorcerer of Brorda's. Maybe he had silver eyes and rode with the wild hunt. Heilyn smiled despite himself, remembering his mother's hair-raising tales, and got up as the gates began to squeal shut in their pivot stones for the night.

Mathrafal had a tavern, he was happy to find. He sat gripping his wooden ale cup and feeling dangerously out of place.

"Offa can't hold the Saxons," someone at the next bench was saying. "Eventually someone will slit his throat while he sleeps."

"Offa dœsn't sleep. Demons attend him all night."

Heilyn took a swallow of ale to hide his mirth. *True. Demons like Brorda.*

"He's an old man. Even a tyrant loses his grip fast enough in a shroud."

"You just pray he lives to a hundred. It's a long swim to Ireland if the border gœs."

"What do you think?"

Silence. Faces turned to him. One of them was the potter from the west gate. What lies had he . . ? Heilyn clutched his ale cup in panic and scrabbled for the right answer — the right answer in Powys — and plunged into treason without a backward glance.

"He'll hold them all until he dies. Why not? He's murdered all the real opposition. Wessex is in fragments with the rightful heir in exile, Kent is a small kingdom backed against the sea, and Offa has a tame archbishop to do his bidding." He gripped his cup for dear life and waited for the accusation. How do you know, *Sais?* Then they would call the guard.

"You been over there?" the potter asked. He didn't seem to care much one way or the other.

"I was born there." Heilyn took a long shaky drink. "My mother said I'd find my way home."

His lie took on truth as he spoke. She had said that, back on the farthest shore of memory. This realization, her voice from behind a wall of silence, unnerved him even more than the question. The others nodded without comment, keeping their thoughts behind unreadable *Wealh* faces. Like his own.

A tap on his shoulder made him leap, and he glanced up at the redhaired guard captain.

"I have something to show you outside."

Another minor mending job, probably, but if it wouldn't make him rich it would at least give him cover. He drained his cup and shouldered his pack.

Darkness had fallen. Heilyn followed the guard captain nervously. In the thatch overhang of the king's hall, beyond the lantern glow at the door, stood a black-haired man. He was tall and tensely strung like a greyhound. Something about the eyes, Heilyn saw, and stopped dead. Silver eyes. No, they were palest grey or blue, the shrunken irises no darker than the whites.

"Lord Gellan, this is the smith." The captain grounded his spear in a salute and was gone.

"Can I serve you, lord?" Heilyn felt the hair prickling on the back of his neck. "A fine weapon? Repairs?"

"As Brochfael's commander, I wonder how you come to be riveting knife hilts in the court of Powys with the tools of an English smith."

Heilyn stepped backward, lifting one hand in an unfinished motion that could have turned a blow. He covered it by hoisting his smith's pack higher and began to explain. Spinning a moving tale of English injustice to a British slave, of buying his freedom, of seeking his mother's people, he took a liar's deep delight in the unassailable truth. But all the while Gellan's light eyes tracked him as an owl watches a mole.

"Your mother spoke well." The commander's face tightened in a smile of reassurance that did nothing to reassure Heilyn. "Smiths always prosper here. Will you stay in Mathrafal?"

"Maybe. Or I'll travel."

Gellan's eyes froze him. It wasn't enough of an answer. "Where?"

"South." Heilyn lied naturally and fluently. "Or west. Anywhere I can find trade, maybe set up a forge before winter." That should shield him in any direction, once he had finished asking here.

"God speed," Gellan wished him. "Is Cenwulf in the west?"

How in God's name should he know where Offa's executioner was? But didn't Cenwulf have lands near Shrewsbury? "Yes. Cenwulf is in the west."

Gellan blinked and turned away.

Heilyn took a long shaking breath and slipped out in the other direction, past Brochfael's great hall with torches hissing in their brackets by the door, between the garths and houses, back to the chapel garth's safety. Curled between a leaning wooden cross and the grassy earthwork base of the north rampart, he tried to sleep. Patience he had in plenty, slavery's best lesson. He lay in the dark, listening to the guards pace and turn on the timber catwalk. By morning he'd heard how much the women loved the guard captain's hairy onion and guessed how much this well-traveled topic bored his second.

In the small hours he had leisure to trace the sinuous paths of his own thoughts. The old smith in Tamworth pranced through his memory, the wine-sodden old goat. He'd sulked when Heilyn left. Time for another boy anyway. He could choose the next one for looks, if the price were right. Heilyn wrapped himself tighter in his dun cloak against a dawn rainfall and planned his forge. Not Tamworth. Maybe

Shrewsbury, where there were others with British faces and galls from English slave collars. But first he needed Brorda's gold.

31 July 793 + Mathrafal

A sea-eagle far from his estuaries swung broad circuits over the plain of Mathrafal. Sunset tufted him in copper and fired his pinions as he drew the land into his rising spiral: a net of streams, a green and golden gameboard of fields, hills crowned with five ancient fortresses. East toward Mercia the highest slopes were rounded in the benediction of amber light. The eagle cried out harshly and stooped into a wheat field. Beyond the rolling plowland lay a far cluster of buildings overhung with blue cooksmoke: Mathrafal.

Brys rode south on a Powys grey, a dark dapple stallion with silver mane and tail, and intelligent dark eyes in a chiselled head. Four gold pieces, a scandalous price even for the famous breed, still left gold and silver in Gwriad's pouch. As Brys rode he watched the shadows and kept his knife loose. It had been less trouble to own nothing worth stealing. The harp was bundled shapelessly behind him, and despite the warm evening, he wore a cloak with the hood pulled forward. His disguised arrival was borrowed from an old tale, amusing but necessary.

South of Meifod abbey the valley opened. Harvest crews were out in the winter barley, singing as they laid the sheaves, hurrying to finish by Lammas eve. He passed a herd boy driving steers into their enclosure. When Brys heard many horses behind, he reined to one side of the track. A handful of Brochfael's guard passed him at a canter, in a glitter of gold and gleaming hunting spears, with hawks gripping their embroidered gloves and groomed hounds loping ahead of the horses. Until his friends were around the bend and into the straight to Mathrafal, Brys kept his head down and held his breath.

Dusk dropped quickly. Brys forded River Efyrnwy and rode south through the river meadow to ford River Banwy. At the west gate a crowd of people were going in with their goods for tomorrow's Lammas fair. The night horn boomed, and the chapel struck compline on its bell of true-voiced bronze. Everywhere he saw the land's wealth, from the green river meadows to the golden hillside pastures sparked with poppies. A haven of abundance, Powys the garden.

At sunset Heilyn lost an argument with himself and headed for Brochfael's great hall. Between the crackling torches an ancient doorkeeper asked him for weapons, waved off the knife and pointed him inside. It was almost disappointingly easy, after he had devised an elaborate excuse to get in.

Heilyn sat close to the door. The hall overflowed, especially at the lower end where poor travelers sat with their packs shoved under the benches, eating their meat stacked on flatbread. Someone brought him food and a cup of bragget. Poor man's mead, ale mixed with honey, grumbled the bald man beside him, but Heilyn hadn't been drenched with enough mead to complain. The dais was above the pillars, half shadowed by an overhanging loft along one side; it was alive with talk and women's laughter. There were also women in the hall, both servants and guests. He drank, watching the high and mighty.

Brochfael must be the stone-faced grey man with the gold chain around his neck. They called the chain a *hual*, a fetter, as though it held a king in bondage to his people. Gellan sat smiling into a jeweled silver cup. Heilyn had no names for the others on the dais. A white-haired man whose cupbearer cradled a harp must be the king's pœt, the *pencerdd*. The old man kept his back half-turned to the king, which seemed dangerous manners. Another man, tall and broad, wore a gold diadem on his black-and-white streaked hair. A sub-king, maybe. In Mercia only thugs and sycophants survived Offa's assassins. What kind of men were these Powys nobles? Did they have imperial ambitions, or did that danger exist only in Brorda's imagination?

Soon the *pencerdd* took his harp and went forward to an ornately carved chair without arms. Even in the murky light the harp looked overdecorated with gold and garnets. The old man sang something Heilyn couldn't follow. He heard the name of Elisedd, Brochfael's father, and thought the song was praise of the rapacious last king's battles against Mercia. After one stanza Brochfael stood abruptly and went out through a guarded door at the back of the dais. A quarrel? If Brochfael had such contempt for the old man, why was he alive, let alone permitted to sing? As soon as he finished, the king returned to his great chair.

"How many will sing?" Heilyn asked his neighbor, the bald man who didn't like bragget. He wished he could get into the upper hall and hear what the high and mighty were saying. Maybe he could pry information out of the guard captain when he returned the sword. For now this was the best he could do.

"On Lammas eve they'll probably go half the night," the man said around a mouthful of bread. "Lots of travelers."

The door slammed behind them, giving Heilyn a start. A gust of summer air shivered the candle flames. Men reached for absent weapons as the old doorkeeper tottered in anxiously. Heilyn, annoyed to lose his conversation, saw a man in a hooded cloak pace slowly toward the dais. By the time he stepped up, he had every eye in the noisy hall. He took the empty harper's chair, pulled forward a harp from under his left arm and unclasped his cloak. All talk died. Brochfael looked stunned. The *pencerdd* was smiling. Heilyn sat forward. Whatever was happening, it looked interesting.

The harper launched into string song while the king was still deciding what to do. Heilyn, knowing nothing of music, knew that this music was masterful. Its complex flights of shining notes seemed too swift for the hands freeing them, too large for the small instrument. The harper himself was unremarkable, just another dark-haired young man in a crimson shirt. He finished the music on a crashing chord and started to talk.

"Where have I been? I've been a mole digging a great ditch. Dead and undead in an earth house at midsummer."

He spoke so quietly that Heilyn soon craned forward to catch every word. It was a performer's trick, he knew, but he didn't care. The words were unimportant, but the voice was beautiful; he wanted it to go on forever.

"Beer in a keg. A knife at the throat. A raven on blood." It was like a riddle. The list went on, and when they were chuckling the harper picked out a few lamenting notes and fell silent. "All of those things. What else?"

Someone called out, "You tell us, Penllyn."

Heilyn dropped his bragget cup.

Brys began to play again, softly at first. If Rhydion wanted ancestral victories, Elisedd with blood on his hands, he would hear them. He built phrase on layered phrase in the taut wire, then broke the music into jarring fragments. Heads lifted at the discord. Brys damped the strings with the flat of his hands and tilted the harp forward. Silence, then a hum of curiosity. These people knew him as Rhydion's student; he had sung in Brochfael's hall many times. Now he was shattering tradition and he would pay for it one way or another. The benches stirred, attentive and puzzled. He spoke quietly, making them lean for the words again.

"Whose graves are these, washed by rain, of men dying without deceit?"

A long wait, no answer. He heard wind fingering the thatch and gate guards calling at the rampart. "Ask me, I know."

"After the wound and the battlefield
And the wearing of armor and white stallions,
This is the grave of Cynddylan."

Cynddylan, and flame in the roof of Pengwern. Brys crashed a chord and pulled a bright scatter of notes from it, sun-shower from a thunderhead. He threw all his anger at the strings, making the metal sing like an abbot's bell. Wordless lament buffeted through his head and took the shape of words he'd heard Offa's pœt sing in Tamworth hall. The thick English came word for word, yet he altered Mercian victory to grief for Cynddylan and lost Tren. It boomed through Mathrafal hall, an invasion. They knew the sound of the English words if not the meaning. By the third alien stanza half the hall was shouting abuse. One man near the door had his face in his hands.

"Throw that shit the other side! Run back to Offa!" And one bellowed an English insult, "Halfwit!"

Some of the guard shouted back angrily; always at each others' throats, they tolerated no criticism from outsiders. Gellan sat among them, studying his hands. Cian was grinning. Laughter drifted down from the sun-chamber. Brys glanced up and saw the queen at the balustrade. Near him on the dais were half a dozen lords. Idris looked angry enough to strike him dead. Brochfael's half-brother Eli, wearing a sky-blue silk shirt and more gold than an altar at Easter mass, nodded gravely. Garmon Penllyn, who had once been his cousin, watched Brochfael.

Brys challenged the insults with the thunderous bronze strings. He threw music across the hall, higher and wilder, until he had silence. Lament beat great wings around the roof beams so the hall itself became his sound box. A last savage flourish, too hard against the tempered bronze above the sister strings. Wire strings, unfamiliar and razor sharp. Blood sprayed from his fingers onto the nearest faces, buying a hiss of shock. He finished righthanded in a minor echo, afraid to look at his hand or the blood-strung harp.

"I shall mourn until I enter steadfast earth, Cynddylan slain with his war host."

The old words fell quietly into the hall, not sung but spoken. They knew Cynddylan's lament well; no need to sing all nine stanzas. *Now, before Brochfael has me thrown out the doors, or nailed to them.*

"Cynddylan stood alone. Alone he attacked Gwynedd, the Cadelling in North Powys, Mercia, all the rest — and he triumphed." A murmur of agreement from the benches. *They like that, warlike Powys alone against all enemies.* "Now Powys stands alone again. Gwynedd is tearing itself apart cantref by cantref. Ceredigion is a nest of sea-raiders we could wipe out in a day. Manaw is half Irish. The south flows with Mercian silver. We have no kinship with these. Powys stands alone. Have you heard this?"

A few scattered voices broke through, then a wave of agreement. *Good.*

"Cynddylan also fell alone, without allies, and he brought down all Powys. One tree is not a forest. One man is not an army."

Puzzled glances. *Something new, unfamiliar and unwelcome.*

"Believe it, if you want. I did once." *No need to fight for silence now.* "Believe it, if you want your children to sing in English and wear rawhide collars. I wore one. Never again."

A murmur was traveling from bench to bench, something about ravens. One voice said clearly, "He flew it at them like a hawk —"

Offa's dyke. Someone's heard about my escape. Brys weighed its usefulness and let the talk travel for a minute. Somehow he was on his feet and the harp lay on its back beside the chair. The two guards at the dais door eased forward to lean unconcerned on their spears, and a handful from the off-duty wings came to stand with arms folded, watching the benches, as a self-appointed honor guard. They could turn against him in a moment. He was fighting fire with fire.

"I'll never wear rawhide again," he repeated. *Now.* "If Powys stands alone, Powys falls alone. Our next war will be our last war. There will never be another, we will be a subject territory of Mercia. Like cantref Tren — the English call it Wreocansæte. Even its name is taken. But we are not alone. We have fellow-countrymen, British allies, all the Cymry."

He looked around and saw doubtful expressions. Confusion. Women lined the sun-chamber balustrade; Adwen the queen was silent. At her elbow, Brochfael's little granddaughter Nest grinned down at him like a squirrel.

"Do I sing war?" he asked the hall, every face turned to him. *No answer. They're cautious now, too many surprises.* "No. What has war given Powys? Terrible enemies. Blood on the face of our fields. Rawhide to bind us in foreign slavery. So I sing peace and prosperity, cattle in barns, sheaves on the threshing floor, honey in the comb. War won't give us this. Alliance will. We need alliance between Powys, Gwynedd, Manaw, others if they choose. We need alliance for trade and unrestricted travel, for prosperity, for peace. There will be a council at midsummer next year. The choice of peace and alliance lies next summer, with Brochfael Powys."

No one moved. People were uncertain, brought down cold. His hand, still leaking a dark spatter onto the dais boards, had begun to sting. No gifts from the hall benches, no praise, and just the first stir of understanding. *First move. Now to see if it sweeps the board.* No alliance existed, not yet — his task for Gwriad was to create one.

Hardest of all was turning to face Brochfael's dangerous mask and Rhydion's black amusement. He bowed and stepped down. Tomorrow, maybe the day after, he would ask to see Brochfael. Give him time to cool. He slung the harp behind him and walked toward the door. A few hands reached out to him, as though he had some charmed protection they could share. He touched them, the least he could do after using an audience so shamelessly. No one barred his way. And no one else would sing in this hall tonight.

Out past the torches, on the forecourt paving stones, he paused to look at his treble hand and saw only neat slices across three finger pads. It felt worse. He took a deep breath. *Weightless, I can lift on a breath of wind and fly like dandelion silk to the star fortress. Rooted in earth, head above the most distant spear of light, body of sea and sky and land.* Ritual words surfaced in his mind. *I was in many shapes before I was released. I was rain in the air, I was the beam of stars, I was a spark in fire. There is nothing which I have not been.* The voice of *awen* roared and tumbled through his head like a river in darkness.

Some time later, not quite sure how he got there, he found the inn outside the gates. He claimed a pallet among the muttering and farts of other travelers, and swept under the raven wing of sleep.

1 August 793 + Mathrafal

The first morning sun and the message arrived together at the inn. Brys accepted the wax tablet in the shabby upper room. As the innkeeper shuffled off, he read it quickly.

"To my cousin Cynfarch, greetings," it began in elegant Latin. *Suddenly everyone remembers I'm a cousin.* The message invited him to a feast honoring the birth of a son after four daughters. The signature was Eli Elfæl.

Brilliant luck. Even if Brochfael stayed angry forever, Brys could still persuade Powys lords to steer the king toward Gwriad's proposal, and this was one way to do it. Eli was the power in South Powys.

Brys would have to tread carefully; Eli mab Elisedd Powys was everything his half-brother Brochfael was not. Some voices in Mathrafal muttered that, despite his illegitimate birth to a woman of the South Powys house, Eli was his father's true heir, not Brochfael.

When Brys arrived at dusk Eli's Mathrafal house was alive with talk, sweet southern mead and early torchlight. It was a small glittering court within Brochfael's own court. Eli, with his newborn heir in the crook of one arm, threw the other arm across Brys's shoulder to bring him inside.

"Cynfarch, you astonished us last night. You shook Mathrafal hall to its cornerstones. An amazing performance."

Brys had no time to reply. Eli's pretty wife took the child and slipped into another chamber, and Elfæl was captured in talk. Friends from the king's bodyguard found him then. They hadn't seen him for months. Brys, fending their questions and good-natured jostling, watched this southern cousin charm his guests.

Eli had striking eyes, blue as a robin's egg, rimmed in white like the eyes of an eastern icon. When he spoke he looked people full in the face, giving his words the weight of truth. He was like something from an older Powys with his golden hair and moustache, his sky-blue shirt embroidered in gold thread, his open hand, his good humor, his love of tradition. Brys smiled to see he wore a golden torc, a fragment of the hero tales worn as casually as a ring. It even had snarling boars at its front opening like his ancestor Cynddylan's.

Eli kept Brys at his right hand when they sat for the meal. After the new son was well toasted he drank to his kinsman Cynfarch, who would be remembered for song for a thousand years. Brys managed a straight face and a graceful answer. Praise was headier than heather mead but likewise not to be swallowed in quantity.

Eli's splendid hospitality brought back half-forgotten days in Penllyn. The chamber blazed with scores of beeswax candles, more than the chapel used in a month, and the candlelight flowed like honey on Eli's gold torc. Around him Brys heard pure Latin with the Irish lilt, women's rich laughter, the mellifluous accents of South Powys. When the candles were spitting in their sockets, a handful of his old guard wing tried to lure him off to a tavern.

Eli put a hand on Brys's shoulder and asked him to stay. "Just the family."

Family. It meant everything to one who grew up without kin in kin-bound Powys. Brys looked down into his glass. The mead surface shimmered dangerously.

When the guests were gone, Eli's wife returned with the baby yawning like a kitten in her arms, and Elfæl's harper Bleddri picked out idle runs in the Lydian mode. He was another southerner, a fair man with grey eyes and broad cheekbones; he had questions about the tuning of the sea-cat harp. Brys settled on a cushioned couch, content. It was civilized. It was a long way from Offa's dyke and the tavern in Rhuddlan and Brochfael's cold rage.

Many in Powys saw Brochfael's discipline as arrogance, his empty treasury as meanness, his pain over his country as anger. Brochfael could use more of his father's flamboyance. He hadn't always been so well controlled, though. Most people had forgotten Elisedd's hotheaded heir Brochfael who strangled a wolf barehanded to test an old song's truth, who gambled an estate on one night with a woman and paid another in penitence, who dropped out of the hills onto Mercia in raids like hammer blows. Now they saw only a wintry king who gave hostages to Offa. Brochfael, as Brys was not alone in thinking, needed to be more like Eli.

Eli poured his mead glass full and asked to know everything about Gwriad's plans. That was exactly what Brys had come to say.

"Easily told." Brys described provision for trade and travel, exchange of manuscripts and artisans, everything he'd talked about with Neithon. "It will take time."

"Everything worth doing takes time," Eli smiled. "But I thought you would go more softly with my brother, after . . . "

After he gave me to Offa as something of no worth? Eli was too diplomatic to say more. Bleddri suddenly found that his sister strings needed retuning. Smoothing over the awkward moment, Eli's dark-eyed wife smiled and handed Brys the child, blue-eyed with a halo of fine golden hair. The baby snuggled deeper into the bend of his elbow, turning his head to suck at Brys's finger when he stroked one soft cheek. The child's slight burden brought back a pang; the last baby he had held was his brother's little daughter. A month later she lay in a new grave, dead of the same FEVER that killed her brother. To have a child lie in your arms trusting and warm one day, cold the next . . . Brys had not visited since. The silence was too painful, like everything else between him and his brother.

"I'll see if Brochfael will hear reason on it," Eli offered unasked, though Brys had been prepared to persuade him. "But we rarely talk. I won't be able to speak openly. A word here and there to various lords."

Brys nodded thanks and drained his glass. He had what he wanted. Time to go. "A long life, a long line."

Eli smiled and said, "Penllyn and Elfæl have interests in common, Cynfarch. Remember Elfæl stood with Penllyn before your father's death. Garmon dœsn't value kinship so highly."

Brys nodded, wondering what he meant. *My father and his cousin Eli Elfæl were friends? I didn't know that.* He would ask his brother sometime. But his brother had no patience with prying into the past.

"Peace and prosperity," Bleddri said over his string arm, "and if ever again we face attack, a gathering point for a war host."

Eli's face tightened as though someone had struck him. Bleddri shrugged. He'd spoken his mind, and who could deny his logic? Brys had said the same thing to Neithon. Others would say it, too, sooner or later.

Eli reprimanded his pœt. "Murmur about war, even think about war, and Offa will be over the border like a grassfire. That will put an end to alliance of any kind."

"Alliance of the kind Gwriad wants can give us true strength, far more than strength in arms. In a perfect world, I suppose we wouldn't need either." Brys got to his feet, feeling the warm glow of just enough mead.

Eli also rose and intercepted a sleepy child wandering out from a dark chamber. He picked her up, a girl of eight or nine with honey-colored hair tangled from its pigtails. One of the four daughters. She fell asleep again on her father's shoulder. Brys, again struck by sudden grief, remembered a honey-haired girl riding a white mare. A bruised face and finery beyond her years. Not much older than this child. He had thought of her many times. He couldn't bear to think of her now.

"Powys can no longer stand alone. We've been living in the past," Eli said in the garth, quietly not to wake the child. Something was in flower nearby, perfuming the summer dark. "Cynfarch, think how it could be. Harpers traveling from Armorica, Ireland, all the kingdoms. Copyists from the right hand and left hand of Britain working in Meifod scriptorium. Builders and glazers from the English lands. Merchants from Arabia, jewelers from Constantinople." Ruefully he shook his head. "Maybe some day. We can have our dreams. But, dear God, first let us have lasting peace."

Brys studied him in the guttering torchlight. Eli's tastes had always run more to heroic song cycles than to psalms. Elfæl read his expression.

"We may see war again, I never deny it. But peace is better. If this alliance can make Powys great once again, I'll back it."

Brys walked back through the quiet palace precinct, smiling a little. Cousin Eli, with his gold torc and his lavish hospitality, wanted to be Cynddylan the Fair in an age of herœs. Instead he was a minor noble in a duller century, the king's bastard brother. Brys felt troubled that he couldn't like Eli as much as Eli seemed to like everyone around him, especially family. Maybe when he knew Eli better.

Silken darkness lapped him with a scent of roses and the distant river. Past halls and outbuildings, granaries on vermin-shielded pilings, bath-house and chapel and well, Brys found his way toward the inn by broken moonlight. It was late. Even the door torches at the king's hall had burned down to blackened stubs.

Near the hall gate, four men moved out of shadow to cross his path with spears. Another four eased in behind, all silently. His first thought was of assassins; his only weapon was his knife. But all were friends, men of Brochfael's guard. There was no threat, but there was also no escape. The spears parted ahead, and an impersonal hand fell on his shoulder. The captain told him that he was detained at Brochfael's order.

2 August 793 + Meifod

Heilyn walked two miles northeast in the broad valley at first light, out to Meifod abbey where the Powys kings were buried. He sat among the carved oaken memorial pillars to think undisturbed. Finally he pulled out his writing materials. He reckoned it was about three hours' walk to the border. The pass stamped with Brorda's seal should convince the border garrison to send this on to Leoba in Tamworth; she would pass it on to Brorda. If they didn't like the pass, that was Brorda's hard luck.

"Saw him in M," Heilyn chewed his quill ragged as he described the rabble-rousing in Mathrafal hall. He ended, "Cause for alarm. Helm."

That night Heilyn found no trace of Gwriad's puppet in the hall, but they were talking about him in the ale house. They spoke of him not as a troublemaker and a disgraced student, but as a great noble's son who had been cruelly betrayed. They couldn't see that he was dangerous, provoking Brochfael's wrath for his own ends. In fact they crowed over Brochfael's discomfiture. It made no sense. But he supposed it did make a good story.

"With these eyes I saw it," an old man with a south British voice was maundering, well in his cups. "He calls his raven down by name and he sings a stillness on us. We can't move a hair, slave nor master. He helps himself to this fine red stallion of the master's and he rides away west with a raven sitting on each shoulder. And Brochfael, bless the name, raises blisters on Offa over it and buys us all but the English."

"Sure he didn't turn into a raven himself and fly away?"

Laughter. The old man took solace in his ale.

Heilyn sat gripping his wooden cup and itching to ask, Where is he now? But the old man left, either sulking or avoiding closer questions about his ludicrous story. Ravens. They'd believe anything. He settled the road dust with more ale, rolled off to the chapel garth, and thought about gold pieces until he fell asleep.

4 August 793 + Mathrafal

Days were segmented not by bells for matins and lauds and the other offices but by the doorkeeper's tread on his plank floor. The planks were also the ceiling of a prison cell not much larger than a coffin. Nights were quieter after Lammas fair, when people had taken their goods and driven their livestock home.

Earthen walls, earthen floor. A faint glow that could be torchlight or daylight filtered between the ceiling planks of the cell beneath the doorkeeper's station. Every day he seized the dry bread shoved through the trap door, depriving the predatory rats and scrabbling insects that shared his darkness. A prisoner again. At least Offa had provided a dry bed.

The first night Brys endured until dawn, waiting to be dragged to execution and dark burial. No one would ransom him, that was certain. Fear of death mocked his sanctuary training and wove grotesque tapestries on the unseen earthen walls. Shame flooded out his fear. Gwriad had overestimated an unmade pœt; he had failed before he had rightly begun. Brys hadn't grasped the depth of Brochfael's wrath, a mistake he would make once only. But why couldn't the king see the need for strong links with other British nations? Anger gave him something to gnaw on. He decided to leave.

The second night, after the day's clatter dwindled overhead, he tested the plank trap-door. It creaked ominously, but he inched it aside and stared up blinking into the dim porch of the doorkeeper's house. A guard sat against a roof post, nodding over his spear. Brys slid past him, quiet on his feet as a hunter, out through the dark hall garth and to the barred west gate. He crouched in shadow in the chapel garth until the watch paced off toward the south corner, then eased up the guardhouse stair and dropped over the rampart palisade to freedom.

Freedom ended among the houses outside the walls when the duty guard caught up with him. His old wing captain Pol had the watch tonight; as they walked back into the court he told Brys a complicated joke about three nuns and a fishing net. Pol spoke with the Armorican accent, slurring the words at the front of his mouth. A dark blade-faced man, he had hired out his sword in some Italian war against Frankia before he drifted to Brochfael's guard. At the gatehouse Pol apologized and strong-armed Brys back into the earthen cell. Kneeling in the dark again, he heard something heavy dragged over the trap-door, then Pol rebuking the doorkeeper and guard.

Brys passed a third weary day working on memory exercises. When he came to the triads on Iâl, he lost his concentration. *Meirwen. Where has she gone? Dœs her sister know yet? Why do I care anyway? Maybe I can still help her — that's all it is. Nothing more.* In Mathrafal he had a girl, one of the queen's weavers, with hair like river gold; she was sweet-natured, small and of good family. She could hold his interest for about an hour. Only one girl held his interest from one year to the next: a freckled girl with a mouth full of thorns, rough-handed from menial work and her silver skill, taller than him if he admitted it, who stole horses. His horse, the first time, when they were still children. Then they had ridden by night across the border, dodging a Mercian patrol. Meirwen led, laughing at the danger. *Where is she now?* He hadn't really expected her to be waiting for him always in Tregeiriog — she had her own life — but where? Brys pounded his fist on the wall in frustration. When he slept, his dreams were a torment of silver and thorns.

Dawn brought more noise overhead and an argument.

"All right, leave him there. You've seen how the king rewards disobedience." It was a clear light voice, familiar and unfamiliar.

"Disobedience?" The doorkeeper, aggrieved, defended his territory. "Brochfael imprisons him, and you want me to believe he sends you to free him? I have my orders."

"Now you have new orders." Triumph with a leavening of laughter. "You recognize the king's seal."

Crouching beneath them in the dark, Brys strained for every word. Who was it? The voice was familiar but changed somehow. Someone who could lay hands on the king's seal, someone who could help him escape. But by daylight?

"This isn't a trick?" The doorkeeper was anxious to please and equally anxious to cover his backside. "I've heard about your pranks."

"If you've heard anything at all, you know you can trust me. Help me move the chest, Tegwy."

Brys relaxed. Of course he knew the voice, though it had dropped an octave in the last few months. Only one person could strike that chord of imperiousness, audacity and laughter. *Cyngen.* Where Tegwy went, you could always find Brochfael's grandson Cyngen.

Thunder on the planks. The trap-door disappeared in a blaze of daylight.

"I'm disappointed in you," said Cyngen. Out of the brilliance a hand reached down to pull Brys up. "I thought you would have shifted shape by now and walked out."

"Easily disappointed." Brys blinked and stumbled across to sit on the chest. "I shifted shape three times as an ant, a mole and a wren. Each time the rats nearly ate me alive. Your grandfather should feed them better."

Brys scrubbed his face in his hands, shook his wits clear of cobwebs and squinted until he could see the porch. Brochfael's fair cupbearer Tegwy was grinning at his foster brother's triumph. Cyngen, grey-eyed and brown-haired like all his house, nodded in satisfaction. At fourteen, an adult at his last birthday, he was already tall and big-boned like his grandfather; no one ever compared him to his unfortunate father Cadell, who was rarely seen at court. When Brys first arrived in Mathrafal Cyngen, a fearless six-year-old, had claimed him as an ally. Usually Brys was the one extricating Cyngen from some predicament while Brochfael turned a blind eye. They went out of the guardhouse, leaving the doorkeeper shaking his head doubtfully.

"Sorry it took three days," Cyngen said on the way to Brochfael's living quarters, Brys's home for many years. "I didn't know until you escaped. Then it took some persuasion."

"How?"

Cyngen only grinned. Brys was too bemused to argue. They passed between the old apple trees and into the arbor, where a few clusters of small tart grapes were ripening on the vines. As they walked through the lattice of apple light, Brys took in the garden smell of high summer, his season. Even here he heard the filtered murmur of the rivers' three monologues.

A guard grounded his spear and opened the heavy wooden door. Inside, in the honey scent of beeswax, Adwen came forward with a finger marking her place in a book. The looms were silent overhead in the sun chamber, unusual at this hour. The queen had sent her weavers and spinners and embroiderers away. Brys counted — today must be the seventh of August. Today he had lived twenty-one years.

In her violet dress Adwen was slender and straight as a girl, though her hair was silver. She had raised her own children until they were fostered, then her grandchildren Cyngen and Nest after their mother divorced Cadell to enter a monastery. She had been good to Brys, wisely not trying to replace his dead mother. Now she had two or three other small souls in hand. Adwen ruled her own realm of orphaned cousins and children bought from slavery; in subtler ways she also steered Powys.

"Mother Adwen." Brys dropped to one knee, avoiding his foster mother's deep blue eyes.

"How pleasant to know that you are alive, Cynfarch."

"I should have sent a message."

"Indeed." Adwen looked mildly from Cyngen to Tegwy to Brys. The mildness was deceptive. "You do love trouble. Keep your distance until you smell better. A bath is poured in the next room."

Brys found it scented but unheated. He folded into it gasping. Adwen could always make her point without wasting words. He scrubbed, swearing at the cold, and washed his hair. Tegwy shaved him with Brochfael's razor after he got out and sat rubbing goosebumps with a towel.

"Out," Cyngen said abruptly. Brys looked over his shoulder to see Nest at the door chewing the end of her braid. "Don't do that, you'll go bald."

"So?" Nest was headstrong at eleven, taking life by storm like her brother. She was brown-haired, and though kings' granddaughters were expected to have milky skin, she was brown from the summer sun. Adwen's beliefs about healthy children didn't produce girls like wilting flowers.

Brys returned to the queen wearing clothes from the saddlebags he'd left at the inn. Adwen, smiling as demurely as a cat, kissed him on both cheeks. Tegwy and Cyngen went outside, dragging Nest by the hand. Nest chose to obey only Adwen and Cyngen and, when she felt like it, Brys. She obeyed her nursemaid only under duress.

Brys ate bread and cheese in silence while Adwen watched, then stood to go. Whatever was happening, he wouldn't find out by asking Adwen. She walked him to the door.

"They're waiting for you in the library," said the queen of Powys. "Your foster father is extremely angry."

"Surely not."

"Save your sarcasm for the string arm, Cynfarch," she said, halting in a swirl of violet skirts. "And whatever happens now, kindly remember that you do have a family, although we are not as entertaining as your cousin Eli."

Brys took his leave, enlightened. Now at least he knew his crime: an evening celebrating Eli's heir, quiet conversation, civilized company. He turned into the colonnade where trailing honeysuckle dappled the morning light on the plaster walls. A woman was singing a plaintive ballad in one of the farther courtyards.

Near the council chamber, a guard came to walk him past the living quarters to the book room; he grounded his spear and disappeared smartly. Brys walked in.

Brochfael sat at the big table where clerks compiled their tax rolls. He was not alone. Brys saw also Idris Meirionydd, Gellan the war commander, Brochfael's sister the abbess Anghenell ferch Elisedd Powys, Rhydion bardd Brochfael, and at the end of the table, stout grey Garmon Penllyn. All glowed in bright linen and silk, all but Gellan wore gold diadems, and all sat as still as the carved statues in Meifod church. *Fair god, I'm on trial.* Brys kneeled and bowed his head.

"Get up," Brochfael told him. His hands were folded in front of him, and he was motionless except for an irregular tic beside his mouth. He let Brys sweat for a while before he said, "I can tolerate your ill manners in singing uninvited in my hall. Your manners are not of interest here. But I do not tolerate open treason. From anyone."

Brys waited. It was not the time to speak out of turn.

"If I wanted to join Gwriad in his fool's paradise I'd have told him so at Tregeiriog," Brochfael went on. "We alread*y* trade with Manaw and Gwynedd. We don't need to provoke a dangerous enemy by carving it in stone."

"I judged otherwise."

"You will judge, Cynfarch," Brochfael said icily, "as I instruct you."

"Uphold the glorious pride of our battle-honored nation?" Brys managed a fair imitation of Rhydion's sonorous hall voice. "If you want a war, there's the declaration."

Brochfael's right fist closed and opened on the table. "You dare to set policy for me? We're balanced on the sword's edge with Mercia, Caradog's slack hand on his nobles could fragment Gwynedd, and you come here singing sedition to my face."

Gellan spoke quietly, with his pale eyes on Brys. "Sedition in an older man. Cynfarch means well but he lacks experience. I know him well, lord. I want him back in the guard. I give you my surety for his loyalty."

Interesting. I'd have sworn Gellan would argue for swift execution.

Brochfael shot his commander a look that should have charred him to ashes. Garmon smiled poisonously at his hands on the table. Garmon had not spoken to Brys, had not even been in close proximity, for eight years.

Idris spoke next. "Clever, Cynfarch. I admired the performance. What did you plan for your next song? Raising the hall to march on Tamworth? I've heard more plausible calls for peace on the battle line."

Then it was Rhydion's turn. Nodding to himself, perhaps lost in the bloody campaigns of his youth, Elisedd's pœt had never fully become Brochfael mab Elisedd's pœt. In the last year his white hair was thinner, and he had spots of pigment on the backs of his hands.

"Explain this warlike intent," Rhydion demanded, looking up over his steepled fingers, much as he would say, Give me three variations in the Æolian mode and analyze each mathematically.

"Powys loves courage and eloquence." Brys was glad of the question, despite his teacher's half-smile which promised him no good. "She hates the colorless and clumsy. I tried for brilliance and a challenge."

"A challenge?" Brochfael repeated. "God my judge, our lives hang by a thread for nine years and you offer a challenge? God knows we need allies . . ." He hesitated too long by a breath.

"So you support Gwriad's idea. You support an alliance of the Cymry," Brys said, taking his opening. When he saw Rhydion's frown, he realized his hands had strayed into his belt and he was rocking on his heels. *Too late.* He didn't stop.

"Support?" Brochfael leaped to his feet. His heavy chair fell back against the shelves full of tax rolls, knocking some to the floor. He pounded the table with a fist. "Support open hostilities with an English warlord, the bloodiest in a hundred years? Support the downfall of Powys? Isn't it enough that your father tried —" He stopped abruptly.

Idris shook his head slowly. Brochfael was white-faced and pinched around the mouth. Rhydion rested his chin on his hands. Anghenell arched one brow and examined a ruby ring on her finger. Garmon, who had been his cousin, shifted weight uncomfortably in his chair. Gellan looked out the window.

"Do you support alliance, Brochfael?" Anghenell folded her hands inside her embroidered blue sleeves. "It's a fair question. You threw Cynfarch in jail for asking, but I'd still like an answer." Anghenell loved debate next to God. She ran her abbey like a warrior queen, they said, but the nuns and monks went about their work smiling. Some called her a saint.

Brochfael glowered at his sister and sat down. "You think well enough of yourself to make my decisions, Cynfarch. Now tell me my options."

"Lord," Brys said. "You can have me beheaded within an hour. Gwriad will send another to say the same thing, if there's enough time. You can ignore all this and try to let the rumors wear themselves out. They won't. Or you can tell your hall tonight that Powys will speak for open trade and peace at the council next midsummer."

"Where?"

"Powys. Unless you'd rather give the honor to Gwynedd."

"Fair and holy God, Cynfarch, don't push me." He turned. "Meirionydd?"

Idris, who had leaned back in his chair and crossed his legs, picked up one of the tax scrolls and tapped it against his boot. Bland as butter, he raised his barrel shoulders. "Who argues against peace?"

"Lady abbess?"

"Your priest should set Cynfarch a penitence for overweening pride. Apart from that —" If Anghenell thought she looked severe, she was mistaken. Unlike her brother, she had a face shaped by fifty years of laughter. " — I fear he has you in the badger bag and has thrown it to a dozen nobles. Of course, you can manage them one way or another."

"Let Offa control his sub-kings by hunting them at each other," Brochfael said sullenly. "I won't play tyrant in Powys."

"Powys isn't governed by delay and doubt," Brys said, impatient with this. *If it's execution, get on with it.* "Since you choose negotiation over war, it's on you to persuade them. For this purpose some kings maintain a pœt." Rhydion smiled ominously at the table top. It did not augur well for his student at their next meeting, if there were to be one. Brochfael got up and began to pace the room with one hand hooked in his *hual,* a gesture he used when the chain weighed heaviest on his neck.

Gellan repeated his words. "'Gwriad will send another to say the same thing, if there's enough time,' Cynfarch?"

"In Mercia I heard —"

Brochfael spun around at the speed of thought and caught Brys by the shoulder in an iron grip. "Be silent."

"We should hear this," said Gellan.

"Hear what the English say?" The king's fingers pried to the bone. Idris looked uneasily from one to another of them, king and commander and troublemaker. "Hear lies to create dissent in Powys?"

Gellan hunched his shoulders in a terse shrug of indifference, but anger wheeled and pivoted behind his expression. He was no man for negotiation.

"If you say more you will die," Brochfael told Brys quietly. "Is that clear?"

Brys nodded and forced himself to hold that iron gaze. It shook him, the most naked threat in eight hard years. Before the king lifted his vise grip, Brys felt him shaking with contained fury.

"I will speak on the wisdom of Gwriad's alliance tonight. And you will say whatever he sent you to say. But I can do nothing more to protect you now."

Brys watched him take his chair and fought the knot in his throat. He had hoped, foolishly, that Brochfael might agree with a high heart and welcome him home, but Brochfael loved only justice and his own vision of Powys. Nothing had changed. Nothing would change.

"Rhydion." Brochfael gave the man as much cold respect as was necessary, knowing a *pencerdd*'s terrible power. "You have more questions?"

"I have." His voice was edged, and he was smiling unpleasantly again. "Come here, boy."

Brys went to him, hackles up at the condescension, even from one with three times his years. That was calculated. He kneeled at his teacher's feet, and Rhydion placed a hand on each shoulder. Brys felt their palsy of anger.

"Tell me the condition and obligation of a student."

His belly clenched. The *pencerdd* was not a court officer but stood above the court. And he could break his student forever. Brys knew the risk at Rhuddlan and consented. That didn't make it easier now.

"A student learns and serves his teacher for twelve years."

"Haste, always haste. You take eight years, and without waiting to graduate in song, you serve a man who will have his way at any cost. Why do this when it robs you of graduation?"

Brys hoped Rhydion couldn't read his sickness. "This is more important. Not next year. Now."

"Tell me the condition and obligation of a *pencerdd*."

Wicked old man, his face had arrogance trapped in its folds and traceries. Brys said, "It would be more fitting for you to tell me."

Rhydion gave a ghost's dry husk of laughter. His breath stank of a bad stomach. "Even your deference reeks of pride. I could graduate you right now. What would you say?"

"At what price?" *Cruel. This is an ugly game.*

Elisedd's pœt smiled slowly, eyes half-lidded like an adder's. He reached for Brys's treble hand and felt the fingertips. "They're saying you made the harp shed its bright blood. I think it was yours."

"Yes." Treble bronze, pulled taut from string arm to sounding board, cut like a knife.

"Clumsy, Cynfarch. It could not have happened had you played properly."

Rhydion slapped him hard on each cheek. The blows carried all the spite of a man who had labored long over a wilful student, only to see his efforts thrown to the wind. Brys got to his feet and faced Brochfael. Idris was reading a tax scroll, maybe his own by his distressed look. Anghenell and Gellan had gone without Brys noticing, also Garmon, who had conveyed his contempt without speaking one word. The ballad-singer outside had resumed her song. The king gazed out the open window with an expression Brys didn't recognize. In anyone else it might have been grief. Idris cleared his throat.

Brochfael turned to him, frowning. "You may go, Cynfarch."

Brys stood his ground, words wedged in his throat. "My loyalty is to you. To Powys."

As he spoke he wondered if Brochfael believed that. Would he believe it if he were Brochfael? Brochfael studied him for a long minute and nodded.

"What did my father do?"

Brochfael faced the window again, locked in his frozen anger. Idris let the parchment roll shut with a snap.

"He died at the wrong time," Rhydion said.

And? No one said anything else, though he waited. Without a word he was dismissed. The trial, if it had been a trial, was over.

Brys went out into the colonnade, fragrant with honeysuckle, and headed for a place by the river. After years in Mathrafal he knew all the places for thinking quietly. Or for hiding.

7 August 793 + Tamworth

The piper puffed his airbag full, and the dancers found sets. Offa, sitting in his great chair in the shade of a canvas fly, watched with an expression he doubtless thought was benevolent as Egfrith and his new bride led their guests in the dance.

Brorda thoughtfully folded the messenger's parchment and pocketed it. At this moment he didn't see the Tamworth palace green with its flags and streamers and dancers in their brightest clothes, or hear the squealing bagpipes and rattling tambours. He saw instead one steading among scores he had burned and seen burned. Thirty years ago, maybe more, somewhere on the Hwicce borderland. He and Offa and their ragged levies arrived to find the house pillars still smoking and ripe wheat smouldering in the fields. No people, no bodies. Given word of Offa's approach, the British farmers had torched their own houses and barns and standing crops. At the field margin a light west wind stirred ranks of crimson poppies, brighter than the sullen flames. He was a young man then, unnerved by people who wilfully and needlessly destroyed their own sustenance. Now he had the same sense, after nine years of peace. There was, as the smith wrote, cause for fear.

"Are you well, lord?" whispered Offa's steward, pouring him mead.

"Yes." Brorda realized he had been scowling at the dancers when he should be smiling and drinking toasts like a guest at a wedding feast. Offa was now leaning on the arm of his chair playing a deadly game with his sub-king Athelbert of East Anglia, who was talking about his nobles' demands for greater independence from Mercia. Offa, grinning like a wolf, stabbed his points home with a forefinger. Offa's queen Cynethryth, still comely despite her plain garments and veil, watched apprehensively amidst her usual coterie of churchwomen. Brorda knew she had suggested Athelbet as a husband for one of her younger daughters. He wondered if the East Anglian king knew his present danger.

He watched Egfrith and hoped there would be more love in his marriage than in his father's. Offa tried to command his quiet son, a wise young man after a few wild years, who endured his father's trespasses with a grace Offa mistook for weakness. Brorda could only guess what Egfrith thought of his father's first attempt to find him a bride.

The Frankish marriage fiasco had started innocently like most of Offa's violent confrontations. Four years ago Charles had suggested that his son should marry Offa's daughter. Offa agreed, but only if his son Egfrith wed Charles's daughter. Charles took offence at this horse trading, perhaps reading all too clearly his peer's broadening ambitions. He withdrew his envoys and closed Frankish ports to English trade. Egbert, the dispossessed West Saxon heir, must have laughed heartily in his comfortable Frankish exile. Egfrith Offason, in the eye of this storm, kept his own counsel. Maybe he was relieved to marry an English girl today. Her veil had flown back in the dancing; she had thick blonde braids looped over her ears and a sweet smile. Brorda raised his horn in a silent toast and drank.

The music brayed to a halt and the dancers scattered laughing. Cenwulf escorted Offa's daughter Eadburh into the shade. A striking pair. Cenwulf was ashen fair and handsome in a way that drew women; Eadburh was reddish fair and aquiline, with looks and height inherited from her mother Cynethryth, certainly not from Offa. Cenwulf leaned attentively, smiling into her eyes as they talked. Whatever these two might find to talk about made Brorda deeply uneasy: an unholy alliance if he ever saw one. Then he followed Cenwulf's quick glance across to where his wife stood with her dancing-partner of a moment ago, a lad newly come to Offa's guard. Cenwulf flirted with as much duplicity as he did everything else. It was only a way to covertly watch his wife's new lover. Brorda, reassured, hoped his other worries could be as easily laid to rest.

7 August + Mathrafal

Idris walked from the colonnade into a courtyard of three sprawling hazel trees. Brochfael followed. One door opened onto this courtyard, no windows. It was a good place to talk quietly in seething Mathrafal. Idris examined a hazel branch. The nuts were still green nubs swelling among green leaves.

"I suppose it's my repayment for sending him to Mercia." Brochfael stood in the middle of the courtyard, looking over the thatched roof ridges to the grey sky. "Now he's made me the hostage."

Idris shrugged. "Gwriad made sense to him. You knew that at Tregeiriog. And he's right. After you weed out the fancy talk and exotic philosophy, stronger ties are a good idea. You're just suspicious because it's Gwriad. And Cynfarch."

"Northern adventurers."

"God's name, Brochfael, it's two hundred years since they fled to Powys. A quarter of your nobles are of Rheged's old line."

"And like their damned ravens, wherever they settle they drive others from their nests. They're a plague, a pestilence."

"That's your Cadelling house talking."

"We ruled in Iâl when the Romans came and left. Where was the famous Rheged house? Quarelling with each other in Carlisle while English pirates overran North Britain from York to the Roman wall."

Idris sighed, impatient with Powys's old quarrels. Cantref Meirionydd couldn't afford the luxury of centuries-old feuds. Nor could Powys. "Where indeed? The Cynferchin were also fighting for Arthur, three hundred swords. Dying at Catræth, thirty swords. Before that they were holding the west coast against the Irish, holding the north border against the Picts. And where was your famous North Powys house? Sitting on feather cushions in Iâl thinking the English would never push west. Don't try historical arguments on me, Powys, I'll always win."

Brochfael wasn't ready to give in. "It was always Cynddylan's thugs, Elfæl, Penllyn, Meirionydd when you had something to gain by it, all against North

Powys."

"Look to your heavy-fisted domination for the reason. Why do you think Cynddylan attacked Iâl? Your Cadelling kin needed to be beaten down. You're lucky he died young."

"May God judge me —"

"May God judge you harshly indeed if you put personal enmity before your kingdom. You'd spend your efforts better by curing this running sore of treason. It's been festering too long. The infection will spread — one day you'll find it's choked the life out of Powys. Don't delay."

"Forget the treason. It will heal." Brochfael hooked a hand in his *hual* chain, the golden fetter of kingship that bound him as rawhide binds a slave.

"Only with surgery. Digain was dangerous. His master is dangerous still."

"Not to me," said Brochfael. "It's useful to have one of them at court. He's a mirror to their plans."

Arrogant words, dangerous words. Powys also had a tradition of kings falling from their own over-reaching pride, but Idris left this unsaid. "Never forget Eli descends from both North Powys and South Powys. He carries Cynddylan's blood, and it gives him a powerful claim. Wait too long and power will shift to your brother."

"I have no brother, Meirionydd," said Brochfael Powys. "Don't provoke me."

A stranger would think we were enemies, Idris thought, not lifelong friends. When Elisedd Powys raised his stag banner all those years ago and savaged Mercia, he had three war captains, heirs of ancient houses. Where were those three now? Brochfael mab Elisedd was as peace-loving as a monk. Idris Meirionydd — also christened Brochfael but called Idris since childhood after his famous ancestor — was his prudent grey counselor. Cadeyrn Penllyn was dead. A strange triad.

Brochfael walked to the bench against the north wall, but stood for a long time leaning against the plaster wall with his back turned. "I can't afford a rift with Penllyn. Garmon's angrier than I've ever seen him. I watched him when Cynfarch was stirring up my hall."

"Garmon's afraid, being a reasonable man. But he knows where to stop."

"Unlike his cousin Cadeyrn." Brochfael turned. "And now Cadeyrn's son. How do I handle Cynfarch, Idris?"

Idris shrugged, unwilling to probe the serpent's nest of Penllyn. Penllyn and her neighbor Meirionydd had once been warring kingdoms; now as cantrefs of Powys they maintained an uneasy peace, a state of affairs that Idris preferred. Brochfael Powys created the problem of Cadeyrn Penllyn and his heir, let Brochfael solve it. " You know best, lord."

7 August 793 + Mathrafal

Heilyn stood against the back wall of the king's hall, jammed between a kitchen girl and a man who smelled of cattle. He couldn't get near the benches. Scores of people were packed like salt pork in a barrel. The same rumor had brought them all. This was an amazing place for rumors, now that he was learning where and how to listen.

An overdressed beanpole, apparently Brochfael's steward, rapped on the dais floor with a staff. Everyone stood as the king came through the door at the back of the dais under the loft overhang. With him were the burly sub-king who wore a gold diadem on his black-and-white streaked hair, and Cynfarch mab Cadeyrn. The rumor about prison could not be true. He walked in lightly, greeting people here and there in the crowd, and stood respectfully while the king took his chair. If he knew who inspired that sudden hush and renewed murmur, he gave no sign. Heilyn stared, trying to make sense of the man. What drove him to this? Heilyn was driven by silver and gold. What drove Gwriad's creature?

Silence was absolute when Cynfarch sang again. No rabble-rousing this time, but praise of Brochfael Powys. Heilyn followed him more easily than the old *pencerdd*; he used ordinary words instead of pœts' fancy talk. It was all about the wealth of the land and its generous ruler, corn in the fields, rivers leaping with trout and salmon, children playing in apple orchards, servants singing by the hearth. *Singing by the hearth, what shit.* Heilyn knew servitude. But the kitchen girl jammed against his left elbow wiped her eyes and snuffled. Cynfarch eased into some lilting tune without words, and people began tapping their feet and laughing. Heilyn watched him play them up and down the scales like a wooden flute. They loved it, loved being teased and flattered, just as they loved the old family tragedy, the sorcerer's ravens, the freed hostage, the alliance. Now he was a bloody hero. Brorda was right. Cold-blooded, calculating and dangerous.

Brochfael came forward after a while and talked to the hall. A heart-warming picture, Cynfarch standing with the king's arm across his shoulders, Brochfael saying what a wonderful opportunity his brother Gwriad offered. He certainly hadn't thought so a few days ago. A white-haired woman in a gold diadem came down from the loft and gave Cynfarch a sword. For the coming war? Brorda would fill his boots when he heard this. Yet Heilyn had to smile when he thought of the brazen madman sitting there the other day singing English while they yelled curses. Someone should try singing *Wealisc* in Offa's hall. What would people do on the benches? Watch Offa's reaction, watch Cenwulf to see if there would be a disappearance? Then maybe an outcry and insults. In Powys they seemed to be ungoverned. Or ungovernable. Each man, each woman even, had an opinion and thought it mattered. Some said Mercia was like that in the old days, but Heilyn had never believed it.

Rhydion, the old *pencerdd*, took a gold arm ring from his cupbearer and gave it to Cynfarch with an elaborate speech about Elisedd. Brochfael stared at the old man, not pleased. Finally the king gave Cynfarch a fold of parchment and said something about a rowan hill.

"Wish someone would give me an estate for raising trouble," said the herdsman. "Even Bryn Cerddin."

It was a place, then. An estate called Rowan Hill.

"There's only one kind of trouble you can raise, and it spoils a girl's waist," the kitchen girl shot back, getting a few guffaws.

Heilyn flattened himself to the wall, afraid hostilities were going to break out around him. Brochfael looked like a man with a toothache, and Cynfarch looked — sad? Strange people, and they seemed stranger by the minute. *Wealas.* He wondered if he would ever fully understand anything he saw or heard in Powys. Around the upper hall, Brochfael's nobles and bodyguard had their heads together like crows on a midden. Cynfarch sat with the sword beneath his feet and one forearm across the harp's upper bar, arrogant as Lucifer like any pœt, wearing the gold arm ring. Pleasant to be an idle younger son wearing gifts of gold and playing a harp strung in silver, accepting an estate with a graceful nod. Heilyn spat into the rushes and headed for the door.

The rain had stopped, but the garths were awash with reflections of broken cloud. Heilyn picked his way toward the north gate. It was time for another stroll to the border. Maybe he should buy a horse. Was a mule cheaper? In the shadows he waited for the watch to come back. Instead he heard two strangers talking in low voices.

"Ravens, shit. He started that story himself."

Heilyn gave a start; it was as though his thoughts had spoken themselves.

"Where, then?" A different voice.

"We'll watch for our chance. If he leaves, we follow."

"Something to give him a bellyache? Nightshade?"

"Maybe."

Invisible as always, Heilyn stood frozen in the shadows. When the guard opened the door they walked out, a tall man dragging his left leg and a shorter one with a black moustache and thinning hair. Both had British voices but not the Mathrafal accent. Stunned, Heilyn came to his senses only when the door slammed. The guard climbed the catwalk and paced off to the west corner.

Heilyn bit his knuckle until he tasted blood. He understood all too well. Brorda didn't trust him. Or things had changed. Now he wanted assassination, not information, and had sent these two to do Heilyn's job and claim his gold. Heilyn could catch up with them, make a deal . . . but that bright metal lying on a Tamworth table held him back. He wanted every gleaming piece. Should he mention these two in his next letter? Better not. But if he failed Offa's minister, how long was Brorda's arm? Maybe he should cut his losses, take the silver in hand, and travel beyond Mercian reach to live in peace. But he thought again of the gold. He would do what Brorda wanted.

Brorda: one day I'll repay you in kind. The imagined dispatches were easier than the real ones. He waited for the guard.

8 August 793 + Mathrafal

Brys left Mathrafal's three-river plain without going to Mæn Pedr. He knew what the priest would say. *Exactly what is it that you want? You stir them up in the hall and then say it's a call for peace. Do you want peace or do you want revenge on the English?* Brys wasn't sure he could convince Mæn. Mæn would say that meant he wasn't sure he could convince himself. A wasted effort.

As he went out the west gate at dawn, the rampart watch hailed him.

"Cynfarch!"

Brys turned with the sea-cat harp on his back and his saddlebags on his shoulder. The man was an anonymous black figure leaning on his spear. Brys shaded his eyes but couldn't make out a face against the bright sunrise.

"Next time let dead herœs lie." A man from the north, by his voice, and smiling. "Sing the living ones."

"The king's guard, by any chance?"

"Are there others?"

"One or two." Brys grinned, exchanging idle talk with a shadow.

"And this talk about peace. Who'd we raid without Gwynedd and Mercia?"

"Your fights would be only half so fine with no one to sing them." Insolent puppy. Satire would take the smugness off Brochfael's hounds in their jeweled collars. All in good time.

"Your task on returning, then, Cynfarch. Take care of those ravens."

Ravens? So everyone knows that story now. Good. The only ravens I have are the worn silver ones on my arm, but no one will believe that once a story spreads. He examined it for perils and found none. *Let it prosper.* He hummed all the way to the stable.

9 August 793 + Cærsws

Cærsws once commanded the meeting of five great western roads. Some tumbled masonry lay below, but mostly the place was reduced to overgrown mounds clawed by bramble and bracken. Alder grew inside the fort, thickly where buildings had stood and more sparsely on the broad metalled streets. The living successor town was north, out of sight. Today brought an easy summer wind, blue sky brilliant above green treetops, afternoon light shattering on River Hafren.

Brys leaned in the ruined wall of the west gate, looking out from the Roman fort to the equally ruinous British town, eating a handful of blackberries. A raven clan moved over the broken brick and grass hummocks outside the gate, picking over the scattered offal of another animal's feast. One, doing sentry duty on a stump, kept a quizzical golden eye on the man who offered no threat. Gradually the birds worked uphill, the sun striking iridescent fire from their jet shoulders and backs, until nine of them fed within a spear's length of Brys. He always liked watching ravens; perhaps it was a family obligation. Curious, bold, restless, they consulted among themselves in brazen voices like trees grinding together in a storm. At last the guard bird asserted his status by gliding down on broad black wings almost to Brys's feet, pretending to pry for grubs while sizing up the motionless stranger.

When the grey stallion neighed, Brys glanced over his shoulder into the fort. Some people feared the Roman places, but if Cærsws held ghosts they had faded past malice to a plaintive breeze over broken pavements. A burst of starlings lifted from the harebells. A fox ran past, belly to the ground, staring back over his rusty flank. Brys folded his arms and waited. Someone was coming, the way he'd come, through from the south gate and the bridge on the Mathrafal road. Quiet as a ghost, but the fox knew better.

A man rode in sight on a bony crock of a brown mare, with a heavy pack on his back. Why didn't he tie it behind his saddle? He had ragged dun hair hanging in his eyes and he looked around him uncertainly. He looked fearful rather than threatening.

"Lost, friend?" Brys stepped out from the gate. The flight of ravens exploded into the air around him, crying out in alarm and thundering their great blue-black wings. *I forgot them. Stupid.*

The miserable mare reared halfheartedly, but enough to fling the rider in one direction and the pack in another. She trotted downhill to the hobbled stallion and began to crop grass. The rider sprawled on his back. Brys walked out and crouched beside him. The man opened smoke-grey eyes, a brilliant burst of gold at the center, and closed them again tightly.

"All right?"

"Where?" He looked up stunned.

"Cærsws. Southwest of Mathrafal." *My fault, playing raven games.*

"Oh." He sat up, feeling the back of his head.

Brys offered his hand. The stranger looked at it suspiciously but took it. Brys pulled him to his feet. "You don't seem to have broken anything."

The dun man walked a few paces and turned, not meeting Brys's eyes. He said sullenly, "I haven't ridden a horse much."

"Anyone would have fallen off. Almost anyone."

The man shrugged and looked around for the mare.

"Come." Brys walked down the slope and took the mare's bridle. She looked as though a gust of wind would collapse her. He folded back the sheepskin riding pad. Old gall scars, healed now, marred her dull hide. He needed more saddle to carry a heavy pack; he would also ride less like a sack of straw. "Where are your hobbles?"

The man gave him a walleyed look and shook his head.

Brys braided and looped a leather thong for him and showed him how to let the mare tighten them on her own legs. Brys felt himself watched as he worked, but the man said little. *Shaken. So would I be if a flight of ravens flew in my face, and my horse threw me.* He walked back up the hill and pulled bread and meat out of his saddlebag. It was the least he could do, and it would be enough delay to check again for a head injury. The other fetched his pack, brought out cheese and apples, and offered his name. So did Brys, which earned him a frown.

"It's a nickname," Brys explained.

"Oh."

"You feel all right? You hit your head." Brys rummaged in a saddlebag and pulled out a leather bottle.

The man gave an owlish nod, chewing dry meat. Odd character. His voice was Gwent with a layer of something else. English? He reached into his pack and pulled out an impossible object. A silver chalice studded with rock crystal and garnet lay glittering on the dusty grass. Brys picked it up and turned it between his hands. Its rim and base were alive with graceful and exact pattern.

"What . . . ?" It was Brys's turn to be tongue-tied. Had he robbed a church?

"I'm a goldsmith. And you?"

"God knows. A pœt," he said absently, looking at the piece. Music for eyes and fingers. He poured some of the mead with a flourish he'd learned long ago as Brochfael's cupbearer and handed it to the goldsmith.

Heilyn met eyes as green as chipped glass — not the muddy hazel most people called green but the green of cats' eyes — and drank. Sorcery. He couldn't stop shaking. Maybe the mead would help. But too much loosened the tongue. *Careful.*

"Your harp?" He nodded at the deep triangular case beside the saddlebags. Cynfarch — Brys? — pulled it over. He wiped his hands on the grass and took out the instrument. Bronze pegs along the top bar held the strings. He did something to each peg with one hand, touching the strings with the other. Tuning, Heilyn guessed, still unable to believe his luck. He had yet to see whether it was good luck or bad luck.

"I've never seen one like that in Tamworth."

A muscle tightened under one eye, that was all, and then he looked down at the harp. That instant of unshielded hatred told Heilyn everything he needed to know. He was in terrible danger, thanks to Brorda's entrapment. But somehow he blurted his mother's story and his own tale of slavery, and Cynfarch nodded with a frown creased between black brows.

"But you've probably seen this." He pulled at the neck of his shirt. This one was white linen, heavily embroidered. How many shirts did he own? Heilyn saw a scar to match his own but newer and angrier, as though the collar had been uncured leather or a bad fit. A good owner took care to avoid that. So it was true about being a slave. That didn't make it true about the ravens. Except that Heilyn had just seen them with his own eyes, had been attacked by them. He took refuge in a shaking gulp of mead.

"It dœsn't alter anyone's worth." He seemed to think Heilyn needed reassuring.

No one could tell Heilyn what altered anyone's worth. Silver and gold scattered on a polished table, maybe. Being auctioned between two weeping children torn from their mother, like him, and an old man too feeble to work out a year, maybe. "A pound of silver. That's what I paid for myself."

"You bought your freedom?"

"I stole some of it." Black humor rose in his throat. Mead was stronger than he thought, not sweet but as dry as captive sunlight. "Some of the silver. I kept it in my shœ. It gave me blisters."

Brys looked startled and grinned. He had white teeth; the front two were crooked. "I stole all of mine. Maybe they're still standing there waiting." He started to laugh.

Heilyn laughed, too, almost pissing himself in fright. Christ have mercy, if Brorda were here . . . Brys picked up the harp and began to play a light and airy tune that wandered from the thick silver strings up to fine bronze and back. He sang three stanzas.

"Who is Cynddylan?" Heilyn asked when he stopped. He lay back in the grass watching clouds sail east. "I've heard of Arthur but not Cynddylan." Except once, unexplained, in the king's hall in Mathrafal. Probably everyone there knew, but there was so much he didn't know.

The answer was relentless grief, nine stanzas of archaic words sung in that unnerving voice. Heilyn closed his eyes and tried to see the sword strife and triumph, the betrayal, the dark burial. It ended on a plaintive run of string music. Then he heard only the river flowing past toward Mercia.

When he looked up Brys had both hands clasped over the snarling cat-head with amber eyes, and the light caught his two arm rings. Above the left elbow was silver in a pattern he couldn't make out; above the right elbow was the gold ring the old man had given him, a stag's head in a net of interlace that flowed from its antlers.

"Why did he attack Gwynedd and North Powys? How did he come to have Mercian allies? Why did they turn on him later?" Heilyn wasn't much interested in the answers, but the more questions he asked the more he might learn. So he tried to tell himself. Maybe he just wanted to hear that wonderful voice. Like mead, smooth and warm, with that hard northern accent. A Penllyn accent, he supposed. How could have Heilyn thought him unremarkable? He saw a pit trap open before him and closed his eyes tightly enough to see red sparks. *Sorcery. Danger. Certain death.* He rolled over onto his belly and forced himself to concentrate.

"It's complicated —"

It was. Brys talked for a quarter of an hour before Heilyn began to see how the pieces fitted together. Historical interlace, not vines writhing over and under and becoming serpents, but lives and alliances and conspiracies going back centuries. Centuries, when Heilyn had enough trouble sorting out the events of this week.

"But mostly you're interested in his sister."

A green stare flew across the harp. "What makes you say that?"

Heilyn shrugged. He wasn't going to say, Because your voice went low and gentle as though you were talking to a lover. The stare swerved away. He ventured, "Who tells you this? How do you know she rode a white mare with red harness?"

Wrong question. Brys got to his feet as though stung. "How do you know the right heat to shape iron?"

That isn't anger, it's fear. What had he said? Could he patch it? Before he could think how, Cynfarch spoke again.

"Every pœt knows about that family. They're an object lesson in tragic error." He was frowning at the distant river.

Like your own family? "I'm sorry. It's none of my business." Heilyn heard the beggar's whine in his voice and felt too dispirited to fight it. He reached for his hatred and loathing of this dangerous man. It gave him less consolation than it had yesterday.

"Good comes of it, if it keeps other people from doing the same thing. No one thrives in isolation and strife." Thinking out loud, he had quite forgotten Heilyn.

"I'll remember to treat my allies better so they won't betray me," Heilyn agreed waspishly, angry at himself for whining, "next time I'm born a king."

Brys looked around and smiled. "Don't tell me that people still believe that in Gwent. The baptized say only cats have nine lives. Heilyn, are you riding west?"

Heilyn was taken aback for an instant. Of course, travelers would band together against brigands. *Do I have the faintest idea what I'm doing?* He couldn't risk saying that people in Gwent, for all he knew, believed the sun was a disk of polished bronze hanging in the world-tree.

10 August 793 + Gwynedd

Bound for her own realm of metal and millefiori glass and stone, wherever it might lie, Meirwen passed through North Powys and into Gwynedd. She learned to stay away from courts, which had their own smiths. In small townships or outlying farms a traveling smith was welcome. When landowners doubted her skill, she shrugged. "If you're not satisfied, you pay nothing." She never went unpaid. Occasionally men assumed her willingness went beyond metal work. Only one went away swearing at the scorch of hot iron on his hand.

After eight weeks Meirwen wore fine linen in three colors and red leather boots with silver strap ends, had three small bars of gold in her pack, and smiled to herself like a cat in a dairy as she hammered and shaped. But the work was much like Tregeiriog work, mostly iron tools, and she had a head full of ideas for fine inlaid bracelets and gemmed chalices.

Life would be perfect but for her sickness every morning from the child growing under her heart. Meirwen lay awake in strangers' lofts accusing herself. Could she have fought Digain harder? When she had tried the first few times, he had hurt her badly. She wasted some anger on him, but he was beyond her anger now. Besides, the child might not be Digain's . . . She refused to think about that possibility. Long ago, another lifetime. He had forgotten her by now. On the edge of sleep, sometimes, she remembered his touch and his laughter, and spread her hands over her still flat belly. Awake, Meirwen searched her memory of physic plants to expel the child and bring on menses. Tansy might do, but perhaps she would wait a little longer. She traveled until the snow mountain Eryri loomed at her back and the island Môn lay before her, green and promising.

Menai Strait she crossed in an Irish trade curragh in exchange for a curved bronze sail needle. A week later, in a morning sea mist, she descended a gentle slope to the hidden murmur where River ffraw's small estuary meets the sea. She had reached the wealthiest court of the British kingdoms, and until the plague a hundred years ago, the most powerful.

The sun burned off the mist and illuminated a sprawl of houses and outbuildings, cornfields and woodland. The place was unwalled except for a low bank; the sea was its rampart. At the end of a dull journey it looked brilliantly lit from within. The buildings were brightly whitewashed, thatched in silver straw and scattered to the banks of the silver stream. There a handful of mounted men rode complex formations, their lances flowing with morning light. Meirwen stood at the edge of the honey-colored dunes and smiled at the sun's warmth on her face. Then she started down again. Maybe prosperity waited for her here in the stronghold of west Britain, the greatest court of Gwynedd, golden Aberffraw.

Two smiths worked in Aberffraw. One, the court smith, had sons to work the bellows and reduce scrap; he needed no assistant. He told her Padrig was the jeweler, and since he was crazy enough to insult the king, maybe he was crazy enough to hire a woman against the king's law. Meirwen laughed, letting nothing dim this morning. She followed directions into a dogleg alley which ended at a house as unlike its neighbors as a cat among hounds. It was plastered and painted the same honey color as the sand dunes across the river and roofed in wooden shingles painted dark red. There was no garth. On the doorstep a cracked wine-jar held a gorse bush sparked with brazen yellow flowers. The door was painted blue. On it coiled a silver-scaled creature with one clawed forefoot clutching an iron ring. It was Gwynedd's dragon, but wearing a fatuous simper. Small wonder Caradog was insulted. Meirwen was admiring its superb workmanship when the door swung soundlessly inward.

"God's teeth." A gravelbed growl from the interior shadows. "flattering as the thought may be, my door knocker will not open my door for you." The owner of the voice appeared, a white-haired man with blue eyes fixed on blue sky above the next house. "But then, a system of levers governed by weights. Could be done. Yes." He nodded. "What brings you, child? I'm too busy to take new orders."

One day a week later Padrig entertained visitors in the workshop. A knock on the door caught her in the midst of granulation and Padrig in the privy; Anna, Padrig's wife, was out talking with a patron, having found a problem in her design for a gold ring. Padrig shouted something about Christ's tœnails and why in hell didn't people knock properly. He swore for good measure in his nasal Greek. Someone opened the outside door before Meirwen could put her tools down. She looked through the open workshop door at two senior churchmen drawing their stiff robes about them as though they saw vermin underfoot and an old man leaning on a bishop's crozier who gave her a beatific smile. When Padrig returned, the bishop said something pleasantly in what sounded like a more elegant grain of Greek. Unimaginably, Padrig looked embarrassed.

He brought the three men in past the flowering courtyard in the center of the house. The workshop, besides its shuttered windows, had a large square of priceless glass panes, its light revealing an unholy mess on the workbench. Meirwen nodded politely and went back to work. Not that she'd achieved much since then, between eavesdropping and trying not to laugh outright. Of course it had to do with the reliquary and the king's penance, but she had scarcely expected Bishop Elfoddw himself to come all the way from Bangor to discuss it.

Caradog's Irish adventure and its inglorious outcome made a good story, at least when Padrig's friend Gwydron had told it, and Meirwen had laughed freely for the first time in weeks. Caradog was lying low in Aberffraw, Gwydron said, to avoid the bishop's wrath. But Elfoddw walked across Môn to deliver quiet censure in person. He told Caradog it was an offence before God to sail raiding and slaving in

Christian Ireland for no better reason than the idleness and avarice that had ruined his ancestors. Caradog was a black bull unbroken to God's yoke, said the bishop. What example did he set his nobles and his people? Elfoddw laid down a penitence, which Gwydron said the king had forgotten by morning. He also extracted the sullen promise of an altar gift, a chest to house the saint's relics at Cær Gybi. On the way out Elfoddw had asked Gwydron whether a grown man had nothing better to do than twiddle harp strings and howl praise at a deep-stained sinner, but Gwydron swore that he lightened these harsh words with a wink.

Now the bishop and his two sour clerics sipped Padrig's red wine, far from its sunny vineyard, and worked steadily toward the impossible.

Elfoddw had a name for miracles — in Gwynedd, not in Powys — and now Meirwen understood why. He did not accept refusal. With God's grace one finds a way, he told Padrig calmly, and unfolded a canny proposal to let a jeweler use carved ivory without carving it. Meirwen, listening with a smile, suspected he would take the same approach to plowing or bookbinding or baking. Of course it could be done. So he was credited with homely miracles by doubters who saw their own hands accomplish Elfoddw's wonders.

Padrig, who cast a stoic's cool eye on both the reward of eternal life and the reward of newly minted Frankish coins, loved the saintly man for his worldly tenacity. By now he was arguing and pouring his best Burgundian for the pure pleasure of philosophical entertainment.

"Filigree, inlay, gems, of course," the smith said. He'd run his hands back through his hair so it stood out like tufted cotton grass. Now he tapped out his points with a stubby forefinger at the end of the messy workbench. "No ivory."

Twenty-five years ago as a young monk Elfoddw poured out his eloquence to lead the British church back into the Roman fold, a dubious blessing it seemed when the frightened Pope ordered the independent British bishops to obey the archbishops of their English enemies. The Powys bishops still defended their older orthodoxy, not just the once Pelagian monasteries which Rome and Elfoddw had declared heretical, but the king's bishops at Meifod and Llanelwy. Today Elfoddw lavished his eloquence on a truculent goldsmith with no patience for bishops' baubles. Meirwen heard Padrig set unrealistic problems for the sake of having them joyfully refuted.

Padrig demanded at last, overcome by rhetorical passion,"Why are you wasting away in this godforsaken land, mouldering in the crypt of the church? You should be with the Moorish scholars in Cordoba, debating the nature of the good."

Elfoddw smiled wonderfully, rolled up his crimson sleeves, and leaned among the silver scraps to draw on Padrig's wax tablet. Maybe he longed for the rough wool robes he wore as a novice working in cattle shed and bean field. The two high-nostrilled churchmen had probably never set foot in a bean field. "This is what I see, Patricius. It must be a showpiece for your virtuosity."

"A year's work," grumbled Padrig.

"I need it by Easter. You should manage with your student's help." And Elfoddw slowly closed one dark eye at Meirwen. So Gwydron told the truth, at least about the wink.

Meirwen's dammed laughter finally broke free and spilled out into the sunny workshop. It flooded Padrig and the bishop, leached reluctant grunts from the sour churchmen, and floated Anna into the room with her sketches rolled under her arm. The bishop spat in his palm and clasped hands with Padrig. Two old horse traders, each grinning at a different triumph. Elfoddw blessed them all gravely and left with another miracle chalked beside his name.

That evening the three of them took their meal into the garden. Out of the sea wind, it produced persimmon and olive, narcissus and rhododendron. Anna, carrying a bowl of last year's brined olives, stopped to hug Meirwen.

"Is the baby kicking yet?"

"It's only three months." Meirwen shyly put her arm around Anna's waist. Her own mother had died at her birth, her father had been distracted and overworked, and an older sister gave mostly pinches. She wasn't used to hugging people in simple affection. "I think you should have this baby, you're the one who's excited."

"It's more amusing when someone else dœs the work." Anna handed her the bowl. She lifted a wandering strand of her hair, which had faded from fair to grey without anyone noticing. One glance at Anna's fine unblemished skin was enough to send Meirwen off to the loft for her lotion, but the mirror told her it was no use. She had as many freckles as ever. "Why don't you stay here? Visit your sister next year."

Olwen's letter had arrived yesterday, water-stained and creased from who knew how many hands, probably passed from smith to smith between Iâl and Aberffraw. Olwen worried, wanted her there, had asked the priest to write a letter and entrusted it to some traveler. The last sentence troubled her. A black-haired man with a fine voice, Olwen said. That took little guesswork. But why?

A dawn wind was stirring when she sieved down to the hot core of her anger and found anger at herself. She could have spoken for him when the king threw questions at her half the night about Digain, about his allegiances and visitors, about his death. Brys had looked at her without anger when the guard took him. She could have spoken but she had said nothing. Some day she would find a traveler bound for Mathrafal and write — what? Forgive me. That was all he needed to know.

Everything else was put away with childhood. As long as she wanted nothing, his rank and her servitude had never troubled their friendship. What had changed? An ugly lesson in the difference between love and rape, and realizing it would be the same if she married, coupling with a man she felt nothing for, bearing his children. If this child had black hair and light eyes, maybe one day Meirwen would tell her she was conceived in love. Maybe not. She would not marry. No one could make her. She wept and fell asleep.

She woke without a weight she didn't know she had carried and found it was mid-morning. They had left her to her sleep. At noon Anna brought her food, crept into bed with her and they both ate apples and bread and told stories until the bed was full of crumbs.

If she truly believed that they wanted another baby crawling underfoot long after their own were grown, she would stay and cast her life in precious metal.

15 August 793 + Ceredigion

The high track crossed into Ceredigion on the broad humped back of the world, where everything folded away green and tawny on every side, and the ancient grass way muffled the hoofbeats so travel was abstract and dreamlike.

As Brys rode, the wind combed his hair, sang small to itself in the grass, dandled cranberries on their low bushes, stirred the mountain gorse spreading sun's gold over south-facing slopes. In places the track plunged them deep in bracken, and they emerged from its green corridors like swimmers breasting rough water. Hares sat up at the mouths of their earth dens, and hawks surveyed the plateaus from slow circles. Between upland farms it was as lonely as any place on earth.

Hill regions are known for robbers. Brys counted their safety in travel by daylight, weapons worn openly and the harp on his back. Often they met only solitary sheep and cattle herders, and once a traveling monk chanting psalms to the swing of his staff. One day they saw no one between morning farewell at one farm and evening arrival at the next, yet they were expected. In sheltered *cwm* or shadowed hillside, there were always watchers.

Sometimes he forgot the smith entirely, he was so quiet. Sometimes they talked. Sometimes he sang. Heilyn seemed to like that, but it was hard to know what else he liked or what he thought.

17 August 793 + Winchester

The embroidered hanging showed a halœd man with his eyes turned up to heaven. His hands were on the head of a woman who kneeled facing him. His garments were in disarray.

Egfrith looked across the room at its excellent needlework, bright colors and two beeswax candles in front as though it were a shrine, and decided the hanging was exactly what it seemed. Eadburh had a taste for the sacrilegious and vulgar; disapproval only deepened her pleasure. Alfflед had seen it too; she was blushing.

"And what brings this outburst of fraternal love and devotion?" Eadburh motioned the servant to pour wine and smiled from her brother to her sister. Having a mirror, she always smiled with her mouth closed. Her teeth were large and brown, but with her mouth closed she was a handsome woman. "I wonder which titbit is going around Tamworth and York. Have I eaten my babies again? Is it my affair with Holy Father? Is it the slave I murdered and buried under the hearth stone?"

At that her serving-woman's hand jittered slightly as she poured Egfrith's glass, and wine slopped onto the polished table. He immediately moved it, spilling a few more drops, and told the woman, "I'm clumsy today. Bring a cloth."

Alffled said, "I was in Tamworth and decided Winchester wasn't much farther. Egfrith had seen enough of the parade ground for a while."

The servant went to stand in the darkest corner of Eadburh's chamber, clasping her hands tightly in front of her. Her lips moved slightly in prayer.

"Our good brother needed reinforcements, in other words. Two church mice coming to bell the cat." Eadburh pursed her full mouth and looked down demurely. "Very touching. But sad to say, my dear ones, I do nothing but good works these days."

For whom? wondered Egfrith, not looking at the indecent wall hanging. And what service do you get in return? This was a witless game for two queens and a king to play. Even two sisters and a brother. Even Offa's children. But the stakes were high. He would speak his sister's language.

"I hate to deny you rumors of your wickedness, but Tamworth has found other fare. How's the hunting on your new estate?"

"Thin," said the queen of the West Saxons. "Southerners see no difference between king's wood and kin's wood. They poach and plunder whenever I turn my back. My noble husband makes excuses, as though they'd never had a corn tax before."

Not at thirty percent, certainly. Was that one of her good works? Egfrith smiled warmly at his older sister, thinking there must be something in her to love. Bertric her husband loved power, never mind whether it was borrowed from Offa or Offa's daughter.

Alffled looked at her hands. No color on the short nails, no rings. Egfrith was always sorry that the younger sister had chosen, probably without thinking about it, to be different in every way from the older sister. And what had he decided to be, without thinking about it? Kingly qualities in Offa's estimation amounted to brutality and avarice in Egfrith's.

"I'm going to hear appeals here tomorrow, Eadburh," he said. "Petitioners have been coming to Tamworth saying they're not heard in Winchester."

"And is Papa terribly angry?" Eadburh said wide-eyed. "Tell the old pirate to come down here himself if he wants to wet-nurse the West Saxons."

Just the kind of answer that would delight Offa, unfortunately. She's strong, he would say, she knows her mind, of course she rubs people against the grain sometimes.

At least she had brought the topic around to Wessex. Egfrith said, "Egbert's in Britain."

"And a dozen other self-styled rightful heirs. Are you telling me this to keep me awake at night?" She yawned and stretched luxuriously, pulling her deep rose gown close against her fine breasts. "Where is he? He's been ill-bred enough not to present himself in Winchester."

"Gone to ground," Egfrith admitted.

"He's certainly not in York," Alffled said to her hands. It took only the lift of one fair arched brow from Eadburh, to subdue her. "Eadburh, he's been in Aachen the whole time father's been quarrelling with Charles. He fought in Frankia's northern campaigns."

"He has gold and mercenary contacts," Egfrith explained. "And I can think of only one reason why he's returned."

"Dearest, if Egbert arrives at the gates with an army of Frankish mercenaries, then I'll worry."

"And an army of Irish mercenaries?" It was not information, not even a guess. "Or Picts?"

"Picts, what a wonderful thought. I hear they paint themselves blue and fight naked." She winked at Alffled, who sighed. Eadburh stood up. "This has been most instructive and entertaining. You'll forgive me if I don't make a sudden appearance in York or Tamworth to tell you how to run Northumbria or Mercia? Whenever you do run Mercia, of course, Egfrith. How tiresome to have such a vigorous old bandit for a co-ruler, and especially when he picks quarrels for the hellish fun of it. As for the West Saxons —"

Eadburh crooked a finger at the servant, who hurried near and bent a knee with head bowed. The queen slapped the woman hard, making a sound as harsh as a green stick snapping. The woman didn't lift her head.

"What's it for?" Eadburh asked the Saxon woman.

Red welts appeared on the woman's cheek. She didn't raise her eyes. "For spilling the Mercian king's wine, lady queen."

Eadburh lifted the glass wine decanter and emptied it slowly over the woman's head, then threw it down. It shattered. A serving woman cost several ounces of silver. The decanter had probably cost two or three pounds.

"Saxons are a spineless herd that can be driven in any direction. Driven, not led. Especially not led by a snivelling Saxon princeling who's been drying his eyes on Charles's skirts. Like cattle, they need a loud voice and a strong hand."

Egfrith, kissing her on both scented cheeks at her chamber door, felt a momentary sympathy for the Northumbrian fratricides. Then he thought of the monster in the new pœm, the one with the ferocious mother. Despite the priests' disapproval of such entertainment, Egfrith was eager to hear the rest of the pœm. He liked the hero, Beowulf, a man of thought and action.

Eadburh, once she'd dispatched the missionaries, opened the wardrobe door and burst into delighted laughter. Her new lover, impatient, had stripped down to his eager erection and his large pectoral cross. There was more than the usual traffic from Tamworth today, and some of it at least was amusing.

31 august 793 + dinas maelor

Sea wind leaped the north rampart of Dinas Mælor, dragging at Brys's hair. On the shore far below, two sand bars folded in toward the land like the claws of a great grey crab. Two rivers joined nearer the sea in a tide-race. Sea westward, mountains eastward. Dinas Mælor was a good defensive site for the court of Ceredigion — until a generation ago part of Gwynedd — risking only sea invasion from Dyfed in the south or Gwynedd in the north. As a maritime nation Ceredigion married, raided and traded by sea.

Beyond the double estuary, ocean swept away to meet the horizon's taut wire of radiance. The day might have been shaped on a jeweler's workbench. The overcast sky had the ashy brightness of unpolished silver, the sea was burnished silver, and tarnished black shoreline rocks were a bezel for emerald and topaz valleys where corn harvest was in full swing. Brys knew more about goldsmithing than he had a month ago. Meirwen had always shrugged off questions about her work, unwilling to believe he was truly interested. After some hesitation Heilyn talked freely about his casting and enamelling.

"Can you see it?" Brys pointed northwest.

A silver knot in the silver wire between grey sea and sky, an unearthly island shimmered like a self-contained source of light. Heilyn looked his question.

"Ynys Enlli," Brys told him. "Some believe it's far Afallach, a heaven floating in time. From land's end they say it's only another island of stones and bracken and sea birds, but as peaceful as heaven in the monks' care."

Heilyn smiled in silence. Strange man, Brys thought. Traveling west to Dinas Mælor they had joined a band of monks who were glad of an armed companion. Once they arrived it was as easy to bring Heilyn into the king's hospitality as to turn him away to cheap lodgings in the town below. In fact he was planning to sleep under a tree, preferably in a churchyard. He was amazingly tightfisted, but this made sense once he explained that every bronze piece or silver bar he spent was a piece of forge equipment he had to earn all over again. Heilyn, with a quick imagination and a wicked wit, was good company — not as easy as old friends in Brochfael's guard but more entertaining than most. He was also a troubled spirit who seemed to trust no one.

Brys went inside when rain swept in from the sea. The windows in the guest house faced inland. He left them unshuttered and watched the rain slant into a courtyard where three children were picking small red apples from an old tree.

"Wood-wisdom?" asked Heilyn.

"No bets, or you'll have my shirt again."

He'd never seen a *gwyddbwyll* board until a week ago when Arthen Ceredigion gave one to Brys. Now he played with anyone he could entrap and won too often for comfort. He had a reluctant hunger to know of his mother's people. For most of his life he'd had no one to ask about history, music, how to say words. Brys answered as patiently as he could, knowing that Heilyn lashed out when he felt threatened, fled when he felt unwelcome. Kindness brought suspicion first, then a smile of uncertain radiance that Brys had more often seen in women. But the smile was rare. The scar around his neck ran deep. Brys asked few questions, understanding that his companion was a refugee from some cantref of hell.

"I didn't understand what you sang last night."

Heilyn sat crosslegged on a floor mat with a handful of small ivory warriors. His hair was hanging in his eyes as usual, but it had been clean and scented with yarrow since Brys described, he hoped not too pointedly, how the British cleaned hair and body and teeth. In payment for repairing a knife he had taken a linen shirt with interlace embroidered at the neck. It was clean. He had even washed it once.

"Why?" It was a cycle on the lady Rhiannon, full of inrhyming and puns. Brys sat on the edge of the sleeping shelf, elbows on knees. The sweet scent of bedstraw rose around him, and rain purred on the thatch.

"I know it was clever because some of them laughed, but it made no sense to me," Heilyn said, not looking up. "If I do that to iron, twisting it this way and that, it breaks."

This was unusually bold for Heilyn. Brys took it more seriously than Rhydion's hairsplitting over pœtic diction. "How should I change it?"

"Use ordinary words and don't tie them in knots."

"All right."

"What do you mean, All right?" Heilyn looked up suspiciously.

"It's easy to be clever. It's harder to be clever and clear and make people sit up and think. I know good advice when I hear it."

Heilyn opened his mouth to argue, closed it and ducked his head. "Oh."

"What do you mean, Oh?" Brys grinned. *Careful, or he'll be off again.* "That's a compliment."

"You're generous to mention it," Heilyn said gravely. So he had absorbed some manners. His smile fell off abruptly as though he'd just remembered a law against smiling. Maybe there was one, for British slaves in Mercia. Brys was increasingly glad he hadn't stayed longer to find out. "Brys —"

"Yes?"

Silence.

Brys looked out the window. One of the children had climbed the tree to peer in at them and almost fell out giggling when he saw her. He put a finger to his lips, miming silence. She repeated the gesture, nearly collapsing in unvoiced laughter.

"How long will you stay here?" asked Heilyn at last.

It wasn't the question he'd started to ask. Brys studied him, but he was intent on the gameboard. The squares of fruitwood were separated by silver inlay, but it was not as fine as Brorda's set.

"Arthen wants to talk to his nobles. If they agree to Gwriad's council, another few days."

"They'll agree," Heilyn said absently. "He spoke out for it strongly enough in hall."

The king of Ceredigion, a dour man with a long sheep's face and a ruminant mind, was cautious about any new idea. And why should he scour his backwater ports of sea raiders? First let Gwynedd control its own pirates, including the king. His pedantic grey *pencerdd* argued against alliance and sulked as long as Brys sat on the hall dais. Chosen for his birth, probably, not for his *awen*. But Arthen could think for himself, and on the whole, he thought alliance might bring more gains than losses.

Brys nodded. "Alliance might keep Caradog from raiding his monasteries again."

"And his court thinks you're Taliesin and Bedwyr rolled together."

"Slow summer, new idea," Brys said, impressed that Heilyn remembered the old pœts' names. He absorbed everything at one telling, dry moss in a summer rain.

"That's a compliment."

Brys shoved him with a foot until he fell over laughing. Heilyn had no grasp of the horseplay that every bodyguard man learned to survive. This wasn't an English deficiency — Brys had seen Offa's household warriors wrestling and joking — but another slave scar. Time to learn, then.

As for Taliesin and Bedwyr — sometimes a pœt or harper captured people's imaginations and set his name in every mouth. Then he usually found a feather cushion in some king's court with an annual gift of cattle and gold to keep his estates. But Rhydion had broken Brys from graduating; he would be lucky to sing at isolated farms if he wasn't too worn out from working their fields all day. Bryn Cerddin, Brochfael's derisive gift, would barely feed a goat.

"Where are you going next?"

"Gwynedd. But first I have a trip inland. To Penllyn." To face his brother's eternal disapproval, for as long as he could swallow it, and the silent house. This time it would be disapproval of Gwriad's envoy. Next time it would be something else. It already made a knot in his stomach. Brys dropped onto the floor and started setting pieces on the board. "Tell me something. Do you know the name of Brorda's son?"

Heilyn gave him the walleyed look, the same look Brys's grey stallion would give a grouse beating up under his hooves. "He dœsn't have a son. Two daughters."

"No son who went on pilgrimage to Rome?" Brys reflected. "Are you sure?"

"Quite sure. A few years ago there was a dispute about the elder daughter. She was joining a monastery, and Offa wanted to make her abbess. Brorda said to let her join as a novice like anyone else. The other one married a North Mercian noble, Cadmon."

Brochfael lied, in the sanctuary.

After a minute Brys realized Heilyn was watching him warily and asked, "Cadmon?"

"Like the old British name Cadfan. They're not, any more, not British." Heilyn looked uncomfortable. "It's wiser to become English."

"Did you feel that way?"

"Yes."

Cat ice. It wouldn't bear any more weight. Brys changed the subject. "How long will this commission take you?"

Arthen's court smith had discovered this morning that the traveler quietly straightening nails for him was a skilled enameller. By afternoon he had a request from one of Arthen's cousins to make a pair of silver brooches.

"A week, maybe. Remelting the glass will be the difficult part, especially keeping the heat up. Brys —"

Brys looked up. There it was again, that desperate hesitation.

"I heard you put a word in the smith's ear. Thank you." Again he'd said something other than what he intended. What ate at him? Some fear of failure?

"You'll be fine. If you come to Aberffraw when I'm there, and if Caradog dœsn't throw me out for meddling, I can speak for you at his court."

"You don't have to do that," Heilyn said, as though doing so small a thing set up a terrible obligation he could never repay. For Brys it was easy, nothing more than opening a door for a friend. Heilyn still had to walk through it and work well, as he doubtless would. But he didn't like to be in anyone's debt. Senseless — but then Brys had felt the same way growing up at Brochfael's court in Mathrafal and Iâl.

"Do you want to tell me what's on your mind?" Brys asked, as he rarely did. "You're working something around in your head like a pebble in your boot."

Questions didn't prosper with Heilyn. His face shuttered closed as he bent over the gameboard, and he asked testily, "Do you want to play or not?"

1 September 793 + Llanbadarn

"The world cannot sing bright and sweet enough, through grass and trees themselves sing your glory, O true Lord."

Heilyn went up soon after dawn to Llanbadarn church, two miles inland from Dinas Mælor. The priest's prayers gave no comfort. Lead weight, dead weight. He had not entered a church willingly in ten years, let alone paid a precious silver penny for a mass. For his dead mother, he told the priest. She had never tried to find him; by that he knew she was dead, forever beyond his regret or his help. And he had never tried to find her, not among the living. At least the chant and blessing let him find tears. If some of the tears were for his own affliction, who was there to care?

"Death is the center of a long life," Brys had said. "Longer than memory." The conversation came back to him clearly.

A few days ago Brys had been restringing one of his short bronze harp strings, sitting under an old apple tree outside Arthen's guest house, and reached for ways to explain the saying. He called it a parable, though Heilyn didn't think it was in the gospels.

"Think of gold," Brys had said. "You want to make something new and wonderful. You break it into your crucible and melt it down, then recast it in a better form."

"More likely lead," Heilyn said with his usual caution. "It's easier to melt, and I can afford it."

"Lead and gold," Brys said, "like your eyes. Do you know your eyes are the color of lead with a bright gold inlay at the center?"

Heilyn shook his head, helpless to say that he had no mirror but Brys. Instead he said, "Once I poured gold, but when it cooled and I broke open my mold there was nothing inside. No gold. It wasn't in the clay and it didn't run out with the wax. It just went, vanished. Sometimes it happens to other smiths."

Brys smiled. "It was translated to something even rarer. Death is the center, the hub of a wheel. Our lives are the spokes. We turn and turn within the rim of the green world. We live and die and return to the sun fire at the hub. But sometimes we escape into perfect nothingness. That's where your gold went."

Heilyn kneeled on cold stone in Llanbadarn church, unable to confess, unable to pray. He needed no priest to tell him he was doing wrong. And he knew his penance: yielding the sweet chiming silver in his little pouch. The one thing that he desired and could have. The rich morning light streamed in at unshuttered windows, making pools of dusty gold on the leaden stone.

3 september 793 + penllyn

The Roman road climbed north through Meirionydd's twisting valleys, then inland and eastward through the mountain passes. Brys rode steadily uphill past settlements and monasteries, with the river always at his left hand. The sea wind out of Ireland at his back chased cloud shadows across the grey heights of Cader Idris. When he reached River Wnion's crossing around midday he dismounted to look over the bridge. One winter the bridge had been washed out when he rode down to buy cattle in Dolgellau with his father and brothers. But today its timbers were solid; the river was low even for September. No reason to turn back.

With a Roman road to ride most of the way, he would reach Dolgarnen by evening. Cadwr wouldn't want to see him. Why was he bothering? His mother and father slept in Llanfor graveyard on the green hillside northeast of Lake Tegid. His oldest brother's stone was there, also, though he lay in a rainwashed grave on the border. He had been a spirited fifteen-year-old, Brys's defender and hero, who rode to war armed with his father's boar spear. Now Brys's sister lay there also with her stillborn child. She had been a pretty girl, fair and gentle like their mother, with their father's gift for music. This was the hardest part of coming to Penllyn. The people he most wanted to see were there, but under green grass, pale brittle bone in the embrace of black boards. Brys checked the grey horse's harness, looked at the sky for weather, and rode on northeast through the passes into Penllyn.

Southwest of the lake was high wild country. Early snow lay on steep scarps on either side of the track. Flat land was beyond sight, beyond imagination in this sea of peaks. Below them high meadows of grass and heather swept down to provide thin grazing for a few cattle. The stream splashed black and icy even in scattered sunlight, and trees grew thick in the valley floor. At farms built and roofed in slate, people came from threshing or cider pressing to ask Brys for news, and gave him warm pulpy apple juice. Some recognized him, for he was much like his father, but they were too courteous to say so.

The valley broadened as he rode northeast, and soon he saw cooksmoke from the houses of Cær Gai drifting northward toward grey Arennig Fawr. When he splashed up out of River Twrch ford near the marshy west end of the lake, heading east, a woman came towards him leaning on a staff. Her hooded cloak shadowed her face. She looked frail, so he rode close and dismounted.

"I'll ford with you," he said, willing to cross again for her sake.

She glanced up out of her deep shadow, an old woman with wildly tangled grey hair, and looked through him with a peregrine's unblinking eyes. Blind? She had the bleak endurance of one doing life penance for a terrible crime.

"Twrch flows into Marchnwy," she said flatly. "Like the border."

"It's a different river. Lady, have you lost your way?" A madwoman, he thought, a wanderer. *Fair god, let Penllyn never be like the border.*

"I know thee."

More likely my father. He held out a hand, but she shook her head slowly.

"I do not cross here, dear son. Nor do you."

Brys pulled off a silver bracelet someone had given him in Ceredigion and slipped it over the end of her staff. If she were blind she would feel it resting on her hand. There was nothing else to do. He remounted and rode away. When he reached higher ground he looked back. She was still standing there, leaning on her staff.

Someone was calling cows in for evening when he forded the last stream leaping down from the hills southeast of Llangywair and rode steeply upward. The track branched through a valley of oak and mossy boulders beside splashing Nant Carnen. The anchorite's cell at the first bend was deserted, with bracken falling through the roof and leaves drifting in at the open door. He shivered, half remembering a dream . . . He rode on up to the rocky shoulder and halted under the crimson berries of the old rowan.

Dolgarnen's fields and grazing filled the narrow valley below, bounded by woodland. The small stream stepped frothing across stony ground below the orchard. Dolgarnen was too high to grow wheat, but Cadwr always insisted on planting. He was lucky to get a onefold yield for the next year's seed. From this height the farm looked prosperous. When he got lower he would see the decaying timber house and outbuildings, the weedy fields. He rode down slowly.

Cattle lifted their heads in mild curiosity, leaves turned on the apple trees. It was peaceful. He dismounted at the gate as a square black-haired man came around the barn leading a chestnut horse. Cadwr looked up frowning and stopped.

"Peace on you."

"Peace on you and on your house." *If you want to give a stranger's greeting, you can have a stranger's reply.* Brys balanced on his feet a moment, then crossed the forecourt to clasp his brother's arm. *I knew I shouldn't have come.*

"Cynfarch! How wonderful!" Angharad at least came out smiling, a round and rosy small woman. She carried a guest cup. It was their mother's great silver dowry chalice, set with rock crystal and emerald; the drink was not mead but Angharad's plum wine. Brys drank and passed it back, and Angharad kissed him decorously on both cheeks.

Brys looked around the farm, realizing everything had changed in three years. The house was recently chinked, whitewashed and newly thatched in wheat straw. Only its unevenly settled timbers betrayed its age. Thorn trees still guarded the door. He saw baskets of apples under the trees, stubble in the field, livestock in pasture, and field workers' houses reoccupied on the far bank of the stream.

"Well?" Cadwr had his thumbs hooked in his belt and was still scowling.

"Not bad." *Miraculous, I should have said. Too late.*

The silence gathered around them like shadows. He could think of nothing to say. What could anyone say about two children stolen by sickness? Last time the little boy had come running out to seize him around the knees, almost toppling them both to the grass, and Angharad had laid the baby girl in his arms. Now everything seemed very quiet. Angharad was quieter, certainly.

Cadwr was the same, frowning and turning away abruptly to lead his horse to the barn.

At daybreak the next morning Cadwr fetched ax and saw from the barn to dress timber for a new calving pen. He said nothing when Brys came after him. The morning was clear and cool. A few leaves already drifted to the grass as Brys followed his brother up to the tree margin. It was easier to carry tools up to bark the trees than carry raw timber down. They worked in silence.

At noon, when they sat on the squared oak logs to eat bannock, the day had turned still and hot. Cadwr looked across his harvest. Half the sheaves were in the barn; three men were hauling the rest. "You must have graduated in song by now, Brys. Was it a hard trial?"

"I didn't graduate."

"Why?"

"Gwriad Manaw needed an envoy."

Now it starts. But Cadwr only digested it in his thoughtful way. *Where do you get that gravity? It's not a family trait.* Brys watched his brother pick up a piece of oak bark and crumble it methodically.

"When will you?"

"I don't know."

"What dœs that mean?"

Brys replied too quickly, "I said I don't know."

"Just a question, Cynfarch."

"It means never." He was jumping at shadows. "Rhydion broke me for taking Gwriad's service ungraduated and without his approval."

"That seems a waste after eight years of your study and his teaching. Maybe he'll just let you stew for a while." Cadwr creased his black brows together and carefully tried his ax for sharpness with the pad of his thumb.

"Maybe." There seemed no point in arguing.

"You know there's always a place for you here," Cadwr finally dropped into the lengthening silence, too well controlled.

"I don't need anything from you."

"You never did." Cadwr got to his feet and pulled his shirt over his head in a single abrupt motion and flung it away. He was brown and muscular from years of working the place alone, harder work than daily weapons training in the bodyguard and a month's farm labor. Dispossession had left them no servants and no wealth, only their mother's summer farm. Dolgarnen was her dowry land. "You don't need anything from anyone."

"What I said," Brys answered with careful exactness, "is that I don't need anything from you."

"The land's half mine, Cynfarch. The house is the youngest son's."

"I'll sign it over to you."

"Same as ever, aren't you? All or nothing."

Cadwr was slow to anger but in his deliberate way he was angry now. Brys frowned across the valley.

"I told you to give that thing to Brochfael." He was staring at the silver arm ring that had been the royal insignia of Penllyn.

"I didn't." Brys got to his feet. *Time to go. Why in God's name did I come here? For old contempt heaped on new resentment?*

"I see that." Cadwr took up his ax and slapped it gently against his boot. "You want to play envoy to foreign kings, please yourself. But let me tell you, in case you've forgotten, that's all past."

"Tend to Dolgarnen, Cadwr, and stay out of my affairs."

"I might, if your affairs didn't intrude into mine."

Cadwr chunked his ax neatly into the uncut log. He took two strides and caught Brys by the shoulder. His left fist exploded square on Brys's jaw and flew him backwards onto the dry grass. Cadwr threw himself down with a knee in his belly and a handful of his hair. Brys, dazed, found the rage in his brother's cold green eyes before he found his own.

"What . . ?"

"That's for murder price."

Brys felt around inside his teeth with his tongue. He had a split lip. He closed his eyes until the knee lifted out of his belly, then launched himself up. Cadwr rolled sideways.

"Not your affair." He spat blood.

Cadwr was quick to his feet. Brys's fist skidded off his cheekbone. They wrestled and fell back. Cadwr was stronger, Brys was quicker; it made for a close match. Brys landed a blow on his brother's chin. Then Cadwr's fist hit him with the weight of the Penllyn hillside. He sprawled into blackness. Cadwr slapped his face until he groaned awake.

"You kill a man, and who pays your fine? The king of Powys, in God's name. And Garmon sends his steward up here to say he has twelve head in-gathered from high pasture to pay your fine himself. Garmon Penllyn, after our father killed his brother." Cadwr sat back on his heels looking at his bloody knuckles.

"After he dispossessed us," Brys accused.

"He had to, or else Powys — never mind that. It's done. And now you. You break me with shame and say it's not my affair?"

Brys closed his eyes. "There was a reason."

"I heard. A woman."

Brys told him everything.

"You're a fool," Cadwr said. Brys flung his forearm over his eyes. *Enough. But Cadwr's got his teeth in it now.* "You're enslaved in Mercia, the girl flees, Brochfael's stung for twelve head of cattle, Garmon's insulted, Angharad's weeping, I'm sleepless thinking you're dead. Fool. Get up."

"No more, Cadwr. You're right, I'm a fool."

Cadwr put both arms around him pulled him to his feet. "Why do you carry it all yourself? I'm your blood." Cadwr patted him like a horse. "All right, all right."

"Is it?" Brys pulled away, bruised inside and out.

Cadwr pulled the ax out of the log. "You'd better find her."

"I've been trying." He hesitated. Another lecture now. "She's landless. She has no family, only one sister."

"And?"

"You're family head."

"Family? Angharad's father is a small freeholder. His grandmother was a slave. Brys, when will you understand there is no family? Dear God, you know what dispossession meant."

Brys clasped the arm ring of Penllyn, sun warm under his right hand, and looked south toward Powys. "What did Father do, Cadwr? After he quarrelled with Brochfael?"

"So you heard about that. Leave it alone, Brys."

"Penllyn always stood with South Powys." He kept it from sounding like a question. "The bond of blood."

"Yes. That's all I know."

More than enough, for now. So they were friends, Eli and my father. Allies at least. "Do you still dam the pool? When we finish we can swim."

Blue dusk was on the valley when they settled by the hearth. A young girl hummed under her breath as she turned meat on the spit. Brys sat on a chest picking splinters out of his hands. The house was well tended: walls newly clayed, two looms in the loft, furs piled on the sleeping shelves. On the age-blackened house-posts twined serpents and greyhounds, vines and leaves. He saw one creature he had carved into the tangled design, one summer long ago, a *gwyniad* with a braided serpentine body and bronze nailhead eyes. It didn't look much like a fish. He would carve others for Cadwr's children. When there were children. Long after they ate, Angharad shook out the quilts and drew the bed screens and went to sleep. The house was silent except for the wind pushing a few dry thorn leaves over the threshold outside.

"I'm going to check the horse," Cadwr said. Brys followed him out.

Outside, the Hunter hung in the southern sky. Dolgarnen's high valley folded away in darkness napped like a black dog. Their boots echœd on the courtyard slates. Cadwr found the door latch and they stepped into the warm scented barn. Brys set down the lantern and felt along the shelf for the candle stub on its fragment of stamped Roman tile, where it had always been. In that moment he loved Cadwr for being what he had always been. He didn't say it. *There's too much I don't say.* Brys lit the candle from the lantern, and light bloomed. The chestnut horse shifted around in its stall, and the speckled barn cat yawned and unfolded herself from a shelf.

"Still hot above the joint, but he's putting more weight on it." Cadwr felt the gelding's leg up and down, talking to the horse all the while.

"Cadwr? Brochfael gave me a few acres of rockslide above Tregeiriog. It's poor soil, I'll be living on venison. But maybe some of that hardy wheat of yours would take." He saw his brother's wariness and plunged on. "In spring will you ride down and tell me what can be done?"

Cadwr smiled. "Don't expect miracles."

For once I've said the right thing. "Nothing more than what you've done here. This place was mostly scrub and bramble when I left."

"There have been setbacks. I lost four head this summer."

"Wolves?"

"Of a kind. Remember the three brothers north of Cær Gai? I caught one of them in my cattle pen. The others were already away."

"You killed him?"

"I tried. He cut my plowman badly. If I'd gone after them he'd have bled to death. It didn't seem much of a bargain. Come back next summer, Brys, and we'll go over and take eight head."

"You'll just start another blood feud that gœs on forever."

"I know you, firebrand. You're not ready for a monastery."

"Gwriad's alliance depends on peace." Brys was acutely aware of the irony of cautioning Cadwr to moderation. It had always been the other way around.

"Your alliance." Cadwr got to his feet and brushed the chaff from his knees. "Will it bring back my cattle or my dead brother?" A shadow dimmed his face even in the poor light, and he crossed himself to turn the unlucky words. One dead brother was enough.

"Will raiding and war?"

Cadwr blew out the candle and flung open the door. Brys went out after him and dropped the bar in place. He leaned on the drystone wall beside the barn, and after a minute his brother joined him. It was cool now, and their breath curled on the night air. Stars were out in countless thousands.

"I heard what you did in Mathrafal hall," said Cadwr. "Garmon's son was here last week. We've stayed friends, though I don't think Garmon knows. Geraint said you were brilliant and dangerous. He said you wanted to start a war in the name of peace."

"It's not true."

"Either way, I hear enough about peace and brotherhood from the priest without hearing it from you, Brys."

"You don't want alliance."

"Maybe. I think it could easily become a war host. You do, too, or you wouldn't argue."

Brys looked up to the mountain wall rising southward in darkness, blacker than the sky, and the folding valleys on every other side. He thought about Egbert, Cenwulf, an unnamed Powys noble, the unknown men Digain spoke of who opposed Brochfael's treaties. Each had the potential to destroy a fragile peace. "I think we're going to have more border trouble. If it's peace, good. If it's war, we're ready."

"I'm glad you know what you're doing. They may be soft-headed in Manaw and Powys, but we never could afford to be in Penllyn."

Brys smiled into the dark. Cadwr had surprised him once again.

"It would have been a good raid, all the same. You could have sung it,"

Cadwr said.

"Tomorrow I'll sing you Cynddylan's raid on Mercia. See what it got him. Broken treaty, burned court and dark burial."

"Still cousin Cynddylan? He was always your lodestar."

"Cynddylan," Brys agreed. *And his sister. No pœt sings of a woman's loss, but who knows grief and dispossession better?*

They walked back toward the house, between the old thorn trees that had spread further along the walls than he remembered. The heavy door swung shut on the night orchard. Brys lay awake for a long time listening to the wolves call each other across the hills.

8 September 793 + Cær Seint

Cær Seint's gate hinges were rusted away to an iron stain and the timber gates were long since rotted to nothing. The old guardhouse was haphazardly patched with mud and rock, like a swallow's nest built onto the enduring Roman stone. Nothing now barred passage to the old city in Arfon.

Brys rode in the southeast gate on a September morning of rain blowing in horizontally from the Irish Sea. Leaves clotted under the grey stallion's hooves. Blackbirds splashed in the street while cats sat by hearths. Cooksmoke hung in layers over the grass streets, now encroached by saplings. Two boys on a sheltered doorstep pointed Brys toward the inn and went back to polishing their oxhide with pebbles. This was where Constantine had sown his seeds of silver, gold and bronze, the story said, so none would suffer poverty. There was no sign here that it had made much difference.

The inn still had one wing with two storeys of reddish stone and a few sheds with their original humpbacked red roof tiles. He led the horse in, clattering past rooms open to the seasons, empty but for leaf mold. In the central courtyard a year's hay was stacked on the pavements within a rectangle of broken columns; tarred canvas was lashed on top. Enclosed by a building yet under open sky, it was a strange place. Three plum trees leaning wearily against one wall made it less a cage. Brys stabled his horse and gave a bronze piece to a red-faced woman who kept shouting over her shoulder about a cauldron. The ale house next door was already doing noisy business, but he would look for the trade captains down in the port. There he could buy his passage across the strait, which would be easier than waiting for the right tide to wade through shallow water across the sands.

Brys walked the rubbled streets to the northeast gate, then descended the track to the estuary. River Seint flowed sluggishly into the grey Menai Strait, where its paler stream disappeared into the current by mid-channel. On the far shore the island of Môn was a low landmass bordered in tawny sandbars and shallows. Over there was Caradog, keeping court in Aberffraw this month instead of Rhos.

The port taverns clustered with the traders' and suppliers' huts near the docks on the east side of the river. A handful of deepsea trade curraghs were blocked up on the shore like beached whales and three large wooden hulls swung at moorings in the Seint. Brys paused in the porch overhang of the tavern nearest the crossroads to shake rain off his cloak. A man came out quickly, looking back over his shoulder. It was Heilyn.

He saw Brys with a start of surprise and offered a distracted greeting.

Brys nodded to the tavern. "I need to find a captain and arrange passage."

"This other tavern is better." Heilyn started down the boardwalk. Something seemed to have shaken him, but he recovered quickly. "Are you going to Aberffraw?"

"Tomorrow, if the weather lifts." Brys walked with him. "What about you?"

"I talked with an Aberffraw smith yesterday. There may be work on a reliquary, the bishop wants it quickly." He was looking over his shoulder again and he had his wild-eyed look. "Brys, I've got to tell you something. I had a dream, a terrible dream, and I saw two men from Powys —"

"Tell me over a meal." Brys was hungry, and food and drink might help calm Heilyn. They went into a tavern and found a place as close to the hearth as they could in the crowded room. Everyone wanted to be warm and dry on the stormy day. The serving boy slapped flatbread and meat on the table, took the bronze piece and came back with a sweating jug of ale.

"I saw them —" Heilyn talked around a mouthful of food. He ate like a starving man.

"First the reliquary." It might slow him down.

"The reliquary. It means months of work for the three of them. I could do the casting and forging. But I'll leave some of my pieces lying around and maybe I'll get some fine work," Heilyn grinned. *That's better.* "She says the bishop wants it for Easter —"

"Who?" Brys poured ale, his hand unsteady, and spilled it.

"The goldsmith. She's here to trade for gems and precious metals. An unexpected order —"

"What's her name?" Brys traced designs in spilled ale on the table.

"Dœs it matter?"

"What dœs she look like?"

"Dark with freckles. She's friendly but she trades hard." Heilyn frowned. "You know her?"

"Where is she?"

"I don't know. They're waiting on the storm."

Brys started to get up and thought better. "They?"

"A man was with her." Heilyn looked unhappy but had the sense to keep talking. "Not a smith, he wears a gold diadem, he's good-looking but not as good as he thinks. Everyone seems to know him, they were joking about some raid in Ireland."

A lord? She's landed on her feet. No surprise, after nearly half a year, and she's one of a kind. Brys drained the ale cup and poured it full again. He pushed the food away and called for mead.

"Brys? I'm sorry." Heilyn looked into his own ale cup, untouched. "I've got to tell you something else."

"Later." Brys drained the mead jug, not bothering with the cup, and stood up.

A dream about two men in Powys wasn't the most pressing thing on his mind. Heilyn followed him out through the inn. He wanted to be alone but he hadn't the heart to push the smith away.

"Where are you going?" Heilyn asked in the rain. The water made rivers of his colorless hair.

Brys pushed his hood back as he walked. The rain felt good on his face. "I'm going to get drunk and I'm going to get a woman." *Drunk, anyway.* "Coming?"

"I don't — No." Heilyn looked even more uncomfortable.

Think I don't, or think I shouldn't? You're as bad as Rhydion and Mæn Pedr. He remembered the smith's earlier anxiousness. "Someone gave you a hard time back at that crossroads tavern?"

"Not really." Heilyn stopped and gave him the walleyed look. "But I don't think you should go in there, all the same."

"Why not, granny?"

Heilyn looked away. He spoke carefully, as though he were the one who'd been gulping mead on top of ale. "A Mercian crew is in there. They were inbound to Chester, bringing some noblewoman back from Frankia, when the storm drove them in. They're drinking the place dry and picking fights."

"There's a thought. You think I'm afraid of English?"

"No." Heilyn met his eyes. "And that's a good reason to stay out. They're the worst kind, a free crew and a noble guard."

"You know them?"

"I saw plenty of their kind in Tamworth."

"So did I."

Brys went on, shook himself like a dog in the porch, and pushed into the crowded ale house. An invisible border ran through the middle of the room. Nearest the door were groups of British, Irish, tattoœd Picts, who watched the other side with varying degrees of hostility. Near the kitchen sat the English, discernible by the cut of their clothes and their drunkenness.

"You again?" one of them bellowed at Heilyn. "Another message for the lovely Leoba?" They all laughed hugely.

Brys walked down the clear area in the middle. He shoved his hands in his belt and looked around. A supercilious young man with an armful of gold bracelets looked like he might be a guard captain. He was flushed with drink. Brys said in English, "I hear you've got an English whore who learned some new tricks in Frankia."

"Sweet Savior," Heilyn muttered behind him. "She's an abbess."

There was stirring on the benches near the door, and some laughter. The innkeeper peered in from the kitchen. The Mercians stared at him in slow wrath.

The man with the bracelets looked at his companions, who had grown quieter, and shrugged. "You're drunk. Get out."

"Know why so many English women take vows?" he asked the benches near the door, keeping his eyes on the captain. "Even the Pope knows it's because the men are too busy using each other as women."

In the same moment he saw Heilyn's look of raw terror and the Mercian leaping to his feet. Benches emptied on both sides of the room. Heilyn went out the door like a scalded cat. Brys pulled his knife and nodded. "You'll do."

Heilyn stood shivering in the rain and watched men and women drift away from the fight in the crossroads tavern. At least this had distracted the Mercian shit from his message to Leoba. It had been a cryptic masterpiece, telling Brorda nothing in a great many words. Wasted effort now probably. Another knot of people pushed past him, headed for other taverns. The fight was none of their concern. Or Heilyn's.

God rot the bastard. Heilyn was going to lose his gold payment and his forge. Over a woman. He might as well head back now to Mercia, or on to Aberffraw. No, he couldn't stomach that now. Reluctantly, slowly, unable to resist the opportunity to meddle, he turned and splashed through the narrow passage between the inn and its neighboring building. There was a back door. The innkeeper, hands twisted in her apron, stood in the kitchen doorway watching the tavern. Heilyn looked over her shoulder and saw Cynfarch and the Mercian captain circling with knives. He seized an empty spit from beside the kitchen fire and shoved between them.

"Get out, slave," the Mercian spat.

"Not any more, you shit." Heilyn crowned him with the spit and kicked Cynfarch's feet from under him.

The place cleared soon once the entertainment was ended. The innkeeper barred the door and started picking up her benches in silence. Heilyn sat on the nearest bench, head in hands. Cynfarch rolled over and got up. He didn't seem drunk or crazy. Heilyn kept his distance, revulsed by stupidity and senseless violence and most of all by raw hatred, which curdled his guts with fear. He was also half English.

"No doubt that's a demonstration of peaceful alliance." Heilyn, without lifting his head, spoke in biting sarcasm. It came out sounding like grief.

"Alliance is for friends," Cynfarch mumbled.

"Liar. Verminous liar. That's not what you said in Dinas Mælor. Even Mercia will benefit. Peace and prosperity. All lies."

Heilyn turned his back to dig into the pouch around his neck and took the woman a silver coin. She gave him a twisted smile. The poor were always the ones who paid, the ones who picked up after the powerful. They knew the worth of pœts' fancy talk. Dog shit. He headed for the kitchen door. Cynfarch came after him. Heilyn couldn't stop him. *Who cares?* Rain still seeped down outside. A dark and weeping land. He walked up the hill Cynfarch had come down earlier.

"Was that practice for one of your hero cycles? Rolling around on an ale house floor?" Heilyn flung over his shoulder. He couldn't seem to keep quiet. All his bitterness burned in his throat.

Heilyn walked through the gateway of the old city and headed blindly along the first street to the left. The houses gave way to ruins. Here people had been robbing the cut stone, if one could rob ghosts, for new buildings and walls. Still most of the old barracks stood shoulder high in the streets of grass, so he could see only ahead and behind except at cross-streets. A cat in a vacant window turned hunting eyes, and small creatures fled away into safe bramble nests. A distant bell clanged nones. Late afternoon. Finally he stopped. Heilyn said, "Go back. Leave me alone."

And do what? In all the years of slavery he had never opened a vein. Always he thought he would buy freedom. Now freedom turned out to be more humiliation. The guard's laughter, Cynfarch's stupid game, his own unbearable dilemma.

"Heilyn. Help me." Cynfarch was leaning against a wall a few feet away, arms folded and head bowed.

"Help yourself. I'm not your servant."

There was no answer. After a minute Heilyn turned and saw him on the ground. He rolled Cynfarch over with one foot and saw the dark stain of blood. His heart lurched. *Good, get yourself killed in a tavern fight, save me the trouble.* For weeks he had been uncertain what to do, but it was clear enough now. Finish the bastard, send the arm rings to Brorda as proof — no, keep the gold and silver and pick up the next ship to Ireland, Frankia, it didn't matter. Heilyn kneeled in the rain, in the attitude, he realized, of a supplicant or a whore.

Brys opened his eyes, green as sunlight through old forest, and closed them again when he saw Heilyn's knife. So he knew or guessed. He always knew too much, scaring the spit out of Heilyn. It had been too late for weeks anyway.

Hating himself, Heilyn felt for the pulse at his throat. It was strong and steady. Where? He found the stab wound high on his left arm, oozing but not spurting. Shock, ale and mead on an empty stomach, loss of blood, that was all. Heilyn used the knife to cut a handspan from the bottom of his cloak, wrung it out and bound the wound. It was a slave trick, this passion for mending broken things. Gwriad could toss him a coin sometime.

Brys's square hand closed around his wrist before he was done. Heilyn's eyes spilled over unnoticed in the rain. If he could mend himself as easily.

"What's wrong?"

Heilyn wiped his nose. "You're a stupid shit is what's wrong. Get on your feet."

8 september 793 + tamworth

Leoba lifted off her blue veil and dropped it on Brorda's polished table. The damned thing made her look like a respectable matron. Bad for business of any kind. She lifted the henna'd ringlets back from her shoulder and smoothed her gown over her legs. She still had good legs.

"How are things in the kitchens, brother?"

"You'll have to lend me a silver piece till Michælmas," Brorda said straightfaced. "I spent my wages on a pit dog, but a mastiff tore out his throat in the first fight."

"You're improving," Leoba said and winked at him. She handed over the parchment that had come to her by a long route from Ceredigion. "My new lover's not so talkative. Maybe we should go west ourselves. At least Offa would hear some good stories."

"Between the two of us, Leoba, we could tell enough stories to reinvent Britain.

Sometimes I think that's a good idea."

Leoba smiled at him with great affection. Years ago Brorda thought it an outright disgrace to consort with one of her calling to meet Offa's demands for information. He'd mellowed. She suspected their meetings were now one of his pleasures as they were one of hers. They shared a black northern humor that few others would appreciate. She'd never managed to seduce him.

The door opened and slammed again. Without looking around Leoba said, "Offa, love, it's high time for you to put your foot down with Eadburh."

8 September 793 + Caer Seint

Brys ate the warm bread Heilyn had brought, probably stolen from a windowsill. Overhead the storm blew in fiercely from the west. They sat in the dry corner of a building that still had most of its roof tiles. The cut was nothing much, he'd taken worse in spear practice. The rest of it he was trying to forget. Heilyn sat with his head on his knees, looking away.

"You had a dream."

"It dœsn't matter."

"Tell me."

Heilyn described it woodenly. A woman in red crouched by shallow ford water, scrubbing at something that roiled long crimson eddies downstream. Heilyn tried to drop his burden to see what she scoured so persistently. She crooned, lifting it, and he saw his own face shredding from the skull. The singing, the singing, stabbed through his head. Then he woke screaming, with someone cursing him and kicking his leg, on a pallet in a portside inn.

Brys felt his skin walking on his back. *If you believe it you'll die.* "Do you know what it means?"

"Yes," said Heilyn. That was all.

"Go to a priest."

"I did. This morning. He said a prayer and took a silver piece."

"Come." One more transgression couldn't make Mæn any angrier. Outside in the grass street, an apple tree had sprung wild and misshapen from a random seed. Below it lay a shallow pool of water, dimpling with rain. He kneeled under the dripping leaves and small fruit and felt Heilyn drop beside him.

"Your pin." It was straight bronze with a rosette head. "Bend it and drop it in the water."

Heilyn pulled the pin out of his shirt opening, bent it and dropped it. It went under silently and sank the few inches. Brys waited until the water smoothed and put his left hand on the smith's head to bow it forward.

"I lift this from you and I cast it down, at the rising and at the setting of the sun. I draw this out and I break it, in the fallow and in the harvest. I bend this and I turn it from you, on the wide waters and in the narrows." Heilyn tensed under his hand as the ritual took hold of him. It would do. Brys stretched it out to the full. "God shield thee and guard thee and surround thee. *Te absolvo, te libero, te levo.* So be it."

"So be it."

Brys got to his feet. It was dusk, and the lines of buildings and streets were hard to make out for a moment.

"I don't know," Heilyn said.

"What?"

"About Cenwulf. What you asked me just now. You're the second one to ask me about Cenwulf. Why would I know anything about Cenwulf?"

Brys shook the mist out of his head and wrapped his cloak tighter. It had almost stopped raining, and the wind was down. He started along the staring barracks row. Briar caught at his boots as he walked. He stopped in what might have been an open square, or a large building reduced to grass and rubble. He remembered something.

"I thought the dream was about two men in Powys."

"No." Heilyn tœd a piece of broken roof tile out of the grass. "That's not a dream. I've got to tell you now."

Brys heard the finality in his voice. This was what he'd been trying to say all those times a week ago. He had also guessed there were things about Heilyn that it might be better not to know. "You don't have to tell me anything."

Heilyn slid his gaze up and away. "Two men are following you. They've been paid to kill you. I saw them this morning. Here in Cær Seint."

"How do you know?"

"I overheard them. In Mathrafal, after the old man gave you the arm ring and the king gave you the estate."

"Mathrafal. You were there?" Things were starting to fall into place, and he didn't like the pattern. Brys lifted the knife in its sheath. Heilyn saw the motion and stopped himself from taking a step backward. "And then you tracked me to Cærsws. Who sent you? Why?"

Silence.

"Why?"

"Brorda sent me. To report on Gwriad's plans, how you would stir the British to war through hatred of Mercia. But he didn't trust me. He never told me about killers."

Brys laughed; he couldn't help it. Finally he knew what was chafing Heilyn. Something like a conscience — imagine that. And he'd thought it was humiliation over his past slavery. He had been so trusting. Fool. Telling him stories. Explaining words. Trying not to bruise his feelings. All for Brorda's spy. The joke was on him, if he lived to enjoy it. Heilyn — was that his real name? — wouldn't be telling him this unless it were all but over. "Wood-wisdom. The game."

"What?"

"The warriors drive the princes before them as they move to attack the king. Where are you supposed to drive me? Or are they here now? Is this where you collect your payment?" Brys started back through the open place.

Heilyn caught his arm. "Try thinking with your head instead of your balls. Because you can't have some woman you're going to throw away alliance. Peace. All that."

Brys shook off his hand. *You're right, and that makes it worse.* "All that. What do you care?"

"It was Brorda I betrayed, not you. I would never — I couldn't."

"Liar." Brys knew he should use the knife.

"Mercia is sick. A leper. Parts are rotting. When Offa dies, Mercia dies, and brutal men will defile the corpse." Heilyn got in front of him and blocked his path, refusing to see his own danger.

Your betrayals make you braver. Brys stepped around him.

"I lied about you, he won't send another. I lied about everything," Heilyn insisted. "To him."

"What was it, gold? Not loyalty, or love of anything under heaven."

"Gold," Heilyn agreed. He spoke slowly, fighting his broad accent as he had tried to do lately, as though it mattered now. "What would you know about gold? About needing it? Brorda told me about you. Amusing yourself with your silver harp strings until you claim your patrimony."

"Three months ago I was throwing drunks out of a tavern and mucking the stable. Brochfael gave me the estate as an insult. It's a goat pasture. But believe what you want." Suddenly too weary for all this, he leaned on a lichened wall.

"Brys —"

"Don't speak my name, *Sais.*"

"*Wealh* in Tamworth."

"Whore."

"Not any more." Heilyn spat at his feet. "Sold into it, sold out of it. You're too old at fifteen."

"Fair god," Brys said.

"But you don't want to know about that, you want to sing your little songs about glory and honor," said Heilyn. "You don't want to know what it feels like to be fucked in the bum when you're eight years old and beaten half senseless and tied up in ribbons and told to dance like a trained dog."

"Stop."

"Make me." Tears were running down his face again. He pulled out his knife. He held it like a butcher, not a fighter. "Is this easier? Don't you think I would rather die?"

Brys shook his head, unable to think straight. Suddenly everything seemed too complicated, yet he guessed he was seeing only a few squares of a larger board. "I won't foul my blade."

Heilyn lunged, leaving himself wide open. Brys slapped aside his knife hand, seized his wrist and flung him into the stone wall. He fell sprawling. The wound on Brys's arm opened, and for a moment he saw everything through a wavering haze of sparks. He leaned against the wall and slid down onto his heels, head in hands. "What did you tell Brorda?"

Heilyn blinked and sat up painfully. "After the first message I told him it was just a trade pact. And I told him what he wanted to hear, that the British could never co-operate on anything. Maybe I told him the truth."

Brys shrugged.

Heilyn looked up at the sky. "You don't have to believe me. Just believe me about the killers. If they're this close they'll try soon."

Brys stood up unsteadily and fell against the wet stone wall. "Good timing. I could fight an army."

"No ravens to help you?"

"Is that a joke?"

Heilyn fidgeted. "Brorda said you're a priest. Not the Christian kind."

"I wonder if all of Brorda's spies are as accurate as you." *What possessed him to send someone like Heilyn? He can't even hold a knife. Curse the man.*

Heilyn blinked. "You have to trust me."

"I did trust you." But he handed back Heilyn's knife, wondering if it would be under his ribs soon.

Heilyn shook his head, all his words flown, and got to his feet. Together, in silence, they walked back to the inn in the old Roman building.

The tavern was full, lit by firelight and smoking tallow candles. Heilyn headed straight for the darkest corner. A few people looked at them and muttered, people who'd been in the port tavern a few hours ago. Brys looked around as his eyes adjusted. No one matched the description of Heilyn's two killers.

"There's your goldsmith."

Everything else is in shreds, why not that? Brys followed his nod. She sat with her back turned, but the faint amber glow of candlelight played on her silver earrings. Talking intently across the table was a slight man in a garish red and yellow hooded tunic. Neithon.

Heilyn touched his arm and turned to the door.

"Stay. It dœsn't matter now."

Meirwen glanced up and pulled her cloak close around her. She had come a long way from homespun. She wore saffron and russet linen, and her hair was coiled and pinned at her nape with silver. Gold rings, silver bracelets, and when she moved down the bench to make room, her feet chimed like her ears. She looked exactly as he wanted to see her. His heart kicked his ribs.

"I found her." Neithon grinned under his red moustache like a fox trotting back from the hen house. His gold earrings danced merrily.

"So you did, Neithon." Not knowing what else to do, he gave Meirwen his most polished courtesy. "I have a message from your sister in Iâl. She asks that you go to her or send word."

"I will." Meirwen turned to Heilyn, chiming. "Especially if you're coming to Aberffraw. From your work I think Padrig will welcome you."

Heilyn mumbled something about going to Ireland instead.

Neithon looked from Brys to the English smith and back with a smile that covered something else. He asked, "You're going to Aberffraw now?"

"Yes."

"Waste no time."

"Why?"

"No one ever knows what Caradog will do next." Neithon shrugged. *Secrets. Enough secrets today to last a lifetime, mostly unwelcome.* The trader drained his ale. "Carnelian and quartz, then, and the gold."

Meirwen said, "You'll take them to Padrig?"

"Next tide." Halfway across the room he threw over his shoulder, "This woman's a brigand at trade. You could have warned me."

"She always knows what she wants." *And gets it, by trade or theft. Horses, hearts . . .* Heilyn gave him a troubled look and left quickly. *Everything's happening too quickly.* Brys stood and looked down at Meirwen. "You're staying here?"

"Near here. With a friend of Padrig's."

"Heilyn told me. I'm glad to see you're well. I'm happy for you." Politeness was wearing him down. It was always more satisfying to argue with Meirwen or make her laugh. The only clear thought in his mind was how much he wanted to touch her cheek and brush back a fallen strand of her hair. But that would be the worst encroachment, to presume friendship from easier days.

"Brys." Meirwen stood up, eye to eye with him, scented with that lotion she made from rose and vervain. She hugged her cloak around her again in a protective gesture that was new, and dropped her eyes. *Shutting herself in, shutting me out. That says everything.* "About what happened at Tregeiriog. I was wrong. I should have spoken for you."

He smiled for her. "You had trouble enough of your own."

"Today's your saint's day," Meirwen said. She wanted to linger, naturally, now that he was desperate to get away.

"So it is." *Not the first thought on my mind tonight.*

They walked out together. The overcast had broken over a few stars. Brys said, remembering, "What's happening in Aberffraw that worries Neithon?"

"Probably Caradog's guest at court. He arrived with only a few friends, but men have been coming to him. Warriors. Mercenaries. People don't like it."

"Who is he?"

"Egbert. The West Saxon heir."

"Fair and holy god. Are you sure?"

"The West Saxons have only one exiled heir, as far as I know. You haven't changed, Brys." She gave him her half smile and walked out into the night.

Brys watched her go. He should walk her to this man's lodging but that he couldn't bring himself to do. Not yet. He leaned in the doorway, wondering what would go wrong next. His heart felt as though it had been squeezed dry, his belly was on his backbone with hunger, his arm hurt and two Mercians were stalking him. Three, if he counted Heilyn.

Brys found the smith sitting at the base of a broken column in the inn courtyard, idly prying up a piece of colored tile with his knife.

"They're in there. I told you." He didn't look up.

Brys walked past him into the inn's sleeping room. The hearths had just been banked for the night. Flames sank lower inside their walls of peat, and the room darkened to an amber glow. The cauldron rested on the bakestone. He scraped out the last half-bowl of stewed meat and crouched in the sparse rushes to eat. The room was a warm fug of wet wool and dirty straw. Not many travelers. Two wagoners talked by the fire. A man and woman with a young daughter were settling to sleep.

Three men already lay rolled in blankets near the door. Two other men sat talking quietly in the far corner. One had thinning hair and a black moustache, as Heilyn said, but they paid him no attention. Heilyn slid in and sat at the far side of the hearths. Brys ignored him, tallying odds. *Two against two? More likely three against one.* He ate slowly, though there was barely a mouthful, and finally the two men went to the far sleeping shelf. Brys dropped his bowl by the cauldron and went to spread his cloak on a pallet.

When the room was finally black except for the red heart of the coals, he drew his knife and pushed aside the cloak. He lay on his back staring into the dark, sweating cold, watching for movement. He tried to think about Egbert in Aberffraw, anything but Meirwen, but his thoughts slid like water on an oiled hide. *Let it be soon.*

An hour, maybe two. Bedstraw rustled near his left foot. Then nothing.

Brys had drifted near sleep. When he rolled on his side, the cut on his arm woke him. He settled his grip on the knife and watched under his lashes. At last a black shape blotted the faint fire glow. A hand on his chest, seeking the mark. Brys rolled right, onto one knee, and stabbed up. Too far, he only grazed flesh. A man cursed. Then another hurtling shape sent him sprawling back on the straw. The room erupted into a cursing struggle. Other sleepers woke screaming. Someone yelled for a light.

Brys shoved the motionless body off him. Where was the other? The room blossomed dimly into sight as someone lit a tallow candle. A man lay beside him, one arm outflung as though to embrace his spread cloak, with Heilyn's knife hilt protruding from his back. No sign of Heilyn. The man with the black moustache crouched near the wall holding his side. Brys stumbled over and wrestled him to his feet. The other travelers shrank against the walls clutching each other and their possessions.

"Thieves," Brys told them and shoved the man toward the door with the knife at his back.

Heilyn kneeled near the stacked hay in the dark courtyard, eyes closed. A slight man stood over him with a hand twisted in his hair. Neithon. Brys pushed his captive against a column, afraid of falling over himself.

"Who paid you?"

"I saw your arm ring, I meant no harm —" Heilyn was right, it was not an English voice. It was South Powys.

"Who?" He held the killer with a forearm at the throat and dropped the knife point to his groin. "He's sent you to your death. Take him with you."

The man shook his head. Brys probed with the point until he flinched.

"Brochfael."

"Liar."

"His man. I swear."

"What man?"

"Dark hair, light eyes. Spare me —"

Brys buried the knife hilt-deep under his ribs, straight to the heart. It gave him a sick feeling. *War is one thing, but this . . . Dark hair, light eyes? Half the men in Mathrafal answer to that description.* He turned to see Neithon twisting Heilyn's head back, exposing the throat.

"And this one," Neithon said. "He's a Mercian spy. He has papers with Brorda's seal in his pack. And I saw a dispatch from Chester."

"Not any more." Brys leaned on the column as the courtyard shifted under his feet and prayed he was speaking the truth. He didn't dare to look at Heilyn, lest he have another attack of confession. "Now he's my spy. Sends false reports to Brorda. Keeps the Mercians calm."

Neithon weighed him a long time before he loosened his grip. "Gwriad said you were clever."

Heilyn got to his feet, looking as stunned as Brys felt. *Clever? Gwriad would swallow his tongue if he knew how clever. I nearly threw the game.*

In the morning, overseen by a bored Arfon judge who waved aside most of the witnesses, the inn servants buried two thieves.

22 September 793 + Aberffraw

Padrig's sunny room opened on a garden protected from the prevailing west wind of Aberffraw. Heilyn was arguing with the smith in his workshop. Meirwen was at the royal church poring over books, comparing her design sketches with illuminations, to Brys's relief. Her cool and withdrawn presence was hard to bear.

Tuning the harp from one mode to another, Brys wondered how to deal with Caradog. Gwriad's alliance would never stand without Gwynedd. But how to sway a king known mainly as a raider and womanizer, fond of his mead? Maybe he should take Neithon's advice and ask Caradog's *pencerdd*. But his thoughts strayed back to Brochfael.

Brochfael. Who has now tried to kill me. And who lied about Egbert. Brys thought about black-haired men with light eyes — himself, Cadwr, hundreds of men — and gave it up. It didn't matter who hired the killers if Brochfael gave the order. And there was nowhere to turn. Only to Cadwr or Eli, though that could bring harm on them. *The bond of blood. South Powys and Penllyn stand together.* He found his hands had carried him into the grim Æolian mode, spinning black and bloody reflections among the strings. Fear had a cold hand on the back of his neck.

Wind rattled over Padrig's wooden roof and boomed in the dogleg alley beyond Caradog's palace compound. The door snapped open suddenly in a gust and Anna came in laughing, with a willow basket under her arm. Fishtails drooped over its rim.

A tall man stepped in after her, his crimson cloak beating back in bright wings. Like a peacock on a hall roof, he wore a rainbow. His shirt was kingfisher-blue silk, darker than his eyes, and his breeches were dœskin dyed green. His hair was as pale as sea foam, paler than the gold diadem that bound it. Brys watched him shake back his fair mane, take note of the sea-cat harp and assess the man who leaned on her string arm. *Why dœs he look surprised? It could mean anything.*

Padrig came in wearing two wool shirts; he said Greece had thinned his blood.

"Weasel, what have you done with my scabbard?" the newcomer demanded.

"Add a week for every time you ask and another for every insult," snapped Padrig. "Why, Gwydron? Do you need it to attack an Irish chicken coop again?"

"I wanted eggs." A grin. Perfect white teeth. The insult washed off his back. "The good sisters were un-Christian enough to refuse."

"That must have been a new experience, women who refused you."

"One week." He clasped the smith with big hands ringed in gold. "Or Bishop Elfoddw will see in a dream that you've lined his reliquary with the cracked bones of unbaptized children."

"Excellent. Relieve me of a tiresome task. His fool of a prior wants more changes. Forget about ivory, he says now. Ask me about the scabbard after Christ's mass."

The blond man laid an arm like an oaken beam on Padrig's bent shoulder. "Three redhaired virgins if it's ready next week."

"Certainly not. Unless they're trained in gem-cutting." The old smith gazed absently from the blond man to Brys, shook his head and drifted back toward the workshop.

Brys stared at the man's gold arm ring. A dragon swallowing its own tail. *Ireland. The diadem. The arm ring. Heilyn didn't mentioned the dragon, thank God.* Brys looked over the string arm at Gwydron, Caradog's *pencerdd*. Meirwen's lover. He should be kneeling as any pœt's student would kneel. Instead, considering their grandfathers had splintered each others' shields, and considering Meirwen, he nodded coolly.

"You took your sweet time getting here, Penllyn." Now his voice was like the blue silk, rich and mellow, with the slightest husky catch.

Brys picked out a fluid run and answered him in a voice for honing steel, cold and sleek. "I almost didn't get here at all."

"Find your cloak, Cynfarch, and lay it over your ruffled feathers. We'll walk out and enjoy a breath of the sea air."

Brys looked at him a long moment, taking his measure, and shaped the first thought of how he might sway Caradog.

Tide was ebbing from Ffraw estuary below the court, and only a trickle of water from Môn's rolling wheatlands wandered between the weedy rocks. The wind grabbed their cloaks as they crossed the timber bridge over the mud flat and pushed them forward with each step. Ahead, the scrubby pasture yielded to sand dunes like a shrunken mountain range against the sea. Gwydron struck out towards them south across the flat. Sand grains in the gale stung Brys's face, he pushed through the wall of wind with his eyes slitted. The first rampart of sand scattered and shifted under their weight, and hares flew away before them to tunnels under the salt grass. On the last rise they looked out on a great curved bay, charging with breaker after grey breaker between green headlands. Gwydron shouted something and flung himself on the golden sand behind the crest of the dune. Brys dropped beside him, and the wind shrieked up and over into the sand country.

"Neithon told me about the assassins," yelled Gwydron. "Who sent them?"

"At first I thought it was Offa." *Before I realized it was Brochfael — but that's not Gwynedd's affair.* "They'd already sent one man to spy, but he betrayed them."

"What did you do about him?"

"Nothing. He's become a good friend," Brys shouted against the wind, enjoying Gwydron's suspicious blue stare.

"Truth, Penllyn."

Call me that one more time, peacock. Give me reason to shove it down your throat. "They were fool enough to send a freed slave whose mother was a British captive. Even his English half has cause to hate Mercia more than I could in a lifetime."

The *pencerdd* spat out sand, scowling, and Brys laughed. The wind tore his laughter from his mouth and flung it east toward the heart of the island.

"Gwriad should have pulled his envoy out of Frankia. This is our only opportunity and it's too important to ruin. There won't be a second chance." *Too important for a young and untried pœt, you mean. Thanks for the encouragement.*

"Too important for you to handle alone," Brys agreed.

"Tell me about Ceredigion and Powys."

As Brys told him what he needed to know, Gwydron looked out over the crescents of grey water, eyes narrowed. "I owe Neithon a gold piece. I should have known better than to match his bet. You've done well enough, considering."

"But now I need Caradog."

"What do you plan?"

"I wanted to ask you that."

"A young Powys hotspur asking advice of the Gwynedd *pencerdd*? I thought you'd come to teach me how to do it." It was open challenge. *Good. Let it stay that way.*

Brys grinned and got sand between his teeth. "Why wouldn't a pœt's student seek out wisdom and long experience? *Even if you're past your prime and in love with your own reflection.*

"You really are a student? I thought that was another of Neithon's tales." Gwydron whistled. "Rhydion will have your guts for harp strings."

"He has already. He won't graduate me in song."

"You don't need it. *Awen*'s enough. If you have it."

"Yes." Brys studied a knot of sandwort on the dune near his elbow. Easy to say as *pencerdd*, hard to swallow as a broken student.

"But he gave you that?" Gwydron was looking at the gold arm ring with the stag's head embedded in forged interlace. "Why?"

"To provoke Brochfael."

"Powys." Gwydron shook his head slowly. "All the same, you took your time getting to Aberffraw. Neithon had me expecting you a month ago."

"I was imprisoned in Mathrafal." *Haven't you been busy enough entertaining your new girl and your English exiles?* Egbert made him uneasy anywhere, but especially in a British kingdom. "And why hurry? You had Caradog well in hand — once you got back from your victory in Ireland." Brys was pleased to see that draw blood.

Gwydron said, "Meirwen told me you were pushy. I'll keep her out of your reach — maybe you don't recognize her worth now, but you might learn. And you've done her enough damage already."

Damage? Digain did the damage. Brys met the arrogant blue gaze and smiled at his own rush of cleansing rage. It made everything easier. *You're going to eat that.* "Tell me if we could hook Caradog with this . . . "

Gwydron listened carefully as Brys laid out the framework and said only, "Dangerous."

The tide was on the turn when they descended the lee face of the sand dunes in long slipping strides. The wind had shifted and now pushed them north toward Aberffraw like a fist in the back.

Brys waited restlessly near the doorway, looking past Gwydron's shoulder into AberVraw hall. It was a sea of colors, with its painted plaster frieze, brilliant tapestries, silver serving dishes, dresses bright as spring Xowers on women leaning at the sun-chamber rail. The door guard shifted impatiently with a faint rattle of his mail shirt. Caradog was late.

Gwydron stroked the hawk on his wrist, smiling to himself. *Smile while you can, peacock.* Heilyn, playing cupbearer, carried the sea-cat harp. Gwydron's redhaired cupbearer was Caradog's foster son. Merfyn mab Gwriad Manaw had greeted Brys earlier as a cousin, never mind that a dispossessed man claims no kinship; no one seemed to care about that. *Only Brochfael, who wants me without kin.* Merfyn's mother Esyllt was the daughter of Caradog's quarrelsome lord Cynan Tindæthwy.

A door crashed open somewhere in the king's chambers and a voice as raw as this year's mead boomed out. The steward hurried to the door. On his heels was a burly man of forty, black-haired and blue-jawed, wearing a yellow silk shirt and the gold *hual* chain. He passed in a cloud of scented oil. This was the man they called the black bull of Rhos: Caradog, king of Gwynedd.

A crash of spear salutes and the rap of the steward's staff on the dais brought silence. The steward spoke his ancestry, and the hall settled as Caradog took his chair.

"Now."

Gwydron sauntered through the door and turned his wrist sharply so his hawk lost her hold and bated, screaming. It drew every eye in the hall, as he intended, and a few people shouted his name. Brys walked in after him. When he reached the dais, he saw the *pencerdd* had tricked him. *Bastard.* He stood near Caradog's chair, unannounced and unknown to the distressed steward, while Gwydron stepped down among the upper hall benches joking with friends. Caradog scowled after him, though he himself was scarcely known for diplomacy, angry at the rudeness.

Brys saw this and walked out to put both hands on the back of the *pencerdd*'s empty chair. *The insult only hits the mark if I accept it.* He flung his voice — harsh enough to shake the far wall.

"In Powys we say the greatest courtesy is to make a stranger welcome." It got silence except where Gwydron was busy charming the king's guard. The blond man's back stiffened but remained turned. Brys gave him a cold glance, not lost on the benches. He turned to Caradog and bowed deeply. "Brochfael Powys sends a greeting with Cynfarch mab Cadeyrn." *That's breathtaking irony. All Brochfael sends are assassins.*

"Penllyn! Chase Gwydron into the sea again. He needs to soak his swollen head," someone shouted, recalling his grandfather's victory. Gwynedd knew as much of Penllyn as Powys did. Why not? In the past Penllyn had been a Gwynedd cantref, a Powys cantref, a free kingdom. Border states have at least the advantage of choosing their enemies and allies.

"But can he swim? His grandfather learned the hard way." Brys called to the man, earning some laughter. *Mark that one for reaction as I sing.*

Caradog Rhos, after a thoughtful pause, heaved to his feet and clasped Brys's arm in welcome. Saving face for his *pencerdd* did not please him. The benches stirred with interest. The steward's flustered servant found a chair and a drinking cup for Brys. Heilyn came silently to stand behind him. Brys tilted the mead cup but drank little. Gwydron had finished his leisurely circuit and was laughing with a woman at the door. He summoned one of the servants and nodded up at the sun chamber. The servant bowed and led the woman to a stair. Her dark hair was pinned on her nape with gold, and she had silver drops in her ears. *Meirwen . . .* Gwydron returned to his dais chair with a shrug of disdain for the guest from Powys. He gave the hawk to a servant and took his harp.

Gwydron put the instrument back to his shoulder, a big golden man smiling confidently around his hall. Gold studs marked intricate patterns on every surface of the harp; any more gold on the string arm and he'd never find the pegs. He adjusted one gut string. What he did next brought Brys up cold. No introduction, no string song. Gwydron hurled his voice like a gleaming spear as he sang. After the stanzas, equally superb string music. Caradog folded his arms to listen, still scowling. Gwydron damped the strings to silence between his hands. Then he smiled at the Powys pœt. *Fair hand of god, how can I ever match that?*

Brys gave Heilyn the drinking cup and took his harp, thinking quickly. He took up Gwydron's string song as though there had been no interruption, duplicating his fluid style and mellow sound. Then he struck the metal strings harder than gut could be struck, ringing them like bells, and swelled the praise to an echoing shout of silver and bronze in Caradog's hall. He sang victory. And then he took the song beyond victory.

He let victory die in the strings and picked out a dark thread of song, faintly, demanding deep quiet. *A good audience. It knows how to listen.* After war's fervor and darkened spears, he sang lament. Lament for whom, did that really matter? He finished with a bittersweet bronze echo of triumph. Behind him Heilyn caught his breath as though in pain. On the benches, faces were thoughtful or surprised.

The silence drifted with a few comments; servants took mead and bragget to the benches. Gwydron dropped Brys a serpent stare across his crusted string arm and yawned elaborately. That raised a murmur. Caradog nodded thanks to Brys. Brys, wrist on his string arm, bowed his head to the king and ignored Gwydron.

"Try another, Gwydron," one of Caradog's bodyguard men taunted and held an arm ring high. "This says he makes a fool of you again."

"Don't lose that," Gwydron shot back. It had the earmarks of an old dispute. "Your wife will beat you."

"I'll match that!" Someone yelled. The bet took hold. Heads bent together. Movables changed hands. A woman in the lower hall called out, "Contest!"

Gwydron ignored the demands and handed his harp to Merfyn. The hall didn't like being ignored, especially not with ill-mannered arrogance. Brys was hard pressed not to laugh aloud. People were shouting now. When Caradog's son Hywel leaped to his feet holding up a fine knife as a bet, he earned ten offers. He took Cynan Tindæthwy's. Finally the steward, fluttering like a wren in a hawk mews, rapped a house post for quiet. Gwydron looked profoundly bored. Caradog gave his *pencerdd* a black glare and nodded to the steward.

"Contest!" the court officer called out. "Who judges?"

"That gilded pheasant owes me ten head," a man yelled. "I want to judge!"

"I judge," Caradog announced.

Gwydron shrugged sullen agreement and offered a challenge. Brys called out to the benches, making the most of the poor hospitality, "Who will shield me from this great lord when he loses?"

Promises flew back to him. Brys took the challenge, more gracefully than it was given, in an end-rhymed couplet. He tuned carefully, allowing the bets and curiosity to build. Sweat prickled on his back and face. Who would lay silver on an unknown from Powys against the Gwynedd *pencerdd*? Brys looked over a sea of Gwynedd faces, all eagerly awaiting his humiliation. And what would that do to Gwriad's British alliance? He glanced up and wished he hadn't. Meirwen was laughing with another woman at the sun-chamber rail. *That raises the stakes too high. But what do I have to lose? Only what I've already lost.* Gwydron recovered his humor and basked in the hall's shouted advice, playing them and playing to them quite shamelessly. He drained his gold-bound blue drinking horn, cast out the dregs and held it high over his head, offering it in wager.

A man in the upper hall matched the bet, and Gwydron flung the horn out trailing bright drops of mead. The hall company laughed, fickle as carrion birds, shouting encouragement and insults to both pœts.

"Cut him to size, Powys, his vanity's overblown like the rest of him," a servant woman called out, and earned bawdy comments.

"I hear no bet from Powys," Gwydron smiled at the rafters. "Why lose anything, if you haven't anything to lose?" He added so only the dais could hear, "Since I already have your woman."

You'll swallow that. Brys said with a great show of solicitousness, "I won't rob you of cattle or land. I'll have your dragon." Caradog leaned forward abruptly but did not intervene.

Gwydron's hand flew to the arm ring. So it was his insignia of rank. *Good.* Then he nodded slowly. "And I'll have your English slave."

Brys stood slowly in a frozen hall, aware of Heilyn's voice at a great distance. The chair toppled backward with leisurely grace. Heilyn's hand slid from his shoulder. The knife was in Brys's left hand. It flew light as a bird to quiver in a dais plank.

"Face price." Brys folded his arms.

"Accept," Heilyn was saying in urgent English. "Accept. Heaven's realm, accept."

Gwydron got to his feet smiling wickedly. Caradog gave a quiet order, and two men of his guard moved between them with crossed spears.

"Face price in truth," said Gwydron, "for drawing a weapon before the king."

"You insult a free man and my friend."

"The dispossessed make friends as they can," Gwydron told the hall wisely. "Slave once, slave forever."

"Accept," said Heilyn and clamped a hand on his shoulder. "If you don't I will."

Gwydron and Brys locked eyes a long moment across the polished ash spear shafts. The hall was trapped in amber light, dead silent. Heilyn's grip opened. Brys looked out across the benches.

"Gwydron bardd Caradog asks me for an unworthy wager. He asks me to set my friend's honor against gold." *Never mind Meirwen, a private matter.* Rapt faces below. He paused just long enough. "Before God, I will have both."

The hall sighed like a single creature. One of the bodyguard men handed Brys his knife. Merfyn mab Gwriad lifted his hands from the back of Gwydron's chair and let out his breath. He'd paled so his freckles stood out on white skin like flecks of blood. Gwydron took his chair. Brys sat after a moment.

"Who takes my bet?" Heilyn asked in his broadest English accent. He held up a silver bracelet — and he was asking the king.

Fair god, pushing it too far . . . But Caradog pulled off a gold ring, making up for his *pencerdd*'s disgraceful insult. Gwydron shrugged and shouldered his jeweled harp.

"First choice?" he condescended to ask Brys over the string arm.

"String music," Brys decided. Gwydron's reputation was as strong for music as for pœtry. It scarcely mattered what he chose. *But I have your measure now, peacock.*

The Gwynedd *pencerdd* flung back his bright hair bound by the diadem and launched into a cascade of melody. He streamed sweet sound through complex changes, running a rivulet around rapid bends. Perfect technique, flowing with light and graceful humor. Brys listened meticulously. When Gwydron finished, the company pounded their feet in the rushes and thumped drinking cups on benches.

Brys laid the snarling sea-cat to his shoulder. *River.* He gave back Gwydron's music once through in a pure torrent. Then he began to weave it double and triple, a rippling interlace in the glittering strings. He cataracted music swift and deep, spread it broad in shallow estuaries, surged it into the strong cross-rhythm of sea. The big voice of the Irish harp's bronze and silver strings boomed out. *Ocean.* He played the cool depth of a washing undercurrent. Gradually he let the sea wash take over the melody, carried the music up through slow black eons of rock grinding to sand, and crashed one last wave to shore. *Competent. Not brilliant.*

Silence. They wanted to hear every note now that bets rode on this. Brys laid the flat of both hands to the resonant wire. Sweat channelled new streams on his face. Heilyn handed him the mead cup with a hand trembling only slightly; he drank, shaken by the hall's stillness. There was a sea susurration out among the hall benches, only an afterthought perhaps, but a treasury of valuables was now changing hands. Gwydron was watching him closely with no further pretence of ignoring him; his expression was acknowledgment as much as threat.

"Overblown," Brys said pensively, stealing the second choice of categories and catching Gwydron off guard. He didn't need to raise his voice. He already had the audience. "A bullfrog can only swallow so much air before he becomes a green leaping fart."

A hush, then an explosion of laughter. Gwydron narrowed his fine eyes, understanding the new competition. Satire. Not the usual fare for a *pencerdd*, more a tavern pœt's style, but Gwydron was quick on his feet.

"Should eleven generations of Gwynedd's royal line waste breath on a hollow reed of Powys?" His voice rode insolent over the silence.

"A bullfrog has breath to spare." Brys smiled benevolently, starting to enjoy this. "And wastes it on twelve generations of royal Penllyn, from the emperor Macsen who set Cunedda Gwynedd in power as one sets a child on a privy pot." *Genealogical warfare on my terms, peacock. That's for throwing my disgraced father's cantref in my face.*

Caradog bellowed laughter at his kinsman Gwydron's expense, overlooking that the insult also struck him. Gwydron flushed and clamped his mouth shut. The first sting to raw skin. Brys threw back his head and laughed for sheer pleasure.

The next round would have thrown Brochfael into one of his white rages. Gwydron said, "Penllyn, the whore of Powys, lifting her skirts to her brother. Cynddylan's sister preferred his bed to the Mercian's. *Satis est,* they preach in Powys churches, praying to Saint Pelagius. But it's never enough once you try it."

An unhappy murmur. Clever, but it didn't work as Gwydron planned. People looked askance at the church politics, though the old story of incest might titillate them. Brys saw one young monk near the sun room frowning in disapproval.

Brys, exploiting their discomfort, shook his head sadly. "Let the one without sin among you throw the first stone. Dœs Gwydron have a sister?"

Uneasy scattered laughter. The young monk cast him a thoughtful look.

Gwydron recovered quickly. "A sly slippery blackened stump with a bag of tricks borrowed from a tinker's lad, and a tatty black cloak so full of feathers from his barn beds that he claims raven shape."

"A frog-fingered belching backcountry boy seeking smaller ponds for his swollen conceit, grunting sorcerers' charms, lacking other ways to lure girls to his flatulent floating embrace," answered Brys. This kind of nonsense he could recite all day; Rhydion had drilled him well, and he had a natural bent. He looked up at the sun chamber. Meirwen looked down, not at the *pencerdd*. It put an edge on his ambition. He smiled at her, and she covered her mouth with one hand. "Lured, they look twice and leap free."

Gwydron followed his glance and flushed a deeper crimson. He groped for new insults as the company hooted and pounded the benches. Caradog roared, and even his kinsmen on the dais laughed at his king's consternation. Gwydron waited too long and lost his chance.

"A peacock parade," Brys told the hall, "A green-faced glass house admiring its own reflection —"

"Chair!"

Caradog's guard raised the shout first, but it swept through the hall's mirth from the dais pillars down to the kitchen. Brys was lost in delight at Gwydron's helpless rage.

"Chair!"

"Penllyn!"

"Judge, Caradog!" It became a chant. Maybe Gwydron had stung them with satire too often; now he paid the price.

Caradog got to his feet, head down like a bull, to give his judgment. He held his gold ring high, long enough to buy absolute quiet, then tossed it to Heilyn.

"He silenced you, Gwydron," the king commanded. "Yield the chair!"

Merfyn seized the gold-studded harp before he flung it at someone. Gwydron jumped to his feet, his face mottled red in incredulous outrage. He swept a hand toward his carved and inlaid chair, offering it to Brys in a mockery of welcome. Heilyn, grinning, went to stand behind it with the king's gold ring on his hand.

Brys stood. Gwydron loomed close and clasped Brys's right arm in a show of friendship that nearly wrenched him apart at the shoulder. Under the noise he said quietly, "Take that smirk off your face, Penllyn, you dung-handed upstart, and do your work."

"Learn the taste of it, Gwynedd. Your grandfather did."

"My father didn't come peddling Penllyn to Aberffraw."

Brys clenched until his fingers hit bone, and Gwydron winced. "Don't leave with that arm ring."

Gwydron pulled off the dragon arm ring, and Brys displayed his trophy to the hall as the *pencerdd* stalked off the dais and vanished out the door in a gust of black sea wind.

Caradog told the steward to bring nine-year mead for the lower hall, twelve-year mead for the upper hall and unwatered Burgundian for the dais. Quarrels over the bets stopped at that. The king turned to Brys in the pœt's chair, pleased with the entertainment and his own open hand.

"What will you have from me, Cynfarch mab Cadeyrn Penllyn?"

"Lord." Brys bowed deeply. "Let me sing."

Caradog rubbed a square thumb across his chin, suspicious of anything so easy.

Rightly so. "Very well. Sing."

Brys settled on the feather cushion of the *pencerdd*'s chair and touched up the tuning on the sea-cat harp. Her eyes shone silver and amber, fierce and lovely creature. He looked over the hall. Restless, changeable, distrustful of anything blown west from Powys or even Penllyn, yet for this minute they loved the dispossessed youngest son of an ancient house. It was all the chance he would have. He planned nothing until he set his hands to the strings, trusting his bright *awen.*

Sunlight on water. A new victory sourced in the shining wire between his hands, a victory of alliance. Brys sang it with subtlety and fire. He sang township and cantref and kingdom, and wove in undying peace, a rampart of hope to fellow-countrymen. The pæan echœd over the benches after he stilled the strings. Meirwen leaned at the sun-room railing; she hadn't followed Gwydron outside.

Heilyn took the harp as though moving with his thought. Brys went before Caradog and kneeled. He waited. Aberffraw hall was soundless.

A strong grip on each arm; Caradog raised him to his feet. Brys looked into deep brown eyes that studied him minutely. His heavy-boned face was shadowed blue and he had a shaving cut under his right nostril. He reeked of some exotic scent. Brys held the hard gaze and saw that this had only been the easy part.

"Two wonders in one night." Caradog's voice was unnervingly quiet. "Disgrace sung on the chief *pencerdd* of the island of Britain, and Penllyn singing of peace for a king of Powys. Is there a third wonder, Cynfarch?"

Ride the wave before it breaks. "Yes, lord. In private."

Caradog said, "In my quarters."

Near dawn Caradog Rhos called for more wine in a voice ground down to gravel. A guard paced the passage outside the council room, eight steps, pivot, ground the spear butt, eight steps. Brys stared along the table border, inlaid with silver wire in an unending tendrilled vine. The bright metal blurred again, and he blinked. First light began to seep through the window shutters, challenging the candlelight.

Caradog slapped the table. His wine cup jolted and slopped. "Alliance for war, I can see Brochfael supporting that."

"Powys lives for war." Gwydron had drifted in after midnight and now sprawled in a chair with his feet crossed on the polished oak table. The room held only the three of them. "And always has."

Brys watched Caradog's heavy face. He was a warlord rather than a king as Brochfael interpreted the word. Gwydron counseled him well, for the most part. He largely ignored his quarrelsome kinsmen. Unlike southern kings, he made his own decisions and rarely called his council.

"Powys lived for war until nine years ago," Brys answered shortly. "We fought three centuries to keep the English at bay. Now we have a treaty and a marked border — whether we want it or not. We keep the peace."

"Who are the Mercians to impose borders on us?" Caradog demanded.

Brys suppressed a shrug. Gwynedd had no powerful enemy on its border.

"Gwynedd is the head of Britain and has been since Arthur's time," Gwydron said lazily, eyeing his dragon on Brys's arm below the Powys stag. "Why would we follow Powys?"

"Powys is the heart." Brys looked at the king, who was rubbing his chin again with a broad thumb. "Gwriad invites you to a council at midsummer."

"Gwydron?" asked Caradog.

"Yes." Gwydron was still performing, but to what extent Brys couldn't guess. "Gwynedd has always defended peace. Besides, think of the novelty of hearing Powys speak for love and brotherhood."

"I'll meet with Gwriad. Why waste all this effort by you two philosophers?"

"You think I would plot with a Powys adventurer to get myself unchaired in Aberffraw hall?" Gwydron demanded sullenly.

"God knows the two of you are cut from the same cloth." Caradog heaved to his feet and flung the door open. The guard gave a hasty spear salute and followed his heavy footsteps down the corridor to the king's chamber. Merfyn appeared, yawning. On his heels trailed Heilyn.

Gwydron slumped in his chair, rubbing his face. "My hall will be unbearable for weeks. Were we convincing?"

Merfyn shook his head. "That was no performance. You were ready to tear out each others' throats."

"Never." Gwydron turned his brilliant smile on Brys. "You knew better."

"Of course. Who could take you seriously?" Brys stood up and stretched until his back muscles creaked. *Time to get on with other matters.* "How's your hunting this year?"

The window looked east, as Aberffraw looked east, over small River Ffraw and the sea of dunes spuming sand into the west wind. Brys sat in the sunny window seat of the inn's upper room, thinking. After a while he sent for the innkeeper's young son, asked questions, gave instructions and sent him away with seven pieces of bronze.

30 september 793 + aberffraw

Meirwen sat on Padrig's garden bench in the cool morning sun with six small objects in a row beside her. Every morning a young boy brought a new one.

The first was a feather with a rainbow locked in its shimmering jet black. The second was a corn wreath, not that she needed a fertility charm. The third was a clay cat, painted in grey stripes with a green collar and green eyes. The fourth was a wooden spoon with a handle carved in interlace. The fifth was a glass vial of oil, the boy told her, scented with frankincense. The sixth had just arrived, a silver ring set with amber.

None of them was larger than her palm. Small things.

Anna came out after a while and sat drawing in silverpoint. She was working on a procession of saints for the reliquary, taking special pains with the draping of their robes. She smiled silently at Meirwen's collection and bent her head over her parchment.

The morning was still and sunny, though last night there had been frost. Meirwen walked between the houses, past the court compound, among the familiar merchants and farmers with their produce, and down the east slope toward the river. At the inn everyone was in the kitchen, laughing and clattering pots in preparation for the afternoon meal. She walked through the empty tavern and quietly up the stair. There was only one upper room. At the top, she had second thoughts and gathered the skirts of her hooded cloak to go down again. But after walking across Britain alone, she was not afraid of one closed door. She knocked.

"Come."

Meirwen walked in. Brys was sitting in the window seat with one leg bent under him, leaning over something. He had his shirt off and his hair tied back with a thong. He wasn't expecting her.

"I thought you were going to Cær Gybi today." Brys reached forward, and the muscles shifted in his back and shoulder. He was still brown from the summer.

"Heilyn went," said Meirwen. "Padrig thinks it's good for him to deal with customers, especially finicky churchmen."

Brys turned quickly and sent sheets of parchment flying.

"I thought . . " He trailed off, forgetting his polished manners.

Meirwen moved farther along the window seat, turning her back on him to look out on the river. "I've interrupted your work."

"It's not important. Trade routes."

"Gwriad's alliance?"

"There's not long to work things out. I'm glad to see you. I thought I might not —" Brys said, "Don't go."

Meirwen pushed her hood back. The wool caught one of her silver pins and sent a strand of hair falling to her shoulder. She tried to pin it back in place, but loosened more instead. Her hands were usually steadier than this. She clicked her tongue and pulled the other two pins as well. Brys went to the sleeping shelf and brought a satchel. He was always neat, as clean as a cat. He handed her a wooden comb with a silver spine; it looked like a gift from a woman.

This would not be easy after all. Meirwen combed her hair forward over her left shoulder, toward the sunny window, in long pulls. She found a knot and worked at it, wondering if he'd gone back to his trade routes. But he sat again, close enough that she felt his warmth against her hip, and lifted the comb from her fingers. He opened the knot and began to comb her hair straight down her back. His touch was very light, as it always was. He kissed her at the base of her neck, and she leaned back into the curve of his shoulder. His arms came around her shoulders, holding her tightly.

Now. Meirwen found herself waylaid by tears, robbed of words. She took his hand and lifted it down onto the new swelling of her belly. Realization took him a moment. Then his other hand was there too. She felt his breathing catch and steady.

"It's not yours, Brys." She managed to keep her voice level.

"Did I ask?"

"You have the right to know. Why I was avoiding you."

"Good. Now I know." He shrugged. "Meirwen —"

"Your gifts arrived each morning. Thank you. You can't imagine how much fun Gwrgi had finding them for you. You've made him a hero to his friends." If Meirwen kept talking she could avoid thinking. Or listening. There was nothing he could say that could change anything. Her tears had come and gone, but they would be back. She had cried more this summer than in the rest of her life together, not especially from sorrow. Anna said it was a change that came with the baby. Meirwen hoped it would depart just as quickly.

"Meirwen." Brys tried to turn her to him, but she held her ground. "Look at me. Talk to me."

Easier now that she had unburdened herself. After she twisted and pinned her hair, she got to her feet, moving more awkwardly now that the child's growing weight confused her sense of balance, and looked down at him. She'd never seen him at a loss for words.

"I can't stay," Meirwen said. "Anna needs me."

"Not for an hour."

Despite herself, Meirwen laughed. He had said that so many times in Tregeiriog, meeting her by the tall stone after dark. Brys looked puzzled, and then color flooded into his face. As long as they could laugh, she supposed life would go on. She touched his cheek, gathered her cloak and turned to the door. Brys was on his feet, reaching for his shirt.

"You look human for a change," she said, lingering. Now that she'd managed her unpleasant task, she felt a vast relief and acceptance. They were friends.

"What dœs that mean?"

"Slightly the worse for wear." Meirwen looked him over. Brown to the waist. Unshaven. Uncombed, too, unless he'd been tearing his hair over his trade routes. Barefoot. But he looked good in every way that counted, though she wouldn't say that; he was vain enough already.

"Glad I meet your approval," Brys said dryly, following her scrutiny. "Now can we talk?"

"Anything you can say in ten words."

Brys made a show of counting on his fingers, which meant he was recovering. He came to take her by the shoulders. "Silver thorn —"

"I like that. Two. You have eight left." It was time to go.

" — I love you. Marry me."

"What?" She demanded inelegantly. "Don't talk dull."

"Brochfael gave me a farm. Bryn Cerddin, you know it. Or we can live with my brother and his wife in Penllyn."

"Penllyn?"

"My mother's farm. My brother gave his consent as family head and waived a dowry. We can draw up a contract and get witnesses. I'll present you to Brochfael at the next high feast."

Meirwen was missing important parts of this conversation. Brys was serious, she realized, or thought he was serious. She owed him a serious answer. "If you hadn't risked yourself with Digain, I would probably be in Tregeiriog right now. I shall always be in your debt —"

"Why not?" Brys interrupted her careful recitation.

"You're used to getting what you want, aren't you?"

"Scarcely."

"You'll marry a cantref lord's daughter or Brochfael's granddaughter. Everyone says so."

"Everyone but me." Brys grinned. "Those are dynastic marriages, Meirwen. I don't want that or need it. I can marry anyone I want."

"Brochfael won't let you."

"Brochfael can't stop me."

Closer to the truth. "I don't plan to marry anyone. I plan to stay in Aberffraw, or go to Iâl if there's smithy work there, and raise my child. A woman's only place in your privileged world is on her back or on the birthing stool. A woman who thinks — and who makes things in metal — has no place in it at all."

"Far from true, but let it pass. I'll make sure you have a place in it."

"I'll make my own place. Wherever I go."

Brys always knew when to stop talking. His mouth found hers, the gentlest brush of lips, a kiss for old friendship. Meirwen warmed to his touch, wanting him more than she had known, longing to spin out a childhood dream another hour —

"No." *Not with another man's child in my belly. Not through seduction. Not with someone so far above me in rank that I can only guess at the rules of conduct.* Meirwen disengaged herself. Brys didn't try to hold her. That, she supposed from his troubled look, had something to do with Digain and what he had done to her. "Not like this."

"Tell me how, Meirwen."

"Too many words." She tried to smile, and failed.

Meirwen got through the door before the tears blinded her, and somehow flew down the stairs without breaking her neck. She didn't look back until she sat by the small window of Anna's loft. By then she had packed her bag and laid her plans.

Brys labored all night, beset by two demons. One was fear of saying plainly what he felt for any man or woman. The other was reluctance to admit that he needed anything from anyone. He took up his tablet and stylus, and wrote all around what he wanted to say. As usual. *Verbal interlace.*

His first attempt was a charming three-line *englyn*, beautifully turned and balanced, for a pale-browed girl with sunny hair and hands like silk. It would have captivated a woman of the court. But Meirwen had a freckled face, rough hands often burned and scarred, hair the color of seasoned heartwood — and she was all moonlight and silver and thorns in his memory. He smoothed the wax, again and again, until the inn began stirring at dawn.

By then he was worn down to a few threadbare words which were inarticulate if not illiterate. As Meirwen would lose no time in telling him.

2 October 793 + Eglwysail

They ran down the stag at mid-morning and cornered him by a stream in a brown pasture. Caradog nodded to one of his young men, who speared the stag through the breast and risked the antlers to cut his throat for a clean death. The stag's last shudder sprayed blood over the first spear's blue shirt, and his friends shouted that it was good luck. Not for the laundress, Heilyn muttered to Brys. The huntsman came forward to *gralloch*, but the hunter shook his head. He spoke to his waiting friends, and they silently went to their horses and rode away. Heilyn looked queasily at the knife flicking at scent glands and genitals, and he also departed. Gwydron steered Caradog after the rest of the hunting party, talking about a boar upstream.

Brys leaned on his spear, once they left, and watched the young man dress his kill. He looked around for a *gralloch*-tree and saw the wild cherry with leaves turning purple on its branches. The huntsman helped them hang the carcass by its hind legs, then gathered his dog boys to try the boar. That left Brys alone with Egbert of Wessex.

"Was Caradog worth your effort the other night, Cynfarch?" he asked. He was a tall brown-haired man in his twenties wearing a gold bracelet; he spoke British with a faint accent of Cernyw, or maybe it was Armorica.

"Song is never wasted," said Brys.

"Time is." Egbert sliced down the stag's belly in one controlled yet savage stroke. He slit the legs one by one and eased his knife meticulously between hide and raw flesh. "Gwydron said you asked for me."

Brys plunged into an indisputable lie which was also probably treason. *If Brochfael knew* . . . "In Powys we remember that the West Saxons have a longstanding sympathy for British affairs." *Overlooking a relentless encroachment on Cernyw and occasional attacks on Gwent.*

"Most certainly," Egbert said with a twist of the mouth that might be irony. His eyes were a cool grey; they could be blue on a hot summer day.

"We share generations of goodwill and one ancestor." *Hard to get that out without choking.*

"A great king of Powys," Egbert said; it was almost more than Brys could hear straightfaced. "But why speak to me of old friendship with the West Saxons, Cynfarch? Offa's son-in-law Bertric rules in Winchester."

"Eadburh and Bertric are riding roughshod over the West Saxons."

"God strike them down for it. I have no greater grief," Egbert said quietly. His lack of passion gave his words all the more power.

"A West Saxon heir in exile is like ungrounded lightning. Many in Mathrafal want you crowned."

"Why?" Egbert's mouth tightened with effort as he hacked through the stag's neck and threw the head aside. He knew the answer but he wanted to hear it.

"Rebellions have a way of spattering in every direction." Brys glanced at the blood smeared up past Egbert's bracelet and splashed over his clothes.

"And some might land on Powys?" The heir of Wessex smiled warmly. His eyes didn't change. "What do you want?"

"Ask instead what we don't want." Brys felt one line of sweat run down beside his spine despite the cool morning air. "A broken border."

"Winchester is a long way from Mathrafal."

"Dœs Cenwulf understand that?" asked Brys, putting his life on his tongue.

The West Saxon reached into the belly cavity and wrenched steaming coils of intestines onto the ground between them. "Who sent you?"

"I think you know." Brys looked down at the reeking mess and fought sickness for a different reason. *Who sent me indeed? Whom was I supposed to tell that Egbert is returned to Britain? Fair god, I'm in this too deep. There's no way back. I have to go on.* "One who says, Wait for the right moment."

"Why would I wait longer? He knows my moment."

"A diversion in Powys might give you Winchester," Brys said, struggling with the shock of that easy answer, struggling to believe this conversation was taking place. "But how long could you hold it after Offa finished with us? The man is formidable."

"Ask me, I know it," Egbert said calmly in the British pœt's phrase. "My father fought Offa at Otford. I fought him at Portchester. It cost me a crown."

"Offa would go through one nation in a month. He would make uphill work of four nations. Powys would be nearly invulnerable with backing from Gwynedd, Ceredigion and Manaw," said Brys. *In fact Offa and Brochfael would do anything to avoid war. Maybe even ally against Wessex. But maybe Egbert dœsn't know that yet.* "It would take him longer. You need more time."

Egbert paused, thoughtful. Brys watched the cool, exact mind take it apart word by word and put it back together. "Your alliance. That's why your kinsman backs it."

Kinsman? Which kinsman of many? But only one of them lies to me about Egbert. Only one sends killers. Brochfael Powys, kin by fostering. "Yes."

"I underestimated him. And I underestimated you, until I saw you handle Caradog and his pœt." Egbert laughed. "He told me you'd be an asset. Another of the dispossessed. In a year, two at most, you'll have Penllyn. You like the sound of that? Cynfarch Penllyn?"

Merciful God. Brys smiled at the butt of his borrowed spear, not trusting either his voice or his face. *Lead us not into temptation.*

Egbert drew out the last entrails and looked at his bloody hands. He walked down to the stream bank, pulled off his boots and waded into the thigh-deep water. There he sat with the current streaming around his shoulders and his breath hanging on the cool morning air. If he noticed the chill he gave no sign of it. Brys sat on his heels and watched the sun lift over the shoulder of Arfon's snow mountains until the West Saxon surged out of the water and shook himself. The laundress's task would be easier after all.

"What guarantee do I have that your alliance won't land an army in Cernyw and cut my throat?" He shoved his feet into his boots and tied the straps.

"What guarantee do you have that Offa won't attack Frankia? Or Charles attack Mercia? Consider how much it would cost us and how little we would gain. Then make up your own mind."

Egbert got lightly to his feet and went to tie his horse under the cherry tree. It pulled back on its reins at the stink of fresh blood and the swinging carcass. At his saddlebow was strapped a *frankiska*, one of the deadly old-fashioned Frankish throwing axes.

"One other thing, though it's none of my business." Egbert hesitated. "Tell him it was a mistake giving his daughter to Cenwulf. The man's vicious. He will use her cruelly and kill her to prevent her from talking."

"I'll tell him. One way or another." *Mair mother of God. Brochfael has no living daughter, not even a bastard. Who if not Brochfael?*

Egbert pulled a chequered cloak from the saddlebag and pinned it with a gold brooch the size of his hand. Brys looked with curiosity at the man's instinctive adaptation. The West Saxon heir, descendent of an English pirate who may or may not have been the son of a Powys king, carried off a flawless imitation of a British noble. He parted the thongs that held the carcass and tied the stag in its hide behind his saddle. Then he turned and offered Brys his arm. They clasped. His hand was bloody again. Now so was Brys's hand.

"Tell Eli that I will delay as long as I can." He hesitated. "He told me Penllyn always stood with South Powys. I'm sorry about your father, Cynfarch."

Brys nodded, looking at the stag. If he met Egbert's eyes he was lost. *Eli Elfæl, of Cynddylan's line, with his boar-headed torc. And his four daughters — or were there five? Eli whom Brochfael hates as only half-brother can hate bastard half-brother. And Eli hates Brochfael more, enough to cut him down in cold blood. That's why Brochfael tried to have me killed. He knows about Eli. He thinks I'm part of it because Eli courted me. South Powys and Penllyn.*

They rode back to Aberffraw through a heavy dew, leaving hoofprints black in the pale grass. The noon sun would burn it to nothing, a half-remembered illusion.

3 October 793 ✝ Aberffraw

Gwrgi arrived disconsolate while they were breaking their fast in the garden. "He didn't want me to find anything this time. He sent this instead."

This package was larger than the others, wrapped in a painted silk stole that had the look of Neithon's trade goods. Inside it Meirwen found his two arm rings, the old silver one with ravens and the gold one that Brochfael's *pencerdd* had given him. Meirwen understood the message quite clearly. *Everything I am, everything I could be.*

"Not bad," Gwrgi admitted grudgingly.

Anna and Padrig were exchanging looks over her head, she knew, and Gwrgi climbed up beside her for a better look. She hugged him once, wordlessly and fiercely, and he ran off to play on the tideflats. Anna put an arm around her and reached for the silk stole after the first few tears fell. That was when the folded parchment fell out at Meirwen's feet. Her name was written on the outside in a clear, open script. Anna picked it up.

"Is this his lettering? He writes a fine hand. Some Byzantine influence, I would say."

"Anna, my dear," Padrig said mildly, on his way to the workshop.

Anna gave her the letter, kissed her and left her alone. Meirwen went back into the garden and sat a long time with the parchment on her lap. Two sparrows returned to peck among the crumbs of the morning meal, made brave by her stillness. As long as she sat here holding an unread letter, her satchel waiting ready upstairs, she was between choices. She could ignore them for a while longer.

Finally she read it. What had she expected? Not this small promise that rolled sweetly around her tongue. *Meirwen, fy miaren arian* . . . My silver thorn, I love you forever. On your terms. Brys.

Meirwen held it for a long time, and decided to leave tomorrow instead. Today she would walk in the sand dunes. A place between was what she needed right now; between sea and pasture, between land and sky. She put the arm rings in her pouch; she could leave them on her way past the inn.

At the inn everyone was hurrying to prepare the day's meal. In any case, gold and silver were too precious to leave with anyone but their owner.

This time his door stood open, and a warm breeze blew through the upper room. Brys stood up from the window seat, washed and combed this time, looking as though he hadn't slept. Meirwen silently closed the door behind her and went to hand him the arm rings. He pushed them above his elbows. Not asking. On the windowsill stood a jointed wooden horse that would fit on the palm of her hand, and a rag doll. Small things.

This time Meirwen kissed him on the mouth, gently, and let herself lean inside the circle of his arms. His light touch on her face, on her hair. Another kiss, deep and warm, lasted a long time. She had almost forgotten. But she was starting to remember.

"I need a forge and smithy." *Not marriage. Not divorce when you marry someone else.* "I'll have those if I stay here."

"Then I'll stay here too."

"Why?"

"Why do you think? But there's Bryn Cerddin. Do you remember it?"

Meirwen was remembering instead how much she liked looking a man in the eyes, especially when his eyes were as green as a willow leaf between long black lashes. Why couldn't she have lashes like that, and thick curling hair? He had wonderful hair; she loved to take a handful. It felt crisp between her fingers and gave off a scent of sage. She closed her eyes and remembered him by touch, straight nose and curved mouth, eyes deepset under straight brows. Forehead and cheekbones and jaw. Square shoulders and back . . .

"What do you think you're doing? Buying a horse? You can check my teeth, too, if you like."

"I'm thinking." Last week she had put aside her belt; her belly still rose gently, but it felt big enough to be in the way of everything. Her breasts were swollen. She felt ungainly and slow. What if he found her unsightly?

"Let me help you think." Brys found her hair pins, and dropped them on the floor one by one with a small clatter. Then her dress pin. "Fair god, you look beautiful."

"Brys —"

"And having lascivious dreams every night for months has nothing to do with it."

"Be serious for once. Everything's different."

"That's the best part." He pulled her dress and shift over her head, taking time to explore her changing body. Then he put an arm under her and carried her to the sleeping shelf. "I want a good look at you both. Is it a girl or a boy?"

"A girl," Meirwen guessed. A girl with curling black hair and light eyes. Loving, high-spirited, full of life. God willing.

Brys was compact and muscular, as graceful as a cat. Meirwen ran a forefinger from the hollow of his throat down the line of black hair into his breeches. The brown skin ended at his waist, she soon found. They had rarely enjoyed the luxury of a bed in three years as lovers. After that her senses followed his touch, light and certain, on her tender breasts and her thighs and the warm hidden places. Slowest was best, it had taken them some time to discover at Tregeiriog. He stretched her like a wire, coiled her and melted her, until not having him inside her was too great a need. She took him in, slowly, so that he held his breath at the intensity. After that she was drawn steadily into the waves of pleasure, breaking, ebbing, flowing. A crease of concentration between his brows gave Brys away. Reciting legal triads, he told her once, to make things last, to savor every sensation at the same time. The more obscure the better.

"What is it this time, corn laws or murder price?"

"Seduction. What else?"

Laughter undid them, not for the first time. He came surging into her, carrying her along with him on another breaking wave. Soon they were spent in a tangle of linens. Brys was quiet for many long breaths and slowing heartbeats. He said something about salt. Was he still doing that? But he was back again quickly from wherever his mind had wandered. He fell asleep with one arm cradled protectively over her belly. Already, he was getting possessive about this child.

When she woke again, it was late afternoon. Brys lay with his head on his arms, frowning up at the thatch. She watched him unnoticed, tallying the changes. His mouth was harder. A new scar on his arm, probably the one Heilyn told her about. His startling green eyes were his only beauty. It wasn't his looks that attracted people. Wit, passion, the name — everyone knew about Penllyn — and the skill. She hadn't understood until Caradog's hall that he was far more than a pœt's gifted student. No wonder Gwriad had sought him out to sing his idea to the kings.

Meirwen's thoughts drifted to her own work: metal and stone, heat and the tempering shock of water, all elements bonding together into a new form. A carved monument lasts a few centuries; song lasts as long as someone sings it. Gold lasts forever, an alloy of time and vision. Her vision was evolving, her skills were blossoming under expert guidance, her ideas spilled in a torrent from her tablets and parchment onto Padrig's littered workbench.

"Meirwen," Brys said. She turned her head against his elbow. He'd been watching her and smiling. "You're thinking about metal."

"How do you know?"

"I read minds."

"If you did —"

A long time later when they lay curved against each other like spoons, warmly linked, he said over her shoulder, "I know because you always chew your lower lip. Come to Bryn Cerddin with me and work metal. Maybe Heilyn will change his mind and come too."

She hesitated. "I don't think so. It would be painful."

"Why?" He sounded surprised.

"Heilyn is in love with you. Didn't you know?"

"It crossed my mind. I love him. Not that way."

"I've never heard you say the word. Love. First me, now Heilyn."

"It gets easier," Brys said. "I love you. You love me. You see?"

"You're an innocent," said Meirwen, rolling into his arms. "Only the rich and powerful can afford love."

"Do you love me?"

"Dearly."

"Then either power and wealth are relative terms, or love is a relative term. Padrig was showing me passages from Lucretius yesterday."

"Whatever for?"

"We were arguing about Pelagius."

"The heretic?"

"Salvation in good works, dœs that sound like heresy?"

We'll be here for a week debating moral philosophy and logic. Meirwen put her leg across his thigh, curious about the relative attraction of philosophical and physical love. It didn't take long to find out.

"Not Penllyn," she said later, answering his question of two days ago. "Bryn Cerddin."

Downstairs, the tavern filled for evening. The innkeeper heard more laughter upstairs and carried up a meal which he discreetly left outside the door.

When Padrig's goldsmith came downstairs hand-in-hand with Cynfarch mab Cadeyrn and they walked out together in the gathering dusk, no one seemed to notice. Of course the interesting news had traveled to Eglwysail and back again already.

7 october 793 + aberffraw

Merfyn held the bets while Brys and Gwydron attacked and retreated across the gameboard. They all sat or sprawled on cushions in the goldsmiths' strange house, where the shutters were closed tightly on the enclosed garden. Russet apples filled a lapis-colored bowl. Heilyn frowned over his drawing in a wax tablet. Under an oil lamp, Meirwen was reading aloud to Anna of Helena who brought down Troy. *As another Helena brought down Pengwern.* Brys's thoughts wandered far from the gameboard, where Gwydron was making steady gains across the cherrywood and ivory squares.

"Pay up, Cynfarch." Merfyn held up the arm ring. "He has you."

Brys handed over the dragon arm ring and Gwydron slipped it over his elbow without comment. Caradog had been hugely amused over his loss. Time to get things back on an even keel.

"What will you do in Armorica?" Brys asked Merfyn.

"King's bodyguard. That's the place for younger sons." Untroubled, Merfyn began setting up the game again. He had two older brothers and would probably never rule Manaw; he was even further from the kingship of Gwynedd on his mother's side. He would do well in Armorica. Or anywhere else. Merfyn had a highly developed interest in rank, ancient rights, all the trappings of power, and he had a cool-headed way of getting around any obstacle. At fifteen he outdistanced Caradog in political sophistication. The blood of old Rheged, the lost north, ran true. Like his father, Merfyn had coppery hair; he also had so many freckles that in Aberffraw they called him Merfyn Frych.

"Do you think we'll see your father's idea come to life?" Brys said, looking at the gameboard.

"Why not? We're undivided in history and language and custom. We're one people. Cymry," said Merfyn. "Are you sure you won't go to Manaw? Take your letter in person. You'd be welcome as a kinsman."

Brys had stopped correcting people about his dispossession. "I'm going to Powys to live on my goat pasture. Now we'll wait for the council at midsummer and see what the kings say to alliance." And wait for Gwydron to find some way, as he promised, to get Egbert out of Gwynedd. Preferably out of Britain.

"Stay here," Gwydron said, looking up from the *gwyddbwyll* board. "I'll graduate you in song."

"Too easy." Brys sipped the pale Rhenish wine. *Tempting. But I was tempted more cruelly a week ago by the English exile. How to tell Brochfael about Egbert without getting my throat cut? Why do I care about Powys though? All my ties are Penllyn, and I can do no good there. Powys is only an idea, a collection of cantrefs and captive kingdoms huddled in defence against the English. It never really has existed. But it can. Powys* paradwys, *Powys the garden.*

"Fine, do everything the hard way." Gwydron shook his head. The diadem flowed with lamplight. And though he had known the answer for days, he asked, "Meirwen?"

"I'll go to Powys."

"Why, when all you two do is argue?" Gwydron demanded, not expecting an answer. "Things will be dull if everyone gœs. Heilyn?"

"I'll stay until the reliquary's finished." He had made peace with Gwydron over the insult in Caradog's hall.

Heilyn's uncertain farewells were made. Meirwen left him a list of instructions, a sheaf of drawings and a sisterly kiss which made him fidget. Brys, never comfortable with shows of affection at the best of times, walked with him one afternoon in the dunes. He tried to say the things that needed to be said about honor and loyalty. No words sufficed, but he gave it his best. He spoke of owing his life to Heilyn in Cær Seint, of the love between friends. If Heilyn wanted more, he didn't have it to give. Heilyn responded with his rare open smile, sullen lead transformed to shining gold, and said that he fully expected to survive.

"If things get dull you can always raid Ireland," Brys told Gwydron.

"You had to say that, Penllyn."

"What would you have done if I'd lost the competition?" he wondered, now that it was over.

"I would have waited for Gwriad's envoy." Gwydron was a sober and intelligent man when he wasn't performing. "No one would have listened to you in Aberffraw again. You knew the risk you took."

Brys nodded. "Did it bother you, losing?"

"Losing what?" Gwydron laughed, but looked rueful for an unguarded moment. No doubt he had another girl in his bed by now. His marriage was political, Meirwen said; his wife kept to her estates instead of coming to court. "Take good care of her, Cynfarch. Don't let her slip away."

Later, when the braziers were pulled in from the corners against the chill, Meirwen and Anna leaned over the gameboard. They were brighter than the small flames flickering above the coals, Meirwen in amber-colored linen and Anna in ruby red. Heilyn and Padrig were debating about the best ornament for the side panels, granulation and enamel or forged interlace. Brys lay among the cushions with a gift from Caradog, a book probably stolen from the scriptorium of an Irish abbey. It was the sixth book of Virgil's *Æneid.* Æneas was in the other world among the spirits waiting for rebirth. Strange pœtry, harder to sing than a law tract; it must have been chanted instead. Yet the words held strength and grace, as the parchment held the faint scent of a cedar book chest.

"The houses of Athens step down the dusty hillsides to the sea," Padrig was telling Heilyn. Meirwen raised her head to listen, one hand curled around Anna's pearwood flute. "All whitewashed and tiled red under that blinding blue sky, and the sea's as dark as southern wine."

In the lee of Aberffraw they could barely hear the waves thundering in from Ireland and the night cries of gull and petrel. Rain stopped at the precious window glass. Inside was an island of warmth, safe from danger and time.

" — Constantinople, where I saw gold work that made me weep. And beyond, a year overland with traders of lapis lazuli and spice and silk, lies India —

Brys bent his head over the book again. *Sunt geminæ somni portæ.* The gates of sleep are twinned. One is of horn, giving easy exit to true spirits. The other shines in flawless ivory, through which the dead send false dreams to the living.

Anna lifted Meirwen's last prince from an inner square, a small figure suddenly dropped into a wider world than the silver-channelled board. Meirwen set the flute to her lips and played the few notes that call hounds from a hunt.

PART II

Anno Domini 794 to 795

Keint rac ud clotleu yn doleu hafren
Rac brochuæl powys a gravys vy awen.

I sang before a bright-famed lord in Severn meadows,
Before Brochfael Powys who loved my awen.

– *Taliesin*

River Teirw ran high all autumn, embattling the lower ford and greening the river meadows, but even in spate it was a small stream. Bryn Cerddin hall looked south from a bench; the herdsman's house stood nearer the river. On the bedrock spurs the rowans that gave the farm its name were heavy with crimson fruit. A smaller stream danced down from the windy moorland, falling through woodland to pasture and tilled fields, and splashed into Teirw.

"How's the game this year?" Brys asked Alban the first time they walked around the farm.

"Stag and a few boar upstream. We may see wolves if winter closes in. Remember the hard winter three years ago? I took a bear, a mangy old sow that tasted like bootsoles. Not many of them left now."

Alban was a big, loose-strung man with thinning black hair and bad teeth. His two brothers farmed together in Tregeiriog; Brochfael's huntsman was best known for breeding fierce falcons and steady hounds. Brys had never really thought about Alban's skill as a farmer. Who thought of Bryn Cerddin as a farm? It was just another of Brochfael's upland hunting halls. Alban and he had always been on good terms. Now the farmer had little to say and watched him carefully.

"Are your hounds ready?" Brys asked, looking over the hayfields.

Alban showed gaps in his side teeth when he grinned. "Ready? I could run them blindfold. You better come look at this."

Brys, braced for trouble, followed Alban to the enclosures where seven black cows and one red bull fed on chopped bracken and gorse. They looked sleek and fat.

"What's the problem?"

"Brochfael sent ten head but they were eating us out of fodder. So I traded two head over at Llangollen for these others. Is that all right?" He'd walked on to another pen of spotted hogs with flop ears and wise, curious faces. "And there's a few sheep."

"Fine." Brys puzzled over it. He also wondered at the tight elm planks of a new threshing floor and at the new plowing and harvest gear stowed under the barn thatch. It wasn't what he expected at Bryn Cerddin, a stony poor farm near a battered frontier.

Meirwen found an anvil in the barn loft and she set about building a smithy shed with Brys's help, until Alban's stout grey wife, Bethan, clucked over her hauling timber and stone. Bethan herded Alban and their two shy daughters into a day-long work party. Soon they had corner posts, thatched roof, rolled oxhide walls, a workbench and a hearth. They kindled it and toasted it with Bethan's new nine-year mead. After that Brys often spent afternoons working the bellows while Meirwen shaped metal, talking and arguing about anything that came to mind.

One day a trader rode in fervently cursing a gift from Gwydron, a brace of loping Irish hound puppies nearly as tall as his pack pony. Meirwen named them after the Irish lovers, Deirdre and Naoise, as she had named the grey stallion Carnlas. The dogs were catapulting around the hall a few days later when Brys and Alban sat near the hearth cleaning harness. Alban jumped to his feet and started up the loft stair.

"Brochfael asked me to show you this. Slipped my mind," he apologized over his shoulder.

Brys climbed after him, stepped between baskets of apples and raw wool, and ducked the braided onions hanging overhead. He'd given the upper room only a quick glance, having slept there on many hunting trips. But Alban walked across the creaking planks to the window and lifted the latch. The shutters opened stiffly, sending rainy grey light over the storage chests and low roof beams. Brys kneeled in a corner to lift a leather war shirt; it tore at his touch like a dry leaf, and a few bronze studs clattered onto the planks.

"Up here."

Alban ran a hand along the roof beam nearest the window. Brys stooped beside him under the slope of thatch and saw the carved letters. At first he thought it was a joke, but the huntsman waited patiently.

With an unlettered man's suspicion, Alban said, "Brochfael said you'd know what it reads. I can see the boar clear enough and the spear through his head."

"Fair hand of god." Brys heard the slow drub of his own heart. The archaic letters were hard to make out. "It's a hunting tally. It says, 'Two years after Cocboi. Condilan I wolf I boar. Panna II stag. Eliud I stag.'"

Brys leaned his forehead on the oak beam, counting. Cynddylan mab Cyndrwyn of South Powys, Eiludd mab Brochfael of North Powys, Penda the son of Pybba, a Mercian king with a British name. They were still allies against English Northumbria then, two years after the great battle of Mæs Cogwy. Maybe even friends, hunting at Eiludd's hall. It wasn't close to the border then but deep in North Powys. All three in young manhood, a hundred and fifty years ago. Years before Cynddylan's fatal raids on Mercia and North Powys. Years before he fell guarding ford and hillside against Penda's treacherous son Wulfhere. Years before Pengwern fell.

This, not the stone-ribbed farm, is Brochfael's gift. It was a wonderful gift, a gift to the heart. Brys stood until the carved letters swam in his vision and wondered how Brochfael could plot to have him killed at Cær Seint and still give him this. *Why?*

"Reckon it was hunted less back then. We might try boar tomorrow." Alban latched the shutters.

In thin December sunshine Meirwen sat on the south-facing door bench while Brys combed her hair dry. The season's last warmth rose from the clayed timber at his back. The speckled barn cat led her kittens on a fruitless hunt through the orchard and finally crawled into Meirwen's lap for refuge while they snarled and tumbled around her feet. Downstream, on the track up from Tregeiriog, a black ant grew into a small man riding a half-wild black pony stallion. Meirwen went inside for the guest cup and Brys walked to the orchard gate.

Cian landed lightly, and when the stallion began to dance on the rein, pulled his bronze knife and hit the pony hard, pommel first, on his proud black nose. Then he took the guest cup and drained it in silence.

"You could always break him, just for the novelty," Brys said, watching him hobble the beast.

"I came for a song." Cian crouched on his heels near the door in the fair family's way, looked up quizzically, then deliberately stood and came to sit beside him on the bench. "My wife is dead."

It was a different message that he wanted to hear, Brochfael's request that he come to Mathrafal. But he was still an exile. Maybe he should just ride south. And walk into another assassin's knife? At least he'd bought time from Egbert, time to decide how to deal with Brochfael.

Brys turned to look at him. Cian's eyes were dark blue, almost black around the iris, and slanted in his narrow face. They yielded no emotion Brys could identify, no clear anger or sorrow, as though all feeling lay beyond reach in their depths.

"Cian," he searched for words. "Times change."

"To show her the way to the island," Cian said quietly. He glanced past Brys to the orchard, where Meirwen kneeled in her physic garden in a sunny corner. She was big with child now. Soon she would have the baby in her arms. Brys had made a cradle from Alban's hoard of applewood; Bethan had been cutting down old linens to fit. The two young girls were making cloth dolls, endlessly dressing and instructing them. It was a good time, waiting for a little son or daughter to dance in sunlight and laugh at the shadows. Cadwr would be pleased. On a branch above Meirwen a small bird flirted its feathers out of reach of the speckled cat.

Brys brought out the harp. Cian was leaning motionless against the wall, eyes closed. In his cupped hand he held a bracelet of braided bronze wire with one smooth white quartz pebble caught between the strands. Even on Cian's narrow palm it looked only big enough for a child's wrist. There was no point asking her name. Cian's own real name was nine syllables, never spoken outside his mother's house. So Brys sang for him of Rhiannon's three birds of forgetfulness, skimming the waves of the western sea, now among the living and now beyond time in Afallach's green island of youth. After the bronze and silver faded to silence, he looked up to see Cian gazing up Teirw's green valley, to the west. His hands were empty.

Meirwen joined them on the bench with one striped kitten. She stroked it as she drew in her wax tablet, smoothed the wax and drew again. It was the design for Bethan's bracelet, silver with one amber oval in a knot of interlace. Cian went out to free his black stallion and vaulted up. He nodded farewell and rode away without a backward glance.

A week after Christ's mass Brys left Meirwen teaching Bethan's girls how to work the bellows and went upstream with Alban after a rumor of wolves. Three days later they came back empty-handed to find Meirwen in labor, weeks early.

Bethan and the Tregeiriog midwife turned Brys from the door. He might assist the Meifod surgeon but he wasn't assisting here. Alban took him in hand, gave him mead and told him about the livestock in a great deal of unnecessary detail. Brys didn't remember much later.

At dawn the next day Meirwen gave birth to a daughter with a fine halo of black hair and dark blue eyes. They thought her name would be Meisyr, like his sister. As they held her, her gaze would wander across their faces as though she could find all the world's secrets there. Her mouth was a pretty bow, triangular as a kitten's when she yawned, and her hands were shaped like stars. She was no bigger than the girls' dolls in her borrowed gowns and blankets. Brys walked her at night, singing quietly, while Meirwen slept. Such a hurry to get here, he told her, and now all you can do is sleep and cry. He wanted her to be a tall beautiful girl, brave and generous and full of laughter. But he knew from the start that she was too small.

In the depth of her third night her breathing grew rough and shallow, though she showed no sign of sickness. In the hour before dawn it failed, and she died in her mother's arms.

Meirwen was silent when they buried the child at the wood margin behind Bryn Cerddin hall and silent when she returned to work. She knows what she needs, Bethan advised kindly. Give her some peace. There'll be another. I lost three. Let her grieve.

Brys went to help Alban shore up the footbridge two days later, and the work stretched into the late afternoon. He returned to find the hall empty. Meirwen was gone, and so was her satchel of tools. Bethan had not seen her go, but the younger daughter said someone had walked upstream when she was in the orchard. Perhaps Meirwen had gone looking for medicinal herbs? So soon after childbirth she should not walk far, Bethan said, failing to hide her worry. Then Alban found tracks on the stream path heading west, up into the moorland.

Brys saddled the stallion quickly. A clear sky promised hard frost for the night. He mounted and dug his heels into Carnlas's flanks, and the grey exploded into a gallop west. Beyond his cleared land he slowed to a canter, looking around him. How far could she walk? She would avoid deep forest, but he halted at the upstream farms to ask. Three had seen no woman walking alone. The fourth was a poor plot of weeds with a single milk goat, where a gap-toothed old woman pointed him further up toward the stream sources. Last summer a girl had walked down from there, she said, a tall girl with metal skill. Brys wheeled away uphill, searching by the stream's shallow pools and sheltered hollows, calling her name. Light retreated west before him. An hour at most remained. Above River Teirw's source the land broke into rolling waves of moor and dense woodland, all dark now that the sun was low. Kites circled overhead. Hunting, he prayed, not scavenging.

In half-light he descended a slope of matted red bracken toward the next ridge. A hut of turf and stone lay at its foot. No light or motion, and the doorway gaped. Deserted. As Brys turned away a raven lifted silently from the piled stones. He saw a pale blur before the door and when he urged Carnlas forward the stallion reared wildly. Brys flung himself down and saw Meirwen curled like a child with her hands pressed over her face. Her old homespun gown was caked with her dried milk and seeping fresh blood. What possessed her to walk so far? As he knelt in the grass at her side, a stench of death struck him sickeningly from within the hut.

Meirwen's face was flushed, her pulse light and racing with fever, as she turned restlessly under his hands. Brys unclasped his cloak and lifted her. She turned her face blindly away as he got her sitting and wrapped thick folds of wool around her.

"I have to bury him." A dry weightless voice, chaff on the wind. She fought his hold without strength. "He blessed me."

Not today. Brys left her bundled in the cloak and ducked his head under the turf lintel, holding his breath. A hermit, probably, dead a month or more by the scattered bones and flesh. Fox and stoat would continue their work, but he thought of the plagues spread from unburied corpses. Outside, he drove a heel at the loose wall of turf and stones. It gave, and another blow brought the dwelling crumbling over the hermit's body. The stink blossomed horribly.

Brys could do nothing now for her internal bleeding and not much later. A small blood vessel could bleed itself out; that was the only hope. He caught Carnlas and got Meirwen on the saddlebow, mounting awkwardly behind her as the stallion shied from the blood reek. She struggled in his arms at first but by the time he handed her down to Alban at Bryn Cerddin she was still.

By midnight infection clawed her belly and drove fever through her. Brys watched her convulse and fight, kept the quilts and fur robes on her despite her will to fling them off, slept in snatches hardly aware of Bethan preparing broth and fever infusions. Meirwen talked, a steady low torrent of tattered sense. Some was about Digain, some about Brys, some about her father and the mother she had never known.

Most of it was conversation with a beloved child, first an infant and then a young girl. At first Brys could not bear to listen. After a time he understood that in some way Meirwen was giving her child life of the only kind possible to her, and the relentless outpouring of her love and grief became a sacrament of passage.

On the fifth day she knew Brys. He held her parched hands and watched the distance grow in her eyes, the same distance that had stolen their daughter. Bethan touched his shoulder as she went out.

"Meirwen." Brys could find nothing to say for her. Mæn Pedr had taught him to help the dying, to go as far as he could on their journey. But now he could think only of the toys neatly lined up on the bottom loft stair by Bethan's daughters. Small things. *Don't leave me, not both of you together.* "Meirwen, live. I love you forever."

She opened bright eyes in an extinguished white face. Death coiled in the house corners, waiting. *A gleam of light over dark water.* Brys gathered radiance from the spring source of his love for this woman and hurled it at shadow. He hunted desolation with spears of light, praying in every way he knew. Shadows flowed together and rose to the roof vent like peat smoke. Meirwen drifted toward sleep.

By morning she was gathering strength. While she slept, Brys weighed Meirwen's life against their small loss and was grateful. All the same, as he remembered his brother's silent house, his thoughts drifted like dry leaves in an empty courtyard.

On the April day when the swallows returned to plaster their untidy nests under the eaves, a day alive with sleek murmuring birds, Meirwen rolled the oxhide walls of her forge and chased the spiders out of the bellows, long unused. Brys filled the quenching trough with peat-filtered Teirw water and leaned on a corner post to watch her sure hands shape bronze. She worked intently and quietly. Grass grew on their daughter's grave-mound, and a transplanted apple sapling flowered there. Brys tried to lift Meirwen's silence but instead only deepened his own.

Cadwr rode down with a sack of seed corn and paced out the fields with him and Alban, showing them how thickly to broadcast and how deeply to set the seed. His gift was for making a garden where there had been waste. Once, he went walking in the rain with Meirwen and brought her back laughing. How did he do that? Silly jokes, Cadwr shrugged. We talked about Angharad. And Dolgarnen. Nothing special.

Sometimes he climbed to look at Cynddylan's hunt tally, touched the crude outline of the boar, and wondered what was happening in Mathrafal. On the outcrops, the rowans blossomed.

9 April 794 + Bryn Cerddin

Mist hung heavily in Teirw's valley under a clotted sky one morning when Brys and Alban wove thorn shoots into hedges between the green pastures. A muffled sound reached them from far upstream and resolved into slow hoofbeats. Finally a grey shape emerged from the wall of mist. A small woman in a pale grey cloak on a grey-dun horse rode near. Brys got to his feet, watching a figure emerge from legend.

The rider reined and pushed back her hood. She had black slanted eyes, and a silver diadem bound her straight black hair. Between her brows was the mark of an old burn scar, white against her tawny skin. Alban crossed himself. The rider smiled faintly. Brys had met her once when Brochfael visited her kindred upstream; she was harper to the oldest woman of the earth-houses there. Her true name was not spoken, but some called her Otter.

"Cynfarch."

Brys said nothing. Alban gathered his fencing tools and hastily retreated. Brys was tempted to follow. Whatever this dark lady wanted he did not want to know.

"Get ready to ride south. You are summoned."

"By whom?" Surely Brochfael wouldn't send a message with one of the fair family?

"By Mæn, Rhydion and me. Mathrafal sanctuary in three days."

Brys had one second in which he could choose to turn on his heel, or laugh, or accept with grace. *So Rhydion will finally break me in a formal trial. A sanctuary trial in the old way.* He bowed his head. "Lady, I consent."

Otter smiled, showing her sharp teeth, and rode into the mist.

On the third afternoon, when Brys came to the old sanctuary in its sheltering hills, Mathrafal was a distant smudge of dwelling-smoke downstream. He rode among towering straight oaks; silver rain gathered on their branches and fell silently to the leaf mold. Small creatures fled away before Carnlas's soft hoofbeats. Once, he rode through a glittering spider's web spanning the track. He dismounted at the sanctuary gate and led the horse into the great oval enclosure. A small wind clattered the gold and silver offerings hanging in the bare oak branches.

Mæn met him at the door after he tethered the grey stallion. He looked the same as always: white hair brushing the shoulders of his homespun robe, bare feet, direct dark eyes. He embraced Brys warmly, searching his face and finding whatever it was he sought. In the largest cell, a peat fire glowed and muttered between its hearth stones. Brys looked around the familiar place, clean and whitewashed and quiet. It was complete, peaceful. Brys, knowing his ordeal, felt himself to be neither.

Otter arrived next, Rhydion soon after. Brys took his teacher's horse, rubbed it down and fed it. Rhydion looked ill. His breath was sour, the hollows were deeper around his eyes and his skin looked as transparent as vellum. After their meal at dusk, Rhydion sat on the sleeping shelf. Otter came to crouch on her heels beside him, and Mæn stood at his shoulder. Three judges. One was an earth-house harper with a face shaped by cruel laughter. The other two he had forsaken last year, to do

Gwriad's work he had thought then. Now he knew his main reason lay in blood and anger, in the unseen scars left by enslavement. Brys hardened himself as their indifferent eyes turned to him. *I am less than nothing, a problem to be solved, unfinished business to be settled.*

"Your name?" Mæn's voice was quiet and cool.

"Cynfarch mab Cadeyrn."

"Why are you here?" asked Otter.

"I am here at your summons to be tried for pœt's recognition." Brys heard anger twist his voice. *To permit you to legally break me.*

"What is your right?" Rhydion's voice was an adder's coiled threat. This was his revenge for Brys's insult in Mathrafal last summer.

Brys looked from one face to another and saw their intent. *These three will not only break me from recognition, they'll break my pride. And what else do I have?* Fear clenched his chest and drove his breath out.

"Eight years' training." His answer barely reached his own ears. Otter smiled openly at his strangled voice. Anger flooded him. *I won't be brought down so easily. If you want to humiliate me, you can work for it.* He forced air into his lungs and let it flow out again. Tension followed it out of his body. He threw his voice. "My skill. And my *awen*."

Mæn went to open a storage chest and flung him something. Brys caught it, a homespun shirt threadbare from many washings.

"You have no name," Mæn said coldly. "You will serve us."

Brys bowed his head. He would be their slave until this ended but he would yield nothing. He took off his clothes, boots, two arm rings, and folded them in the chest. He pulled the coarser garment over his head. A priest's long shirt, it had no belt. Barefoot and barelegged as a slave, he waited. In the bell of shifting firelight, he saw the three judges blur into a single shape. If he let them alter his eyes' evidence, he would never stand up to them. He blinked away the illusion.

"See to the hearth. We shall sleep now."

He kneeled to bank the fire in peat bricks, then laid the three straw pallets and linen and pulled screens across the sleeping shelves. As they settled, he took the eating bowls outside. The wet grass was cold underfoot. He dipped water from the rain barrel and sand from a tub beside it to wash them. As he worked, he slid his thought and feeling out of reach between layers of awareness; otherwise he would shatter on their icy contempt. *Survival.* He clung to that idea.

Without a blanket he curled near the central hearth. An hour before dawn he groped his way outside to split log rounds at the woodpile. He stirred the embers to life and swung the cauldron over the flames. To break their fast he gave them hot barley sweetened with honey. He crouched in the porch when they were done, eating their scraps. *Not much. Tonight I'll be more generous so there'll be some left for me. It dœsn't take long to start thinking like a slave again.*

Inside they had each taken a chair. Brys found his balance and faced them, knowing he would stand for hours. Mæn was prepared to wait forever. Rhydion smiled into the banked hearth.

"History."

It was all the instruction he would get. Brys spoke half the morning of origins, invasions, kingdoms that were only names now. Rhydion waited for him to run dry and grasp at nothing, but one triad keyed another, and each keyed a chapter of the past. Finally the *pencerdd* nodded that it was enough. Brys stood motionless, shifting small muscles in his back and neck one by one, as Mæn had taught him, to ease his tension. He managed to keep his hands still at his sides.

"Laws."

Brys had a pœt's knowledge, not a lawyer's, but a pœt could be called on for judgment. He recited laws of land and inheritance, compensation for theft and murder and rape, obligations of family and kingdom. He had sweated for months to learn these, sitting crosslegged in a darkened room, and now he would never need them again. Most of the laws were in archaic language, full of strange prolific syllables, and he worked hard not to stumble on the words. All the while they watched him, a grim old man and a serene young one and a powerful stranger of an unknown race, waiting for him to fail.

"Genealogies."

Powys had enough genealogical pitfalls to keep him reciting all week, but he picked his footing through variants that accounted for Brochfael's ancestors and the other supposedly incest-tangled line. Rhydion, still Elisedd's pœt more than he was Brochfæl's, scowled at his evasion. Otter pursed her thin mouth, perhaps amused at genealogies traced through men. Only women know their children's fathers, she might say, and why would they tell?

Darkness fell outside. Mæn released him with a curt nod. Brys built the fire, grateful to work out his stiffness. And this was only the start of his trial.

Brys gave them barley flatbread, smoked trout and withered storage apples, and then cooked honey cakes full of sliced apples on the bakestone. *They'll trip me sooner or later, make me fall from the weight of my pride, but meanwhile I'll do it with grace.* Mæn almost smiled over his sweet. Brys kept his eyes down and waited for the leftovers. Less than this morning. Rain blew into the dark porch as he ate. He heard their voices, Otter's cool suggestion and Rhydion's deep response, but none of the words carried. Brys found himself staring into the layered shadows of the sanctuary, barely aware of the cold, and pulled himself together. He needed strength, not a light head. He ate every chewed scrap and went inside.

"Languages," Mæn demanded. "First Latin, then English. Description of the chief kingdoms of Britain, with political analysis of relations between Mercia and Powys."

Unusual. Brys searched their faces. Few west of Frankia used Latin for diplomacy, and only the English used their own language. He suppressed a shrug. Mæn Pedr, who among other things had been a novice at Meifod abbey, looked pained at his slow and awkward Latin. English was better, though his accent sounded doubtful even in his own ears. But they only nodded, not allowing him even the measure of his failure.

"Powys," said Otter. "Cantref by cantref, with detail."

Brys managed not to smile at this question from Otter, to whose people Powys was a passing thought. He spent an hour answering. Brochfael had mentioned enough about tax renders and allegiances to fill all the blank margins of Meifod gospel book, if he were ever rash enough to put it in ink. He knew the hatreds, the illegitimacies, the secret murders and pacts. He knew far more than his judges, he saw in their shocked expressions. Maybe he should go back to Gwynedd after all with information to buy a place at court; the twisted humor of that appealed just now. Penllyn had not always obeyed the king of Powys.

Rhydion said in his razor voice, "Kindly instruct me in the rights and obligations of a *pencerdd.*"

Brys's stomach clenched. *Breathe, breathe. I slid out of this question in Mathrafal last time. Not this time.* He began, "*Gwnaf it glod.* I will make fame for thee. A *pencerdd* sings praise on his lord, maintaining his strength and the land's wholeness. A *pencerdd* counsels his lord to wisdom and courage. Powys —"

Powys paradwys. Powys the garden. His eyes swam with exhaustion and his helpless love for an idea. Feeling had surfaced, he had dropped his guard, now they would strike. But when he looked up Rhydion also had a distant look. Though never Brochfael's *pencerdd* in any sense of the word, once he had been Elisedd's finest weapon.

"— Powys still bleeds from the heart. Our present is without form. We have lost our way between past and future."

"Don't dribble half-baked metaphor. Specify. How shall a Powys *pencerdd* deal with this?"

"That is for you to say, lord." *I didn't mean that as it sounded . . . He'll tear my heart out. But he will anyway.* "Hope lies in Brochfael's justice and *braint,* his ruling right. It lies in the bitter price we paid for peace."

"How?" Silk over iron.

Nothing to lose, not really, not any more. "Why glorify dead Elisedd's savagery that cost us dearly? The time for that has passed. And why keep a shrivelled silence about Brochfael's courage and vision and painstaking stewardship?"

Otter drew in her breath sharply. Rhydion rested his chin on his folded hands, looking into the fire. His expression could be a bitter smile or a grimace of pain.

"I had no idea you loved Brochfael so well," the *pencerdd* said cruelly. "How?"

"By keeping faith with the king. Defending the people. Guarding the land."

"How?"

Brys swayed on his feet, back and legs afire with strain. The room floated a little in his vision. Midnight, maybe later. Now they would try to crack his defence. His eyes slid closed for an instant; his eyelids were a sandbar. His back muscles were seared meat.

"With *awen*."

"*Awen* is no answer," Rhydion snapped. "*Awen* is nine parts sweat. Leave the tenth part to the god. How?"

"If the god speaks in me I listen," Brys said rashly. "I make pœms. As my brother makes a farm. To seed the ruined wasteland and make a garden. If I sing it, it will be so."

They exchanged glances. Mæn said, "See to the hearth."

Brys swam the stream between sleep and waking, thought moving out on either side like ripples of current. His judges were emptying his mind; when they finished he would be a dry well. He would never again need this knowledge, these skills. One part of him still refused to believe, but when they brought him down he would have to believe. But now he dreamed of small River Teirw, sourcing on the windy moors and flowing down through green valleys into lost cantref Tren, and he awakened refreshed in a rainy dawn.

14 April 794 + Mathrafal

At first light Mæn brought a harp from another cell and motioned Brys to pull a stool into the center of the room. The others had eaten what he cooked, leaving no scraps. This time he went hungry.

Brys took the narrow harp. Its unornamented oak and willow were black with age, yet it was strung in bronze and silver like his own. A priest's harp, from the long-ago time when pœts and seers and celebrants were three orders of the same priesthood. Now the distinctions had blurred. He ran his fingers quickly across the strings and found it tuned up and down from the sisters in the usual way. Mæn watched with an expression near a smile.

Brys needed no instruction for this part of the trial. He settled the instrument across his knees and loosened the string pegs one by one, freed the strings by reaching into the hollow sound box to pull them through from the back, coiled them carefully and laid them aside. Gently he pulled apart the three elements of pillar, string arm and sound box. He examined the joints for rot and insects; he found only a scent of beeswax. They fitted together again smoothly, so he restrung and tuned until he was satisfied. Then he rested his wrist on the string arm, waiting. When had they last tried a student? There were never many in any Powys generation, trained by hall harper or *pencerdd* or the pœts' schools that occasionally sprang up and died with their teachers.

"String song," said Otter.

All the measures and modes and variations came easily, after so many years. After each, Rhydion demanded a mathematical analysis. Before Brys was half done, boredom took hold. His fingers twitched toward improvisation. *Patience. Freedom soon.* After this he would play only for his own pleasure. When he finished, sunlight showed golden through the eaves' vents and around the closed shutters. Birds were loud in the trees outside. Noon. His belly rumbled. He wiped sweat off his face with the back of a wrist.

"Pœtry," said Rhydion. "Sing of Brochfael in the style of Talhæarn."

"No." Brys was starting to enjoy himself. He felt light-headed. *What can they do but throw me out? They're going to do that anyway.* "Talhæarn was a pompous ass. I think too well of Brochfael." *Better than he thinks of me.*

Rhydion and Otter exchanged glances. Otter looked extremely sober, which possibly meant she was privately awash with laughter.

"In that case," Rhydion suggested bitingly, "honor us with the style of a pœt for whom you can muster some degree of tolerance."

Brys thought of a northern pœt who served a king of Powys, though some now thought he was a Powys pœt. He found his mode and shaped his stanzas on Brochfael. A useless exercise, and the pœt would roll in his rain-washed grave with rage at imitation. Then Brys had a better idea. Stanza on stanza, he built a suggestion of a quarrel between pœt and king, and topped it with a begging verse. This pœt had been famous for insulting kings and apologizing to save his skin. Brys ended it and picked out an afterthought in the bronze strings, a small query. *Who am I?*

"'I sing true.'" Otter smiled. "'Taliesin sings it.'"

"'I can tell more than you can ask.'" Brys nodded. Taliesin had not been known for modesty, mildness, chastity or love of the church — among other esteemed qualities — and he was unhappily skilled at driving away those who loved him, including an earlier Brochfael Powys. But he was the god's own darling of a pœt.

"Nine *englynion* on a Gwynedd battle," Rhydion snapped, "for a Powys lord."

Brys found his seven notes in the bright wire, three times repeated. *Englynion* were his chosen form. Each one he rhymed and in-rhymed, breaking the beat for effect, giving the words sense and sympathy in the string song. He sang all a Powys man's disdain for Cadwallon, a long-ago Gwynedd king driven into exile by his own English foster brother Edwin, and made the last *englyn* an elegy for Griffri, Ieuaf, all the other Powys men who died under Gwynedd's dragon standard.

"Now for a Gwynedd lord."

This time he kept his protest behind his teeth and did it. After that it was all the *beirdd gwaywrudd*, the red-speared pœts of three centuries. Then the four branches of the world's youth, their stories and *englynion* a bright weave of words and music. Then season songs shot with the light of godhead. Then grave stanzas, cycles and improvisation after improvisation in pœtry and story and music. Long training carried him through, but Rhydion probed closer and closer to the fault line of his skill. By early evening his arms and back ached. His fingertips felt raw. They broke off for a meal. Again no food was left when they finished. If they couldn't wear him down, they would starve him. One way or another they would grind him small.

"Praise."

Taliesin had sung a king's praise in ravens, sharpened spears and English dead lying open-eyed under a wide sky. *The bloody past. It has to be different now. We may have to fight and kill but we can also build . . .* Brys sang Brochfael, but more than the cold grey man who loved only justice. Brochfael might be his enemy but Brochfael was also his king. He sang war and the end of war, regrowth, peace, a just king in a fair country. Rhydion listened with a hard mouth, looking at his hand on the chair arm.

"Satire."

Sharpening his tongue, he sang Elisedd as a warlord, a brutal fool reaping the wealth of the country and sowing only bastards, jabbing at young Offa like a hunter provoking a bear cub. But bastards become rebels and young bears grow strong; both take their revenge. Rhydion yawned. *I can sting you, old man.* Brys added a last stanza on a feeble pœt with his harp strings still pegged to Elisedd's rotting corpse. Who could wonder at the discord?

Rhydion's face mottled in anger. "Lament," he said and smiled evilly. "For Cadeyrn Penllyn."

One string needed tuning, and Brys took that moment to absorb his shock. *I could sing any son's acceptable lament for a father, but what good is safety? Truth is never safe, it lives out on the hard edge of fear and pain. I'll give you lament, Rhydion.*

Brys found music like a wandering hill breeze in the bronze strings and sang of a king's son who loved his country enough not to be king, who kneeled to a Powys warlord, who stood by his friend Brochfael until his fatal error cost his kingdom, his kindred, his son and finally his life. Brys sang no embellishments, no graces. Almost as an afterthought he sang of the man he remembered: a black-haired man who laughed often, fought fiercely, loved passionately and taught a young son to play this mountain air.

There he ended. His face was tracked with tears as well as sweat, but his hands and his voice were steady. He was very tired, past hunger. Was it midnight? He had lost the memory of morning. Mæn was wiping his face on his sleeve and Otter had an inward look. Rhydion studied the floor boards between his feet. He looked up slowly, smiling.

"Humor." The coiled adder struck.

I cannot . . . But Brys picked out a prancing insolent tune. He sang the lady Rhiannon riding her pale horse past Pwyll who was slow to seduction. Black humor lit a tongue-twisting run of the lady's invective and the southern lord's bleating excuses; he punned wickedly on Rhiannon's hardness and Pwyll's lack of it. Angry enough to raise blisters on ice, he smiled lightly and finished the silly piece. Rhydion looked put out.

"War."

Easy. No one wears a slave collar without thinking of revenge. But what war . . ? One yet to come. Brys sang a border-breaking, the Mathrafal bodyguard and nobles' warriors riding east with their foot levies to bring the English down. Knowing Brochfael's hall hounds by name and ways, it was easy to sing their attack. As he sang he knew it for his own bloody dream, Mercians falling before Powys spears, and his intensity of wanting it made him sick and afraid. When he finished he touched the harp's oaken pillar to avert the evil. Mæn watched with his mouth clamped as though in pain, as he had last year.

Finally Rhydion nodded and scrubbed at his face with both big-knuckled hands. All three of them blurred and shifted in his weary eyes. Time to stop for the night, surely. Otter, who'd watched him steadily from slitted black eyes, looked into the fire and up. Brys followed her gaze toward the thatch with the faintly blue peat smoke, weaving, plaiting, fading . . .

Brys dragged his eyes away. *Too close.*

"Bring water," said Mæn quietly.

He stumbled outside and kneeled by the spring, perhaps for a long time.

My name? I have none. Later than midnight; the Swan was almost on the east horizon. An hour to cockcrow. *Birds rustle on barren branches, warning: Territory, get out. Cold bitter grass. Kneel by the murmur of the living sweetwater sanctuary spring. Clay water jug. Reach for the still heart of the pool and stop with arm outstretched. Whir and swoop of a hunting owl. Sweep across the dark and layered shadows. Shadows become light. See everything: Mouse. Terror. Flight through a rattle of frosted leaves, crouch quivering in the dark reeking mouth of a fox's earth. Crimson talons plunge outside in the night. Fox, a dream of fat hares, curls around his tail in sleep. Wings roar summer thunder. Death rises. Sanctuary. Fox guardian enemy mother fear earth trembling man scent. The jug falls. Explodes the surface of the spring, a sheet of black water, arm and face. Who? I am the mouse the owl the fox the earth the water the grass the jug the Swan the man.*

Icy water ran out of his hair and plastered the shirt. A double handful of black water numbed his face. Fair god, awake again, shivering.

Brys filled the jug, pissed against a tree and went inside.

Mæn motioned him to put the jug on the floor planks and to sit on the far side. The harp and stool were gone. Brys sat crosslegged and centered on his breathing. Otter lifted one hand slowly, floating on shadow, and the sun rose in it. *Most beautiful* . . . Brys shook his head. It was only a gold ring set with amber. *Almost. But I am stronger than your illusion. You haven't broken me yet.*

Mæn sighed.

"Do you consent?"

No. He stared. They were going beyond anything he knew of trial. Was it an older rite? He was afraid; he was also irresistibly drawn into his fear. "I consent."

"Contemplate the colors of water."

Brys frowned and relaxed. They waited. He let his vision drift down to the clay jug in front of his bare legs. He looked at its beaded rim and the rivulets on its sweating grey flank. Inside, ring within ring of blackness rippled the water surface, faintly moving and smoothing. The outer curve of each gradual ring held all colors within black, springing new from darkness and emitting brilliant light. A long time he was with it, until the water lay motionless in its rough clay. Its voice rose restless and waiting. *A hundred years I could listen . . .*

"Speak." A voice from the other side of darkness and light.

Words sourced in the water, sweeping from beyond darkness and rushing through him to radiance. *Englynion* formed on his tongue like honey, like sunlight, and a great burden lifted from him with the weight of the fettering words. It was a stranger's voice he heard, a beautiful voice but raw with grief, speaking the stanzas. They were terrible, they were desolate. Blood on the fields, a swordland by fire, a plow wrecked in the furrow, dark houses, fair lord, the land's lover and sacrifice. Salt, precious and bitter. Ravens, flights of ravens, stitching a blue-black seam between earth and hell. After them a kindred of wolves. And all of these had names.

An old man cried out denial. Another wept. Brys fled from that borderland of blood and salt and fire. The narrow oaken boards rose with terrible slowness to surround him and swallow him, but instead they struck him a bitter blow for his pride. He sprawled face up. His eyes stared open and sightless like a dead man's before the first raven.

Otter shuddered. Rhydion wiped tears from his face with a shaking hand. Mæn opened his eyes and crossed himself. Outside birds began to shriek at the daylight. Dawn.

"'I can tell more than you can ask.' Are we judges? Or are we the accused?" Rhydion looked at the priest.

"Clear surface, muddy depth," Mæn said. "This may be vision or dream, true or false. They come to us with equal force."

"Everything he describes is in place now," Otter said. "Don't talk to me of dreams and visions. This is truth pieced together below his awareness. We know its truth. We cannot let this happen. We cannot let him live."

Brys heard the words, but they made no more sense than the birds' cries. A narrow tawny face hovered over him, and a hand went to his throat. *No.*

"He's breathing."

"Bring him back," ordered Rhydion.

"His spirit may take flight," said Mæn. "It must be treated as the falling sickness."

"*Awen* is no sickness. Do it."

Otter slapped his face. Brys closed his eyes and opened them. The three judges watched him get slowly to his feet. A stain on the planks. Not urine. He had spilled his seed. It humiliated him as they had failed to do.

"When did you last take communion?" asked Mæn.

Why dœs a sanctuary priest care? "A year ago, before we rode north to meet Gwriad. At Meifod abbey."

"Why so long?"

Brys hesitated, but it was easier now. "I have been sick. In my spirit."

"You'll be well soon." Mæn smiled, which only deepened his regretful look.

"Now tell everything you have done since then."

"A confession?" *In the sanctuary? When I have committed no grievous sin?*

"More than confession. Everything, without omission. You are privileged by trial. Nothing gœs beyond us."

Why? Brys searched their faces and found only a kind of finality. It would be over soon. As he talked, despite long training, sometimes he had to go back and add detail. He was unaccustomed to talking about himself, especially in this naked way.

Then they had questions. "Who sent these assassins?"

"I have only a dead man's word."

"Who?"

"One of Brochfael's men. I don't know who he was." He still couldn't bring himself to say, at Brochfael's order.

"You have told Brochfael?"

"No."

A long silence.

"You have married and made a child, although a student is celibate."

"Yes."

"Until you graduate in song all your obligation is to your *awen*."

Let it be. My awen. *My child. My loss.* Brys waited until they shifted in their chairs and looked away. Finally they went on.

"Do you remember your *awenydd* words?"

He never did remember much. Knowledge from that subterranean river would eventually surface. Sometimes, like a blood-stained bone splinter rising through torn flesh, it thrust into his pœms. This time he remembered something about fair-haired Cyngen and the land. Brys frowned. Cyngen had brown hair. It was Cynddylan who was as fair as wheat in August. And salt, a place of salt. A woman turned to salt.

"Kneel."

Brys dropped to his knees on the cold planks. What else could they do to him? Even before Otter approached with the bronze knife naked in her hand, he knew. Now that he had told them everything, they could silence him. Someone had said, before, *We cannot let him live.*

The blade was newly honed and bright as copper along one edge. Rhydion came near. Mæn was doing something to the hearth. *One sick old man, one small woman, one priest who refuses violence. I could strike you down and escape but I never could escape the shame of doing so.*

"Do you consent?"

No. But training keeps its grip. "I consent."

Pride held his tongue as Otter twisted a hand in his hair and the blade came in slowly, slowly.

"Close your eyes."

The knife point came to rest at the hollow between his collarbones, lifting with his pulse. He tried to find a prayer, a point of balance or an image, but he failed.

A searing pain, not at the throat but on his forehead between his brows. The smell of scorched skin and hair. Branded. What had he consented to? And he understood. A shock of cold water splashed on the burn and ran down his face.

They stepped back a pace. Otter lifted the knife, cut a lock of his hair and threw it onto the fire. Again the stench of burning hair. Someone placed his hands around a cool hard object.

Brys opened his eyes and found he was holding a plain silver chalice full of dark liquid. Rhydion nodded for him to drink. Cool and bitter, like medicinal mead. Not poison. The other three drank in turn, and Rhydion took the chalice away. Once he would also have been immersed in spring or cauldron; maybe it was enough that he had read the water last night. Otter sheathed her knife and slapped him, first on one cheek and then on the other, hard enough to rock him back on his heels. She seemed amused again. Then she took his right hand and pulled him to his feet, kissed his right cheek and embraced him. She passed him to Mæn, who did the same thing, and Mæn passed him to Rhydion. Brys stood dazed.

"You are to make the three pœms you told of last night," said Rhydion. "Not for Brochfael. For Powys."

Brys shook his head, frowning.

"When you need to remember, you will remember." Mæn smiled.

"Remember what your Greek said. Our words should be easy to speak and easy to hear," said Otter. "Don't let the *pencerdd* tell you simplicity is vulgar. Sometimes there's more power in a tavern ballad than in a king's elegy."

"Your pœtry is too straight and your music is too convoluted," Rhydion said, glaring at Otter. Then, offering a rare concession, he added, "For my taste."

"You may join me here with your wife and child," Mæn said. "Or you may take another sanctuary."

"Our daughter died. She was born too soon." His own words caught him by the throat.

Mæn came to embrace him. "Do you need me there? Or Otter?"

Brys shook his head. "I have a farm to run. My wheat is up, and the calves should start next week."

Otter's dark eyes seemed kinder now. "Pride, ambition, anger. Learn to govern them. Until you do, you will be a danger to yourself and to many others. We hold you in our thoughts."

"Go."

It was over. Brys pulled on his own clothes under their quiet eyes. Rhydion smiled when he returned the golden stag to his right arm, the silver band to his left.

"Duw gennyt, Cynfarch."

Brys answered their blessing and started home.

30 April 794 ✝ Bryn Cerddin

Three silver chains, each with a different link, bored Meirwen thoroughly before they were done. Now she knew how flat link and triple coil went together. The idea, the design, the first realization in silver or gold were exciting. After that it was all dog work. Brys said the same thing, hammering out *englynion* syllable by syllable, making harmony and melody fly wing to wing. But it had to be done, or an idea remained just an idea. She pinched the last silver link closed and took the chains outside to examine them in daylight. All they needed was a polish. Rain was blowing in from the west. It would be a wet Calan Haf.

Meirwen saw the dogs loping down the streambank, as fast as racehorses and almost as big. In a minute Brys came in sight driving the cow that always escaped to the high pasture. She made her break at the orchard gate this time, and Brys sprinted after her waving his arms. The cow was getting smart, but so was Brys. He penned her and came down to the smithy.

"Think you can light fires in the rain tonight?" she asked over her burnishing.

Brys put his arms around her from behind, rested his chin on her shoulder and told her whose fires he planned to light and how.

"Talk's cheap," said Meirwen, polishing her silver.

Which is why he rolled down the oxhides and they made love precariously on the edge of her workbench near the banked forge hearth as rain spat on the roof slates and oiled oxhide. He smelled of cows. Later she couldn't find her silver chains. Brys found them under the work bench.

"Wear these tonight, silver thorn."

"I hate the sight of them. They took me days and they're boring."

But he pulled her hair forward over her shoulder, frowning in concentration, and wrapped the chains loosely around it. She kissed him on the forehead, where the burn scar was fading to pink. Whatever else his examiners had done to him, she was grateful.

By March she had been planning her departure. What point could there be in staying? Losing the baby was sorrow enough without his ingrown silence. But he came back ready to laugh instead of curse when he had to chase the cow, slept without nightmares, told Meirwen all she wanted to hear from her lover, sang and told jokes as awful as Cadwr's. Someday another baby might watch the forge work from a basket on the smithy work bench. She decided not to go.

Meirwen wore the chains in her hair when they went up through the rain to start the Calan Haf fires high on the grassy south-facing bench. Only a few people were there when Brys started the first fire, but they had enough to drive the cattle through for protection against disease. As Alban and his daughters were taking the last cows down, the others from upstream came in silently.

A woman of about sixty came first, wearing a silver knife and a silver spindle at the belt of her grey gown. Meirwen watched as she offered Brys three flat loaves of barley bread, three skins of their powerful liquor and three wrinkled yellow apples. He thanked her and took them, though he looked surprised. Beside the old woman was a younger one in a silver diadem with a harp slung on her back. She came to embrace Meirwen and to smear her forehead with an aromatic herb she didn't recognize. Then they faded back from the firelight, the fair family with their jewels of sun gold, moon silver and night jet. They were motionless, almost invisible, in clothes the color of earth or grass. Meirwen thought they were like earth shadows reflected from the wet grass and the stone ribs of Bryn Cerddin.

Cian rode up from the stream crossing when the fires were mostly ember. He went first to kneel at the feet of the old woman, who rested a hand on his head. Then he came to Brys and said something quietly about Brochfael and Rhydion and fighting on the border. As he spoke Meirwen knew it was not only the end of winter, it was the end of everything. She would need to pack her gear and mend her boots after all.

1 May 794 + Tamworth

Snatches of singing reached Brorda through his open window late in the afternoon. In a hidden palace courtyard, his only remaining servant sat drinking stolen ale with another slave. In the morning he would be sick and clumsy; Brorda would chastise him for intemperance. Probably he should lash the man, but he would feel his own skin tighten with every stroke. It was an old understanding. He didn't grudge the servant his ale, even his off-key singing, and the man accepted the price of his pleasure.

Brorda got up to latch the shutters. He had never bothered with a house in Tamworth. Lately he had spent more time on Offa's travels through southern England than on his own estates, north or south. His large room and two smaller ones in the palace wing were bright and comfortable, with carved and painted beams and a few good tapestries. His older daughter, the nun, was a fine weaver and needlewoman, with a rare blend of skill and imagination; the younger one throve on her farms in Elmesæte. Brorda left management of the estates to her and her husband for as long as Offa needed him. Mercia was enough to worry about for the present. He stooped under the lintel and went out into Tamworth.

Instead of going straight through the palace compound he walked the long way around the perimeter, as he often did, especially on returning from travel. He sidestepped two pigs tearing at a pile of offal on the boardwalk. A salt wagon rumbled past on its way south, armed guards riding beside its precious cargo. A barefoot Irish monk gave him a blessing; he was probably bound for Frankia, where scholars were eagerly welcomed.

Brorda paused at the timbered corner of a house, a brewery smelling of yeast, and watched people throng past. Offa would say his minister was wasting time now, but Brorda thought Offa should do more idling. He always noticed the British faces and voices when he returned from the south. The earliest Mercians were largely British, of course; their royal house and nobles and great landowners had married in Powys. After two centuries the British were still a visible presence, maybe even a majority. Some men and women wore rawhide collars, some wore gold and bright linen; most looked as prosperous or poor or harried as anyone else in Tamworth.

Yesterday he had returned from London, where he had seen the latest Italian fashions — clothes, weapons and adornment — and heard the latest Frankish rumors. Most news from the continent came by way of London and Southwark and Rochester but it soon reached Tamworth. The latest rumor was about Egbert. Again. That thought broke Brorda's reverie and pushed him onward.

Outside Offa's council room the guards stayed in shadow, but he counted three by the glitter of mail shirts. The outermost dropped his spear across the door until he had had a good look at Brorda's face. Offa had seized power years ago after Athelbald's assassination; he did not intend to lose power the same way. A brief wait in the anteroom while candlelight slid under the door and quiet voices went back and forth. An inner door closed softly, and Offa called out. A guard opened the door for Brorda and shut it behind him.

Offa sat in a ragged circle of light from a wall sconce, flicking through sheets of parchment on his writing desk. Egfrith smiled a welcome. His hair, as fair and fine as a child's, framed his thin face. All he needed was a tonsure to look the perfect young monk. He was as well-read as a monk, as well-versed in lore as a pœt. But would he flourish as king in his own right? Brorda wondered. Offa set a stack of tablets aside and folded his hands, himself momentarily achieving an unlikely air of benevolence. He motioned his counselor to sit and slid a folded parchment to him across the desk. It was written in open letters with the short risers of a British monastic hand, but the signature was a complex knot that spelled out the name of Gwriad. Brorda read it and looked up, waiting for an outburst.

"Has Gwriad lost his wits? Or have I lost mine?" The air of benevolence shattered as Offa sprang to his feet and paced the confines of the room.

"It looks straightforward to me. He's offering an incentive to increase trade and discourage attacks on British shipping," Brorda said. In his shadowed corner, Egfrith nodded. Brorda folded his arms and watched the king pace.

"Why? Have there been recent attacks?"

"No."

Offa sat again and picked up a pen. He turned it point over plume, thinking. His crown and rings lay at the edge of the table, and his hair was ruffled from combing it with his hands. Brorda recalled the morning's pageantry of sub-kings ratifying a charter, a bishop blessing the transaction, ordered ranks of landowners adding their signatures as witnesses, clerks hustling in every direction. Offa's daily court thoroughly impressed most people. In truth Mercia and the southern English were ruled here, as officials and clerks and others came and went, in a cramped and heavily guarded room by night.

"It's their damned alliance. What shall we do? Egfrith?"

"Accept the offer," advised the younger king. "The worst that can happen is that it will collapse and prices will remain what they are."

"Curse Gwriad to eternal flame," Offa said mildly. "Why dœs he feel this deranged need to forge quicksilver?"

Why do you? Brorda could have countered.

"We shall see." Offa thrust the pen into its stand. End of topic. "Athelbert of East Anglia. Keep him on the throne, or discipline him?"

As they talked, Brorda's thoughts drifted. One island, one nation. A poignant fancy for tough-minded Offa, yet the idea still struck Brorda bone-deep with love for the man and his dream. Offa wouldn't live to see it, perhaps not even Egfrith. It was probably impracticable, maybe deranged, to impose one rule on this thieves' nest of languages and races and allegiances. That didn't mean it wasn't worth trying.

2 May 794 + Mathrafal

Wind prowled the flowering branches of a hawthorn tree outside the window, captured a few blossoms and flung them away.

If Brys looked at the tree and listened, Rhydion's voice was a young man's. The scent of thorn blossoms masked the room's sour smell of sickness; the green wind that searched the boughs could lift memory and deny death. But Rhydion coughed, and Brys glanced down. The *pencerdd*'s sunken skin showed the shape of the skull beneath and his hands trembled on the bed coverlet like exposed oak roots. He had been ill for the past month, Brochfael said, and he was getting no better. Brys needed to talk privately with Brochfael about Egbert and his supporters. Today. Before some irreversible damage was done to the border and the Mercian peace. He still didn't know how to begin.

"Play," Rhydion ordered, no more gently than he had asked for anything in the last forty years. "Your touch is light. I like the southern ballads."

Brys unslung the harp case, still spattered with mud from the road south, and sat on a bench in the *pencerdd*'s quarters. Brochfael, greyer and grimmer than a year ago, sat in a chair near the window staring at his own clasped hands. Brys lilted music from the strings, willing to serve the headstrong old man.

Maybe Rhydion should have fallen beside his king Elisedd rather than fading away like parchment in the sun. Warrior's life, warrior's death. Maybe it was simpler when Rhydion was a young man. Maybe not. Now the border was broken and nothing was simple.

Brochfael had sent a letter to Tamworth protesting the destruction of four border farms. The first messenger came back through Cær Digoll gate tied to the saddle of his horse. Idris said the mutilation was done after death. Brys saw the face of the dead man, who had been a friend, and thought otherwise. Brochfael waited, saying little. This morning he sent another messenger, while his captains readied the three bodyguard wings, and rumors ran through Mathrafal like crowning wildfire. The favorite rumor, now that Brochfael saw how Mercians kept a treaty, was war.

Rhydion's eyes were closed. Thinking he had fallen asleep, Brys let his hands fall still.

"I'm going home," Rhydion said abruptly. "Back to my farm. Brochfael's finally rid of his father's *pencerdd*. He never had enough courage to throw me out."

Offensive to the bitter end. Brys said, too quietly for the king to hear, "He had too much honor to throw you out."

"You love him more than he loves you, boy." Rhydion snorted. "Now he hates both of us more. I have named the next *pencerdd*."

That choice was not Rhydion's any more than it was Brochfael's. Pœts competed for the position; pœts decided the winner. There had been no contest to Brys's knowledge. And, though a *pencerdd* was not a court officer, in courtesy the king usually had right of refusal. Trust Rhydion to leave a last vexation for Brochfael at a difficult time. *But a new* pencerdd. *Maybe if I humble myself, get approval to work again toward graduation in song . . .*

Rhydion reached out and caught his wrist. "I named you."

Cruel old man, cruel humor. Brys tried to free his wrist, but Rhydion still had a good grip.

"You don't believe me?" Rhydion raised his voice. "Brochfael."

Brys felt blood rise to his face in anger. This was too far to push an evil joke. He gathered himself to get to his feet, too late. Brochfael walked over to the sleeping shelf and looked down at Rhydion with only mild distaste. Less than he deserved.

"Tell him," Rhydion ordered his king.

"It's true." Brochfael turned on his heel and went back to the window.

Brys shook his head as though it held a blizzard of thorn blossoms. *No sane man makes a king's pœt, a nation's chief of song, of a broken student. No sane king accepts it.*

"Lord Rhydion —" Words fled. "I failed my trial."

"Did you?" Rhydion was enjoying this. "We graduated you last month."

"You said —"

"We said you were steeped in pride and ambition and anger, as I recall. It did you no harm to wait a while."

Fair-handed Lleu. Blessed virgin Mair. Merciful God. He is serious. "But there was no contest, no invitation to compete —"

"You won Gwriad's approval." Rhydion couldn't resist a spiteful jab. "And we heard that you chased Caradog's *pencerdd* out of his chair in Aberffraw. These seem sufficient in troubled times."

Thin reasoning. Do I want something I haven't earned?

"You're a fighter. Do what must be done." Rhydion smiled faintly at his choking silence. "Don't stare like a fool, boy. Would you rather turn monk and bray Latin?" The hand tightened on Brys's wrist. "Do you consent?"

It didn't take any thought. Brys said, "I consent."

Rhydion's hand fumbled up to his elbow and touched the gold arm ring with the stag in its interlace. His eyes closed and his voice dropped. "Elisedd gave me this when he named me. Remember it's not Brochfael you serve. Kings inherit, we are chosen. You are the land's guardian. You serve Powys."

After a while Rhydion slept, having dropped a last net of trouble on Brochfael. The king stood by while Brys packed his harp and walked with him to the court chapel.

Brys spent much of the afternoon on his knees confessing to bad-tempered Father Bened and suffering his admonitions, silently raging because there were a hundred other things to do. Rhydion was too sick to attend the ceremony that evening, but others crowded into the chapel. Some of the guard came in war gear and left their weapons at the chapel door. Garmon Penllyn arrived with Brochfael, both of them bleak-faced. Bened blessed the arm ring as his insignia of rank, handling it gingerly as though it might scorch him, and committed Rhydion's malice and Brochfael's risk into the hands of God. Brochfael raised his new *pencerdd* from his knees, coldly gave him the kiss of peace, and in a reversal of the usual roles, spoke his rank and honors. That didn't take long for the son of a ruined house. He spoke mainly of Gwriad's envoy.

"Cynfarch bardd Brochfael," Brochfael ended, and the others echœd it. Brys saw himself reflected in their faces, his only mirror, as *pencerdd* of the oldest nation in the island of Britain, of Powys the garden.

Brys managed in his daze to thank friends for their good wishes and sidestepped the guard's insistence on celebration. He needed to talk to Brochfael. *Now.* He detached himself from their noisy throng and saw the king watching his new pœt from the doorway, his expression impenetrable.

Brochfael, having reached some decision of his own, nodded for him to follow. Brys went out into the colonnade where the honeysuckle was still in tight bud. The sky had cleared on a starry May night.

In the library, books and tax scrolls littered the table until Brochfael pushed them to one side. Idris lit a beeswax candle from the door guard's torch. Three other silver candlesticks held down the corners of an untrimmed parchment which bore the traceries of a map. Idris touched the braided wicks one by one until candlelight swayed across the bookshelves and the tired faces. Brochfael, Idris, Garmon Penllyn, Gellan the commander and his captain Pol. The other two bodyguard captains were already at the border with their mounted wings and a few local foot levies.

Brys felt their gaze on him as he looked into the candle shimmer. Idris was amused, exasperated, maybe curious. Garmon was suspicious. But all that mattered was Brochfael's coldness. Did it mask tolerance for Rhydion's choice, or a promise of sudden death? He had threatened it last year in this room. *If you say more you will die.*

"Two wings north and south of the Rhiw confluence, where they raided last week." Idris pushed a forefinger across the map. "Another tomorrow."

"Under strength," said Gellan. His pale eyes were fixed on Brochfael, and he seemed even more tightly strung than usual. Pol nodded agreement.

"They'll do," Brochfael said. "Wait until we hear from Tamworth. They may be isolated incidents."

"Lord—" Gellan said, then shook his head.

Attack now, he wants to say, hit Tamworth while Offa's unprepared. But he knows Brochfael will never do it. The commander shrugged abruptly, his mail shirt glittering dully with candlelight. He went to the map and pointed out known Mercian patrol zones of other summers. Brochfael nodded.

"I'm riding out tonight to make the field camp at Cær. Cynfarch can ride with me," said Gellan.

"Another place. Not Cær. It's too vulnerable between River Hafren and the border. The ford's dangerous after rain," Brochfael said. "And Cynfarch has other plans."

Other plans? Brys tried to ignore the chill at the back of his neck and kept his eyes on the map. Idris's big hand tightened into a fist on the parchment where the two rivers Rhiw flowed together in ink.

"Farther west, then." Gellan turned away quickly, a thin man lent bulk by the iron shirt. He was out in the colonnade before the door guard could ground his spear.

Pol bowed his head to the king, grinned at Brys and went out after his commander.

Idris ended the silence with a question about provisioning the war bands and levies. If they were called. Everything was still *if.* Everything depended on the second envoy to Offa. Brys remembered sitting in Tamworth wondering how long he would survive, this time last year, and thought about the ugly death of the first envoy a few days ago. And he heard Cenwulf's voice in a stable by lantern light. *Dump him on the west bank.* Brochfael needed to know everything. *But he tried to have me killed. Or did he? If I tell him . . . If.*

"I can provision them for now," Brochfael was saying. His estates in nearby Cæreinion grew wheat and he had cattle herds in Iâl.

They talked more. Garmon had overwintered more steers than usual, having more fodder than usual. Idris offered corn. Brys listened to their quiet voices and looked at the wealth of books and scrolls on the library shelves. Brochfael had allowed him in here while he was fostered, yet still he had read only a quarter of them. It would take months to read them all. Would he ever have a chance?

Idris left. Garmon lingered. Brochfael turned away and began searching for something on the shelves.

"Cynfarch." Garmon cleared his throat. He looked uncomfortable in his heavily embroidered blue shirt, which sagged across his shoulders and pulled across his belly. His blue eyes, always unguarded, now avoided Brys. A long time ago Garmon had been an easy-going second cousin who told good jokes and once showed him the grave of Cynddylan's sister near Rhiwædog. He was almost fifty now, his hair grey and thinning. He hadn't spoken to Brys in nine years.

"Lord Garmon?"

"Just want to offer good wishes." Garmon pulled a silver ring from his smallest finger and offered it.

Brys took the gift and put it on. It fit his bass second finger. Garmon had big hands. A blurred glimpse of its vine and leaf interlace design. "Thank you, lord."

"You know my name."

"Garmon. Thank you."

Garmon Penllyn held out his right hand. Brys looked at it stupidly, then up at his face, and clasped it. Garmon's left arm went around his shoulder, and he felt the rasp of his shaven cheek as he gave the kiss of kinship. On impulse Brys put both arms around him. They embraced a moment, then Garmon stepped back with a nod and went out the door without looking back. *Nine years.* Brys went to lean on the wall and wiped his eyes.

Brochfael had given up searching the shelves and sat at the table frowning over a tax scroll. He looked up after a while and let the parchment roll closed on his hand.

"I would have liked to give you a feast. Rhydion picked a difficult time," he said stiffly. He was never a man to soothe soft words over an old enemy, even one who was dying. He folded his arms and looked down at the pitted floor planks. "I've deeded over to you my estate Cilwen north of Meifod, and you have quarters at court. Tell me anything else you need."

"Nothing, lord. You are generous." *Nothing including an estate, in God's name.* Brys stood by the wall, frowning at the brightest candle flame, thumbs in his belt, rocking on his heels.

"Your father used to do that."

"I know." *Why else would I do it? You'll never be given an opportunity to forget, not while I live.*

Brys saw himself in Brochfael's weary expression: cocksure and dangerous. And even through the iron mask he saw fear. *At least we're afraid of each other.* He dropped his hands. *How much to say? And where to start?*

"Lord." Brys glanced at the closed door and swallowed. "In Gwynedd I talked with Egbert of Wessex."

Brochfael remained motionless, watching him. A muscle danced in his cheek.

"I had to know what was happening." Brys held his eyes. *This is a confession of treason.* "After I survived the assassins."

"Assassins?"

"Two men from the south. Ergyng or maybe South Powys."

"Who sent them?" the king asked, as Rhydion had asked.

"You. I thought." *A paid killer's word against — what?*

"God my judge." Brochfael digested it. "You believed I could do that? To you?"

"You were angry." *And I wouldn't be the first, would I?* "I had pushed you into meeting again with Gwriad. And I had talked with your brother. Eli probably wanted you to think the worst. I didn't know then . . . "

"You didn't know what?" Brochfael said softly. "Sit down, Cynfarch."

Brys took a chair across the table from him. Its scrape across the planks was loud in the quiet room. He said, "I didn't know my cousin Eli was conspiring against you with the English. As he conspired against you nine years ago with my father."

Brochfael scrubbed a hand over his face, slowly. "Idris said you knew. I didn't believe him."

I don't know enough, not yet. Maybe not enough to survive knowing some. "Lord, this border trouble. Egbert said it was part of their plan."

"That dœsn't make it true." Brochfael looked down at the map and spread his hands flat on its margins. "They say he's a clever man. Why did he speak freely to you?"

"I said enough to make him think I knew more."

As you're doing right now, said the king's expression. "My half-brother is a bitter man. He believes he's dispossessed. In a way he's right, since my father Elisedd seized South Powys and Penllyn and Meirionydd. But Eli loves Powys."

"Eli loves Powys enough to take it from what he sees as your mishandling. Just as he probably thinks that if Offa and Egfrith fall, someone like Cenwulf will be easier to handle. He's wrong."

"It's all theory." Brochfael was looking at the map. Powys. Mercia. All the kingdoms of Britain. It was an old map; some of its boundaries had been scraped out and redrawn. "You have no proof."

Proof? We could all be dead or enslaved before you see proof. "What proof can you expect? A signed document from Eli laying out his plans?"

Brochfael shook his head wearily. "I'm glad you told me this, Cynfarch. But there's nothing more you can do now. Leave it alone."

You won't listen. No choice but to leave it alone—for now. But there was one other matter. "Lord, I apologize for my dangerous behavior last year. I put you in a difficult position."

"Accepted. Maybe alliance will be a good thing. Gwriad writes that Offa agrees to lower tariffs and seems untroubled by all of this. We'll see soon enough." He hesitated. "Cynfarch, about your father."

Brys waited, looking down at the map between them. The thick kingdom border separating Penllyn from Powys was erased, replaced by the thinner line of a cantref boundary.

"I loved him as a brother. So did Idris. Cadeyrn was everything Rhydion loved to praise. But he was wanting in some things."

"Yes." *I couldn't have admitted that once.* "Balance. Patience."

"And a sense of history, of how patterns repeat." Brochfael looked up. His eyes were darkly shadowed, as though he hadn't slept in days. "We learn by our mistakes. I made sure you understood those things, Cynfarch. You've had the best education I could arrange without making you a monk."

Why? Brys didn't ask. He found he was holding his breath and forced himself to take in air.

Brochfael said, "Powys and Mercia, that border will stand as long as sane men rule. The real division lies through the heart of old bitterness, old dispossession. Penllyn, Meirionydd, Elfæl, their loyalty to Powys is our survival. You are the border."

"I'm not Penllyn." The words came out as a whisper.

"No. And Idris thought I was a fool to temper a dangerous weapon by bringing you here. He said you would turn on me, perhaps turn on Garmon."

"I didn't."

"Why not? You swore revenge."

Brys remained silent. Brochfael, of all people, knew.

"*Braint.*" Moral right and legal right and love of country. Penllyn, Powys. Brochfael's face thawed a little. "So be it. And now you're my *pencerdd*. Powys's *pencerdd*. If you were Taliesin I'd ask you to sing a binding spell, but I'm afraid it won't be that easy. All you face are years of hard work. Not tearing down but building and planting."

"Powys the garden." Brys said to the map, his voice a husk.

"We've always had a huntsman," Brochfael said. "Now we need a gardener. A sanctuary keeper."

Brys looked up warily.

"I have eyes. And ears. It's a disgrace that you're not Christian—"

"I am Christian."

"Bened thinks not." Brochfael lifted his shoulders, making the *hual* chain flow with candlelight. "I leave that on your soul. And a great deal more."

"I consent."

Brochfael nodded and looked down at his map, awkward with the emotion. *Elisedd's heavy hand at work there, as brutal with his only son as with his enemies. Give no quarter. Take no prisoners. Elisedd would not have fostered an enemy's son, not for long.*

"Whose squadron will you ride with?" the king asked stiffly without looking up. A king's *pencerdd* stood equal to his nobles, above court officers, effectively beyond a king's command. Brochfael was following the letter of the law.

"Yours," Brys said. "How bad is it, the border?"

"Four raids last week. Random destruction, livestock run off, buildings torched at three farms. Everything slaughtered at the fourth."

"Is it always the same band of raiders?"

"Not known." He sounded like one of his own terse dispatches. "We may know more when the messenger returns."

If the messenger returns. "Counter-strikes?"

"Under no circumstances. We're not robbers preying on Mercian farms. There's been too much of that in the past."

Three wings of the bodyguard, three hundred armed horsemen, were sitting on the border straining to start the hunt. Brochfael trusted his own hand on the leash.

"Tell me what happened at the last battle ten years ago. Mæs Derwen."

"Why?" Brochfael turned away.

"A gardener must hunt to protect the garden. I need to sing praise on you." *And displace bloody Elisedd in your people's eyes.* "They say your strategy and your courage won the battle. The battle won us an agreed border instead of endless war."

"Sing something else."

"Mæs Derwen balances the sword and the parley. A reminder to keep your hounds from hunting all the way to Tamworth."

"Mæs Derwen was an ugly defeat for both Powys and Mercia. It was the bitter end of a ragged campaign. It was almost winter. Our levies were hungry and frightened. So were theirs." Brochfael took a deep breath and went on. His voice was unsteady. "I sent in men with sickles and clubs. I sent in your brother, Cynfarch. He was fifteen years old. I saw him die in your father's arms. He wanted his mother."

As my father died . . . "Was it different for Arthur at Mount Badon?" Brys said evenly, when he would rather have put his face in his hands. "It bought our peace."

"With too much blood."

"Peace is always bought with blood. Victory at Mæs Derwen didn't lie in shedding more blood but in the peace it bought." *A sting of anger, a rush of arrogance.* "If I sing it as victory, it is victory. If I sing you as a hero, you are a hero. I sing true."

"God my judge." Brochfael slammed a fist on the table. Molten wax spurted from one of the candles onto the sanded surface. "I warn you, Cynfarch, if you sing war, if you divide Powys —"

"Your grim peace divides Powys right now, Brochfael. Eli is right about that much." The king scowled. So easily they quarrelled. Brys drove on. "I could sing war, I could fling them on Tamworth by week's end, and enough nobles would sweep after them to devastate Powys with the backwash. Instead I'll sing the tarnish off your name. I will make fame for you."

Brochfael leaned forward on both fists. The *hual* swung free, casting four faint shadows on the map. "You shall hear about Mæs Derwen until it sickens you. Tomorrow."

"Lord." Brys nodded, shaken. *I pushed too far. No sleep since Bryn Cerddin and it's starting to tell.* He got up stiffly, walked around to Brochfael's side of the table and dropped to his knees. The king watched him coldly. "I give you my loyalty and my life, until I lie in narrow oak." *Another Powys* pencerdd *said that — Meigant — mourning his lord Cynddylan. Pray we don't come to their end.*

Brochfael's hands fell on his shoulders and raised him to his feet. Iron hands, iron eyes. He smiled, though it looked more like pain. "God protect us from your arrogance and my anger. I ride from the south gate at dawn." And before he turned to the door he kissed his pœt on the forehead like a beloved son.

Brys stood motionless in the small room until one of the candles spat in its pooled beeswax and winked out. He hugged his arms across his chest. The parchment map still lay on the table, ready to spring into a scroll when he lifted the candlesticks.

Powys was a garden torn raggedly along the eastern frontier, battered and impoverished. Brys leaned with hands spread on the table either side of the vellum, looking at the altered borders of the old map. For all Elisedd's brief strength against Mercia, one part never had been redrawn, the almost obscured line that flung a loop eastward around Amwythig and Cynddylan's capital of Pengwern. Cantref Tren. Wreocansæte. But the time was past for reconquest. *Now we have a different border to hold.*

Other maps, in Mæn's books and in Meifod scriptorium, showed all the world anchored on ocean stream. Those were abstractions; this was a shrunken picture of his own country. Brys ran his forefinger along River Dyfrdwy's flow east out of Penllyn to Offa's frontier. Then he traced the border from Tegeingl south to Elfæl. Many fords were marked in red. Powys battles were always at fords or the roads commanding them. Once Heilyn had dreamed of the goddess Madron washing her corpses by a crimson-flowing ford. If any fords ran blood, they were Powys fords.

Gwynedd in the northwest was relatively safe as long as the Irish didn't resume their sea raids. He frowned, thinking of Egbert spinning his silver web from Caradog's court, casting out strands to Cenwulf and Eli. *I could tell Brochfael everything — not yet, not without proof.* But if these raids were part of Egbert's plan, why weren't they striking further south as well? There were no reports from Gwent's border with Wessex, only from the Powys border.

On a shelf he found the small sheaf of Meigant's work, all that remained. So much was lost from that black time of betrayal. He turned to Cynddylan's lament, nine *awdl* stanzas in Meigant's powerful wordcraft. *Greatness of swordplay . . .* He recited aloud, but memory took over after the first stanza, and the pages fell closed in his hand. The pœm, like much archaic work, hid as much as it revealed. Why did Cynddylan attack his Mercian ally? What passions drove them to bitter conflict?

What did they think, what did they feel? Brys shook his head. The old praise pœms never told. How people responded to misfortune — surely that was the heart of any story. Listeners ignorant of the history could only guess about the Lichfield stanzas. What would they make of "A brother did not escape the battle caused by his sister?"

Some blamed Cynddylan's sister later for refusing the alliance marriage, for choosing to live her life. But should she have allowed herself instead to be led into Mercia like a captive? What did she feel? What did it cost her to watch her choice destroy her family and her country? Cynddylan's house had supported Pelagian monasteries; his sister would not have shrugged off the disaster as God's will. The Pelagians maintained that we save ourselves not only by faith but by taking every opportunity to do the good. *I did it,* she would say. *My tongue did it.* And another voice came to him in the silent room.

Wyf Heledd. I am a place of salt. Salt tears, semen, sweat, payment, commodity, precious condiment, a bitterness too great to swallow, a land laid waste, fields sown with salt. A girl on a white horse, beaten and probably raped, with madness as her only defence, led into Mercia alone to further ruin. Egbert had warned of Eli's daughter in Cenwulf's hands. Was that the girl he saw? Her likeness, he finally realized, was less to Eli's sleeping child than to Nest. They would be cousins. *Where is she, in Magonsæte? Wreocansæte? Tamworth?*

Brys straightened at last. Fading ink still scrawled across his vision when he closed his eyes. Border patrol tomorrow, and he still had to join his friends' celebration. He returned Meigant to the high shelf with a nod. Brothers in arms. Darkness grew softly as he pinched the wicks one by one, savoring the honey scent which rose to lighten the room's dry air of books and strategy.

8 May 794 + Tamworth

The young man's brown hair curled to his shoulders and his smooth face was flushed. A handsome boy. Cynegyth's taste was as predictable as her lack of caution. It wasn't his wife's lovers that troubled Cenwulf, it was her indiscretion. Evening was near, and it was getting dark in the inn's back room where they faced each other across the cloth-draped table. The boy's hands tightened and relaxed on his mead cup; he was having trouble concentrating on Cenwulf's offer of a farm stewardship at Northampton. That was part of the game.

A Persian trader in London had played this game with Cenwulf a long time ago, though he had refined it since. As they had sipped some sweet concoction and negotiated the price of a Damascus steel sword, two whores were under the table between their legs, working with their busy mouths. The game was to keep a level head and a straight face. The boy was managing neither. Cenwulf, having paid three times the Damascus sword's worth, had lost the game only once. Now he sometimes added his own flourishes.

"The estate is a holding of Saint Mary's, on parchment," Cenwulf said, "so I pay no tax. I name my own man to run it. I need a steward who can be discreet about the occasional compromise between church law and private interest."

"That dœsn't sound too difficult," the boy said, closing his eyes.

Vain little fool. An hour ago, before the mead and the whores, he had sounded more intelligent. It didn't take much. Cenwulf reached under the table to twist his girl's hair. That sent a wave of warm sensation through his groin, and he grew stiff at last. Both girls knew Cenwulf's game; Leoba had thrown them into the street over it, but they'd landed lucky. The boy had a glazed look. Soon.

"And it's a good place for privacy," said Cenwulf. Almost as good as this remote inn where he paid off the innkeeper regularly. He didn't want to end like the West Saxon king years ago who was murdered while he plowed the furrow of a friend's wife. "I'll have you freed from Offa's bodyguard."

"As you like." The boy's smile suggested Cenwulf was overly sensitive about the affair by Tamworth standards and would do anything to get him out of sight.

"I'll ask something of you first." Not something anyone would freely give. The boy thought he would play and win? He was so outmatched he didn't know there was a match.

"Oh." The boy opened his mouth like a fish and knocked over his mead cup. "Oh."

Cenwulf read everything as it happened in the handsome young face. The boy's eyes closed blissfully. They flew open again as the whore set her sharp little knife to his scrotum. Then the amusing part. A sobering shock of fear, then a flood of entreaties. He had meant no harm. He would do anything, give anything . . . Indeed, he would. After he had spent enough time babbling out his remorse and had reached the silent glassy-eyed terror of a steer in the shambles, Cenwulf nudged the whore under the table.

She castrated him with a surgeon's precision. The boy screamed in disbelief. Agony. Rage. Pain and redemption and revenge and triumph. It was powerful medicine, just what Cenwulf needed, and his ejaculation filled the other whore's mouth. He had won again.

The game's aftertaste of faint disappointment still lingered when Cenwulf rode into Tamworth. A servant waited for him at his door.

"A visitor, lord, waiting inside."

"Tomorrow."

The man shuffled uncomfortably. "It's Brorda, lord."

Coincidence? Cenwulf dismounted. Egbert's outraged message yesterday, Brorda's visit today. Both set his teeth on edge.

"Get him wine."

Cenwulf smoothed his beard as the man hurried inside. He had already washed off the blood. Confession tomorrow.

"God's greeting to you, Brorda." He went in smiling warmly and extended a hand. Brorda didn't take it.

"Cenwulf."

Brorda stood by the central hearth, ignoring the food and drink the servant had placed on a table. He had a healthy Mercian fear of poison. Cenwulf studied him, this opportunistic noble of an ancient Elmesæte line, many years in Offa's service. There were few like him, at least few who still lived. Brorda had made himself a tool, instead of a victim, of Offa's obsession with securing Egfrith's succession. Brorda was a survivor. Cenwulf admired that. But just once it would be entertaining to hear him drop his aristocratic bearing and talk bluntly of how for nearly forty years they had set landowner against noble, sub-king against bishop, and engineered the farce of creating an unnecessary new archbishopric in Lichfield to secure Mercian supremacy. All of it, all of the manipulation and outright murder.

Cenwulf drew up chairs, and Offa's closest adviser sat stiffly. Why didn't he say something? Coincidence. It had to be coincidence.

"I have a letter from Alcuin in Aachen." Brorda didn't glance up from the fire, where applewood logs burned merrily.

Cenwulf laughed. Was that all? "Condolences. What have you done to draw the famous admonition?"

Brorda shook his head slowly. He was frowning at Cenwulf's heavy gold pectoral cross, making Cenwulf uneasy. Could he know it was Egbert's gift? "This wasn't an open letter, though you know how Alcuin likes to sit at Charles's feet telling the world how to run its affairs. And this is a private question. I came to ask you about the last war against Athelbert of East Anglia."

"Certainly. Anything." Cenwulf's relief made him gracious. Coincidence. So Brorda wanted quiet counsel without telling Offa. That might be worth leverage someday. And he was prudent to seek advice, since the Northumbrian monk's letters to Offa ran heavily to censure for cutting down the noble Mercian houses. Like Brorda's.

"Athelbert's nobles want independence from Mercia," said Offa's oldest henchman. "Alcuin wants me to restrain the king from a new campaign against another Anglian kingdom."

"An East Anglian war is worth avoiding," Cenwulf agreed sagely. Sweet Savior, it could throw his own western plans. On the other hand, it might be useful. God bless the interfering monk. Meanwhile, maybe the *Wealas* should ravage one of his own estates, causing tragic personal losses to Offa's loyal kinsman Cenwulf. Cynegyth was there now. Two birds with one stone? No, it would look suspicious to bring the children away and leave his wife. And the witless girl, he wasn't ready to give her up yet. One of Ceolwulf's holdings would have to do. Most of the slaves were *Wealas* anyway.

"But how to avoid it?" prompted Brorda.

"Athelbert listens to his counselors." Cenwulf stroked his beard. "But they're weathervanes. They've badgered him about having a Mercian overlord, but if he tries for freedom and fails they'll kneel meekly enough to Offa." With the right hand on the rein.

"How can he be discouraged?"

Discouraged? That was a nice turn of phrase for termination. But this man was no milksop like Egfrith. He knew exactly what he was saying.

"Only edged iron will stop Athelbert once he gets an idea into his head. And—Cenwulf found an expression of diffidence which suggested, Who am I to advise the Lord Brorda and my distant royal kinsman Offa? "— another might rule East Anglia better. A Mercian." One of Offa's distant kinsmen, for example, in case Egbert's scheme failed.

Brorda got awkwardly to his feet, a big man with fading hair and deepset blue eyes, frowning. As though in forty years his hands had never touched blood. Cenwulf resisted the temptation to again look at his own hands. He sent Brorda out with a torch-bearer, though he knew the northerner disdained his courtesy. That added to the piquancy.

Cenwulf was turning to his door when he heard the rampart guard making a commotion, shouting something about a messenger from Mathrafal. That at least, after the clear if unspoken message he had returned with the first messenger, was not coincidence.

23 May 794 + Maelienydd

At the top of the grassy bank of Offa's dyke, Brys lay looking east across the border. Mercia was as hilly as Powys here, south of Ceri ridgeway, where a long arm of hills reached into the lowlands. Cloud shadows drifted across a far hillside where a shepherd sat with a black dog at his knee watching a small flock. A stream trickled north through the trees into rough grazing. At the wood margin a band of armed men were making their way north. Mercians.

"Another patrol," said Pol, chewing on a grass stalk at Brys's right elbow. Cian stirred restlessly at his left side. These were not raiders; raiders would move quickly under cover, not openly along a border track. The raiders could almost be invisible, yet they had destroyed three farms in the last two weeks, without warning and without survivors.

The Mercian captain wore a mail shirt and rode a tall chestnut horse. Another twenty or so men walked in loose formation with spear blades floating in a dull gleam over their shoulders. They carried knives and long-bladed *seax* knives and round wooden shields, and their war shirts were plain boiled leather. Not Offa's bodyguard or even a noble's bodyguard but hearth warriors from some minor landowner's hall. As they walked they looked west, but the sun was against them. It was the second patrol today.

"More every day." Brys asked, "But why?"

Cian said, "Watching. Like us. They have orders not to cross. They want to."

"Or are they building their strength until they can attack? Now that our forces are scattered from River Gwy all the way north to Iâl." Pol was a quiet man when he wasn't telling one of his complicated jokes. Narrowing his dark eyes was usually enough to freeze a quarrel. No one wanted to cross swords with Pol.

Brys shook his head, watching the patrol come closer. The afternoon sun beat on his back. Even through harp case, quilted jerkin and shirt he felt the scorch of each bronze stud riveted to the boiled leather war shirt. He looked over his shoulder; Pol's squadron held to the treeline on the west side of the dyke, watching the captain, ready to ride up at a signal. Brochfael was rarely with them, having too much to hold together in field camp and court. His absence always increased the temptation.

"So who's raiding?" Pol frowned at the Mercians.

Invisible men. Brys had seen the devastation. Raiding was the wrong word, but he didn't know another. The raiders burned houses and granaries and barns, cut down livestock instead of running it off, left mutilated bodies and wrecked household goods. Theft he understood, not destruction for its own sake. And Brochfael's patrols always arrived too late, as though the raiders knew their every movement and could vanish into the air. "Border patrol?" someone spat this morning. "We're not a border patrol, we're a burial party."

With each attack, it grew harder to hold back the squadrons, from May into June, harder to stay on this side as Brochfael ordered. Offa denied all knowledge of the raids or the fate of the first envoy, and predictably suggested that Brochfael failed to recognize civil war in Powys when he saw it. Brochfael's second envoy was well-treated and had an armed escort back to the border. Brys watched the English come closer and thought of the burned farms and the slave collar's gall. It was a dark metallic taste, revenge.

"We could take them," Pol said around his grass stalk.

Brys looked at him uneasily. *Something new, a contagion that we've all caught. I've seen it grow with each quarrel, each burned farm.*

"No."

"Who would know, Brys?"

"One too many. I would." Cynfarch spoke, Brochfael's pœt, not Brys who had ridden the border with Pol's squadron for five summers and shared their anger now. The dark taste rose in his mouth like blood.

Pol looked over his shoulder at his men, sitting their horses in the shade of the oakwood. No captain could hold free men in the field too long without retaliating against a violent enemy. Much longer and some would start slipping away to do their own raiding eastward, burning off their anger, or suddenly ambush an English patrol. If Offa didn't hang them Brochfael would.

"How long do we have to wait?" Pol spat out his grass.

They slid down the west bank into the border ditch and walked back toward the squadron. Brochfael's guard were all mounted; a Frank would call them light cavalry. Pol used stirrups like an Arab, claiming they gave stability in a charge. Brys found them clumsy, but maybe one had to get used to them. He remounted the grey stallion, took his spear from a friend and settled the shield on his right shoulder as they rode south again. *How long?*

That evening Pol's men were unusually silent over their cooking fire. It was Elgan's turn to cook bannock and the two snared hares spitting below the tripod. This morning, unasked, a farm woman had given them a bag of milled flour and her last storage apples.

"Cynfarch bardd Brochfael."

Brys glanced up. He would get used to that eventually, no doubt, but not in Addonwy's speculative tone of seeing how far he could push it. Redhaired Addonwy was always willing to make things livelier. He was small and slight, with peaked eyebrows and a peeling sunburn; he entertained himself by stirring trouble.

"When will Brochfael Hostages get off the privy pot?" Addonwy flashed white teeth in the summer dusk. He knew quite well he spoke to the only hostage. A mutter of anger from the others.

"Don't tell me you've got the runs at both ends now."

Pol leaned forward intently, ready to intervene.

"But why—"

"Shut your face, you sly troublemaker." Elgan scowled up at him from turning the bannock. He was another Penllyn man, big and slow-moving, with a black shock of moustache across his face. He looked as though he would cut a stranger's throat to own his boots but he was mild except in attack.

Brys glanced thanks at him. It was easy enough to puncture Addonwy with a pointed answer, but behind his provocations he was a friend. Most of them were. After a strained week of deferring and calling him Cynfarch they had thankfully fallen back into old habits, though they were more protective, somehow. "Proud of you," Elgan had growled offhand one day as they rode. Maybe the mark between his brows and the faint rawhide gall on his neck made a difference.

"Earn your keep," Elgan told Brys before Addonwy could turn his injured innocence to further mischief, nodding at the harp case under his elbow. "Give us some music."

One rainy morning they rode through new bracken and bright gorse, silvered and shaking under the downpour. Deep in South Powys, Ceri ridgeway linked with other ancient tracks above the river sources, up in the territory of hawk and kite. Rain veiled the farther hills as they crossed the spine of the world between rolling ground mist and low-lying cloud.

Their patrol area was from sleepy brown River Clun north through Ceri and Argœd to the open valley of small Cæbitra stream — from southern Cydewain into northern Mælienydd — then south again. By now they could ride blindfold the track on the Powys side of the border and knew each township and farm within a mile or two west. Much of their area was hilly and unsettled. They heard the raids were worse south and north, in the richer valleys.

In the rain on Ceri ridge they sat their horses and watched a Mercian patrol also halt its southward march on the far side. The captain with the chestnut horse led it. Pol swore in an unknown language and ordered them forward. That day Brochfael was with them. *Otherwise . . .*

June twelfth or thirteenth? Six weeks on the border. Gwriad should soon be in Mathrafal.

19 June 794 + Ceri

Seven weeks. Seven weeks of watching English patrols, burying strangers and friends, moving refugees, swallowing the blind anger of people whose farms lay ruined or untended, obeying Brochfael.

One afternoon Cian pointed south across a wooded hillside. At first Brys saw nothing more than a shimmer of midsummer heat, then a pillar of smoke against the hot blue sky close to the border. A second pillar of smoke rose near the first. Brys pushed the harp case further behind his back, settled the shield on his right arm and lifted his sword loose in the scabbard. Pol turned in the saddle and nodded.

An easy canter swallowed the grassland, then they leaned to take the flank of the ridge. Bright dappled oakwood surrounded them briefly, until they cleared the other side. From the gentle height they looked down on ripening cornfields to the farm that had given them flour and apples a week ago. One house was in flames; people moved through the smoke and fire haze. Gaining speed from the slope, they dropped through the rough grazing into the corn.

The raiders' watch jumped up out of long grass by a turf wall, his mouth open, but a spear laid him under the hooves before he could shout a warning. They swept past the wall of smoke toward the barn, and a handful of raiders faced them in the cobbled yard. Brys set his spear for the chest of a shouting man, but another horse swerved too near and threw his aim. The raiders scattered and the patrol dismounted. It became an ugly game of pursuit through smoke and flying sparks. Behind him somewhere he heard the insolent blat of Marc's blue hunting horn.

Brys followed a raider past the whitewashed barn, stumbling over dead cattle and once a man's body, and recoiled from an explosion of heat and flame as the threshing floor caught. The man turned to face him, flushed with stolen ale and flourishing a spear. Brys speared him in the belly and saw another lurch around the burning barn with blood streaming from his hair. He ran forward with a *seax.* No time to reclaim the spear. Brys turned the first *seax* stroke on his shield rim and drew his sword and drove in. Their shields clashed and caught. The raider gave ground until he felt the barn wall at his back, then leaped forward again in panic. He thrust wildly and grazed Brys's sword arm. *Enough of that.* The man was no trained fighter. A feint to the throat. He lost his guard long enough for Brys to plunge the blade up under his ribs.

Running sweat, Brys looked around. No time seemed to have passed, but he saw only a few raiders scrambling toward the oakwood with Pol and some of his squadron after them on foot. He pushed through the billowing black smoke and found the others had gathered around the dead. *None of ours.* Two men in mail shirts, three others barefoot and ragged. *Seax* knives, leaf-bladed English spears, British swords, one square-headed British spear probably taken in an earlier raid. A strange collection. One thing was reassuring: they were not a Mercian border patrol.

"Farm people?"

"In there." Addonwy nodded at the burning house.

Too late once again. Brys turned away and nearly walked into Cian.

"Barley field." Cian showed his teeth, not smiling.

Brys followed him past the burning hay barn, then a wattle granary on pilings. Maybe they could save that, they needed the grain — Cian hissed and leaped past him into the smoke. In the same instant Brys saw hurtling bright iron. A thrown wood ax thunked into a granary piling. He ran forward and found Cian with blood on his short bronze sword crouching over a dead man.

"Bodyguard?" Brys's sarcasm fell flat. Cian gave him a narrow blue look and walked on.

The story told itself as Brys vaulted the gate. A litter of broken ale jars, a feather quilt flung across the green barley. Marc and Elgan had disarmed two men. One stood sweating and pleading for a quick death. The other had his breeches around his knees and was repeating something in English. Brys didn't bother to understand.

"Cut their balls off," someone suggested.

Brys didn't look to see who said it. He didn't want to know or to yield to the temptation. He ordered instead, "Kill them."

The first man murmured to Wotan and leaned to meet Cian's sword. Elgan gripped the other one from behind and cursed him when he fouled himself. Addonwy swallowed hard and cut his throat. Then he went to lean on the stone wall and vomited.

Brys walked into the barley field. Cian came silently after him. Last week there were two daughters whispering in the hay loft as they watched their mother bring out the food. The older one had come down shyly to pour buttermilk for Pol's squadron as they sat their horses in the cobbled yard. She had glanced up once at fair-haired Marc, who was a handsome man. Now she lay naked with a slit throat and her eyes open to the sky. Tears still tracked her face. They'd dropped an ale jar on her belly; ale dripped down the curve of her ribs.

The little one curled on the trampled corn, thumbing a broken tooth out of her bloody mouth. She was nine or ten, younger than that other girl who rode the white mare. Cian frightened her. She flinched away from Brys, clutching an amber bead on a thong at her neck. *Amber for protection.* He sat down beside her and talked awhile, not about anything that mattered. Cian brought a striped cloak from somewhere, and Brys wrapped it around her. She was dry-eyed in shock.

"Where are your kin, child?"

She pointed west, up the valley, never taking her eyes from Cian as he kneeled to plunge his bronze sword into the soil, then wiped it carefully with a handful of barley stalks. Brys picked her up and carried her back toward the horses. The gate stood open now. The buildings were burning down to a few standing posts and a core of flame and smoke. Pol and his handful had come back, and a few were passing around a ale jar.

"Too young for you, Brys," a man called out.

Elgan raised a fist but only knocked the jar away to shatter on the ground. Beer foamed over the cobbles. Pol's black eyes took in the potential for a quarrel; he sent the mouthy one to find a shovel and bury the other girl. Any bodies in the house would be ash by now, and ravens could have the stripped raiders. They were already cawing appreciation from the nearest treetops. Pol split the band and sent half with Brys.

The girl shivered in his arms as clouds swept over the sun, darkening the wooded knolls westward. Above the treeline they forded a stream barely a spear length wide, tumbling down through beds of rushes, and climbed to the ridge track. Riding west they passed through the upper grazing of one of Brochfael's English settlements, dating from the years when Mercia had claimed this region. Farm people sighted the riders and clustered in their common garth, ready to flee or defend. Brochfael's protection was too sparse to save them from either English raids or misplaced Powys revenge. Brys sent Marc down to tell them the bad news.

They dropped north into a shallow valley overhung with blue cooksmoke. Only then the child pressed her face against his leather war shirt and began to cry silently; he smoothed her tangled hair and wiped the salt from her face. *If we'd been quicker.* People came from the fields and buildings and asked where. Not who. Brys lifted the girl down to a weeping grey woman and watched her turn to the house. A young man took Carnlas's bridle and frowned up.

"How long will you let this happen?"

"We're bound by treaty." With an effort, Brys kept his voice even and quiet.

"Peace treaty?" Hot eyes, a mouth twisted in anger.

"Peace treaty," Brys agreed, swallowing bile, or maybe despair.

The farmer spat, dropped his hand from the bridle and turned away.

Brys said to his back, "Tell your kinsmen any raids into Mercia can touch off open war."

He pivoted angrily. "Why should we sit here while they pick us off farm by farm?"

"When did you rebuild?" Brys nodded toward houses and barns.

"After Mæs Derwen." He took the point — full-scale war would be more devastating by far — and glanced around at them. They were tired and dirty, one or two blood-stained. "Need anything? Food?"

"Patience."

"Send word if you need help, Cynfarch. I can call out ten spears."

A black mood settled on Brys before they reached the grazing. The wind that usually scoured the cwms of the high country had fallen away to still heat. His war shirt clung to his back through sweaty linen and wool, he stank, and his arm throbbed and itched. As they rode east to rejoin Pol, they followed the small stream downhill through meadows full of ripening bilberries and bees in the thyme. The water grew loud in a stony riffle and curved into a pool that might be good for trout. He turned in the saddle and found Addonwy watching him cautiously, for once holding his tongue.

"We'll water the horses," Brys told them.

Brys dismounted and led Carnlas to the riffle, watching the brown water slide toward Mercia. They were a good mile from the border. Why not? He shed harp, war gear and clothes and walked into the pool. The water was icy. Half of them waded in while the other half kept watch; the pool brimmed a handspan higher against the roots of an overhanging alder. In a while the water numbed him to the point where it felt warm, and fingerling trout brushed his legs in the peaty water. Brys clambered out with water streaming from his hair and took watch while others went in. He didn't feel clean.

A raven glided east overhead on broad ragged wings. Before he was out of sight, a single rider came upstream at a canter. Tegwy, now Brochfael's armor-bearer, restrained his dancing bay mare. His fair hair was plastered sweatily on his forehead;

he gave the pool one regretful glance.

"Cynfarch, the king wants you. Gwriad has arrived."

Brys turned to get his comb, clean clothes and some linen to bind the gash on his arm. He rolled his war shirt inside his shield and strapped it to the saddle. As he pulled on his clothes, Tegwy eyed the scars on his chest and arms, most of them from training. Brochfael wouldn't release Tegwy from fosterage to the bodyguard for another year. Brys remembered being fifteen and counting the days to sixteen.

"Mathrafal?"

"The field camp at Aberriw. They wanted to see what's happening on the border, not that they're seeing anything. Gwriad dœsn't understand the raids. Caradog is talking about how Powys loves war, even imaginary war. Arthen's nervous. Brochfael's angry."

Brys shaped a soundless whistle. Not a brilliant start to a peace council. *Imaginary war, is it?* Thoughtfully he folded the unused linen bandage back into his saddlebag. *Let it bleed. Caradog can see some imaginary blood.* Arm rings. Gold left, silver right. Then the war shirt after all, bronze studs clashing. Sword belt, harp case on his back, shield on his shoulder.

Carnlas was restless with the mare near. As Brys mounted, the stallion shied and leaped forward, and he vaulted into the saddle with an unplanned flourish that should have landed him like a fool on his backside. As he fought the rearing stallion down he saw Tegwy's wide blue eyes. His companions had the manners not to jeer. Brys would have laughed another day.

19 June 794 + Aberriw

Brochfael started down to the river when he saw the two riders take the ford at a plunging canter. Others in the Aberriw field camp stopped what they were doing and drifted after the king. Cyngen came to help Tegwy, who managed not to grin as they led the winded horses away.

Brys walked up to meet the king. He saw Gwriad's red head among the tents, and Gellan arrived from the picket lines, frowning over a handful of tally sticks.

"Lord king." Brys dropped his saddlebag and went to one knee, playing to the gathering audience, and stayed there until Brochfael nodded. He rose.

"Raiders?" demanded Gellan.

"At a farm south of Ceri. Too late again. We got most of them."

"Did you take prisoners?" The commander's light eyes were intense and unblinking, an owl's eyes.

"No." *New orders? Take prisoners with a farm burning around us?* "Only two were left after the fighting. I had them killed."

Gellan frowned down at his notched sticks.

"Did you need to fight?" Brochfael asked quietly, aware of others near.

"Maybe not." Brys put an edge on his voice. "We could have let them finish with the girl and go upstream to the next farm —"

"Shut your mouth." Brochfael looked sick, and a muscle was pulling in his cheek again. "It's untimely."

Untimely? Brys thought of several sharp answers and instead said quietly, "Don't pretend it's not happening. Rumor's taken care of that already."

Brochfael studied his pœt a moment. "Have you left me a choice?"

Gellan's eyes sharpened. He bowed stiffly and left for the horse lines. The others had started drifting back to the tents.

"How shall I help you here, lord?"

"Some advice on handling Caradog and Arthen. God my judge, a swaggering pirate and a grey hand-wringer. I can talk sense with Gwriad and Bishop Elfoddw at least. What have you dropped on me, Cynfarch?"

"Alliance —" *For Powys, and damn your pride.* "— lord."

"Something else?" Brochfael was looking at him too closely.

"If we'd been half an hour earlier —"

"No. You'll break your teeth on it." The king looked across the field camp, fighting some emotion behind his iron mask. "They're my people."

"What in God's name is happening?" The words leaped out, not what he had meant to say. "What is Offa doing?"

"Holding court in Hereford, I hear, since Easter. Admonishing Bertric and Athelbert of East Anglia. There has been talk of rebellion."

Hereford. Offa rarely went there, though he traveled often to his other sub-kingdoms, cathedrals, abbeys, nobles' seats. Hereford was nearer than Tamworth to restless Wessex and Gwent — and nearer to Cenwulf's holdings. *Is he there because of this border trouble? After claiming it's nonexistent?*

"Egbert's rebellion?"

Brochfael shook his head. "We meet formally tomorrow. Discuss this with me this evening."

Brys watched him away across the ruined farm that was the field camp. A sprawl of bramble and nettles almost hid the standing wall of the ruined house. It had fallen to one of Offa's attacks a generation ago. In the last month it had grown into a town of leather and tarred canvas tents. A squadron of Gwyddien's wing were in from the north and Idris had brought out his own Meirionydd bodyguard for border duty. Brys saw banners of half a dozen other Powys lords, but most of the people were from Manaw, Gwynedd, Ceredigion. He shouldered his saddlebag and started toward the tents. Someone came up on him from behind, and an arm like a cruck beam fell across his shoulders.

"I see Brochfael's getting extra service from you. Is Powys so short of warriors?" A voice like blue silk, clothes in a rainbow of colors, fair hair curling under a gold diadem.

"Gwydron." Brys smiled. It was impossible not to smile. "See for yourself."

"I see well enough." Caradog's pœt surveyed the picket lines and tents and armed men, then looked at Brys. "Cleverly done, Powys, you have blood on your *pencerdd*'s arm ring. A walking metaphor."

"Good for you, Gwynedd. I wasn't sure you knew the word metaphor."

"You haven't changed." Gwydron's smile might have had a spiked bit in it. He gestured around the camp. "What in God's name is this intended to prove?"

"Treachery."

They walked on together. *Another metaphor. Gwynedd in silk and gold, Powys in dust and blood.* People got out of their way.

"Treachery by — ?" Gwydron prompted, as though he were coaching a student.

Brys shrugged. *It's not Gwynedd's business.* He shifted the saddlebag to his other shoulder. A weight of weariness had settled on him. "Where's Egbert?"

"Gone. Maybe back to Frankia, I don't know. Forget Egbert. We have to talk, you and I and Gwriad. Will Brochfael bring Powys in?"

"Yes. And the lords want it." Garmon, loyal to Brochfael. Idris, weighing Meirionydd's advantage as well as Powys's. Others, afraid of Offa or his successor. Eli, drawn to the flame of power. And Egbert was gone from Gwynedd, vanished. *Ungrounded lightning can strike anywhere.*

"What happened out there?" Gwydron was suddenly cold and exact, not performing. "Cynfarch, tell me."

Brys looked east past Rhiw and Mæn Beuno to River Hafren, past Hafren to Mercia. "Raiders. They had English spears but British swords. Some wore mail, some wore rags."

"I see. I hope to God *you* see," Gwydron said to his back as he walked away, "before it's too late."

When Brys left the bubble of lamplight in Brochfael's tent it was dark outside. At one of the fires someone was singing in Irish, probably one of the Manaw company. Familiar faces were everywhere. Caradog had brought his quarrelsome kinsmen; it was one way to keep them from tearing Gwynedd apart in his absence. Among Gwriad's redhaired sons Brys found Merfyn.

"I thought you were going to Armorica," Brys said as they clasped arms.

"Soon." Merfyn grinned down at him, taller now by a handspan, and led him over to a whitehaired man. "Cousin Cynfarch. My kinsman Edern is father's envoy to Charles in Frankia."

Envoy to Charles? Brys nodded, curious. This was the man Gwriad had planned to send with him last summer. Edern shared Merfyn's height, and his hair still showed traces of rust. He was impeccably dressed, but his clothing seemed oddly like a Frankish tailor's attempt to copy British garb. Probably it was.

"Charles dœsn't recognize Manaw, of course," Merfyn added coolly. "All he knows of the British is his Northumbrian adviser Alcuin's evil talk. True, Edern?"

Edern smiled. "Give me time."

"How long have you been there?" asked Brys.

"Seven years. Diplomacy is slow work."

Gwydron appeared between the fires then, and soon they were all sitting in Gwriad's tent. Brys looked around at the russet heads, thinking the ghosts of the old north would laugh to see their scattered house gathered once again to plot the future of Britain. Manaw was of red Llywarch's line and Penllyn was of black Owain's, but apart from Gwydron they were all Cynferchin, all the remaining blood of Rheged. Brochfael would not be amused. They worked quickly, discussing the trade routes and port tolls.

Sometime before dawn Brys woke disoriented, reaching for his sword, but he wasn't in a border camp. He was asleep in his clothes in the tent Tegwy had cleared, and the cloak flung over him was clasped with a gold brooch in the shape of Gwynedd's dragon. *Alliance.*

In the morning they gathered in the largest tent with the walls rolled up to catch a crossdraft; it was already hot. Brys stood among the Powys nobles behind Brochfael. After Bishop Elfoddw's prayer Gwriad spoke of his kinsman and envoy Cynfarch carefully enough not to offend Brochfael. Gwriad was cautious, diplomatic, maybe wise. Reading about Greek philosopher kings had done him no harm, but he had the sense not to quote Plato.

"Alliance is not a new idea." Gwriad had a pœt's trick of fixing on faces one by one, drawing people into his cool passion. "For four hundred years we've fought the English together. What is new is the idea of alliance for peace."

Elfoddw, having striven all his life for peace and conciliation with mixed results, gazed off into a kinder world. *Not Britain,* Brys thought. *You'll find your eternal peace only in the city of God.* Outside, the banners of four earthly kingdoms stirred lazily in the warm wind of high summer.

Gwriad laid out his proposals for trade and Elfoddw's suggestions for safer traffic between monasteries. Caradog scowled over folded arms. Arthen's eyes hunted shadows around the carpets spread on trampled grass. Brochfael watched without expression. Each was cautious in his own way. *They're oil and water, nothing can make them flow together.*

But Gwriad was clever. He talked about the dangers of raiding and suspicious isolation and soon stirred angry words between Caradog and Arthen; Gwynedd had raided its former cantref of Ceredigion a few years ago. Arthen asked pettishly why he should get involved in Powys's interminable wars; Brochfael told him icily that Powys held the border for Ceredigion as well as Powys. Other lords spoke up quietly at first but were soon shouting. The king of Manaw sat back in his chair, not quite smiling into his parted red beard, as though their argument were just the thing he wanted to hear.

"Offa knows of this alliance." Brochfael was harder to provoke than the rest. "He'll assume we plan war."

"British alliance in the past has helped Mercia. If Gwynedd and Powys and Mercia hadn't joined forces six generations ago, this island would be Northumbrian. Offa knows this alliance will do Mercia no harm and can do good," said Gwriad.

"The English have short memories. How do we remind them what dear friends we all were once?" Gwydron asked lazily, playing his part.

"Friends?" A tight voice behind Brys, and a hand fell on his shoulder. Gellan. "Ask Gwriad's envoy Cynfarch about these friends. He fought them yesterday on Powys soil."

Brochfael didn't turn in his chair, but his back stiffened. Every other face was on Brys; Gwydron's expression said, Get yourself out of this one. Gwriad looked uneasy. *If I describe the raids, Brochfael will flay me. If I deny them, Gellan will flay me. Create a diversion.*

Brys borrowed Gwydron's lazy voice and twisted it with humor. "Last year I took a close look at Offa's frontier. You wouldn't want to look any closer, I promise you." Some laughter; his enslavement had already entered the fireside tales. "Despite this, I think Offa has had his fill of war with the British. Powys patrols the border every summer, as Mercia dœs. Yesterday we drove raiders from a Powys farm, not for the first time."

Brochfael's iron head nodded, and Gellan's hand squeezed his shoulder. But Gwriad's mouth quirked. *It's an art, talking without saying anything.*

"Offa could gain economically from this too. Brochfael, what do you trade with Mercia?" Gwriad asked, as though the idea had just crossed his mind.

"Cattle and cured hides. Some exotic goods coming out of Armorica. Barter on a small scale at every border gate."

"Manaw and Gwynedd both move Frankish and Irish goods into the port of Chester. We're paying five percent duty." Gwriad leaned forward. "I've proposed giving up ten percent on any of our goods going into Mercia in exchange for dropping the tariff. Offa is in favor. Others can try the same."

Brys, having last night reminded two kings of different merits of this idea, held his breath.

Brochfael was interested. Caradog made plain his distaste. Why trade when you can raid? Enough in Powys clung to that idea from an earlier century. But Gwydron could handle his king.

Gwriad at least didn't worry about soiling his hands with commerce. "We can also suggest Dyfed and Gwent try the same idea with their West Saxon and Mercian trade . . ."

While the others finished their evening meal, Brys and Gwydron walked the trampled riverbank. The Gwynedd *pencerdd* pulled a slip of parchment from a belt pouch. Brys looked askance at the angular English letters spelling British words, then read and laughed. It was from Heilyn.

Heilyn wrote that he was rich and famous, at least by his own humble standards, and since no one in Aberffraw was still willing to play *gwyddbwyll* he'd have to go to Constantinople and play chess instead. Or maybe India, since he'd always admired lapis lazuli. Maybe he'd go by way of Gwent where all his troubles started. Your friend, Heilyn.

"I tried to take him on as my smith—" Gwydron broke off abruptly.

On the southeast bank of Rhiw, a single rider in war gear was approaching the ford on a spent horse.

"And this time," Gwydron took the thought from Brys's mind, "it's not the Powys *pencerdd* playing hotspur."

Brys ran for the ford-stones and took the horse's bridle as the rider vaulted down. He staggered as he tried to stand, and Brys caught him. Under the dust and sweat he recognized a man of Rhirid's wing.

"Get Brochfael." As Gwydron sprinted up toward the tents, he stood clear. "I'm all right. I rode straight from River Gwy."

Brochfael came with a knot of his nobles; the others hung back in a show of courtesy but they were within hearing.

"Lord king, Offa murdered Athelbert of East Anglia. Weeks ago, in Hereford."

Brochfael motioned the others closer. "How do you know?"

"Traders and farm people. The Mercian garrison always lets them through." The bodyguard man was still catching his breath. "First there were confused reports of fighting in Hereford and talk that the West Saxons would rise. Finally they beheaded Athelbert while Bertric stood by under guard. Offa told him he'd meet the same fate if he couldn't control the West Saxons. Now they say Offa martyred a holy man, a sacrifice for his people."

"Not Offa himself?" Brochfael looked stunned.

"By his order, but one of his kinsmen saw to it. Cenwulf."

Gellan's pale eyes tracked from Brochfael to the rider and back again. "Lord, we can bring out all of the nobles' bodyguards and raise the levies."

"No," Brochfael said. "Not unless the West Saxons rebel against Offa."

"The West Saxons won't rise yet," said Gellan, "but we should be ready."

Brys considered Brochfael's war commander. The river rush seemed very loud in the silence, full of voices. *You know what I think of this border,* said Cenwulf in a stable at Y Drefwen. *I never deny we may see war again,* said Eli at Mathrafal, holding a sleepy child. *Tell Eli I'll delay as long as I can,* said Egbert with his hands deep in a stag's blood. And the river brought him a fourth voice, a southern voice in a Roman courtyard in Cær Seint: *Brochfael's man. Dark hair, light eyes.* No one had lighter eyes or darker hair than Gellan. *Brochfael's man. Brochfael's commander. Gellan, who said, The West Saxons won't rise. Yet.*

Idris asked something. Brochfael answered. Their words swept past Brys like leaves on a fast current. The messenger had taken his stumbling horse off to the picket lines. Gwriad had drawn the others up the slope of the overgrown field, back to the remnants of their meal. *Egbert. Cenwulf. Eli. Gellan.* And Gellan controlled the king's bodyguard which was the only standing army of Powys, their ranks swelled by foot levies and nobles' bodyguards in time of war. *The West Saxons won't rise. Yet. Gellan can say that with confidence because he knows the plan. When will they rise, then? How long do we have?*

"I'll send reinforcements tonight to double the patrols, at least," said Gellan tersely. His eyes flicked to the river and back. "Eli's bodyguard is standing by in Elfæl."

No doubt. With Egbert and a company of mercenaries?

Brochfael shook his head. "No more men on the border. Send half the Elfæl band here and leave half with Eli."

And Brochfael knows.

"Lord —" Protest rose as far as Gellan's mouth and stopped.

Brochfael nodded pleasantly and walked back to his guests. Gellan stared after him from a narrow black point at the core of his pale grey eyes. He turned to Brys.

"Cynfarch, will you ride a message to your cousin in Elfæl?"

Anything, any reason to turn him down. The first lie that comes to mind. "I would go gladly. But Gwydron has asked me to join his meeting tonight with Brochfael. You have met?" *God only knows what Brochfael and Gwydron have to talk about. Pray Gwydron's as quick as he seems.*

Gwydron nodded to the commander. "I've been trading with Ulster for hides. I'll do better trading with Powys instead if Brochfael agrees."

Gellan wished him well in his venture, his thoughts already on finding a messenger, and headed for the horse lines.

Brys turned. Gwydron and he stood alone again by the river. *None of this has happened, I wish I could believe.*

"Cynfarch, in God's name—"

"I know." Brys felt cold sweat on his face, mercifully now and not when he was lying to Gellan. "Later."

Gwydron was white-faced. "I'll set up a talk with Brochfael. About hides. Or something."

"Friend." Brys clasped his forearm.

Gwydron smiled too brilliantly.

By evening the four kings and their nobles bickered their way to something like a trade agreement. Brys listened, stored it all in his trained memory while his thoughts were miles away. Alliance was a good thing, certainly. But now peace seemed beautiful and fragile, like a wildflower that blooms for one short day before frost strikes its mountain garden.

22 June 794 + Aberriw

"'Lovely on the mountains are the feet of the herald, proclaiming prosperity and peace.'" Elfoddw turned from his traveling altar and blessed Gwriad, his smile brighter than a benediction. A shining host stood in the river meadows, yet many glittered darkly with the weapons of war. What is Cæsar's must be given to Cæsar, Elfoddw would say. Others, nuns and monks from four kingdoms, raised a chant of pure soaring praise.

On the altar behind Gwynedd's beloved bishop and the bishop of Meifod, between golden cross and silver chalice, Padrig's marvellous reliquary—Anna's and Meirwen's and Heilyn's marvellous reliquary—gleamed in the morning sun. Brys had examined it earlier. Anna had drawn most of the figures for the panels, Gwydron said, but Heilyn had drawn two "saints" for the procession. The tall woman had a stubborn mouth in an oval face and wore complex earrings; she carried a small mallet. The man was shorter, with fine direct eyes, and at his shoulder projected the bulk of a harp case. Now Brys and Meirwen faced eternity in hammered gold, though sainthood was not likely to follow.

Benediction, then dismissal. The congregation stirred and became a worldly company again.

Father Bened and a handful of Meifod monks, at a trestle table in the council tent, lettered words on parchment. The priest's rosy face and tonsure glowing with sweat made him look like a testy cherub. His pen scraped across the distant shouts of orders and laughter in the field camp. Kings and bishops signed the agreement beside their names, then the witnesses. Careful to avoid a lefthanded smear, Brys signed with satisfaction. Brochfael's son Cadell signed next, and they went out together into the still sunshine.

"Rhydion died last week," Cadell managed without a stutter.

"I thought it would be soon." Brys wouldn't lie by saying he was deeply grieved. For Elisedd's pœt he had felt a grudging respect but little warmth.

"He asked me to — to wish you well."

Brys nodded. Crooked Cadell, people taunted Brochfael's son in Mathrafal. A brutal grandfather, a cold father and disastrous fostering to one of Elisedd's nobles had misshapen his spirit more than childhood illness had twisted his back. Cadell had few friends. His wife had become abbess of a Tegeingl monastery, according to gossip, to get as far from Cadell as she could, leaving Adwen to raise Cyngen and Nest, her children by Cadell. Some thought Cadell stupid, but he had been kind when Brys first came to Mathrafal, a boy shocked with grief at losing both parents; he could have been cruel instead. Brys, remembering that kindness, always treated the man gently.

"How is it on the border?" asked Cadell.

Brys made him laugh over the discomforts and kept the terrors to himself. It was surprising to see Cadell here; usually he shunned any court duty. A king's son usually at least captained a wing of the bodyguard. Was it Cadell's choice, or Brochfael's, to keep him at a distance? "Hunt sometime, Brys?"

"Good idea." Brys watched Cadell away until he saw Brochfael come out of the tent. He caught up with him in the meadow. With a hand on his shoulder, a familiarity he rarely took, he drew the king out of earshot toward the ruined farm house. Brochfael eyed him closely but came without protest.

"Act now before it's too late," Brys said without preamble. "On Gellan."

"Gellan is a troublesome man, Cynfarch. War is a matter of honor to him, and he thinks it's a solution now. I can't allow that." Brochfael kept his voice easy, making it a frank explanation. It wasn't. *Something else in your voice. Relief. What were you expecting?*

"Now I know more than I told you before," Brys said desperately. "It was Gellan who tried to have me killed in Arfon. He's conspiring with Eli. We don't have long."

Brochfael turned so that the sun stood behind him, shadowing his face and striking full in his *pencerdd*'s eyes. *Voices are easier to read anyway, and I learned yours years ago.*

"It's not your trouble." *Impatience.*

"You don't trust me much," Brys said.

"I don't trouble you with things that don't concern you." *Cool warning.*

"Your death by treason concerns me, since I won't outlive it," Brys said bluntly and heard the king draw in his breath sharply. *I've gone too far again, but that can't be helped.* "Gellan is plotting with your brother and the English to overthrow you. The raids cover their troop movements and also invite counterattack. The first time some border patrol strikes back — and our squadron has come close to it, I promise you — there'll be outright border war to cover the start of civil war in Powys, Mercia and Wessex."

Brochfael made another sound that might be laughter. "Your imagination runs stronger than your strategy, Cynfarch."

"Every word is true. You know that. Why deny treachery that can kill us all and destroy Powys?"

"Your father was a troublemaker." *Bitter amusement.* "I could have guessed you'd be worse."

"My father was broken by grief at my brother's death, misguided, tempted too far, it dœsn't matter. I'm not my father. I'm your man."

"Are you indeed?" *Cold to the bone.* "Yet you meet by night with other northern-spawned malcontents to direct Powys policy. You and your Cynferchin cousins overlooked only Eli."

"We also discussed Manaw and Gwynedd and Ceredigion policy. Not all Gwriad's concessions yesterday were freely given. And why would we deal with Eli? You're king of Powys." *Now we come to it. The old hatred between North Powys and South Powys, with Rheged thrown in.* "Act now."

"I cannot act on anything without proof."

Radiant god. You'll die of your own justice. "And if I give you proof?"

"What proof?" *A whip crack.*

Brys balanced lightly on his heels and left it hanging.

"You have no proof, Cynfarch. That's all you will hear of it and that's all you will say of it."

"The sacrifice consents." Brys let his gaze drift downstream with a skein of cooksmoke. "Deadly nightshade, or will it be a knife in the back?"

"Don't provoke me." Brochfael started away angrily.

"One more thing, if you're going to court disaster," Brys put an edge on the words and flung them at the king's back. "Name your heir as Offa has done. Name Cyngen. Then send him somewhere out of sight before he dies of your inaction. If Eli tries for the *hual*, he'll cut down Cyngen to end the succession." Cadell was out of the question anyway.

"You dare —" Brochfael spun back to him, his fist raised. He opened his hand deliberately and let it fall. "Very well. I give you charge of Cyngen. See that he prospers."

Brys watched him walk away. *Try to shock some sense into you and you drop this on me.* He was shaking.

The pœts of the Powys lords had also come to the field camp. It was too good an opportunity to miss but not a welcome one. That evening Brys exercised his right to call them together and found himself sitting by a campfire with eight men of high *awen* and higher arrogance. Eli's harper Bleddri was absent. Brys was the youngest by three or four years. *A belly flutter of performer's fright. Keep it simple.*

"When did Rhydion last gather you?" *I should know these things. Rhydion told me nothing.*

They looked at each other. The greyest said, "Before the last battle, before Mæs

Derwen." *Ten years ago.*

"What do you need from me?"

Brys looked around, expecting amusement. Instead, raised eyebrows. No one said anything. The Arwystli man began tuning his harp. A long silence, growing longer. Idris Meirionydd's pœt, a tall and faded-looking man with a drooping moustache, cleared his throat. Monks were writing his pœtry in the margins of Tywyn abbey gospel book, he said. It was clearly an encroachment on the pœt's trained memory, yet it preserved the work. What should he do? It gave Brys something to answer, and mercifully, something for them all to discuss. Another needed to know standards for graduation in song, since his student was nearly finished. And another suggested they meet in Mathrafal at Michælmas.

Without planning to, Brys spent an hour smiling to himself at the backbiting and boasting and effortless wit of those who lived by words. He listened more than he talked, knowing he was on trial as much here as he had been in Mathrafal sanctuary. When he stood they got to their feet around the fire, an unnecessary courtesy, and the nearest offered his arm. Brys clasped it. Then the rest. As he walked away there was laughter at some joke about ravens, but he heard no malice.

Moments later Cyngen and Tegwy materialized out of the summer dark together. Cyngen said, "Grandfather says we're in your charge. What time are we riding out tomorrow?"

Impossible. Surely Brochfael didn't mean immediately . . . Brys nearly killed the idea, then thought twice. Where was Cyngen safer, in the steaming entrails of Mathrafal court politics or surrounded by Pol's squadron? Better if he were named heir, but that could only be Brochfael's decision.

"Do you have arms?"

"Of course." Cyngen spoke for both of them as usual.

Brys looked from one to the other. Cyngen grinned, and Tegwy tœd the dusty grass. Waiting for any chance to get to the border. Brys managed not to smile. *I can order them out of any fighting. At least Cyngen's a good hunter.*

"Meet me at the horses at dawn." He walked on toward the fire where he saw Gwydron and Merfyn and Edern, then turned. For the two boys at least there would be something to celebrate. "Coming?"

Edern was talking about Offa's daughter Eadburh, the West Saxon queen, as they settled on the grass. Gwydron levered himself up on one elbow to pass a mead bottle and a cup.

"I met her once in Quentavic, the Frankish port, where she'd stopped over on pilgrimage to Rome. So nothing she's done among the West Saxons surprises me." Edern glanced at Cyngen and his foster brother.

"Don't stop there," Gwydron ordered, to their delight. "You can't say anything these two haven't heard before. Even about Eadburh."

"She was selling herself in a dockside tavern with the port girls and turning her trade on an ale house table for all to see. For amusement. Apparently."

Tegwy gaped; Cyngen shook his head, mainly at the betrayal of rank. Already at fifteen he drew Mathrafal women like moths to a flame; if he didn't marry soon he would scatter as many bastards as Elisedd. Cyngen sighted Merfyn across the flames and got up to offer his hand. They stood for a moment balanced across the fire like wrestlers before the signal: redhaired Merfyn with his fighter's face and cool eyes, deliberate movements, promising still greater height; Cyngen growing from a boy to a rawboned young man, with straight light brown hair and a long face shaped by laughter.

Brys lay back with his harp case for a pillow, hands folded on his chest. *Let someone else talk. My tongue's brought me enough trouble today.* A man was singing at the next fire and someone played a wooden flute, more breath than melody. Brys looked up past wisps of smoke to the star dance. Deep ocean at midnight, a sea of darkness lapping the shallow inverted bowl of Powys hills, floured with brilliance like the phosphorescent flash of creatures under a ship's hull. Sea floor, sky floor. *To be at Bryn Cerddin. In summer with the eaves vents open. Trees in the wind outside. A bar of night sky showing under the thatch. Meirwen.*

"You were in Rome?" Cyngen was asking Edern.

"Following Frankish Charles on pilgrimage, as Gwriad's envoy," Edern told him. "Keeping myself under Charles's eyes. Eventually he'll take notice and give an audience."

"Did you talk with Holy Father?" Cyngen leaned forward eagerly.

"Pope Hadrian has old debts to Charles and he fears Offa, so it's not in his interest to hear any appeal from the British unless Charles or Offa assents. He's probably never heard of Manaw or Powys. No. I didn't talk with Holy Father." Edern didn't seem too put out. An impatient man or an optimist would lose his reason as a British envoy to the great void.

"So when Bishop Elfoddw brought the British churches back to the Roman way it didn't mean anything," said Cyngen. Edern shrugged.

"Spiritual comfort," Brys said, keeping other thoughts to himself. Twenty-six years of spiritual comfort since Elfoddw's peacemaking didn't add up to anything good in Powys, which was ordered to obey the Mercian archbishop, but Elfoddw was much loved and respected in Gwynedd.

"Maybe if Gwriad threatened to boot the Pope off his earthly throne as Offa did, you'd get an audience. I hear Hadrian is profoundly courteous to Offa," suggested Gwydron.

"But there's a British school in Rome," Cyngen frowned.

"It's not like the English enclave, which is under the Pope's own protection and provides him with bodyguard soldiers," said Edern. "The British house is a flea-bitten pilgrims' house where travelers are at equal risk from thieves and priests, who are sometimes indistinguishable."

"We'll change that," said Cyngen.

Edern looked up in surprise but decided not to challenge the boy's promise.

Brys watched with hands wedged behind his neck, feet getting too hot at the fire, too lazy to move. Cyngen, leaning with brown hair falling straight around his face, drew something for Merfyn in the scuffed earth. Two boys on the blade's edge of manhood, making their own alliance. Brys already felt the weight of his guardianship.

"Cyngen."

A light voice from beyond the flames. Brys saw nothing past the brightness and sat up abruptly with hair prickling at the back of his neck. But it was only Nest who walked into the firelight. She wore a blue dress, none too clean, and her brown hair was straying from its braid.

Cyngen straightened. "Did grandmother bring you?"

"I took my pony for a ride and got lost."

"You're never lost, little hawk. Even at midnight. You sneaked out and lifted a horse."

Another one who stole horses. Brys, trying not to laugh or get caught up in family politics, plucked a piece of grass and folded it around a finger. Cyngen gave his sister her marching orders: if she found a bodyguard man to ride with her the eight miles back to Mathrafal he wouldn't tell. Nest's attempt at persuasion was lost on an older brother. Tegwy watched, clearly her captive. Brys felt sorry for the boy. Nest would be old enough to marry soon but she would marry far above a small landowner's son. Cyngen introduced her to the others.

Gwydron levered himself onto one knee. "Not the lady Nest ferch Cadell? I thought you were Boudicca come to take charge of the bodyguard."

Nest nodded gravely, taking quick measure of Gwydron with her rainy grey eyes. "Next year. Bring me your sword if you want to drive the Romans into the sea."

"Lady, my heart's pierced now. Make me your pœt."

"I have Cynfarch as my pœt," said Nest. "And so I have no need of another."

Gwydron flushed to his diadem, sat back on his heels and shot Brys a stunned glance. Brys grinned. *No one underestimates Nest for long. If Cyngen will found a British enclave at Rome, Nest will command swords and drive someone into the sea.*

Cyngen stood up. "Let's find someone to take you to Mathrafal."

"Brys." She drew herself up, all royal house. "Ride with me."

"I'm taking your brother and Tegwy to the border at dawn. I'm not riding all night even for you, my girl."

"Take me to the border, too, then."

"You're worth a squadron, true. The English would flee before you," Brys admitted. "But not this year."

"But Brys—"

"Nest," said Brys. "Enough. Go."

Nest gave him one glance of speculation or conspiracy or defiance, he wasn't sure, but for once she chose to do what he said. She led Cyngen and Tegwy into the dark toward the horse lines. Hard-headed Merfyn looked into his cup bemused as though a fish had just surfaced in it, drained his mead and left with Edern. Brys took the mead jar from Gwydron and poured himself one cup more than he needed.

"How old is she?" asked Gwydron.

Brys thought about it. "Probably twelve."

"Boudicca. She'll be a beauty." Gwydron shook his head. He tipped a head of wild grass between thumb and forefinger and watched its dancing firelight shadow on his knee. "What's this Brys?"

"A nickname. As far back as I can remember. Even my parents used it."

"'Haste' — it suits you, Powys."

"Penllyn." *Much more mead than I needed,* he realized. *Rain on the four-square stones in Llanfor churchyard. A smiling woman with light brown hair framing her face, a dark man who looked much like Cadwr and much like me. A memory of loss: that's all I have of Penllyn.* He poured out a few drops of the amber mead, an offering.

Gwydron tossed the grass stalk into the fire, where it flared for an instant on the dying flames. "Did you talk with Brochfael?"

Brys nodded. *It's not Gwynedd's business.* He said quietly, "Cyngen worries me. He's too old to foster, too young to be in the king's bodyguard when there's a chance of war, too hot-blooded for a monastery."

"Merfyn's going back to Macliau of Bro Waroch, in Armorica. He's some distant kin to Brochfael. Send Cyngen there."

"Neither Brochfael nor Cadell will make that decision."

"Edern can arrange it so Brochfael can't refuse. A welcome guest, further education. Something like that. I'll take care of it if you want."

"All right." Brys poured another. *I'll regret this at dawn.*

"And I'll take your letter to Heilyn. I'm starting to feel like your courier."

"Good. Make yourself useful." But he had no heart for insults tonight.

"About your traitor."

"Which one?" asked Brys bleakly. *Eli. Gellan. My father.*

"Give him an accident."

"It throws the game."

"Throw the game, then." Gwydron shivered, maybe. "You can be attacker or defender, hunter or quarry. You choose."

"An accident is not my way."

"Survival is your way. See that soon or you'll be carrion."

"I need proof." Brys, aware of the irony of singing Brochfael's refrain, dropped his forehead onto his clasped knees. There had been too much of this today.

"Don't let honor stop you. *They* have none." A ringed hand fell on his shoulder and shook him lightly.

"When I have proof."

"Penllyn." Gwydron yawned. "Remember. Survival."

17 July 794 + Maelienydd

The border was quiet. Past midsummer into a wet July they rode patrols until their backbones felt threaded with fire. There were no raids.

"Alliance," Addonwy tried, one morning when rain dripped from the forward edge of his cloak hood, and they all rode muffled like old men against the unseasonable cold. "If this is alliance, why isn't Caradog out here wearing the lard off his backside?"

No one bothered to answer. Monotony, soaked chafing clothes, weapons that rusted almost before the whetstone was lifted, all prodded Addonwy to work for an entertaining quarrel. More often than not he got one. Tempers were fraying.

English patrols now were as regular as sunrise, glimpsed eastward in the open grazing and scrub. In folds and spurs of wooded country they disappeared from sight of the Powys patrols, then emerged at small ungarrisoned crossings of the ridgeway tracks before they turned to retrace their steps. Sometimes they were mounted bands, probably nobles' bodyguards.

One dusk sweetened by recent rain, an English patrol waited where the new border intersected with the old Ceri ridgeway. On the top of the bank, their captain sat his chestnut horse and held up his shield woven over in green branches. Despite the peace signal, Pol halted his squadron just beyond a spear's cast. They loosened spears and settled shields. Pol called Brys, and together they rode up the path angling across ditch and bank. Cyngen and Tegwy started forward, but he motioned them back, being responsible for their safety.

"Cyfaill." Friend, the black-bearded captain called out in British as they drew near, looking as though friendship were the last thing on his mind.

"Wine," Brys answered him in English. The captain had angry dark eyes and made a great effort not to level the long-bladed spear. *Many things but not friend.* "What do you want?"

"Ask instead what you want."

Not an exchange of longwinded English riddles. But the captain turned in his saddle and called out to one of his men. Then he said, "We have some of your people."

"Raiding?"

"Making trouble."

His second brought forward a scruffy pair and prodded them over the bank. Brys knew them on sight, a Gwent *crwth* player and his bony woman who had spent a night by their campfire a week ago. Food and small objects were missing the next day. Easy to guess what kind of trouble. The man shot Pol a ferret look and the woman began to weep noisily behind her hands.

"Stealing, cheating at dice or hurting your ears?" asked Brys.

"You know them?" A smile briefly threatened the Mercian's face.

"Enough to send them packing."

Brys turned to repeat the exchange to Pol, who herded the pair into Powys cursing Gwent dock rats who strayed from their verminous home. The English captain turned his horse, but Brys rode forward until they could have clasped arms.

"Have your border villages been raided?" he asked quietly.

The black-bearded man on the other side stared narrowly and finally nodded. "Not for a month."

"Who were they?"

A flare of anger in dark eyes. "*Wealas*."

I was afraid of that. "If you take any, bring them here alive. I will buy them."

"Why?"

"They're traitors, treaty-breakers."

"No ransom," the Mercian answered haughtily. "If I find them, I will give them."

"Hwæt!" It sharpened the captain's attention, the English pœt's cry to silence a

hall for song. Brys gave him a line from one of their grim laments. "'Worthy the one who keeps good faith.'"

"Good faith? Not from *Wealas*." He wheeled away.

The *crwth* player and the woman went on their way sullenly after bolting a meal that would have fed five. For a week the rain lifted and the ground began to dry. Whenever they passed the ridgeway crossing Brys looked for the English patrol. All he saw was the first purple bloom on the heather and larks rising out of the warm grass.

Cyngen and Tegwy carried their weight without complaint, always first to find firewood or rub down the horses. Brys began to find his gear polished to mirror brightness and his spare shirt washed before he thought of it. One afternoon when the two crouched to examine deer spoor in the soft earth by a spring, brown head and blond head together, Marc turned to Brys with one of his oblique looks.

"They'd rather track English. They're bursting their hides to prove themselves to you."

"Pol's the one they should worry about," said Brys. "And he's pleased with them."

"No." Marc smiled slowly. "You remember being fifteen. They live in the song cycles and think you stepped out of one. Three red-speared pœts in the island of Britain, and a fourth is Cynfarch bardd Brochfael."

Brys swore at him. Grinning, Marc slouched away to pull his mare out of the lush grass before she bloated. Tegwy might be dazzled, eager to join the bodyguard. The squadron groaned at his practical jokes and applauded his gift for mimicry. Cyngen's road would take him further; though Brochfael had named no heir, Cyngen knew his own *braint*. He traded gambling wins with the bodyguard men, heard about their wives and girls in Cærsws and Llanarmon, settled arguments, dealt with minor injustices subtly enough that no one objected. Brys watched him study his companions, the countryside and the English. Elisedd would have broken this stalemate, Cyngen said once, and only shrugged when Brys said Brochfael was wiser than Elisedd. Cyngen admired warlike Elisedd. It was tempting, bound by a frayed peace, to mistake war for a solution. The sooner Edern arranged an invitation from Macliau the better.

Lammas arrived. They kept the harvest festival at a township south of Clun, among farm people and stock traders in for the cattle fair. They bent custom by coming armed to the fires, and Pol posted a guard overlooking the eastward track. No one complained. There were sweet Lammas cakes, dark ale, golden mead and light-hearted company for the first time in weeks. Brys danced the circles and chains until a dark-eyed girl put a hand on his arm and suggested they walk by the river. He turned her aside gently, half wishing he'd drunk more, and retreated to the standing stones where some of the squadron sprawled with a mead jar.

Barley harvest now at Bryn Cerddin. Someone at the fires was singing a bawdy tune about the rod that women love. Brys lay looking up at a cloudy shoal of stars and thought of Meirwen at Calan Haf, with her dark hair netted in silver chains. He rolled onto his belly and watched the dancers over his folded arms. A cloistered monk had more sense. Cyngen disappeared into the dark with his hand on the curve of a girl's hip. His friend looked after them, blinking, and went back to the dance circles to try his luck. *Waste no time, Tegwy, life is short.*

At dawn they saddled the horses, choked back dry bannock and stale ale, and rode out northward.

Three days later they passed the dogleg join in the frontier dyke that always inspired great humor about the eyesight of Offa's surveyors. Leather war shirts or mail laced loosely in the drowsy warmth, they rode north as afternoon light curved the hills of Powys to the west. Cian slipped back among them. He often strayed and returned with hares for the evening meal; once a hind fattened on summer browse. This time, empty-handed, he went straight to Pol.

"In the birches, forty men and some women."

"English?" Pol began to tighten the lacing of his mail shirt, and the others stirred with interest.

Cian shrugged, holding his jibbing black pony stallion on a tight rein. "There's a guard sitting above the stream. I watched a while. They're waiting for something."

"We'll wait with them." Pol turned to give the order. "North, then cut across from the track."

Brys easily interpreted the look that passed between Cyngen and Tegwy. *At last.* And he was their guardian. Should he tell them to stay here? Order them to stay clear of trouble? But they were probably safer with the squadron.

The wooded country rolled steeply until they reached the old rutted ridgeway which led west to open moorland. Briefly they were skylined on the high ground, then Cian led them down into more woodland on the north side. Pol had the squadron wait in a shadowed hollow, then he and Brys followed Cian on foot to the head of a steep valley thick with scrub birch. From a tangled bilberry thicket, Cian pointed silently across the crease. Almost invisible in shadow beside a rock spill, a man crouched with a square-headed British spear across his knees. Below, where trees and shadow were denser, a few people moved busily. Brys watched a man on a white horse giving orders. He looked suddenly uphill as though he heard his name, a light-haired man with a flat southern face.

"Something new," Cian pointed below.

A handful of people worked busily around a four-wheeled horse-drawn wagon. Harvest gear? Had they come skulking under cover just to watch a traveling harvest crew get ready for tomorrow's reaping? Then a British voice called an order, and people shifted enough to reveal the wagon's load: spears, knives, swords, shields. Cian pointed out a few horses and some tough hill ponies. Pol studied the activities below with a hunter's meticulous care. This was something they had been desperate to intercept, a raiding band preparing to move from Powys east into Mercia.

The sun sank below the western hills. Another hour, flat in the grass. Finally, close enough to dark that movements below were shadow on shadow, the raiders gathered and started down the narrow hillside stream. They would travel the long way around the moor's shoulder, adding a mile to avoid the settlement to the west—

not that a few farm people could stop a band this size, but they could sound the alarm — before they bore east for the border.

Twilight boomed with early owls and rustled with foxes as the raiders disappeared out of sight at the first bend downstream. Pol nodded. Brys and the other two picked a silent route back up through the scrub, then ran like hares once they reached open ground. The captain gave orders quietly: mount, follow the raiders and move in just as they cross the border. In minutes they were cantering south on the minor grass-grown track that skirted the old fortress and clung to the heights.

They waited a long time in a shadowed *cwm*, holding the horses as still as they could, but there was no movement on the streamside track far below. Pol motioned to Cian, who dismounted and loped off into the night. He returned panting from a long run.

"Not moving east. West."

Raiding into Powys, from within Powys. Fair god.

Pol swore quietly in his own language. He motioned them to turn around in their tracks. Ahead, a steep track branched down a slope. It was the fastest way. They led the horses down with a clatter that would wake Arthur in his glass island, then remounted at the bottom to ride upstream.

A moonless night. Changing hoofbeats told their passage over grass, three crossings of hill streams, loose rock. The lie of the land started to look familiar. Cian found them a ford and led up through a hazel coppice to a ridge. From the top they looked down into a hollow of plowland and farms. It swam with flame like the bowl of an oil lamp.

People swarmed between the buildings. Even up here they heard the roar as walls caught from the thatch. Pol signalled for Marc's horn, then with its warning still on the air they swept down through the wheat stubble. The charge plunged them through a handful of mounted raiders, and Brys left his spear in a man's shoulder. Pol was yelling for the farm people, and a knot gathered at the orchard gate.

Raiders abandoned their looting as the Powys squadron dismounted and went after them. Brys shouted for Cyngen and Tegwy to stay close, the best he could do. They pursued a handful of shadows through the garths, hand-to-hand with a scattering enemy. Dirty fighting. A few fought like cornered wolves, but most were rabble. When the snarling face of the *crwth* player loomed up in shadow, Cyngen coolly speared him. His verminous woman flourished a *seax*. Brys ducked her wild sweep and stabbed her in the throat. As he turned, a holly throwing spear hissed toward him. Cyngen leaped and staggered, catching it in his shield with the point jutting under his elbow.

Cyngen laughed and flung the shield away, springing toward another man. *I'll never get them out of this. And we need every blade now anyway.* Brys flung himself in as the man's *seax* sang in the air, but Cyngen ducked aside grinning and let Tegwy take him. Then the two of them were off across the barnyard, Cyngen with his brown hair flying like a banner and yelling, of all things, "Elisedd!" Tegwy pounded on his heels. Brys gathered himself to follow. To one side, a blur of white. One of Pol's men flew toward him with arms spread, a spear in his back. Behind him the spearman wheeled his white horse and drew his sword. He was a fair man with a southern face, broad in the cheekbones: Eli's harper Bleddri.

"Sing, Cynfarch." He vaulted down.

Brys lifted his sword point and took the first swing on his shield rim, barely turning it from his face. Bleddri backed him toward a house wall before Brys could return a stroke, driven before the man's superb skill. The world closed in to the arc and stab of Bleddri's flickering blade. Brys stayed out of reach, barely, in a deadly dance. He fought panic. *I'll never take this man. Think. Quickly.* He leaped back suddenly and got the house wall on his sword hand. Bleddri came on, but the wall hampered his right hand with the sword. Brys sliced air near his shoulder.

"Why?" He had to give ground again. "Why's Eli doing this?"

"Changed sides, have you? You have no honor, hostage." Bleddri chopped sidewise.

The sword nearly split his head. Enough talk. Brys tried to edge him toward a burning shed. He rang his blade on the harper's iron shield rim, doing no damage, not coming near. Bleddri smiled, taking his time, and started backing him up again until he felt the orchard wall at his back. He had nothing to gain from waiting. Brys took the risk and shouldered Bleddri aside. Bleddri spun and gave him the shield in his face. Brys sprawled headlong, dazed. *Risk taken, life lost.* He twisted under the glittering curve of the descending sword, too swift for prayer or regret.

Then Bleddri kneeled slowly, opened his mouth on a gout of blood and fell forward onto him with a hilt between his shoulder blades. Brys stared in wordless shock as Cian crouched to retrieve his blade. His belly knotted and he rolled away vomiting. When he was done Cian gave him a hand up.

"Bodyguard again?" he asked shakily.

"You did not consent."

Brys started to laugh, too nearly hysterical, and shut his mouth. *Harp.* He'd landed on his sword arm, not his back, but he reached into the case to be sure. Sweet-voiced and whole. Cian smiled, showing his sharp dog teeth. Brys got to his feet spitting out bile and leaned against the orchard wall on unsteady legs. *Ten years' terror burned out in a quarter hour.*

The fighting was now scattered. Together they pursued raiders among the houses. Brys stabbed one too late to save a farm boy with a hunting spear. He looked around for more. Figures black against flame, some of them running uphill. He yelled at Cian, and they sprinted up through the wheat stubble. Elgan and a handful more came after them. Three men turned to face them up at the edge of the hazel coppice, a thick barrier against flight. One of them took Elgan's spear in the throat, and Cian finished a second. The third found a way between the hazels and looked over his shoulder once as he slipped into their shelter. Firelight painted his sweating face for an instant. A tall young man, ashen fair, whom Brys had last seen on Offa's hall dais in Tamworth. Cenwulf's younger brother, Cuthred.

Brys went in after him, out of the smoke and firelight and into a different hunt. Shadow on darker shadow. Scent of leaf mold. Leaves sighing a little in the night wind. No other sound. He walked quietly, hair lifting on the back of his neck, both hunter and prey. He stood a few minutes in the deepest shadow. Wings beat further along the ridge: birds lifting from a tree. Then a sound that could be one hoof striking root or stone. But when he walked on he found no trace. Disappointment sat on his tongue like metal, like revenge. He turned and went back to the settlement.

It was over. Some of Pol's squadron had joined the settlement people beating out flames with their cloaks, trying to save the outbuildings at least. The captain was giving orders near the orchard gate. Brys drew him aside.

"Do you understand this?" he asked quietly.

Pol looked over at Eli's dead harper. "It's hard not to understand."

"I'm riding to Brochfael. Not a word about any of it. You or anyone else." *Heavy-handed, but I can't help that.* "Otherwise, civil war."

Pol only said, "I know."

Brys found Cian sitting under an apple tree, cleaning his sword. "Take Cyngen and Tegwy—"

"Brochfael's at Rhyd y Grœs, not the field camp."

"— until I get back."

Cian nodded without looking up. Brys found his charges with the farm people, gathering wounded and dead. Cyngen was helping Tegwy bandage a gashed thigh. No worse damage, thank God. Brys motioned to them and steered them out past the orchard wall with a hand on each shoulder to where Bleddri lay. He rolled the body over with his foot and looked to make sure Cyngen knew him. The dead man stared flatly up at them, blood smeared beside his mouth.

"You answer to Cian for now. No fire-eating."

Cyngen nodded and twisted his mouth around something. "They were *Cymry*, British. Outlaws and fugitives, from Gwent and South Powys. They—"

Brys squeezed his shoulder. For a moment Cyngen looked as though he might weep, or heave his meal like his guardian; but he steadied, and clamped his mouth shut.

The white gelding trailed its reins nearby. Brys wrapped Bleddri in his cloak and together they hefted him up across the saddle and tied him in place. Tegwy brought Carnlas and tied the white horse behind. A line of blood trickled down to blight the dead harper's barley hair. *One of the Powys harpers, too close to kinship. Salt. The taste of desolation.*

7 August 794 + Rhyd y Groes

Brochfael rode into the clearing an hour after dawn and sent the messenger back to the Rhyd y Grœs garrison. He sat his horse for a moment looking at Brys. The clearing was cool with morning shadow and swam with honeysuckle scent and the pulsing drone of bees. As soon as the rider was out of sight, Brys dismounted stiffly and walked back to the white horse. He pulled the cloak away from Bleddri's head.

Brochfael dismounted and crossed the wet grass, leaving dark footsteps through the sheen of silver. He stood for a long time with one hand on the saddle bow. The dew breeze stirred the white horse's mane and the king's grey hair.

"He was leading a band of raiders. British, armed with English weapons. They attacked one of our settlements north of River Clun. Cenwulf's brother was with him but escaped." *No reaction.* "Here's your proof."

"Proof of what, Cynfarch?"

Brys shook disbelief out of his head. *Still denying it?* "Eli's pœt leads a raid against a Powys farm. Gellan tries to kill me in Arfon. Cenwulf has me ridden down in cantref Tren. Egbert exploits anyone under heaven to recover his patrimony of Wessex. They use murder and brigandry to mimic Powys raids into Mercia and Mercian raids into Powys. An army's probably gathering in Elfæl, and another in Wessex or Mercia. The border will finally break before long. There will be civil war in Mercia and Wessex. And now that Pol's squadron knows the truth, civil war will be inevitable in Powys."

"Go on," was all Brochfael said.

"Eli will attempt to usurp. He has Elisedd's aura and a gold *torc* like Cynddylan, in God's name! All you have is your ice-bound self-devouring pride."

"Are you finished?" asked Brochfael, looking at Bleddri again.

"Yes." Brys leaned at Carnlas's shoulder, catching his balance as the grey stallion shifted weight. *Is this all?*

Brochfael looked at Brys and took a handful of Bleddri's bloodied hair to lift his head, but rigor mortis gripped the body. He knifed his hand to the back of the neck and broke it. The head twisted unnaturally upward. Blood had drained into the face, giving it an ugly black stare.

"Look well, Cynfarch, a mirror. Do you know why it isn't you?"

Too late now for denials and threats. Brys took the reins and turned to mount Carnlas. But Brochfael caught his shoulder and spun him around, and the other hand pinned him. His face was transformed. Without its impassivity it was a different mask. Flushed, pinched white around the mouth, eyes glittering. Anger. Mostly pain.

"You want to know everything." Brochfael made a fist of one hand but kept it on his shoulder. "But you can't live with the knowledge."

"Try." *Not my voice. A shadow.*

"Proof," said Brochfael. "Sometimes there is no proof. How did your father die?"

Ask me, I know it. Who could know better? "A fight."

"A knife fight at Lammas fair in Cær Gai. How did it start?"

Brys shrugged under the fist. He didn't want to argue about this, not right now. "He had a hot temper, he was easy enough to provoke."

"Before that — why did he kill his cousin, Garmon's brother?"

"Dœs it matter?" What had mattered was the ruin and death that followed.

"Maybe not." Brochfael dropped his hand and looked away. "What happened to Cynddylan's *torc*?"

"The English took it from his body at Tren ford. Probably melted down years ago." Brys put his face in both hands a moment and rubbed. His eyes were grainy with fatigue. His mind was crawling with illusions. Proof. Belief that proof could make a difference. *Cynddylan's* torc*? It's just part of Eli's game from the hero cycles, playing Cynddylan with the help of Mercians. Enough. No more lies and evasions.* "Get another *pencerdd*."

"I can't dismiss you." Brochfael said bleakly. "You're too dangerous. You know too much."

"Everyone knows my ambition, people keep telling me." *Out on the razor edge of fear, suddenly.* The risk took his breath. "Egbert offered me Penllyn. 'Cynfarch Penllyn,' he said, 'how do you like the sound of that?' Not as a cantref of Powys or Gwynedd. As a kingdom."

"God my judge." A dry whisper. And nothing more. The sun lifted between the trees at Brochfael's back.

"Instead I took the kiss of peace from Garmon." Silence. Brys looked blindly into Brochfael's face, dark against the gold and green morning sun. *Another risk.* "Release me. You can trust me that much."

A voice like driftwood, all the life leached out of it. The real man for once, maybe? "I loved your father. I trusted him . . . I trust Idris. I trust you. God help me."

"What will you do?"

"You want me to say, march into Elfæl and attack Eli. Do you really think a civil war will cure this sickness? I will do nothing. And trust Offa."

Laughter seized Brys. Trust the deadly enemy, fear the kinsman? He closed his eyes deliberately and opened them on the bright dappled clearing. "I have no heart for lies. And no *pencerdd* can help you if you won't act."

"None has tried," said Brochfael quietly. "I hold you to your oath of service, freely given."

"To Powys."

"I am Powys."

Brochfael walked away across the grass. The dew had begun to steam. Sun shifted between the leaves of high summer. A wood pigeon sailed soundlessly overhead. The king stood by a willow clump for a while, then came back and again put a hand on Brys's shoulder. This time gently.

"A taste of ashes?"

Brys eyed him warily and nodded over a knot in his throat.

"Powys builds on ashes, an old tradition." Brochfael's voice caught on the words. "This is where your work starts. It's hard work. Help me build."

"If you will act—" *I have to gamble, though I have nothing to wager. He'll curse my meddling. First throw.* —"on Cyngen."

"I can't name him heir," Brochfael said quietly. "He's fifteen, too young to hold Powys alone."

"Send him away, then." Brys went on, not giving him a chance to argue. "You'll argue that he's not safe in Britain and if you send him farther he may never return.

But there are ways. Have him disgraced and exiled. Speak no more of him. Call him back at twenty, clear his name and make him heir."

Brochfael considered it. "Possible."

"You should hear from Macliau soon."

"Christ in heaven." Brochfael's head swivelled. "You take too much on yourself, Cynfarch."

Second throw. "If you won't attack, at least assassinate Gellan and Eli." *My cousin Eli. Family. The only one who showed me kindness in Mathrafal last year, whatever his reasons.* "Then take Eli's son as a hostage."

"No killing. I can control them."

"Only in death." *Have you lost your edge? Or hasn't Eli pushed you far enough yet?*

"It offends my honor."

"Honor is mist, it thins to nothing in daylight." *Words I never thought to say, least of all to Brochfael Powys. This strangling grief. Salt.* Brys looked at Bleddri. "He spoke of honor. Died of it. Forget your honor or commit this to my conscience."

"Enough blood." Brochfael sighed. He went to put his arm around his foster son and pœt in a rare gesture. "We can make peace. We can make Powys a garden. Give me your help and your prayers."

"You have them." *Now we'll see about trust.* "Eli seems to think I'm with him. Maybe it's better that way for now."

"I'll tell Idris."

Trust. "I don't think there'll be any more raids. They'll see that they need a different approach." Brys was resigned to Brochfael's justice. Eli would kill as he saw the need, like his father Elisedd, but blood only brought more blood. He turned away to take the body into the garrison. *Rictus humor. Eli's pœt will be buried bent double or broken straight. What dœs that do for honor? We're all hostages, Bleddri, every one of us.*

Brochfael kept the patrols on the border another two weeks without raids, then said the matter was settled with OVa. To Brys's knowledge no messenger went to or from Tamworth. Brochfael went to spend a month at his court in Iâl.

Soon after that the king's *pencerdd* took a handful of the bodyguard to assess the damage on the border and to tell the farm people Brochfael Powys would send them dressed lumber now, then seed corn and breeding stock in the spring.

Some farmers agreed to rebuild. Others decided to let the house posts and orchard walls crumble back into the land; they would move west to join kin or to break new ground. This always was the mark of the borderland, weed-choked fields and ruins tangled in thorns.

8 September 794 + Mathrafal

The sound of River Banwy flowed, always through Mathrafal, an undercurrent to the life of the court.

A west wind lifted rain through the old scriptorium's windows. Brys set his harp down, but as he got up to bar the shutters, sun again lit the raindrops on the plank floor. He left the shutters open, welcoming in the September weather. Winter soon.

No one had come yet. Impatient, Brys walked around the room, stared out at the first leaves falling from the hazel tree, went to look at the faded wall-painting of the apostle Marc, who held a quill pen in mid-air, apparently lost in thought, gospel pages spread on his lap and a winged yellow cat crouched at his feet. The small room held only a few books and scrolls; the copyists now worked mainly in Meifod abbey's larger scriptorium with its tall windows and many oil lamps. The voices of the gate guards calling to each other came faintly to Brys above the gusts — and an earthy fragment from a harvest song. He settled again with his feet propped on a table. *Maybe no one's interested. Or maybe they know enough to fear the idea of joining the* pencerdd*'s guard.*

Raising a guard was one way to protect his back from Gellan and Eli; last night he dropped the invitation over his string arm in hall. Elgan agreed to be his captain. A *pencerdd* had the traditional right to raise thirty men; Brys and Elgan agreed on twenty.

Elgan came in yawning after a while and dropped a wax tablet on the table. His laziness was illusory. A quick mind worked, mostly in silence, behind his dark eyes and heavy face. Elgan knew. This would not be merely an ornamental guard. Any trouble and they would guard the king as well as the *pencerdd*. They needed seasoned fighters, loyal men with heart, glitter and fire. Like the *pencerdd*, they would have to be performers.

"You're early," said Elgan.

"No, I'm not."

"All right, you're late." His captain smiled behind his moustache. "Don't worry, they'll come."

They started to trickle in as the court began to stir. Mostly they were bodyguard men, with a handful from nearby townships. Word had traveled. Elgan spent an hour asking questions while Brys scratched names in wax, and in that time they could have raised forty. Eleven were Penllyn men like himself and Elgan. Of Pol's wing he took Marc and Cian and, after some thought, troublesome Addonwy. When they were done Brys struck hands with his captain like a horse trader and proposed the ale house. As they dropped the door latch, Cyngen and Tegwy appeared in the colonnade. They were both taller than him now, growing straight as hazel saplings.

"Lesson in an hour," said Brys, knowing quite well what they wanted.

"We've come to join the *pencerdd*'s guard." Cyngen folded his arms.

"Ask me again next year." Brys spiked his cloak at the neck and turned the silver ring brooch until the pin caught. The morning had turned sullen again, laying plans for autumn and winter. Elgan wisely kept quiet.

Tegwy set his mouth stubbornly. "We are legal adults and we have men's rights."

"Certainly. And in time I shall consider you."

"Then consider us now." Cyngen's smile lit his face, making things harder. "I caught a spear for you, remember?"

"No one questions your skill or courage, either of you."

"So what do you question?" Cyngen demanded, ready to debate. *Give him a chance and we'll leave here with two extra men.*

"When you can disarm Elgan at sword practice, carry a man for a mile your back and spear-vault onto a cantering horse, we'll talk. With permission from your father, Cyngen."

"My father." Cyngen looked blank. No one spoke much of Cadell, as though the unfortunate man were dead or cloistered. Whatever his failings, he could still permit or forbid his son's sword service.

"Your father. Cadell mab Brochfael. And be glad you have one." Brys threw the cloak back from his shoulder, hooked a thumb behind his silver belt buckle, and stepped into the colonnade with Elgan.

"Cynfarch mab Cadeyrn," Cyngen asked formally, "May we walk with you?"

"As far as the gate. But you have my answer." They went through the courtyards to the hall garth and past the doorkeeper. When they reached the empty chapel garth, Cyngen stopped.

Brys turned, frowning. Enough was enough.

"Grandfather put me and Tegwy in your guardianship this summer." Cyngen's voice was unsteady, though he had learned Brochfael's impassive face.

Elgan moved to walk on, a discreet man, but Brys signalled his captain to stay.

"Three days ago my red bitch died when we were out after boar. She died in convulsions after I fed her meat from the kitchen. Last night a drunk blundered into me outside the hall. It was too dark to recognize him, and the doorkeeper was inside for a message. When I drew my knife he ran. He dropped something."

Cyngen nodded to Tegwy, who cautiously held out an object between thumb and forefinger. It was a jagged bronze triangle with a bluish stain on the narrow end. Brys took it with care. *No scent. Monkshood? A scratch brings slow and terrible death.*

"What about the meat?" asked Elgan quietly.

"It looked purple and smelled sweet," said Tegwy.

Nightshade. Brys passed it to Elgan and stood rocking on his feet. There was really nothing to decide. Among twenty men Cyngen would be as safe as he could be in Mathrafal without more obvious precautions. Tegwy was incidental, no threat to anyone. Elgan put the poisoned bronze in his belt pouch without a word.

"Poison is an ugly death. I'm sorry about your hound." *A coward's weapon.* Brys, waiting for his anger to subside, looked at them. Shoulder to shoulder, pale but steady. So nothing was left of childhood. "It was God's hand the first time, quick thinking the second. Dawn tomorrow on the training ground."

When Marc rode home to Llangollen for his cousin's wedding, Brys gave him a message for Meirwen. *Mathrafal is a good place for a smith to work,* he wrote, *either in the court or at Cilwen.* A week later Marc returned, worn out from celebrating, and said Meirwen had left Bryn Cerddin in June. Bethan thought she had gone to Iâl. She left no message.

What dœs that mean? Boredom, anger, family visit, trouble from someone, sickness, another man, flight? Meirwen walks away from anything she dœsn't like or trust.

If I could find a few days to ride to Iâl, I would know. Do I want to know? Meirwen knew her own mind, Brys decided unhappily, and would come south if and when she wanted. He fell back into a half-hearted affair with a Mathrafal woman. But he couldn't debate with her, her brother was angry, and after the first pleasure of shooting his bolt into a warm body and not into his hand, it was nothing. He drifted out of it again. He sidestepped others who waylaid him in the court or sent him gifts. *Maybe another letter.*

Cyngen played passably, as any well-bred man played when the harp passed along the bench, making treble melody and the simplest undercurrent of bass. He played from his head, not from his heart; that would either come or it would not. Impulsive Tegwy often forgot bass entirely in his rush to carry a melody to the end. But they were coming along well enough; Brys wasn't training them for graduation in song.

History, pœtry, logic and rhetoric were their other lessons from the *pencerdd*; he and Elgan also drilled them in weaponry and thus steered them away from Gellan. Bened gave them arithmetic, grammar and scriptural studies. They were learning all the arts that ill-chosen fostering and Brochfael's absences and isolation had denied Cadell.

This afternoon, wind stirred the leaves of the hazel tree outside the scriptorium, and the sun flooded across the writing table and the wooden floor. Brys listened carefully as Tegwy played the lament of Bedwyr Nine-strings for Gwenhwyfar, his lover and Arthur's wife. The piece was cleverly made to sound one-handed; slow cadence rippling in runs, pause for a change of hands, and suddenly the dark hand carried the melody. *Fair. He's been practising.* It was time to move them from the buzzing horsehair student harp he'd excavated from a storeroom to the gut-strung hall harp.

"One more."

It was Cyngen's turn. He quickly tuned down into a different mode and began to lay down a dark undercurrent in the long strings.

"Blood was under ravens, a raw stirring.
They split shields on spears, sons of Cyndrwyn.
I will mourn until I am in my earthen bed
Cynddylan slain, lord fully honored."

As Cyngen sang, Brys looked out into the courtyard, past the hazel tree and into lost Pengwern. Cyngen sang it as victory, then stepped down a mode at the end to give it a last minor echo. He damped the strings with efficiency and grace and rested his wrist on the string arm, pleased.

Brys turned to the room again. So brown-haired Cyngen's eyes grew bright when he lamented fair Cynddylan, who died with no heir. *Time rolls on toward its starting place. Eli thinks he is Cynddylan's heir, after six generations, but Eli is wrong. Cynddylan's heir is Cyngen.*

"Why did she do it, his sister?" asked Tegwy.

"Refuse the Mercian marriage? There are different stories." Brys hesitated.

"One is that she loved Cynddylan. Not as a sister. Some say she loved another man, or that she was promised to the church."

"Didn't she understand Cynddylan needed the alliance?"

"How would you like to be sent as a gift to your enemy? To sleep with him, bear his children and die unloved in a foreign land? How do you think Nest would like it?" Brys asked, trying not to sound as impatient as he felt. *How do you think Nest* will *like it?* A certainty, not a possibility. It weighed on Brys's heart as well as Tegwy's to think of little Boudicca traded for peace. It would happen soon.

Tegwy flushed and looked away. It was heavy-handed, but he took the point.

Cyngen looked out through the window, frowning. "Did you see Pengwern? When you . . ." He was reluctant to say, when you were a slave.

"I saw Y Drefwen." Brys crossed to bar the shutters. Lesson over. He could hear Banwy and maybe distant Efyrnwy under the wind. At the door he looked back and saw their young faces, open and waiting. "Grown over with thorns, beside a Mercian town."

As he stepped into the colonnade, the wind shifted and touched his neck with cold and the river rush swelled to a voice full of tears. *Once I had brothers. They grew as straight as hazel saplings. One by one they all died.* She was making herself at home in his dreams and his imagination, the woman whose name was salt.

If he went to the sanctuary and prayed for a healing dream, perhaps he would be freed of her voice and her sorrow. Or was it all his own? The thought of no longer hearing her voice in the wind and rushing water was desolate. *Stay a while longer, sad wanderer, lost Heledd.*

And the girl on the white mare, if she were indeed living flesh, could not be found anywhere.

Elgan worked them all hard every day for weeks before he stopped growling. Brys joined them, practising with spear and sword, running circuits of the training field beside brown Banwy, riding formations on horseback. Brys made sure Elgan spared no one to turn them into a deadly fighting force. If they needed to fight, they would have no second chances.

Brys was pressing advantage in a sword match one clear afternoon when a man rode onto the training ground on a fine red roan. He sat his horse, watching. Brys disarmed his man and took Elgan's usual reminder that a cool head won more fights than a hot head. Then someone said the rider wanted him. Brys picked up his shirt on his sword point and went over, prepared to turn away another who wanted to join the guard.

A young man with glossy brown hair smiled down at him and said, "I'm on my way to India."

20 September 794 + Mathrafal

Heilyn slid off his horse and watched Brys and his guard finish their practice. A score of men stripped to the waist, sinewy bodies gleaming with sweat in the September morning, moving with precision and harmony. Like dancers, except for their deadly purpose. After a while the captain shouted and they gathered to him for orders. Brys said little, a word of praise here and there. They called him Cynfarch when they thought of it and Brys when they forgot; he answered to both names. Heilyn studied their faces. Respect. Loyalty. Affection. An edge of something else, some disquiet. Brys came and embraced him sweatily.

"Not bad horseflesh, for Gwynedd. Let's get her to the stable." They walked downstream beside eloquent Banwy. As they reached the outer paddock, a man brought Brys a fold of parchment. Heilyn glimpsed a broken red wax seal stamped with some ornate design and a few lines of writing in an English hand. Brys read it and swore with unusual crudity.

"I leave for Gwent tomorrow," Heilyn said. Obviously there was bad news; best to keep moving. "I'll be at the inn tonight if you have time to share a meal."

"Why don't you stay here? With me?" Brys looked offended: a slight hardening of the mouth, one green glance, a downward gaze under long black lashes.

Nothing had changed. Heilyn found his balance and asked dryly, "Do you really want the latest gossip about the altar silver of Bangor church?"

"Any gossip, as long as it's about you too." Brys stopped and put a hand on his shoulder. His smile showed his crooked front teeth, and Heilyn was helpless not to smile. "I saw your reliquary when Elfoddw was here. It's wonderful work. Will you make me some arm rings?"

"Ask Meirwen."

"Meirwen's in Iâl. Or somewhere. Will you?"

"I don't know." Being here at all tested his courage; staying too long would shatter it.

"Payment in silver," Brys said, misunderstanding. "Brochfael gave me another estate, a wealthy one. Come with me tomorrow and we'll have a look."

"You haven't seen it?"

"I've been on the border all summer. Why didn't you come with Gwydron? I looked for you."

"Ask Gwydron. He's the one who left me sweating over a set of decorated harness." It was one of several answers. *I couldn't bear to. I nearly did.*

Brys walked toward a long building behind the king's hall. An armed guard stood at a covered walkway screened in honeysuckle vines. They went on through a grape arbor where a few small bunches still hung. Brys opened the door on a large room and dropped his sword on a storage chest beside the harp. Chair, table, bedding on the sleeping bench, nothing else. Not living in splendor. Did Brys notice? Probably. He just wouldn't care. Maybe it didn't matter if you'd grown up in two royal households and now couldn't find time to visit your estates. Brys stood with his hands in his belt, looking at the cauldron hanging over the banked fire by a chain.

"Cold water all right for a wash? It takes time to heat. Or we can go to the bath house."

"Cold water," Heilyn said quickly. Anything to avoid the jostling and ogling of a public bath. "Give the English hot water and they think it's soup. Bathing is unhealthy, they say." Brys still assumed a traveler's first need was wash water. Heilyn had caught his habit. Now he felt dirty if he didn't wash every day.

Brys laughed and shoved the folded parchment into the back of his harp's sound box. "Good. You won't be tempted to drink this."

Heilyn watched him pour water from a pitcher into a basin and add some liquid from a bottle. Brys stripped, put his boots side by side, folded his clothes and washed himself meticulously. Heilyn pulled his clothes off and left them where they fell. He had been horrified the first time Brys shed his clothes in Ceredigion, not so much by his obsessive washing, as it seemed then, as by casual nakedness. They were a different people, a strange people, his own people.

Brys scrubbed his back for him and handed him the cloth. Like the water, it smelled of sage. Heilyn washed his friend's back, rubbing between the shoulder blades where sweat gathered in the pores. It made him hunch his back in pleasure, which gave Heilyn a small contentment. Did Brys ever guess his thoughts last year as his back was scrubbed in Ceredigion and Gwynedd? Walking among the dunes at Aberffraw he had spoken clumsily, with heartbreaking kindness, of love. Heilyn understood. Restraint. Like cell enamelling. There was the boundary. He didn't cross it, choosing instead to keep a friend.

Brys threw him a linen towel, and when Heilyn reached for the clothes he'd traveled in, delved clean clothes out of the chest for both of them. Luxury. Clean clothes in plenty. Dressed, Heilyn tied his hair back and found his earring. It was a new teardrop of lapis lazuli, as good a way as any to use the hole in his earlobe that once marked his slavery. Brys brought out a leather bottle and two clay cups, and they sat on the edge of the sleeping shelf.

"Sweet Virgin." Heilyn gasped after a good swallow. "What is this?"

"A drink like mead. From the earth houses."

Heilyn grinned. "You spent a night in the hollow hills with a beautiful girl and found a hundred years had passed? I missed that story in Aberffraw. But I heard all the others about you."

Brys was combing water from his hair. "You know better."

"Sometimes." Heilyn remembered what else he had heard. "I'm sorry about your daughter. And I was looking forward to seeing Meirwen."

"Yes. Thank you." He looked down and there was a long silence.

Heilyn studied the cool depth of his cup. Meirwen was in Iâl. Or somewhere. Because of the child's death? And Brys was in some distress he couldn't reach. A buried splinter was the worst. Heilyn decided a friend would try to draw it, even knowing his clumsiness. "I watched you in practice today, with the sword. You're skillful."

"I was almost killed a few weeks ago by a man three times better. My only advantage is the instant's surprise that I'm lefthanded."

Heilyn saw that he was glad of the change of subject, away from the personal. But he could be as devious as Brys. "When you fight you're there in the blade."

"Everyone is."

"Don't laugh at me, Brys, I'm telling you something important. You have courage. You take risks. You leave yourself open. You do unexpected things. You're the same when you sing."

"Elgan's trying to cure me of it. What are you trying to say?"

This is a bad idea. "Never mind. It's none of my business."

"Spit it out."

"You should deal with people as you fight. Take risks."

"Example?" Brys gave him a green glance, not amused. The Penllyn stare, Heilyn had come to think of it. Cool, challenging, biding time, waiting to take it all. His hair was curling dry.

"I've never seen you run after a woman."

Brys gave him one astonished look and exploded into laughter. His laughter was always infectious; they both gave way to it. "You're an authority on that, are you? Women?"

Heilyn looked him in the eye, refusing to be embarrassed. "No. But it's true all the same."

"I was supposed to be celibate for eight years as a student. Then there was Meirwen." His past tense sounded regretful.

Heilyn said, "I can guess how celibate from watching Gwydron. But you wait for people to come to you. Sometimes they don't. You have to go to them. Take risks."

Brys got to his feet abruptly. He went over to his harp and stopped with one hand on the pillar. He wanted to look at his letter again, Heilyn saw. Alone. Heilyn drained the cup and stood. Slave thinking: if it's broken, fix it. He would make apologies later.

But Brys turned to face him. "You're right, not that I like being told. You don't know how I've missed you."

"You said." Heilyn leaned on the house post and looked in his empty cup. "In your letter."

Brys smiled and was present in himself, right there. As in the blade, as in the song. How did he do that? He had his arms folded on his chest, gold arm ring and silver arm ring against brown skin and white linen, and he balanced on his feet like a dancer. "You're in good form. What have they been teaching you in Gwynedd?"

Heilyn recognized an invitation to quarrel and silently declined. "I learned how to raise relief on a gold panel. Anna did most of the drawings, fortunately."

"Did you find a lover?"

"None of your business." Heilyn put the cup carefully on the edge of the sleeping bench. Whatever had stung Brys, Meirwen or that letter in the sound box or his own meddling, he needed to leave now. Anger and undirected energy made a dangerous combination.

"Love me then."

"That's not what you want." Heilyn flushed hotly, not as shocked as he should be.

"How do you know?" Brys walked close to Heilyn. His hair smelled of sage.

"Go find a woman."

"I didn't say fuck me, I said love me."

Heilyn closed his eyes, most afraid of what he desired most. Two warm hands on his shoulders, sliding down to his own cold hands. A warm mouth against his own for a heartbeat. And that was all. Brys stood back. Heilyn looked at him, helpless to speak, and turned away.

Heilyn walked out through the west gate and down to the talkative river where he had fled a year ago, routed by an old woman with a rusted kettle. There was a place where he could sit and skip rocks. In the cool evening he felt molten, at once translated into another state and locked in the certainty of his own being. His careful plans, all his cells to contain feeling and action, were overrun. Yet he felt unreasonable gladness.

Deepening cold, as the first stars pricked out in a clear night sky, finally made itself known. He was shivering. And he had reason to worry about a good friend. If he skipped another nine pebbles, on the tenth he would know what to do.

Brys read the letter again. It was worse the second time, now that he'd considered the implications. The letter thanked Brochfael's brother and heir Eli Elfæl for the military commitment he had made in the interests of old Powys friendship with the West Saxons. It was signed in the looping scroll of Egbert's hand. A marginal note said that it came from the westernmost British kingdom of Dyfed. *Eli claiming to be Brochfael's heir?*

After a while he put the letter back in the sound box for return to Brochfael and looked around. Heilyn's traveling clothes lay in a heap on the floor, his pack and saddlebags near the door. Where had he taken himself? *Everyone flees from me as though I have the plague. Meirwen. Heilyn. A plague of stupidity.* Brys knew what Heilyn's self-control cost; he should have respected that. But at the same time he felt a spark of injured virtue. *Take risks, is it? I took a breathtaking risk, little good it did me.* Now God knew how long it would take to rebuild Heilyn's trust.

Dusk outside in the scented courtyard. Usually he was on the dais in Brochfael's hall by now. Maybe later. He closed the door behind him and went out. Heilyn wasn't in the chapel garth, or the inner courtyard with the hazel trees, or in the hall. Brys found him sitting by Banwy, skipping pebbles as though he hadn't a care in the world. He looked up with that unshielded smile. "How did you find me?"

"I know every hiding-place in Mathrafal. I was a hostage here for years." Brys sat down. "Fostering, they called it."

"Did they mistreat you?"

"I had to fight almost every day. I was beaten a lot. Then I learned how to hold my own."

"I only learned how to run," Heilyn said.

Brys laughed and put an arm across his shoulders. That seemed to be all right.

"Hostage," Heilyn tried out. "I suppose that's a kind of slavery."

Brys shook his head. "A slave, however badly treated, is part of the process. A hostage is removed from the process, sometimes forever. A king who takes an enemy's son hostage often kills him. It's the easiest way to solve the problem."

Heilyn shook his head. "Hostages, alliance marriages, children given to the church. And I always thought the powerful enjoyed lives of ease and security."

"I thought the humble did. Sometimes, anyway," Brys said, interested in this change. Once Heilyn had been unable to view that gulf between worlds without anger and suspicion.

"Huh. Little did you know."

"But I found out," Brys smiled in the dark. It was good to sit talking companionably. Heilyn was almost the only constant in his shifting and uncertain situation.

In his quarters, Brys found linens and unrolled a second pallet at the far end of the sleeping shelf. All across Ceredigion last year they had shared a pallet; often he had awakened with Heilyn's arm across him or his across Heilyn. Now it was different. Heilyn had fallen asleep before he pinched out the candle.

22 september + mathrafal

Preoccupied with in the forge's rhythm at dusk, the court smith was a wizened man with an unforgiving mouth and eyes like cherry pits under sparse grey hair. He disliked young men with high-nostrilled Gwynedd accents as much as he disliked Penllyn upstarts. Heilyn said nothing but pulled pieces out of his pack.

Brys watched the court smith look over an enamelled bracelet in rare cerulean blue, a knife blade inlaid in the English way, four amber medallions cut to size for a brooch, plaques of carved ivory. Heilyn nodded to himself. He knew his skill. Good.

The old smith produced a reluctant smile, short on teeth. "Very fine. Where did you learn?"

"Tamworth. And with Padrig and Anna in Aberffraw."

"Ah." As though the names evoked Lleu, god of all skills. "Maybe I can give you some simple enamelling. A trial."

You old devil. He'll be running the place in a week.

Heilyn said he thought that would be a good idea.

The lord of Buellt died suddenly with stomach pains in early September. Eli made the lord's three young sons his guests in Elfæl and ruled Buellt on their behalf with the old Roman title of protector.

After Brochfael had told them this news, Idris paced the library for an hour laying out reasons why they had to act now. Eli had seized territory and hostages and probably committed murder. It was open aggression, so why would he stop there? Now he would try Mathrafal.

Brochfael watched coolly across the usual scatter of tax records on the table until Idris ran out of arguments. Then he said only that at Calan Gæaf they'd see whether or not Eli paid tax to Mathrafal for both Elfæl and Buellt. Idris sat down heavily, shaking his head. Brys said nothing. What was there to say?

Afterwards he walked down the colonnade to the grape arbor. It was before the third hour of a cool September morning. Last night's rain sloughed from the bronze leaves, and his breath hung on the air. Blue sky above the wooded hills around Mathrafal's three-river plain, now golden at harvest's end. In an hour the dew and rain would burn off, leaving a flawless day of late summer. *Brochfael's right, more's the pity. A move on Elfæl would mean open war, and that's what the conspirators want. So they found the new approach I predicted: Eli absorbs the southern regions, Egbert sits spinning his plans in Dyfed, and what about Cenwulf?*

How much time do we have?

Heilyn was sitting on the door bench shaded by a courtyard apple tree, examining a rectangle of silver. Brys stood near a colonnade pillar to watch him for a moment. His light hair fell forward across his face, watered silk, and his long brown fingers turned the silver, bent it, straightened it. Totally absorbed. Brys walked over, earning one of his shining smiles. Lead-and-gold eyes. Startling, beautiful. When he sat, Heilyn's arm was warm against his own in the cool morning.

"The arm rings will call for about five pounds of silver any way I count. Are you sure you want to do this?"

Brys took the silver rectangle from him. "If you can stand the boredom of forging them one after the other."

"Each will be a little different."

"Good. Ready to go?"

They forded River Efyrnwy and rode the two miles northeast to Meifod, letting their horses race on the straightaway. When they passed the abbey gate the brothers were ringing for mass, and the doorkeeper raised a hand in greeting from his porter's cubby. Cilwen began half a mile on, climbing from the main valley into a broad saddle of cornfields and grazing and managed woodland. A herd of leggy colts lifted their heads as they rode past the turf field wall, then streamed away in a flourish of flying manes and tails. They passed cattle and sheep on grazing, laborers' houses clustered by the stream, barns for livestock and corn. Cilwen was wealthy, even by Cæreinion standards, with revenues from food rents, cattle and horse breeding, tolls paid by a harness-maker and blacksmith, and sales of fine woollen cloth. Brys went in to greet his steward, then rode on to the weavers' shed.

The stout head weaver led them to the wool room, away from the noisy looms, and listened to Brys with her hands fisted on her big hips.

"Twenty-five cloak lengths with not a day's warning? It will take us a week just to thread the warps. A fortnight to weave. A week to dye. Respectfully. Lord."

"All right," said Brys. *You'd like to box my ears or swat me with your spindle.* "You know your trade. Will you send word when they're ready?"

"And another thing." She tucked her chins obstinately. "I'm not stripping the looms to start this. We've got orders to meet."

Heilyn, tœing a wool puff around the floorboards, said quietly, "Can you weave a different border on each? You've got to splice the weft anyway."

"Extra trouble."

"What share do you take?" asked Brys as he turned to the door. Under the sighing rhythm of the looms, a girl in the far corner was singing in a shaft of sunlight as she threw the shuttle.

"Thirty percent." The head weaver scowled.

"Take forty."

"And that barely feeds us, I promise you."

"You're not listening. I'll tell the steward. Forty percent."

"But . . . " She looked grieved, deprived of her argument.

Brys smiled and saw that Heilyn was trying not to. "I'm proud to wear your work. The flannels, but especially the heavy weights. Who's your dyer? She's an artist."

She blushed like a girl and held up piebald hands. "I think we can manage in a week. Or two. Maybe. Lord."

The wind was rising as they rode back, beating the sweet woodsmoke low over the court. In a field upstream, someone was burning stubble against all of Mæn Pedr's advice to let it nourish the soil. In the orchards, fruit trees swayed under their weight of apples and late plums. Leaves were beginning to rust out and run in restless packs along houses and orchard walls.

That night Brys thought again about Egbert's letter as he stripped and folded his clothes. Should Brochfael respond? Anything he wrote would provoke Egbert and tempt Eli. He crawled under his quilt and lay with his head on his clasped hands, looking up through the eaves vent. A square of night sky, a scattering of stars. He watched their slow journey across the small window, prepared for a sleepless night. *Military commitment — what's Egbert planning? Is he ready to move yet?* Then he found himself walking through the burdock and thistle of a ruined wheatfield. He knew he dreamed but he remained aware. One crumbling wall stood, and one weathered pillar. On it someone had crudely carved a creature in interlace, a fish with bronze nailhead eyes —

"Brys, Brys. It's a dream, that's all."

Brys lay, unable to speak, trying to center his breathing. Heilyn kneeled beside him, dimly outlined against the starlight, touching his face. He found the tears and brushed them away. Brys said, "A dream."

"You were talking about salt and blood."

"No."

Heilyn lifted his hand and straightened. "Should I stay?"

"Stay." *A breathtaking risk.* "Hold me. Please."

Heilyn slid under the quilt and put an arm over him, saying nothing, asking nothing, trembling. They lay this way together until the nightmare faded back into the mist it rose from. Brys reached up and found his face, his smooth hair, and kissed him on the mouth. Heilyn caught his breath.

Heilyn gathered himself to pull away.

Brys took his hand and drew it downward. "This is least important. I told you at Aberffraw."

A long moment of perfect stillness. Then his kiss came back to him, tender and passionate, and the distance was closed. Brys explored Heilyn's body with his hands, slowly, enjoying its hot willingness contained by will. Heilyn carefully moved his hands away.

"Show me," Brys said. "How to love you."

Heilyn gently took over, seeking out every hidden sensation and pleasure. Whenever he made Brys's back arch and his breath catch, he found something new to explore.

"Are you planning to torture me all night?"

"Don't do that," Heilyn said. "I can't concentrate."

"That's why I'm doing it."

Then smooth heat surrounded him, and Brys plunged into in a tightening spiral of movement and unbearable sensation. An intensity of release, the heart of the sun. Incapable of thought or motion, he exploded through light and fell back into a spark-ridden darkness.

Heilyn's cheek rested on Brys's chest. He heard Brys say something about a river. He was warm, solid, a rock. Heilyn kissed the hollow of his throat where the pulse beat fast and strong. "Sleep now."

Brys only laughed and turned his own skills back on him with ruthless tenderness. Heilyn was quickly lost in a hot flood that swept across all boundaries. Then strong arms held him. No one had ever held him while he wept.

Heilyn woke in his arms at dawn and found himself under scrutiny.

"What about India?" Brys asked.

"Some day. What are you thinking?"

"My arm's gone to sleep." Brys yawned. "Did you think I would lose my reason over loving a man?"

"It happens." Especially to a man so clearly interested in women. Heilyn had watched Brys training among his guard, intent on their skill but not on their physical presence. But when a woman walked by on some errand from the court . . .

"Not to me." Brys resumed his appraisal. "You have a beautiful body. Lean and quick as a greyhound."

Heilyn smiled; he knew beauty well. Brys's body had the economy of a weapon forged for strength and grace. Nothing extraordinary apart from the eyes. Beauty lay in how he inhabited this: his presence in the moment, his quick reflexes, his quick mind.

"Why do you have all these small scars on your arms and chest?"

"Weapons training. We use staves only in the boys' class. No one can afford to miss a stroke because a spear or sword has the wrong heft. You'll see in about —" Brys glanced toward the bar of brightening daylight under the eaves. "— an hour. Will you join my guard?"

"And get cut to ribbons?" Heilyn snorted. "Do you really think you can make a soldier of me?"

"Your courage runs deep. There's no one I would rather have at my shoulder."

"Maybe." There was nowhere Heilyn would rather be than at Brys's shoulder, even if that meant holding a spear. "I can try."

"You need to know something first." Brys hesitated. "Powys is threatened by civil war. I raised my guard mostly to have a last rampart of iron around Brochfael. And Cyngen."

"That letter you had last week."

Silence. "You're better not knowing."

"I heard there was trouble with Brochfael's half-brother. And the bodyguard commander, the one with pale eyes. And Cenwulf."

"Merciful God, how do you know all that?"

Rumors and guesswork, Heilyn told him, but others could make the same connections, and the knowledge was dangerous. "And even in Gwynedd everyone knows Penllyn stands with Elfæl."

Brys freed his hands and scrubbed his face. "Garmon is Brochfael's man."

"But is Cynfarch? They wager in Aberffraw that you'll seize Penllyn by winter. Everyone knows about your guard. You also have a secret army in the hills north of Llanycil waiting to join you. In case you didn't know."

Brys laughed and sobered. "I'll tell Brochfael. He's already dealt with one Penllyn rebellion."

"Your father."

"Sometimes I think everyone knows more about it than I do."

"You attract stories, my dear. Your brother made his choices, but you are the last of a famous line, dispossessed by your cousin, a warrior, a pœt—"

"Don't forget the ravens." Brys grinned, taking delight in this.

"— a sorcerer. And ambitious."

Brys brushed the hair back from Heilyn's face, suddenly serious. "There's been enough blood. How could I displace my cousin Garmon and think I had the *braint* to rule Penllyn? By doing that I would lose my right, not gain it. Are you coming to training?"

"What about this?" Heilyn kissed the nearest bare skin, an arm.

"Other men love each other. The church hisses, but I'm already in disgrace for my apostasy, as Bened likes to call it. As usual he has everything backwards."

"Gwydron told me." Heilyn touched the small new scar between Brys's black brows. "What dœs this mean?"

Brys frowned, creasing the scar. Was this something not to be asked? But he said, "I interpret dreams. Pray for troubled spirits. Study birds and animals to predict weather. Advise on crops, though people still follow superstition before sense. Perform simple surgery— I don't like that much. It hurts us both too much, surgeon and patient. Assist in rituals. Everything changes. The old way and the new way work well together with enough goodwill. I am Christian, never mind what Bened says. I could as easily join a monastery as a sanctuary."

"Not soon, please."

Brys touched his cheek and sat up. "Time for training."

29 September 794 + Mathrafal

At Michælmas the harvest crews raced rain and frost to get the wheat into barns. Many sheaves came in wet; the corn dryers roared day and night for weeks until mold overtook them and made the effort useless. South-sloping Cilwen did better than most farms, but the steward nearly wept over his tallies. Two-thirds of normal, unless rot claimed even more. Brys told him to slaughter and salt most of the bullocks, the older cows and half the intended replacement heifers, remembering some of Cadwr's advice: better to healthily overwinter a small herd than watch a large herd starve by spring. The steward regarded him with new interest and did it. Dogs were kennelled, horses were stabled.

By then the *pencerdd*'s guard were wearing their green cloaks and silver arm rings with ravens somewhere in the design. Elgan worked them hard every day with spear and sword, on foot and mounted, even on mornings when grass stalks were stiff with frost on the training ground. They grumbled until they found the king's guard mocking their devotion, then worked twice as hard.

After the first tavern brawl, Elgan gave them a quiet talk; they could afford no friction. Blades were always loose in scabbards, and Cyngen was never without company. Elgan took Heilyn in hand, first because Brys asked, then because of his promising skill with a throwing spear. One evening Brys caught Tegwy tasting his food and Cyngen's before they ate; he only shrugged at Brys's reprimand.

Since time out of mind Powys had drawn pœts and harpers, storytellers and *crwyth* players. Brys's Powys pœts and harpers gathered at Michælmas, argued and sang and boasted, competed in the contests he set, quarrelled over the winners, and went their ways. Others came to Mathrafal expecting Rhydion and were surprised to Wnd an open-handed young man who made the hall his own sound box for laughter and for praise of Brochfael Powys. Some cast a cold eye on his glittering harp strings and left feeling slighted. Some came with stories about Cynfarch and his ravens and embroidered them further. Brys was amused, knowing that stories collapse of their own weight like foam under a waterfall.

On wet afternoons when wind pried at the thatch and buffeted smoke back down the roof vents, he sat with the travelers giving song for song. Once or twice his own pœms came back to him in the mouths of strangers, which swept him with laughter and something like terror. Often they sang old work with stanzas missing, and he filled the gaps to preserve them in memory. A *crwth* player from far Ystrad Clud sang an elegy unknown in the south, lit with Taliesin's spare imagery; she left with gold on her arms.

His training gave Brys a compulsive dread of losing or corrupting the early pœtry. Only its accurate transmission preserved the history, genealogy, pœts' art, storytellers' craft, laws, creation myths, spiritual wisdom, practical lore even down to the season songs and planting days. One stanza lost or changed picked one thread out of the weave, diminishing its truth. One pœm lost or changed altered reality itself. *Our lives and voices lost forever. Will we never have lived, never have sung? Will our history be written by enemies in an alien tongue?*

Parchment burned. Wax melted. Even the most dedicated recording monk wrote down only a few tattered words, poor fragments torn from a great many-colored page. Inscriptions in stone captured at most a phrase or a sentence. Only by passing the great lore voice to voice, mind to mind, could they preserve it in memory for those to come. War and destruction would come again; book cellars would burn, monks would perish. Often Brys sat crosslegged on the sanded planks of the old scriptorium, shutters latched, reciting triads and stanzas to fix them in memory. *We speak across the silence. Listen well.*

Mid-October brought unseasonable cold, and the cold brought game down from the hills early. Brys rode hunting with Heilyn and men of his bodyguard, taking deer and boar, lean hares and mottled red grouse. One evening Cadell leaned to him on the hall dais and said wolves were taking stock on his estate upstream in Banwy meadows. Brys agreed to bring Cyngen hunting the next day.

At dawn, as they stamped cold from their feet in the stable yard, Brys made apologies for Cyngen to his father. His current dalliance was five years older and married, an open invitation to trouble, but his lapse was worse than embarrassing. Father and son barely knew each other, repeating the barren gulf between Cadell and Brochfael. The hunt could have thrown them together, if not in friendship, at least in acquaintance.

"Oh." Cadell heard Brys's apology quietly, standing hunched and gazing at the frosted ground. His stance was less from his malformed shoulder than it was a kind of self-protection, Brys thought, like a hedgehog's curled back. Cadell said nothing else. He never said much.

Grooms led out Carnlas and a buckskin gelding, and they rode west in the glimmering grey dawn. Frost lay as thick as snow on the higher ground, and Cadell's two hounds kicked up crystal plumes as they bounded before the horses. Brys set his teeth against the cold that crept insidiously through two wool tunics, fur cloak, gloves, felted wool liners in his boots. The tunics' colors alone should warm him, flame red and saffron yellow, the personal gift of his head weaver. But the wind pried through each layer. Heilyn would be curled warm under a quilt, fair hair spread on the pillow, sleeping until the forge hearths were fired. Heilyn had better sense.

"My field men have marked out one wolf and tracked a second." Cadell reined at the forest margin.

Small icicles chimed on branches in the wind. If this was October, what would January be like? Another rider was approaching through the woods, and he saw the dark gleam of a spearhead between the grey trees. A lean black-haired rider on a tall black horse. *Gellan.*

"Cynfarch."

Brys greeted him pleasantly, trying not to shiver. *Gellan had Cadell invite Cyngen to hunt. Weak Cadell, easily led. Thank God Cyngen is safe between a woman's thighs. I never questioned—fool.*

They rode upstream through the stillness of first light, past sleeping farms and fields pale with frost. Under the hooves the stiff grass crunched. A blackbird singing near their path seemed unnaturally loud, and Carnlas shied. *Find your nest, sister, or freeze to the air.*

Ahead, the huntsman and his dog-boys cornered the wolf within sound of the river in a hollow of frost-rimed fallen leaves. Cadell took first spear; the animal resisted with only a snapping of blunt teeth after a brief lurching run. A savage pride flickered in her yellow eyes as the blade plunged home. She consented. Hunger, bad teeth and age had probably driven her to try cattle, Brys decided as the huntsman skinned her. Still it was unusual so early in the autumn. Brys leaned on his spear watching blood seeping crimson, then fading to pink crystals on the frost. The man bundled the hide; the meat wasn't worth taking. Carrion crows rustling in the oak branches cheered that decision.

Brys became aware he was trembling. It twisted him tight so he mounted stiffly and worked his shoulders around under the cloak to stir some warmth. *Hate the cold. Summer is my season. August.* He raged at the cramp in his hands and the tremor on his shoulders and knew it was less cold than fear.

Gellan was watchfully silent as they leaned to the horses' plowing climb out of the dip and back onto the track. They rode east. Brys leaned to test his girth on the off side. As he straightened, he loosened his knife in its sheath. *Poison seems worse than a hunting accident only until the moment of naked blades.*

Cadell looked from Gellan to Brys and gathered his reins. "My horse is favoring one leg. I'm going to try him on the straight."

The track crossed the lower pasture of a scattered township, where a few cows bunched near the barn and smoke rose in tight columns above silvered thatch. Brys reined around to Gellan's left, distrusting the commander's knife hand. Cadell urged the buckskin into a canter and rode leaning forward on the withers to ease his weight. Brys watched him turn at the far field boundary, making sure he also had a clear view of the commander. He gave the horse its head and cantered back. As it slowed he leaped down lightly, forgetting his need to be clumsy for once, and bent to run his hands over the right foreleg. Gellan wheeled his black horse closer to Brys.

"Cynfarch, it's time."

"Well?" *This is the price we pay for Brochfael waiting, delaying, not taking Gwydron's advice or my own.*

"We're grateful for your word to Egbert. Eli was pleased that you saw the need and spoke. Last summer's border raids were useful."

Brys nodded. *A dawning of sick realization. If I'd kept my mouth shut to Egbert, farms would be unburned, lives would be unscathed. I thought I was defending them, and instead they should have been defended from me. Merciful god, lift this from me. Pale-eyed Gellan. A maggot in the gangrene of Powys. I can raise the spear, kill him now. But Cadell will take me, or at least have me killed. Or will he? How deep is he in Gellan's plans? What if Cyngen were here? Something strange about this. Something else.*

Cadell vaulted onto his horse again, casting an uncertain look at the commander.

"I'll tell you what we need from you now," Gellan said. "Start singing satire on Brochfael. Subtly at first. Then break him."

On the off side Brys raked Carnlas's ribs with his boot heel, snubbing in the rein at the same time, and the stallion obligingly began to snort and rear at this mishandling. It saved him from having to answer. *Do you really think it all slides past unnoticed? Assassins, monkshood, Eli as heir in a letter from Egbert? It takes a fool to think everyone else is a fool. But a dangerous fool.*

"The timing is bad," Brys objected. *Why? Think of a reason. I can't be backed into promising satire or anything else. It will have to be one more lie to spring on Brochfael who has enough on his shoulders.* "From now until Christ's mass Brochfael will travel the cantrefs, reviewing taxes and renders."

A small muscle began to tick beside Gellan's right eye. "After Christ's mass, you're saying."

"Not before." Brys fought down the frantic stallion, growing wilder in response to his boot.

"Cadell?" asked Gellan, with a look like an owl's pale stare on a busy vole.

Cadell huddled in his cloak, staring at the frost sparking on his horse's dark mane. He looked lost. Finally he said, "It dœsn't really matter to me."

Then what dœs? Your son? Your daughter? Not power, or you'd reach for it yourself instead of handing it to Eli. Eli won't let any crumbs fall from his table. And Cadell, poor rudderless Cadell, thinks I've sold myself to this. To buy power in Penllyn. That means Garmon's in danger too. It stung Brys from sick fear to a cold rage.

Gellan looked at Brys, narrowing his eyes slightly. *First doubt. First concern that all's not as Eli says.* Brys ached to strike his chalk-white face.

"It's dangerous to be here together," Brys said curtly. *Irony and understatement.* Laughter almost ravelled this ludicrous performance. "We'll return separately."

Gellan nodded, pleased by the command in his voice, and wheeled his black horse. Brys held Carnlas a moment longer and looked at Cadell. *Are you really part of this?* Brochfael's only son studied his own gloved hands on the reins and at last lifted his chapped red face. Grey eyes, unfathomable pain.

Brys left them at the township's east boundary. Three miles to Mathrafal he cantered through woodland and plowland, churning up leaf mold and water full of ice crystals. He shook with rage now, not cold, though the fur cloak dragged back from his shoulders and water tracked stinging back from his eyes. By the time he pounded in sight of the ramparts, he was sprayed in foam from the stallion's working mouth and numbed by the stream of bitter air. He jolted down onto the frozen mud of the stable yard and headed for the king's quarters.

Cyngen must go to Armorica immediately. Pictland. Ulster. Anywhere.

Brys told him everything, all but Cadell's involvement, too uncertain to mention. Brochfael heard him out politely and said that he would wait.

18 October 794 + Mathrafal

Brys sat in a favorite spot under the wind, out of sight of the rampart, where only a few people knew to find him. His back to a lichened rock, he plucked a rose hip and turned it around in his fingers. Afternoon sunlight without warmth speared through the alders into the river's steady flow east toward Mercia, amber shafts through peat-brown water. His thoughts flowed in the same direction with the same somber hue.

He couldn't concentrate on *englynion.*

Brochfael still delayed, or refused to act, but his chill for Eli and warmth for Offa made more sense now. Brys could understand Egbert; Egbert wanted his patrimony restored. Cenwulf he could not understand, not fully. That dark voice, savoring others' fear and pain. A devout man, he was said to give many alms, altar gifts, even estates to the church. Anxious to float out of hell on a river of gold? Brys hadn't needed Egbert to tell him Cenwulf was vicious. And some unfortunate girl was his hostage. None of Eli's daughters was missing. *I have asked everyone, God knows, thereby confirming every rumor about my supposed dynastic affairs. Who is she? Someone's daughter. And if this man gets his hands on Cyngen . . .* Brys looked down and found he'd shredded the rose haw to its fibrous core. After the flower, the bitter fruit. Could he work that into an *englyn*? No. Nine other pœts had used it already. New imagery was a matter of pride.

Heilyn came silently between the alders and sat next to him on the cloak. Brys tossed the rose hip away and put an arm around his neck.

"Progress?"

"No." He'd been telling Heilyn about his new cycle on Brochfael's ancestor Llemenig, known for ferocity in war and justice in peace. He thought he'd talked of it during his trial in the sanctuary.

Heilyn leaned into the curve of his arm, and Brys dropped his forehead on his friend's shoulder. *Friend, lover. I'll never love another man this way. Only Heilyn, Heilyn's way. Meirwen, before she fled, Meirwen's way.*

"Don't fall asleep on me."

"Why not? Anyway, I was thinking." Brys yawned. Heilyn's hair clung to his cheek, and he brushed it back. Fine and silken, it had many colors to each strand in the low light, mostly gold, copper, bronze. It smelled of yarrow from washing. Fine hair, fine bones, steadfast heart. The first time Heilyn faced him with a sword Brys thought he would drop it and run. Instead he kept a cool head, provoked Brys until he lost his temper, and drew blood.

"I'm going to Llandinam about the chalice. I'll be gone five days."

"I'll come with you."

"No." Long silence. Heilyn's eyes were closed but moving within their own darkness. He kissed the hand on his chest. "Brys, this is everything I am."

"What dœs that mean?"

"It's only part of what you are — No, don't argue for once. Go north and bring Meirwen back."

"She won't come."

"How do you know? Go and find out."

"Why? Don't you think she knows what she wants?"

"You'll find out."

"Don't be cryptic." Brys sat up, vexed. "I'm the pœt."

"And full of yourself too."

Brys was quiet a long time, looking at the brown river. No one had commented about Heilyn. They were discreet — growing up at court, one chose early between discretion and disgrace — and most people believed what they wanted to believe about anything. Mathrafal women liked him and he was not known for abstinence. The favorite Powys scandal was incest, anyway, if you listened to Gwynedd stories. *Which cousin shall I marry? Or maybe a sister?* He realized he was holding his breath and let it out.

"Why?"

"You put me in a ridiculous position, telling you this." Heilyn closed his eyes. "Because you love her, and she loves you. But she's a fine artisan and a proud woman."

"And so — ?"

"Lackwit. You're a performer, don't you know performance when you see it?"

"Meirwen knows her own mind."

"And her heart?"

"Fair god, you're hard on me."

"I am." Heilyn smiled at the river. "So is Meirwen. Brochfael and his family. Mæn Pedr, when you argue for the sake of argument. Elgan. Your guard. People who love you."

Brys put both arms around him and held him tightly.

"Do you think this is easy?" Heilyn asked. "A day without you is nothing. Cinders. Ashes."

"Why this sudden selflessness?"

Heilyn reached up to touch his face. "Love is rarer than you think. Never leave it to wither."

"And afterward?"

"I don't know. Neither do you. But remember about taking risks."

Brys shredded another rose hip and flung the pieces toward the river. But the wind had shifted, and the fragments flew back across him and Heilyn. Bitter fruit, but it had flourished and fallen in its season. Now it held the memory and seed of its flowering. Past and future. Loss and promise. That image might work.

"Will you go?"

"Yes." *There must be something wrong with this. Why dœsn't it feel wrong?* "Because I love you. And Meirwen."

"Aren't you getting brave," Heilyn needled, risking wrath.

Brys said, "I seem to be taking lessons."

20 october 794 + llandegla yn iâl

Two days later he reined at Llandegla crossroads in early morning rain, less certain of his destination. The shallow valley lay green and golden in the afterglow of harvest, bordered by the grey Clwydian Range to the north.

If he cut west through Llanfair and followed River Clwyd, he would end up at Rhuddlan instead of Llanarmon. Maybe Neithon would be in port with news and messages from Gwriad. Or he could stay here at Llandegla, spend a few peaceful days with the old surgeon, take a cell in the monastery and pray for understanding. Perhaps he should take the cure too. Or should he just turn back south? This was probably a fool's errand.

Finally Brys took the righthand road down past the small whitewashed timber church, past the grove of the sacred spring near swift River Alyn. He crossed at the ford.

An hour after that he sat by a farmhouse hearth with a small boy leaning tentatively against his knee. Carnlas he left tied outside the door, not accidentally. No surprises. Servants and an elderly aunt were working around the house and Meirwen's brother-in-law was shouting at the door about a missing harness. The aunt announced that Meirwen was off delivering cheeses and ironwork to the North Powys court of Llanarmon, where next month Brochfael would bring judgments and meet with his tenants and landowners. Brys put the boy on his knee and sang silly rhymes to him until they both laughed. The old woman came over to correct him on two verses, pleased with her memory.

An oxcart squealed to a stop outside soon after midday. Meirwen came in briskly, walked to the hearth and picked up the child. She wore homespun and had two braids tied together at her back like a farm girl.

"What's the man telling you?" She picked a leaf out of the boy's hair.

"Stories." He was suddenly shy again.

Meirwen sat on a bench, her freckled chin resting on the boy's freckled forehead. Olwen's child, by their likeness. Brys suddenly kneeled to straighten the banked peat at the hearth. Otherwise he might never breathe again. The last time he had seen Meirwen holding a child . . . It brought back too much: the slight warmth of a little daughter in his arms at midnight, an apple sapling in flower on a grave-mound behind Bryn Cerddin hall. That pain hadn't stabbed as often lately; now it stopped his heart.

Meirwen set the boy down on the rushes. "Go straight to your mam, not to the cow house."

"Meirwen." Brys found his voice. "Walk with me."

Olwen was in the barn yard when they came out together. When she saw them, the dairywoman dropped her bundle of straw and went down on one knee. Brys, thinking she had tripped, went to take her hands and raised her. But Olwen studied the muddy ground, refusing to meet his eyes.

Meirwen shrugged. "I told her who you were."

Brys still held Olwen's hands. "Do you remember me?"

"I do, lord." She didn't raise her head.

"Why did you give me buttermilk last year?"

"Any traveler is welcome, lord."

"Olwen," he said. Eventually she looked up. "You gave me buttermilk because I was hungry and ragged. My name is Brys."

Olwen shot Meirwen a straight look under her russet brows, so much like her sister he could have laughed. Instead he put his hands on her shoulders and kissed her on each cheek. She gave him a hard look, nodded gravely and headed for the barn with her straw.

"We heard at Bryn Cerddin that you were *pencerdd*," said Meirwen as they went out through the stone gate. "Brochfael has some judgment after all."

"He'll be happy to know someone thinks so," Brys said, but it didn't make her smile. She had her mouth set stubbornly. They walked down the gentle eastward slope, along the margins of stubble fields, to River Alyn. He offered his hand at a stile, but she chose not to see it and climbed over unaided. The rain had lifted, leaving the riverbank sodden wet. They stood looking at the black water flowing north. Leaves and branches drifted, caught, freed themselves, drifted on.

"I sent you a letter."

"Did you," Meirwen said. It wasn't a question.

"It was still at Bryn Cerddin." Brys gave her the letter. *What to say? Whatever I expected, it wasn't this frozen stillness.* "I'm glad you came here. You have your family, though Bethan misses you."

She broke the seal and read the letter. Then she folded it and tucked it in her belt without a word.

"Will you come to Mathrafal?" Brys put a hand on her shoulder, but she moved out of his reach.

Meirwen looked at him steadily. Brown eyes, freckles, eyebrows like the wings of a bird on a rising spiral. A new crease on either side of her mouth. Pain or laughter? She said, "I hear you have enough company."

Heilyn? Was there talk after all? "It's yours I want."

"Who is she?"

Caught off guard, Brys laughed. *Stupid.*

Meirwen looked away across the dark river. "It is ironic, isn't it? I never thought I'd say that."

"Tell me which scandalous rumor you've heard."

"You're betrothed to Nest ferch Cadell. You're living with a married woman, a blonde from somewhere in the south, and she's carrying your child. Her husband killed himself in grief."

"And you believe that?" It sounded like an ale house ballad of a particularly maudlin kind. Can't people credit me with some sense?

"Look at you. You're wearing scented oil. New clothes, a woman's taste. Someone's been cutting your hair well. And you're different. Quieter."

"I remember sitting in a Cær Seint tavern while Heilyn told me you were traveling with a handsome man wearing a diadem. I thought I was going to die of it. And it turned out to be true."

"I said it was ironic." She looked over the river to the hills.

"The woman who gave me this shirt is a great-grandmother, my head weaver at Cilwen. Nest ferch Cadell is family, at least by fostering. You'll like her — she steals horses. In a few years she'll marry in Gwynedd or maybe Ceredigion. A young woman whose waist is still small spent a few nights and went back to her family. Her brother was angry but feared to challenge Brochfael's *pencerdd*. It was a heartless and stupid thing for me to do."

"Now you want me. For how long?"

"Yes. I want you. Always." Brys watched foam eddy on the black water. *Is anything ever easy, with Meirwen? Maybe that's why I keep trying.* He hesitated too long.

"But," Meirwen said and let it hang.

Brys stooped for an alder leaf on the wet grass and spread it on his palm. A ragged oval leaf, faded to golden brown now the sap had left it, with strong diagonal veins. Beautiful. He turned his hand and let the leaf drift down the still air. *No avoiding this.* "But Heilyn."

"In Mathrafal?"

"I sent a letter with Gwydron this summer. Asking him to come."

Meirwen turned and looked him in the eyes. "Don't hurt him, Brys. He loves you more than anyone deserves."

"As I love him." *Black water, deep and swift. Too late not to plunge in.* "As I love you."

"Am I supposed to be shocked? It seemed so unfair in Aberffraw."

Brys took her hands and kissed her mouth. Cold hands, cold lips, a small exhalation. Different. Familiar. He dropped his hands and stepped back. *No seductions.* "Silver thorn, I can't see my way through this. Help me."

"You're asking me — ? What on earth do you want?"

"You already know what I want. I want you. I want a house full of children. I want Heilyn. I want my birthright. I want Powys to —"

"You want everything." Meirwen shook her head, and her earrings chimed. "How flattering to be one of your many desires."

Brys let the silence grow between them, trying to think ahead of her for a change. "It tore my heart to see you with Olwen's boy."

"Yes."

"Dœs it hurt you still?"

"It happens to almost everyone. We go on."

Another silence. The river's sound.

"If you marry me, your children will be my heirs. That will protect you and them if I'm dead."

"No." Meirwen was looking across the river again but she drew her gaze back, allowing him to see her eyes shining with unshed tears. A measure of trust. "There will be no children, you know that. Not after childbed fever and hemorrhage. And Brochfael will ask you to marry a woman from one of the great houses."

Brys pulled her close again and rested his chin on her shoulder. The dream about his brother's house, his house, surfaced, but he shut it away quickly. "Brochfael won't ask anything. He trusts me, more than may be wise after my father's betrayal, to make my own decisions. He also knows I'm like Egbert the West Saxon, ungrounded lightning."

"Don't tempt the god, Brys."

"I'm also nothing but the words in my mouth." Brys shrugged. "Heilyn is working with the court smith. Your work is superior in iron and brilliant in precious metals. Come to Mathrafal."

"Heilyn and I are friends," Meirwen said. "Don't try to come between us."

Whatever reaction he expected, it wasn't this. And it was no help at all. But there was a time to stop talking. Brys kissed her mouth, making some warmth in the cold day. Meirwen put her hands on his shoulders and kissed him in turn. Her touch left traceries of fire on his back and arms. Familiar and different. Her waist was thicker since the child, her breasts fuller. The flare of her hips, a slow dialogue of thigh and thigh. It had always been this way, a shared flush of heat and desire. Better than stealing horses, once they discovered it.

A year ago they would have spread their cloaks among the bare willows and made love under the grey sky. That at least had changed. Brys took her by the hand through the fragrant fields, between the farm buildings and into the house. The chamber was empty; Olwen was in the dairy and her husband was in the hay barn. No one was going to object. If there was ever a time to take advantage of rank, real or imagined, this was it. The old woman gave them a bawdy wink as they closed the chamber door.

When they emerged at dusk, no one appeared to take any notice. But the rumour would be in Mathrafal by tomorrow. *Good. Saves me the trouble.*

29 October 794 + Mathrafal

Toward the end of October, late for sea travel, an Armorican trader came to Mathrafal and spent an hour with Brochfael walking by River Banwy. He left the next day. Brys waited all day, then all week, for the king to tell him that Macliau had written to him, that Cyngen would go to Armorica. Brochfael said nothing.

Light flared with cool brilliance as the days shortened, edging the leaves on the apple tree in the courtyard outside Brys's quarters. One by one they abandoned their hold on the branches and eddied to the grass. Brys, Meirwen, Heilyn, and his bodyguard often gathered there, sitting on the bench and the doorstep, eating plums and pears while wasps snarled over the windfalls. Sometimes they played wood-wisdom, though with Heilyn only if he played defender. Tegwy rescued a speckled kitten the cook was about to drown and gave it to Meirwen. They ate the last bruised culls and picked over the best apples for storage.

Father Bened admonished Brys about keeping a mistress. Mæn Pedr expressed his pleasure that his wife had rejoined him. Cyngen tried to seduce Meirwen, to her high amusement. Elgan and Addonwy took her hunting; she was a daring rider and loved the pursuit. She argued and worked amiably with Heilyn.

Meirwen brought south her recent work: shirt pins, cloak pins, belt buckles, bracelets, rings and ornamental combs cast in lost wax. She forged a tuning key with a handle of uncut rock crystal netted in silver interlace and hung it on a silver chain around Brys's neck as a gift. Brys wore it, a jewel in its own right, on the hall dais. Best of all her work was a great flexible necklace of gold. Its many pieces were beaten as thin as parchment, linked in a net of apple branches and birds in flight and waves rolling to an unreached shore. It whispered of Rhiannon's realm beyond time in the western island.

Brys asked once, "Where do you get these ideas? I've never seen anything like this."

"Where do *englynion* come from?" Meirwen wondered. "Word *awen,* metal *awen.*" She went back to work smiling.

One day Brys carefully gathered the jewelry and the tuning key and her evenly drawn harp strings into a dœskin bag and took her to meet the court smith. Heilyn looked up from his work bench and grinned, knowing the game. Brys spread the necklace over the litter of iron and bronze scraps. The old smith took it to the daylight and held it swinging and flashing golden reflections in every direction. Meirwen glanced uneasily at Brys, torn between pride at her skill and wanting to escape.

"Constantinople, but the jeweler has worked from a British drawing. A wonderful piece. A fitting gift for a pretty woman." The smith gave a stiff little bow in Meirwen's direction.

"Would you hire the smith who made it?" asked Meirwen.

Brys saw Heilyn trying not to laugh in the corner.

"My dear, a prince of smiths made this. If he came to Mathrafal from the golden east, a month of his time would break the treasury. And how could I ask such a man to forge shield bosses or bucket rims?"

Meirwen smiled warmly and pulled out a sheaf of silverpoint drawings. "Maybe we can come to some arrangement."

Brys saw understanding widen the man's small black eyes, closely followed by confusion and dismay. He nodded farewell and left Meirwen to her work.

Heilyn and Meirwen, when they weren't in the smithy, often worked by the window overlooking the colonnade and courtyard, with their design tablets and wax balls for carving scattered around them. In the evenings they polished pieces by the hanging oil lamp, speaking their own language of alloy and temper and granulation, their faces intent over sanded sheepskin and dull metal. In the clatter of the smithy they forged hœs, knives, awls, once a plowshare; between times they cast their names as jewelers. Brother and sister, some people thought, by the way they squabbled over their enamelling and filigree. Soon their work began to brighten the *pencerdd*'s guard and Brochfael's bodyguard, then their women, then court officers and their families. The court smith happily took credit for his good judgment.

Brochfael's court enforced a social precedence as exact as the layers in a drystone wall. Heilyn found acceptance as a smith and a bodyguard man. He wasn't the only one who had slave years behind him, absent-mindedly swore in English or lacked a father's name to put behind his own. Brys brought Heilyn to the hall dais, where Brochfael greeted him civilly, but Heilyn preferred taking his gameboard to the bodyguard benches. He had sleeping space in the old smith's loft but spent most free hours in Brys's quarters.

But Meirwen met a wall of ice from the wives of nobles and court officials, who disdained her as the *pencerdd*'s mistress. When they understood that others saw her as an artist, they thawed to the consistency of spring runoff water, cool and murky. If the proud ones scorned a smith's daughter from Tregeiriog, that was nothing new; Meirwen shrugged and went back to her latest piece in silver or gold, set with amethyst or garnet. Brys, seeing this, took Meirwen to the queen's chambers one day when Anghenell was visiting. Adwen understood without a word spoken. Brys left unnoticed while Meirwen was telling Nest about Aberffraw shining in the morning sun and Anna's courtyard garden. At midnight she came home singing. After that she sometimes went to the sun chamber, where the court women sheathed their claws as much as necessary, and at Adwen's suggestion she took Nest riding on the three-river plain and its surrounding hills with a guard riding discreetly behind.

Geraint mab Garmon came to the old scriptorium one day to pass on Cadwr's thanks for the breeding stock and fodder he'd sent to Dolgarnen. Brys's cousin was dark-haired and blue-eyed like most of the Penllyn house, already bulging over his belt like Garmon. He told a joke that Brys had heard three times, then grew serious and fidgeted, and invited him to join his sisters and parents in Rhiwædog for Christ's mass. Brys excused himself with other plans, thinking Geraint's kind heart would draw Garmon's anger. It was enough that he made the offer. When he left, Brys gave him one of Meirwen's rings in silver and amber. Geraint had always treated Cadwr well, not letting dispossession come between cousins who were friends.

On the last night of October, Calan Gæaf fires sent a roaring pyramid of flame into a clear night at Cilwen. Piled high with stumps from land clearing, they would smoulder and rekindle all winter. Brys watched his herdsmen drive cattle between the fires. This was meant to protect them against disease and barrenness, but would anything protect them from starvation? Most of the *pencerdd*'s guard were here with Cyngen and Tegwy. A few couples made the old marriage by walking between the flames to clasp hands with one another; they were kinless or forbidden by their families to marry. Then flutes and drums came out, and dancing began, and it was possible for an hour not to think of danger and treachery. Later Brys prodded live coals into a clay pot and walked down with Heilyn yawning and Meirwen singing to relight Cilwen's extinguished hall hearth.

Next sunset at Mathrafal, as though to prove the accuracy of the season songs, the wind rose and swept shrieking down from the north for three days. It flung the last spent honey bees and dry leaves across the courtyards. When the wind fell again in a sour yellow dawn, most branches were bare grey. Winter now. The scents of woodsmoke and apples gave way to odors of turned earth and deep leaf mold.

November settled on the three-river plain. On cold mornings mist filled the broad valley like milk in a bowl, lapping against heights as insubstantial as smoke. The fields lay grey and quiet. Life gathered indoors. In barns, cattle stamped and breathed steam in the straw-scented air; in houses, people stayed near hearths where peat and logs hissed far into the night. Friendships were remade in the dark season of the year, old stories were retold, weapons and tools were tended by lamplight. Old men and women claimed overflowing harvests, the coldest winters, the hottest summers, dragons of fire in the night sky, great victories, all long ago. Brys listened smiling. Who could deny them now?

Brys closed the scriptorium door behind him one dull afternoon after Cyngen and Tegwy had clattered off to find Elgan. At the end of the colonnade, the honeysuckle and grape vines were bare. Brys stopped and leaned on a colonnade post to look into an inner courtyard. Weathered timber walls, drab winter grass underfoot, a spreading tree of smooth grey branches that retained a last few bright amber leaves. Hammered copper, sunlight through honey, a tree of small flames in a dark day.

"Striking. Will we hear it in an *englyn* tonight in hall?" asked Idris's gravelly voice behind him.

Brys didn't look around. He trusted Idris with his back. "Winter and decay aren't the imagery I want right now."

"Decay's the problem, no doubt about that." A different voice.

Brys turned, saw Garmon Penllyn standing there also, and bowed. These days it seemed wise to make a point of allegiance, *pencerdd* or not. Garmon was his kinsman and his lord. He knew everything. *He trusts me. I think. I hope to God.* "Lord Garmon."

Garmon blinked. Idris folded his arms. This was not an accidental encounter with two powerful northern lords, not a week after Brochfael returned from his circuit around the Powys cantrefs. Brys waited.

"In the north we had no time to parch the corn. Farms north of the lake had to harvest and thresh wet. There's a blight on the rye. People who eat the flour have visions of burning hell and go mad. One has died," Garmon said.

Idris added, "Mountain snow is already deep in the passes, and we're a month from Christ's mass. Hunting is poor. Some farms are already on their salted meat."

"A hard year." *We all know this. Why are you telling me?*

"Some are saying Brochfael's unlucky, a coward, and blights the wealth of the land. He's under a destiny," said Idris.

Brys said, "You don't believe that."

"No. That's not the point."

What is then?

Garmon said, "The harvest was good in the south. In Buellt and Elfæl."

Driving the wedge deeper. If Brys knew how to tip the balance further than his praise of Brochfael could . . . It was all so slow. One sharp war would cure this Powys disease, a terrible irony. "What can we do about that?"

Idris sidestepped. "You're doing well with song. Given enough time, you can remake him despite his dourness. And I like your watch on the boy. But there may not be enough time. People must see his good fortune and generosity *now*."

Brys scrubbed his face, suddenly weary though he'd done nothing today more strenuous than training. *Give it everything and it gets worse. No. Don't even think that.* "Make an altar gift. Dedicate it in gratitude for some occasion of Brochfael's justice and generosity. Ask others to do the same. Have Bened say masses. Make a show of wealth."

Garmon looked at the ground. "Of course. And an offering to the old sanctuary."

Brys stood forward from the post and turned to go. "If you want. Talk to

Mæn Pedr."

Garmon's hand fell on his shoulder. "Pedr is a good man, a healer. But he's not a performer."

"I won't provoke the church or the king by taking part."

"We speak for others," said Idris and named two other nobles.

"What do you have in mind?"

"Gifts. Ritual of purification."

Brys nodded. *I can do that with some fire and glitter. Make sure my bodyguard men are there with their wives or girls. Cilwen people. Pœts and harpers. Anyone who's not going to lose sleep over the church's censure.*

"And sacrifice," Idris said.

Brys wanted to turn away. Instead he shoved his hands in his belt and stood his ground. Garmon read his expression. The hand tightened on his shoulder and fell away.

"A bull," Idris added.

"Why?" It was traditional, of course, and displayed strength and virility without offering Cadelling stag or Cyndrwynyn boar. But why the dark rites? The church was bad enough with its red offerings on the altar. *This is my flesh. This is my blood. Shape shifting, all of it, one way or another. Blood rites. And in this case I'm the one who holds the knife.*

"A substantial offering," rasped pragmatic Idris. "And there'll be meat to share out."

Brys rocked on his heels, torn between amusement and distress. "At the request of a cynical handful of the baptized who want to sponsor a performance for the credulous."

"And for my soul's good, teacher," said Idris and heaved his big frame down onto one knee.

Fair and holy god, Meirionydd. Brys hauled him to his feet, angry enough to strike him, but he saw no cynicism. Desperation, maybe. He shook his head. *We're all losing our grip.*

"Lord Garmon? Do you ask this of me?"

"Teacher." Garmon's blue eyes were without defence or deceit.

"Then I ask something of you." *Bargaining over it, but in a good cause.* "Give recognition to my brother as you did to me."

Garmon cleared his throat, glancing at Idris Meirionydd, and said, "I did that a month ago. Invited him to Rhiwædog. And his wife."

Brys nodded thanks and turned away before his cousin could see his eyes flood.

If Brochfael knew why his *pencerdd* fasted for three days and was gone for another three, why a red-eared white bull disappeared from the Cilwen herd, why Geraint mab Garmon gave his cousin Cynfarch a well-trained falcon as a personal gift, why Mathrafal seethed with more than the usual gossip for weeks afterward, he gave no sign.

Elfæl, Buellt and two other southern provinces, despite fair harvests, had still sent no taxes by the end of November. In council one evening Brochfael looked up from his records and told Gellan, "Send a squadron south with the steward."

Gellan agreed with only a token argument. *Maggot.*

Brys sang honor on Brochfael, tried part of his new cycle in the hall and returned it to his thoughts for more shaping. He watched his back, and Cyngen's, and his king's.

He sat in the old scriptorium one rainy afternoon, idly tuning the sea-cat harp from one mode to another. *Do I tell Brochfael his son is conspiring with Gellan, maybe against Cyngen? What if I'm wrong? Cadell has never had anything to do with palace intrigues. For all I know he thinks Gellan only wants to set Brochfael on the right road. How many others will throw in with Eli? Who's next? Who's weak or gullible or starving? And what's the delay with Macliau?* Brys had tried asking and met silence. Yet the king treated him with warmth and generosity, took his advice on policy, even agreed to Brys's request that he spend more time with his bodyguard. Assassinations came from bodyguards; an assassination had enabled Offa to seize power in Mercia. Brochfael had seen to everything his pœt asked, everything but Cyngen. Brys, thinking about that and what the result might be, broke a bronze string. Five above the sisters, he'd replaced it last week. The strong, well-pulled wire should last years. *Shit.* Cynfarch bardd Brochfael, swearing in the crudest English. What would Taliesin bardd Brochfael have made of that? Of any of this? Probably a worse mess.

Brys pulled the wire's end out of the sound box and went home. If he stayed he would break another. Meirwen and Heilyn had a bench drawn under the small window and sat with their heads together over a wax tablet. Brys came up behind them and put a hand on each shoulder.

"Let me guess," said Heilyn.

Meirwen said, "You've snapped another string."

Mathrafal also was like a harp string about to snap.

12 november 794 + mathrafal

Next morning Brys found Bened laboring over a letter in his sacristy, his round face flushed. His tonsured hair flared out around his head, rusty red with the first few threads of silver. A clerk showed Brys in and latched the door softly. Bened looked up and found Brochfael's *pencerdd* sitting across the writing table. He rammed his quill into his ink jar, glaring up, then colored more deeply when he realized his temper was on display.

"A reprimand to a monk in Llangurig. He vowed chastity, then fathered two children. Why do people promise things they can't do?"

"Ask instead, why don't people do the things they promise?"

Bened scowled and shook his head. Brys shrugged. *So it sounds like sanctuary lore. Take wisdom where you find it. Do good as the chance comes.*

Bened sighed and pushed the parchment away. "One way or the other."

"Do you have children, Bened?"

"Two boys and a girl. The older boy is from my wife's first marriage. No bastards," Bened, caught in his thorny honesty, blinked pale red lashes. "That I know of. And you?"

"No." Brys hesitated. "Father, I want to make an altar gift to Meifod."

The priest's face froze in suspicion but he recovered quickly. "Very generous, my son. What would you like to give?"

Brys pulled out a scrap of parchment listing Cilwen revenues, figured quickly and told him how much he would give in cattle and silver rods. Bened stared. It was a large sum. He cleared his throat, got up abruptly and went to straighten the gospel book on his shelf. He sat again and combed both hands though his flaming curls.

"Why?"

"You think I'm destined for hell anyway?" Brys smiled. It was too much to expect that he also refrain from provoking Bened.

"After what you did last month in that pagan place? Do you think I don't hear these things? By the Trinity, if your great wish is to be excommunicated —" Bened broke off angrily and bowed his head for a minute. "Forgiveness awaits all those who repent in Christ, my son."

"I want to confess, Father." Brys heard the unplanned edge on his own voice.

Bened looked at him closely, took up his traveling gospel and his crucifix, and moved effortlessly into his role. He was a good man, despite all his ranting. Brys leaned on the chair arm with fingers biting into his forehead and talked out his sinful pride and complex passions and devouring fear. The Powys matters must remain between him and God. Even so Bened drew a sharp breath more than once, though he said nothing beyond setting penitence. *This changes nothing,* Brys thought. *The priest in me has only cool disdain for easy regrets. Deep water flows under all; church and sanctuary are only words that skim the bright surface.* But he felt anxiety lift like a rain curtain, to let in hope and love of living. The Christian priest's beads clicked softly, and the responses dwindled. "So be it."

"So be it."

Halfway to the door Brys turned back into the sacristy. Bened stood behind his table, hands resting on the scarred wood. He looked tired.

Brys knew he would draw another blast of anger, giving them both more sins to confess, but said, "Father, I can help people sometimes. Will you tell me if you have need?"

"I don't know."

No blast. Brys nodded and went out the door before either of them had time to turn it into an argument.

That night he dreamed that he played wood-wisdom with Tegwy under the apple tree in summer. Somehow they strayed from the board's silver paths into ancient forest. King and princes and warriors fell behind them among the silent trees. In the deep green shadow a horned hunter with silver eyes loomed before him and reached down with remote curiosity, trying to tear away the clever mask of his face.

14 november 794 + mathrafal

Cyngen didn't turn up at training one grey morning. No doubt he was with a girl, yet it wasn't like him to sleep late. At noon Brys went in search. Tegwy didn't know.

Cadell had been upstream for days. Gellan was buying a horse in Trallwng. Brochfael, like his grandson, was absent. Brys sent his bodyguard men to taverns and private houses, Meifod abbey where Cyngen sometimes read in the book cellar, anywhere the others suggested. By mid-afternoon he was sweated dry and out of ideas. It was probably nothing. But when someone touched his arm in a dark passage near the west gate, he spun with his knife half out of the sheath. Marc nodded with a slow smile, blond hair falling over one eye. *We're all jumping at shadows. Now we're jumping at each others' shadows. Damn Cyngen.*

"The queen wants you to play in the sun chamber."

"Did she know where Cyngen is?" Whatever Brys needed right now, it decidedly didn't include an hour in the sun room providing light entertainment.

"No. But she didn't seem worried."

They walked toward the court compound. Near the chapel, three bodyguard men came in from the training ground, wearing salt-caked leather war shirts and shields slung on their backs. As they passed, the nearest shouldered Brys so that he sidestepped, fighting for balance. The man turned and apologized, making it an accident, but as they walked on laughter floated back. Marc turned with his hand on his knife hilt, but Brys clasped his shoulder and steered him onward. They were men of Rhirid's squadron, Gellan's favorites. *What dœs it mean? Gellan has decided I'm not to be trusted? Or is it just king's bodyguard making trouble with pencerdd's bodyguard? Or nothing? And where in flaming hell is Cyngen? He's an adult, God knows; he's already acknowledged a bastard. I can't watch him like a child. But if I don't . . .* Marc asked him something, shook his head when he missed it and went off to question the grooms.

Brys got his harp from the writing room and walked down the colonnade, where the wind sighed in the grey and barren grape vines. Maybe a distraction wouldn't be a bad thing anyway. The man on guard duty grounded his spear and passed the *pencerdd* in. As a servant woman took his cloak, he heard laughter floating down from above. Brochfael's family lived in the rooms on the ground floor; Adwen ruled upstairs. He climbed the stair into the sunny weaving room. One window shutter was open on the south wall, out of the wind, but bright afternoon light filtered through the parchment stretched over the west windows. The big airy room opened onto the gallery overlooking the hall.

Brys had always liked visiting this woman's realm. Long ago Adwen had furthered his political education more than once by contriving to forget that he sat in a quiet corner while she talked freely with her women. Here they settled marriages, lovers, children, priests, inheritances, all the affairs of kingdom and cantref, despite the best efforts of the church to lock women between weft and warp. Adwen had been making sure Brys never overlooked the power and subtlety of women. He learned well; he always had to stay on his tœs in the sun chamber. The minds here were often sharper than those below in the hall and by necessity more devious.

"Cynfarch. Rescue us from boredom." Adwen came through from the sun chamber in a rustle of blue silk and took his hands. Brys dropped to one knee, and she raised him smiling. It was a gesture they set aside among the family, but with outsiders Adwen liked a show of respect. "Cold hands, my dear. Come and warm them. Mead or wine?"

Her sister-in-law the abbess Anghenell sat, bright as a cherry in a red dress, among a rainbow of pillows on a cushioned bench. Nest leaned in the curve of her great-aunt's arm as she talked with three local landowners' wives and a nun from Meifod. A brazier glowed in a corner. Adwen poured Brys a cup of her pale wine, last year's harvest from the grape arbors, and no sweeter than ever. It suited Brys's mood. *Can I ask about Cyngen? No. Not on Marc's heels.*

In a cushioned window seat Brys tuned his harp. Near the parchment-covered windows two girls at tall looms were throwing the shuttle across the weave, one warped with fine white linen and the other with a cloak length of russet and gold squares. They had fallen into rhythm: throw the shuttle, block the thread, tug straight, throw the shuttle. He picked it up in his own shining warp of bronze and silver strings and made them a song woven from their own work. Laughing, the younger girl dropped her shuttle; she darted a cautious glance at Adwen but found only a smile. Brys laid her moment's hesitation into his melody, then played on. Warmth rose from the hearth below; laughter and light strung the looms. As his hands grew supple some of his worry lifted.

Brys asked Adwen for her request. Adwen tossed the choice to her sister-in-law, and Anghenell tossed it to Nest. Nest looked out through the open window, where a light wind was driving woodsmoke east across the green hills of Cæreinion, and said that she would like a song about the queen Boudicca or about Cynddylan's sister, the one Brys sang about in hall.

"Something on the saint Melangell will do," said Adwen dryly. "I won't have you riding about the country like Cynddylan's sister with her amazons."

"I've never heard that," Brys said, looking up quickly.

"Please, *nain,*" Nest asked her grandmother.

What was her name, Cynfarch?" asked Adwen.

"Helena," Brys said. "Or maybe Heledd."

"Heledd." Nest shivered, tasting the name of sorrow. "Tell us, *nain.*"

So, instead of a song, they heard the queen of Powys tell about the hawk-proud girl, ungovernable and wild. The two weavers fell still to listen, expecting no reproach. Two of Adwen's orphan children, now young women, they sang at their looms all day.

Nine of them, said Adwen, nine amazons. Two or three were her sisters, but Heledd was their captain and always had some bold plan. Run cattle by night and drive them a few miles for sport. Dazzle a stag with a horn lantern and hunt it from the rolling lowland forest into the western hills before letting it escape. Kidnap a younger brother or a farm boy and frighten him out of a year's growth by dawn. They held no malice and did little damage but it was disgraceful conduct for a royal woman who should have been at her letters and her prayers. Heledd was a motherless hellion, Adwen said, and see the price she paid. Brys glanced at Anghenell, who was smiling into her wine. Nest was rapt. If Adwen meant the story to show her the error of anyone's ways, it failed.

Then Pengwern fell, Adwen said. Then it was all ended.

In the silence they heard the wind brushing the thatch. Then three women spoke at once and laughed, and the silence splintered. Nest smiled out into the grey late afternoon, off on her own hunt. Today she barely resembled the ruffian who trailed her brother to the field camp this summer. Instead she was the king's granddaughter in a deep blue dress with pale blue needlework at the borders, brown braids looped at her neck. Growing up. Still she would rather be the warrior queen Boudicca, or maybe headstrong Heledd.

Is the old story true? Brys wondered, not for the first time. *They lived at Pengwern, lost cantref Tren, died one by one. That much I believe. But the rest? And why do people keep telling this story of broken love and bitter words and fatal outcome? Why dœs Powys remember? Our own, they were brilliant. Too proud, they met destruction. And can I tell it better?* Heledd lay silent in his thoughts, giving him no help tonight.

"'Three songs to the queen in her chamber' are your right, Mother Adwen," said Brys. "What will you hear?"

Debate followed, then consensus. They wanted Arthur.

"Ask me, I know it."

Brys sang of the Arfon cavalry captain, fostered in Penllyn, who became king. He lifted color and warmth from the clacking looms, the books and needlework, the soft laughter and hard politics filling Adwen's loft. It was pleasant to sit with a window at his back chinked against prying wind, a brazier throwing heat to augment the fire below, soft voices, food and drink. The weaving girls locked their shuttles into the warp and went out. The landowners' wives and the nun started home. The window parchment faded until Adwen lit candles and the flames flickered brighter inside than the last light outside, and Anghenell went to shutter the south window. *South. Elfæl and Buellt. And Eli's in the south. Plotting? Listening to Egbert's plots? And where's Cyngen?* He couldn't concentrate on Arthur. But if Adwen didn't worry maybe there was no need for him to worry. Three royal women sat in the couch's bright meadow of cushions, talking quietly. Brys ended his song, far beyond the three songs of a *pencerdd*'s obligation, and reached for the otterskin harp case.

"Not yet," said Adwen quickly. Brys looked up and found her eyes bright and grave. So she was worried too. She amended, "Not long. Play, if you see fit. Anything of summer."

Brys put the harp to his left shoulder again and played his own northern airs, spiralling like a summer breeze in the mountain chalice of Penllyn. Adwen rose to open the shutter and leaned out, looking west toward the dark river. Rain slanted in past her shoulder. She wasn't usually so restless. Brys played through dance airs, slow airs, harvest songs and rowing songs. Anything of summer. *August. At Rhiwædog we kept a boat on the lake shore a mile away. Drifting under the August sun, under the looping swallows. Trailing a line or net. Too lazy to stir when the* gwyniad *fins below the hull. Summer. August. Home. Near there my mother's body washed up, floating in the reedbeds . . .* The memory came unbidden and painful but after all these years no longer unbearable. Still too close to lament. He lilted into another dance tune.

Nest came to stand by him after a while, watching his hands. "May I try?"

Good. Brys had awaited her request for months, even wondered how to provoke it. A royal woman should never lack this art, but she had never studied with Rhydion.

"No." If Brys encouraged willful Nest, she would lose interest in minutes. "You may not."

"Why?" she challenged.

"It's not a toy."

"And I'm not a child."

Brys shook his head smiling and played on. *True.* Her round child's face was narrowing and refining to a young woman's, and new breasts pushed against the embroidered blue linen. *Dream on about warrior queens, little hawk. Soon you'll wound hearts more tenderly.*

"*Nain,* can't I study the harp like Cyngen?"

"Cyngen sings in hall, my dear." Adwen looked closely at Brys. "And Cynfarch needs his time for more important things."

Brys played, watching the candlelight flow on his strings.

"Please, Brys."

"Nest," said Adwen. A warning.

"You'd like it for a week, my girl. Then you'd grow bored and stop practising," Brys told her across the string arm.

"No! Let me try, just for a minute," commanded Nest. "I would practise, I promise."

"How many strings can you span?"

Nest came to lean at his left shoulder and spread her fingers over the stretched bronze. Her small hands were still brown from summer. She announced, "Nine strings."

"You're a match for Bedwyr Nine-strings then. And unlike him you have the use of two arms." Brys moved over on the window seat, and when she settled, put the harp on her knee. The roughened hide he had glued on the base of the sound box gripped her blue linen, and she leaned the instrument cautiously to her shoulder. "What will you play?"

"Ask me, I know it." She began to pick out a song in the light bird voices of bronze, one-handed like Arthur's harper. Brys reached to give her a simple undercurrent in the dark-sounding silver strings. She finished the stanza and laughed up at her grandmother. "You see?"

Adwen turned from the window and met his eyes with a smile. Brys gave her a questioning glance over Nest's brown head. Adwen parried it like a swordsman. She knew the girl's hand on his harp strings held power far beyond a *pencerdd*'s; she also knew Nest's dreams of warrior queens were giving way to dreams of her grandfather's warrior pœt with his flamboyant bodyguard and his name from northern legend.

Adwen's face flashed sudden humor. "Nest, don't annoy your foster brother any more."

Foster brother? Maybe, by some stretch of imagination, foster brother to Cadell. Some kind of foster uncle to Cyngen and Nest, if there were such a thing. That'll teach me to match wits with Adwen, who casually deploys the chimera of royal incest. I'd sooner corner a mountain wildcat with kittens. Brys reclaimed his harp, smiling.

"If Cynfarch has the patience, you may study the harp," the queen said, having won her duel.

Brys was halfway through another song, wondering whether he could leave, when the door crashed open below. Night air swept in, batting the candle flames and making the brazier coals glow redder. Brochfael spoke to the servant downstairs and a lighter voice added something. *Cyngen.*

"Come," called Adwen.

Brys felt huge relief, then anger. Had Adwen known all along? Never mind. He was safe. Brys cased the sea-cat harp as the king and his grandson clattered up the stair, dripping, pulling at cloak pins. Brochfael saw his pœt getting to his feet and lifted a hand.

"Don't go, Cynfarch." Brochfael's face was grey with cold and he looked ten years older than yesterday.

Adwen rose to kiss her husband and unpinned his cloak, spreading it over the loft rail to dry. Brys leaned on the wall, arms folded, watching Cyngen gravely hang his gloves in the loops of Nest's brown braids. Brochfael sat on one of the weaving-stools and took mead from his sister. Rain ran from his leather riding breeches and boots, making rivulets on the floor-planks.

"Cyngen has been judged guilty of murdering a traveling monk, accused by a Llanfair landowner with three confused witnesses. It was easily done. I pray when the time comes it's as easily undone."

"God willing," said the abbess, one arm around watchful Nest.

Brys nodded. *Thank God. Long overdue but better now than later.* "And what next?"

"I leave for Armorica tomorrow." Cyngen looked subdued but not much put out. "Four years."

"From a northern port?" asked Brys. *Any way but south through Elfæl.*

"Sailing from Rhuddlan. The Llanelwy monastery ship will carry him." A winter sea voyage was dangerous, but Eli was much deadlier.

Nest looked around at them silently. She hadn't known but she understood. Even a young girl heard too much court rumor not to understand. She went to stand by her brother, who captured her by one braid.

Adwen called for the evening meal. None of them would go to the hall tonight with a family tragedy at hand, half created and half real. Brys headed for the stair, but the queen called him back. They sat at the table in the lower room, trying to talk about Mathrafal and Armorica and Frankia, but all their words fell into a gulf of silence. *In four years Brochfael will be greyer and grimmer. Adwen will be the same silver pillar of calm, Brochfael's heart. Anghenell will be merrier. Cyngen will be twenty. Nest will be sixteen, married with her own child. I'll be . . .* It was an unlucky game, guessing these things.

Cyngen's thoughts were already halfway across the southern sea. After the meal

Brys embraced him, foster brother and ward and bodyguard warrior, as he left for his own quarters. Cyngen mab Cadell mab Brochfael Powys had all of Elisedd's fire, all of Brochfael's cool reason and all of their hopes. *God's speed going, God's help returning.*

In a silent winter dawn two weeks before Christ's mass, Cyngen left Mathrafal without looking back.

In January famine struck Powys for the first time since the Mercian wars had ended ten years earlier. The northern cantrefs went hungry. Brochfael Powys sent oxcarts of corn north to the Clwyd hills and Mechain. His pœt sent Cilwen's surplus corn to Penllyn. Mountain snow piled into drifts; this snow and the mud that followed it kept the carts from traveling freely.

A few houses starved. Tegeingl children appeared for sale in the Chester slave market when parents made the cruel choice between losing their children to starvation and losing them to foreign bondage. South Powys had surplus corn, yet Eli Elfæl sent no more tax to Mathrafal after one of Brochfael's squadrons seized a few cartloads of corn in November. Cattle starved in northern fields, unable to forage through crusted snow, and soon fed the kites and ravens. Brochfael's oxcarts, those that got through, brought wheat and barley for milling, but there was no grain to spare for cattle feed. Many farmers slaughtered their skeletal breeding stock; some cursed the king for his half-measure.

At the end of February, a few days before Saint David's feast, a courier killed a horse under him bringing news: through the sparse settlements of Mælienydd, north of Elfæl, moved a large armed band of Mercians.

Predictably, Brochfael's messenger to Offa brought back denials. Predictably, Mathrafal seethed with rumors of war.

1 March 795 + Mathrafal

Brys left the council chamber after midnight scrubbing gravel out of his eyes; they had argued for hours. Idris, Garmon and he agreed they should throw three wings of the bodyguard into South Powys — Eli was at his main court of Glascwm in Elfæl, Gellan was at his southern farm — and swear treason against both conspirators. Brochfael heard them out patiently and said he would take one wing to Mælienydd instead to deal with the English.

English? More likely this was another smokescreen or another attempt to wear down Brochfael's resources. Brys went out silently cursing someone's careful timing at the thin end of a hard winter. Eli, probably. Gellan was no strategist, though he had taken one wing south on exercises without permission. Brys prayed, *Let it not be Cenwulf or Egbert.*

An hour later on the training ground, Elgan gave the order that they would ride south tomorrow at first light. One more round of practice would shake their nerves out, then last checks on harness and horses.

Brys reined aside from a charge to watch his ravens. Who had started calling the *pencerdd*'s guard Cynfarch's ravens? Someone who knew the tales of his northern ancestor Owain, whose three hundred ravens, his warriors, fought for Arthur. His guard were quick, confident, fit enough to run fully armed to Meifod and then fight. Their horses were hardened to winter exercises. They pounded past, some of them grinning at the prospect of first action. They had what he wanted: fire, glitter, heart. Green cloaks lifted over leather war shirts and a few mail shirts; a better harvest would have given them all mail. Next year.

Heilyn wheeled past among the others. At the turn, his roan mare stumbled and he sailed off over her shoulder. Brys could only sit twisting the reins unnoticed; Carnlas jigged. *What have I done? I should have left you in your smithy, making beautiful things.* But Heilyn vaulted back onto his mount and rode on. *I hope to God you're laughing a month from now, my dear.* At the end of the field Heilyn flung his holly javelin and pierced the man-shaped target through its straw heart.

By noon Brys and Elgan were satisfied and sent the guard off duty, though the captain warned that he would personally horsewhip any man with a hangover in the morning. The rest of the court clattered with mounts, weapons, orders, servants racing with messages that would be forgotten in an hour. Brys, walking home through the windswept court compound with Heilyn, saw them preparing for war. And whatever Brochfael might hope and fear, Powys had always been ready for war.

At the court forge, Meirwen squinted over her repair to a mail shirt. It was holed over the chest, and though the red stain was rust and not blood, it made her queasy. This was a jeweler's art, riveting new links into the pattern. At least she had a boy to help her coil, flatten and cut the iron wire and pierce its ends. She linked each piece, easing the rhythm of her hands into the rhythm of the war shirt's design. Flexible and light, it flowed like cold water over her hands as she turned it. She could have made one for Brys, stronger than boiled leather. She had never thought of it. She had hoped they would never see war again, a foolish dream. Meirwen riveted the last link and was reaching for the next repair when the boy came to say a man wanted her outside. Probably Heilyn had returned from training to help in the smithy. But in the stone-paved yard she found Brys's friend, the whitehaired young priest from Mathrafal sanctuary.

"You are a boneset," said Mæn.

"I collect medicinal herbs for infusions and poultices. I have set bones when I must," Meirwen said. *But why ask me? Your skills are far greater.*

"Can you ride a horse?"

"Yes."

"The Meifod surgeon and I will accompany the squadrons to the border. We need others."

She carefully retied her apron belt, unwilling to see his face. "Not me."

"Men may die."

"Why? I'll only be helpless against terrible injuries."

"Pride is a good thing," Mæn said, "until it gets in your way. You can achieve something like perfection in metal but not in healing. Our bodies aren't perfect. Medicine is even less perfect."

"No."

Mæn's brown eyes looked troubled, she thought, more over her fear than her refusal. What did he expect? *I didn't join the bodyguard. Why should I mend their damage?* Heilyn was right about fixing other people's destruction; it was a slave habit. If the powerful wanted wars, let them deal with the bloody outcome.

"Why do you make weapons of war?" Mæn glanced toward the smithy. "When you know what they do to human bodies?"

"I'm a smith." Meirwen turned and went inside, feeling the priest's presence in the yard as a blow to her back. She knew where that logic carried her. She worked with weapons because she was a smith; she set bones because she was a boneset. But she wasn't a carrion crow, flapping to the border to perch on the bodies of the dead and dying.

Long after darkness fell, Meirwen finished riveting the sword hilt and reached for the next repair. Brys had come to help. He passed her tools, held the lamp close while she cold-hammered and finally fetched her away. Heilyn said he would stay another hour to finish riveting a sword hilt. Let the others work all night if they wanted. She knew the work was never finished. She also knew she shouldn't have walked away from Mæn, but she couldn't go. Wouldn't go. She leaned on Brys as they walked home. His step was light, as though he had set down a burden.

"How long?"

"A few days." Brys stopped, letting passersby sidestep, and put his arms around her to kiss her forehead. He was warm, but her hands rested on cold stained leather and bronze studs. It was like embracing a scaled sea-cat, his whimsical beast. "Meirwen — if things ever turn bad, go to Aberffraw. Not Iâl. Don't look back."

A bitter price for coming to Mathrafal, seeing men ride away to war and never knowing if they would return. As helpless as any other woman. Waiting on a man's warfaring was not her way. Her way was silver and gold, amber and crystal. A cool ribbon of eternity, not a hot flood of wasted blood. One week. If he wasn't back in one week, she would go. Iâl, Aberffraw, it didn't matter. Too desolate to argue, Meirwen nodded, and they walked on hand in hand. When they got home she had no will to eat. Brys sat her on the end of the sleeping bench and crouched to turn flatbread on the bakestone. He fed her bread and cheese and sweet wizened apples, then washed her soot-smudged face and bundled her under the quilts.

"I have another council." He kissed her and wiped crumbs from her mouth.

Not so easily. Meirwen linked her fingers behind his neck and drew him down. Firelight was gentle to his face. It shadowed the sweep of dark lashes, smoothed the break in his nose, sculpted his mouth. Sword belt and war shirt slithered cold against her skin; she wanted the warm man inside them. The buckles were a clumsy design. She would forge something better. Brys slid under the quilts, muttering about seduction, but he was never difficult to persuade. After he left, Meirwen curled sleepily with her hands spread on her flat belly, trying to recall the small weight of the child in her arms.

Mercy and weakness *look much the same to some men, especially to predators and their scavengers.* Brys sat with his feet propped on the table and watched the light of one candle flicker on the painting of Marc Sant on the scriptorium wall. The saint looked ready to set down his book, step across the winged yellow cat that crouched like a small flame at his feet, and walk out into the room. It was full night outside. Brochfael would send someone to fetch him for the council in a few minutes.

You would understand the difference, Brys resumed his silent and one-sided conversation with the saint. *Mercy springs from strength. But people must see that strength to know it. Brochfael's mercy, as invisible as his strength to many eyes, falls on frozen ground.*

Steps outside. When the door opened, it wasn't a servant but the king, who rarely came to the old scriptorium. Brys got to his feet, but Brochfael closed the door quietly behind him and came to sit down. Outside, the guard paced off down the colonnade.

The king propped his elbows on the chair arms, linked his fingers and looked at his pœt. "It's time to act on Eli."

"Yes." *At last. Finally he's pushed you too far.*

"I thought he would come to see his folly. How could I move against my brother?"

Brys waited. Brochfael had never acknowledged *that* before either.

"I thought of letting him have South Powys, but we need to stand together against Mercia. Now he's paid only part of his tax and that at swordpoint. The only way to deal with him is by force."

"Now?" *Every day is another day closer to trouble.*

"First we'll see what's happening in Mælienydd. It sounded like English landowners' bands out lifting cattle. It's been a hard winter. Nothing too serious," Brochfael offered his wintry smile. "Despite court rumors."

Now, Brys wanted to shout. *Forget the raiding party, go straight to Elfæl now.*

"Cynfarch. You've done everything I asked of you." Brochfael looked down at his linked fingers, then up at the saint as though seeking his counsel. "Don't let Idris or anyone else compare you to your father. God knows I've had enough of that in my life. You can be more than Cadeyrn ever could have been." Brochfael looked up. "Dœs that make you angry?"

Brys shook his head. *Not angry, extremely wary. What's coming?*

"You were never able to talk about him at first. Nor about your mother."

"It took time to understand," Brys said slowly. If Brochfael was bending a little, maybe because Cyngen was safe in Bro Waroch, so could Brys. "That she couldn't bear any more sorrow."

"None of it would have happened if I'd . . . allowed him his pride. In the end what did it matter, cantref or kingdom? I feared losing Powys region by region."

Brys looked at him, lost for words, lost even for an emotion. The silence grew uncomfortable. The candle flame dipped, wavering the saint's image. His voice finally came out twisted raw. "You would have. Lost everything."

"Not if I'd crushed Eli and forgiven Cadeyrn."

"You share a bond of blood." *Irony. Brochfael confesses, I offer absolution. A year ago*

I would have taken this as my defeat. Now . . . "You did what survival demanded." *Your survival. Not ours. But I would have done the same, put my kingdom before my friend.*

Brochfael studied him, weighing his response. *For its* braint*? Compassion? Sincerity? Justice? What do you want, the kiss of peace or retribution?* Whatever it was the king wanted, he seemed to find. Finally he nodded. "Your brother wrote to me. He's hard-headed like your mother's kin."

"And I'm not?"

Brochfael smiled, "You're a northerner, my dear, from your name to your anger."

"Coming from your house that should be an insult."

"Remember: the Cynferchin sailed into River Clwyd from the ruins of Carlisle and took land, gold, power — from the Cadelling."

"We gave more than we took," Brys said warily, leaning to push some wax around the dripping candle rim. *This cuts close to the bone with Brochfael, even after two centuries.* "Saints, pœts, formidable protection in war."

"So you did," Brochfael said. "But what you took was ours."

"And Carlisle was ours before the English took it." Brys saw the king's mouth quirk and realized the parallel he had created. North Powys and the English, both enemies of old Rheged.

"You brought new blood. But don't ask the old blood to forget."

"Brorda told me about his grandfather's falconer in Elfed," Brys said after a while. "He said the man taught him to speak the British tongue."

"That archaic accent of his."

"Brorda said that he was of the royal house but happy enough as a falconer."

"Then he was not of the royal house. He could be content as an abbot or hermit serving God, perhaps, not as a falconer serving an English lord."

"Yes." *Royal blood dœs not forget. In Elfed, in Powys, in Penllyn.* He looked up, meeting Brochfael's iron stare and perfect understanding. "What did Cadwr want?"

"He thanked me for Garmon's recognition, having somehow formed the idea I had arranged it." Another direct look, a challenge. "And he told me to have Garmon name you heir of Penllyn."

Brys felt the color rising to his face. "That's not hard-headed. That's an insult, a matter for face price."

"Hard to know which sometimes," Brochfael agreed dryly. "Garmon will name his son Geraint or another cousin as heir. It's his right. I won't interfere."

No one asks it. No one but Cadwr. Cadwr who said, That's all past. Brys looked into the candle until he saw a bright host of flames and finally got up to open the window shutter a hand's width. It was cold outside.

"Now I need you, Cynfarch. You are my weapon in reserve," said Brochfael quietly. "Now I must raise you against Eli. Will you bind Powys together or split us apart?"

"With my guard of twenty men? Or is it my secret army north of Llanycil?" Brys turned and leaned on the shutter.

"No." Brochfael smiled, but his smile was brittle.

"Eli's the one gathering an army, Brochfael. I make songs. I make legends. I can make an idea of Powys as a bloody wasteland or as a flowering garden."

"So I've seen. Which will it be?" Brochfael made his question sound cool and dispassionate.

"Both."

"God my judge, don't play with words."

"You've heard my *englynion* on Llemenig? Light and dark, blessed and cursed, abundant and stricken, loyal and treacherous, peace and war. The tension between opposites drives the cycle."

"Llemenig as both warrior and peacemaker."

"Powys loves war, everyone says. Maybe it's true," Brys said quietly. This wasn't the kind of thing Brochfael liked hearing. It was safer talking about old wars and old kingdoms. "Maybe she still hasn't fully understood the cost."

"She?" Brochfael looked up, amused.

"Sometimes I think so. Like Cynddylan's sister. Heledd."

"His betrayer. Was that her name?"

"No one seems to remember. It was a dark time in Powys."

"Heledd. Salt on the fields. Even the name is tears." Brochfael paused a moment. "Did you know I wed Powys?"

"No." *Brochfael had followed the old ritual of king-making?* Brys felt the chill on his back, prying between the window shutters. "I didn't know."

Brochfael nodded, watching his face. "Bened took my confession. I am a simple Christian. Yet some things must be done." He shrugged it off, a pragmatic man. "Sing both, then, peace and war, Brys. Play with fire."

You also, in trusting me. "To shed light."

"Let's get through this council." Brochfael got to his feet.

Brys stood, hesitating. "Brochfael. About Cadell."

Brochfael frowned at Marc Sant. "What about Cadell?"

Either you know and don't want to hear, or you'll never believe me. I can't say your son's plotting with your bastard brother, do you blame him? You scarred him as your own cursed father scarred you. But maybe you did all you could do in a dangerous time. "He means well. You should know him better."

"Should I?" Bleak humor. "Perhaps I should invite him to ride to Mælienydd."

You know. Brys watched him go out, and thought of Heledd. *That fatal Powys pride and passion, careless of destruction. No, insisting on destruction. Both of our houses share that compulsion.* He crossed himself and went to collect his weapons.

3 march 795 + muletun

Rain on a sullen east wind swept the borderland. Cloaks dragging sodden, wet gear in saddlebags, weapons speckling with rust overnight: these were three good reasons to avoid winter campaigns.

"Even the English should be too smart to make war in March," Addonwy griped as they rode south through border farms already gathered for flight.

Two wings of the bodyguard rode south, with the small *pencerdd*'s small guard and some of the household warriors of the lords of Mechain, Meirionydd and

Penllyn. They had about two hundred and fifty men. After two days of slow travel on washed-out tracks and through swirling fords in the cold rain, sleeping on ground frozen under a glaze of mud, it seemed likely to be a false alarm. Why would anyone come out in this? Some Mercian quarrel, at most, thought Brys. The only one who never complained, seemed even pleased to be here, was Cadell.

A scout from Mælienydd met them the second day and said armed men had been seen moving through the English settlements within Powys, an hour to the south. Brochfael called his captains to hear, but the scout could only say a farm boy spotted about twenty men on foot yesterday. Twenty men was scarcely a warband.

Brochfael said he would question the landowner and gathered a small escort. Heilyn rode beside the king to act as translator if need be. As they rode, Brys tried to make sense of it. The English landowers paid tax to Brochfael Powys but were exempt from military levy. More of Eli's provocation?

South of Muletun they forded a hill stream surging high in its banks with rain; last summer Brys had often crossed its dry trickle with Pol's patrol. They dismounted on the south bank to lead the horses precariously up the muddy trail, then rode upstream through an English village's mast-woods and hazel coppices. A striped sow lumbered away from them, evading her swineherd. When they halted on the ridge to look down again, Brochfael fell silent.

Brys came up beside him and sat Carnlas with sleet blowing forward over his shoulders. *They went back to Mercia, that's all. Burned the buildings to leave nothing behind, abandoned the farms, went back to the fat lowlands. A few did that, after Offa's treaties.* Brys tried to believe it, until Heilyn drew in his breath raggedly. Then the reality came home. He sat locked in the pitiless instant of knowing something has changed forever and can never again be the same.

The timbered earth enclosure stood empty. Houses, barns and outbuildings had once clustered inside. All had fallen to ash and black ruin. But it was the half-plowed strip field that shouted loudest. No farmer abandoned his plow overturned in a suddenly jagged furrow, leaving slashed harness to stir listlessly in the wind.

No one spoke. Brochfael shook himself as though he'd been sleeping and heeled his bay gelding forward, though Idris reached to catch his arm in warning. He dropped his hand and shrugged at the king's stony stare. As they rode into the enclosure, ravens lifted.

Outside their destroyed hall a man lay on his back with his arms spread. His skull was split. A hound lay dead at his feet. On watch, perhaps. Most of the people had probably died in the charred waste of the hall or in the smaller huts, denied any escape from the smoke and flames.

They dismounted. Brys searched cautiously through the blackened tangle of beams and picked up a shapeless lump of bronze that had been a nail or bracket. For a short time the place had been an inferno, but the bronze was cold and so was the ash when he bent to touch it. Idris walked silently into the middle of the hall. Brys turned away abruptly, skin crawling on his back, sensing all too clearly the place's death terror. Two days ago, judging by the birds' work on the man and the dog.

"What do you make of it?" Brys asked Heilyn quietly.

Heilyn looked unhappily at the dead man. He was an ugly sight with most of his face pecked to the bone. "An ax blow from horseback. He didn't struggle or give the alarm. Maybe it was someone he knew."

Or at least someone he trusted. "The English don't use axes in war, not that I know."

"Free levies would bring their wood-cutting axes," Heilyn said.

"Maybe." But Brys also remembered a narrow-bladed Frankish throwing-ax hanging at Egbert's saddlebow.

Brys walked on to the stable, and Heilyn came after him with his spear levelled. But nothing was alive here. The horses were dead in their stalls, their big carcasses bloated under a layer of ash. A stench of scorched hair and hooves hung over the whole place. Heilyn walked out again with a hand over his mouth. Everything was unnaturally quiet, even the ravens and one sea eagle watching, waiting on the granary roof. Brys rejoined the others in a silent knot near the hall and remounted. Pol swallowed dry and gave quiet orders. Cadell was as pale as tallow.

Cian, who had been walking the inside perimeter, came and told Brochfael there had been two hundred men here, maybe more, mostly on foot. Not twenty. Brys looked up to the ridge treeline and the scrub willows farther upstream. *Two hundred? Where are they? Back across the Mercian border? South in Elfæl? Watching us from dense cover up there among the hazels?*

"Send a rider to Tamworth," said Idris.

"Not until we know." Brochfael was ashen-faced. Rain fell from his grey hair and beaded on the gold *hual* chain. He looked around the destroyed village as though he had to commit it to memory. "We'll wait. Make camp where we left the others."

"Then let's return to Mathrafal, raise levies, pull the other wing in from the south." Idris sounded extremely reasonable, knowing Brochfael wasn't going to listen.

"I'll send a man south to bring Gellan and Rhirid's wing."

"And when Gellan arrives?" Brys asked. His shield turned idly at his right knee as the stallion shifted weight. Rain slid between his numb fingers and the reins. *Do we join Gellan or attack him?*

"Ask me then, Cynfarch."

Brochfael turned his horse, and Idris let out an angry breath. Bened, with his traveling gospel held carefully under his cloak, got to his feet from beside the dead man and remounted. Pol gave a quiet order to keep weapons ready, with the king in their center. They climbed the ridge to the dripping coppices. Brys shivered, looking a last time at the plow skewed at the end of its muddy furrow.

They gathered the main force and rode south across Ceri ridgeway into Mælienydd, halting in a wooded valley that offered some shelter from wind and sleet. Brochfael's two servants unloaded the packhorse and pitched a tent; it would be another miserable night. Brys was crouching by a reluctant fire with his bodyguard when the upper sentry cried a challenge, and one of their scouts rode sliding and clattering down into their camp and straight to Brochfael.

"Mercians, lord, north of Cæbitra stream. They're east of the border, settled in for the night but ready to move out fast. Well armed, well organized." The scout slid down off his winded pony.

"How many?"

"Three hundred."

Miles north, at their backs. Was it the force sighted four days ago to the south, or a second one? And Rhirid's wing was in the south, as was Eli. *A trap. We've walked right in and kicked it shut behind us. Retreat north, and they'll be on us like wolves. If the Mercians slaughtered the Powys English village, they won't stop there. If they didn't do it, they'll be ready to slaughter whœver they think did it.* Brys felt sweat prickle his back under the clammy leather, colder than the rain on his face. Brochfael heard it all in glacial stillness, with the fading light gleaming on his iron shirt and gold *hual*.

"Pol," he told his captain. "Find a man who knows the area. Send him south to Gellan's estate to bring up Rhirid's wing, then on to Glascwm for Eli's bodyguard."

Eli and Gellan? Better outnumbered than trapped and betrayed.

"Lord," Idris began and gave up at Brochfael's look.

"Brochfael, use your head," said blunt Garmon Penllyn and walked forward with his son. Geraint dropped a hand on Brys's shoulder. It was a warning. "If we return to Mathrafal we can take counsel there and gather a force. Take your two wings back tonight under darkness. Leave the packhorses and ride light. We'll take rearguard with our men and Cynfarch's guard."

"Do it, Brochfael," Brys said, catching Elgan's nod. *Garmon didn't bother to ask. He trusts me enough . . .* But the sweat began to slide down his spine like cold grease. *Rearguard, suicide guard. One attack ends the house of Penllyn, all except Cadwr.*

"I'll go to the English as your messenger. Tell me what you want to say," said Heilyn quietly behind him and to make his point he repeated it in English.

Fair god, Heilyn. They'll skin you with blunt knives and kill you next week.

Brochfael shook his head. "You wouldn't live to carry an answer."

Pol was back with a freckled Elfæl boy leading a horse.

"If you send a messenger south they'll — wait for morning. We need them tonight," said a hesitant voice at Brochfael's back. It was Cadell, blinking at the sleet on his pale eyelashes. "I'll go."

Brys heard rain hiss on the small stream. *Not the hunt, the snare.* Brys stepped forward and gripped Brochfael's forearm, warm under his cold fingers. The king turned his eyes first to his *pencerdd*, then to his son. Cadell stood with his arms folded under his cloak, one shoulder twisted, rain tracking in his lank hair.

Brochfael clasped his son's arm. "Tell them to hurry. We could be under attack by morning."

Brys bit back another warning and watched Cadell vault onto his horse's back. He climbed the south track at a scrambling canter. *Will he go south? Or will he disappear until the ravens have picked us clean?*

Brochfael smiled around at them. Garmon looked blindly after Cadell, now out of sight. Pol was intent on a pebble in his boot. Idris's face was frozen in dismay. Brys wondered if he looked as sick as he felt. *Eli and Gellan. Coming to our aid. Fair God.*

The night was bitterly cold, sodden wet and endless. Brys pulled the garish

Mathrafal hall harp off a packhorse and sang by the fires. First he sang wicked satire to let them laugh out their nerves, then lament to free them from fear and loss. No bloody hero cycles; those were best left for safe winter nights in the hall. Long afterward he lay rolled in his cloak beside Heilyn, feet to the guttering fire, drinking someone's mead and hearing about Elgan's girl with curling brown hair in Pentreduldog. Eventually sleep was less effort than talk, but soon it was dawn and the camp was stirring.

4 March 795 + Argoed

Mercian scouts picked them up near Ceri ridge soon after sunrise as they rode north. Skylined briefly between leafless trees on the heights, the riders turned lazily and dropped out of sight. Brochfael's scouts reported that the English force had crossed west of the border and now waited near the burned village. There was no sign of Cadell.

Early sun pierced scattered clouds over Mercia and curved the Powys hills with gold. Winter still had a grip on the air, but spring touched the land. As he rode Brys saw the land's renewal. Primroses were in flower at the dripping woodland margin, white catkins puffed on willows, moist green scents rose under the horses' hooves. Brochfael rode wrapped in his wintry silence.

They descended the undercut slope of Argœd hill toward the stream. The British farm under the brow was deserted, its people hiding upstream at sight of warbands. As they emerged from the trees among farm pastures Brys caught a first sight of the Mercians. They were gathered in the broadest part of the small valley on this side of the stream, willing to risk a downhill assault from the smaller Powys force. Brys counted at least three hundred. They massed on foot; a few horses were tied among trees by the stream. When the Powys force cleared the trees the English raised weapons and lapped their shields, then started forward. That was how they fought best, advancing in close ranks when they were ready, breaking attack after attack on their shield wall, letting their enemies do the work. It was infuriating and effective.

Brochfael quickly ordered his two mounted wings to form up on a north-sloping fallow field. He grouped the smaller guards in the center, perhaps trusting them more. The east wind turned the golden stag banner writhing in the hands of his standard-bearer. Brys sat Carnlas, bumping knees with the king on his right and Heilyn on his left, and for the first time in his life faced ordered ranks of English warriors. They were a sight to chill the blood, walking steadily uphill under the bitter wind. Many had mail shirts, a few wore iron helmets. They looked like a noble's bodyguard or maybe several landowners' guards. *Not Offa's bodyguard, thank God for that much. But whose?* A lord more ruthless than Brochfael would have sent Heilyn last night to find out.

The waste farms of the Powys English lay just out of sight upstream; the English force had positioned itself as though to defend or avenge their ruin. The commander's silken standard twisted and fell straight long enough to reveal the Mercian eagle, not Offa's black eagle but a gold eagle on a red field with wings lifted for the stoop. Was it some member of their royal house? Brys searched the front rank behind the painted and bossed shields, but in the stinging wind all the faces blurred to a likeness even without the helmets. *We should attack now, before Eli has a chance to come to their aid.* But a rider came down Argœd hill at a breakneck canter, bareback on a mud-caked hill pony. It was Cadell.

"Gellan's on my heels. Eli's a mile south." He slid down and staggered against the spent pony. Someone brought him a horse.

Shouts on the ridge. Gellan and his captain Rhirid led the third wing stumbling and splashing down the track. They were spattered with red border mud and worn from riding half the night, but Gellan's lathered black horse caught enough of the commander's nervous energy to seethe around under him like a wild colt. Brochfael motioned Rhirid's wing to the left, upstream, and called Cadell to his side.

Brys waited for the command. Why did Brochfael delay? They were still outnumbered, and now the English had crossed nearly half the distance. Hair whipped across his face. Too late now to tie it back like Heilyn's. The throwing spear balanced light in his left hand, the shield rim rode companionably against his right cheek, cold fear tied knots in his gut. *Come on. Before Eli gets here.* At last Brochfael signalled his standard-bearer to blare a challenge on his bronze trumpet, and at Elgan's nod Marc answered on his blue hunting horn. The sound floated out over the shallow valley, and they spurred the horses beneath it, downhill.

The charge swept from trot to hand gallop, but when they were still a spear cast distant the English line suddenly broke and leaped forward. The English stopped abruptly, grounded their spear butts under their feet and angled them to meet the charge. No room remained to turn aside. Impact. The battle line boiled with horses screaming and lunging on the long-bladed spears, trying to pull away, but the second line was still coming in at their backs. A spear gouged a shallow red track on Carnlas's neck, and the stallion lifted to lash with forehooves. A Mercian went down. Brys hurled his spear, but it fell among the ranks doing no damage.

Now the English pressed forward again, deflecting the Powys charge away toward their flanks in a confusion of spears and hooves. Brys was carried away from the center among his guard. Better than being caught between English spears and Powys spears pushing in from behind. Heilyn stayed beside him, clinging like a burr. He saw one of his own guard go down with a spear through his shoulder, but there was no way to drag him free. Pushing downstream, the captains were yelling to dismount. Up on the ridge someone was sounding a hunting horn again. At last Brys broke away, buying room to swing down and draw his sword. He took one glance uphill at their backs.

Eli and about fifty men sat their horses up at the dark treeline, motionless as though they were watching a training match. The morning sun lit the links of Eli's iron shirt and the blade of his drawn sword. He had pinned his cloak low; the boar-headed torc glowed at his neck in radiant gold under his yellow hair. He made a flawless picture of a warrior prince riding to his brother's aid. *Stay there. You're less dangerous.* Eli was playing at Cynddylan the Fair again, but Cynddylan would have made short work of Eli. Brys's back itched under the war shirt where he couldn't reach, right between the shoulder blades where he could take a traitor's spear.

Elgan gathered them at the flank of Pol's wing and led them in on foot against the immovable English shield wall. It was less sword fight than shield fight, they were jammed so close. Heilyn was at his right side, muttering in English, and Tegwy at his left. They gave ground again quickly as the Mercians moved forward in a solid wall, forcing the Powys men into their English style of fighting. Brys stumbled back over the body of one of his guard, yielding ground, trying to stay clear of wounded horses flailing their hooves in agony and terror. The slope rose under his feet behind him. Elgan yelled for them to hold their ground. *How long?* If they were backed up against Eli — Brys risked a glance over his shoulder. Eli was still there, dismounted now. And up there with him was Cadell.

"Brys!" Heilyn yelled.

A *seax* blade sang past his cheek. He shielded blows and gave more ground. *If we break, Argœd hill runs blood.* A spear scored the leather on his chest, and he slashed to splinter the shaft. One less weapon. His sword was dulled, not much blooded. Maybe they could push upstream. He saw Brochfael's stag banner lean drunkenly and pass into another man's hands. Brys's line wavered, fell back another step and then stiffened with new men. Garmon had brought in his Penllyn bodyguard. Friends and cousins. Geraint appeared at Brys's left hand, singing tunelessly to himself and using his sword to good effect. Gaining ground, not much, they heard the horn sound again on the ridge, and Eli's bodyguard dropped downhill. Elfæl had chosen his side. *Powys. Why?* With Eli there would be a good reason. Cadell and Eli fell on the scattered Mercians below by the stream. Their flanks crumbled inward and they lapped their shields. The English pressing on Brys's guard and Garmon's men fell back. A few stumbled and went under on the rough slope.

Someone shouted an order in English, something about the border. Brys looked along the fight's roiling line of confusion. *That dark voice.* The man under the eagle banner wore an iron helmet with cheek flanges and nose piece but he was tall and his hair was ashen blond. *Cenwulf?* Then Geraint staggered against him and went down. A Mercian with a bloody spear blade grinned in his beard. Brys stabbed him in the throat. Another order in English. The Mercians closed ranks and began to retreat as coolly as though they were on exercises. Off to their left Idris was shouting.

Brys let his guard pursue and kneeled on the wet grass beside Geraint. Garmon was already there. The spear had gone through Geraint's cheek and up into the brain. A quick death. Brys said the words for his cousin and closed his eyes. Garmon swayed wordless in the grip of his anguish. Another of Penllyn lost. Grief would come later. But they were too late anyway. The English were in the stream bottom reclaiming their horses and those on foot were making an orderly retreat to Offa's earthwork. *Why?* Then Brys saw they had what they wanted. Brochfael was down.

Brys sprinted across the fallow to the stag standard, Garmon behind him. Idris kneeled beside Brochfael with Mæn Pedr and the Meifod surgeon, but Brochfael motioned them away impatiently and got to his feet. A blow to the sword arm, both bones broken above the wrist. His face was chalky with pain and shock.

"I'll take the bodyguard after them," said Gellan.

"They'll reach the border first," Brochfael told him, biting the words short. "Let them go."

But Gellan spun away calling for his captains and ran for the horses. Brochfael watched him long enough to take one breath. Then he looked at Idris, Garmon, Brys, Cadell.

"Stop him."

Brys was off before the others moved, leaving Elgan to gather the *pencerdd*'s guard, who still only half-understood what was happening.

He caught Carnlas upstream. Gellan was well ahead, with Rhirid's squadrons lashing their horses toward the border. Brys got astride and caught one glimpse of Brochfael holding his bay horse. Let Idris stop him. He galloped east riding low on the stallion's grey neck and whipping with the flat of his sword blade, careering downstream through rough pasture and scrub. The stallion flew, hooves barely touching the brown grass, and he came level with the rearmost of Brochfael's guard.

He drew ahead until he rode knee to knee with the commander and shouted down the streaming wind. Gellan looked over his shoulder and spurred his black horse faster. Ahead the Mercians were climbing the slope of Offa's dyke in knots but stopped to watch this pursuit. They stood outlined on the crest in a dark ragged line. Brys swung Carnlas hard against Gellan's horse, breaking his gallop.

Gellan wheeled with his sword drawn and threw himself across his saddlebow to stab for the groin. Brys jerked back sharply, and the sword point drove into the saddle leather at his thigh. The commander wrenched it free, and the black horse reared screaming with murderous hooves lashing out.

Brys circled. Elgan and his guard were pounding in, only a spear cast away. The sun stood halfway up the morning sky, east over Mercia. He needed the left hand's advantage, his sword arm to the commander's shield arm, and he moved sunwise. Gellan narrowed his unnatural eyes at the light, his bloodless lips drawn back tight against his teeth. He spurred the black horse forward and slashed heavily at Brys's unshielded sword arm. Brys twisted out of range, accustomed to fighting lefthanded, and parted the cloak over the commander's shoulder. Mail glittered underneath. He would have to strike above or below the armor, if he could get close enough.

Heilyn's voice floated to him, and Garmon's. Gellan circled. As they shifted Brys saw the English watching motionless from the dyke. The *pencerdd*'s guard and the bodyguard wings were taking formation. Brys felt a sick jolt of shock. Their formation had nothing to do with the English. Pol's wing, Gwyddien's wing, Garmon, Elgan, Idris and Cadell had moved together. And across the rough grazing Rhirid's wing and Eli's bodyguard were drawn up, ready to attack them. *Their own.*

Brochfael drove his horse between his commander and his *pencerdd.* Brys could have wept for the lost chance. Gellan's death was the taste of metal on his tongue. Too many deaths, too much treachery.

"Cyning!" A shout from the border, calling out to the king.

Brochfael Powys turned. The broken arm was strapped to his chest, and the other managed the horse. No weapon, no shield. Brys kicked his mount forward, and strangely enough so did Gellan.

Too late. As Brochfael looked up into the morning light, the spear caught him full in the chest. It pierced iron links as though they were linen and went deep under his breast bone. One long still moment Brochfael sat the horse, and then he toppled backward from the saddle. On the crest of the earthwork only two English stood now. One still had the spearman's forward stance. The other had pale hair and an iron helmet looped over his arm. They turned and vanished.

Brys stared into the sun. Grass swept flat under the wind and stayed motionless. Clouds stopped in the pale Mercian sky. Sun spilled as from a goldsmith's crucible. Frozen. A painted icon.

"Brân!" A hoarse voice tore the silence. His own voice.

Ravens stooped to carry him forward. A creature of light, without substance. Slow as a grey sea wave, Carnlas plunged down into the ditch, up onto the dyke, wheeled on the height. The Mercians eastward were mostly mounted and away. A white mare with red harness remained. A honey-haired girl sat on the horse; her face looked bruised though it was unmarked. Yellow silk blew across her hanging feet. She cried out his name.

Cenwulf turned from the white horse's bridle and dropped the chiming scarlet reins. Brys laughed and sent his shield spinning up through the stopped sky like a child's toy. And Carnlas swept down toward the single scorched image of a handsome face with eyes like blue smoke. Brys rode straight toward him and smashed a boot into the ashen fair beard and soft mouth. Cenwulf shouted from bloody lips and drove a fist at his face. And he was gone.

Words. Bird voices shrieking the unknown language of starling and wren. Words, feathers, tumbling up into the bright air. Frozen. Empty. Raven dark descended. A long time. Clouds raced across a cold blue sky, cold earth lay underneath. Cloaked figures stood up there. A dark green cloak swung near his face. Not English. A name came to him. Elgan.

Elgan spat, signed the cross and kneeled beside him. Over his shoulder he told someone, "Not a scratch. *Gwyllt.*" Crazy.

"The girl." Brys took Heilyn's hand and got to his feet. "I need to find the girl."

Elgan looked at Heilyn and shrugged. "There's no girl here."

Brys walked west blindly. Someone touched his hand for luck. Creaking overhead, a raven rode the air current west. Brys shuddered and looked around him. No English. Away to the northeast, cooksmoke rose from a thatched hall among narrow strips of plowland. They were in Mercia. At the horses he took a leg up and crossed the border westward after his raven, up the dyke and down into the ditch, up again into Powys.

Brochfael lay straight and still now on the brown grass, hands folded on his chest, the spear drawn. Bened kneeled with his traveling gospel between his hands, praying quietly. Idris crouched with his head bowed over his grief, one big hand splayed on Brochfael's shoulder. Cadell kneeled beside the priest, lost in whatever unknown pain his life inhabited, looking down at his father. The *hual* of North Powys had fallen back of its own weight, a few links of blood-spattered gold chain drawn tight across a dead man's throat. Brochfael's face was more than ever an iron mask in death, though once or twice he had put aside that mask. Brys felt tears flow down his face, but his heart was locked in the king's winter. Even now, with hate and fear no longer needed, for his father's sake he could not admit he also loved Brochfael.

Eli got to his feet, looking handsomely distressed, wearing the gold torc of South Powys. This small ugly knot of coincidence had to be his handiwork. Cenwulf's also, and maybe Egbert's, but unlike his allies Egbert was clever enough to be invisible. And now Powys lay fallow, without a king, without an heir. Gellan and Rhirid moved forward on either side of Eli.

The east wind ruffled Eli's yellow hair and lit the gold torc. Brys couldn't take his eyes from it. Massive, it was finely crafted in an archaic style of forged spirals where a modern smith would engrave interlace. It was dented near the right boar's head, scratched but glowing with gold's secret light. Brys knew at last that it was not copied from the old songs. That was what Brochfael had been trying to tell him at Rhyd Y Grœs. *What happened to Cynddylan's torc? Ask me, I know it.* Behind Eli stood Gellan, never taking his light eyes from the *pencerdd*'s face.

"Cadell Powys," said Idris Meirionydd clearly. He got slowly to his feet, Brochfael's badger, with black brows drawn down over blue eyes. He was a dangerous man for traitors. He drew Cadell to his feet, clasped his arm and gave him the kiss of peace.

Gellan looked around sharp-eyed. "We need a proven leader. Eli —"

"Cadell Powys," said Garmon quietly and put one hand on Brys's shoulder. With the other he took Cadell's hand, which Idris passed to him, and kissed Cadell's cheek.

Eli looked at his cousin Cynfarch, Brochfael's pœt. The others looked also, all of them waiting. Brys felt it sink under his ribs like a blade, a death threat. He took Cadell's hand from Garmon and kissed his foster brother. He saw Eli's look of shock and betrayal, the menace of Gellan's pale eyes, as he said from the dry husk of his voice, "Cadell Powys."

Bened stopped praying to lift the *hual* over Brochfael's grey head.

Cadell kneeled trembling as Idris settled the gold chain around his neck. Crooked Cadell, trying to find something to do with his awkward hands. Cadell Powys.

14 March 795 + Meifod

Three things make a king in the island of Britain: the hands of his kinsmen, the embrace of his land, the sacrament of his church.

Cadell accepted the *hual* three times. The first time his father's oldest friend placed it around his neck, while cold rain washed his father's blood from the gold links.

A woman placed the *hual* a second time on a frost-rimed night in Mathrafal sanctuary. At the gate in the thorn hedge she greeted them — Mæn Pedr was still helping with the wounded at Meifod — and led them in under the chiming trees.

Brys kneeled with her by the clearwater spring. She was a springkeeper, from the south by her voice, and she knew what to do. Less was asked of Brys, though he had never before acted as king's priest in the old way. It was a deeply clouded night, and they worked without light. The others in the sanctuary, a dozen or more, were only dark shapes that moved sometimes against a darker wall of trees. Brys and the springkeeper readied cup and king stone with the old many-cornered words. *Fair hand of god, give us good fortune. Otherwise — Eli is here, God help us.* Cadell was a risk in this ritual as in kingship itself. His wife had left him years ago; he kept no mistress. Court rumor explained both with a choice of evils, but in truth Cadell had as few evils as virtues. He was never groomed for the *hual*, and Elisedd's choice of heavy-handed fostering had broken his spirit. But he knew the rite and he consented. As the king's priest Brys brought Cadell to stand on the king stone with its maze pattern uncovered and all but worn away.

Brys filled the silver chalice with herb-flavored liquor and blessed it. He gave it first to Cadell, who drank deeply and passed it to his right. Eli spoke for Elfæl, and Idris for Meirionydd. Lords were there from Cæreinion, Mechain, Arwystli, Mælienydd, most cantrefs of Powys. Two women from the earth houses gave unlooked-for allegiance. Garmon was in the north burying his son; at his cousin's wish, Brys spoke for Penllyn. The sanctuary's old silver chalice passed hand to hand until everyone had tasted the dark liquor.

Brys sang Cadell as a lord of truth and beauty in a fecund land of springing corn, teeming rivers, fruitful herds. The words were old beyond measure, older than Powys, from a time when the king danced this rite in a stag's antlers and the woman danced in a white dœ's hide. He sang the marriage of king with kingdom. Other voices gave him the responses and fell silent. He led Cadell from the kingstone to the springkeeper, who offered herself as sovereignty. Any failure would be devastating. Everyone was somber and quiet. A man lay with a woman under the sheltering trees of the sanctuary, a king lay with his kingdom. When it was consummated they both cried out, and a shiver ran around the witnesses. Cadell Powys had wed the land.

Afterward the springkeeper uncovered her horn lantern, and Brys saw a mild-faced woman with dark hair hanging to her waist over a pale dress. She set the *hual* on Cadell's neck, turned to the others, and said quietly, "There is fulfilment in the land. There is a lord. There is truth."

A DAY LATER, nine days after Brochfael's funeral rites, the consecrated *hual* lay on the altar of Meifod church as the procession approached from Mathrafal. The muddy track was bordered in early wildflowers. Monks carried a processional cross and the stag banner of Powys. Cadell, who would accept the *hual* a third time today, walked next between two bishops. Brys followed them with Gellan at his left and Idris Meirionydd at his right. Crooked Cadell managed to hold himself as straight as anyone could under the weight of stiff layered robes.

At the abbey gate the monks resumed their chant. The cross-bearer led them in past the whitewashed hostel and cells to the timber church. Monks, laborers, people from the court and outlying townships, court officers and travelers gathered near the yew-wreathed church door. The last plangent *Kyrie, eleison* fell away, and as Cadell stepped inside, the jubilant *alleluia* boomed around the painted church walls in many voices. Brys silently congratulated the abbey's song-master, who had a pœt's instinct for timing. The bishops of Meifod and Llanelwy led Cadell forward to the altar which gleamed with gold and silver. A few new pieces carried Heilyn's enamelling or Meirwen's engraved interlace. Brys kneeled with the others, bowing his head under the bishops' murmur of prayer. He absorbed the psalms, the incense, the perfume of beeswax tapers, the echo from the porch where a priest repeated the prayer for people gathered outside. The Meifod bishop turned to speak of the king's consecration to God, placed the *hual* and anointed Cadell Powys.

"*Vivat rex in æternum, Cadell Rex Gratia Dei Pouisi, in nomine Domini.*"

"*In nomine Domini,*" the response came back.

"So be it."

The bishop nodded at Idris Meirionydd, who went to kneel at Cadell's feet. Cadell raised him, and Idris spoke the king's obligations to his people. Cadell repeated them and added his own oath of service. He hesitated once, but it could pass for effect. Next he raised Gellan, who buckled on him the jeweled sword of Elisedd, which usually lay in the treasury.

A monk handed Brys a carved oak staff, cautiously, as though in the *pencerdd*'s hands it might burst into flames or flowers. Cadell raised him, and he gave the king the staff for eloquence, wisdom and generosity. Brys began the genealogies that supported Cadell's *braint,* his right to rule Powys. Cadell met his eye and smiled suddenly as though they shared a joke, nearly startling Brys from his place in the chain of generations. He recovered, speaking to Cadell but throwing his voice to the corners of the church and beyond, and invoked the ancient honors and rights of Powys in service of prosperity and peace. The bishop nodded when he was done and resumed his mass. Brys kneeled on the fragrant new rushes, head bowed, wishing it were all as easy as prayer.

Blessing and dismissal. Meifod abbey's great square bell of bronze clanged, and across the three-river plain the Mathrafal chapel bell answered. Cadell Powys walked among his people, whose hands reached out to touch their king for luck. Brys stood at his king's shoulder, blinking in the bright sunlight and praying again silently. *Maybe he can succeed. Let him succeed.*

The valley was alive with birds, and spring washed the air.

23 March 795 + Mathrafal

Eleven of twelve cantref lords came to Cadell's first council at the end of March. Curiosity brought them, Brys thought, leaning on the council chamber wall; he usually put a wall at his back these days when Gellan was near. He watched Cadell Powys fidget at the door while Eli, sleek and golden, charmed the nobles. It was the first council Eli had attended since Elisedd died.

The steward rapped his staff for silence and they found places at the table. Cadell Powys sat at the end of the table looking ill-at-ease despite a new blue silk shirt and the *hual.* He had a stack of parchment and scrolls before him like a clerk. Candlelight caressed Cynddylan's splendid old torc as Eli took the chair at the opposite end. *Neatly done. Now which is the table's head?* Gellan quickly took the chair at Eli's right, and three southern lords clustered near. The steward looked queasy, all but wringing his hands at this frayed protocol.

So let's reverse things again. Brys caught the steward's eye and walked forward to hold chairs at Cadell's end of the table for Idris and Garmon, then the other northern lords, making it a lesson in Powys geography. Idris coughed, trying not to smile. Brys sat at Garmon's right hand, halfway along the table. Let them puzzle over that. It was not a solution; it was a challenge. North Powys and South Powys, facing each other across an expanse of gleaming waxed wood. In Cynddylan's time they had faced each other across shield rims.

Now what? Brochfael had held councils at first, trying to lighten Elisedd's tyranny, but he called fewer and fewer as Offa's attacks grew more savage. Offa wasn't his only reason. Every Powys dunghill had a lord, and every lord loudly claimed rights and privileges. In the southern kingdoms, elders held councils, advised their kings and went about their business. Powys, like a runaway horse, needed to be curbed. Elisedd had understood that, Brys once heard in a rare admission from Brochfael. The steward went out, looking glad to escape.

"Cynfarch, You have done well as my father's *pencerdd,*" said Cadell without preamble, looking not at Brys but at Eli. *For approval? For prompting? That alone is enough to chill the blood.* Cadell didn't make decisions. He ignored his father's chief adviser Idris. Brys had waited two weeks asking for, but not getting, an hour's talk without Eli murmuring in Cadell's other ear. "I want you to continue."

Brys nodded, stunned by the clumsiness. *Do you remotely understand what I was doing?* He fought down the temptation to ask. Cadell wasn't stupid, just graceless. A competition between invited pœts was the correct procedure, but too late now. A king might ask but not command a *pencerdd. I can make you or break you, and if you bruise my honor it's an easy choice.*

"This is for you." Cadell slid a parchment scroll down the table. "Will you do it?"

Trying to buy me like a whore? Let's see the coin. Brys read and was suddenly coldly angry. This showed Eli's touch; it was a deed to an estate near Llandderfel in Penllyn. Bloody Elisedd had seized Garth Teyrnog from Brys's grandfather's kingdom, enslaving free tenants, plundering the hall, raping the steward's daughter. Penllyn did not forget. To have this tossed across the table now . . . Brys held the scroll open long enough for Garmon to read. Garmon said nothing but his breathing changed.

"I cannot accept your gift, lord," Brys said quietly. Cadell looked distressed. He didn't even see that it was an insult and an attempt to set Brys at Garmon. From the corner of his eye Brys saw Eli shake his head slowly, and under the table his cousin nudged his ankle. *Patience, Garmon.* "I cannot accept it myself. But I gratefully accept on behalf of Llanfor abbey. I'll grant the estate in your name and in the name of my lord and kinsman Garmon Penllyn. And I will continue as your pœt. We can talk tomorrow." *Without any of your eager advisers. I hope.*

Cadell nodded and smiled, still oblivious. Let Eli chew on that. Across the table, Idris decided not to wipe the sweat trickling down his heavy face. Things could get exciting.

Worse than exciting, Brys thought an hour later. *Heartstopping.* He listened to Cadell Powys flounder under his nobles' questions about the British alliance which Brys could easily have answered. Then he wanted to know what ores came from the mines on Halkyn ridge in Tegeingl.

Owain Tegeingl, whose cantref was still flirting with Powys as well as Gwynedd, looked at the new king for a moment in pure astonishment. He flattened both hands on the tabletop reflections of the candle sconces, and for a dark little man prone to sudden humor and rages, he spoke with precision and restraint. Owain explained that his landowners, some of them English settlers who served as border watch and travelers' guides, sold some Halkyn lead to Tamworth mint and forged some silver into currency rods.

"And Chester?" Cadell was tearing at a hangnail. "Do we trade there?"

Where was Cadell when Gwriad offered Mercia special tariffs? Brochfael's oversight was stunning. But Brys bit his tongue instead of leaping in.

Owain looked at Cadell closely, as though waiting for the joke. "Chester is our main port for Ireland and Mercia. Our traders deal there under sanction and escort." Owain read Cadell's blank look and went on. "Trade rights are granted from Tamworth, usually on request, with a toll. We counter that with tariffs on trade into Powys. Both have dropped as a result of British alliance and Mercian treaty. The port supplies a Mercian guide and witness. It's the same kind of arrangement West Saxons have in Gwent and Frisians have in London. We get fair treatment in Chester."

"A city lost through Gwynedd treachery," Eli said in a low vibrant voice which carried admirably. *A hundred and eighty years ago!* This was the most bizarre and frightening thing Brys had heard yet.

"A wealthy city," Cadell said, keeping his eyes down and toying with a scroll.

"A wealthy Mercian city," said Owain too loudly.

"Chester was always ours. We'll raise the tariff and — tell Offa to lower the toll," said the king hesitantly.

And cantref Tren was ours, once, before events converged to shatter the old Powys. Do you plan to ask Offa for cantref Tren too? Sing fair Cynddylan from his dark burial and Heledd the wanderer from her last sanctuary? Don't ask me to make the song. If I could sing up the dead this room would be full. Brys shivered. A draft through the window shutters, and the sound of three rivers flowing east through the fair broad plain. Brys was again looking into a wavering candle flame and again was listening to Mæn's voice in the sanctuary: *When you need to, you'll remember.*

Cadell, incredibly, was talking about Dyfed. All this was starting to make ugly sense. Eli was leading the new king to his own destruction; the sooner he fell, the sooner Eli would take over. Sitting there in Cynddylan's archaic boar-headed torc of South Powys, at his own head of the table, he was ready to be king on a minute's notice. *Not while I live.*

"— Maredudd asks for military aid against Irish raiders in Dyfed."

Egbert's present refuge. Brys said quickly, stung from his restraint, "When have you ever heard of Irish raiders in Dyfed?"

"Now our pœt is a strategist," Gellan chuckled.

"Survival is the best strategy," Brys said. "For the survivor. I await your next lesson, commander."

"You won't wait long." Gellan turned and looked at him across the table, perhaps for the first time since Brochfael's death. His pupils were dilated in the dim light, so only a thin well of pale grey surrounded them, and his mouth was a slash; it was a lethal expression.

"The Irish don't raid Dyfed — Maredudd and his family are half Irish," Brys told Cadell. "Worry instead about these northern barbarians who burned Lindisfarne monastery two years ago, killing the monks at their own altar. They drive their keels upriver, strike at midnight and take to the sea by dawn. We may see them here — but not the Irish."

Cadell Powys stared at his own busy hands on the table. Another hangnail, or the same one? He made it bleed and shoved his hands out of sight in his lap. He had twisted in his chair so that his silk shirt rucked up behind his neck. *You haven't thought it through, my friend. Who offered you this neat package? Tear one corner, and out spill maggots.*

But Cadell redeemed himself when Eli put forward the last item, saying a kinsman of Caradog asked to marry Nest, making a useful tie with Gwynedd. At whose suggestion? Brys found Eli's eyes on him, waiting. He made sure he yielded no reaction.

"Nest is twelve and full of life, this man is forty and a sour malcontent. I want her to marry a younger man, someone she likes," Cadell said plainly. "And I want my son Cyngen back in Mathrafal."

Brys saw Eli's smile slip and recover at that. Cadell was a puzzle. He rarely mentioned his children. *Concern for your daughter's happiness but poison and a deadly hunting party for your son? A strange collection of fragments you make. Do I know you at all?*

Cadell struggled on through the gritty sediment of law, tax, court administration and trade. Finally he spread his hands in a gesture intended to show they were done; it only proclaimed his helplessness. In the silent room, Brys heard a candle wick hissing against molten wax and the snarl of winter's last wind outside the shutters.

At midnight, barred with the skeletal shadow of an apple tree in the chapel garth, Idris spoke quietly. This was one of the safer places to talk in Mathrafal. "Cadell likes you. He hasn't many friends."

"He has more than he needs now. Men who never gave him a thought before, all dancing attendance."

Idris looked like someone with a broken tooth, unable to stop worrying at it but getting no pleasure from doing so. His hair was still thick under his gold diadem but more than half white now, and his face had weathered to a tolerant cynicism. *You'll watch the game out with those hard blue eyes, probably pack up the board on the rest of us players.*

The moon hung in a low branch, brightening the cloud which drifted across it like sheep's wool pulled on a thorn. The grass was bone cold even through bootsoles, pale with a light spring frost. Idris stretched for a dry leaf clinging to a high branch and crumbled it between his fingers.

"In a night he's unpicked the weave of Brochfael's lifetime. We warned Brochfael to give him some preparation, in case . . ." Idris opened his hand, scattering the powdered leaf across the night.

"Cyngen." Brys watched an owl glide overhead. She banked briefly to inspect them with great golden eyes, pale light washing her spread wings. *No prey here, sister, and nothing to scavenge. Not yet.* She slid west, out toward the open plain of Mathrafal. "We must not let him return."

"My youngest son leads a wild life." Idris let his gaze follow the owl. "A week's prayer will do him good. And the sea air. Perhaps at Tywyn monastery."

"Prayer and a message by ship to Cyngen in Bro Waroch?"

Idris nodded. "But, dear God — Cadell insulting Offa. Think of his ridiculous letter about Chester on top of border fighting last month. Offa has a nervous sword hand at the best of times. He's been distracted lately by Charles, but they say Alcuin has nearly convinced them both to mend their quarrel. Maybe if we sent a delegation to Charles — No. He hates the British."

"Leave Offa to me," Brys said quietly.

"Dangerous." Idris twitched his cloak forward and looked up under thick black brows. *Brochfael's badger. Brochfael's counselor, as I was Brochfael's pœt. But we still serve Powys.*

"Think of harvest, Idris. August. Heat haze on the cornfields, mountain streams down to a trickle, lying with a girl in the long grass. I won't give it all up for a treacherous maggot and a pretender in a gold collar. It's time to think of survival."

Idris smiled a little. "Survive, then. But watch your back in Mercia."

"Offa's not the gravest danger. We'd all do better to watch our backs in Powys." *You know a great deal. What else do you know? All the rest are dead now.* "Idris. Why did he have my father killed at Cær Gai?"

"If you know that, you know why." Idris was quiet a long time. "What do you remember?"

More than I want. A man running away, pushing through the crowded Lammas fair, a stranger. My father's torn throat, bright red blood spurting under my hands. Trying to stop it, I couldn't even slow it . . . life rushing out in waves like the tide. My mother, dry-eyed in shock. They were lovers to the end. Oh merciful God. "Not much."

Idris turned his face to the occluded moon. "Brochfael talked your father around. Eli realized he was betrayed. I think he sent a killer."

"No." *Don't lie to me, Meirionydd. I'm not a child. I haven't been since that day.*

"It's as close to truth as you'll ever hear now." Idris walked out of the chapel garth. Brys followed him onto the boardwalk. "Let it be, Cynfarch."

Footfalls sounded behind them. Idris looked past his shoulder. Brys turned and saw Garmon, quiet on his feet for a man sinking heavily into middle years.

And why are you here, cousin? A small wind moaned south out of hilly Mechain, and from the chapel a homespun monk came out yawning to sound the Nocturne.

"Good work," Garmon said under the bronze clamor and dropped a thick arm across Brys's shoulders. "So you're staying."

Brys heard the emphasis shift in his words. If these two pillars of Brochfael's Powys planned to leave Mathrafal, perhaps it was too late now. "You're not staying?"

"Myself," said Idris, sparing Garmon, "I may soon find that I'm urgently needed in Meirionydd. You'd be wise to do the same, Cynfarch. Go to Gwynedd or Manaw, let all this die down. Remember. If things get out of hand, I'll be in Tywyn."

"You can't shelter exiles in Meirionydd, Idris." Brys tested it.

"No. Not in cantref Meirionydd."

But in the kingdom of Meirionydd . . . Brys understood.

"Garmon?"

"I see to my own people first," Garmon said.

Meirionydd and Penllyn, the first fracture lines? The first kingdoms carved out of what was briefly a strong Powys? Twelve Powys cantrefs could drift into twelve warring kingdoms, each barely a spit across, and ultimately twelve English territories. Tren was already called Wreocansæte. *First we lose our names, then our rights and honors. Then we lose even the idea of a kingdom of Powys.*

"Cynfarch." Garmon found a long splinter on the edge of a board and pried at it with his boot. "That girl you asked about. It seems Eli has another daughter after all, a bastard. I'm told she's with the nuns in Llanfair."

Brys nodded thanks. Idris walked on a few paces, creaking the frosted boardwalk. The moon rode out from cloud like a blossoming thorn branch. It gave Idris a diadem of silver in place of gold and silvered his barrel shoulders and the last black in his hair.

"Lord Idris, cousin Garmon." Wormwood words, bitter on the tongue. "Stay. Don't break Powys apart. We can survive this if we act together."

"Tell me that next year, Cynfarch." Idris walked on. Garmon embraced him in silence and followed. Brys could read the marginal note: *If we're all alive.*

3 April 795 ✝ Mathrafal

After morning training Heilyn woke suddenly in the curve of Brys's arm. Sweet Savior, he wasn't supposed to fall asleep. It was the only time Brys was unwatched. Guards prowled outside all night, against Brys's orders but following Elgan's, and friends were at hand all other times.

Brys lifted his arm. "Work late last night? Or have you found another lover?"

"One's enough." Heilyn sat up yawning. "No hot water?"

"Your turn to heat it." Brys propped his head on his elbow. "Dœs it bother you?"

"Sharing? No." That surprised even Heilyn sometimes.

Brys closed his eyes. "Why can't I give Meirwen a baby?"

Heilyn, recognizing a rhetorical question, rose to stir up the banked fire. Meirwen said she was barren, but there were also his brother's dead children, his dead sister with her stillborn child, the eldest brother who died unwed.

Meirwen was at the sanctuary upstream this morning, no doubt arguing with the priest about theology. Why not? She argued with him about enamelling and with Brys about pœtry. Meirwen never failed to surprise Heilyn. He had watched first Cyngen, then Rhirid, try to seduce her. Cyngen got a sisterly talk. Rhirid got a burn scar on his hand. Brys got everything except the child that he, not just Meirwen, wanted. Come to think of it, that was more likely why she was up at the sanctuary. Not arguing theology, arguing medicine, which he reckoned was as close as Meirwen came to prayer.

Time for some slave meddling. As he laid new wood on the hearth, Heilyn asked carefully over his shoulder, "Did you ever think of having someone turn the curse?"

"It's nothing. A song that went around the ale houses."

"Part of you believes it. You were twelve years old and everything fell apart in one year. What did it say?"

Brys opened his eyes and looked at the thatch. "When we save from destruction the house that destroyed us, we're free of the curse. Sentimental nonsense. Bad verse too."

"Radiant god. What house?"

"I need your help." Brys sat up suddenly. "Where's our parchment and ink?"

Spring sunshine reached tentatively into the courtyard an hour later. Swallows rolled in the air overhead, translucent shoots probed up through the thin yellow grass and the apple tree was bursting with buds. Heilyn sat beneath it, working at a chunk of wood with his knife. Turning, marking, shaving off long curls that would brighten the fire tonight. The parchment still lay blank, the ink jar was stoppered, the quill fluttered on the grass with each breath of wind.

"What is it? A drinking cup?" asked Brys.

"Would I waste apple heartwood on a cup, when I can get by with Ravenna rainbow glass instead?" Heilyn mocked gently. "It's a mallet head. Meirwen needs a new one to raise her silver chalice for Meifod monastery. She needs just the right shape to raise the rim. The abbot liked the hanging bowl in the chapel."

"You two probably outweigh Mathrafal treasury by now."

"I hear that's easily done." Heilyn saw no point in asking what help Brys wanted. They'd get to it eventually in his lefthanded way. But did he want help from the smith? The slave? His bodyguard man? His English spy? His friend?

"More's the pity. Cadell sent a letter to Tamworth this morning," Brys said quietly, though no one could overhear. He picked up long curls of ruddy wood as they fell from Heilyn's knife. "Accusing Offa of conspiring to break the border. He can't grasp that the destroyed village was English, under Powys protection, and he made noises about raising trade tariffs. Offa will laugh himself sick."

"Offa's more inclined to revenge than humor. Brorda dœs his laughing for him. Cenwulf and his brothers do his killing." Heilyn leaned to blow small coils of shaved wood from his work. They flew across the pale grass and lay trembling.

"Brorda. You hate him."

"Brorda's a man of justice and compassion. They say. His landowners in Elfed revere him. Alcuin writes to him from Charles' court in Aachen for advice, and the only other advice Alcuin asks is God's. A dubious honor for both God and Brorda." Heilyn slicked the knife blade across his thigh and tested the edge cautiously with a thumb. Still sharp. "But he played me against my own fear and greed and sent me here under threat of death."

"Ruthless."

"No doubt that's a virtue for Offa's minister."

"What's his view of Powys, do you think?"

"Don't kick the hive, fence the beeyard. It's Offa's view, but Brorda adds compassion. His daughter married into a British family. Many of his nobles and landowners are British."

"I know." Brys absently watched the steady scrape of the knife-blade without seeing it.

Brorda. So that's what you want to know. "You want to write Brorda a letter telling him Offa should ignore Cadell's ill-advised nonsense, that you're working on him, that he'll smarten up."

"No. Yes." Brys put his face in his hands, a rare gesture. "More than that. Heilyn, would you throw away hundreds of lives to save thousands — ?"

Heilyn waited, knowing there would be more. This was not a rhetorical question.

"— and maybe aid a creature like Cenwulf by doing it?"

"Yes." *If I found the courage for such a choice — then I'd slit Cenwulf's lying throat as a service to humankind.* "So what do you want to say?"

As they talked, Brys combed both hands through his damp hair, which only made it curl more fiercely. It was getting long. Time to borrow scissors again.

"Good. We can write it now."

"Don't sign it."

"It needs all the weight I can give it."

"You could always sign it Alcuin."

"There's a thought." An attempt at a smile.

Heilyn set down the apple heartwood, sheathed his knife, and took up the pen. Brys spelled out the unfamiliar words. The second draft looked good enough to send, so he copied it from the wax tablet to parchment in his best hand.

Brys lay back on the grass, head in hands. "Remind me. What's the English word for hero?"

Heilyn told him three words. "There are dozens. Why?"

"A different one."

"Hæleth —"

"Yes! That's the one."

"— means warrior more than hero."

"Listen —" Brys sat up abruptly. "Hæleth in English. Heledd in British."

"Close, not identical." Heilyn said. "The English sound is broader, and the ending is harder. Do you want them to sound the same?"

"I want to know why they do sound the same. Close anyway." Brys got up and started pacing the courtyard, thinking out loud. "What dœs *heledd* mean?"

"Something about salt. A place where you dig salt, I think."

"A salt pit. What dœs salt mean? Anything that comes to mind. Quickly. Don't think."

"Trade. Work. Slaves. Blood. Sweat. Semen. Tears. Precious goods. Conservation. Cooking. The woman who looked back and was turned to salt. Sorrow—" Heilyn ran dry.

Brys sat down crosslegged in front of him again and was silent. For an unnerving length of time he twisted his new signet, the tree with ravens that Meirwen and Heilyn had cast in gold, around and around his thumb. Heilyn went back to carving Meirwen's mallet, paying no attention. Another lefthanded conversation. He would get to the point in his own good time.

"Mair mother of God," Brys said eventually. "Was her mother English, married to Cyndrwyn as a peaceweaver? Cadwallon Gwynedd married Penda's sister, they say. Why wouldn't Cyndrwyn Powys marry another sister? And all of her children were blond. Cynddylan and his brothers. Heledd. Wulfhere killed his own cousins. Avenging the insult—because she refused to marry him. Good choice, my girl."

Heilyn put down mallet and knife. "You're starting to believe your own story. You told me her name was Elen ferch Cyndrwyn but you thought she should be called Heledd instead. Salt. Tears. Hero. Brys, you're falling in love with a woman who's been dead for a century."

Brys grinned. "I had a dream."

"More than one, I assure you. You still talk in your sleep."

"But what dœs it mean?"

"It means—" *For one thing, there are too many women in your life. Meirwen, Heledd, Nest, the others who send small gifts and invitations. And you're slightly addled, just as we all thought.* But Heilyn saw real distress and answered soberly. "What do you think?"

"I think I should go to Llandegla for the cure."

That wasn't at all what he thought, from his expression. Heilyn decided it was time to be rational. "Let us suppose that the holy well dœs cure epilepsy or at least unusual dreams. You might banish a true sending. If it is a true sending, no doubt you're receiving it for a reason. You're meant to do something."

"You don't believe in those things."

"Did I believe the lady Madron washing at the ford?" Even the thought made him shudder.

"Sunt geminæ somni portæ," Brys said.

"Latin. Something about doors. Go on."

"Virgil's Æneid, sixth book. The gates of sleep are twinned. One is of horn, giving easy exit to true spirits. The other shines in flawless ivory, through which the dead send false dreams to the living."

"Which gate do you have your ear to, horn or ivory, is that what you're asking me?"

"Yes." Brys looked elfshot, as the English said, as though he'd seen his own ghost.

"Brys—" *Only you can answer that. You're the priest. Ask Mæn Pedr who understands such matters. Ask Father Bened, who will cast out your beloved demon. Go to Llandegla. Leave off this business.* Heilyn knew those answers were wasted breath. Meet madness with madness. "Have you asked Heledd?"

"Heledd won't tell me. On the border when they killed Brochfael. You came over after me. What did you see?"

"You were lying face up on the ground beside your horse. Your eyes were open. I thought you were dead." He tried to say it lightly.

Brys gripped his wrist. "Nothing else?"

"I wasn't looking—I saw the English warband, a few spear casts into Mercia, marching east. Two on horseback had almost caught up."

"Yes. Describe them."

Heilyn squinted up into the apple branches, trying to call back the bare glimpse. "A man in chain mail. A boy wearing yellow."

"Gate of horn." Brys touched his cheek. He looked all right now, not addled at all. "A girl wearing yellow silk. I've got to free her. I promised."

Brys stamped the sealing wax with his signet. Heilyn considered asking if there could be an easier way to do any of these things, guessed the answer, and held his peace.

That afternoon in the sacristy Brys looked at fresh ink stains on his hand and down at the parchment with the text for Brochfael's memorial stone. This time he was the clerk and at Bened's command.

"Whœver shall read this handwritten stone, let him speak benediction on the soul of Brochfael mab Elisedd mab Gwallog, who held his patrimony of Powys with—" He glanced up frowning. "Not 'the sword.' 'The Grace of God'?"

Bened sat with his hands folded across his stomach, watching the hazel tree sway outside the sacristy window. A thrush settled like a stippled leaf on the sill, lilted a compact *englyn* of song, and lifted again into the air.

"Grace of God is as good as any other easy phrase."

"*Gratia Dei.* You doubt my Latin, Father."

"*Super animam,* not *anima.* I not only doubt it, I despair of it."

"Do we put your name on this?"

"Name and pride are your preserve, Cynfarch," Bened snapped. "I am a simple priest."

And what is your preserve? Righteousness and quick temper? Who hears your confession, little man? Bened took great satisfaction in being a king's confessor. Brys lifted one eyebrow as he dipped the quill for the last words and glanced up to see Bened color. But ascetics were rare these days. Bened's austerity lay in owning only one estate, wearing somber colors and refusing to hunt on saints' days.

"As a simple priest," Brys suggested, "you'd be under scrutiny for putting your name on it instead of your bishop's. The *pencerdd*'s name is more expedient—*Hoc lapidem Conmarch pinxit.*"

"A bitter tongue, Cynfarch. Complaining of the church, a heretic. I've warned you once you'll be excommunicated if you keep pagan rites." Bened was working his way to anger. So it was the kingmaking that ailed him.

"We keep custom, Father." Brys leaned back in the chair, the wording for the memorial stone forgotten on the table, and smiled at the priest. "Powys is the oldest kingdom in Britain, whatever people say in Pictland or Gwynedd."

Bened blinked his pale lashes and looked angrily away. "The English sacrifice white horses and eat the flesh, and hang their unwanted children in ash groves. That's custom too. I expect penitence and a disavowal of this apostate savagery. Hell burns for eternity, my son."

"Yes, Father." Another quarrel, another tentative milepost toward something like tolerance. Bened should be much angrier. But he'd already confessed two kings of this supposed sin of wedding the land. Maybe he was getting used to the idea. Crimson and scowling under his rusty tonsure, he loved argument only slightly less than he loved God. *A little provocation, then.* "If it's the flaming lake of hell again, give me radiant Lleu who suffered in an oak tree for his people."

Bened hissed and crossed himself. *Too much.*

"Bened, if you cast out every woman who has her children blessed at a spring, you won't have a flock. If I took your narrow view—"

"Don't you see the risk to your immortal soul?"

"I fear more for my mortal body." Brys pulled the parchment near again and dipped the pen. Too near the truth, it spoiled a fine argument. He drew the letters round and open for the stone carver to copy. "*In æternum.* When will the mason cut the pillar?"

"Meifod has a blank ready, but the mason's working in Lichfield until midsummer," Bened said absently. "Do you really—"

"No." Brys got to his feet and shoved the stopper in the ink jar, then laid the pen neatly alongside it on the scoured sacristy table. He looked at his smeared left hand. *Better avoid monastic life. In an hour they'd have me out of the scriptorium and into the turnip field.* As he turned to leave he saw Bened's anxious face shaped to speak but frozen in silence. Brys lowered his eyes, one hand on the door latch, and turned back to face the room. "Father, give me your blessing."

Bened sighed and crossed the sacristy to his book shelf. He came back with a carved ivory box the size of his palm and delicately lifted out a blackened wood splinter. Brys kneeled and bowed his head. The priest marked the points of the cross with a murmured prayer. All the slivers of the true cross, if assembled, would provide enough timber to build a fleet of ships to sail to Jerusalem. But why say so?

"So be it."

"Cynfarch. Remember the olive branch."

"It dœsn't grow in Britain, Father." Brys got to his feet and for an instant rested his hands lightly on Bened's stooped shoulders. "*Duw gennyt.*"

"Cynfarch." He hesitated and flushed an even deeper red. "That honey salve. A small pot would be welcome."

"Maybe you'd also like instructions for mixing it? It's excellent for keeping poison from wounds and sores." Mæn Pedr, always seeking better relations with the church, would be pleased.

Bened nodded thanks and disappeared back into his sacristy. But the priest's troubled look stayed with Brys through the outer room, where a clerk dozed at his writing table in a cataract of spring sunshine.

Outside in the gable overhang, a handful of the king's bodyguard fell silent. They were men of Rhirid's first squadron, Gellan's men. He heard a few quiet words, laughter, mimicry of a crow cawing. Brys greeted them, and they nodded awkwardly, trapped in their mockery. *I could raise satire, barbed and sleek-shafted, to pierce any one of you, or drop a raven shadow across your face lefthanded. But a curse, like a misflown falcon, always comes back to trouble its sender.*

Nest ferch Cadell waited in the writing room. She was already tuning his sea-cat harp at her shoulder while her old nurse looked about suspiciously. Nest loved his mythical beast with its ringing voice, and he hadn't the heart to banish her to the buzzing horsehair-strung student harp. Not that it mattered now. Barely begun, already finished. She would go north tomorrow with Adwen to Anghenell's monastery, out of Cadell's reach and Eli's. It was best, but he would miss her brown fingers on his bronze strings. Brys listened to her lessons and smiled. Nest had Cyngen's discipline, Tegwy's passion and a clear singing voice. Her shining brown hair was coiled over her ears, framing an oval face. Grey eyes under long lashes, a sweetly curved mouth. *Little hawk, do you still dream of warrior queens?*

"I have a gift for you." Brys took the sea-cat from her and opened a storage chest. His gift was still hidden. Nest would have looked, but not too persistently under her nurse's eyes. He pulled out the new harp and put it in her hands, then sat on the writing table, smiling, to watch her discover it. Bronze strings, who would have anything else after hearing them? The soundbox was ornamented with three-armed sunwheels, and he'd had interlace carved down the front of the pillar, a two-headed tailless fish with bronze nailhead eyes. "It's a *gwyniad,* our Penllyn fish."

"I'll learn all of Taliesin's songs." Nest looked up with shining eyes. "I'll practise twice a day."

"Taliesin might be a little bloodthirsty for the nuns. And one practice will do." Brys kept a straight face. *Don't promise what you can't give. The sisters will have other plans.* Thank God abbess Anghenell was a civilized woman who wouldn't try to break Nest's spirit.

There was a knock at the door, then the voice of her escort from the bodyguard. A king's daughter faced threats beyond murder. If she were raped, she married the rapist or took vows. Either way she ceased to be a piece in the game and left the board. Wood-wisdom was on his mind today after writing that letter. *Fair hand of god, that letter.* "Now you must go, Nest."

The nurse clumped off down the colonnade, belaboring the guard about their travel preparations. Nest slung her instrument at her back like any harper and paused at the door. Only a few fingers shorter than Brys, she was growing like a river willow. Tears brimmed in her eyes, ready to spill, and whatever she wanted to say her father's pœt didn't need to hear.

"Go, little hawk."

Nest chose not to listen. She nudged the door with a tœ and put her arms around his neck. *No you don't, my girl. Not at thirteen.* But as Brys reached to dislodge her, she linked her fingers and kissed his mouth, softly and awkwardly. *Dear God.* Quickly he stepped back.

"Absolutely not," Brys said severely. "Do you want to see me beheaded before you leave?"

Nest's tears spilled. That was one reason he leaned against the closed door and pulled her into his arms to kiss her slowly and thoroughly as a desirable woman. She was a slender pliant shape pressing close, a mouth alive and warm. The intensity of his own desire for her took his breath and left him in terror. Suddenly there was one figure too many on the board. Nest left smiling.

Brys barred the door and sat a long time at the table with his head down on his arms, shivering like a birch leaf. *What have I done? Ask me, I know it. Set in motion something I may not be able to stop.*

5 April 795 + Rhayadr

Early this spring morning, when dippers were diving through and under the great falls in the river, a mountain wildcat sat in the young bracken. His brindled fur and the ringed tail curled around his forepaws made him part of the barred shadows, and his furious green eyes were almost the color of the new bracken fronds.

When the man stirred awake the wildcat crouched but didn't run. This was his territory. He watched the horse shift around, snorting nervously as the cat scent came downwind under the rush and spray of the waterfall. He watched the man get up, make fire and sear the fish he had captured last night. The wildcat opened his mouth a little at the smell. He waited.

After he ate, the man licked his hands and wiped them on the grass, then brought out a small flat piece of wood. It had a bright red spot on one side, and the man gave great attention to the red spot. He wanted to move it without killing it. Finally the piece of wood doubled into two pieces of wood. A smell of beeswax came from inside: marks were scratched into the beeswax.

The man's hand touched each mark, and he made meaningless sounds: *cynfarch the young woman you mention was withdrawn from llanfair monastery two years ago the abbess dœs not know where she is now she is his acknowledged bastard and eldest child her name is gwladus ferch eli yours in christ anghenell.*

The man lifted his shoulders, held a burning stick from the fire near the wood, and pressed the red spot hard with his hand. Before the shadows moved much farther he was on the horse's back and out of sight downstream.

The wildcat padded over and found the remains of the fish among the embers. Bones, fins, tail. The man had left nothing. He pissed on it and leaped away with a howl of rage as steam spat at his back legs. He stalked slowly into the bracken, sniffing carefully at each frond, so that no watcher would think him afraid of fire.

The coughing fit lasted longer this time. Offa, mottled and enraged, wiped his mouth with the square of linen. No blood this time. "Well?"

Brorda searched for a discreet way to suggest the elder king should go to bed and call the Spanish physician. He hesitated too long.

"Gather your wits," snapped Offa. At the writing table he perched like a predator, yellow-skinned and fierce, clawing his parchments into orderly piles and scattering them into new disorder. Not a Mercian eagle, this creature of prey; perhaps a merlin, slow to reconnoitre and quick to stoop for the kill. "Next?"

Egfrith looked up from his shadowed corner, caught Brorda's eye and nodded. Between his father's outbursts and spells of coughing, he was scratching words on a parchment scrap, maybe notes for his planned Mercian supplement to Bede's history.

Dawn had flooded Tamworth an hour ago and they were still deep in reports from the reeve, an earlier handful of officials and priests, and Leoba who had left a few minutes ago. Called without ceremony from their beds to advise the king on Irish port tolls or the Northumbrian king's new mistress, no one refused Offa's summons. Outside, beyond the shuttered window and barred doors and pacing guards, stablemen already called to each other over the clip of hooves on cobbles as they took the horses out for exercise. At the distant river, the water mill began its creaking rumble. Shouted orders came faintly from the parade ground where the bodyguard men were at early training.

Dawn, and they were still mired in yesterday's administration. One day the work would quietly stretch from one sunset to the next, but Offa would never notice until he dropped. His tireless energy was waning but he was driving harder than ever, harder than his body could tolerate. Offa knew his time was short and he wanted Egfrith's succession to be certain. Brorda, whose old slave last week lifted his heels and ran away with the wife of a traveling Kentish leatherworker, could tell him nothing was ever certain. And now there was this riddle to answer. He handed Offa the folded parchment.

"Almighty God, they've all gone mad." Offa read it a second time and threw it down. "What is this document?"

"As you see, it's a letter written in Latin by an English scribe and signed with great flourish by a British noble," said Brorda calmly. Since its sender was a lettered man who spoke English, all this was a message in itself: a neutral language, English help at his disposal and a reminder of his power.

"How many names dœs he need for everyday use?" Offa scowled and shoved the parchment to Egfrith across the table. The younger king read it and gave it back to Brorda.

"Three," said Egfrith sleepily. "His father was a sub-king put down by Brochfael, his grandfather was a king: and he is ambitious."

"How ambitious?" Ambition always seized Offa's full attention.

"He is not of the royal kindred." Brorda hoped the answer would satisfy Offa, who had less grasp of *Wealisc* ways, better than it did him. He stared grainily at the Latin, remembered Egfrith telling him that the British had hated the Romans when they were in Britain but now thought they were Romans.

"What dœs he want then?"

"With this letter?" Egfrith asked absently. "Read it again, Brorda."

"Greetings, good wishes, a reminder that I promised to play a board game with him and now we're well begun," Brorda interpreted. It was all somewhat nonchalant for a clear act of treason. Offa beheaded men for less. "West Saxon war this summer unless you leash your wolves and drive the prince from Rheinwg. Treachery here will cross silver and knock three kings off the board. No sanctuary for the raven. Cynfarch mab Cadeyrn mab Teyrnog Penllyn, *pencerdd* Powys, bardd Cadell."

"Lunatic babble," said Offa irritably. "What is he, a pœt?"

"More than that," said Egfrith, who understood the British. "Pœt, historian, envoy, priest, right hand and voice. King and *pencerdd* live at each other's mercy."

"You remember him? Brochfael's hostage." Brorda propped his head on his hands. His eyes were full of sleep; he was tired to the marrow of his bones.

"You sent a man after him. Their damned alliance." Offa's own gathering of nations depended on conquest, not consent. He twisted in his chair, provoked by this freakish overturn of his calculated order, and suddenly laughed in a dry snort. "You wasted your silver. You could have written him a letter."

"I wasted time, not silver. I got poor information, then no information, then polite apology from my smith that there was nothing to say about a nonexistent threat. He sent the silver back from Aberffraw."

"With interest?" Offa asked, sniffing for blood. Egfrith stared into the hissing oil lamp's flame and yawned with his mouth closed.

Brorda shrugged. It was all long past; they had other things to worry about now. But why had Cynfarch risked this letter? He was afraid, and there must be some good reason. *Think.*

"Idiot Cadell didn't approve this letter, not after writing insolent threats under royal seal," said Offa. "We could send it to him in answer."

Brorda looked thoughtfully at the folded parchment. "There's meaning in this. Listen. There will be war in Wessex this summer unless you control your troublemakers and drive Egbert out of Rheinwg. That's part of Dyfed in the southwest. Egbert's a guest there. Treachery here will cross silver . . . "

"Treachery where?" demanded Offa.

"Powys. Egbert was courting one of their discontented southern nobles." He scrubbed at his face, driving off the sleep that stalked him, then froze with his hands still raised. "My God. Think of the diversion."

Brorda stared blindly, knowing his delay whipped Offa to rage. The king hadn't learned patience in sixty-odd years, and it was late in the day for new lessons.

"Stop ravelling. Speak."

"Rebellion. What if they staged simultaneous risings, this South Powys noble in Mathrafal and Egbert in Winchester? Listen again. Wolves in Mercia means some unnamed rebels here. Silver boundaries, as between the squares on a gameboard. I think he means the border. We had a rash of border raids last year and another incident last month just before Brochfael's death. He thinks they'll start trouble first on the border between Powys and Mercia. Egbert is their captain. If we knock him out we can control it. That's what he's telling us. Bring down Egbert."

Offa was leaning forward on the table with fingers spread over his narrow gold crown and thumbs probing the hollow above his eyes. Pain again. It meant sending for the Spaniard, over the usual objections from the king. But Offa looked up calmly. "There's only one way to drive Egbert out of Dyfed — how, Egfrith?"

Egfrith had learned his father's catechism well. "Tempt him."

Offa smiled grimly. This was his favorite game. "And Cadell needs a lesson in the virtues of diplomacy. He'll learn it best as a sub-king."

"Remember the battle at Akenfeld — in Powys they call it Mæs Derwen. It was a near thing," Brorda warned wearily, for perhaps the hundredth time in ten years. "And the border is barely marked in the north."

"No sanctuary for the raven?" Egfrith glanced up.

"His own life is in danger. Or he risks his life to tell us this because of its importance."

"Why?" Offa was suspicious.

Why indeed? Brorda chanced a liberal interpretation of a talk two years ago. "He admires elements of your statecraft, lord. And he wants Powys to survive."

Offa snorted. "Strange allies. Get him out safe and give him lands. Somewhere we can control the cursed *Wealas* without fighting them. Wreocansæte, maybe."

Brorda agreed, since it was the easiest way to end discussion, knowing Cadell's pœt would see any such offer as a deadly insult. Egfrith, half amused, avoided his eye. Offa's minister dropped his head into his hands again, thinking about wolves. Wolves in general, wolves in metaphor, and specific wolves. And one particular half-pound of worked gold which went missing from the treasury two years ago. No one outside this room had official access. There was always unofficial access to anything, and some men were better at it than others.

"They must never regain their lowlands." Offa was thinking aloud. "Especially Cynddylan's old court at Pengwern."

"There's nothing there now," Egfrith said.

"All the more important then. The place has symbolic power," Offa snapped, an unusual perception from a pragmatic thinker. "And a powerful Powys threatens us."

No doubt that was the view when Mercia absorbed Elmesæte years ago, Brorda reflected. *Cut a small kingdom adrift, then absorb it, then slowly break down the rest.* Elmesæte, Elfed, had been a kingdom long before Penda's time, when Mercia was only the refuge of outlaws and border brigands, an ungovernable mixture of Powys adventurers and Anglian warlords fattened on Pengwern mead and Iâl beef. In an independent Elmesæte, Brorda would not be a Mercian *ealdorman* heeling to Mercian commands — but there were more important things. Peace first among them, then a vision of a greater polity. Penllyn to Powys, Elmesæte to Mercia. Prince to king, warriors in pursuit, all across the silver-channelled board.

Offa was studying him too benignly. His thoughts had wandered from the missing gold; in Offa's presence daydreaming was a dangerous error. What could he say? Only drop a name. "Several members of the *witan* council, among others, have received rich gifts from Cenwulf."

"Cenwulf will ask something in return, never fear." The king rubbed his bloodshot eyes. "He's never satisfied. Dangerous. Remember it," he threw across the room to his son. Yet another lesson.

Egfrith nodded, sparing needless words. He had set aside his diadem; his hair was ruffled like a child's. His own young son, six months old now, had hair as white as new cream. Egfrith smiled more and fretted less these days, even about Eadburh's abuses, but he was still a mild and thoughtful young man. Could he hold Mercia alone, after Offa? Probably, if he took his father's advice in some things, among them the handling of his distant cousin Cenwulf.

"Cenwulf has a year," said Offa.

They were silent a moment. A death sentence, a year for Cenwulf to curb his ambition or go the way of all the other rebels over four decades. But could even Offa bring down Cenwulf now? He had been drawing in younger sons and dispossessed men who had nothing to lose and everything to gain. If any man was worth cutting down before it was too late, it was Cenwulf. But then, God willing, no more.

"Cenwulf is a kinsman," said his son quietly. "His father's kindred was not powerful. He has prospered only with your generosity."

"All the more cause for his hatred."

Enough, thought Brorda from his depth of exhaustion. Egfrith's pained gaze fell on him, then on the parchment rocking slightly on the table. Offa watched keenly as his minister carried the letter to the corner brazier, laid it on the coals and stirred until the last charred fragment became ash. *But, once it begins, there never is enough.*

They had learned that in the wreckage of their last Mercian battlefield, thirty-eight years ago, facing the usurper Beornred. Another ambitious kinsman. Someone held a torch over the kneeling man, rain spitting and crackling against the flame; the executioner's ax was ready. Offa saw defeat in the man's bloodied face, thus no need for the death blow. Beornred died in exile three years later. Maybe it was the last time Offa was merciful. *Wyrd* gave him few more chances. Yet even now he awakened shouting the man's name. The others never walked in his dreams, the ones who found not exile but death, not even after his own archbishop had Offa kneel in penitence at Hereford for killing Athelbert of East Anglia. People now said, not murdered but martyred.

Enough. Offa's own nobles, and the Saxon and Anglian sub-kings, were all angry and fearful in the clenched Mercian fist. Offa created his archbishopric at Lichfield purely to advance Mercian power, anointed Egfrith as king without asking the *witan* council, took whole kingdoms under his direct rule and murdered Mercian nobles to make Egfrith's rule safer than his own. Every other good work weighed less in the balance. Soon these sores could fester into insurrection and death, an old story. Egfrith's reign would be more merciful, God willing. Brorda sat with his head in his hands watching the morning light wash further across the room and realized it was a prayer. *Merciful lord of heaven's realm, forgive us our excesses. Give us the grace to halt bloodshed, show us a way to create peace instead. Let it be enough.*

7 April 795 + Mathrafal

The sunlight was as thick as honey and warm enough so the ravens shed their plumage for morning training. Brys stood between matches to watch the *pencerdd*'s guard at their deadly play. Elgan and Addonwy were stalking each other with sword and shield, a match Elgan would win unless Addonwy tricked him again. Heilyn, showing a new man the heft of the holly throwing spear, made the spear a projection of his reach and let it fly to the heart of the straw target. He still shied from close work with the sword. Light brown hair tied in a thong slapped his bare back as he jogged up to the target to reclaim his weapon.

"Good throw," Brys called out.

Heilyn smiled, more at ease these days but still English enough to be suspicious of happiness.

Beyond the training ground, in the stable pasture, Cadell Powys and Eli talked with a groom over the upturned foot of a brown horse. The king mounted, controlled the horse well when it tried to rear, and heeled into a canter around the pasture wall. A pity he couldn't learn to handle people with the same skill as he handled a horse. Eli shouted something, too far away to hear, and Brys felt the familiar knot in his belly clench tighter. Then Elfæl went into the stable and Cadell cantered on toward the training ground. For weeks Brys had sought an hour's talk; the king sidestepped and obviously would do so as long as Eli advised him. But now Cadell was approaching on his horse. Brys sheathed his sword as the king leaped down to run the last few paces at the horse's side.

"Cynfarch." Cadell Powys grinned as though he hadn't a thought in the world. Probably he hadn't. Eli would see to that. "I want to talk with you."

"Certainly, lord king." Brys had a sudden flash of guilt. Was this about Nest? Or had Cadell merely been sent to deliver a message from a southern cousin? Brys went to Carnlas and pulled his shirt off the saddlebow.

Cadell swung back onto his horse and headed over to the ford. Still in boyish high spirits, God help him. God help them all. Brys followed him through the brown waters of Banwy and onto the Meifod track. They rode in silence until they passed the saint's grave up among the trees on their left hand; then the king halted. At least he was clever enough to know where he couldn't be overheard, a first step toward surviving Mathrafal.

"Garmon has gone north to Rhiwædog," said Cadell, intent on wrapping his rein around his big knuckles. "And Idris says he's going to Meirionydd after Easter."

"Yes."

"My uncle thinks I should order Garmon back."

Drive the wedge deep, split Powys like kindling. Eli's advice is predictable at least. "And what do you think, lord king?"

"I — don't know." Cadell looked nonplussed. Didn't anyone else ask what he thought? Eli certainly wouldn't think it important to his plans. Cadell knotted his reins, unknotted them, and finally looked up. Unlovely man, he was always flinching as though he lacked an outer layer of skin. "That's why I'm asking you, Cynfarch."

Brys shook his head. *Whatever I say will go straight back to Eli.*

"You won't advise me." Cadell looked at his hands and swallowed hard. "He said from the beginning that you wouldn't. I didn't believe him."

Trapped. Poor crooked Cadell, blind to the difference between old friends and new enemies. All right, cousin Eli. Listen well. "It's not a good idea to order Garmon back. First, he won't come, so it makes you look powerless. Second, he'll withdraw Penllyn from Powys. Idris will do the same with Meirionydd if you cœrce him. You can't afford to fight to retain the northern cantrefs. And if Powys weakens we can't withstand Mercia."

Cadell stared. *You really haven't thought of this?* "Did Garmon tell you that?"

"No." *Not in so many words. But it's exactly what I would do.* "It's likely all the same."

"Why is Garmon going to Penllyn?"

Good man, that's the right question. "What dœs Eli think?"

"To raise a warband."

Garmon? Brys bit his tongue and didn't laugh. "Garmon's more interested in his kitchen than in his bodyguard. He likes to hunt, watch horse races, eat well, drink well and hear good music. If he were angry enough and under attack, he might defend Penllyn against Powys. But he would never attack Powys."

They dismounted and walked on toward Meifod. In the distance the abbey bell clanged for morning mass.

"Was he angry about Garth Teyrnog?"

Two good questions. A glimmer of Cadell's common sense through Eli's wall of dung? Handle this carefully. "Your generosity touched me deeply, but Garmon deserved to know you were giving Penllyn lands to the son of his brother's murderer, whom he had dispossessed and sentenced to exile. I prevented him from being angry by giving the estate to Llanfor church."

"Your father was a dispossessed murderer. You're not." Cadell frowned, furrowing his brow. He had some kind of skin rash; as usual, his face looked chapped and angry.

"My father was more than a murderer. He was a traitor. He killed his cousin, Garmon's brother, over the question of breaking away from Powys. He died for his wrongdoing."

"Oh." Cadell looked shocked. *How could anyone in Mathrafal not have heard that? What possessed Brochfael to keep his only son in such isolation? Was he bent on repeating Elisedd's brutality to Brochfael? More likely the opposite. Preoccupied with the survival of Powys, he left Cadell with the vicious foster-father Elisedd had chosen and later let him go his own way. Now we pay the price of Brochfael's misjudgment.* "I'm sorry."

"It's long ago now." Brys stopped and looked up through the trees toward the saint's grave. "About Garmon. And Idris. And me."

"Yes?"

"We are loyal to you. We know the administration. We can counsel you. Yet you've kept us all at arm's length for a month. That's the main reason they're leaving. If they're not needed here, they might as well see to their own affairs."

"That's not what — my uncle says. So whom — do I believe? Tell me that." *A cry of distress or fear. If it's fear there's still hope.*

Brys stopped and faced him. "You'll hear different advice from everyone you ask. Always. But you have all the answers you need in yourself. You're an intelligent man."

"I doubt that," said Cadell. It was not bitterness but a plain statement. *His honesty is devastating, the worst enemy of diplomacy. Eli must fear for his sanity trying to make Cadell an accomplice in his own downfall.*

"You tell me what you believe, and I'll tell you if you're right — in my view, which may not be Eli's view."

"Very well. My uncle wants something." Cadell worried at doubt like another hangnail.

"What could he want?"

"Not gold. I've given him gold and lands. What then?"

Brys tœd a white pebble across the muddy cart ruts but said nothing.

"Power," Cadell answered himself. "He wants me in his power."

"Yes?" Brys felt sweat stand out all over his back and start to trickle. Where it touched his shirt, the cool breeze made icy spots. He resisted shivering.

"But he wants to rebuild Powys to greatness. He says. Like Elisedd. Put Offa in his place."

Merciful god. "What will happen then, lord king?"

"Brys." Cadell looked up uncertainly. Few people used the old nickname now. "Don't call me that. You're my foster brother."

"Cadell, what will happen if you provoke Offa?"

"War. To — put an end to the border raids."

"Who raided the border?"

Cadell frowned. "Mercia."

"You're sure?" *I feel like a monastery schoolmaster, patiently guiding a student through lessons — as Brochfael used to do with me. Now I repay him.* "There were no Mercian prisoners, not a shred of evidence. Brochfael knew. Cadell, your father died of treachery within Powys."

"Treachery." Cadell tasted that and looked up shaken. "It wasn't my idea. The wolf hunt."

"I know whose idea it was," Brys shot back, stung by anger. *Why didn't you stop it at least? Brochfael would be alive, Cyngen would be in Powys.* "How did you slip the leash today?"

Cadell angrily drew himself straight. "I didn't come to you for satire."

"And why exactly did you come to me?"

"Damn you, Cynfarch, don't stand there in your arrogance and question me like a tutor. I need your advice."

Brys swallowed his temper. Cadell was right. "Forgive me."

"Yes." Cadell smiled with the clear warmth he'd found for a moment in Meifod church, the day he was anointed. "What about Dyfed?"

"Who asks?"

"I ask." Cadell gave him a hard look, a brief battle of eyes. "Who else would ask?"

"Someone who's already sent me one assassin and will try again," Brys said quietly and let it sink in, wondering if he were signing his death order.

"No." Cadell flatly denied it.

Brys waited, holding his tongue. *If I say more I'll have to speak of the attempt on Cyngen. Let him stay hidden, forgotten, as an exiled murderer in Bro Waroch. Cyngen's too important. Cyngen can rule Powys. This man might learn to with enough help and enough time. A great task, since he has to govern himself as well as his country.*

Cadell was pale. "What can I do?"

"Stay away from Dyfed. The sole purpose of any campaign there is to put Egbert in Winchester at our expense. Cadell, you're walking between staked pits. Miss a step and Powys falls."

"Dœs Eli know?"

Brys said nothing. They had come to a farm's boundary stone, almost lost in rampant nettles.

"I promised to send a force to Dyfed," Cadell said. "Christ in splendor, either way . . . "

Now some help. "Give no one else power to make your policy decisions. Lean on your father's counselors, they are the strength of Powys. Your steward is as vain as a cat. Let him advise you on clothes and grooming. I'll bring you some salve for your skin. Take a mistress. Put your *pencerdd* to work to make your name. They call you Crooked Cadell now."

"I know." A miserable twitch of a smile. "I am."

"You are as I sing you." Brys put a hand on his shoulder. *Shaking. Frightened out of your mind. Good. That's not a bad place to start.* "You have a generous spirit, and I love you for it. You've shown your wisdom today. Your courage is common talk at court, riding all night to fight and win a hopeless battle." *And if it's not common talk now, it will be soon.*

"And then all will be well." Doubt corroded Cadell's rare dry humor.

Brys looked him in the eye. "Unless we work quickly, my dear, all will be blood and betrayal."

A FEW DAYS LATER, as Brys and Meirwen and Heilyn came in from Cilwen, a scuffle broke out among travelers inside the south gate. As it erupted in their direction, a sweet-faced Glasbryn dairy girl walked past them. The girl put a hand to her neck and looked around in confusion as the quarrelling strangers scattered like dry leaves. *Too much ale too early in the day,* Brys thought. The guard would be working hard by nighfall. They were under the gatehouse when the dairy girl began to shriek, then fell to the ground outside, rolling in helpless agony. Brys held her hand until it convulsed into a claw. In minutes she was dead, beyond any help but Bened's prayers. There was a fresh scratch on the girl's neck. On the ground where she had passed near them, Heilyn spotted a jagged bronze triangle with a purple stain on the sharp end.

Idris found Brys leaning at the north rampart half an hour later, looking down across the three-river plain. News traveled quickly in Mathrafal.

"Get out with your life," Idris said. "That was meant for you."

"Not yet." Brys felt strangely calm, as though he were the one poisoned and dead, not a cheerful young girl. Now he felt beyond all these fears. *I know what to do now.* "Not quite yet."

"Lord have mercy, Cynfarch." Idris gripped his shoulder in a gesture that could be friendship. "Go now. Don't wait till tomorrow."

"Idris, if I weren't here, would you stay to advise Cadell? He's wiser than you think and begins to doubt Eli."

"If I could," said Idris bluntly. "Eli sent a letter to Offa this morning in Cadell's name, without his knowledge, saying the border will have to be redrawn. Not at Halkyn but all the way south at River Dyfrdwy. He's demanding territory that Mercia's held for generations."

"Now everyone is writing letters to Offa," Brys said absently.

"Cadell might as well be wearing a feast garland as the *hual* of Powys. Eli controls every move."

"I know. It's going to change."

Idris swore eloquently. The duty guard turned at the northwest corner and came back, footsteps hollow on the catwalk. Brys climbed down the stair, aware that Meirionydd was following like a shadow. He walked out through the gate, down toward the houses. People passing into Mathrafal, apart from monks who were gaunt with Lenten fasting, wore brightly colored clothes and eager looks. Good Friday tomorrow, Easter feast on Sunday. Moist earth gave under his bootsoles and the air held a promise. Everything was untarnished, growing, alive.

"Cynfarch," Idris began in the ale house porch.

"Don't worry. I'll take care of it."

"Poison?"

Brys shuddered. *Answer enough.*

"One man with a knife then. I can find someone —"

"No."

As they ducked under the door lintel, an old ballad in a woman's husky voice settled on them from an upper window. Inside, the smoky light halœd a knot of Cynfarch's ravens in one corner.

"You have a better scheme?" Idris challenged, hands in his belt so his russet cloak flared wide in the crowded room.

"Yes." Brys smiled, anticipating Idris's rage. "I trust my *awen*."

14 April 795 + Mathrafal

Easter was Cadell's first high feast, and he broke Brochfael's austere tradition by making it celebration and ceremony. Mathrafal hall was crowded above the pillars and packed solid below. In procession came the stag insignia of beaten gold on red silk, then Cadell with his nobles. As part of the ritual, the war commander carried in the *pencerdd*'s harp; Brys half expected Gellan to drop it, but he contented himself with a congealed stare. Brys waited through the formalities of precedence, prayers, and gifts and recited Cadell's lineage. One of the king's gifts was on his back, a yellow silk shirt with gold embroidery three fingers wide at the border. The silk felt alive, sensual, smooth but for the slightest catch at the skin, like a lover's touch. He settled to watch the company. They were just as he wanted them: restless, excited, curious about the new king.

Rain had washed in from the west and now hushed on the roof thatch. Tegwy, self-appointed as his cupbearer tonight, filled his green glass drinking cup with twelve-year mead for the toasts. At the sun chamber railing, Meirwen was laughing with the steward's wife; she had silver combs in her hair and a new dress of russet silk. Tegwy had undertaken to fall in love with Meirwen in Nest's absence; he looked up and blushed when she smiled at him. Near the dais the *pencerdd*'s guard made an island of green cloaks and silver near the other bodyguard men.

Heads went together, raising a murmur, when Brys took the sea-cat harp from Tegwy and sang praise of Cadell Powys. He made no false claims but built on the man's courage and generosity, his willingness to take up his father's justice and a new promise for Powys. It was unconventional, but so much the better. Then he idled out runs until he had what he wanted in a demand from the benches.

"Sing the border," someone called at last.

"The border has its stories, who can say their truth?" Brys shrugged and asked a question in the shortest bronze strings. "Ask me, I know it."

Smiling around the hall, Brys kept a light touch on the strings and amusement in his voice. Men and women on the benches, leaning on the pillars and walls, drank their mead and bragget and relaxed. *Entertainment.* He found a bouncing little melody and worked on it, adding some insolence.

"A cattle border. Offa is kind to us. Now we can drive English stock in comfort from Hereford to Tegeingl." A question in the strings, mimicking the human voice. "Is it true?"

"It's true." A few obliging shouts. They liked riddles and jokes as a relief from old laments.

"An English border. Grasping people, they fence themselves to spare us their greed for land." He played the light question. "Is it true?"

Answers flew thicker. They were picking up the game.

"A mole border. One night in rut a Mercian mole dug it." He cocked his head. "Is it true?"

"Offa! The mole's called Offa." Grinning faces, waiting for the next round.

"A kite border. There's always a feast. Carrion eaters and their captains can wait out battles, then pick the winner. If the right man dies." Question in the string song. "Is it true?"

"It's true," yelled a few who didn't understand or were lit with mead.

Shocked comprehension on a few faces below. Mostly silence. Some leaned to their neighbors or stared up puzzled. Brys could feel tangible silence at his back, on the dais. Gellan was behind his right shoulder, Eli was directly behind at the king's right hand. He needed a mirror. Elgan was frowning slightly at Brys. His expression said, I know what you're doing but not why. No result yet.

"A miraculous border. Some see it and some don't. Visible to peace-loving kings, invisible to wolves who run at night. They slaughter their lords for rank and power." A light tone kept them uncertain until he moved his string music toward discord. Only a little uneasy laughter now.

Elgan's gaze fixed behind Brys and slid right. *First blood.*

"A moveable border. It leaped west of a Powys farm, foreign fellow-countrymen cut down at their door." He strutted his little tune down the strings. "Is it true?"

One man answered but stopped suddenly as though someone had slapped a hand on his mouth.

"A bauble border. It loves a gold collar even on a sow." Eli could fit that around his neck with his boar-headed torc. He cooled his voice and dropped it. The rain on the thatch was loud for a moment. "Is it true?"

Silence.

Brys dropped hard into the black Æolian mode but kept his tune and his high-stepping rhythm. Yes. That works. A buzz of comment swept the benches; names were passed around. Eli, Gellan. They knew his target. *Good.* Elgan moved restlessly and set down his drinking horn. He looked right, to where Gellan sat behind Brys.

"A treacherous border. It tricked men to murder. Honor has fled."

Elgan glanced around his ravens, gathering them. *He understands what I'm doing now.* Brys stopped the string song suddenly and tilted his harp forward. Tegwy took it from him.

Now. Satire. Brys edged his voice to strike sparks from ice, to split green willow at the root, to blister faces with shame. "A maggot border. A white-eyed maggot finds his way to corruption. A maggot leaves a trail of monkshood and nightshade. In his slime track, royal blood."

"Face price," said someone behind him and to the right. *Wait. You've barely heard the start.* Tegwy, who had once almost suffered poison's agony, far worse than any insult, stood behind the pœt's chair again and laughed under his breath.

"I know a maggot who mimics honor but lusts for the flesh of his dead country. I know a Powys maggot who hates Mercia but earns Mercian gold."

Elgan's glance snapped forward, warning Brys. *Warning of what?*

Dais planks creaked at his right shoulder, and Tegwy drew in his breath sharply. Brys didn't turn to look at him but took his cup from Tegwy and drank. Gellan walked out in front, almost at the edge of the dais, with his hand on his knife hilt. *Fool. All attack and no subtlety. Draw a weapon before the hual at a high feast and even the king will call for face price. Do my work for me. If you're disgraced before Cadell in a way he can't ignore, you're off the board. Out of play.* His white eyes had an extra rim of white, between grey-white pupil and pallid flesh. Most men flushed at satire. Gellan paled.

"Maggot," he said to the war commander, low and clear. Then he threw a ringing voice out to the hall benches. "Gellan! Do you know this maggot?"

Gellan made a shapeless sound and struck the drinking cup out of Brys's hand. It flew up and shattered somewhere behind. Idris told someone quietly to leave it. *Face price to the* pencerdd *before the king on the dais, four head or two gold pieces, say the laws. The man's deranged. But what if he's deranged enough to find a weapon?* Elgan was on his feet. Brys got to his feet and glimpsed Cadell leaning forward open-mouthed, with Bened's hand holding him in place.

What happened next was too rapid to stop, like three steps in a dance. Brys put a hand on Tegwy's shoulder, intending to send him down among the safer benches. There was a flash of motion from Gellan behind Brys's back. Tegwy flung himself forward. Brys turned. Gellan and Tegwy stood face to face, wordless and still as two figures in a wall painting. Then the commander drew away. In his hand was the smeared knife. Tegwy put both hands on his chest, his startled blue eyes on Brys. He kneeled heavily, blood welling over his hands, and folded sideways.

Brys fell to his knees beside him, almost throwing away the life Tegwy had bought him. This time he saw Gellan's blade and rolled out of range. He got up with his own knife in hand. Gellan swung again, and if he hadn't danced back, would have taken him under the ribs. Instead Brys met the stroke on his knife hilt in a grinding clash of metal. The next blow was high, singing past his ear like a blue iron dragonfly. He let another pass by, studying the commander's style. He knew it well enough; the man was his own weapons instructor. *Stiff, maybe from anger, and too sure of victory.*

As though afraid of coming nearer Brys feinted near Gellan's chest, backstepped, circled, kept his distance. The hall held a shocked stillness. Brys saw only a space of planks sanded clean for the high feast and a pale-eyed killer. *Tegwy . . . Maybe he missed the heart.* Gellan stabbed in again, and Brys barely evaded the stained blade. Fear jolted him like a fist in the belly and made him suck in air. Then everything slowed in his eyes, slow as poured honey, slow as noon. *Now I have forever. You have no time left.*

Gellan edged aside. Brys watched the thoughts march through his face. A deceitful man who couldn't mask his deception. When he leaped in, Brys stepped back and left him attacking empty air. Brys reached casually and scored across the man's ribs. Pain and first doubt stung Gellan. Brys danced a stately pace, savoring his knowledge of death. But that made him think of Cenwulf, enjoying others' pain, and the thought sickened. When Gellan made a lunge that left him unguarded Brys ended the dance. He leaned to give him Tegwy's blow, hilt-deep to the chest. Gellan twisted over the blade and took it down with him onto the dais boards.

Brys stood a moment with empty hands and felt only a great lightness. Then grief dropped on him like a fowler's net, like night. He stooped to see Gellan was beyond pulse and pulled the knife. A first murmur from the hall. Elgan had his guard up at the edge of the dais, a silent line ready to defend. Brys went to kneel beside Bened, at Tegwy's head. Bright eyes empty as sky, bright life fled. *Tegwy, Tegwy. I took you into the* pencerdd*'s guard to protect your life, not mine. You served me too well.*

He found his harp and slung it at his back. Idris had a sick mouth but steady eyes. Cadell was speechless. Eli at his right elbow talked busily enough for two. *Eli.*

One of you left. I'm already deep in disgrace — one blow to the throat above that radiant torc would end most of Cadell's worries. But a kinsman. A king's son. Cold-blooded murder. Curse Gellan. The cub is taken but the wolf is still loose. Brys went to kneel before the king. Penitence started here.

"Lord king —"

"Spare me your excuses, Cynfarch." Cadell's mouth was twisted in pain.

Excuses? For being attacked? It stung him sharply. He had a taste of the sea in his throat, for Tegwy, and a great ache. Satire was not murder. He couldn't say it. He bowed his head.

"All of your kind," said Cadell. His voice broke and strangled as though it were his grief, his loss. Brys had spoiled his high feast, that was all he could see. "You. Your father."

Brys looked up, and the current of anger rose and swept him forward. "You're not *your* father, Cadell, that is certain. Before you're done with Powys and Powys is done with you, you will bring the land to ruin and mistake it for peace."

"Insult," Cadell got out with a choking sound. Eli's expression, hovering at his shoulder, shifted from sorrowful dismay to something less palatable.

"Face price for a faceless man? I'll sing you back into a skulking misfit, Cadell, and who will care?" *Too far — Cadell, foster brother, let me gather the words back — too late. God never created such a fool as me.*

"Your arrogance and ambition I can bear, Cynfarch," Cadell said quietly, with more dignity than most kings could muster in the face of shocking and bloody disaster. "But Powys will not bear the destruction of a king. Go."

Straight truth from twisted Cadell. The death of a maggot was nothing; insult to a king was everything. There could be no reparation. *May God forgive me. I know you cannot.* The bleakness of that was a rain-washed grave for everything. Everything but pride. Black and bloody pride drew him to his feet.

"You threaten me? Set a hand on me and you die." And it was true. Elgan would avenge him with his own death, a loyalty Brys no longer merited. He glanced at Eli. "And guard your crooked back, Cadell. It has a crooked shadow."

Cadell's face with its terrible toll of hurt stayed with Brys as he walked out of the silent hall with his guard protectively near. He wanted to send them back, tell them to make their peace with the king. Pride held his tongue. Pride and anger had driven him for ten years since he was a frightened boy, Brochfael's hostage, and he was still in their power.

No one moved in what had been a feast hall. They went out unchallenged into the soft spring rain. Meirwen met them in the colonnade, where the honeysuckle was putting out tender leaves. She had pulled on riding clothes but left her hair twisted high in its silver combs. Brys kissed her and put his head down on her shoulder. Wanted to rest there forever. *Silver thorn.*

"Not Aberffraw," she said, reading his thought.

"Ireland?" asked Heilyn. "Manaw?"

"No."

They ransacked chests and shelves, threw gear into satchels and saddlebags, pinned their cloaks. So half an hour's work destroyed a life's effort. As they finished, Idris filled the doorway.

"There were easier ways, *pencerdd*."

"Were there?" *No one will ever call me that again.* Brys looked up from wrapping his sea-cat in her outer case of oiled hide. "I accept your offer of refuge in Meirionydd for my guard."

At the end of the colonnade, long before they walked through the gate and rode northward through the three-river plain, Brys knew it was a heartless and cowardly choice. But the miles stretched onward and he did not turn back.

PART III

Anno Domini 795 to 796

Gwnav it glod.

I will make fame for thee.

Marginalia

Destruction is sometimes strategic, but this destruction was a needless obliteration of learning and lives. Offa was in a rage about the burned abbey and the slaughtered monks; Egfrith knew that even his father's rage could not rebind books from ash or breathe life into corpses.

The library had been here, between these charred apple trees. Book cellar, the fat librarian monk had called it last night, suggesting that books were fine vintages to be laid down gently for future pleasure. Egfrith, sick at heart, stooped over the warm ash and charcoal. Impossible to locate anything in the burned shell of a timber and clay building. This wing had blazed the brightest of all with its fuel of wooden covers and parchment pages, its treasure of gospel books and histories and commentaries by classical and modern authors. Last night Egfrith had come here to read the abbey's meticulous copy of the *Liber Sancti Germani;* today he came to salvage anything that survived. He found nothing to salvage.

The younger king of Mercia straightened at last and looked across the densely forested Tywi valley to the sunset. Offa and Brorda were still on the far side of the river, hunting stragglers. A few columns of black smoke rose from clearings among the trees, the ruins of farms. The oaks were showing their first bronzed green leaves.

Egfrith had expected Dyfed to be like Powys, a few soft valleys in a hard stony land that bred warlike men. But Dyfed was a fair and smiling country, full of gentle meadows and eloquent rivers. Who could expect this beauty? Especially now that it was forever scarred. *Mercia did this. No, Egbert did this, marching his rabble east from here through British Gwent to Mercian Hwicce.* Mercia had intercepted Egbert's force and pursued it west, back into Dyfed. There had been no choice, Egfrith admitted dully.

"Lord king." His bodyguard captain, smeared with soot and dirt and still trickling blood from a bandaged sword arm, looked as spent as Egfrith felt. "I couldn't find Cenwulf, though they say he's back from the coast. Only the brothers. You want them in headquarters?"

Egfrith had taken over the nearest farm house, the occupants having wisely fled. "Bring them here."

He looked across the abbey ruins to the cornfield that sloped down to River Tywi. Now their battlefield was muddy, the winter wheat trampled under and rusted with blood from the scattered bodies. War was no victory, Egfrith knew, but a failure.

Egfrith saw Ceolwulf and Cuthred stop in the battle wreckage to talk with a man stripping a body. They were in no hurry. Heat beat against his face from the embers in one standing wall as he walked out of the abbey ruins and down into the field.

Ceolwulf kneeled, and Egfrith motioned him up. But Cuthred kept talking to his companion just long enough to be insolent and finally walked over smiling. Like his brothers he had blond hair with a greyish cast in the dwindling light, and his square face was handsomely bearded. He bowed perfunctorily to his king. "We chased the Saxon downstream but he reached the ships and got away with his tail between his legs."

"How many?"

"Three keels, lord king." Ceolwulf looked alarmed by Cuthred's incivility, as well he might. "Maybe a hundred and fifty — Egbert and some of his Frankish mercenaries. He left the *Wealas* to us. It took us all afternoon to track them. Only the Powys and Dyfed bodyguards turned to fight. The rest scattered like hares."

"Bring me Cenwulf," Egfrith said, curious to see how deep the insolence ran.

Egbert's escape was inexcusable — he'd fled barely ahead of his pursuers — and disastrous. How had Cenwulf let him slip away? Egbert was the most dangerous man in Britain. *Or, God help us all, out of Britain.*

"Later," said Cuthred. "He's busy."

Ceolwulf looked angrily at his brother. "Lord king, he's questioning a prisoner."

"West Saxon or British?" asked Egfrith mildly, aware that his captain itched to strike the mannerless whelp's face. Cuthred relied too much on Cenwulf's following in the *witan* council and the size of his bodyguard. Not only was he insolent, he was foolish enough to let it show.

"Dœs it matter?" Cuthred shrugged.

Only to the man screaming under the hot iron, or whatever aids Cenwulf asked his questions with these days. *Necessary*, Offa said, *we live or fall by knowing everything.* Egfrith had learned to hold his tongue and keep his gorge down. Some things would change soon.

"He's in the monastery gate house." Ceolwulf's hand fell on his brother's mailed shoulder. His squeezed warning didn't escape Egfrith's notice, nor did their hasty withdrawal.

Egfrith walked in that direction, stepping carefully among the dead. No survivors here. Many had slashed throats. It was a kindness to spare the fatally wounded, friend or enemy, the agony of splintered bones and festering wounds. Who were they? Egfrith looked at the stripped bodies as he crossed the littered field, and apart from a few swarthy bearded men who had to be Egbert's Frankish or Italian mercenaries, he could rarely tell English from British. He swallowed down a sudden knot of grief.

Cenwulf had taken over the gatekeeper's shed for his interrogation; his white stallion was tied outside the door with a pretty white mare. Egfrith ducked under the low lintel and looked around the dim interior. Nothing. Egfrith's captain motioned him through the other door into an enclosed courtyard, where Cenwulf stood with his priest. Always with his priest, as though he needed more intercession than other men. Egfrith looked down at the body sprawled on the cobbles in the boneless way of the dead. The man was fair-haired, naked, missing his genitals. His hands were twisted and broken, his eyes bulged as though he had suffocated, and blood was smeared around his mouth. *Merciful lord of heaven's realm.* Egfrith suppressed his reaction, knowing Cenwulf; horror and protest only fed his cruelty. The priest had blood on his hands and an uneasy smirk. A young woman with light brown hair stood alone in one corner, praying silently. Her eyes were flat with shock.

"Regrettably he was too badly hurt to tell us anything," said Cenwulf in his deep, improbably gentle voice.

Egfrith felt his stomach heave with nausea, but God willing, not here and now. *Give me strength to endure the hour. And give me strength, when the time comes, to end this evil without committing greater evil as my father did.* But not yet. Not while there was a chance of losing everything by challenging him. Offa refused to acknowledge that danger.

"In my headquarters. Now." Egfrith, arms folded across his mail shirt, managed to keep his voice and face calm. At this moment he wished he had Offa's clear conscience for sudden and expedient murder.

Cenwulf hesitated, then caught the priest's eye. Together they went out through the gate house. Egfrith's bodyguard captain, a veteran of Akenfeld and Portchester and a dozen other battles, took a closer look at the body. He walked across the courtyard and leaned against the whitewashed wall to vomit. This gave the king obscure comfort. He sent the captain to get his wounds treated and turned to the gate. He wanted to hear his captains' reports before Offa returned from the chase.

Egfrith remembered the young woman. "Are you captive?"

She continued her prayer, head bowed and lips moving without sound, until he repeated his question in British. At that she raised her head and nodded. She was very young.

Egfrith saw now that she was Cenwulf's concubine, the deaf-mute girl he had dragged along on this expedition. Not deaf— British. And now that Cenwulf had gone, she was weeping as silently as she prayed. The younger king of Mercia shook his head and turned away.

28 May 795 + Armorica

The storm hurled the monastery ship out of the grey Atlantic with her oaken planks creaking on their pegs and her leather mainsail split. Tide and current caught the beamy lapstrake hull and carried her southeast. Again the wind quartered and drove her northward, until the dark grey smudge of the south Armorican shore loomed above the rolling grey sea. The Tywyn monk who was their captain fell to his foredeck and raised his hands in thanks to God. If a westerly had swept them into Frankish waters they could have faced slavery or ransom. Brys watched from a blind heaving depth of seasickness; even the thought of dry land made him retch. By afternoon they coasted into calmer waters before a gentle breeze.

Sailing into summer, they passed open meadows, forests breaking into leaf and tawny stretches of sand with occasional farms visible beyond dunes of salt grass. The next afternoon they slid into Bro Waroch's glassy Morbihan gulf, where the bottom seemed only an arm's reach below the surface. The breeze fell away. A sailor called the channels from the prow of their ship as islands of honey rock, studded with standing stones and pines, floated past the dripping oars. The sweet bronze voice of an abbey bell welcomed them in to the port of Gwened. Orchards and early crops surrounded the stronghold which overlooked a river outlet; the houses were squares of wheaten thatch within the rampart walls. They were sailing into history. Brys, leaning at the gunwale between Meirwen and Heilyn, looked up at the citadel that so long had withstood Julius Cæsar and still defied Charles the Great.

Arrival was noisy and malodorous. The inshore rowers shipped their oars at the last moment as the outer rowers dipped theirs, and the captain's second leaped onto the stone quay to take the lines. Then confusion: smells of pitch and smoke and exposed pilings, a small boy shouting that his mother's inn had empty rooms, cats prowling underfoot for fish offal, a brown-skinned Moorish ironworker calling out the praises of Damascus steel, hasty farewells. The captain blessed them, as well he might after the fee he charged for passage from Tywyn. Brys started up through teeming portside streets that wound like canyons between buildings two and three storeys high, toward the court. Although his legs insisted this was still swelling ocean, he was suddenly ferociously hungry.

"It'll make you sick," Heilyn warned when he bought them meat rolled in bread from a street pedlar.

"Too bad, granny." Brys licked his fingers.

They were exchanging glances behind his back again. He wished they would stop treating him like a glass cup that someone had dropped, waiting for the first fracture lines. *I fled my obligation, I betrayed Cadell's trust, I did wrong beyond hope of forgiveness. But it's done. Now we go on.*

The grey steward who met them at Macliau's court was as keenly diplomatic as his lord. He smiled a noncommittal welcome and appraised them. He saw a harper wearing salt-stained silk and a good deal of gold, speaking the archaic island dialect of Powys in a nobleman's voice. Macliau's ancestors came from Powys; so did this recent talk of British alliance. What else of value might come from there? The steward bowed from the waist and led them to the king's best hostel in a sunny courtyard. There Meirwen and Heilyn dropped their possessions and went to find the Moorish steelsmith.

Brys walked up through the town and found Cyngen riding exercises in a stone-walled pasture among orchards. He folded his arms on the gate crossbar to watch ten young men riding formations like a flock of swifts, wheeling at their captain's shouted orders. This famous light cavalry protected three small Armorican principalities from crushing Frankish assaults, year after year. The troop cantered to the far wall and turned, throwing-spears held ready, to thunder back toward him. Turf sprayed under iron-shod hooves, tall horses galloped neck and neck, and the ground heaved like a drumhead. They passed so close to the gate that Brys smelled lathered horses and the greased wax dressing on their harness and heard the chink of the riders' mail coats. Cyngen rode three from the left beside Merfyn, eyes slitted against the speed that whipped back his brown hair. Across the flying manes he saw Brys. When they finished the manœuvre he spoke to the man with the captain's bracelet and cantered over. As he vaulted down Brys swung over the gate timber and dropped into the training ground.

"I had a letter from Idris a week ago. What now? No one makes an early voyage with good news." Cyngen set his mouth, waiting. His grey horse nuzzled his mailed shoulder.

"Tegwy is dead. He took Gellan's blade, intended for me. I killed Gellan." Bad news first. But there wasn't any good news.

"Tegwy would like that. A hero's death." Cyngen said coolly, but Brys saw the tremor around his mouth until he clamped his jaw. When he controlled his face like that he looked uncannily like Brochfael. Level grey eyes, a hard mouth. He stood a handspan taller than his guardian now. "Why are you here, Cynfarch?"

Brys told him. Cyngen listened and looked across the pasture without expression: a tall young man in unbleached linen and the serviceable mail of a foreign king's bodyguard, the last of the Powys royal house.

"You will go back," ordered Cyngen when he had finished.

"I will not." Brys knew it for another betrayal; it grated deep inside like broken bone.

But Cyngen just turned to look at him, eyes narrowed slightly against the sun, and shook his head. Brys watched a hawk that skimmed a slow circuit over a blossoming orchard, it stooped suddenly with a backswept blur of brown pinions. Or maybe the blur was in his vision.

"Not for my father." Cyngen frowned, not pleased to ask twice, but doing it all the same. "For Powys."

"Powys is lost between a past that never existed and a ruinous future," Brys said. *No prince commands a* pencerdd, *even a broken* pencerdd. "An incestuous whore, a mad wanderer."

"Dœs anger help?" asked Cyngen, curious.

"No." Brys looked at the grey horse, barely seeing it. Not a Powys grey, almost black with a strange tarnished sheen. *Braint* had settled on Cyngen like a diadem, like the hero-light of the old tales. "Nothing helps."

Cyngen nodded wearily, more than ever like Brochfael, and reached a decision. He laid his arm across Brys's shoulders and started toward the stable, the tall horse pacing behind. Brys went numbly where he was led. For a man said to be ambitious, he had committed the most extravagantly pointless act of his life. All for anger that no longer served any purpose and pride that seemed to have taken on a life of its own. Now he had to find a way to live with the consequences.

Macliau was called Count of Lesser Britain in Charles's court but in Bro Waroch he was a British king. Despite his clipped black beard, Frankish clothes and jeweled crown, Macliau ruled a strong country without demanding vassals' oaths, as no Frank could do. Visitors found a welcome, especially if they were skilled or scholarly. Brys was welcomed as Gwriad's envoy — news floats farther than it walks — and as Cadell's pœt. Never was there any mention of quarrel or exile. Rifts mend and exiles return home. Macliau cultivated his relations with distant Powys as he did all his relations. Bro Waroch was a small country crushed against the iron ribs of the violent Frankish empire, holding a threatened border for his ungrateful neighbors. Macliau was a careful and subtle man, a survivor.

Guests from the other two British Armorican kingdoms of Cerne and Domnonia, never too closely defined as envoys or hostages, had the freedom of the

Bro Waroch court. This year the Avar hordes were hammering Frankia's eastern borders, so Charles was too busy to make a new war on his British enemies. The king of Bro Waroch took this opportunity to charm the Frankish counts bordering on his kingdom, marrying a daughter to one and sending rich gifts to another, in the interests of peace. Sometimes Brys thought of Powys, another small nation bordering on a powerful nation and surviving by diplomacy, and put the thoughts aside.

Everything he tried to forget by day surfaced in his troubling dreams. It was not only Cadell and Powys that he had betrayed. Dreaming, he cried out to a honey-haired girl on a white mare, a girl beaten beyond tears and led captive into a cruel land. Always she was too far from him.

One dream brought an old memory in its wake — a small girl met on a long-ago visit to a Mechain monastery, a girl with a cap of blonde curls and dancing hazel eyes. He had been more interested in plundering the orchard than in meeting yet another cousin. His father had cosseted the child — angry at his kinsman's neglect, Brys guessed now — but on their departure she had clung weeping to Brys's mother.

It had to be Gwladus ferch Eli he remembered. What if his betrayal of a promise broke that passionate spirit shielded by madness? His lost cousin Gwladus, like lost Heledd, tangled deeper into his *awen* and his *braint,* giving him no peace.

Brys hunted and trained with Macliau and his sons — though the short recurved bow still seemed to him a coward's weapon, letting a man kill without so much as looking into his enemy's eyes — played wood-wisdom, learned new songs and sang for any who asked. He still had the *pencerdd*'s habits, in keeping with the stag arm ring he hadn't yielded. As *pencerdd* he served only Cyngen, Merfyn, Meirwen, Heilyn, a few other wanderers from the island of Britain.

By midsummer they were no longer strangers in Gwened. Meirwen and Heilyn worked with the court smith sometimes. The Moors refused to give up the smelting secrets of their hard Damascus metal, which scarcely needed sand and whetstone. Heilyn insisted it started as plain iron, later treated by some unknown process; it was not the magical substance that some claimed.

One day Brys rowed Meirwen across the gulf in a borrowed curragh to Carnac sanctuary, where they walked among the stone circles and avenues. As a leeward shore surged with the sea, Carnac surged with the sun. Golden gorse and a violet haze of heather hid some fallen grey slabs, but hundreds more marched in open ranks through woodlands and farms. They made their offering and walked in the sun silence. If he closed his eyes Brys could believe this was a south-facing Penllyn hillside. Wild thyme, sweet blackberries. But they walked east of that garden, east of Powys. He made Meirwen a garland of dry lavender, full of salt shore and southern sky, which she still wore when they rowed back into Gwened port.

Two long deepsea curraghs were skimming into harbor on silent oars as he lifted their own skin vessel onto the quay. Painted eyes guarded their prows in the Gwened fashion. A black African held the tiller of the first craft, but sunset gave bright fox-red hair to the small man steering the second. Brys was not much surprised when the captain shouted greetings in a Manaw accent to the king's port warden. As the gunwale kissed the quay he sprang ashore. Brys took Meirwen's hand and they went to meet Neithon.

West Britain took shape under Neithon's stylus as he drew his map on the wax tablet. The Manaw trader had chunks of raw amber swinging in his ears and he wore a hooded tunic in violent purple and blue. Sitting on a bench near the guest house's banked hearth he drew, step by step, what had happened in Dyfed.

Brys looked out the open door through the rustling grape vines, where tight green clusters showed among the leaves, into the warm evening. The grapes were sweeter here than in Powys; even their wine tasted of summer.

Each word stabbed deep. First came raids, Neithon said, then open skirmishes on the South Powys border. Offa called local bodyguards and levies north to deal with Powys. The southern border, apparently undefended, seemed no obstacle to an exiled heir with an army of West Saxon rebels, British allies, outlaws and foreign mercenaries. Egbert marched from Dyfed toward Wessex, believing Gwent and Glywysing would join him to bring down Offa. Instead they chose to preserve their Mercian trade. Angrily he let his rabble cut a swathe of destruction eastward through the British kingdoms. When they reached the border, Offa and Egfrith met them with a large and disciplined army.

"Why was Offa there, conveniently waiting?" asked Cyngen.

"Obviously he knew something." Neithon glanced around the pleasant room and his gaze stopped at Brys. He sipped cider from his clay cup and went back to the sketch. "Why else would he sit there for two weeks, pretending to oversee border construction which was long finished? Offa tempted Egbert to make his move with rumors of his own illness and an undefended border. Somehow Offa knew exactly what Egbert planned."

Brys, gazing out into the dusk, thought of the fair and wealthy British kingdoms of the south laid waste by Egbert. He looked at Heilyn, but Heilyn carefully avoided his eyes. Meirwen was occupied over a bronze buckle she was polishing with sanded wool.

"So they fought here." Merfyn pointed over Neithon's shoulder to the wavering line of River Tywi in the golden wax.

Gwriad's son had grown into a tall, big-shouldered young man with hands and feet that promised even greater height. His red hair had lightened to the color of new copper and his freckles were darker than ever in this sunny land. Meirwen's trout speckles looked delicate by comparison; after one look at him she had bought a broad-brimmed hat.

Eadburh, Offa's daughter to the bone, had taken arms herself and brutally crushed an uprising in Winchester while her husband the king hid behind the cathedral altar. The men and women whose bodies fed carrion birds on the ramparts were the fortunate. For captive rebels Eadburh had ordered torture and slow death.

Offa and Egfrith had given Egbert a day's lead to retreat west while they called out the Ergyng warbands pledged by treaty; for once the British borderers were angry enough to rush to Offa's aid. The Mercians marched straight through three British kingdoms, scrupulously avoiding pillage.

Until Offa and Egfrith made their lightning strike, some said Offa had lost his grip. Not afterward. On the banks of River Tywi, the exiled West Saxon heir turned to fight two Mercian kings. Egbert's rebel army was scattered, retreating, already defeated once, composed of the mixed dregs of several kingdoms. The Mercian army was disciplined, fresh, angry, already victorious once and built around the kings' formidable bodyguard. The result was slaughter. The campaign — from Egbert's first move to Offa's demand for tribute and hostages from defeated Dyfed — took nine days.

Cyngen asked quietly, "Was my father there?"

"Cadell delayed and finally sent two wings of his bodyguard. They arrived in time to fight at River Tywi." Neithon set his empty cup on the bench beside him. "Not many survivors."

Cyngen laid a pine twig on the banked hearth. It shrivelled slowly, smoked, then spat into small angry flames.

"Thank God Cadell delayed," said Brys. "After his threats to Offa, any greater commitment could have looked like full-scale Powys attack on Mercia."

"We expected Offa to invade Powys over it, but he stayed his hand," Neithon said carefully. "Still he sent a warning to Mathrafal."

"Namely?" Brys watched the curl of ash fall out of sight, rather than meet Neithon's probing gaze. *My tongue did it. I was the land's guardian. I betrayed her, betrayed them all.*

"Cadell had made some claim about the border in Tegeingl which angered both Offa and Caradog. Offa said any more Powys involvement with enemies of Mercia, and any more border shifting, would be acts of war."

In the silence Brys heard the distant wash and pull of tide at the river docks. Cyngen stared blindly at a bird in the grape arbor. Meirwen polished and polished her bronze with a small grating sound that overlaid the river flow, and glanced at Heilyn. Heilyn looked away.

"Where's Egbert?" Merfyn's cool voice brought them all back to the room.

"Aachen."

"Clever. Leave the British to pay the price of West Saxon rebellion while he asks Charles for advice on making peace with Offa," Brys said.

"But why was Offa waiting?" Returning to the heart of this, Merfyn shoved the bright hair from his forehead. Some of the story remained untold, he knew. "Someone must have warned him."

"Offa has spies. Some of them are dependable," Heilyn answered, too sharply to Brys's ear.

Is that what I am? Offa's spy? Brys resisted the temptation to drop his face into his hands. But the others laughed, knowing Heilyn's brief career as Offa's spy. Heilyn glanced across the room at Neithon, perhaps remembering Neithon's knife at his throat in a rainy Arfon courtyard. Neithon began studiously rubbing out his wax map with a thumb.

Merfyn frowned, working it out. "A British spy then. Someone in Powys, if Offa only warned Cadell instead of invading."

"Egfrith and Brorda restrain him," Heilyn said quietly. Meirwen gave him a long look and forgot to polish her buckle for a moment.

Neithon, Gwriad's own messenger and spy, pulled at his moustache and turned to Brys. Brys had the sense to be watching Meirwen's hands. He couldn't be sure of guarding his eyes.

"But why?" Now Cyngen was on the scent, following his friend's lead. "No one in Powys would do that. It unleashed Egbert on the southern kingdoms and brought Maredudd Dyfed to his knees before Offa. Death, destruction, humiliation."

Merciful god, I did it, Brys wanted to shout. But he couldn't allow himself even the bleak satisfaction of confession.

Neithon raised his brightly clad shoulders; this time he didn't look at Brys. *Keep guessing, friend.* The trader closed the wax tablet with a small click and got up to lean in the doorway. Gentian twilight had fallen on Gwened. It was quiet enough to hear a homing bat twitter overhead. Neithon said, "Think of the alternatives. Powys at war with Mercia. Egbert as king of the West Saxons, threatening the Mercian imperium and Offa's British treaties. Maybe Offa and Egfrith overthrown. How long would Cadell hold Powys? And then how much death and destruction?"

No doubt. Any number of good reasons. Brys looked out into the grey courtyard, blind to the evening's sensual beauty. *Reasons. Alternatives. Justifications. Betrayals. I have become adept at compromise. All the lives lost. Yet I would do it again, even if they were Powys lives. For Powys.* He glanced up to find Neithon watching him with something too close to compassion, and Heilyn watching Neithon with his old walleyed look, and Meirwen watching Heilyn . . . *God have mercy on us all.*

"What about the alliance?" Brys asked.

Neithon found a leaf on his garish tunic sleeve and picked it off carefully before he answered. Gwriad's man liked gathering information but disliked parting with it. "Letters flying around Britain, I understand."

You more than understand, my friend. A state of chaos, in other words. Caradog harassing Cadell over disputable Tegeingl, perhaps also over disputable Penllyn. Cadell seething with rage and confusion, caught between Eli's smooth counsel and his own timid good sense. No one to advise him, no one to guard him or the land. And bloody Egbert no doubt drinking Alsatian wine in Charles's best guest house. Cenwulf's ally. Eli's ally. No man's ally. Clever, persuasive Egbert. Now Cadell Powys was in Eli's grip with a diminished bodyguard, no allies, no *pencerdd*, no heir.

Cyngen's frown traveled from Neithon to Brys. Cyngen and Brys — Brochfael's students, both blood and bone of Powys's ruling families — knew the terrible hazard. Yet both their lives were under threat now. It was not the time to return to Mathrafal. Brys nodded dully when Neithon made his farewell and slipped out into the dark courtyard. Silence held the others a minute longer, until Meirwen dropped her bronze buckle on the floor and sighed. Brys picked it up. Most of the piece still carried its forge tarnish; only one corner was polished to mirror brightness.

"You'll be welcome here," Brys told Meirwen and Heilyn.

Meirwen looked up under auburn brows, wings of a falcon on a rising spiral. "A smith can earn passage anywhere. Including Frankia."

"Two smiths," amended Heilyn.

"And a bodyguard." Cyngen tapped his arm above the elbow. Like Heilyn, he still wore his silver arm ring engraved with ravens. Cynfarch's ravens. The *pencerdd*'s guard, with no *pencerdd* and not much guard. Brys shook his head, humbled by their undeserved loyalty.

Merfyn looked around at them one by one, weighed the idea coolly for advantage, and made the rational choice. "Not me. You're all mad. Whatever you think you can accomplish . . . Never mind. Cousin Cynfarch, hand me some parchment. I'll write you a letter."

11 July 795 + Domnonia

As they rode north through Bro Celien sanctuary, the wildwood seemed endless and timeless. The grass roads swallowed hoofbeats as the fluent tree canopy swallowed the wind. Game trails, cart tracks, wide roads with the ditch and broken metalling of Roman construction — all netted the forest, knotting together at crossroads over the pale clay soil. Bro Celien could engulf an army in blind silence, let alone four riders on unshod ponies. It took them two days to traverse, another two days to reach Domnonia's great port on the north coast, Machlou Sant.

A salt wind whipped south from the island of Britain to the windward shore of the granite island; offshore curraghs and wooden hulls were lashed gunwale to gunwale across the harbor. There it was easy to bargain passage farther north into Frankia.

Late summer gales and their Frisian captain's refusal to forego one silver dinar stretched their journey. Five weeks he coasted north and east, halting at every estuary to trade his wine, weapons, Kentish cheeses and East Anglian wool. They rode out a storm in Seine mouth while smaller vessels pushed upstream to show their goods at Saint Denis fair near Paris. Quentavic, with its high port tolls, they avoided. Finally they slid between green islands barely lifting out of the sea at Rhine mouth and rowed up the broad waterway. As they pulled above tidewater the land scent changed from salt tang to mild forest and pasture. By then the lashed plank hull seemed like home and the Frisian language came naturally, especially to Heilyn. At Dorostat docks he bargained passage for them on a riverboat trading upstream through low hills and wooded valleys to Cologne.

Two weeks later, in a boisterous company of laborers, craftsmen, farmers, monks, merchants and pilgrims walking south to Rome, they came dusty-footed through the late September calm of woodlands and farms, through the unfinished city wall and laborers' hovels and nobles' mansions, to Aachen.

29 September 795 + Aachen

"Nothing is as it seems, you will find," Edern said reluctantly, looking down at his empty gameboard and the pieces Brys had captured. For an hour he had managed to avoid his guest's eyes.

Gwriad's envoy to an unwelcoming Frankia combed a hand through thinning white hair which he wore in the Frankish way, cut short across the back of his neck. Edern's face was deeply shadowed. He shifted weight often in his elegantly carved chair, easing his stiff leg, which gave him more pain on cool days.

"What ever is as it seems?" Brys walked over to stand at the open window.

Another wagon was lurching down the rutted royal street of Aachen, its axles groaning like every tormented soul in hell. Slaves dragging their feet behind it somehow found energy to leap clear as a block of marble jolted out. Everyone avoided the whips cracking air over the ox teams; there was no point in arguing right-of-way with Charles's building foremen, who were notorious thugs. Free craftsmen were also hired from every land north of Africa and west of Persia. In Aachen the city's birth took precedence over all else. Even over human decency, Brys thought, watching an old woman beg for food in the gutter below. He would go hungry before one of his tenants begged. But that was an idle thought. He was as dispossessed as the beggar, with his estates forfeited to Mathrafal treasury. *Two gold pieces and one silver rod left.*

"I had hoped to be gone within a month," Brys said. A month had passed already, and Edern was too much a diplomat to say he would never achieve his purpose.

"Charles is accessible, certainly," said Gwriad's envoy wearily, reminded of his own failure to obtain diplomatic acceptance by Frankia and the Pope, which could protect British borders. "If you have letters of introduction from Offa and his archbishop, or a purse of gold for each of the seven doorkeepers. The Empress Eirene in Constantinople has her cordon of eunuchs, Charles has his seven doorkeepers."

"But you have talked with Charles."

Edern levered himself to his feet and crossed his Persian carpet to a wall cupboard. He halted back with a painted wine jar and two fine goblets of colored Italian glass and set them on the inlaid table. Brys watched the ritual he made of pouring, a ritual of delay. He could guess what Edern was thinking. *You haven't a chance. Don't meddle with years of delicate manœuvring by crashing in like a boar in a thicket.*

"I have talked with Charles three times in eight years." Edern passed one glass and sketched a health. "I was among other foreigners the first time. He said my presence enriched his court and that we would find a chance to talk. Perhaps we would hunt sometime. I think he was sincere. I can't imagine Charles not being sincere." Edern was quiet a long time.

"And?"

"The second time Alcuin the Northumbrian was at his shoulder like a grey ghost. No invitation to hunt. The third time we met in the west porch of the old church, the one they'll tear down when he finishes his new church up on the hill."

Brys nodded. He knew the new building, an upended cauldron of pilfered

Ravenna marble.

"You've heard of Charles's rages? From a distance I once saw him reduce a bishop to tears. Others have fainted. The third time I talked with him, he had just fought one of his Armorican campaigns and Alcuin was with him, so I was braced for thunder and lightning. He confined himself to a monologue on the perfidies of the British race. There wasn't going to be any meeting. He knew exactly what he was saying and that I knew, all without malice."

"Why?"

"It was stanza and line from *Saints of York*."

"Alcuin's Latin pœm? I've heard of it."

"Required reading for British envoys to Charles, but I'll spare you the boredom. Alcuin is no *pencerdd*, Cynfarch. It's bad pœtry and worse history — the swords of the righteous English cleansed in the blood of British savages." Edern's words defined a depth of bitterness under his polished manners.

"But wasn't Alcuin singing of pagan English and Christian British?" Brys turned against the window frame, frowning into his wine.

"Don't ask me to explain his logic." Edern shrugged. "He hates the British. Blood flowed when British kings — your Rheged ancestors among others — tried to reclaim Northumbria from Anglian rule. The Irish he accepts, but the Irish have never been a political threat to Northumbria. And God knows wretched Northumbria has long had its wœs with interminable rebellion and murder. The point is that Charles follows Alcuin's lead on British matters."

"Dœs it change anything for us that Charles and Offa are smoothing over their differences?"

Edern sighed. "More Frankish trade into West Britain. More pilgrims and church traffic going both ways. But on the whole it will probably make things more difficult. Charles's friendship greatly strengthens Offa's position in England, Rome, everywhere. That naturally weakens our position."

Outside, an oxcart rumbled up the street toward the great unfinished stone octagon that was Charles's pride and delight. A single marble column lay lashed on its bed. When Brys pulled the glazed window shut, Edern's room grew quiet.

"Charles must have something to gain too. He didn't pull his father's kingdom from the fire and build it into a great empire by being credulous."

"Certainly not. He calls Offa his beloved brother, plays peacemaker between Egbert and Offa, soothes Northumbria and Kent, talks sweetly about peace and harmony in Britain. In other words, he keeps a sharp eye on a dangerous situation."

"And they all rub shoulders here without murdering each other? Anglians, Saxons, Jutes?"

"Even some British." Edern permitted himself a smile. "It's an Aachen phenomenon. Not friendship but a kind of exiles' truce."

"Alcuin." Brys sipped the pale wine. The Northumbrian monk and scholar was Charles's counselor on church and state, his spiritual adviser, his children's tutor, and a vocal self-appointed chastiser of every public figure in Christendom. "Is there any way to work through him?"

Edern laughed abruptly. "If you walked on your knees to Pedr Sant in Rome and back, he might favor you with a sanctimonious reprimand for the sins of your ancestors."

"The sin of defending their land from barbarians? And small success they had preaching the peace of God to the invaders of it." Angry, Brys dropped into the second cushioned chair. A Rheged kinsman two centuries ago had baptized Edwin of Northumbria, who responded by laying waste to Elfed, Mercia, Powys, Penllyn, Meirionydd and Gwynedd before the British-Mercian alliance brought him down. And Edern had endured eight years of this resurrected bile from Alcuin — he must have a strong stomach and a tight rein on his temper.

"If you were Irish or Persian you could present a petition. If you were Frankish you could at least sing to entertain his table." Edern shook his head. "Cadell will soon fall from power anyway, it seems, so you can spare yourself an attempt on the seven doorkeepers."

"If Cadell falls we face Mercian war. Offa will cross the border within days and Mathrafal will go the way of Pengwern." Brys got to his feet and reached for his cloak. *Only one way remains for the land's guardian to serve the land.* "We could survive with Charles's support."

Edern saw his guest to the door and watched him cross the courtyard. Cynfarch threaded between the travelers, merchants, monks, laborers, all the polyglot mix of an Aachen crowd.

Near the gate a big red-bearded man in mail, some count's bodyguard warrior, gave him a shoulder. Edern winced as Cynfarch's hand flew to his knife. Wearily he shifted weight in his doorway. This one would last a week if he were lucky.

But then the Frank threw back his head and slapped his helmet on his thigh, roaring with laughter at whatever Cadell's pœt said. Cynfarch sauntered off pleased with himself and the world. Sometimes things are not as they seem. Not entirely.

The blue-jowled Burgundian abbot who supervised smiths at the new church site said he had enough metalworkers to rebuild Rome. He waved away the newcomers with a plump hand and rolled oV toward the forge sheds.

Heilyn kneeled in the builders' rubble returning samples of work to his pack. They'd heard this so many times. But he looked up to see Meirwen on the man's heels, asking him in Latin about the oversized bronze door hinges. A splendid design, she was telling him. The abbot's trapdoor mouth softened. Heilyn smiled into his pack. It had cost him a pitcher of ale to discover the abbot's greatest vanity was his design skill. Crimson and gold flashed in Meirwen's palm as she produced the brooch. The Burgundian looked over his shoulder in alarm, not wanting to take a bribe — or perhaps not wanting to be seen taking a bribe.

"A sample of our work to aid your memory when you need skilled smiths. For your altar, Father."

The abbot turned the garnet brooch to the light, nodded and cached it somewhere in the habit he wore kilted up over his cross-gartered Frankish leggings. A warm farewell and blessing. Wonders never cease. The brooch was garish and monotonously symmetrical to Heilyn's taste but beautiful to Frankish eyes. Heilyn would remember to tell Cyngen and Brys: alms were acceptable but not bribes.

"Tomorrow," Meirwen said offhandedly when she sauntered back. As though there were never any doubt, as though they had silver for another week's lodging. "Foreigners get two-thirds of a Frank's pay."

"What are we?"

"English." Meirwen grinned and the silver chimed in her ears. "I'll fall back on my natural feminine reticence and let you do the talking."

"Huh. I'll believe that when I see it," said Heilyn. "I'll handle lies and deceptions. You handle bribery. You seem to have a talent for it."

Lies, deceptions and bribery neatly summed up Aachen. A wonderful place for the wealthy and powerful, a dreadful hole for the poor, much worse for the foreign poor and especially British or Armoricans, thanks to the Armorican wars and Alcuin. Brys was crazy to keep trying . . . Meirwen offered Heilyn a hand up and lifted her satchel from the muddy ground. Together they started across the open area that would soon be the forecourt of Charles's basilica church.

An hour before sunset, the masons were getting slower by the minute. A few had found a patch of sunshine away from the foreman's eyes and were dicing for yesterday's wages or tonight's ale. Their job was like any mason's job, somehow blending newly quarried stone with blocks and ornament plundered from ancient buildings. The main body of the church was of dressed local stone, but the decoration came from the old city of Ravenna, which Charles, with the Pope's blessing, had mined for its arches and sculpture. Heilyn wondered if the people of Ravenna had given their blessing.

A new Rome in the northern forests, Charles claimed. Even in stolen marble it wouldn't outshine old Rome. Anyone in search of empire looked not at the building sites but at the ale houses. A patchwork of languages, nations and religions drank together, bearing every skin color from Avar tawny to Irish fishbelly white to Ethiopian charcoal. It was exciting, Heilyn admitted grudgingly. In Aachen you can hear the world's heart beating like a drum, he'd told Meirwen yesterday. She had put an arm around his waist and told him he was spending too much time with pœts. Only one, he had answered. Bitch, Meirwen said, pinching his arm. He'd kept a cool silence for three steps, then grabbed her and danced another three, laughing themselves breathless. It was contagious.

"If we work bronze tomorrow we'll be fine for equipment." Meirwen looked around as they passed the nobles' houses and best inns, then the large guest house Charles built for his cherished foreigners, the ones he invited. None were Armorican or British. "If we work iron let's hope they'll provide the furnace, crucibles and molds."

Heilyn listened with one ear, tracking a familiar sound behind them: English spoken with the Tamworth Anglian accent. Two men passed them from behind, with their own glance of curiosity for the woman speaking British in Aachen. Hair prickled on the back of his neck. Stupid. He couldn't go through life wanting to spit at every Mercian. They were just traders or craftsmen minding their own business.

What did Edern call it? The exiles' truce.

"If we hurry we'll catch the baker and the cheese woman," said Meirwen.

Otherwise it would be windfall apples again tonight; they couldn't afford inn meals. But now they would have silver dinars to jingle. Brys had been open-handed for years, now they would keep him instead. How would he take that? Money was nothing, of course, this was about power. Brys was born to it, liked it, used it well and now had walked away from it. Meirwen found the cheese stall and bargained for a slab of pale cheese. No stale bread. Apples again.

They walked on to the inn, a crumbling Roman ruin shored up with noisome timber and plank lean-tos. They shared close quarters — even with Cyngen gone most nights they had to be careful not to get in each others' way — and fleas were everywhere despite the pennyroyal and rue Meirwen laid down. Not the best inn, but at least the back courtyard didn't have a slave merchant or brothel.

30 September 795 + Aachen

Two gold coins, one silver coin, Meirwen's necklace of linked gold pieces, four arm rings and an enamelled gold brooch lay together on the floor. Brys considered them, glittering in the dim morning light filtering through the closed shutters. Cyngen, also crosslegged on the floor pallet, yawned. *Serves you right, rutting around Aachen all night.* Brys replaced his arm rings. Those were not his to melt down. One belonged to Powys, the other to Penllyn. He put aside the two silver raven arm rings; maybe next time. And they would be criminal to reduce Meirwen's necklace, her finest work. He pulled it aside. The sum of their wealth was a brooch and three coins.

Brys went to the chest and pulled out his finest shirt, Cadell's last gift of yellow silk embroidered with gold wire. He washed, shaved and dressed carefully, to Cyngen's amusement, then poured more hot water from the cauldron at the hearth.

"Your turn. Then dress yourself to be cupbearer to a king's envoy."

Cyngen was on his feet in one fluid effortless motion. "Whose envoy?"

"Where are your wits?" Brys grinned. "Cadell Powys."

The rubble of old Aachen and the stockpiled building materials of the new Aachen were sometimes identical. The last summer fireweed, its flowers mostly gone to silk, colonized broken stone that workmen had temporarily abandoned. Charles had levelled the earlier kings' timber hunting hall and moved his family into an immense stone building which crowned the hill above the church. Rising out of muddy chaos, within its high wall his palace covered the elegant ruins of the old Roman spa town and the posting station. Brys and Cyngen passed timber houses, stone houses, a wall of Roman brick incorporated into a mud hovel, churches, shops and stables, and finally came to the new gatehouse.

The mailed Frankish gate guard bit the silver dinar, flipped it neatly in the air and called a gatekeeper. The gatekeeper listened to Cyngen's elegant Latin — he had studied his *Colloquium* well with Bened, though his syntax wouldn't bear much strain — asked careful questions and led them up a tiled staircase. In a crowded alcove they found a clerk with a handful of scrolls pushed through his belt. Seconds later, a gold piece poorer, they had an appointment in two days with Ercambald, head secretary to Charles.

For the rest of the day they walked the unfinished city walls, listened carefully in taverns and markets, and stopped to watch construction at a dozen sites. Masonry was a rare skill in Powys, which had only a few stone churches and monasteries; seasoned oak was more available and outlasted mortar. When they came to the new church, still rising course by course in stone and brick, good luck met them halfway. Charles was visiting his building site.

The king strode about demanding reports from supervisors and often stopped to talk with awestruck laborers. His retinue followed close on his heels, wheeling together like sparrows in flight. Each movement was a brilliant flurry of brocades, embroidered silks, hats of exotic fur trimmed with feathers and ribbons. Many favored long tunics and sandals in the Roman style, with the short Burgundian cloaks Charles detested; he complained that they left his backside cold in the privy. A handful of monks stood out for the simplicity of their bleached woollen robes but they fluttered along with the rest of the flock. Brys, shadowed by an arch, saw that the king dominated their chatter with a word, an eagle among songbirds. Cyngen watched Charles, as one king recognizing another. Charles the Great was as splendid as everyone said, undimmed by his rage and occasional cruelty. People would walk a hundred miles to say they had seen him and many went home with a silver piece or a kind word.

Brys also watched with particular care, storing his impressions against future need. The king stood a head taller than all but a few of his bodyguard, and his hair and moustache were golden even in his fifty-third year. He was vigorous and strongly-built, with an expressive face that flew easily to anger or delight. Not a subtle man, Brys thought, but evenhanded. One rumor was true; Charles scorned his counts' imported silks and dressed like a Frankish farmer in shirt and leggings. His own daughters were said to weave and stitch his clothes.

Charles beckoned to a carpentry foreman, a one-eyed Friulian who terrorized the ale houses. The man kneeled meekly until the king pulled him to his feet and embattled him with questions. His voice was surprisingly light. The wind flapped at Charles's blue cloak, revealing his only departure from austerity, a Roman long-sword with a gold hilt jeweled in blue and violet and yellow. He left his hardbitten foreman laughing like a boy and forged on to talk with a group of masons' hod carriers. Other workers stopped to stare in fascination at this towering presence. It was like encountering Æneas or Arthur or that prophet the Moors revered. Brys, bemused, saw Cyngen smiling like a dairy cat. Was Alcuin among that feathered flock? He eyed the courtiers and monks. There was Einhard, the jeweler and scholar Meirwen pointed out last week, running around with messages like an ant on an oven. But no one here looked like a scholarly Northumbrian monk. When Charles left for the palace, the building site dimmed as though a cloud had covered the sun.

Ercambald's office adjoined the council rooms above the new gatehouse. Brys and Cyngen arrived an hour after dawn the day of their appointment and found the anteroom crowded to the doors.

Country people had come to appeal harsh judgment. A woman whose son died in last summer's Avar campaign was asking help to buy a milk cow. Two monks from Pavia sought Charles's support in founding a new monastic order. There were many others. The petitioners soon overflowed into the chilly corridor. Brys watched as they were called inside one by one, wealthiest and most godly first, to disappear as the heavy door clicked shut. Most were out again in minutes. A moulding of fine stucco work, shaped with grape vines and intricately painted, decorated the door frame. Brys had most of the day to study its detail.

In late afternoon they were hurried in to the inner room, where two clerks huddled wearily at writing desks. Ercambald's drooping eyelid gave him an unlikely air of conspiracy. A sinewy grey man, minimally tonsured, he wore excellent black silk. Haste and pressure were so stamped into his face that Cyngen pared his Latin introduction to a few short sentences. Brys presented the parchment he had carefully lettered for the king's eyes. Envoys from the royal house of Powys, it said simply, seek the wisdom of the great Charles to maintain peace with Offa of Mercia.

"I shall convey your request to my lord the king." Ercambald took the petition and got to his feet smoothly, smiling just enough. "God be with you."

"And with you."

The door clicked softly at their backs.

Thunder startled them the next morning from a clear sky. Brys and Cyngen followed a surging Aachen crowd to the east road. At first the wagons looked like any other convoy of lumber or stone, a common sight on the city's churned streets. Four plodding oxen drew each one, cart after cart with oiled hides or canvas lashed over their loads. But with these wagons rode the dusty rearguard of Charles's army, returning from victory against the Avars a full month after the king. This was the royal treasure train, each wagon and pack piled high with plunder.

Fifteen wagons, scores of pack horses. Even foot levies wore a ransom in gold and silver loot and some had lashed gold drinking bowls and silk banners to their spears. The legendary treasure of The Ring, the Avar court, had been looted in turn from every city the grassland hordes had raided between Bavaria and Samarkand. Now their king was dead. At swordpoint his son had kneeled to Charles and Christ. But the crowd at the east road was less interested in politics than in the fabulous wealth, the wealth of half a world, rolling into Aachen. The wagons threw dust onto the dark fir branches overhead and drove new ruts into the road with their sheer weight. Brys guessed each wagon held enough gold to plate the walls of Mathrafal treasury and catapult Powys out of danger forever. It was enough to hire, train and maintain a mercenary army for generations.

At sunset the rearguard troops came off duty with a thousand-mile thirst and a flood of silver. By midnight Aachen was awash in sweet Frankish ale. The next day saw many hangovers, guards on double duty and little progress on the new capital of Frankia. Brys had no word from Ercambald's office that day.

A month later he still had no word.

In the tranquil countryside, beeches flared as yellow as gorse blossom, and the last corn went to the barns. Estate stewards ordered their last grapes from riverside vineyards, and harvest ale spilled like liquid gold through the last of summer. *Windumanoth,* the wine month of Charles's beloved Frankish tongue, was a bloom on the land. *Herbistmanoth,* when farmers flailed their corn on the threshing floor, frosted the bright beech leaves to a fading forest carpet. Winter wind touched the oaks; soon they were a grey mist against the dark evergreens sparked with scarlet holly berries. In Penllyn the hill streams would be foaming down green hillsides to the lake.

Brys woke one night with Cyngen's hand on his shoulder, and yellow flame blossomed as Heilyn lit a candle from the banked fire. Words hung in the air; salt tracked his face. He rolled over on the floor pallet and dropped his head on his arms, avoiding their eyes.

Another nightmare. *Nights are worst. Days I can put on a good show.* He had dreamed of Dolgarnen, with thorn leaves blowing past the broken shutters and gaping door, wind lifting the thatch away in grey handfuls. Some nights he dreamed of children playing in the sloping orchard, but they were children of some other generation. *Cadwr. Would Cadell dispossess him in revenge? Eli might try. If you harm my brother . . .* But he could do nothing about it here in the ruins and imminent splendor of Aachen.

"Count Gereon enjoys new people and new ideas," Edern said over wine one rainy afternoon as Brys played the old slow airs for him. His slow smile deepened the folds of his face yet paradoxically made him years younger. "I taught him to play wood-wisdom. He wins much too often."

"We should send Heilyn to see him then."

Brys had no intention of scratching at Frankish door posts for the privilege of singing pidgin to brawling revellers. In the island of Britain he would sing freely, gift or no gift, but here they paid pœts and musicians in coin as though they were laborers. They would rather watch fire swallowers and jugglers, anyway, like children. He nodded and forgot it, as Edern talked about Charles's gifts to Offa from the Avar treasure. Once again he marvelled at Edern's information. The envoy made it his business to hear everything. Maybe that was why he never seemed to tire of Gwriad's mission in Aachen. *Year after year. After two months I'm already sick of playing envoy to the void.*

Edern insisted on limping to the door when Brys got up. His white hair had lost its last rust stains and he used a walking stick now. Leaning on the door frame, Edern handed him a wax tablet. Brys took it, half afraid he would find coins inside. But it was only a brief note of introduction to Count Gereon and directions to a house with a stag carved over the door. He slipped it into his harp case.

"He's having a banquet tomorrow night. Unfortunately I cannot attend."

Brys smiled at the man's delicacy. Edern clasped his shoulder for a moment before he turned to the stairs.

Envoys from Italy were arriving at Charles's guest house as Brys passed on his way to the poorer quarter. He stood among the crowd to watch the king's chief steward greet three men with fur robes clasped over their jeweled silks. A swarm of servants unloaded their gifts and baggage from a wagon. Milling together to watch the latest spectacle was an Aachen pastime, more like a passion. Brys clamped the harp tight under his elbow in the jostling crowd, his breath rising in plumes on the November air. He wished he hadn't sold his fur cloak. This was only the start of winter.

"Cynfarch mab Cadeyrn Penllyn." A warm and mellow voice behind him.

Brys turned, and instead of a friend's unexpected face he saw a tall bearded Frank smiling and extending a ringed hand. No, not a Frank, despite the Frankish dress. The voice was West Saxon but the eyes were coolly without nation. Brys's hand moved for the old iron knife at his belt, then he forced himself instead to nod. *The exiles' truce.*

Egbert made pleasant talk about the Avar gold and the hot springs. He didn't mention the island of Britain, or hundreds of British and English and other lives lost in Dyfed. One stab to the throat, here in a cold Aachen street, would avenge them all and buy peace from Offa. As Brys hesitated, Egbert made his farewell. He gathered his sleek, cold-eyed West Saxon companions and went to greet the Italian envoys. Brys watched him take their hands, kiss them on each cheek and ask in flawless Latin about Holy Father's health.

11 october 795 + aachen

The juggler, a Sicilian dwarf, was amusing and deft. He flirted his drinking glasses in an arc, found a bright handful of strawflowers in his sleeve and floated them across the table to land only in front of the women.

Count Gereon's guests had nearly finished their meal. Brys arrived with the bleak expectation of being a servant and found he was a guest. Now he sipped Alsatian wine and studied the other guests. Men and women were deep in lively conversation. Curious, ambitious, wealthy, they were constantly probing and testing each other. Their comments were frequently witty, to judge by the bursts of laughter. Avar jewelry adorned a number of men and women. Some churchmen were here, including the famous pœt Angilbert. Although his Latin was improving, Brys made only fractional sense of a ribald story the woman on his right was telling.

Brys began revising his ideas about Franks. Gereon's guests were eclectic and powerful, far from a rowdy gaggle of merchants and bodyguard men. All of them dressed with a love of color and precious things that would be at home in any British court. Chiselled dark faces like Gereon's from the Gallic south and fair men and women from the Frankish north gave proof of Charles's astonishing feat in forging a score of small fiefdoms into the alloy of Frankia. *Theodisc,* the dialect cobbled together from a handful of their languages, mixed on every side with fluent Latin. A woman with red hair piled elaborately high was quoting Bœthius. A soldier was arguing that pagan ethics were higher than those of the Christian fathers and defending his claim with Greek philosophers. The Sicilian juggler made a last flourish with jewelry borrowed from three laughing women and sat down to drink wine and charm his companions. He had already taken Brys in hand, naming the guests and pointing out likely patrons.

Gereon traveled among the tables, sampling the dishes and the conversation. He was a tall man with large dark eyes and brows meeting over an aquiline nose, his black hair and beard trimmed short in the Aachen fashion. A favorite of Charles, the Sicilian said, since Aquitania's rebellion a generation ago. It had seemed Frankia would crumble back to a handful of hostile provinces, but Gereon's family stood by the crown. The comfortable town house, two storeys in stone, was the king's gift.

Another course, this time preserved cherries and figs. *Merciful god, they'll founder.* The servants withdrew to the tapestried wall.

"Song, my friends, will lift our hearts," Gereon said in three languages, smiling with a southerner's warm melancholy. His hint to the singer was to try something light.

Brys took his harp to the stool he had requested. Among his audience instead of up on a dais, it was as easy as joining friends on the hall benches. He would try that in Mathrafal some time. If ever again . . . He wandered through his tuning melody and leaped into string song.

Arthur was a good choice, he soon saw. Setting aside Arthur the Saxon fighter, he gave them the high king in his golden court, his faithful companions and his faithless lady, his hounds and his horses, his hawks and his magic gameboard. *Englynion* limped in Latin; rhyme and metre fell as hard as a mason's hammer. But these Frankish nobles leaned eagerly for the words, sensitive to bright triumph and bleak loss. Between stanzas he lifted music from the shining strings. Only a few carried on their conversations.

Women were his best audience, he saw, attentive to the story of Gwenhwyfar and her lover Bedwyr. Brys saw lingering glances between lovers around the tables. Abbot Angilbert was speaking a silent volume to a blonde girl, some countryman's daughter by her simple homespun dress which closed at the neck; many other women's garments were more revealing. Brys smiled across his string arm, weaving sweet regret into the strings, and met several pairs of pretty eyes brimming with invitation. *If other means failed, perhaps I could reach the court by way of the bed chamber. But among these huge golden women?* He finished with a rippling tide of string song and a pœt's suggestion of another story to tell another day.

"We shall hold you to your word," Count Gereon stood, stiffly thanks to an Avar lance this summer, smiling warmly. His guests echœd him, apparently sincere. The Sicilian winked. Gereon handed Brys a small ivory jewel box with a hunting scene inlaid in silver. It was fine Frankish work, not Avar loot. Brys lifted the lid without thinking, saw silver pieces stacked inside, and looked up quickly. Gereon, deep in talk with another guest, courteously failed to notice his surprise.

In truth their recognition was payment enough; Brys had missed this after months of singing only for friends. Perhaps that made him no better than a juggler — but the juggler was trading *ex tempore* Latin couplets, satirical epigrams drawn from Greek history, with a bearded Jewish scholar. He wondered if Gereon would let him read in the book cellar Edern had mentioned. His own learning and lore seemed threadbare in Aachen.

As guests drifted away, servants cleared the food and removed the trestle tables. The many candles and raised hearths sent light dancing across the bright room. A painted frieze of Frankish hero tales travelled around three walls and a tapestry hung on the fourth. Brys found a bench, rested the harp beside him and accepted a cup of dark wine. He sipped incautiously. The spiced wine scalded his mouth and left something as hard as a nail sitting on his tongue. He bit it, and his mouth was instantly numb.

"Nomen sancte, don't swallow that. It will make you sick." A light hand on his shoulder, a low husky voice, a simple dress of cream wool, a crown of golden braids: it was Angilbert's girl. Woman, rather, since she was bountifully swollen with pregnancy. Her blue eyes widened in amusement at his expression. "It's a clove."

"Clove?" Brys stood courteously, as though she were a woman of good family and not a concubine. She could be both. Who knew the customs of a strange country? She stood a good hand taller than him.

"To spice the drink," she said in pure Latin with a startling Northumbrian accent. "Also excellent for sweetening the breath and for toothache."

Brys smiled at her, recovering his balance. "I worry when I bite strange objects in my wine."

"Especially at court?"

"Only at court." He picked the clove out of his mouth and flicked it into the nearest hearth.

"But if it were poison you would never taste it."

"Thank you, that's a great comfort."

The woman laughed in her husky voice. So the abbot's mistress, with her braids and country clothes, had some understanding of the court. She was a rare beauty. *Lucky Angilbert.* She read Brys's assessment in his eyes and color crept into her cheeks.

"I came to examine your harp. It is quite different from ours. You are Italian, I think? You look Italian."

"British. The harp is from Ireland."

"Your Arthur is also British?"

"Three centuries ago he was. He kept the Saxons from swallowing Britain whole."

"We fight Saxon enemies too."

"Then we must be allies," Brys smiled.

Charles might think the British were beyond redemption, but at least one of his subjects was sympathetic. Taking her elbow, Brys settled her on the cushioned bench and sat beside her. He leaned the harp to his shoulder and picked out a minor run. The blonde woman reached to touch one vibrating bronze string as though she could absorb the music through her fingers.

"Will you show me? My sister Gisela would like this. She plays the lute."

Brys liked her unassuming charm. And why offend Abbot Angilbert, a powerful man, by refusing? He pointed to the two central strings. "All tuning is from the sisters. Some tune sharp for a plangent sound, but in truth that's easy enough to create with the modes . . ."

Gisela's sister bent her head attentively and questioned Brys on his modes for lays, laments and love songs. She knew more about music than her sister told her across the lute; of course a woman educated in Latin had probably also studied music.

"Try the notes." Brys set the butt of the sound box on her thigh, leaving her to deal with the obstruction of her belly.

"It is lighter than it looks." She picked out a chord, note by note, then three notes together.

Short fingernails and a shuttle callus on the side of her forefinger. A weaver. Surely her lover could afford loom servants? Brys looked across the room and saw the abbot talking with Gereon. Fair, bearded, tall, dressed in silks and furs and jewels as luxurious as this woman's clothes were plain, Angilbert was watching her with warm amusement. But Gereon at his shoulder slid his dark gaze from Brys to the blonde woman and back again, a clear warning. *Do you think I plan to seduce Angilbert's mistress under his eyes?*

As she raised a royal shimmer of sound from the strings, Brys caught his breath in sudden understanding. He knew why she dressed plainly, had loom calluses, spoke Northumbrian Latin and knew the court. *Fair hand of god. Charles's daughter, Berta.*

"Don't be hesitant." Since she sought no recognition, Brys gave her none. "Irish harpers grow their nails long to strike the strings like a bell. Otherwise you must work harder."

She found a few more notes and said, "You have not eaten. I won't keep you hungry."

"Music first." He reached across her to pick out a tune he remembered his mother singing in summer twilight. He had sung it to his own little daughter. "Now you do it."

She began slowly, then gained rhythm as the melody took shape. Brys gave her a simple undercurrent from the long silver strings. Music sprang from the shining wire. Heads turned. Conversation fell away. Gereon's face struggled between humor and perplexity. Angilbert's radiated pleasure. The Sicilian juggler did two handflips across the room and bowed with great flourish. Berta flushed deeply but played on to the last harmony of light hand and dark hand. The guests clapped their hands when she finished.

"Berta! Long life and many children!" someone called, bringing mild laughter and a few raised brows.

Berta smiled. Not even Alcuin dared to criticize the love, or the love child, of Abbot Angilbert and Berta. Brys reclaimed the harp as she stood and from long habit sat with his wrist across the string arm. When she offered her hand, he clasped her warm fingers for a moment. Then she thanked him in her low voice and crossed the room to her lover.

Brys took another mouthful of the spiced wine, more careful this time of the floating cloves which were not poison after all. Across the room Gereon lifted his glass in a silent health and in a few minutes came to join his guest. That at least was predictable.

"Edern says you may be in Aachen for a while."

Carefully phrased. *What else dœs Edern say?* But if anyone was sensitive to political nuance it was Edern.

"Charles is a difficult man to see," Brys said.

"The city takes much of his time," Gereon agreed. "When our enemies permit. He has readings or music every night with his meal. The Lady Berta likes your skill. She has her father's charm, though her voice is sweeter."

Brys nodded and swirled the wine in his cup. Berta's name was on every tongue in the island of Britain five years ago, after Charles refused to let this daughter marry Offa's son Egfrith. Taking Offa's proposal as an insult, he blockaded English ports and threatened war. Now letters were flying back and forth between Aachen and Tamworth, Edern said; Alcuin's smooth words had almost healed the rift.

"Still unmarried?"

"In his devotion, the king won't let his daughters marry," said Gereon. "But life is too short for convents and denials."

Frankia had also seen too many royal children scrabbling after the throne. The children of three married daughters, let alone legitimate and bastard sons, could split Frankia too many ways. Charles loved his daughters; he also planned an undivided kingdom.

"The Lady Berta outshines the Avar gold," Brys said. "Beautiful, cultured and generous. Few royal houses are so fortunate."

Gereon's nod told him the compliment would travel onward as intended, and a faint flicker of amusement reminded Brys that he spoke as one familiar with royal houses. Given time, Gereon would pursue it. A razor edge lay behind that warm and worldly southern smile. *I like this man. Well enough to forgive him for paying me in much-needed silver coins.*

"We share an insignia." The count was looking at the gold stag on his arm ring.

"The stag is the emblem of the king of Powys. I am his pœt." *If Cadell has chosen someone else by now, I don't know it yet.*

"And are those ravens?"

"The ravens are my own house. My father rebelled against the king and failed."

"Your king is a forgiving man." Gereon's charm remained, but the next question was blunter. "What is a British king's pœt doing in Aachen?"

"Singing for a meal." Brys chanced his good humor. Gereon smiled. This also could fall into the right ears if he chose. "And hoping to talk to Charles the gardener, who believes in pulling weeds to let the worthy plants flourish."

The count needed no explanation. "Another rebellion in Britain."

"Three rebellions. Unless someone stops them, we'll be at war with Offa of Mercia," Brys said. "Charles has a name for advising peacemakers."

"For God shall call them his children." Gereon smiled at his silken carpet and steered Brys toward a hearth with a hand on his shoulder. "My southern bones tell me winter is near. Tell me of Powys and I'll tell you of my golden Aquitania."

Lefthanded luck, Cyngen called it, over the inn's best ale and venison stew at midnight.

Three days later a stone-faced servant in the livery of the royal household brought a message to Gereon's house, who sent it to Edern's rooms, who sent it in turn to a shabby inn. It was an invitation. Berta the daughter of Charles would be honored to sponsor Kinmarcus in providing music for the king and his guests at dinner.

Humbler than an envoy's role, Brys thought, but humility was among the lessons of Aachen.

16 October 795 + Aachen

A small dinner with Charles, his family and a few friends, the chamberlain told Brys on the stairs. Cyngen, playing cupbearer tonight, carried the sea-cat harp. They climbed to the palace's upper floor in unnerving silence, since each footstep fell on carpets of silk knotted in complex patterns. Gereon had one of these Baghdad rugs; Edern said it cost a year's revenue from a small estate. Candle sconces all the way to the high ceiling cast a daylight brightness. Servants took their cloaks at the top of the stairs, discreetly exploring for daggers and knives. Charles had survived two assassination attempts in recent years, one by a bastard son.

A corridor opened on the large reception room with painted plaster walls and windows that threw jeweled winter light through colored panes. Brys tried, and saw Cyngen trying, not to stare at the sheer opulence of the room and the king's guests. He recognized Count Gereon, the king's secretary Ercambald, busy Einhard the scholar, Angilbert. And Egbert. Cyngen's and his own jewelry and clothes were modest amid the glitter of gold, pearls, plumes, brocades and the rainbow of jewels.

Charles's small family dinner would have filled Mathrafal hall. Brys sipped sweet wine, watered because of Charles's dislike for drunkenness. Rumor had not exaggerated but understated this room. Wall panels were painted different colors, and around the top a frieze showed the deeds of earlier kings and of Charles himself, all in sequence like a pœtry cycle. Hanging silver candelabras turned slightly in the warmth rising from the hearths, dancing their lights across the pieced silk tapestries, the hide of the white bear from the deep north and three solid silver tables. So those also were real, not an ale house story. Their surfaces were carved with maps of Rome, Constantinople and all the world within ocean stream.

Shouted orders, and a crash of spears in the corridor. Six royal guards, heavily armed and mailed, escorted the king's family. Charles wore his countryman's clothes and a golden crown. His mistress Liutgard followed, beautiful and smiling, as beloved as his last wife had been hated. Berta, splendid tonight in blue silk, led in a handful of children. One of the girls would be Gisela, the lutenist. Another blonde daughter was a little older, and two young men fell in age between Cyngen and Brys. All of Charles's children were here except a son who was studying statecraft in Italy and the other, never-mentioned traitorous son.

Charles walked straight in among his guests, taking people by both hands, stooping to kiss their cheeks in the Roman custom. A prow-wave of affection ran before this golden giant. Charles had murdered five thousand North Saxon hostages in one day's revenge and made swordpoint Christians of thousands more, burned out the eyes of rebels, made kinsmen disappear. As a dangerous enemy he evinced terror; he commanded love as a brilliant friend. He came near Cyngen and Brys to embrace a barefoot Irish monk. For a moment his large blue eyes fell on them in a smile of dazzling directness, sun reflecting from a wave crest. Then he signalled the steward, who moved guests toward the long dining-tables of saffroned oak inlaid with silver.

The ponderous blessing was in Northumbrian Latin. Brys glanced at the thin grey-haired man who gave it, unobtrusive at Charles's right hand. Alcuin had set aside noble birth and church power to become a simple monk, but this simple monk directed the greatest power in Christendom from the footstool of the Frankish throne.

Dinner was a parade of platters and bowls, heady aromas and foreign spices. An hour ago Brys and Cyngen had shared bread and apples with their friends; most of Gereon's silver had paid the landlord. Brys ate little and sipped his wine as slowly as mead, surrounded by the clatter and conversation at the tables.

Berta leaned across her sisters to tease Alcuin, who gravely answered something that had them pounding knives and cups on the table in applause. Angilbert capped the joke, earning more laughter, and Alcuin explained for the puzzled Irish monk. The quiet girl, Berta's older sister, asked a riddle. After guesses and more laughter, she tossed a bunch of grapes to the winner. Charles smiled benevolently at all; Brys assumed nothing from that benevolence.

Most of the dishes were cleared when Berta leaned murmuring at her father's shoulder. Alcuin gestured dismissal, and Charles frowned.

"But you will enjoy a song," she smiled at Alcuin's obstruction. "We all nodded off yesterday when your student read homilies. We cannot spend every hour dreaming of the city of God."

"Dear child, to make you happy I would listen to the grunting of an ape," Alcuin said in a carrying voice. His warm smile for the king's daughter cooled when it fell on Brys. Cyngen drew in a sharp breath. Gereon glanced at Angilbert. Egbert examined the back of his ringed and manicured hand.

Berta gave the monk a crimson silk poppy from the bunch pinned at her throat, leaving him looking slightly ridiculous with the pretty ornament. Then she came around the table, her blue skirts in full sail over her belly, toward Brys's chair. She smiled brilliantly and extended her right hand. Brys took her warm fingers and got up. Cyngen handed him the harp. *Greeted by kings in splendid halls, never by a royal woman glowing with beauty and generosity.* Berta's firm grip tightened as she led him to Charles.

"Forgive me for not meeting you earlier," she said as they walked, as unpretentious as she had been when she tried his bronze strings. "The correct style is 'lord king.' I hope you will sing of your Arthur."

Forgive you? Anything at all, golden daughter of a golden king. Berta spoke his name, and he kneeled beside Charles's chair and bowed his head. At a touch on his shoulder he looked up into the wide blue eyes, clear and innocent, and the king's reedy voice welcomed him. Brys gave him a Latin couplet in gratitude. *Did I get the endings right? No one winced.* Alcuin pushed a wedge of pale cheese around his silver plate, staring into his wine. Candlelight polished his tonsured head.

"I am honored to meet the scholar of York also." The words were a razor on his tongue, cutting any way he spoke them. "All the world knows the great king's teacher and peacemaker."

Charles nodded, pleased. Alcuin looked up reluctantly and glanced away. *Leave well enough alone.* Brys bowed to Charles and again to Berta and went to the armless musician's chair set apart from the table. Cyngen kneeled beside him as he tuned and began to play.

Arthur as king, adventurer, soldier, betrayed lover, he could give this audience. Here Arthur was an almost unknown name, but did it matter? His subject could be Ingeld, Roland, any other hero radiant with greatness and mortality. Brys sang the stubborn Latin regretfully; in his own language he could make words fit the sense as skin fit an apple. They listened well, even the big swarthy man who'd been cracking his knuckles all evening. The story shifted subtly as he sang. Only a few here knew or cared that Arthur's true enemies had been Alcuin's and Egbert's ancestors. As he sang Arthur became a force of justice far beyond his own kingdom in a golden age, a realm of wisdom and generosity, and the enemies became nameless eastern pagans. Charles's expression sharpened as Brys steadily reshaped the story to a reflection of this room, this greatness. The king smiled.

Brys ended on a flood of string song and damped the strings. It was a court pœt's offering, cleverly shaped and smoothly delivered. In the sudden silence he heard a hearth mumbling over its fuel as a river mutters in a logjam. Then the guests stirred and nodded, and a few pounded the tables with open palms. Alcuin sat motionless, unsurprisingly. Brys bowed, and Cyngen took the harp. *Now what? I need a path.*

Berta rose again with a hand on Angilbert's shoulder, laughing at something her lover said, and sailed toward the musician's chair again in a sigh of rippling blue silk. She thanked him graciously and dropped a prettily embroidered pouch clinking into his hand. Brys stood smiling and saw his opportunity. Before she could tack away, Brys took her elbow to escort her back to her place. Unusual, by her expression, but he turned a difference of customs to his advantage. He seated the king's daughter and instead of retreating he kneeled again by the king's chair. Charles looked at him closely, and a burly servant took one step forward from the wall. *Mair mother of heaven. I never considered being taken for an assassin.*

"To sing before this company is a great honor." Brys opened his hand on the embroidered coin pouch. "But, wisest lord of men, I ask something more precious than silver. I ask your advice."

Alcuin stirred forward sharply at Charles's right hand.

"Ask freely," said Charles. *Was that expression amusement? Doubt?*

Brys lowered his voice. "About Offa of Mercia."

The king's benign gaze traveled over his head to the Northumbrian monk. He nodded. "On my way to bed in an hour I pass the assembly hall. Await me there."

The servant left the candlestick on a polished table and went out. Two of the royal guards stood silent in the shadows by the door. One shifted weight and his spear shaft tapped his shield; the sound echœd sharply around the cavernous hall. Then silence reclaimed the assembly hall, and Brys and Cyngen settled to wait. An hour passed, long enough for a lifetime of contemplation.

Then Charles swept in with another pair of guards and took his throne, his big hands clasping its inlaid arms. Alcuin followed him and stood beyond the reach of candlelight, a grey man-shaped deepening of shadow. Kneeling, Brys and Cyngen stood at Charles's gesture.

"Lord king, I ask your leave to present Cyngen the son of King Cadell, whose country of Powys borders on Mercia."

"Welcome, boy."

Cyngen bowed, brown hair spilling around his long face.

"Son but not heir," said a narrow disembodied voice from behind Charles. "Among the British any kinsman can inherit."

"Cyngen is named in intention," said Brys and dropped his hand onto the shoulder of his ward. *And student, bodyguard man, kinsman by fostering, lord.* "He was out of the country when his father took the throne."

"And you?" Charles dropped his chin onto one fist, frowning.

"I am Cyngen's guardian, Cadell's pœt."

"They are both princes in exile," said the thin Northumbrian voice.

"Is everyone far from home an exile?" Brys gazed into the shadow at Alcuin, also far from his home. Northumbria's bloody feuds had left most of the royal house dead or in exile, he was tempted to say, but this was no time to provoke a dangerous enemy of the British. Alcuin was just testing the water anyway; he himself taught that it was better to choose service in exile than death at home.

"We are here by choice." Cyngen couldn't pull his eyes from the big golden man. "But it is always exile to be out of Powys."

"Powys," murmured the detached voice, turning the word to cool venom. Cold fingers on the back of Brys's neck. "There lies the heart of trouble."

Charles stroked his square chin under the drooping moustache, considering them with large eyes in his open face. Getting impatient. Time was shorter with every word.

"Powys the garden, we sing. And we hear even at the edge of ocean stream that the great Charles has a gardener's skill." Brys read the king's expression more carefully than he had ever read the mood of a hall. A suggestion of a smile. Brys felt as tight as a strung bow. *Breathe, breathe.* "Mercia and Powys may be at war by year's end. All Britain will shatter into small troublesome kingdoms, British and English, with lives and wealth and church all undone."

"The British formed an alliance recently. Dangerous," murmured Alcuin.

"For peaceful trade," said Brys. *Let's not stray too far along that road.* "Some of the trade is with Mercia."

Charles cleared his throat, and impatience put an edge on his light voice. "If you have rebellion among your nobles, you know my advice now. No garden has sun space for weeds. No nation has room for traitors."

"Lord king. This gœs beyond Powys. Some of the traitors are in Mercia. I fear for Offa and Egfrith."

"If Offa wanted my help he would ask."

Doubtful, but why debate the likelihood? "Lord king — if he knew to ask."

"And you claim to know what Offa dœsn't." Charles's golden brows drew together angrily and his voice hardened.

"I was Offa's hostage two years ago." *Never mind how briefly. I'm walking unknown ground or no ground at all. Quicksand. A hand signal, and one of those spears leaps twenty feet to spit me.* "And I was another king's envoy to speak for this British alliance. These are dangerous times in Britain. I have survived assassins, poison and disgrace to tell you this."

"What do you ask of me?"

Hope was a cruel shock after months of patient waiting. Brys's heart sped.

"Lord king, send a mission of official envoys to Mercia and Powys to reinforce our imperilled ten-year peace." *And drop a few quiet words to Offa on gardens and traitors . . . but no need to mention the obvious to Charles.* "This will happen only with encouragement from Frankia's great moral force." *And the unspoken threat of military force.*

"Boy?" Charles turned to Cyngen. "What do you want?"

"Peace, lord king. Only peace allows a kingdom to pursue the riches of Christian learning and godliness as Frankia dœs."

Charles nodded thoughtfully, and Brys tightened his hand a little on Cyngen's shoulder. *Well said.*

"Cadell can rule Powys well," Brys said. "Cyngen will rule with greatness. Either a splendor of peace or a devastation of sword and fire. Help us."

The king frowned. *You may not like it but you've seen it often enough to know it.* Alcuin stepped forward into the shifting sphere of candlelight to look closely at Cyngen, but his words were for Brys.

"Choices are rarely so clear, pœt."

Brys saw, within the candlelight, Padrig's warm room in Aberffraw with the winter storm beating around it. It made him smile.

"'The gates of sleep are twinned. One is of horn, gives easy exit to true shadows. The other shines in flawless ivory, through which the dead send false dreams to the living.'"

"Virgil." Alcuin took another step forward. "You know your Virgil but you use it to claim you see the future. You are a worshipper of demons like all your kind."

"I see probabilities as do you." Brys gravely crossed himself. The Northumbrian blinked and said nothing. *Waiting for me to disappear in sulphurous smoke?* "My house was Christian two centuries before my kinsman converted your Northumbrian king, little peace it gained us, and for two centuries since."

"Paulinus, not your Rheged heretic, converted Edwin. And you likewise are no Christian."

"*Magistre,* if God speaks to me in sacred water I do not question the choice of language."

"Faith is everything, my son." It sounded pure and remote. The grey man, having seen enough, moved back into shadow. "Keep your true faith."

Charles nodded approval at his churchman's sound advice, missing their silent struggle between the dispassionate Latin words. He turned his head slightly toward Alcuin. "Traitors in Mercia?"

"Always, lord king." Alcuin sighed deeply, and Brys thought he passed a hand over his lined grey face in the dark. Surprisingly, when he went on, the monk's voice brimmed with grief. "Your beloved brother Offa has spent his strength buying Egfrith's succession, partly by reducing the great houses of Mercia. He is like a man who cuts three legs from a table so it cannot rock. He has spilled the blood of loyal countrymen. Yes, certainly there are traitors."

Unexpected support. Brys saw Charles's hand on the chair's arm. It flattened as though to strike a blow, then made a fist. *Not promising. If I speak, that famous rage . . . But what can he do? Humiliate me? I've already lost everything. He won't harm Cyngen, he didn't harm the son of his Avar enemy. He is a just man, the guardian of the exiles' truce.*

"Lord king," Brys said. "Three traitors provoked war between Powys and Mercia last summer to cover rebellion in my country and in Wessex. It failed. The West Saxon heir is in exile. The Mercian rebel is sitting in Tamworth at Offa's right hand, waiting for his next chance."

"And you are in exile too." A weary voice from the shadow. "This Mercian and you — you are the conspirators."

"Merciful God, no." *Raw shock. How could he believe that? Surely Alcuin would not know Penllyn's tangled history. Has Egbert told him this? I'll strangle him barehanded.* "For two years I tried to control the traitor in Powys. I could kill only his lieutenant, weeding the garden. Then I fled here."

"Why did this rebellion fail?" Charles was looking into some other room of memory, recalling Frankish treason. He was closing and opening his big hand on the chair arm as though it hungered for a weapon. He met Brys's eyes and deliberately rested his chin on his fist.

"Lord king." *Fair hand of god, guide me.* "I sent a warning to Offa."

Cyngen jerked under his hand like a stung colt, startled out of his usual cool self-possession. A breath of laughter from the shadow rocked the nearest candle flames. So Alcuin was capable of humor as well as homilies, at least at another's expense. *God knows I see no humor in my costly act, in the blood on my hands.*

Charles suddenly dropped his hand and put aside his statesman's mask of pleasant neutrality. The iron king, they called him in war. Brys forced himself not to flinch from his terrible eyes.

"A warning to your enemy?"

"Yes, lord king. My great and beloved enemy." *Not what I intended to say. Curse Latin. Frozen word planks that won't bend around a meaning.*

Charles smiled unreadably under his moustache and stood, a golden monument to his own greatness. "I shall give your request my most serious consideration."

1 January 796 + Aachen

Snow drifted over the stacked lumber and water froze in the forges' quenching troughs. Laborers worked with hands cracked and raw from the cold; construction slowed nearly to a halt. At Christ's mass Pope Hadrian had died; Charles and his family went into deep mourning. No guests, no entertainments. Brys calculated an extra month before he could expect the king's decision on sending envoys to Britain. Aachen was quiet, though there were still parties and banquets and hunts almost every day. When a fresh year blew in off the frozen Avar steppes, it was Anno Domini 796 by the new way of reckoning years.

Brys drifted from host to host as a curiosity, like the Sicilian dwarf and a Greek who did fine wall paintings. He visited Gereon's book cellar often and attended dinners as both guest and performer, an idea some Franks found strange. After he repaid one insult with satire and Gereon spread some exotic story about his family, the invitations grew. Song was his only real purpose now; he would have worked the taverns for silver as long as someone wanted a song. He always sang of Britain, as though he could sing it into existence in the minds of these people, or in his own mind sing it out of oblivion.

News in February raised Brys's hopes. A Frankish mission would travel to Northumbria by way of Mercia, strengthening the intermittent relations with both Anglian kings. But a staggering ten gold pieces bought him the intelligence that the rapid journey through Tamworth to York would allow no time for a secondary visit to Mathrafal, no time for detailed discussion of British affairs with the Mercian kings. Charles was still worried about his own uneasy standing with Offa. The envoys would return in June. In June Brys would be waiting with another ten gold pieces, unless the price of news had risen again.

Through *Lentzinmanoth*, the Lenten month, the snow melted by day and the meltwater froze by night. Brys visited Ercambald's assistant week after week, leaving poorer by a silver dinar each time, only to learn there was still no message from Charles. Would they have to wait as long as Edern? Brys tested his patience as an otter tests his weight on an undercut bank. Not much left to rest on.

Slowly the fight for every day's survival lifted its talons from his neck. Life went on. He felt guilty until he saw this also took a burden from his friends. Meirwen went to consult the keeper of Charles's great physic gardens on remedies for Edern's leg. Also for barrenness, Brys supposed unhappily. After their first suspicion of a woman not in holy orders, the monks were eager to instruct another herbalist. She and Heilyn were learning new metalworking techniques and pulling in profits. Cyngen practised cool-headed Merfyn's philosophy: change what you can and ignore the rest. Until Charles made a decision they could do nothing, so why worry? Brys shrugged off the worst of his fears and began to enjoy Aachen. The Franks were open-handed. He began to wear their gifts: longer Frankish tunics, leggings, gold-buckled shœs and short Burgundian cloaks. Heilyn laughed and Meirwen grumbled when he grew a beard and had his hair trimmed short by the street barber near the inn.

April arrived. In Penllyn primroses would bloom under the leafless oaks, and streams would surge with runoff water from the hills under a high spring sky. At Bryn Cerddin the lower meadow would be flooded and new lambs would be bleating. The plow would open the fragrant earth for the seed. But Brys had lost Bryn Cerddin with its old hunting tally, lost his fragile link to Cynddylan. Brys dreamed sometimes of a girl who rode a white mare with red harness, a girl who was not Heledd ferch Cyndrwyn or Powys incarnate, whose name and nature were salt on the fields. Someone shook him awake most times. On those nights he would rise and walk the moonlit half-built city, with the watch crying the hours on the walls and wolves howling far beyond in the black northern forest.

Heilyn occasionally played cupbearer at banquets. At one he watched two women give Brys costly gifts and later gleefully reported on his eavesdropping. *Intriguing young man. Charming manners but so touchy. Did you see the silver mirror Anna gave him? Her last lover's gift, can you believe it? He would be amusing in bed, I can always tell.*

"If you broaden your repertoire, we can afford a better inn," Heilyn suggested sweetly.

"Tell her you're my lover," Brys grinned. "She can join us."

"This place is going to your head. Besides, she would."

Brys kept the silver mirror and the other gifts and in return gave only his warmest smile. Meirwen came to the next dinner on his arm, a tall auburn-haired woman with a splendid gold collar glittering over her gown of russet silk. Heilyn complained that now he had to protect her too from Frankish mercenary captains and lascivious churchmen. Meirwen asked whether, since he had apparently taken a vow of chastity, he would kindly take a vow of silence also. They didn't speak for most of a morning.

12 May 796 + Aachen

Egbert made a dazzling appearance at Gereon's first dinner after Easter, arriving with a count's daughter and a large retinue of English and Frankish warriors. Rebuilding his mercenary force, Brys decided over his string arm. Soon the exiled West Saxon heir, after talking soberly with the nobles and charming their women, came to bring Brys wine and greet him as a friend. Gereon watched carefully, sensing that even under an Aachen roof this mixture of British and English could be as volatile as Greek fire. Cyngen, here with a dark Frankish beauty, watched Egbert as though he were a coiled adder; Brys shook his head slightly in warning. A small dinner next week, Egbert suggested. Perhaps we can hunt boar soon. *I'd sooner ride with the wild hunt than the man who unleashed mercenary rabble on British kingdoms and drew Offa's wrath onto Powys. I could avenge them here and now in West Saxon blood — but you're safe in the exiles' truce.* Egbert, with guarded eyes and a new depth of weariness in his smile, seemed to understand. Brys talked with him over a current of string song but neglected to drink the wine.

Cyngen left early; he would resurface in a day or two when his mistress's husband returned from his trading trip. Brys walked home alone as the watch changed for midnight. The taverns were slowing down as men remembered work at dawn and the whores saw their last customers. Heilyn and Meirwen would be asleep. *Who has the floor tonight? It's more comfortable than the sagging bed anyway, and warmer near the hearth.* Beyond the royal street, among the dark shops and warehouses, a guardsman joined him bound in the same direction. Armed company was never unwelcome on a dark night.

"Quiet evening?" Brys asked in *Theodisc.*

"Quiet for three days after payday," the guard answered in Mercian English.

Brys contained his surprise. Charles had Northumbrians and West Saxons in his guard, why not Mercians? *Heilyn could identify that accent. Too narrow for Chester. Tamworth? Breedon?* Brys asked in English, "How long in Aachen?"

"Not long." The man slowed as they passed a dark alley between two warehouses. Under his shallow Frankish helmet he was round-faced with a dark patchy beard. "Brorda sent me, Cynfarch."

"Yes?" *I wondered if Brorda would repay my letter with a knife in the back. Now I find out.* Brys shifted the harp strap on his right shoulder and loosened his knife in its sheath.

"There's new trouble in York, and Egbert will try taking Winchester again this year. Brorda wants to prevent Eadburh from falling. You can get near Egbert, Cynfarch. It's worth your trouble."

"How much?" Brys tried to sound tempted. *Offa would want to maintain his hateful daughter in power, certainly, but by such indirect means? Brorda knows I'm no assassin. Something is out of place here.*

"Gold. A hundred mancuses."

"Not enough for the risk." *Enough to build an Aachen mansion. Fair god, Brorda would know the insult of that. What is this?* Brys realized they had stopped in the darkest part of the street and walked on. The Mercian followed a pace behind, making his back crawl.

"A hundred and fifty, if I put it to him special," said the guard. "Ten to me for my trouble."

"We had an arrangement for when he sent a man. A password," Brys said ingenuously. *If he invents one, he's not from Brorda. Who else would want Egbert dead apart from bloody Eadburh? But if he has no password, what dœs that prove?*

"Sweet Savior, I forgot. But the password's changed since you left. Dyfed, that's what it is now."

Liar. Who sent you? Brys said angrily, "Last time we talked it was an estate in Ergyng. Why has he changed his tune?"

"Gold. Buy your own estate. Ergyng, Frankia, he dœsn't care."

Brys swore silently. *Who?* "When and how?"

The guard pursed his lips thoughtfully, pleased with this promising reply. "That's up to you. Sometime before Charles musters his army in three weeks for summer campaigns. Egbert likes you, I hear. Maybe take him to some woman and stick him in an alley."

You've had good luck with that method, have you? Three weeks is all I can wait for Charles's decision anyway. Once he's off to fight Avars or North Saxons, it's a long wait to autumn. I've had enough. The void can struggle on, one envoy shorter. And three weeks is long enough to arrange a quiet departure—for Bro Waroch, I suppose, or Manaw. Time to go.

"Well?" The guard was tapping his sword hilt, already playing taskmaster now that he thought he'd bought an assassin.

"I'm thinking." *Say yes and you'll stay off my back. Say no and you'll find someone else, then try to kill me. Egbert needs to know—but why should I warn Egbert?* Somewhere under his feet, under the frozen mud of Aachen, flowed the blood-warm water of a holy spring. Brys stood, letting himself listen. Only the wind. The subterranean surge of his own blood. And a name. *Gwladus ferch Eli, given into the power of a brutal enemy. God knows I have tried to find her, my unknown cousin. So instead of avenging Dyfed by killing Egbert I'll save the whoreson, because he once warned me about a cruelly betrayed daughter.*

"Yes or no?"

"No." *No man will say he's bought me. In the end it all comes down to black pride.*

The Mercian gaped, then turned on his heel and ducked between the two nearest houses.

Brys walked on toward the inn, half expecting an attack from the next pool of shadow. *Probably I should have agreed, kept him waiting. But the taint would be twice as bad. We bought him and he didn't keep his word. Now I need my bodyguard again in earnest—but I can't tell them, just get them out quickly. I will tell Egbert. If only I could be as generous to the people I love as I am to my enemies.*

14 May 796 ✝ Aachen

Meirwen looked up from the heat shiver of the forge, crouching with her skirt tucked around her boots, and brushed back a strand of hair heavy with spring rain. Rain beaded on the wax of her design tablet as she drew.

"Guess who."

"Let's see." Heilyn took it from her. He had a new burn on his forearm; their forge was crude but the best they could do. The interlace she'd drawn was all knots and impossible connections, one ribbon ending here and reappearing there divided into three and writhing into new knots. It was unworkable in metal and only a flight of fancy in malleable wax. Heilyn frowned over it for a while, kneeling in the muddy inn courtyard, tracing the ribbons with a finger. Finally he laughed, spotting the knot with a raven's head. "Brys."

A game, it was something to pass the hours. All Heilyn's ribbons ended in dragon heads biting their own backs. Was that funny? Maybe not, but true. Hers were optical illusions, simple curves that took one equally simple twist somewhere and turned up where least expected. Clean, bare, barren. Cyngen's, as drawn by Heilyn, looked like rods disappearing into fur clefts. Cyngen attracted women like a beacon. Jealous? she asked Heilyn once. Why? he shrugged and drew an outrageous folly of one-eyed serpents. *We've all lost our reason.*

"How much longer?" she asked.

"That's the question, isn't it?" Heilyn handed her the crucible, still warm from their silver pour, and packed sand firmly around the mold for cooling. "A few minutes. Don't step in it this time."

"You jostled me."

"Thank God I never had a sister."

"Thank God I never had a brother." Another game. Brothers and sisters were rarely such good friends. "What's the next order?"

"Enamelled bracelet. Tomorrow."

Since things had slowed down at Charles's new church, they'd been taking private commissions for jewelry. Orders were steady. One look at Meirwen's gold necklace or Heilyn's innovative enamelling was enough. A great deal of disposable wealth flowed through Aachen right now, thanks to the Avar campaign. Often they melted down fragments of gold horse harness, rings, unknown ornaments looted from India or the land of silk. Their small forge hearth occupied a corner of the inn courtyard. The landlord kept a weather eye on the guard who could always choose to enforce city fire laws; he liked their smithy, which brought in travelers needing their gear mended.

"I'd better fix the pin on the brooch. Maybe we can deliver it while the buckle's cooling."

"Soon." Heilyn circled back to their earlier conversation. "But why worry? It's his business if he wants to sing ballads to Franks."

"It's changing him. I didn't think it would."

"Frankish dress? That's nothing." Heilyn shrugged.

"But he wears it like a shield. He knows he shouldn't have left Powys. I'm the one who runs away from things, not him. Mæn always told me I was punishing myself." Meirwen turned the clay crucible between her hands, not seeing its tarnish of silver around the rim. Not seeing anything. Raw wind and tears blurred her vision.

"All right." Heilyn laid his tongs aside and sat back on his heels. His voice took on its reasonable tone. "You think it breaks his pride, but I promise you that river won't run dry. As for Powys, either Cadell will mess things up so royally he'll call Brys back to Mathrafal or Eli will get him into a war with Offa."

"But Charles."

"Cyngen impressed him," said Heilyn, still reasonable. "Charles understands exile. If he didn't mean to consider it, he would have dismissed the idea out of hand."

"Edern has waited nine years."

"Edern is from Manaw, which dœsn't border on Mercia as Powys dœs. Peace in Mercia is vital to Charles. He's afraid of Offa, with good reason. No one else west of Constantinople could mount an attack on Frankia. The King of the Franks dœsn't keep an eye on Mercia out of Christian brotherhood. He dœsn't want someone else's war spilling over his borders."

"You think he'll agree to send envoys? Intercede with Offa?"

Heilyn was looking around for something. Forgetting to be reasonable, he said waspishly, "If he's smart enough."

"Heilyn — what if we told Brys that we're going back to Powys?"

"Brys would stay. If he needed to."

"Don't you miss it? Home?"

"I left Tamworth and Aberffraw and Mathrafal." A rare smile lit his face under his sleek hair, darkened with rain. "I'm three times an exile. Brys is my home."

Bluntly spoken for you, my dear. Meirwen touched his wrist. He looked down, never good at guarding his eyes.

"Where's that brooch? Don't tell me you're squatting on it."

Meirwen found it under the hem of her skirt. Finished now, it had given them nightmares in planning and execution. Six emeralds in a symmetrical design with only a hint of interlace but plenty of granulation. She'd nearly fainted when the Jewish trader tipped the green stones into her palm and described a gold brooch, something pretty for his youngest daughter. They had lain awake nights worrying about applying heat. They had questioned other smiths and tried a dozen designs. He liked the six-point star. Once in a lifetime, with luck, one could set flawless stones of that size. Now they were almost done. In an hour the merchant would have his brooch, his daughter would have her gift and they would have their fee.

"I was just keeping it dry," she explained.

"Never trust a redhaired woman, my mother said. I suppose you thought you'd sell it on the sly to some count."

"Redhaired? You weasel —"

Heilyn grinned in delight. *Trapped again.* Meirwen snorted and tossed a small kingdom's worth of emeralds across the muddy yard. They drew wire for the pin, soldered, buffed the piece front and back, put their tools and the cooling mold in their room and set out across the grand squalor of Aachen.

"It's always ice or mud or dust," Meirwen complained as they picked their way over the ruts of the south road. April was mud. May might be dust if they were lucky. June would be dust and flies.

"Walk faster and don't look back," said Heilyn quietly.

Meirwen searched his face for the joke but found none. They were walking close to one of the houses under construction. No laborers were at work right now.

"Thieves?" She whispered, resisting the temptation to clutch the precious emerald brooch in her belt pouch and run. Such a huge sum they could never pay back. They should have waited for Brys and Cyngen. Before Heilyn could answer, three men came up from behind and stopped in front of them.

"Helm. Brorda sends his greetings," said a blond man conversationally. In English.

"I seriously doubt that." Heilyn sounded amused. "If it's the silver, I paid him."

"You get another chance," said a thin man with a mop of red hair. "There's been bloodshed in York, and Brorda being a man of peace, he wants to keep it from spreading to Winchester. You can get to Egbert."

"So can you." Heilyn took Meirwen's arm and started away, but the English blocked them again.

Meirwen considered the small knife at her belt. The blade was only three inches of iron. Throat, heart or eye. Could Heilyn hold off the other two long enough?

"Only with an army." The third man laughed in his scrubby dark beard. "He's a shy man when it comes to Mercians. But you can mix with that lot."

"What do you want?"

"Kill him."

"All right, let's talk about this seriously." Heilyn used his reasonable voice once again but he had a dead pallor. "It would never work. I'd never get a blade out."

Stalling. But Meirwen saw the Jew's house was barely in sight and the guards were somewhere out of the rain. The few passing shanty people didn't care about foreigners who came to feed on Aachen prosperity and brought their quarrels along with them. *No help. Nowhere to run.*

"So put poison in his drink."

"No." Heilyn shook his head slowly. "I won't do your shit work. Not even on Egbert."

Delay. Buy more time. But she had no chance to try. The blond man punched him in the face, lurching him against Meirwen. As she slipped her hand back to draw her knife, an arm came around her throat from behind. Something sharp probed at the base of her spine. She flinched but couldn't pull away from the blade. The bearded man twisted Heilyn's arm behind his back until he gasped with pain. Not the subtlest persuasion.

"Drop the knife, darling."

"English scum."

A blow behind her left ear. Roared through her head. She blinked, looking up at grey sky from the muddy ground without any memory of sprawling there. Heilyn cursed them by Christ and Cerne and Wotan in a tight stream that should have crawled the skin off their backs. Another blow stopped his words. Now a trickle of blood ran down from his mouth. Meirwen got to her feet unhindered and shook the dizziness out of her head. The blond man seized the back of her neck and began to gently caress it. Digain had done that. She forced herself not to shudder, not to breathe. Heilyn's captor shoved him to his knees and reached for a knife.

Thunder at their backs. Someone swore. The hand lifted from her neck. The English walked away. That was all. Gone.

A loud crack in the air behind. Someone was shouting. Meirwen turned to see a lumber wagon bearing down on them, its driver flourishing his bullwhip and yelling for them to clear the road. She pulled Heilyn to his feet and dragged them both out of the way, close enough to see foam flecking the red oxen's muzzles and stubble on the furious carter's face. She could have kissed him. And the wagon was heading south. Ignoring his threats, they walked alongside it until they could run across the broken ground to their patron's house.

The talkative old merchant admired the brooch as they gratefully drank his sweet wine. His daughter liked her gift. She brought out a bowl of strange amber-colored fruits which she said the Moors grew in Spain: *oranges*. Soon Meirwen and

Heilyn left, each with an orange.

In the inn courtyard, afternoon shadows reached halfway across the cracked paving tiles. The puddles were drying under a warm spring wind. Meirwen sat on a bench against the sunniest wall, watching Heilyn test the buckle mold for coolness.

"What did he mean, bloodshed in York?" Meirwen asked.

"Murder, rebellion, who knows? There's always trouble in Northumbria. The king is Offa's son-in-law and not well liked. But what has that to do with Egbert? And I can't believe Brorda would pick off Offa's enemies under Charles's roof."

"Who else hates Egbert?"

"Eadburh, I suppose. They say she's bedded with Cenwulf."

"What about their voices?"

"Slave, maybe freemen. Not landed men."

"But from where?"

"Magonsæte, maybe." He frowned at that and visibly put the whole thing aside. "What's the next order? Those damned cloak pins? They'll look like some fisherman's trinket to catch pike. Garish and vulgar."

"Then we'll make them better." Meirwen let the exotic fruit roll from her fingertips down to her elbow and caught it with her other hand. *We should tell Brys. Or should we?*

In a wash of pale sunshine, surrounded by tablets and tools and ale cups, they worked through the next design until Brys and Cyngen sauntered in with their boots caked in Aachen mud. Brys crouched at their feet smiling. *Something is in the wind, but what?* Heilyn waited, humming to himself. Meirwen handed Brys an ale cup. He drank and wiped his beard, as clean as a cat even in these outlandish clothes.

"Come to Edern's rooms tonight," Brys said. "He has a visitor from Britain."

"We're meeting the woman who wants the brooches." But her explanation was lost, even in her own ears, with the arrival of the messenger in the king's livery.

Vesper bells boomed softly through cool twilight as Brys came to the old timber church. People were Xowing inside for evening service. He followed his directions to the sacristy door, where two royal guards showed him into a room little brighter than the dusk outside. A sconce held two beeswax candles; their Xames batted when the door closed at Brys's back. A tonsured clerk got up hastily and went through another door into the church.

Charles stopped pacing the small room like a caged lion. Alcuin was nowhere in sight. Was that a good sign? Even in the poor light Brys could see the king's high color. He kneeled.

"Stand." The king stood with arms folded across his ermineskin jacket, staring at Brys. "Explain this tragedy in York."

"I have no news from York," Brys said carefully. *The envoys must have returned early. At least I save ten gold pieces by hearing my news from the only impeccable source. But the Mercian who claimed Brorda sent him, two days ago, also spoke of trouble in Northumbria. Decadent, vicious English. What have they done now?*

Charles scowled for a long moment and went back to his pacing. "King Athelred's own nobles have murdered him in York. Even now they are clawing for power in that stained and violent nation. Where they went to offer the kiss of peace, my envoys found only rebellion and ruin."

"Yet again." Brys shook his head. Like dogs returning to their vomit, Northumbrians always came back for more murder and chaos. But what had this to do with Powys?

"You are not troubled by this?" Charles halted, accusing.

"I am dismayed. Any king overthrown in Britain is a disaster for all. It creates imbalance and threatens every nation. But I had heard nothing, lord king. To us Northumbria is a far foreign country. It has no kinship with Powys."

"All kings have kinship under God." Charles began at a bare whisper and roared toward a breathy bellow. His thin voice gathered volume and substance, a breeze twisting into a whirlwind. "Murder of a king is only less monstrous than the murder of our sweet Lord and Savior Christ. God himself chooses kings to intercede for their people as Christ intercedes for all men."

Brys nodded, denied the opportunity to speak.

"A wicked and infamous act of godless men." Charles's famous rage beat around the cramped sacristy like a trapped demon with a life of its own. The voice alone did not make people tremble; it was also the white-rimmed blue eyes focused slightly apart, the towering height, the threatening stance, and a name for ruthless cruelty in the exercise of power. "All Britain should serve penitence in shame. All Britain should weep for murdered Athelred and the treachery of his people." At last he stopped for breath.

"His people, not mine. We do not slit our kings' throats by night in Powys." Brys bit the words short. *Dœs anyone cross him in his rage and survive?*

"You claim Powys is without treachery?" Charles strode off across the room, a great golden man charged with angry life, and back again to scowl down at Brys. "Powys has attacked the Mercian border, claimed a Mercian port, interfered with frontier construction that your own king negotiated, and aided a West Saxon rebel."

"A lie bought Cadell's aid, but he gave it anyway to save his honor." Brys shoved his hands in his belt and rocked on his heels, staring back up at the king, which never improved his temper. *What's all this about? A Mercian port? Dear God, is Cadell claiming Chester?* "And you now shelter that rebel."

Egbert, who was a gravely shaken man this morning when I told him of the assassins.

"To reconcile him with his lawful king." Charles roared.

"Is that why?" Brys was acutely aware of the two guards outside the door with razor-sharp swords at their belts and ears sharpened for raised voices. *Or is it to keep Offa's power at a manageable level? Greater power would make him a much more formidable enemy than he is now a formidable ally. No doubt that was why Charles had tolerated his own presence here — keeping a watch on Offa and Offa's enemies.*

"I have no patience for the sordid struggles of Britain," the king said more quietly. "Steeped in crime, stained in the blood of murdered innocents."

"Drowned in blood by summer's end, if Cadell has challenged Offa," Brys said wearily. *One more try.* "Lord king, help us. Help Britain. Help Powys and Mercia."

"God will punish the British for withholding his holy word from the English."

Fair god, that lie is centuries old. I hear Alcuin's voice in this. "Did the Avars convert you to their religion? We converted thousands at risk of our lives."

"You do not talk to your own king this way."

"No, lord king. I am a good deal more forthright."

"Then you shall tell your king that he will have no aid." Charles glared and angrily pulled his fur jacket closer. "He has broken faith."

Charles knows exactly what he's saying, just as Edern once said, and he knows that I know. What he's saying, behind the smokescreen of outrage and old church politics, is that he won't risk playing peacemaker between Offa and the British right now. He'll have enough on his hands keeping Offa from seizing Northumbria. Their combined strength could threaten Frankia.

Charles turned toward the door, having pronounced his censure. But Brys had more to say. "My king dœs not say one thing and mean another. My king is Christian in his actions as well as his words. Though every country has its traitors and fools, my king is a free man who rules free men. Free men honor their kings not with flattery but with truth."

"A free man dœs not serve his king well in exile." Charles paused with his hand on the latch. His bluff face wore a frightening expression for a man of vast power and scant subtlety: no expression at all. He raised the latch and opened the door a handspan. Candlelight sparkled on the mailed shoulder of one guard outside. "Now why should I allow you any further freedom after your insolence?"

"Ask me, I know it." *If I'm to taste iron, I'll strike first.* "Because I taught your daughter a cradle song."

"Is insult natural to you, or do you cultivate it?"

"My art and livelihood, lord king."

"Get out."

Brys bowed as much as necessary and walked out through the dark churchyard, unburdened of all hope.

14 May 796 + Aachen

"So are we going to Bro Waroch? Or Powys?" Heilyn was unruffled by this as by most things. One leg folded under him, he sat on the bed polishing the new buckle with sanded sheepskin. The oil lamp on its shelf cast a glow over his brown hair and sparkled on the silver.

"Cadell might throw me out again, or worse, if I go back to Powys." Brys pulled clothes from the chest and dropped them on the end of the bed. Not much to carry. They could ride to Cologne, get passage down the Rhine, sail down the coast to Machlou Sant and then — "What do you think?"

"Powys," Heilyn said. "You belong there, and we're ready to go back."

"Charles told me the same thing. Twice over it must be good advice." Brys's laughter sounded bitter even in his own ears. Still recoiling from Charles's blow, he was unsure whether he felt anger, fear or relief. Probably all three.

"Finished," Heilyn said with satisfaction.

Caught with his thoughts adrift, Brys realized he meant the buckle. He reached for it and turned it around. Too asymmetrical and curvilinear for Frankish tastes, its whorls knotted into a crouching man, a leaping hound, leaves and branches, depending how he looked. Meirwen had been coaching Heilyn in interlace. "No enamel?"

"I planned to enamel it." Heilyn's hair slipped over his eyes as he leaned to trace the complex silver curves with one long finger. "But look. I touched up the rough cells from casting with some granulation. It's more interesting like this. Why muck it up with color? I like the purity."

"You found the truth in the silver. It's beautiful." Brys returned it. *And you know it's beautiful. I'd like to wear that but I can't afford to pay you for who knows how long. You'd want to give it to me anyway and I can't let you.*

Heilyn flipped it in one hand. "Yours. I'll finish polishing later. And don't hand me any rubbish about not accepting it."

Brys absorbed the quick brilliant smile which had grown more elusive over these difficult months. They'd had little time together, even less time than he and Meirwen, living like salt herring in a barrel. "Sorry to leave?"

"I dream sometimes about Aberffraw. About walking in the dunes of the sand country."

"Alone?" *A bleak dream, if so.* Brys realized it was Mæn's student who asked, the interpreter of dreams.

"No." Again the radiant smile.

"Good." *So many things we don't need to say at all any more.* "Tonight, dream about River Banwy. Dream us home to Powys."

"All right." Heilyn tried the buckle tongue for straightness and sat admiring his own work. "I should go. Meirwen's already on her way to this woman who wants the brooches. Aren't you supposed to visit Edern?"

"I'm going. Why don't you come along later?" Brys got up and rummaged through his clothes for a plain linen shirt. Everything was heavy with gold thread, heady with perfumed oil. Generous gifts, fine garments, but not what he wanted right now. Nothing Frankish.

"No politics. I've had a bellyful of the Mercian kind."

Brys rubbed his chin, wondering if his beard needed a trim, and laughed aloud. A better idea. He was tired of wearing a rug on his face like a herdsman. He took out his razor and poured water, still hot for washing, and settled on the chest to shave. Heilyn watched in amusement.

"Brys, have Egbert and Cenwulf fallen out over something?" Heilyn's smile dropped away. "Maybe over Eadburh?"

"Is that Aachen rumor? Why Eadburh?" *Cenwulf— of course. He could want Egbert dead for several reasons. And he'd like to think of me doing his dirty work and blaming Brorda.*

"Cenwulf and Eadburh are supposed to be lovers."

"*Nomen sancte.* They deserve each other." It added whole new stanzas of deception and treachery. Brys hesitated, looking down the narrow blade of his grandfather's razor. *I should warn you, my dear, but we'll be gone tomorrow. And some things are dangerous to know, especially for a one-time Mercian spy.*

"Is there a Northumbrian connection?" Heilyn sounded troubled.

Northumbria again. Twice in one day. "Charles told me that King Athelred has been murdered. I can't see a Mercian or West Saxon connection except maybe as an excuse for trouble."

Heilyn shrugged. "Stop that, you're drawing blood."

Brys lifted the razor. Heilyn came over clicking his tongue in annoyance and kneeled in front of the chest. He carried on more efficiently and a good deal more gently.

"Hogs are easier to shave," Heilyn reflected as he scraped. "You can boil them first to loosen the bristles."

"You wait till you have a blade at my throat to make cheap insults," Brys said carefully under the rasp on his skin, looking into Heilyn's intent face. Lead and gold eyes. It was an inlay possible only to pœts, never in the practical realm of metalwork.

"It's a trick I learned from you." He swirled the razor around the bowl of water, dried it and admired his handiwork. "I think I recognize you now. Aren't you the Powys *pencerdd*?"

"Wandering ballad singer. There must be a likeness." Brys put his hands on Heilyn's shoulders and rested his chin on his smooth hair. *Why should I go to meet some trader or monk whose only distinction is being British? I could stay.*

"No, you don't," Heilyn said. "Get going. Things would improve around here if you were as punctual as you are clean."

Brys laughed, got up stretching and threw on his least ornate shirt. He slung the harp behind his shoulder, pinned his cloak and started out the door. *Something else. I've forgotten something.* He turned frowning to Heilyn, who watched from the faint amber bell of lamplight.

Heilyn told him gently, "Go."

Aachen on a spring evening was almost beautiful. Brys rambled across the streets toward Edern's rooms, past ale houses spilling over with sweet song. Upstairs the girls leaned as remotely tranquil as maidens at vigil; one of them blew him a kiss. Cloud wisped thin between the early stars. The weather would change tomorrow.

Edern's door was open, so Brys thumped the jamb and went in. Edern smiled from his chair, deep in cushions and sensible enough not to get up. Cyngen faced him across a wood-wisdom board; a third man stood looking out the window. A dark wiry man, presumably Edern's visitor from Britain. Brys set down his harp, no need for it here after all, and hung his cloak by the door. Cyngen bounced to his feet and poured wine. *New girl? You're full of something.* Then the man at the window turned, a friend in a strange land.

It was Cadell's bodyguard captain Pol.

Brys went to embrace him. "Have you come from Mathrafal?"

Pol glanced at Cyngen under his black brows and came to a decision. His cat smile, always suggesting a private joke, had transformed over the last year to a twisted frown. His hair was streaked with white. Brys saw now that most of his left arm was missing. Was that from Cadell's misadventure in Dyfed? "I'm on my way home to Domnonia. I have letters for you, Brys, but first tell me what you know about Northumbria."

Three mentions of Northumbria now. "I heard they murdered another king, the bloody savages. Why dœs that concern us?"

"Charles is planning an invasion," said Edern, not looking up from his crackling hearth.

"Never." Brys found space on a couch, took the wine glass from Cyngen, and looked around at their faces. Edern was badly shaken. Cyngen was excited. Pol was weary and subdued, as though something had burned out in him. "Offa might do it, not Charles."

"Did he mention it, Cynfarch?" Edern studied the carpet fringe he was neatly aligning with his cane.

Word travels. Brys glanced at Cyngen, who nodded. If Cyngen thought they needed to know, so be it. "He told me about the regicide — in a shrieking rage. But it was the rage of a man who has spent his anger and drags it back for warmth. He said nothing about invasion."

"Athelred was Alfflæd's husband, Offa's son-in-law," said Edern. "Charles says honor requires him to protect his beloved brother's interests."

Brys laughed abruptly, then thought of Heilyn and sobered. *He heard something about this too. Ask later.* "In other words, Offa is worrying Charles more than usual and he's decided he needs a presence in Britain. Next perhaps he'll convince himself Britain would prosper under Frankish rule. Offa's not well and Egfrith's green."

Pol frowned more deeply. "That's why it affects us. Why would Charles stop at Offa's border? Powys and Gwent wouldn't stand against him for long. And he hates the British."

Brys thought of Charles pacing his church sacristy. "Fears us, distrusts us, misunderstands us, fights us in Armorica. I don't think he hates us."

"Certainly it puts the British situation in a new light," said Edern. "So it's especially alarming that Cadell has taken Powys out of the alliance."

"What?"

"After he quarrelled with Caradog over Tegeingl."

Brys listened, head propped on his fists, as Pol described Eli's destructive advice and his relentless eclipse of Cadell. *My fault. If I had stayed . . . You are the land's guardian, Rhydion said. You are chosen. Not chosen to run away.* Brys scrubbed his face in his hands.

"Go back to Powys," said Edern, looking at his gameboard.

Obviously. Even without the advice of two wise friends and an equally wise enemy, if that's what Charles is. But how? "Cadell will have me killed or imprisoned if I set foot in Powys."

Pol reached into the breast of his shirt and brought out a parchment square secured with cord and wax. It bore Cadell's seal. Death or lifelong exile would be the message if Eli held the reins. This thwarted Brys's plan to quietly return and talk sense into Cadell. Brys broke the red wax and opened the package. Two letters. One was a brief note in Bened's scrawl. It crackled in his hands as he smoothed it out. "When you have served your penitence of one year's exile for provoked manslaughter you may return to Powys. Have your confessor give you communion. Benedictus." Brys read it again. Church complicity in politics always made him uneasy. Confessor? He hadn't seen the inside of a church in a year, only Carnac sanctuary.

The other letter, almost as short, was in Cadell's own cramped minuscule hand. It began, "Cynfarch bardd Cadell, Eil Penllyn."

Heir of Penllyn? He frowned up at Pol, who was rubbing his shoulder above the amputation. The Meifod surgeon used to say amputees could feel the missing arm. "Do you know what's in this?"

Pol shook his head. "I left in the middle of the night like a thief."

Brys read them the neutral words, which yielded no hint of Cadell's own feelings. *Is this bitter necessity? An act of friendship? Disciplined forgiveness? But how can Cadell forgive me?* He knew the answer. *For Powys.* The letter simply noted that his estates and Mathrafal quarters awaited his return. Bring Cyngen back for retrial, Cadell wrote, since on investigation the witnesses seem confused about his alleged crime. At the bottom in even tighter script Cadell wrote, "This letter represents my wish and no one else's." *Eli didn't know. Under siege in his own court by his own uncle? Not the first.* The letter was dated three weeks ago. Pol had delivered it at lightning speed.

Brys looked up. Edern's pensive expression made him think of Gereon. Cyngen, frowning into the glowing fire, jumped when a fir log slumped on the hearth in a spark shower. Brys brushed away the live coal that spat onto his forearm and instructed Cyngen, whom he had lost the right to instruct, "You will go to Bro Waroch for now. Not to Powys until I assess the situation." *Not while Eli lives.*

Cyngen glanced at Pol, then at Brys. "All right."

"Pol, did you come through Dorostat and Cologne? How's the shipping?"

Pol's smile twisted deeper. "Cadell chartered an Irish trader to bring me right up to Cologne, paid a ransom in Frankish port tolls. It's docked there waiting to take you to Tywyn."

Cadell knew I would come. Brys glanced at the letter again. One stumbling block. "He can't buy me, especially at Garmon's expense. It's for Garmon to name the heir of Penllyn."

"Garmon stood up in Mathrafal hall after Cadell threw you out and said it was a disgrace the heir of Penllyn had to exterminate vermin because no one else had the belly for it. Then he rode for Rhiwædog before Eli could lay hands on him."

Garmon was never strong on subtlety. "We can leave tomorrow. Pol, why are you going to Armorica?"

"I'm going home." The captain made an abortive gesture with his left arm.

He was always proud and touchy but now he'd lost some of his edge. *Let's find out how much.*

"Did Cadell send you away?"

"Anything but," said Pol, recovering a shadow of his cat smile.

"What about the other two wing captains?"

"Rhirid died in Dyfed. Gwyddien is at his wits' end with conflicting orders from Cadell and Eli." He shot an apologetic glance at Cyngen, who only nodded.

"Who is war commander?"

"Eli acts as one."

Merciful God. "So you decided it's too late. You think Powys will go under."

Pol shrugged. Edern picked up a white prince and turned him around and around, frowning. Brys could read his expression. *Don't push too far.*

Brys walked over to clasp Pol's right wrist. "This is all you need, my friend, with your left arm behind a shield. You always could fight better one-handed than the rest of us with both hands. Come back to Mathrafal. Help me in Powys."

Pol looked down at Brys, hesitated and turned to look out the window. When he faced the room again he looked younger. "I'll give you my answer by morning."

After another hour they made their farewells. Already deep in Mathrafal affairs, Cyngen and Pol started downstairs together in search of a tavern. Brys lingered at the door with Edern.

"So you burned my bridge to the king," Gwriad's envoy said calmly, leaning heavily on his cane. "Or maybe you built a new one. Angilbert told Gereon that you amused Charles."

"Wonderful. I beg Charles to help Powys survive and instead I amuse him." Brys laughed bitterly. "It's a good lesson, Edern. Take yourself too seriously and you fall face down in dung."

"We all learn that way." Edern looked out over the empty courtyard. "Cynfarch, if you want a long life, stay out of English political intrigues."

"Fair god, I'm trying." *Everyone knows something I don't. Time to get out of this place. For one thing, while I can't stomach murdering Egbert, I can't stomach him alive either, no matter how shaken about assassins on the loose, no matter how grateful with his, 'Cynfarch, I'm in your debt for life.' As Heilyn would say, piss on Egbert.* "And you, Edern?"

"Maybe nine years is long enough. But Manaw's a smaller world." He smiled, a courageous man trying hard not to stoop under his growing burden of pain.

Edern would be here in another nine years, playing wood-wisdom with Gallic counts and growing stiffer each winter. He was too fond of being at the center of the world. Constantinople and Rome were backwaters to this half-built city here in the fir forests.

"Duw gennyt," Brys blessed him, taking him by the shoulders. He felt more fragile than he looked. Maybe less than nine years. Edern embraced him and returned his blessing. Brys left without looking back.

Rain glistened on the boardwalk below. At the bottom of the stairs in the inn courtyard, Cyngen had paused to banter in atrocious English with a Kentish noble who had incurred Offa's wrath. Another exile. Brys declined the tavern. Cyngen sauntered off, the girls of Aachen forgotten forever, to learn British news from Pol over the foaming ale of a strange country.

Brys headed for his own inn, stalked by a longing he'd kept at bay for months. Mud and unfinished marble. In moonlight the skeletal city looked much like a ruin. Powys had its ruins, especially on the border, but there abandonment was kinder. Briar and grass and earth's burrowing creatures soon covered the burning of a timber house and brought new life. Scars vanished from the land; not so easily from the heart. At Bryn Cerddin an apple sapling would be in flower near the wood's margin. A hawthorn would be in flower at Tren ford, where Cynddylan had died to nourish the earth that nourished him, where Heledd would be always mourning, always wandering west. *And tomorrow* we *start west.*

Outside their threadbare room, lamplight washed past the unlatched door onto the broken paving tiles. Dimly it danced in shadow as it guttered to the end of frayed wick and cheap oil. When Brys pushed the door, it thudded against some obstacle. Two messy smiths. They would have their gear scattered everywhere as they readied for the journey. He edged around the jammed door and saw the dark pool spreading on the packed clay floor. Against the wall, at the terminus of a black smear he had dragged across the room, lay Heilyn.

Brys dropped to his knees. The harp sang out a sweet random echo as it hit the floor unheeded. Heilyn lay motionless, curled as though he slept, black with blood from chest to groin. While his eyes and his heart tried to deny it, Brys's hands were already seeking signs of life. Warm. A weak shudder of pulse at the throat. Through the torn shirt he could see enough to discourage any attempt at healing. He was disemboweled, an agonizing death. Nothing to be done. Brys unpinned his cloak to cover him and brushed the hair back from his face.

"Heilyn." *Kinder not to call him back, maybe.*

But Heilyn opened his eyes and tried to say something. He had no breath to push the words. Even that effort brought beads of sweat to his face, colored like the clay under him.

"Who was it?" *You knew when you asked me about Northumbria. Radiant god, why didn't you tell me? Or come with me? And where's Meirwen?* Brys leaned close for the words but he had to listen twice.

"No more killing." Heilyn was silent for a while. "They wanted you. Go now while you can."

"Tomorrow," Brys agreed. "Who were they?"

"No more deaths. No revenge." In British, then again in English. *Wandering. A long journey to the shores of the island. In the end we all go alone, but I'll go with you as far as I can.*

"I promise." Brys lay down beside him with both arms around the seeping cloak. Heilyn turned his face against Brys's shoulder.

"Mercians."

"Cenwulf's men?"

"I think so. Magonsæte."

Exiles' truce. Fools' truce. Why would I bother taking revenge on hired assassins? It's Cenwulf who owes me one life too many.

"Under the apple tree," said Heilyn. "In Ceredigion. Remember? Gold and lead."

"I remember," Brys whispered. *Now, I'm the one who cannot speak.*

"When the gold is gone, nothing left but the clay mold."

Brys tried to quiet him.

"Most of us value the gold. Not the absence. Not the idea of gold. But it's not gone. It's somewhere else."

"I know, my dear." But that belief was easier for the dying to accept than the living.

Ragged breathing. Hideous pain. It could drag on for hours of agony. *And I can do nothing but watch. Could I put the knife to your throat?* Brys held him close and shut his own eyes against the leaden days ahead. He found one cold hand and pressed it over his own steady heart. *If I could give you my strength, my warmth, my blood. If I could return some of your constancy.* A fainter pulse now.

Brys found his voice. He talked about Powys the garden, about Penllyn, and Heilyn calmed to the flow of words. "At Dolgarnen we'll set the hives up in the heather. We'll try the trout under the logjam. The children will pick wild flowers, they always take too many. My sister will have chicks as yellow as dandelions, and my brothers will train the new colt." Carnen rushed clear brown over its pebble bed as he talked, hidden valleys pooled and dappled with August sun, and the old timber house settled more comfortably into its years.

Somehow he sang for a while. Somehow he talked again. He spoke of life spinning like a great wheel through the green world, the silver star fortresses turning in the black heavens, the undying sun driving the years onward. Turn and return. Brys smoothed the shining hair drabbed with blood. Even now it captured summer, a scent of yarrow and sage. Heilyn's eyes opened and his gaze wandered the room, returned to Brys's face. The singing, the birds, the wash of waves on a western shore. Brys held him, cheek pressed to his cool forehead, until his pulse faded to nothing and his eyes were dark.

Stone silence. Brys realized with one remote rational part of his mind that he was covered in blood, that someone would come in eventually and think they were both dead. It took all his remaining strength to rise from that dark shore. Cold. Stiffly he got up and kneeled, dull blood-soaked clay like the floor beneath him, like Heilyn's empty body. He closed Heilyn's eyes and laid him straight, since he was beyond pain now. Then he washed in the cold water, changed his clothes and kneeled again to keep vigil.

Meirwen came in. Then Cyngen. Then guards and smoking torches and questions and the landlord wringing his hands. Cyngen kept an arm around Brys's shoulders and fended off the worst.

"Foreigners," the guard captain told the innkeeper, surveying the ransacked room. "Must be the change of wind, they've all gone mad. Why the king lets them behind the door and clasped its cool curves of interlace that shifted shape to man or beast or sea wave. They ended their questions and were gone.

In the rainy morning Cyngen found a priest to bury Heilyn in the foreigners' corner of the graveyard. Wrapped in his green cloak, wearing his silver arm ring with its Penllyn ravens, he was not the first to depart the *pencerdd*'s guard for black boards and cold earth. The slow northern spring was alive with birds, fragrant with evergreen sap. More people came than Brys expected: a Burgundian abbot, a Sicilian juggler, the landlord of their shabby inn; Gereon, Edern, Pol, the Jewish trader and his quiet daughter. Other exiles. Egbert had the sense to stay away, if he knew or cared that a man had died, a man who would make no more beautiful things. Brys heard the prayers and the priest's kind wishes. He stood looking down at Meirwen's flowers clumped on the raw fir coffin. The old merchant had given her narcissi, mostly in bud.

Brys stooped for the handful of earth and threw it in, since the gravedigger leaned nearby on his shovel. He turned away, clay clotted between his fingers, to start the journey west.

15 May 796 + Tamworth

Around midnight, Brorda handed the letter to Offa and waited for an explosion of rage. Offa read and handed it on to Egfrith, then sat examining his seal ring as though he had never seen it before, as though it had just fallen onto his writing table from a clear blue sky.

After a minute Egfrith dropped the parchment. "First Cadell has his minister make insolent claims about Engelfeld and Chester, now he wants to talk further about them. He's lost control of either his minister or his mind."

Brorda nodded. "The former, I regret."

Offa got up and went to open the shuttered window. It was warm for mid-May. The room was stuffy after a few hours' work. He leaned on the sill, asked the mailed guard outside what he thought of the weather, walked around, stretched and sat again. "He wants to talk. We will talk."

Mellowing in old age? Brorda wondered. More likely just Offa's insatiable curiosity. So much the better. Now they would find out how to deal with Cadell, unless he sent this man Eli mab Elisedd who conveyed or created the insolent claims. But one problem at a time. They would settle this problem and the next, and with any luck Brorda would be home by dawn.

Egfrith was studying the letter again, tilting it to the candle sconce. "This is a different hand from his other letters."

"Different clerk," Offa said impatiently.

Brorda, already reading the reports of new trouble in Kent, shrugged.

Egfrith wasn't put off. "His priest writes openly, untidily. Eli's hand is exact, like a well-trained schoolboy's. This one is tight and painstaking, the hand of someone who dœsn't write much. I think it's Cadell himself."

"So?"

who dœsn't write much. I think it's Cadell himself."

"So?"

Egfrith smiled up, pleased with his analysis. "So he can think for himself— and what he thinks is reasonable. It's a good sign. We may not have to do anything about Engelfeld. Tegeingl."

Brorda thought Egfrith was unduly optimistic, but after nearly forty years of Offa's grim pessimism, he would share any available hope. And Egfrith could see reality well enough. Brorda remembered what the younger king had told him in Dyfed about a prisoner mutilated and killed, a slave girl forced to watch. Two tortures. Torture was distasteful, but Brorda had more serious concerns about Cenwulf. Conspiracy, for one. Egfrith agreed and said, "We must relieve him of any power or influence." Since his unstinting attack on Egbert and his British allies, Offa was, unfortunately, choosing to overlook Cenwulf's plots and deceptions.

Cenwulf had strong support in the *witan* council; and on the excuse of border unrest, his bodyguard and his two brothers' guards together now outnumbered the kings' guards. With Cenwulf in Offa's good graces for the present, they could do nothing until the next violent incident. Inevitably there would be one.

"The lord in Engelfeld is sick of Powys and wants nothing to do with Gwynedd." Offa shoved his signet back over his knuckles. "We can use that. Do we have documents to sign?"

8 June 796 + Mathrafal

Summer was full-blown in Mathrafal's three-river plain. Apple trees were dropping their flowers, plowlands and woods were green, as they rode downstream toward the court. In Tywyn the three travelers had grown to twenty-three; the *pencerdd*'s guard was returning from a year's sojourn in Meirionydd. Not one man had left, Brys was surprised to learn. Elgan offhandedly quoted a triad on faithful warbands, pounded the breath out of him in greeting, and went to collect men and horses.

Late afternoon was falling when they dismounted outside the Mathrafal stables. Brys found it strange and sad to return with Heilyn's gear tied to his roan horse. Grief had subsided to a dull ache— like Pol's missing arm, he supposed. *I keep finding him and losing him every place we've been together, at Dorostat docks, Tywyn monastery, the high moorland track. A small shock of pain each time.*

Meirwen had wept more bitterly but recovered more quickly, a hard-headed smith. She went upstream to tell Mæn Pedr, which also meant she wanted to reflect further in solitude.

Brys left Elgan to make stabling arrangements and took Pol straight up to the court, before swift rumor could inform Cadell. Outside the west gate, a whitehaired woman sat in a boneless huddle over a begging bowl. She seemed blind. Brys crouched on his heels and tried to talk with her, but she began singing. He found a silver dinar in his belt pouch and dropped it in her bowl. Singing, she looked in his direction. Her eyes were unclouded and golden like a hawk's. He blessed her and went in through the west gate, feeling the first chill of evening. *Mathrafal has never had beggars. What will I find inside?*

The honeysuckle in the colonnade was all green tendrils and amber flowers. No guard outside the council room door. Brys glanced at Pol, but Pol was avoiding his eyes. He knocked. The door creaked inward, unlatched. Cadell Powys looked up wearily from a drift of parchment across the table and returned his quill pen to the ink jar.

"Lord king." Brys bowed his head. Pol echœd him.

"Cynfarch." Cadell put both hands flat on the table. He didn't know what to do or say. "Pol?"

"Pol realized that he is most useful in Powys." Brys set down his harp beside an empty chair and added a strong hint. "I knew you would be pleased to see him back."

"God knows I am. Your wing will be too," said Cadell. *Radiant god, has he left it without a captain for two months? Ineffectual, ill-advised, or waiting for rescue?*

Pol, having made his appearance as asked, excused himself. Brys closed the door behind him quietly and leaned against it for a moment. There was no easy way. He dropped to his knees and bowed his head. If he had learned one thing in Aachen, it was how to kneel. "Last year I shamed myself and injured you. Lord king, I ask your forgiveness."

"Since I'm not my father or my grandfather, thank God, I forgive you," said Cadell bluntly, with a twist of humor or irony. Brys, staring at sanded floor boards, couldn't tell which it was. "You are what you are, Brys. I've always known. . . Get up."

Always known what? Brys took the chair Cadell pointed him to. He sat, uncomfortable, as the king scrutinized him over his steepled fingers.

"I can't control you," said Cadell after a while. "I watched my father try to keep you on a tight leash, both as a boy and as his *pencerdd*. He couldn't, could he? You did Gwriad's work and Powys's work and everything else exactly as you pleased."

"Not entirely." *But an interesting observation. So you did notice some things in Mathrafal beyond hunting dogs and horses? What do I know about you? Not enough, it seems. You've lost the worst of your desperate uncertainty, perhaps burned off like morning mist by your disasters. What else have you lost and gained? Maybe in one way I served you well by leaving for a year. Except I could have kept Powys men from dying in Dyfed.*

"So I'm not going to try to control you," Cadell said. Brys waited for an explanation but saw that he would have to ask. Cadell had absorbed at least some of his *pencerdd*'s lessons. "Where is Cyngen?"

Where is Eli? That's a better question. I'm on trial in some way, invited to lose my temper or push you. Is that Eli's idea? Brys answered mildly. "Cyngen is serving in a king's bodyguard in Armorica."

"I want him here."

"Why?"

Cadell frowned. *None of my business. But I'm less worried about courtesy than about Cyngen's safety.* "I love my children, Cynfarch, though I suppose it's too late to become their father. And I will not make my own father's mistake in not naming an heir. Cyngen is seventeen. Is he ready?"

Brys hesitated. "Ready to be heir." *Not ready to be king. Don't ask, not now. I would have to say he's too lost in admiration of Elisedd's bloody solutions to Mercian problems. Even to Cadell just now that might seem a virtue and not a liability.*

"Write to him. Tell him I will send for him this year. He will believe you."

"All right. What's to be done here?" *You've called me back, now put me to use, if you know how.*

Cadell rustled through the parchments, wax tablets and tax scrolls pulled from their shelves to litter the table. A plate holding the congealed remnants of a meal sat on a law book. As Cadell searched through the documents, a breeze stirred the leaves of a plum tree outside the window and lifted his thinning brown hair. He found what he wanted and read it to himself, following the words with one finger. A fly settled to feast on the abandoned food. Finally the king leaned across the table to hand him the letter. Brys looked first at the signature, centered on a large and ornate E. Under it were the words *Rex Merciorum et Anglorum*. It was Egfrith's seal. Its Latin spelled out cool acceptance of Cadell's proposal to further discuss Tegeingl. A tœhold of hope on a sheer cliff.

Cadell looked up, blinking. "Will you carry my message to Tamworth?"

A sick jolt in the belly. *I'd sooner go to the flaming lakes of hell. Going isn't the difficulty. Returning is. But . . .* "Yes, lord."

Something in his expression caught Cadell's eye and he smiled faintly. *Irony, definitely.* "Not as a hostage. As my envoy, accompanied by your armed bodyguard. I'll write to Egfrith."

"You're writing your own letters." Brys looked at the quill and the ink jar. "Why not Bened?"

I don't—" Cadell showed some of his old hesitation and looked across his rampart of parchment. "I'm tired of flattery and lies. I don't always know—whom to trust."

Brys nodded. It was a rational fear in Mathrafal at the best of times, but Cadell's solution was extreme. *What am I doing here? If I wait for you to get around to telling me . . .* "Cadell, are you asking me to advise you on these matters? Is that why you called me back?"

Cadell nodded stiffly. "If you will."

"Trust Bened and his clerks. He keeps them in terror of hellfire, though he's a kind soul at heart. And trust Idris." *I still don't know if he sees himself as cantref lord or king. Idris offered no help in defining his status, the crafty old badger.*

"Idris won't return. I asked him three times."

"Idris should be here tomorrow. He'll try to bring Garmon. But any foolishness from your other advisers and he'll turn on his heel."

"I suppose you mean Eli. He's not here," Cadell said, taking the bait. He pushed back his chair and went to the window, then walked around the room in fits and starts. The story likewise came out in awkward bursts. Eli, at home in Elfæl when the border raids became skirmishes last year, had taken his bodyguard to Egbert's aid in Dyfed. Survivors of Rhirid's and Pol's wings who limped back to Mathrafal said his force fled the Mercian attack. Traitor to Powys or to Egbert, either way Cadell told his uncle he was unwelcome in Mathrafal. Brys shaped a silent whistle. *Well done. He'll be plotting furiously in Elfæl but let him plot while we get things in order.*

"My bodyguard is still at two-thirds strength after Dyfed." Cadell turned from the plundered book shelves. At his neck the *hual's* perfect links gleamed dully. Dusk was gathering outside and birds were singing. Cattle were bellowing somewhere near the river.

Two-thirds strength, yet you challenge Offa? Remedy that quickly, both the numbers and the challenges. "I heard they were in Dyfed. So did Charles. It provoked him to rage."

"So it was true." Cadell looked at him with curiosity. "You were a guest at his court."

"Arm in arm with Egbert? Scarcely. I stayed at an inn where the fleas outnumbered the paying guests a thousandfold. I talked with Charles twice."

"No one's going to believe that. You're a legend in your absence."

"Legends fall of their own weight. I'm much less interesting in reality, when I'm here doing my work. Your work."

Cadell sighed and combed his hands through his unruly hair. Not a graceful man, but some of his fretting nervousness had worn down as though adolescence had finally ended. *Maybe.* Their eyes met, the king's pained and his *pencerdd*'s wary. Then Cadell walked over and put a hand on Brys's shoulder. Cadell never touched anyone. Brochfael's harshness had scoured out any feeling, at least any outward show of feeling. *You've come a lifetime in a year, my friend.*

"Brys, I missed you. As a brother."

"I'm not your brother."

"Let go of your pride, Brys, you don't need it any longer." Cadell's hand tightened for a moment and lifted. It was a gesture of Brochfael's, with him also a rare gesture of affection. "You're my foster brother, my pœt and my trusted envoy to Charles, if you listen to court talk."

Brys nodded, beyond surprise, and unexpected regret clamped his throat. A year wasted.

"I cannot control you. We both know that." Cadell took his chair again, back to business. "You'll have to control your own ambition and arrogance. What I need is your deft diplomacy, your courage and your compassion." Cadell glanced down at his documents, then up at his *pencerdd*. He had no more guile or guardedness than a child, God help him. "And your love for Powys."

Brys looked across the table at him helplessly. This was infinitely more humbling than any imagined reprimand.

"I've called a council in a week, which gives us time to persuade as many lords as possible to attend. Here, you write the letters. They'll come out of curiosity."

"You're deft enough without me," Brys said. "What else?"

"My daughter is running wild. Discipline only makes her worse."

"Nest?" So Adwen had decided Mathrafal was again safe enough for the girl, a good sign.

"I have only one daughter," Cadell said owlishly. "Daily lessons in music and grammar, anything else you advise. Without Cyngen you should have more time to teach."

"Lord." *More time, more trouble. Fourteen now.* Brys occupied himself with the flap on his harp case, tightening the buckle. When he looked up, Cadell was staring out the window.

"I want her to marry this year, next year at the latest. And I don't want her trapped in a loveless diplomatic marriage."

"If you're careful, her marriage can forge a useful link with another kingdom." *So why dœs it knock the breath out of me?*

"Perhaps." Cadell looked at Brys over his linked fingers again. "I know that a third person customarily takes this role. I could have asked someone to approach you but I wanted to see your reaction first."

Brys nodded, battling the weariness that had overtaken him on the road from Tywyn. More traveling. Gwynedd or Ceredigion would be best for Powys to bind in alliance, or maybe Manaw. There were also the southern kingdoms. "After we clear things up with Mercia certainly I will speak for you."

"That's not—" Cadell hesitated and looked at his big-knuckled hands on the scattered parchment sheets. Whatever he planned to say next he put aside. "Very well. Read these render tallies and tell me what you think."

An hour later Brys leaned, forehead on fists, among the books and scrolls and documents. They sieved through the minor problems and isolated the crises. *Not as bad as Pol warned and I feared. Where Eli left his mark I see chaos or a mantrap. Where Cadell puts his own stamp on things I see good sense but a terrifying naivety.* Evening at last spilled a friendly scent of cooksmoke into the room. Cadell gathered his parchments and told Brys to get some rest.

A pleasant thought . . . "I'll have to be in the hall tonight."

"Why? You've traveled all day."

"You tell me why." *Better if you work it out.*

Cadell bit a hangnail until he saw Brys watching and dropped his hand. "I don't see what . . . Oh. Everyone will know you're back. If they don't see us together in harmony they'll invent the worst explanations."

Brys smiled—a habit he'd lost lately. "Yes. So I'll give my best performance and so will you. Show generosity in ways people can grasp. Put on your finest clothes, pour your best mead, make some gifts. Pol has earned something of worth." He went to the window but before he latched the shutters, he pushed back the short Burgundian cloak so the last light glittered on the *pencerdd*'s arm ring. A reminder.

"All right." Cadell looked bemused. "Do you think we can do it?"

"Can we—? Yes."

"I have to believe you, don't I? You sing true."

"Always." Another smile for Cadell's cautious venture into humor. "If it's not true when I start, it is true when I finish."

The hall was half empty and unusually quiet when they arrived together. The guards slouching at the door grounded spears and straightened when they saw the king's companion. *Careless and insolent. That will end.* A visibly reduced bodyguard, only one threadbare *crwth* player waiting to sing, a few farmers, no cantref lords. The *pencerdd*'s guard made a familiar island of green and silver: Elgan smiling with deceptive laziness behind his black moustache, Marc with his blue hunting horn slung under his arm, Addonwy trying to raise a bet. Over his mead glass in his dais chair, Brys watched the benches slowly fill to the back wall. Word was traveling. Soon landowners, court officers, monks, laborers, weaving-women, nuns and most of the hall servants crowded in. Cadell gave his gifts, made his performance and nodded to his pœt.

Brys tuned the sea-cat harp, out of voice from her long journey. He sang Cadell's strengths of generosity and quiet courage, making no extravagant claims. It was easy, it was true. The hall gave him back too much praise, too much misplaced affection for a troublesome man who had deserted his king and his land. Fickle, they only saw Cynfarch returned with Frankish silks and new stories. So he sang them a double-hinged satire, throwing *englynion* together on the wing, about his year and a day in hell, which some call Frankia.

Still laughing, they turned to see more people flood into the crowded hall. *Merciful God, not Eli. Not yet.* But it was Idris Meirionydd with two sons and a large retinue. Owain Tegeingl and a handful of his English landholders. Garmon Penllyn — with Cadwr of all people. Two other northern lords. *Idris's doing — the old badger has turned fox.* Brys kept a straight face and watched Cadell Powys offer a fair welcome. Then he went down to embrace Garmon and his brother, who swore at him for no good reason and wiped his eyes. *Now we can get to work.*

15 June 796 + Mathrafal

Two couriers returned to Mathrafal on the same sunny morning a week later. One brought back Cadell's letter to Caradog, never opened. Still angry over Tegeingl, which he considered a Gwynedd cantref despite Owain's protest, Caradog refused to receive Cadell's messenger. The second courier, returned from Tamworth, said Egfrith's envoy would be waiting in Tegeingl. Not at the planned border terminus near Gwenfrewi Sant, not at the construction site, but six miles northwest at Llanasa, a British monastery which Offa now claimed was within Mercian territory. Cadell wanted his own envoy there without delay.

Brys found Meirwen propped on her elbows under the apple tree, a the last few pale apple blossoms speckling her green dress. Her hair hung in dark strands, freshly washed. Sleeves rolled to the elbow, chin cupped in one hand, totally absorbed in her Ovid, Gereon's gift. Brys crouched soundlessly at her feet and closed a hand around one bare ankle.

"Caught it!"

She yelped satisfactorily, so he dropped onto the grass in apple-filtered sunlight. Green leaves, sun, swallows swooping down from their nest in the eaves. Summer. Meirwen rolled lazily and sat up yawning. A few petals lay wilting on her shoulders. He picked up the silver comb he had given her in Aachen and began to work it gently through her wet hair.

"Did I sing you from rose and vervain and apple blossom?"

"Mmm. When do you leave for Tegeingl?"

"Noon."

Meirwen leaned against his braced right arm and closed her eyes. Her speckled cat appeared, no longer a scrawny rescued kitten but a sleek green-eyed hunter soon to produce kittens of her own, and settled in her lap. As he combed, her hair dried and lightened to its dark bronze. He wrapped it around his hand, admiring the copper lights in it, and kissed her neck where the freckles had already started to multiply as they did every summer. Speckled cat, speckled woman, green grass in speckled shadow from the fragrant tree. After a while she leaned forward to braid her hair. One strand escaped and caught in her silver earring, which chimed faintly when he lifted it free. He watched her long sure fingers in her dark hair, her slender neck curving above the embroidered green linen. When she had braided halfway, he captured her fingers, then the rest of her. They stepped over the cat and went inside. Lately they had been catching up for the last year, rediscovering old pleasures.

Later, he found Meirwen watching him from her shuttered quiet. Sun and shadow still flew across her like open cloud, but at last she had unpacked Heilyn's half-finished work. She had given Mæn Pedr the seeds from Charles's physic garden in Aachen. After debating with him whether it was too late to plant, they planted half. No shoots yet, she reported, but there was time. Mæn especially welcomed the seeds of red poppies, from which Charles's physicians derived a concoction to ease pain, and the vial of poppy syrup. She spent days in the sanctuary helping the priest. *We heal ourselves in different ways.*

At noon Elgan walked whistling into the colonnade and found them on the door-bench. Brys opened one saddlebag as an afterthought and shoved in his gameboard. They walked together to the north gate, where the rest of the *pencerdd*'s guard waited with the horses. After Brys mounted and the others started away, Meirwen came to lean by his knee. She took his hand and kissed the palm. Something new from Meirwen, his silver thorn. Brys brushed an apple blossom from her freckled cheek and started north.

18 June 796 ✝ Rhuddlan

Three days north of Mathrafal they sat their horses west of Rhuddlan ford at sunset. Across Clwyd, under the early darkness, lanterns swung in front of the river taverns on the quays. Five miles northeast lay Llanasa where Offa's envoy waited.

Brys remembered the river tavern where he had worked three years ago stacking kegs in the storeroom and rolling drunks out the door. *Tempting to go in and buy ale for all, but the innkeeper might slip a cog and put me to work again.*

He turned west through the flat river meadows and halted at the first farm big enough to quarter twenty-odd men. In daylight, he realized later, he would have seen the low-lying clustered houses and strip fields. He pounded on the unlatched door and walked in. And stopped short, staring down the smooth shaft of a cross-braced boar spear.

"Stand where you are, peacock," said an English voice, speaking British. Its owner stood three steps below, on the sunken floor of the house, a beamy man with sharp blue eyes and a greying blond beard.

Brys glanced down into the dim house. A handful of sons and farm workers had armed hastily at a glimpse of armed riders. Women and children huddled in the loft. The man at the other end of the spear was one of Tegeingl's English landowners. *Stupid mistake, but it's too late to back down now.*

"Is this your best welcome for Cadell Powys's envoy?" Brys let the spear's kiss against his chest help him sound aggrieved.

"Prove it."

Cautiously he pushed the cloak back from his right arm to show the *pencerdd*'s arm ring. The spear lowered a slow inch, then the man grounded it and offered a mild welcome without apology. Brys, breathing again, clasped his arm.

"We thought you were Mercians," the landowner said with no hint of irony. The young men behind him silently replaced their weapons on the wall pegs. Children tumbled giggling out of the loft.

"I've come to talk with Offa's envoy at Llanasa."

"Good. You and Brorda can winnow Cadell's chaff for him."

Brorda? That's hopeful. The English landowner called over a son and gave orders. Brys went outside.

"Addonwy, not one quarrel — Marc, not even one glance at a girl," he warned. "Or you go back to Mathrafal in leg-irons. Your host's name is Rendil Osmodson."

A slow grin from Elgan and a ripple of surprised comment. One of the new men muttered, "Now we're part of the performance." Addonwy told him if he didn't like it he could go back down to the king's bodyguard. Brys left them unsaddling and took Elgan in to drink Rendil's mead, which his white-blonde daughter poured with a pretty flourish.

At dawn Rendil's youngest son rode a message to Llanasa and brought an answer back: the day after tomorrow, with three unarmed men as escort. *Brorda is letting me know I'm a supplicant. I hope we don't all perform so well we lose sight of our purpose.*

Rendil's south hayfield was ready for cutting and Elgan said the guard needed a workout. Brys nodded. Let them burn off some energy and pay for their keep. The farm boys scythed circles around them with the sweeping strokes of long practice, taunting them for being idle aristocrats. Glances of speculation. A few bets changed hands. Most of the *pencerdd*'s guard were farm-bred in Penllyn. Stripped to their breeches, they all put their backs into the scythes until grass and chaff flew. By mid-afternoon both sides of the field were levelled and the long windrows raked out, and both teams sprawled in the scented shade of the dog roses.

Rendil's daughters and servant girls brought bland English ale, their morning's baking, a braid of onions, a wheel of hard yellow cheese and wizened apples. Together they sat down to eat. Brys pricked his blisters and lay down in the long grass, watching clouds drift overhead. He closed his eyes and heard English and British, random mixtures of both, and laughter. *It could be like this always. English in Powys, British in Mercia. Maybe some day we won't even need a patrolled border.* By the cool of evening, when they were pulling on shirts and picking up the tools, Marc was walking hand in hand with Rendil's daughter. So much for his dire warning. Later Marc told Brys her father said they could marry. He fidgeted and asked Brys's permission.

I'm not your kinsman to give you permission, Brys almost said, then remembered Marc was a nun's son. He grinned. "Will you invite me to the wedding?"

The second day Brys and Rendil walked to the estuary and spent the afternoon crouching on the floorboards of a net-curragh to jig the oarweed beds for flounder. Brys would rather be tickling trout by a sunny riffle, but at least this would raise a blister on Brorda when he heard. Rendil was good company, full of stories. Their sack bulged with fish wrapped in seaweed when they went home.

21 June 796 + Llanasa

To Elgan's disgust, Brys dressed carefully the next morning. "What if they take you hostage? Or kill you? At least wear my mail shirt."

Brys dropped a tunic of heavily embroidered blue silk over his white dœskin breeches and pulled on boots of fine green leather. Then came finger rings of Avar gold, bracelets, the gold-mounted sheath Meirwen had made for his old knife, the belt with Heilyn's last silver buckle. He pinned the cloak of white Burgundian wool with a silver ring brooch as wide as his palm and rubbed a drop of scented Syrian oil in his hair. Elgan shook his head when Brys dropped his gameboard in the saddlebag.

"Three unarmed men can't save me anyway. Lead with the king if you want to turn the attack back on the attacker."

Brys rode east through Rendil's open woods and river meadows to Rhuddlan ford. Ravens circled above the shallows and the reedy river margin, drawn by something dying nearby. River Clwyd swirled against its red eastern bank, high with runoff water, and he made a slow and cautious crossing. As Carnlas's hooves clipped the paving stones on dry ground again, four riders came through the willows on the Mercian side and descended to the ford in a cloud of reddish dust. Their captain spoke British with Brorda's strange accent. Brys rode east with them past the old stronghold of Cær Hiraddug toward a low and uneven ridge. At its southern end was Halkyn, with its lead-silver mines. Southeast beyond the ridge lay the survey markers and the raw first trench of Offa's border where construction proceeded despite Cadell's claims. At the northern end, in an east-sloping crease, lay the small whitewashed timber church and monks' cells of Llanasa.

Brorda came from the largest cell with a full-hide parchment map rolled in one hand. The monks were at mass; plainchant rose from the small church. Brys dismounted and his escort took Carnlas. Brorda's clear blue eyes were steady and noncommittal. His hair had lost its last color but he stood straight and solid; he was still a fighting man, not a soft Tamworth counselor. He noted Brys's fine clothes, his gold and silver, but his gaze lingered on his face. In his own good time, he smiled.

"No harp? I thought you might honor me with song," he said in English.

"And hear that I sang an enchantment on you? Too easy. We'll have to talk plainly like other envoys." Brys tapped the embroidered bag under his arm with a ringed forefinger. "But our game has been delayed too long. The stakes have risen."

Brorda showed Brys inside, stooping for the lintel. Sleeping shelf, beams carved with interlace, rushes on the floor: everything was sweet-smelling and clean. Llanasa was a British church with British monks — one of Brys's northern kinsmen had founded it two centuries earlier — for all that Offa now claimed it lay within the boundaries of Mercian Engelfeld. The broad Dyfrdwy estuary flowed tidally a mile east, out of sight and sound, and the Irish Sea lay about the same distance north. Brorda's choice of locale was calculated provocation.

Brys sat in one of the two fine inlaid chairs, probably the abbot's best. Brorda settled in the other. A servant brought wine in a sweating clay jar and set it on a table. Then he stood sullenly waiting for an order. Brys saw the loosely plaited leather collar on his neck and the raw hatred in his eyes. A slave, and recent.

"Pour," Brorda told the slave, exaggerating the word and pointing as though the man barely understood English. A British slave? Another reminder of Mercian power in Tegeingl, as deliberate as Brorda's British bodyguard captain. At least Mercia still respected the southern border Offa and Brochfael drew years ago, despite Cadell's ill-advised bluster and Offa's answering rage. The slave paused just long enough to be insolent, filled their wine cups and scowled at Brorda's nod of dismissal. Offa's minister frowned; his slave's look alone was enough to poison the wine.

Brys allowed himself no reaction, denying any advantage to Brorda. Instead he brought out his board of cherrywood and ivory, his gamesmen set with red amber and silver. Brorda admired a few pieces, then began to place them within the squares' silver boundaries. In Tamworth he had disavowed knowledge of the game; this was a different match.

"You are my guest in Engelfeld," Brorda said. "Choose for color or first play."

Brys took it with a prince. Foregoing the advantage of attack, he chose, "First play."

Brorda took the attacking white army. Brys lifted a red prince with silver eyes and made a deliberate assault on the white host while his king was still safely surrounded. Offa's minister smiled and mobilized his warriors. They played a fast game, wine forgotten at their elbows.

"You learned the game in Elfed?"

"From my grandfather's falconer. He would bet his favorite merlin on a game, though I never took her."

"The man who said he was of the royal house."

"I always wondered too," Brorda said.

The white warriors' opening strength became their vulnerability as the red princes flung them from the squares one by one. Slowly the ivory army was halved. Brys made a phalanx of his red king and his princes, though Brorda would clearly see their undefended backs.

"Fine artistry," said Brorda, studying the king. Without lifting the piece from the cherrywood square he touched the small silver *hual* chain around the gamesman's neck. "Maybe better for show than for play. This could go astray and then who would know where the power lies?"

"Good players always know." Brys captured another ivory warrior, wide silver eyes in a pale bleak face. "It's in the blood."

"So they say, Penllyn."

The white warriors held their silver-bordered territory in a shrinking shield wall. Brys sent out his red princes against the white host in a series of risks he would never have needed against a poorer player. Brorda knew his game, but luck was singing in Brys's veins. He held his king in sanctuary and sacrificed his princes one by one until the last ivory warrior stood alone. Brys sipped cool wine and waited for his opponent to make a pointless move, his only choice now. But Brorda resolutely moved his warrior between the last cherrywood princes, forcing Brys to pull him down. Brys laid the grim little figure beside the board, where a few drops of wine had jolted from a cup. The English noble gravely raised his cup in a health.

"We neglected to lay bets."

Brys swirled the bitter lees in his cup and flicked them out onto the rushes. "I'll be content with the truth."

"I read your letter." Brorda filled their cups again.

"And I heard about Dyfed. You went gently through the south, for which I thank you and curse Egbert. As for Offa's threats to Cadell, my lord had given his word to aid Dyfed."

"Cymry, fellow-countrymen. But Dyfed is not even part of your alliance." Not a sneer, it sounded more like sadness.

"You find that strange?"

"Among your people *or* mine, Cynfarch. We see you all as *Wealas* and you see us all as *Saeson.* A distant view blurs the internal fractures that we see clearly ourselves. We each need a mirror to reflect back to us all the image of a single people."

"You've built that mirror."

"Offa's border?" Brorda laughed wearily. "An overgrown ditch that couldn't keep out any warband but for Brochfael's goodwill. Now we have Cadell's goodwill, despite his dangerous kinsman, and a peaceful border with Powys. Yet Kent and the West Saxons keep rebelling, and Northumbria devours itself like a serpent in a hero saga. And your alliance is dissolving."

"Not for long. We make alliances when we need them, though we love to quarrel between times," Brys said over the wine cup. How much would he listen to without insult? "Take a lesson from our text, Brorda. We draw together mostly through marriage and mutual gain. The English draw together mostly through war and conquest. Which will survive?"

Low voices passed outside. The monks had finished their offices and were returning to their fields.

"God knows. Offa thinks he knows." Brorda looked past him to the open door. He had drifted into his archaic British, apparently without noticing. "We are uneasy enemies — we might as well be uneasy allies. I doubt we can strike the ancient fear and hatred into each other again. But we would only truly co-operate against an outside threat."

"Is that what you think? Our alliance is a response to a threat?"

"Certainly. So do you. Mercia is the threat now. Your talk of trade is only a marginal gloss. Offa will never provoke the British without reason, but what comes after Offa?"

Brys looked thoughtfully into his wine. *True, all of it.* "Egbert."

"Egbert means the certain death of Mercia," Brorda said. "He cannot be allowed to return to Wessex, though it is his rightful patrimony. No doubt you realize that you should have killed him in Aachen. For once Cenwulf had the right idea."

"You knew?" *How much?*

"Only afterward. I'm sorry about your friend. And pleased about your return. Now you will be lord in Penllyn."

Brys looked up, stung by anger. "I'll be my cousin Garmon's loyal man. As I have been always." He poured again and raised his cup. "To a threat serious enough to make us allies."

"Charles of Frankia has denied us one opportunity," Brorda said dryly after he drank the health. "His plan to invade Northumbria was mainly fear that Offa would do it first. And indigestion. He swallows too much hot air with his news of Britain. Alcuin is a good and wise man but . . ." He let it hang.

"A poor historian."

"I was astonished that he talked with you."

"So was he, Brorda."

The man's big honest laugh, straight from the belly, hadn't changed. Offa's minister clicked his cup down on the table and leaned forward. "In truth there is another threat, these sea raiders we've fought off every summer for three years. They call themselves *vikings* as though they were out sailing for pleasure. Thieving and burning and slaving are bad enough, but they also torture and mutilate. They act without pity or restraint."

"Unspeakable savages," Brys agreed, remembering tales of long-ago Anglian raids.

"Gwriad is vulnerable to raids on his island of Man. I hear his eyes are on Gwynedd."

"Gwriad is not strong enough to seize Gwynedd, however weak Caradog is." Brys frowned at the sweet bedstraw under his boots, thinking aloud. "Maybe with his Irish cousins? No. I don't think so."

"His older sons are married," said Brorda. "The third will marry in Gwynedd. Or Powys."

And only one royal woman remains unwed in Powys. Nest, who once linked her brown fingers around my neck . . . Brys looked out the door. Noon. The shadows lay bunched under the fruit trees. A monk was raking grass in the orchard, singing off-key. After a while he asked, "Dœs Offa know that you talk to an enemy this way?"

"Offa thinks you're a friend of Mercia after reading your letter. He instructed me to reward you with estates in Wreocansaete."

Brys kept the lid on his anger. "My Latin is not strong, Brorda. I told Charles that Offa was my great and beloved enemy. At the time I thought it was a clumsy mistake — now I think the river spoke." He weighed Brorda's puzzled look. "The depth and not the surface. Do you understand me?"

"Wyrd."

"If you like. What shall we do about Tegeingl?"

"Nothing, I would like to say. Egfrith agrees — let bygones be bygones. Let Cadell capitulate in some minor way. The old borderline stands and we get on with construction. But Offa is still angry and he wants Cadell to know it. I have instructions to wait for his courier. Another hour."

Brorda went to talk with his captain. Brys drained his wine and walked out of the cell. The British slave leaned beside the orchard gate, arms hanging listlessly at his sides.

"Where from?" Brys asked.

Brorda's slave deliberately spat between them. Brys saw himself in the man's pinched mouth and narrow eyes: a Mathrafal idler laughing over wine with an English noble while another bore the gall of an English collar.

"Stay angry, friend, and you can survive it. I did." Brys walked away. The slave's sullen look was a blow to his back.

The monks' orchard was a bright jewel in its green bowl of plowland and woodland. Apple blossom still whitened the boughs, here in the north, and the plums were small and green. Foxgloves and eyebright crowded around the grey trunks. For an hour or more Brys walked among the trees with Brorda. Dew clung in silver beads to the shaded grass; their steps through this peaceful place left a dark trail. A flight of ravens flew up from a field margin below and lighted on the church's thatch. The monks must be gentle souls; ravens never settled where people tormented them.

Brorda stopped once near the east gate to look over the garden. "What do you want for yourself, Cynfarch?"

Summer days. A house full of children. Meirwen. Penllyn. To be sung a thousand years, the only immortality. All notes of one chord. "Peace. And everything it makes possible. And you?"

"What else can a sane man want, after forty years of blood that only bought more blood? Why in the name of Our Savior need it be anything but peace?"

Brys heard his anguish and briefly clasped his shoulder. "Perhaps now all we can hope for is armed truce, an equal balance of power. Someday we could be allies again." *We could be friends, you and I — instead of enemies playing a dangerous game on territories divided by raw earth instead of silver wire.*

Brorda reached and pulled down a white-freighted apple branch, careful not to destroy the flower and thus the fruit. "In the end we realize, if we have any shred of wisdom, the unimportance of race and territory."

"What is important, Brorda?"

"What men make of themselves. What they do when their backs are to the wall, whether they do good or evil or carelessly do nothing at all."

"Women and men. If you overlook women's power you're missing half the players."

"God knows I've learned that lesson from Eadburh."

"But why should we wait until we feel the wall at our backs?" It was a question Brys had debated with Mæn. "Then *daioni,* virtue, becomes accidental. There are only two ways, not three. Doing nothing must be one thing or the other, good or evil. Rarely is there a middle road — never, if we wait until we're forced to a decision."

Brorda released the branch gently, and only a few blossoms showered to the grass. "You're saying we are obliged to make an opportunity for good?"

Brys smiled at him, deliberately dropping his guard. "Another Pelagian."

"Your family was, I remember."

"Generations ago. Not our worst sin."

Brorda shook his head, which could be agreement or regret. "Yes, we must create good. But we must also do good when the opportunity arises."

"You have a pœt's tongue. I'll borrow that."

"Otherwise think of the cost. All too often we learn what we should have done by doing the opposite. Then we reap naught but sorrow."

"Sorrow not to do good as it comes. Another English riddle, back to front and inside out."

"Yours to solve, my friend." Brorda dropped an arm across Brys's shoulders as they walked on, a familiarity Brorda rarely offered and Brys rarely encouraged. After that they talked about dogs; Brys promised an Irish hound pup from the next litter at Bryn Cerddin. He invited Brorda to visit after the next border parley. Both of them knew there would never be a visit.

A long stillness held the monks' quiet orchard until the bell clanged out nones at mid-afternoon. Then Brorda's captain came to say riders were approaching from the southeast, where the English were building a church at Basingwerk. Together they walked out through the orchard gate.

Brorda impassively watched the riders dismount in front of the church. One man was salted with road dust and streaked with his mount's sprayed foam. Another twenty were fresh, wearing war gear except for the hatchet-faced priest. And Cenwulf. Why Cenwulf? Offa could have sent anyone, unless he had finally murdered all his other kinsmen. Brys looked for Gwladus ferch Eli, but perhaps he wasn't foolish enough to let her venture into British territory. Or perhaps she no longer could. *Am I too late?* The raven clan circled the church and the hillside, cronking their discontent, then settled among the blossoming orchard trees.

Cenwulf dismounted and took a packet from the courier. He looked at it, dusted it on his thigh, walked slowly toward Brorda. Drawing out the moment, making them both wait, as though Brorda also were an enemy. On the letter, through the dust, Brys saw the large square monogram of Offa and Egfrith.

"You have made great haste to hesitate now," Brorda told Cenwulf in a voice of northern ice.

Brys looked at the two men. An aging noble who had spent a lifetime in Offa's service, a young noble who gave no true allegiance to anyone. *Not friends, not even allies.* A darkness shivered the air on every side. *Brochfael, Geraint, Heilyn, maybe Gwladus. How many other lives have you stolen?* Cenwulf looked at Brys and away. Enjoying his game with Offa's message, savoring his own fear. His priest edged to his side. Brys smiled. *Oh yes, I understand. Devout Cenwulf with his fear of sorcery.*

"My ravens are waiting for you," Brys said quietly.

Cenwulf stiffened but refused to look over his shoulder into the orchard. He touched the scarred left corner of his mouth with his tongue, just where a boot caught it last year on the border; Brys had never understood why, when he had a sword at his belt, Cenwulf had only given him the fist. Proving his strength? A weakness lay inside that strength, craving displays of terror and dominance. A big man, strong and tall, who liked to cause pain and fear.

"Not in the orchard." Brys felt the skin tighten above his eyes and across his shoulders. "At the river."

Cenwulf stared at him for an instant, then leaned to the thin priest's murmur and handed over his letter. Brorda read it, glanced once at Cenwulf and gave it to Brys.

Brys scanned its long-tailed English script. The border would remain where Brochfael and Offa drew it. *Good.* Cadell Powys would provide work crews for the northern section and build according to Mercian specifications. *We can live with that. I can even put a good face on it over the string arm. See our goodwill? We also take responsibility for the border.* And a hundred pounds of Halkyn silver in tribute; that was more than Halkyn had produced in a century. *I can find something else to call it. Construction costs. Humiliation is a small price to pay for peace.*

"Acceptable." He nodded at Brorda and said in English, "I shall convey these demands to my lord king."

Brorda clasped his arm. The British slave brought Carnlas and lifted a saddlebag flap to show the gameboard inside. He had not found a smile but had gained some black satisfaction. Brys swung up and rode out past the whitewashed church, past silent monks leaning on their hœs at the orchard gate.

At the first field marker he nudged the grey stallion into an easy canter. A few strides on something hissed past his left elbow, tugging at his cloak. Ten paces onward a leaf-bladed English spear thrummed into the grass track.

Brys took up the spear without breaking stride and brought Carnlas around in a rearing turn. A warrior beside Cenwulf in the churchyard still leaned from the right foot in the spearman's throwing stance. At such close range he had thrown wide, having some sport with the *Wealh,* but only a little wide. Cenwulf watched in predatory curiosity, not quite smiling. *Fool. Risking your king's peace on an empty threat. Never by your own hand.* Brorda had one hand splayed white over his eyes. Brys balanced the shaft. *I can take aim, let fly and escape beyond hope of pursuit.* Instead he reined Carnlas to a walk and returned to the church with the spear point dropped in truce. Mercian spears levelled as he came close. Brys plunged the blade deep into the grass at Cenwulf's feet. Cenwulf took an involuntary step backwards into his priest.

"You cannot kill me," Brys said quietly. "I am your death."

A creaking overhead. Cenwulf refused to look up. *All the better. Fill your sky with ravens.* Brys turned Carnlas away at a walk. This time he counted every pace of the endless distance from their silence — to the orchard wall, to the first field marker, to the end of spear range. Awash with cold sweat, he finally rolled into a canter, then a headlong gallop toward Hiraddug and River Clwyd.

At the ford, ravens were still circling and clattering over the red earth bank and the reedbeds. *Your feast is taking a long time to die, little brothers.* Without realizing it he stopped in midstream, staring across the noisy shallows. *River voices. Raven voices. Men's voices carrying across the ford. A river flowing with armed riders and blood.*

Elgan rode up to seize his arm and rode knee to knee with him through the crossing, urgent with concern, asking if he were all right.

Brys told his captain slowly, as though his mouth were full of river stones, "Everything will be all right in the end."

1 July 796 + Mathrafal

Meirwen had told the head smith Heilyn would not return, hung her gear on the pegs over her bench and started work. Repairs, which required few decisions, earned her the head smith's undying gratitude. She worked through his backlog for a week until she was thoroughly bored. Then she started drawing, but everything she drew reminded her of Heilyn. The interlace they had laughed over in Aachen, the enamelling he taught her, granulation like his fine silver buckle. She wasn't ready for that yet. When Brys came south from Tegeingl pleased at buying back Cadell's squandered peace, perversely she thought of war.

She put aside her design tablets, measured his old boiled leather war shirt when he wasn't looking and started to pull iron wire. With no one to help her prepare the links, she worked slowly. After a week she had enough links for a mail shirt. She spent another week linking and riveting, bad-tempered and bloated because her menses were late. A week after that, she sang as she worked. The old smith told her with some bemusement that he had never noticed she was such a long beautiful girl. "Have your eyes been troubling you?" she asked and patted his cheek. That was the day she finished the mail shirt. When Brys came in late from the council hall, she gave him his gift.

"Do you know something I don't know?" Brys asked as she fitted it over his quilted jerkin and laced the back for him.

"About what?" Meirwen blushed, but fortunately his back was turned. She tugged. "I haven't done this since my old aunt died. 'Lace me into my bodice, my dear, and lead me to the men.' Don't laugh, Brys, I can't thread the thongs."

"About a sudden need for mail shirts when things haven't looked so promising for a year."

"I was going to make you one last year but we went to Aachen. You'll want heavier quilting underneath or you'll be black and blue after every training fight. Mail is stronger than leather but it gives more under a blow."

Meirwen turned him around, pulling here and there for fit. The shirt hung to mid-thigh and nearly to the elbow, as she planned. Not bad for a first try.

"Where's your mirror?" Brys asked.

Meirwen looked at him in surprise and collapsed in laughter. "Vain creature. You're worse than auntie."

Brys grinned and found the mirror which a Frankish noblewoman had given him for services not rendered, Heilyn had told her, and squinted into its small reflection by candlelight to admire her handiwork. His hair was growing to a decent length again, covering the back of his neck, and he was brown from border diplomacy, which had somehow included hay-cutting and fishing. Twenty-four this summer. She would be twenty-one in the autumn. She loved him as she loved life and at last she had what she wanted most. She had thought she would never carry another child under her heart. Brys looked up, intercepted her smile and kissed her.

"It's good. Unlace me?"

"What's it worth to you?"

This led to a demonstration that he could unlace it himself with some reaching. They discovered other things about mail: for one thing, a weight of iron links is little impediment to amorous intent. By the time they fell into bed Meirwen was helpless with laughter and Brys kept her that way for a while. Sweet revenge. When should she tell him? In a few weeks, when she could be sure.

The next morning Meirwen walked upstream to the sanctuary to look over the sprouting physic garden. She found Mæn claying one of the guest cells where a falling oak branch had damaged a wall. Most of her herb shoots were at the two-leaf stage, though a few hadn't pushed through the soil at all. Mæn sat on a sunny bench with his homespun sleeves rolled up and his hands as pale as one of the statues in Meifod church, caked in dry clay.

"I'm planning to build a water wheel," he said, looking at her closely from his deepset brown eyes. He knew something had changed. "Brys gave me some drawings of Offa's mill at Tamworth and I've been talking to travelers. Will you forge the metal parts?"

"I'm going to visit my sister. Show me your plans and I'll tell you what I can do before I go."

Mæn rarely asked personal questions. All he did was wait for answers to the questions he didn't ask. Meirwen soon found herself talking about the best midwives and about why she hadn't told Brys yet.

"I'm not running away from anything," Meirwen insisted, although Mæn hadn't said so. "I'm going to visit my sister."

"Good," Mæn said. "No one can outdistance fear. We all contain death as a wheel contains its hub."

"Death is the center of a long life," Meirwen repeated the saying. She looked across at the silver and gold and bronze offerings chiming among green oak branches. "But—"

"Whatever happens, you can't escape it any more than I can. You just run and keep running until it overtakes you."

"Anyway," Meirwen said, "I'll only be gone a few weeks. Anything I can't forge now I'll do in August. If it can be forged."

Mæn smiled. His white hair and unlined brown skin were most startling when he smiled. His smile was sad and merriment underlaid his gravity. His greatest kindness was his thin iron scalpel that hurt cruelly. His life centered on death and he believed that when people died they would live. By asking no questions he heard answers.

"I wish I had studied with you as a child," Meirwen said, surprising herself with her own bluntness.

"You will study for the rest of your life, my dear. It comes out the same."

"Teacher." She bowed her head and stood up. The sun had traveled toward late afternoon and the honeybees were drowsing home to their basket hives. Olwen might still be visiting in Tregeiriog; she would be happy to see Meirwen. Not running from, running to. *"Duw gennyt."*

Mæn answered her blessing as he walked with her to the sanctuary gate, and with his hands still caked in clay, went into the oratory to pray.

10 July 796 + Mathrafal

Tribute and hostages. Work crews, reparation, call them whatever you like, but yield hostages and tribute to Mercia once and you'll do it forever, said Owain Tegeingl. He shouted and pounded the council table, but Cadell only watched wearily, looking at his calculations on a wax tablet flooded in sunlight.

No one else objected, not even Idris. Powys had created this mess and now Powys would right it. Brys held his breath, but that was the end of opposition. The Powys border construction crews had already been in place for two weeks, working under a Mercian planner.

"We all want to get this over with. Even Owain is disputing mostly for show," Idris growled later as they walked out into the sunny morning.

"None too soon," Brys agreed in the colonnade. Honeysuckle blossoms still brightened the courtyard and scented its air. He pulled off one of the amber trumpets and bit its end to taste the bead of sweetness. "Once the border is completed north to the estuary we can start calming down Gwynedd."

"Cadell has to learn everything the hard way. It's not a bad way to learn, if you have time." Idris lifted his diadem from his hair, now iron-grey as Brochfael's had been, and wiped his brow. *Sitting heavily on you? That's your price for playing cantref lord in Mathrafal and king in Tywyn.*

"Any news of Eli?"

"Eli is still sulking, thank God."

Brys watched Idris away, a canny old player testing a new game. Brochfael's badger, his own father's friend, one of the last of his generation. He thought of Brorda and wondered which of these two would win at wood-wisdom.

Brys worked with his harp for an hour in the scriptorium under the painted gaze of Marc Sant and his winged yellow cat. Meirwen was off to the north with her far-traveling look, in flight again. Running from something? Heilyn's death? But she seemed happy when she rode out a week ago with Marc, who was visiting his cousins at Llangollen, which meant his girl at Rhuddlan. This was a slow time. No hunting — the king banned hunting when game animals bore their young — and training was done for the day.

At noon Nest arrived for her lesson alone, having dodged her maid. Come back tomorrow, Brys told her. In return he got a long look under long lashes. This new ploy was no great surprise; for weeks she had been working on him much more intensely than she worked on her harp. Brys was in full retreat, which amused Meirwen. Nest was now a slender young woman of fourteen, striking rather than pretty, with her family's long oval face under shining brown hair. Lately she sang well, played well and constantly provoked Brys to startled laughter at her unexpected comments on history or music. A year in a monastery had made Nest no more reverent. Often she was wrong but at least she did her own thinking. Now she hung in the doorway, asking questions she knew the answers to, making Brys thoroughly wary. Lately she had brought her maidens out to watch his guard at morning weapons drills. A few romances had blossomed, Brys noted with amusement, but Nest herself watched only her father's pœt.

"Go or stay, Nest. I'm not going to order you like a child." *Emphasis on child. Legally she was a woman.* Brys set the sea-cat harp on the table. A clatter on the sound board. Distracted, he had forgotten the tuning key was on the pin. He rubbed the gouged sound board with a forefinger and sat back in his chair.

Nest looked at him for a moment and came in. She leaned her harp by the door, pulled it shut behind her and leaned against it. When she stepped into the room he saw she had silently slid the bolt behind her back. *Is that what the nuns taught you between embroidery and plainchant?*

"Why are you here alone? You know Adwen's rule." Brys crossed one leg over the other and tapped his boot with his crystal tuning key.

Nest hesitated, revealing a child's vulnerability on a young woman's face. Then she tucked her chin and narrowed her eyes — the same look his recruits wore the first time they hefted a sword. *Boudicca.* She smoothed her long fingers on her yellow skirt, a gesture which in another girl would be nervous. She walked forward until her hip leaned against his arm, scorching through his linen shirt, and rested one hand lightly on his shoulder. Brys was torn between caution and curiosity: how far would she push this?

"My father wants me to marry Merfyn mab Gwriad Manaw."

"Or one of the royal houses, certainly." Brys noted his own turn of phrase; she would marry a ruling house, not a man.

"I won't."

"Your father is a civilized man, he won't stand between you and a monastic life." *Even if it plays havoc with Powys diplomacy.*

"I want to marry, but not Merfyn," Nest said, as easily as she discussed modes and tuning.

"Merfyn is clever and ambitious. You would do well together."

"Penllyn has a royal house."

Now it's out in the open. Better this way. "Penllyn is a cantref of Powys, Nest. Pay more attention to your history lessons. I am heir, not lord. And I am married."

"No, you're not. Only by custom."

"Your marriage to another kingdom will be important to Powys." *How can I be losing this game? Is it because I want to?*

"I don't like Merfyn. He's cold and arrogant and careless of people. He has a mistress and a child in Armorica. And I love you."

"Love dœsn't count for much against a kingdom, little hawk." *One square ahead of me again. Not many people can claim that.* "I think you should go now."

Nest only laughed. Her light fingers brushed his shoulders, leaving lightning tracks across his senses. He wished fervently that her maid would catch up with her, the guard would knock with a message, anything. No doubt she'd made sure they wouldn't. Brys got to his feet and started for the door. *Strategic retreat.* But he made the mistake of looking back.

Nest flew into his arms like a falcon returning to the glove. Passionate as a hawk. Brys kissed her lightly, then deeply. He pulled the gold combs from her shining hair and it tumbled around her shoulders. Moved by something stronger than good sense, he let her draw his hand to the ivory buttons that closed the front of her dress. Small round breasts, made to fit the palm of his hands. Nest pulled up his shirt and her fingers drew cool fire across his back and chest and belly. Their bodies carried on a slow dance of invitation and promise. He half-tried to keep her light touch from wandering further. One isolated corner of his mind told him he was being seduced, even told him the grave consequences. *I can stop this.* Behind closed eyes he saw northern night skies, summer, a curtain of fire.

"Nain says you're my foster brother," Nest said into the hollow of his throat. "Shall we have some Powys incest?"

Incest? Surprise tripped Brys without warning. Bright waves close to agony. He hadn't been caught out like that in years. Reprieve. Nest had no idea what had happened, only that he stepped away from her; he didn't propose to further her education. *Incest, indeed.* Shocked amusement returned his wits from wherever they had dived to. He held her at arm's length.

"Has anyone told you that you're old beyond your years, Boudicca?"

"Show me." She was flushed with desire, in disarray and quite beautiful.

"No, Nest. Go find your nursemaid." It was both cruelty and kindness.

Nest pensively coiled her hair up and replaced her gold combs. *I'm not fooled. We both know you just took the game, the board, the player, everything.* She leaned to kiss his cheek and went out silently.

Brys lay face down on the bench, sweating and grossly uncomfortable, cursing himself for every imaginable kind of fool. Merciful god, he had been a hair's breadth from deflowering Cadell's virgin daughter. He didn't know which was worse, that his body thought he had, or his mind knew he hadn't. He groaned and rolled over.

Early in the evening he went to collect Cadell on his way to the hall. The guard pacing outside the council wing grounded his spear smartly when Brys walked past. As Cadell's war commander, Pol had brought the three wings nearly up to strength, imposed as much discipline as any Powys bodyguard would take, and restored the polish to their tarnished pride.

"Have you heard from Gwriad about Nest's betrothal to Merfyn?" Brys sat on the sill of the open window. Summer was already half flown.

Cadell shook his head. "Not yet. It should be another three or four weeks before word comes back from Bro Waroch. Is there a hurry?"

Yes. No. If I allow myself to think about Nest as anything but a political marriage . . . not Boudicca. Nest. Brys said, "We need to smooth over our troubles with Gwynedd next. I plan to go to Aberffraw —"

Brys held up a hand and they both listened. Running footsteps. Good news walks.

Someone was talking urgently with the door guard outside. Brys opened the door to find a man of Cadell's guard with a frightened boy in a novice's habit.

"Lord king, I rode since yesterday morning. They told me not to stop till I reached Mathrafal." He kneeled to Cadell in the doorway and lurched when Brys pulled him upright. A northern voice. They were all accustomed to bad news from the south, Eli's direction. "The work crew on the new border. Mercians attacked them. One of them came to us at Llandegla. Our abbot sent to Penllyn and Tegeingl for help. Coming south, I saw smoke and fire on the border but I didn't stop."

"You did well." Brys got him to sit down. They needed to know quickly and the boy would soon be in tears of sheer exhaustion. "Where did you see smoke?"

"Near River Ceiriog."

The door guard brought ale and looked over the boy's head as he drank, mouthing a question. Brys nodded. Soon Pol came in wet-haired, pulling on a shirt. Idris and Owain and three southern lords were in Mathrafal. By the time they and the court officers gathered, the boy had told everything he knew.

Cadell was too stunned to take it in. "But we met Offa's demands."

"Offa and Egfrith have no part in this," Brys said.

"What can we do?" Cadell's voice was raw with panic.

"First we throw them out of Powys."

"I'll send a protest to Offa in Tamworth," Cadell said. "And bring in the lords' bodyguards. Eli has the largest —"

Pol and Idris exchanged glances. Owain was ranting that this had been planned from the start, that Cadell was a fool and Offa was a demon. Brys told him to hold his tongue. *An attack in Tegeingl I can understand, after all the claims and disputes, at least if I think like a Mercian troublemaker. But why the north border? Why now? Where in hell are Marc and Meirwen? Marc should be back, Elgan only gave him a week. Meirwen should be safe in Iâl by now. Unless she stopped in Tregeiriog or Bryn Cerddin . . . near River Ceiriog.*

In another quarter hour all the guards were mounting. The chapel bell was sounding steadily: warning, gather in. An answering clangor came back from Meifod abbey, then from other churches up and down the broad valley. Brys armed himself as he ran to meet his guard at the north gate.

11 July 796 + Tregeiriog

At mid-morning they rode north over the windy moor and down the wooded river valley into Tregeiriog. The outlying farms were deserted, with cold hearths and food still on the tables; their people had fled. From the height, the green fields looked unchanged in the indolent sunshine. But they dropped down the steep track into a layer of smoke, sweeter than forge smoke and denser than hearth smoke, which drifted above the orchards.

Below the smoke they rode among livestock randomly slaughtered and a litter of goods looted from the houses. Brys surveyed the ruin of smoking timbers at the hall, fruit trees withered, the whitewashed orchard wall scorched in ragged black waves. Stable, granaries, smithy and houses were reduced to charred leaning timbers and white ash blowing steadily toward Mercia on a west wind.

A crouching figure stood up suddenly beneath one of the desiccated apple trees as Brys rode toward the hall. Pol beside him hissed in shock. A white face with huge black-circled eyes, three vertical gashes on the forehead; Cian wore the mourning marks of the fair family. He had been scouting ahead. His black pony stallion, tied to a tree, was sidling away from the other horses. Brys dismounted in the trampled orchard, unable to read emotion in Cian's blue eyes within their great charcoaled sockets.

"Maybe fifty English, trapped upstream," Cian said. "My brothers and your brothers drove them there." That could mean earth-house warriors and Penllyn.

"Your family is safe?"

"We hide well."

"But you mourn."

"Your people and one of ours," Cian said. "Bodies are in the churchyard."

"I'm going down."

"Not wise, raven lord." Cian looked around the squadrons sitting their tired horses among the ruins, indifferent to the crosses and horns covertly signed in his direction.

"Cian." Brys put a hand on his friend's shoulder, wanting the support. "Meirwen. Is she here?"

"Not now."

Here yesterday but not today? Here but dead? Brys dropped his hand. It was enough answer for the fair family, with their mutable sense of time, but not enough answer for him. He swung onto Carnlas again and told Pol, "A few minutes."

A standing cross leaned drunkenly at the crossroads. One wall of the church and the priest's cell stood. Some of Cian's people stood silent as shadows beside the grave trench they had been digging. Brys walked among the bodies on the grass. The old doorkeeper, two weaving women, the priest, men and women and children lay there. A young man of Cian's kindred lay among them. And there was a dark-haired woman with freckles showing plainly between smears of soot and blood.

Brys kneeled beside her, cold and clear-headed, to lift her tangled hair. No silver at her ears, not even pierced for earrings. Not Meirwen, her sister Olwen. Relief swept him, then dismay at feeling that relief. Olwen with the baby on her hip, the little boy at her skirts, handing him a dipper of buttermilk. Where were her children? Head bowed, he yielded to a flood of hot tears.

The fair family had closed Olwen's eyes but left something clenched in one hand. Her fingers were cold and rigid but he opened them enough to spill out a shimmering web of gold, a necklace with the Lady Rhiannon's birds flying forever between apple-trees and waves of the western sea. Once Mathrafal's head smith had admired it while Meirwen stood poised between pride and flight. *I should have stayed you from flight a week ago, found out why you were running.* Why was Olwen here? And where was Meirwen? Burned to ash in one of the houses? Dragged somewhere only carrion birds knew? Captive? At Bryn Cerddin? In Iâl? Carefully he clasped the necklace around Olwen's slashed throat and stood up.

The woman who had given him Calan Haf tribute once at Bryn Cerddin stepped forward, a small grey-haired woman in a grey dress, a queen without territory. Brys kneeled before her and thanked her for the burials. One hand settled lightly on his head. On his forehead above the burn scar he felt three swift claw tracks of her silver knife.

"Not Meirwen. Her sister," Brys told Cian, needing to hear himself say it. "Where are the English? Back across the border?"

"Some. Some found mead. They are above Teirw, near the hermit's cell." *Halfway to Bryn Cerddin.* "Your brothers want to fight them in the open. My brothers stalk them one at a time."

Brys's skin lifted at the thought of being stalked by the fair family, who rarely fought for Powys lords, only to protect their earth houses. He remounted and rode back into the ruined township. The squadrons were there with the *pencerdd*'s guard. Elgan and his guard looked uneasily at his face and the new mourning cuts. Pol sent half of his wing north, first to the border downstream and then over the ranges to Tegeingl's northern border. The other half he kept. *Now we hunt.*

On Teirw stream they kept to the narrow river track which Cian assured them was safe, though it passed under a steep height ideal for ambush. The English, unfamiliar with the terrain, had come over the back road on the other side of the hill. In the deepest oakwoods Cian motioned them to leave the horses and led them up the rocky outcrop through thinning birch and rowan. From the top they looked down on the hermit's cell. The old woman's oratory was burned, her garden trampled. A kite and a flock of carrion crows were quarrelling over a body at the edge of the trees. The rowans were in full leaf, past their creamy blossoms but not yet crimson with fruit. A small wind sang across the height, and somewhere a blackbird was warbling, heedless of any territory but his own.

Garmon and his bodyguard lay waiting among the stunted rowans, watching a cleft below. Cadwr was there, too, wearing his father's mail shirt and carrying an English spear taken in some forgotten war. Two of his herdsmen. A handful of Tregeiriog men, bloodstained and exhausted. Three of Cian's wary kinsmen with arrows nocked in their short hunting bows.

"Your friend tracked them," Cadwr told Brys when he slid alongside, putting an arm across his back. *Still the protective older brother. What are you doing here if Penllyn's unguarded?* "Their captain broke through an hour ago with a few men." Fleeing eastward, leaving his followers to die.

Garmon took his bodyguard over the hill; one of the fair family showed them the way. Pol passed orders. In a while they heard a fair imitation of the blackbird's whistling call, three times together, and Cian nodded.

They moved downhill, an iron net dropping from above. Sounds escaped from them, boots slipping on rock and the clink of weapons. The earth-house warriors sent a murderous hail of arrows into the trees until their dog-skin quivers were empty. Only a few of the English had mail and swords; the rest had boiled leather war shirts, plain *seax* knives and spears. A noble's hall warriors. Brys recognized two men with a likeness of wiry height and pale hair: Ordric and his son Wulfric, a long way from cantref Tren. Cenwulf's men.

Was that why they broke the border here, because Cenwulf knew his lands? *A*gain he felt the shock of the Mercian spear driving into the turf at Cenwulf's feet. *I am your death.* Revenge sat on his tongue like a coin for the boatman, heavy and metallic.

The English came out to meet them and linked their shields; though they were outnumbered they took the attack steadfastly. Soon an armed tide of men flooded the hollow, pushing inward elbow to elbow with barely room to swing. The English spears licked over the bossed shields to keep the British swords at bay. Brys fought meticulously, using his shield to bear down the spear points, hacking at the ash shafts and reaching inside their guard for the life. Though the milling struggle soon thinned, he continued to shield and thrust, killing efficiently. The fight was strangely silent except for the clatter of weapons and the screams of the wounded. Away uphill the blackbird still sang.

Giving ground in their shield wall, the Mercians turned to see Garmon's men coming in from the back of the hill. They closed ranks, fighting on with unnerving endurance as their number was halved and quartered, until at last they crumbled inward. Some broke formation to make a run. Pol's men engulfed the few who stood and Elgan shouted the *pencerdd*'s guard into pursuit. Brys ran along his own familiar game trails into the deeper shade of oakwoods, hunting down the last man who turned to face his death. Then there were no more.

Brys leaned on an oak, feeling the rough bark even through his mail shirt, with his feet planted among the last few bluebells which shook silently in the light wind. Green leaves rustled over his head. The sun filtered through. Warm. His sword arm was blood to the shoulder, but none of it was his. Distantly he heard the roar and rasp of his breath.

A knot of his guard crashed through. Addonwy, diligently troublesome as ever, shoved a prisoner before him at sword point. Not Ordric or Wulfric, he'd seen them go down. This man was wounded in several places beyond his mail's protection, struggling to keep his feet, finely dressed, wearing a silver bracelet with one oval of amber caught in a knot of interlace. It was the bracelet Meirwen had made for

Bethan two years ago. Brys met the blue stare of a middle-aged man who should be tending his affairs in Mercia.

"Who is your lord?"

"Who can say? We have many great men." His gaze traveled over Brys and caught on the gold arm ring.

"Cenwulf?"

"'Lasting honor shall be his, a name that never shall die beneath the heavens.'" It was a line from one of their cycles, spoken in a clear trained voice with fine inflection. A pœt.

"Why?" *Not that you'll tell the truth or perhaps even know the truth.*

The man flared with anger. "You ask that? After you burned Bassa's church?"

"Not us, not Powys. Someone lied to you." *I hope to God.* Brys set his teeth and said, "Make your peace. It will be quick."

Eyes as deeply blue as the flowers considered him a moment, disbelieving. Then the Mercian crossed himself.

Addonwy held the man's shoulders. Brys plunged the blade deep into his throat, and he slumped to die in a rush of blood among the bluebells. The others went down to the dead and wounded, leaving him alone at last. Downhill, water trickled from a spring. Brys pushed between the trees to wash his blade in the icy water. Then he kneeled with his face in his hands, buying a moment's delay before he confronted the worst. After a while he looked up again.

A woman in a grey cloak with the hood pulled forward stood on the other side of the spring, watching the nearly silent bubble and braid of water. Watching him. She raised her head, face in shadow, and the hair lifted on his neck.

"I know thee, cousin." She spoke in a voice as dry and lifeless as a husk. *I hear it in dreams between wind and rushing water.*

"No." Brys looked up at her grey shape, wordless in shock, unable to look away. She wandered homeless, she had no consolation and no resting place, her name was salt.

But the woman lifted a smudged hand to push her hood back, revealing a young girl's face, bruised and tear tracked, not the face of a crone or skull. Hair and eyes the color of heather honey. "I ran away from him. I came home."

"Gwladus." Brys got to his feet and held out a hand. She clasped it long enough to prove that she was warm flesh. "Come with me. You're safe now."

But she shook her head gravely and turned away. "They'll find me if I stay."

Madness still held her hostage. *Or is the madness all my own?* Gwladus walked away through the grass and bluebells, crushing some under her shœs of fine blue leather with many small gold buckles. Brys stepped across the spring to follow her, but she sprang like a young deer into the oak undergrowth and vanished.

Cadwr found him there.

"The girl." Brys turned frowning. "I promised to bring her back."

"Soon." Cadwr put an arm around his shoulders. "Come quickly."

Garmon sat with his back to the hermit's plum tree, sword across his knees, a stout grey man resting from his labors. Smiling, eyes closed. A man of the

Penllyn bodyguard kneeled beside him, fingers on his throat. Others stood or crouched silently around. When they came close Brys saw the bloody wound between thigh and groin, under the edge of his cousin's mail, and the grass sodden and floating with blood.

"Gone." His bodyguard man opened one hand in a gesture of helplessness. "We couldn't stop the bleeding."

Brys kneeled and took Garmon's big hand, still warm, and dropped his head to rest on it. Cadwr's hand was on his shoulder, squeezing. *Nothing. No pain or fear. No feeling. Not yet.* Cadwr was saying something. *None of the words matter.*

Brys stood up abruptly. "I have to go. To Bryn Cerddin."

Cadwr nodded tersely. Angry. Brys started for the horses, aware of the king's bodyguard and Elgan's men and Garmon's Penllyn guard standing in silence to watch. *They'll say we quarrelled.* He turned back to embrace Cadwr. *Only two of us left.* A wall of fear hit him, like pain after shock. They held each other tightly, Brys with his eyes closed and face pressed hard against the links of his brother's mailed shoulder. At last he stood back. Elgan shook his head in warning to someone behind him. Cian had brought Carnlas. He swung up and headed for the rowan trail upstream, and at the edge of the trees he looked down.

Stone-poor and lovely Bryn Cerddin had known its last harvest. The house stood charred and gutted; only two blackened walls remained. Cynddylan's hunting tally was now reclaimed into the past that had briefly yielded it to his sight. On his daughter's grave the little apple tree was seared and twisted; if it flowered again, it would flower in solitude.

Alban's family had been in their house by the stream bank, which Brys found ransacked but unburned. Bethan lay across the doorstep with her throat cut, arms reaching as though she had fallen struggling to get inside, but she had been unable to help her daughters. Her two shy girls sprawled naked on the house floor, cruelly used and stabbed many times. Alban was pinned to the outside of his house with his own hunting spear, hands and genitals hacked off, bloodily blinded. The Irish hound lay nearby; the bitch ran whining between her dead mate and the dead man. She came anxiously to lick Brys's hand. Though he combed both houses and the orchard, he found no trace of Meirwen.

In the house he pulled sheets from Bethan's rue-scented linen chest and covered the girls. Outside he levered the spear free, threw an embroidered coverlet over Alban and carried him into the orchard. Cian had brought shovels and a pick from the barn. His guard and some of the others rode down from the trail and helped him dig one wide grave.

When his people were buried and the prayers spoken, Brys heard himself quietly giving orders for his livestock in the barn. The rest could fend for themselves a while. As though from a great distance, he heard Cian calling the hound bitch, Elgan warning him there might be Mercian fugitives in the hills, Cadwr saying something urgently about Rhiwædog. Their words fell away behind him as he rode uphill. The hound bitch came loping after him.

"Deirdre, stay. Go to Cian."

But she wagged her tail uncertainly and trotted at Carnlas's heels up the hillside path. Once she turned to whine for her mate. Brys rode up through his west pasture, where a flock of his sheep scattered away to watch suspiciously. Then the oak canopy threw cool stippled green over him in the quiet between day and evening. After another bank of woodland he reached the open moor.

Up among the stream sources a west wind blasted steadily over the high country. It flattened the sedge, tumbled a torn gorse branch end over end and drove a glossy lapwing almost under Carnlas's hooves. Sunset threw long spiked shadows out from the heather and gorse clumps and bathed the rolling sea of moors in russet light.

Brys gave the stallion his head and narrowed his thought down to the wind keening past his ears and the fall of hooves on the rough grass. Sun thudded onto the mail on his shoulders, its warmth stolen by the wind, and shimmered over the moor. A honed awareness clung after the fighting. The high scoured world on every side held a depth of clarity. He let the fear go. Allowed himself to feel the sting of the mourning cuts. Breathed. Loose with exhaustion, he put his head back to watch a kestrel tilt her hunting pattern against the deepening blue sky. And let go.

A dizzying spiral. Distant below but perfect in every detail, a dark glittering rider on a pale horse, a tawny expanse of land stretching to the green rim of the world. Updrafts, more spirals, long level passages from the mountains and the sea. He soared a long time with the hawk's flight, saw the rider again, plummeted and stooped. His familiar body. An ache of simple weariness. Carnlas took another step forward and stopped. Deirdre lay down with her brindled muzzle on her paws in the long grass. Brys dismounted. He found his feet light on sacred ground and walked west until he came to a small spring source in a grassy hollow.

Awen. Seeking his own source, he walked further west, deeper into earth until he stood rooted beneath old grassland and stretched his arms along the red sun path. Darkness lay behind. Brys waited with infinite patience until the spring's purl and trickle swelled to a rushing river torrent of radiant sound and beat about his head in wings of song. *I have lived since the world's beginning. I will be here at the world's end.* He cried out, falling headlong into the sun's road, and the land struck him a terrible blow.

You are the land's guardian, murmured the stream source. *Do you consent?*

No. He scoured his face against the harsh grass, his mouth full of earth. Day darkened to black seamed with silver and crimson. He would die of it, drown in it, forget the word and truth of light. *Consent to what? Never what it seems.*

Do you consent?

Face upward to night. Time passed. Stars stabbed down from a deep dusk sky, singing in crystal voices as they wheeled through heaven. No end to their song and no beginning. In their dance they were center and surround, hub and spokes and rim, as death was center in life.

Awen. Silence. *I can tell more than you can ask.*

The singing was distant, not his own but a dry whisper of wind in reeds, a rush of sweetwater springs, words breathed into a cup of gold. He knew that singing from the western shore. *An offering to the river. To consent is to become an offering. Too soon.* And at last grief came home. Crushed him to the land, seized him by the throat, blinded him, shook him and wrung him dry. He wept for his tangled garden, undefended, luckless, desolate.

I consent.

Full radiant night offered its sacrament. Brys lay face up on cooling moorland grass anointed with the first dewfall. His terrible and lovely land had struck down her guardian and raised him up, a consecration. Away west toward the unseen island a rim of purple sky lingered. Above him spun a star dance of jeweled silver and jet. Nothing came back to him from memory. But it would. Memory was a bone splinter rising to pierce the skin, a lark springing from the grass, a wheel turning.

Brys got to his feet. Carnlas turned dark eyes on him and Deirdre bounded across the grass to lick his hand. Familiar with every path and game trail, he rode the raven's high track west until he came into Penllyn.

13 July 796 † Rhiwædog

Torches burned at the gate of Rhiwædog. Brys followed their yellow flicker through the trees and up the gentle slope to the court. The talkative river stepped down through the fields among night smells of cattle and hedgerows. He hadn't seen Rhiwædog in twelve years. If he closed his eyes, no time had passed. *The old gatekeeper will tell me I'm late again, I'd better have a good story for my father . . .* The illusion wouldn't hold. At the gate Brys dismounted and tied Carnlas to the post near the mounting block. The Irish bitch sat panting beside him. Rhiwædog was enclosed only by its orchard walls and clustered buildings; the gate was more an idea than a defence. The gatekeeper was a sleepy boy who, when Brys asked to see the lady Onnen, quite properly demanded his name.

"Cynfarch mab Cadeyrn Penllyn?" Starting to wake up, the boy blinked in alarm.

"Cynfarch bardd Cadell." Brys followed the boy inside. People were coming and going among the timber buildings even now, an hour or two before midnight. *No one I recognize. A strange homecoming. Maybe I've slept a hundred years and everyone I know is dust.* "Is my bodyguard here?"

"With the Penllyn bodyguard, lord, in Cæ Cynan."

One of the large pastures, it lay just downstream on River Hirnant. Someone was planning well; they could need to ride out again at short notice. Elgan, probably. Garmon had acted as his own war captain, a dubious plan that was suddenly disastrous. The boy led him to the lord's house, separate from the hall, and pounded on the door. A servant brought Brys to the sun-room, murmured to the big grey-haired woman standing alone by the hearth and closed the door behind her. When Onnen turned with a poker in her right hand, Brys had the fleeting impression she held it as a weapon. Then she deliberately dropped it clanging on the hearth flags.

"Lady." Brys kneeled stiffly. *Sleep soon. First this.* The sword scabbard caught by his right knee and the shield slapped his back. One good push and he would fall over. "I regret your loss."

"Do you indeed?" Onnen sounded more curious than hostile, but the currents ran together in her voice. Her eyes were as hard as Dolgellau slate under her gold diadem, and she was struggling to steady her trembling mouth. "Get up, Cynfarch. Why have you come here? When my son invited you last year you couldn't be troubled."

"To help in any way I can, lady." *Don't make this harder. Last year my only thought was to stay alive from one day to the next. Garmon knew it.*

Onnen made an impatient sound. "And what help can you give?"

"Lady, that is for you to say." No help, clearly, against this anger and resentment. But now the offer was made. "I want to keep my bodyguard here until we know the state of the border. I'll have the cost of keeping them taken from your food render to Mathrafal."

"Very well." Garmon's wife walked past her tall looms to the window. She opened one shutter, looked out on the moonlit hillside, closed it again. Brys stood, hands shoved in his sword belt and eyes falling grittily shut, until she came to stand by the hearth again. "My husband named you heir. You can understand that it sits badly with his kinsmen and yours. He had no right to make that decision alone."

Brys bowed to her and started for the door.

"Where are you going?"

"Cæ Cynan." He would ride to Iâl in the morning. *Meirwen will be there. Almost certainly.*

Onnen said angrily, "And have people say you found no welcome here?"

No welcome that I can see but all that I expected. I haven't wit or energy to argue. And your argument's not with me, it's with death. Brys said quietly, "You have enough to worry you, lady Onnen."

"You shall eat with me and you shall stay here."

Hospitality at swordpoint. Brys was dangerously near laughing from sheer exhaustion. "Thank you."

Garmon's cook was as good as her reputation, but Brys might have been eating boot leather instead of braised veal, drinking marsh water instead of fine mead. He needed food and so he ate. Onnen ate lightly and pushed her plate across the table. They didn't speak. Outside there was more noise; more people were coming and going. Midnight by now. He couldn't remember when he had last slept. Two nights ago? Someone tapped the sun-room door.

"We can go now."

Onnen walked out with him herself instead of sending the servant. The guest house lay in the other direction, but after twelve years, who could say what changes there had been? A flea-ridden straw pallet would be a gift from heaven right now. But Onnen walked past the timber hall, where the torches were now extinguished, around the corner to the book cellar.

Inside, two trestle tables were pulled together. Light from three candle sconces washed and wavered on the faces of about fifteen men and women. Kinsmen and friends. Most of them he hadn't seen in twelve years. Elgan's father Iestyn, a landholder near Llanycil. Two distant cousins, men of good family from the Penllyn guard. Cadwr. *A family council. I can't deal with this now. And I'm the only one in war gear, unshaven, dirty and dishevelled. A savage among the civilized. Well done, Onnen.*

Onnen shut the door and sat at one end of the table. The chair at the other end was empty. Brys found space on a side bench opposite Cadwr.

"Garmon Penllyn named an heir," said the oldest man in the room. He had pouched blue eyes in a deeply lined face. A great-uncle? Brys couldn't remember. "The youngest son of a disgraced murderer who went whoring Penllyn to Gwynedd. A traitor."

"A traitor?" one of the Penllyn bodyguard men threw back at him. "For trying to keep Penllyn out of Powys's grip?"

History. Let it go. But they settled in comfortably to argue about things that had happened a generation, a century ago. This could go on all week. They could still be here arguing about who was lord in Rhiwædog and Cær Gai when the Romans left, while the Mercians overran Penllyn to the mountains of Eryri.

When they'd threshed it fine enough, Brys finally stood up and leaned against the table. "You know why Garmon died. The border is broken. Who is your war captain? Have you raised the levies? Who is organizing food and supplies if you have to fight? Is there word from Mathrafal? When you have taken care of these things, then choose a lord."

Another round of argument, but it was argument in a more useful direction. No one had raised levies. No one had arranged supplies. But they would now. Cadwr looked across the table, considering, and nearly smiled. *Careful.*

Lady Onnen told them what she knew. Cadell's bodyguard wing was on the border, half at Dinas Glas and half farther north. All was quiet. Refugees had been coming south and west. No word had come from Tamworth. Cadell was asking his nobles' bodyguards and levies to stand ready, and Onnen was doing it. She folded her hands on the table. Her husband was lying cold in Llanfor church and she was running Penllyn. Brys gave her a nod of encouragement. She looked at him angrily. *Good. Keep fighting.*

"What has a Powys war to do with Penllyn?" someone asked. "Meirionydd has the right idea, making a king." Another bitter dispute. But now they were asking the right questions.

"Let us waste no more time. Penllyn is without a lord," said Onnen. Others nodded. "We all know that my husband spoke without consulting the family."

"Cynfarch was his chosen heir," said one of the Penllyn bodyguard men, undeterred.

"No," Brys said.

A long silence, a few glances exchanged around the room. Let them chew on that a while.

Garmon's widow turned hard eyes on him. Less hostile, more curious.

"Why not?" asked Iestyn. He was balding but had his son's sleepy dark eyes and heavy face. "Garmon thought you were the best choice after Geraint died."

"Garmon didn't ask me. I did not consent." *Wind on the high moor and a voice under the wind, something about his offering to the river* . . . Brys stared at a candle in one of the sconces, watching one river of wax fall and pool on the sanded wood. He glanced up and saw Cadwr watching him again with something like pain. *You don't need to know, my dear.*

The great-uncle looked around anxiously. *Of course. You've outlived two or three lords, now you think it's your turn. If they choose you they deserve you. Onnen's doing well. What's wrong with a woman as lord?* The argument went on. Names were tossed across the table. Objections outweighed names.

"I've heard enough of this. Magpies quarrelling over crusts." Iestyn heaved to his feet and walked around the table to the door. The Penllyn bodyguard men exchanged glances and followed him. Cadwr shifted weight but stayed where he was, frowning at Brys. *Good man.*

Onnen flung her voice after Iestyn. "You're not making this easier."

"I've said my piece." But Iestyn stood with his hand still on the latch and the two younger men stood with him. "Garmon named Cynfarch. Do any of you know Cynfarch better than Garmon did? Are you saying Garmon didn't know the meaning of *braint,* lady?"

Fair god, go easy. She's had enough for one day without a lesson on honor and ruling right. But Onnen stared at him, then around the table, measuring them all.

"What's the objection?" asked Iestyn. "Apart from the fact he had a father, unlike some of you?" It drew out some laughter.

The great-uncle pursed his mouth. "He's young and untried."

"You're old and untried," said Iestyn, drawing more nods. "Cynfarch has been Gwriad's envoy to the alliance, Cadell's right hand and his envoy to Charles and Offa, and *pencerdd* of Powys for two years. Where have you been? Dozing in the sun?"

"Lady Onnen," the older of the cousins in the bodyguard ventured, "What is your objection to Cynfarch?"

"What makes you think I have an objection? I merely want to see consensus." Onnen smiled coolly, pushing Brys's respect further. *We both know your objection. I'm not Garmon, I'm not Geraint, my father killed your brother-in-law, I'm a stranger and I have a name for ambition.*

The two bodyguard cousins exchanged glances again and went to sit down. Iestyn sighed heavily and did the same. It took another quarter of an hour, a rapidity unknown in the rare Penllyn councils. The only voice of objection was the great-uncle, who buried his disappointment under querulous warnings.

"Cynfarch," said Iestyn. A few voices echœd him.

"You heard him." Cadwr spoke for the first time. "He said no."

All the heads turned toward Brys. He was less of a stranger than an hour ago.

"I haven't set foot in Rhiwædog for twelve years. When Geraint invited me last year, I had all the invitations I could handle — I also had to turn down both death by stabbing and death by poison," Brys said. *Shocked silence.* Onnen paled. Cadwr looked as though he had a barbed hook in his mouth, afraid to swallow it and unable to spit it out. "Lady Onnen knows the administration. If she will take charge until the border settles down, then we can choose."

"You're not refusing?" Iestyn asked, pleased with himself. "In principle, do you consent?"

"Do all of you consent? In principle?" Brys threw it back to them, looking into their faces one by one, a hall pœt's trick. "Any one of us could govern Penllyn. Do you consent?"

Iestyn looked around. "I consent."

"I consent." A murmur from the others. Even Cadwr, bemused.

"I consent," said Brys. "Lady, until there is a decision will you run the affairs of Penllyn?"

Onnen was trying to reach back her anger, even her curiosity. Instead, fighting to keep her eyes from flooding, she managed only a curt nod. *A proud woman. But we've all had enough today.*

Brys got to his feet and wished them a good night. No one else moved. If they wanted to talk until dawn, that was their affair. Onnen came out into the courtyard, softly scented with dew on the grass. Stars overhead. They walked to the family quarters, not the guest house, and Onnen showed him into the large room adjoining the sun-room. *My parents' room. We used to sit on the end of their bed like four noisy starlings before morning mass, sunlight flooding the floor rushes. We must have driven them to distraction. But they loved us all dearly. A long time ago now.* But it hadn't changed much. The sleeping shelf was made up with a bed of scented linen, the open windows let through a faint glimmer of starlight, the carved pillars and beams shone with their inlaid bronze and silver.

"This is your own room, lady." Lost in the past, he realized it at last.

"You will please me by using it while you're here," she said quietly. "I keep vigil at Llanfor church tonight."

Gracious, after her first reception. "Thank you, Onnen."

Onnen looked out through the open door into the courtyard with an apple tree. Her eyes were shining again. "Cynfarch. What will you do with me?"

"It's not for me to decide," Brys said.

"In principle — what would you recommend?" she asked with the slightest edge of mockery. "My choices are my elder sister in Ardudwy or a monastery."

Brys scrubbed his face. *I smell like a slaughterhouse.* "In principle — I think the next lord could have no better adviser. If you would stay on."

"I'll consider it." She turned, wanting to say something else, but couldn't. Then she was gone, silent on her feet for a big buxom woman.

A yawning servant brought hot water and padded out. Brys kept his eyes open long enough to strip, wash himself and fall onto the linen. *I'll pull the sheet up. In a minute.* And was asleep.

Darkness still held the room when something woke him. Sound or movement. How long had he slept? Not long. His eyes were still full of gravel. Brys reached for his knife, but it lay with his sword on the chair. *Fool.* A small clatter as something was dropped or put down next to the bed. He rolled to the far side of the bed with a groan as though turning over in his sleep. Weight on the pallet as someone sat down. He reached suddenly, causing a gasp of fright. *Good. That's two of us.* Touch told him it was a woman. Not Onnen, surely? No. She was younger, slighter, with long curling hair. He dropped his hand. *Radiant god, what is this?*

"What do you want?"

"The lady sent me with a drink."

"In the middle of the night?"

"I'm to drink some to show you it's not poison." She sounded young and desperately fearful.

Brys sat up, awake now. "If it's a sleeping draft, the best thing you could do is let me sleep and not frighten me out of my skin."

A breath of laughter. Brys could see the curve of the girl's shoulder against the window. She found his hand, put a metal cup into it and raised his hand with the cup to her mouth. He felt her drink and swallow. When she raised it to his mouth, he drank. A dark herbal taste, not quite bitter, as strong as earth-house liquor. Warm in the belly. She put the cup aside and leaned against him. *There's more to this than a drink. Of all things I don't need right now, a girl. Hospitality can go too far.*

"The lady sent you?"

"Yes." Hesitation. "And I asked if I might come."

"Why?" *Strange drink. Not poison, or I would be convulsed by now. But a tingling in the limbs and an intense awareness. Linen under my thighs, the scent of sweet bedstraw, my steady heartbeat, the nearness of the girl.*

No answer. But she put a hand to his face and brushed back through his hair to the nape of his neck. A flame of desire followed her touch. Brys caught his breath and pulled her down with him. She was naked inside a wrapped sheet which fell away. Senses in riot at the devastating softness of breasts and belly. Her rich scent of woman and clean hair. A torrent of colors swirled behind his closed eyes. *The drink. It has to be the drink.* He plunged deep into her slick heat and thought he would explode. When he rolled onto his back she rode astride, after a second's hesitation of surprise or protest, and he brought her with him to a blinding completion. She gasped but caught herself. Afterward he held her in his arms and asked her name.

She kissed his mouth and rolled out of his embrace. "Penllyn."

By the time it struck home, candlelight flickered across the chamber walls. Brys, driven to his feet by anger at the trick, saw a redhaired girl standing in the middle of the room wrapped in a linen sheet. The room was full of people.

"There is fulfilment in the land," the girl said clearly. "There is a lord. There is truth."

Cadwr led Brys forward to stand on the largest hearth flag with its worn sun wheel pattern, put his sword in his left hand and a wooden staff in his right, and spoke of the ancient marriage of lord and country. A lord was the land's wealth, the land's good, the land's protection. A lord must love the gods, do good and act with courage. *Where did you learn those words?* Lady Onnen set the gold diadem of Penllyn on his head and smiled at him wearily. A dozen kinsmen were here. The great-uncle was making the best of defeat. Elgan. Iestyn. Cian, and surprisingly, the old woman of his earth house who had put the mourning-cuts on his forehead. Even more surprisingly, an abbot in a homespun robe. The pretty female cousin and her mother blushed and carefully looked only at his face.

"Mother Onnen," Brys said. "This is not how cantref Penllyn makes a lord."

Onnen shook her head slowly. The bodyguard cousins leaned in the sun room door, grinning at each other. Cadwr folded his arms and smiled at the floor.

"We live in uncertain times, Cynfarch." Iestyn shrugged.

Brys looked around at his half-remembered family, realizing exactly what his consent had dropped onto him, and consented again in silence. He put aside sword and staff, went to take Cadwr's hand and gave him the kiss of kinship. Then he turned to Iestyn. One by one he embraced them all, his regained kindred. A few tried to kneel, but he held them on their feet; *braint* sprang not from his people's obligation but from his own.

First light paled the sky eastward over Edeirnion when they filed out by ones and twos, satisfied with their night's work. Cadwr kissed his forehead and was gone. Onnen went out with a hand on the girl's shoulder, speaking of a celebration once the border was quiet. Elgan and Iestyn, cousins and uncles, all walked out into the shallowing end of night. At last Brys sat on the edge of his parents' marriage bed, quite alone.

This was the lasting loneliness. The path across the king stone led in one direction only; there was no returning. He had his birthright, he had what he wanted, and he had nothing. Those who could have lightened his burden, making this a joyous hour, had been borne onward. His father, dying under his youngest son's helpless hands. His mother, singing as she braided her fair hair before this same open window on the last morning. Heilyn on his journey toward lead and gold and oblivion. Meirwen running to some place he could never reach, perhaps following a small girl's laughter between spokes of shadow to the heart of light. Or perhaps she was leaning into the bow spray on an Irish trade ship. Moving onward, away from his life. He sat numb and frozen with loneliness.

In the morning, Llanfor church buried Garmon Penllyn and anointed Cynfarch Penllyn.

15 July 796 + Mathrafal

The north gate of Mathrafal was shut when Brys rode near, though it was midafternoon. His Penllyn guard and the *pencerdd*'s guard together numbered more than a hundred. The watch captain on the crowded ramparts gave an order over his shoulder. Brys sat Carnlas, waiting. A lazy wind lifted some of the summer heat from the three-river plain and tugged the banner straight over his head. Penllyn ravens, northern ravens, black on green silk. The gold diadem held the heat against his brow and the mail shirt scorched like a gridiron where his forearm rested on his thigh. Elgan glanced at him, questioning. Then the gate swung open. Brys dismounted and walked in alone.

Cadell Powys made a better student of performance than anyone had a right to expect, including his pœt. The king stood spear-straight in a pool of sunlight between shaded courtyards; he wore a crimson shirt, the heavy gold *hual* of Powys and the narrow gold diadem of Iâl, the home cantref of his North Powys house. Behind him were ranked his court officers and a handful of nobles. One of them was Idris Meirionydd, looking unusually apprehensive. *What did you expect?* Brys walked up to Cadell, studied his face long enough to see the dread of new pain and kneeled on the dusty paving stones. *My grandfather kneeled here at swordpoint, my father kneeled from bitter necessity, I kneel for love of Powys.*

"Lord king."

"Brys." Cadell raised him, giving him the kiss of peace and his warm smile. Then he passed Brys's right hand to Idris, who kissed him and passed him on again. "Cynfarch Penllyn."

On the rampart, the guard pounded their spear butts on the timber catwalk. The noise swelled from a dull boom to a thunderous roar and then trailed off. The shouting kept on. Brys looked around the courtyards and byways and ramparts, unnerved by the crowd as he rarely was by a hall audience. Acceptance. More than that. Approval. Affection. It made a knot in his throat like a hot stone.

Reality came home to Brys in the council an hour later. The clerk read the letter aloud, then cleared his throat in embarrassment at the long silence that followed. Eli wrote that he saw no need to commit men or supplies to a border dispute in North Powys.

Cadell, tearing at a hangnail, said, "What are we going to do? We need Elfæl and Buellt. We're going to have to patrol the border heavily through the summer."

Offa, of course, denied any knowledge of an attack on Powys work crews or farms.

"Do without," said Idris. "What about Gwynedd?"

Caradog had finally accepted a letter and returned a scorching answer. If Cadell Powys had problems on the north border, entirely of his own creation, let him settle them with the aid of Owain Tegeingl, who was under the mistaken impression that a Gwynedd lord could shift allegiance to Powys under cover of night as a farmer moved boundary stones. As for alliance, Powys had ruined Gwynedd's Mercian and Irish trade. Let Cadell Powys not consider himself part of any alliance that included Gwynedd.

"It's only bluster," suggested one of the lords.

"No," Brys said. *I've seen Caradog bluster, I know the difference.* Cadell looked unhappily at his newest cantref lord.

Then Pol brought word from a wheelwright who had returned from Mercia two days ago. A Mercian army, including the kings' bodyguard and local foot levies, was gathering west of Chester, poised on the Tegeingl border. There was strong feeling in Mercia about a Powys attack on Bassa's church. If there had been an attack, Pol shrugged, it had not come from Powys.

No one bothered to question it. *We've all been waiting to hear this.*

"Mobilize Powys," Cadell told his war commander woodenly, as though a long-awaited blow had fallen. "All the fighting men we can raise. Bodyguard men, levies, any mercenaries we can pull together quickly. Gather the host in Tegeingl."

17 July 796 + Caer Degannwy

"Easy, child, it will only take so much force." Padrig shouted his warning over the smithy din and turned back to his own work.

Meirwen looked at the shield boss under her hammer and saw that a few more blows would beat it as thin as a dry leaf. Padrig was right. He was usually right about metal. Her mind was wandering. She reached to touch his forearm in thanks. Thin and wiry under dry old skin, he was growing no younger. Padrig had a hunger not for food but for silver inlay and filigree of gold, papyrus, pœts and philosophers from his dark Greek seas. He was misplaced in Cær Degannwy, called out with the other Gwynedd smiths. Anna had laughed at Caradog's war commander, saying she answered only to Bishop Elfoddw. Torn between them, Meirwen had gone with Padrig. If this blew over, she was closer to home in Degannwy. But it wasn't going to blow over. Training, military exercise, whatever Caradog wanted to call this, clearly it preceded an attack on Powys.

A tall shadow blocked the door light into the stronghold's cramped smithy. Meirwen turned in irritation, but who could scowl against Gwydron's good humor? He lounged in the doorway, shedding as much brilliance as he blocked. He wore an Avar's wealth of arm-rings, a diadem of gold darker than his hair, a blue-dyed sword-belt over his mail shirt. She looked closely at the mail. Hers was better.

"So Caradog has found the secret of getting an honest day's work from smiths," Gwydron said lazily. "Lock them in the dark."

"A dark room is better for cooling a pœt's overheated wits than for a jeweler's eyes," Padrig snapped, swallowing the lure.

"Don't worry, you sly old dog, I haven't forgotten my gold."

"Caradog would have my head for a spear target if he knew I was wasting forge time on your gaudy toys."

The jeweler searched among leather scraps and rags until half of them were on the packed clay floor. Meirwen reached under the buffing cloth and pulled out the gold strap-end. Padrig was unbelievably messy. This morning he'd looked absently for silver bracelets among the shield rims and blue glass *millefiori* sticks behind the work bench, all the while explaining why Aristotle was wrong about the nature of honey bees. Eventually she had found the bracelets outside on the spoil heap.

Meirwen gave the strap-end a final buffing and admired it for a moment. Gwydron stooped under the lintel to claim it and dropped one arm around her shoulders. During her few days in Aberffraw and a week here on the mainland, she had expected challenges and questions. But no one was turning away Powys refugees; they were quietly sheltered by Caradog Rhos, who did few things quietly. Meirwen didn't want to be in Gwynedd despite Gwydron's and Padrig's kindness. But Powys was crumbling west, no one knew what would happen in Tegeingl, and she had to protect her child. Brys had always said, go to Aberffraw. By now he should have both messages she had sent, one from Tregeiriog and the other with Marc.

"Speechless in the presence of art?" asked Padrig tartly as Gwydron tilted the strap-end to catch the light in the dim shed.

"More than art, friend. It has life."

Padrig grumbled but even he could ask no higher praise. The strap end was a stag's head frozen in gold interlace, antlers swept back to clasp the strap leather, with all the wild alertness of the beast on the hillside. She and Padrig had toiled over each minuscule ball of granulation, peering through his crystal, which made everything look three times its natural size, to decorate the pebbly brow tines. It was good.

Gwydron unbuckled his blue leather sword-belt and laid it on the bench. Meirwen removed the plain iron strap-end with pliers, then took up the smallest hammer. On the dyed leather it looked splendid. She handed it back. "Too fine for exercises, Gwydron."

"So I've been saying." He slung it carelessly over his shoulder.

"What's this game of Caradog's?" demanded Padrig.

"No game," said Gwydron, losing his smile. "Caradog has had enough of Offa and Cadell playing tug-of-war with Tegeingl. It's a Gwynedd cantref."

"Mathrafal dœsn't think so," said Meirwen. "Neither dœs Tegeingl."

"Powys." Gwydron shrugged. "You've heard about Penllyn?"

"No," she said, too abruptly. From time to time Gwynedd also claimed Penllyn.

"Penllyn, my dear, has made a king."

Meirwen frowned. "I can't believe that. Why would Garmon bother?"

"Garmon died on the border a few days ago." Gwydron nodded and ducked out through the doorway.

Meirwen stared at Padrig, whose gaze found some point in space or time far beyond the forge shed wall. She untied her oxhide apron and went outside. Gwydron was leaning lazily against the storeroom opposite, waiting. They walked out to the west rampart overlooking River Conwy's broad winding mouth. Leaning on the sun-warmed timbers he told her what had happened at Rhiwædog. Meirwen listened without much surprise. So Brys had regained his patrimony. Not Brys. Cynfarch Penllyn. Let him have the sense to stop at Penllyn.

River current and tidewater roiled together below at the sand bars, where a few curraghs were working the fishing nets. Over on the west bank rose wooded hills; Caradog's army was ranged here on the east bank in a tent city between the fortress and the town. People were hustling about their business down there now, working like ants . . .

Abruptly Meirwen clutched Gwydron's arm. Well offshore, between iron sea and oyster sky, rode four long keels, sails furled and slender oars running silver in the dull light. The two nearest were graceful lapstrake hulls of a kind rarely seen in these waters, with watchful eyes painted either side of the bow stem and war shields hung outboard from the gunwales.

"Hell fire," breathed Gwydron. "Frisian?"

"Armorican." The other two beamy deepsea curraghs Meirwen would know anywhere: Neithon's ships. "And Manaw."

Gwydron shot her one brilliant glance and sprinted for the rampart stair yelling for the duty captain. Meirwen watched the sleek craft slip under screaming gulls into the changing current. The sun lit Gwydron's bright hair and blue sword-belt as he ran down to the river jetty.

Dusk settled quickly. Meirwen worked in deeper shadow as the evening wore on. Regret had overtaken her happiness for Brys. If she lost this baby, too, there would never be another. He would marry now, he would need an heir. If only Heilyn were here. They could work together, share ideas, squabble. . . . Now what would she do? Olwen would welcome her, but the farm's constant busyness distracted her from work. Instead she wanted to flow into her own alloy, lose herself to sinuous interlace, become a sinewy old woman demanding thieves' prices for the best jewel-work between Ireland and Ravenna, or so she would say. And some day, somewhere far away, she would build a house like Padrig's with a flowering garden at its heart and all the windows facing inward.

"Well?" asked Padrig mildly.

Meirwen had missed another question. She shook her head and stared through a salt blur at the shield boss.

"Go along, child. You're too tired to work."

Meirwen fled to the west rampart, to a place above the storage sheds where she could lay her forehead against rough timber, hidden from casual sight. Down at the jetties, lanterns swung from the masts of the Armorican ships, swaying their light over floorboards and in ripples across the river flow. Though distracted, she knew that it was beautiful. Once she would have watched until she saw the pattern in it, then sketched until she captured it first in wax and finally in metal. Forever and unchanging. Meirwen turned her cheek on the splintered timber and bit her hand so she wouldn't cry out.

"Are you sick again, lady?" a small voice asked.

A mouse shuffle of feet. Meirwen opened her eyes to see the servant girl who shared her cramped loft.

"Sick of pounding sword blades."

"I come here sometimes, too, when the cook gets beery and beats me," said the child wisely. "A priest wants you. Should I bring him here?"

She nodded. The Degannwy priest had asked earlier about a door latch. The girl darted, brown braids flying.

"Meirwen." A familiar voice. Mæn Pedr came to lean beside her at the timbered wall. "You are well?"

"Why wouldn't I be well?" Mæn didn't ask empty questions. His silence lasted one breath too long. She turned and searched his face in the twilight. "What is it? What's wrong?"

"Tregeiriog and Bryn Cerddin have been destroyed. Your sister is dead."

"Olwen." *One more day with my friend, then home,* she had said. *I miss my children after only a week, isn't it silly?* Meirwen leaned toward the sea, longing for wings. "Olwen."

Mæn put his arms around her, talking quietly until she was able to find tears. They scorched her spirit like cautery but offered no healing, only an agony of loss. Death was life renewed, Mæn believed; Meirwen saw only the blood and suffering. Olwen. Bethan, Alban, the girls, who else? And she was untouched. By one day.

"You didn't come from Mathrafal just to tell me that," she realized at last, standing back to wipe her face.

"I came from Llanelwy — Cadell's army is hosting there. There have been raids on both sides of the border. Offa has sent threats."

So Powys was caught in a trap between Gwynedd and Mercia. Caradog would pick up any scraps that Offa let fall. Inept, shortsighted Cadell had brought this on his own people.

"I want peace," Meirwen said, knowing it as she spoke for a child's querulous refusal.

"Peace lives in our hearts." Mæn looked out on the bobbing masthead lanterns, taking in the scene's beauty with a small frown as though he had to commit it to memory. "Meirwen, I need your hands in Llanelwy."

"No."

"There will be fighting. There will be blood and pain and wounds we can't heal, and carrion birds will feast. Come with me to make more work for healers and less for ravens."

Meirwen turned away angrily. Let someone else go. She had to protect her child. She would defend what she had now, not go looking for ways to meddle. Brys would say she could have it all: her baby, her lover, her art, her reluctant satisfaction at helping Mæn. Meirwen knew otherwise.

"Will you come?" Mæn tried once more, though her answer already lay heavy on his voice.

Meirwen looked up into the priest's shadowed face, where she saw all her flights and all his sadness at them. The silver chimed in her ears when she shook her head. She watched the river for a long time, the yellow light dancing on the surface of the dark waters. When she turned again he was gone.

22 July 796 + Llanelwy

Be at Mary's well at noon, said Onnen's messenger. Alone. Brys rode south from Llanelwy abbey on the west bank of slow River Elwy, leaving Elgan and his guard on patrol. He borrowed a brown mare, deciding to be inconspicuous; this sounded like trouble. Two Mercian scouts flanked him on the east bank, just out of spear cast among the river willows, then veered away east above the fish weirs. Cropland closed in to a grass track through shady oak forest. Brys rode steeply down to the small timber church by the river, uneasily aware that the densely wooded cliff was a good place for an ambush. But a monk came out and pointed him into the broad river meadow, where a man in a blue shirt stood holding a white horse. Sun lit his brassy yellow hair and gold collar.

"Cousin Cynfarch." Eli smiled warmly, as though no shadow had ever fallen between them.

"Eli." *Fifty paces to the nearest cover, well within spear range.* Did Eli have men in hiding there? Or did he somehow believe they were still allies?

"Forgive me for borrowing the lady Onnen's name." Eli was charming and punctilious even in deceit. "Now you have Penllyn, Cynfarch. Now you can achieve your father's purpose."

"How?" Brys dismounted, wanting a clear look into his cousin's face. Eli had one minute to talk sense.

Eli studied him and gave a small nod of satisfaction. "You've done well with Offa. I never thought to use the English as leverage against poor Cadell. And Cenwulf promises cantref Tren. Here's what I offer. I take the southern cantrefs and cantref Tren south of River Hafren. The northern cantrefs and Tren north of Hafren are yours."

"I see." *All too well.* "Seven rich southern cantrefs against five poor northern ones and troublesome Tegeingl."

Eli looked across the river meadow to the glittering silver ribbon of River Elwy, his eyes narrowed a little in the bright noon sunshine. "Take all of Tren then. I can do without Cynddylan's country."

No doubt, since Tren is ungovernable. "When? And how?"

"Egfrith will cross River Clwyd the day after tomorrow to drive Cadell out of Tegeingl. Make sure Penllyn has a place in the left wing. We can fall back after the first assault and attack Cadell's center."

"Egfrith alone? Where's Offa?"

"Offa is sick, maybe dying. Thank God, Cynfarch. The man has been a terror."

"What about Egbert?" Impatiently the mare nuzzled the mail shirt on his shoulder.

"In Rome, I hear." His eyes slid. *Liar. You don't know or you know otherwise?*

"Where will you be?"

"Cadell and I are about to have a touching reconciliation. Elfæl and Buellt and my West Saxon mercenaries will be in the left wing with Penllyn."

In the left wing where you can savage Penllyn's unguarded flank, ending any competition? Would you really yield six northern cantrefs so easily, cousin, if you could have them all?

"And by sunset Cenwulf will have Mercia and we will be kings in Powys."

"Yes." Elfæl looked pleased.

"I don't like it," Brys said.

"You have a better idea?" Eli chose to indulge his ally.

"Too much can go wrong if you suddenly order a mixed force to attack the men they've been fighting beside. Instead, wait a mile upstream until Egfrith and Cadell have engaged. Then ride in to attack Cadell's rear. Less damage, less risk of failure."

"You have a point." Eli nodded thoughtfully. "All right. Upstream. About cantref Tren—"

"About your daughter," said Brys. "Gwladus."

Eli crossed himself and considered Brys with swimming eyes. "Gwladus died three years ago. Lovely child. But my next girl is quite a beauty and will be twelve soon. You won't regret this, Cynfarch. You've waited a long time to buy your honor, from Cadell if not from Brochfael."

Brys looked at Cynddylan's great torc with its South Powys boars snarling in old and battered curvilinear gold. He tried unsuccessfully not to look. *Splendid beauty, an aura of the heroic past, a secret life and light of its own. Offa should have melted it down. Without this cursed and radiant thing, would we be talking again of a divided Powys?*

"So you knew about my father and Brochfael."

"How could I not know, when Brochfael Powys tried to place blame on me?" Eli laughed bitterly. "Brochfael's justice. Where was his justice when he had your father murdered?"

"At Cær Gai." Brys vaulted onto the mare and turned her toward the wooded hillside. "I was there, remember."

Remember I grew up in Mathrafal as the hostage of my father's murderer. All my inheritance was fear, despair, a barren hope of vengeance for my betrayed father and my mother who took her life in sorrow. Remember? God knows I can never forget.

"Cær Gai was a terrible day for all of us, Cynfarch," Eli said with great gentleness. "Soon it will be avenged."

Next morning Offa's courier brought an ultimatum south to Llanelwy. The Mercians had made camp at Cær Hiraddug east of River Clwyd in a bold territorial claim. Refugees flooded west through Rhuddlan ford. Offa's message said there had been enough insolence from Powys, enough raiding. The border of Mercian Engelfeld would no longer be along Halkyn ridge to Gwenfrewi Sant but at River Clwyd five miles west. Cadell would demonstrate good faith by giving hostages and tribute.

Cadell sent the answer that if Offa wanted hostages and tribute, he would have to take them. Bravado. But Brys dipped his pen and wrote it. Who could say the outcome? Nothing was ever as it seemed.

As he sent the courier off, the monks were dragging a body out of River Clwyd. Pol went to look, then sent for Elgan and Brys. The man had been blinded and mutilated in Cenwulf's chosen ways; Brys would not have known his friend except for the blue hunting horn still hanging under his arm. *How far did the river carry you back to us? Someone will have to tell Rendil and his daughter that Marc will never marry. Was Meirwen with you? No trace of her anywhere else. Better not to think.*

Late afternoon lit the thatch of the abbey buildings when a scout galloped in from the north coast. Four ships were standing off Clwyd mouth, he told Cadell at the abbey gate, and a large company without standards marched east on the old Roman road from Cær Seint in Arfon.

Cadell, fighting panic, looked quickly at Brys. Beyond the monastery's timber arch, their war camp spilled across the nearest pastures. Drovers leaned on the shady side of supply wagons; steers milled in makeshift pens beyond the tents, field forges and horse lines. But there were not enough men. They couldn't withstand Mercia, let alone other unknown enemies. Gwynedd, and now who else?

They took a squadron north through woodland and marshland alive with water birds. The track ran straight to the sea, though River Clwyd wandered in its brackish estuary. A strong wind met them at the river mouth, singing harshly in the reeds and spilling them golden under the slanting light. They rode among stunted hawthorns bent inland by years of storms and came to a last long dune tangled with white burnet roses and dark juniper. There they reined and looked north over the Irish Sea.

Two long wooden hulls rode at anchor, unloading by inshore curragh. On the beach their crews had piled their gear on the tawny shingle. Out in the roads beyond, swinging between tide and river current, were two deepsea trade curraghs that looked much like Neithon's.

"Manaw," Brys told Cadell. "And Bro Waroch. Four fifties of warriors."

But what were they doing here? Had they come to aid Powys or Gwynedd? Or did they plan to wait for the outcome before they decided? Cadell didn't question it so closely. *It's a costly burden to sing true. The stakes on each throw rise beyond hope of settling.*

Armorican outposts on the beach sighted Cadell's riders on the skyline. A knot of men gathered between tideline and silvered logs and climbed the slope in loose formation. Their spears tossed iron light from blade to blade as the day faded bronze. Cadell Powys dismounted, then his companions. Brys left his shield hanging at his saddlebow. The spears came toward them, a thorn thicket sprung up in the salt grass. Cadell, hands working nervously at his sides, walked forward. As Brys walked beside him he loosened his sword in the scabbard.

Cyngen came first; at his heels was Merfyn. A stone's throw away their Armorican guard halted and grounded spears. Cyngen walked forward alone. Brys heard burnet spines catch on his boots and sandy soil crunch at each step. Where their arms brushed, he felt Cadell trembling. *Steady.* Forever until the gap closed. Sea wind lifted Cyngen's hair from his long face, all golden in the low sunlight, and the brightness across his eyes made him frown. A tall young man with borrowed mail and a plain-hilted sword. *Cyngen Powys.*

"Elisedd. He is the very likeness," said Idris, maybe to himself. Few others now remembered Cyngen's great-grandfather; neither his brutality nor his appearance.

Cyngen took his time looking them over: his father, Pol, Idris, Brys wearing the diadem of Penllyn. His look was a question and he read the answer in Brys's face. Cyngen pushed the shield behind his left shoulder and drew his sword. Brys stepped forward and put his hand on his hilt. Cyngen levelled his blade so russet light flowed from hilt to point and back again. Then he smiled with a brilliance that only he could command, threw the sword at his father's feet and kneeled.

Cadell raised his son from the salt grass and embraced him, casting one ironic glance at his *pencerdd*. Brys dropped his sword hand and let out the breath he hadn't known he was holding. *You young brigand, I'll have your hide for that performance.*

Then everyone began talking in noisy relief. Pol and Brys went down to greet friends. The Bro Waroch guard had a glow that was only half the sunset; not one of them looked older than eighteen. What had Cyngen done, raided the boys' class? But they had all cut their teeth on Frankish swords and many carried a weapon little used for war in the island of Britain, the short composite bow.

Merfyn stood with arms folded, looking intently into the sunset. A flock of gulls wheeled shrill circles over the marsh, and pale dust rose on the west road. It looked like the dust thrown up by an army on the march. Merfyn saw the direction of Brys's gaze.

"I brought half of my father's Manaw bodyguard. And Caradog is leading the war host of Gwynedd."

"Alliance," said Brys.

"Alliance," Merfyn agreed coolly.

"Cadell knows his error," Brys said. "Maybe now we won't all die of it."

Merfyn joked about Cynferchin cousins saving a Cadelling king's skin yet again and congratulated Brys on Penllyn. Then he went off to find his friends. Brys watched him away. Nest disliked Merfyn for his cold arrogance, and now Cadell was in Merfyn's debt. *Nest. Boudicca. Warm lips, cool touch—* Uncomfortably he turned to find Cadell's gaze steady on him over Cyngen's shoulder. He understood then the nature of the choice. Perhaps Cadell had even given Nest her head, watching to see where her heart led her steps, creating a brief mirage of freedom. He had done her no kindness. Nor had Brys, he knew too well. And now he had chosen.

Caradog, Merfyn and Macliau's dark-eyed youngest son brought their fighting forces into the fields of Llanelwy abbey and planted their banners. Over the evening meal, with less argument than they discussed trade routes two years ago, they heard the scouts' reports that Egfrith would attack the next morning. When Pol set a battle order, Brys readily agreed to place Penllyn in the left wing.

At nightfall, when the first torches smoked and spat outside the abbey gate, Cadell Powys went into a brief council with his officers and nobles. When he came out he named as his heir Cyngen Powys.

Celebration flooded the camp. Amidst shouts and weapons clashed on shields, Bened managed to get enough quiet to raise a prayer. The news swept through the camp like sheet lightning. Wearing the diadem of Iâl which Cadell gave him, the diadem Elisedd Powys once wore, Cyngen, fierce as a summer dawn, walked among the night fires.

Later, Brys lay in his tent with his hands behind his head, listening to the camp grow quiet and looking through the open flaps at the new moon. Sleep eluded him. A few days ago he had caught Addonwy working with sanded sheepskin to brighten his shield rim and the links of his mail shirt. Meirwen's work, maybe her last, as Heilyn's silver buckle had become his last. The sword Adwen had given him and his father's old knife were freshly honed. Almost nothing was left to do now. Gwladus had found her freedom, though perhaps not safety. That left only the *englynion* yet to do. *I made only a few* englynion *of her cycle. Next year, if there is a next year. We may survive tomorrow but will we be fighting rearguard for years? For generations? Forever? What is the point in endless resistance while we fall back step by step, cantref by cantref, slowly bled white?*

On the opal shore of sleep, where knowledge and vision flowed together like tidewater and sweetwater, the part of his mind that was Heledd answered her pœt. *We always survive. We endure. If some day we go down into terror, we can leave a rushlight to show others the way on past our fall. We can show that we lived with love and died with courage. In the end that is all we can do.*

The night smelled of roses and horse dung and the mildness of slow-flowing fresh water. *Awen. You swept me here too swiftly.* Outside a man passed by singing and the song was one of Cynfarch's. Brys considered immortality and was asleep before the next englyn.

25 July 796 + Caer Hiraddug

Offa jolted across the tent hacking blood into his crumpled linen. The heat was oppressive. Sweat trickled from Brorda's hair into his beard and plastered the shirt on his back. The physician, a Spaniard who had grown sleek on Offa's patronage, watched anxiously. No doubt he saw his own prospects dwindling with each cough. The fever was worse. Offa would not lie down, would not even sit for a quarter of an hour at a stretch. His color was bad, flushed over sallow, and his eyes were fever-sunk and bloodshot.

"You're certain? Cenwulf himself broke the border?" Offa was grilling his son in a voice like a rusted woodsaw, flinging himself around the tent.

Egfrith had answered the question too many times to bother answering it again.

"And lied about it," said Brorda. Cenwulf had run out of time. It meant more blood, one last time, at least if they could strike at Cenwulf past his bodyguard and his brothers' bodyguards. Cenwulf had acquired a survivor's cunning that Offa himself could envy.

"I thought we might get out of this with tribute and a new treaty." Offa paced and spun, pounding his fist in his palm as though it were all he could find to punish. "Cenwulf has torn that. You know what *Wealas* are like when they want blood. Murderous savages."

The same platitude would also no doubt excuse Cenwulf in a retaliatory push into Powys; he had been whipping up his supporters about a punitive expedition for years. Punishment for what, Brorda hadn't gleaned. But it didn't need to be logical, only to provide an excuse for attack.

"After the battle." Offa stood still and fixed his stare on the place where carpets overlapped, his heat suddenly banked for a cold threat. "He's not above the law. Not any longer."

Brorda glanced up, but Egfrith's gaze deflected away. Sweet Savior, Egfrith knew what Cenwulf was. This was no time for qualms about charity and forgiveness. He wiped his sweating face. Outside, beyond the door guards and royal standards blowing listlessly around their gilded poles, a sullen knot of sub-kings stood waiting to be called in to council. Hostages. They knew it, as they knew this attack on Powys was staged for their enlightenment: observe what happens when you defy Mercian power. The Saxon and Anglian levies and bodyguards were as sullen as their lords.

"This *Wealh.*" Offa sat abruptly and pulled the crown from his fever-damp hair to fling it clattering on the table. "Elisedd's bastard. How the dead rise to haunt us, Brorda. Was he the one who fled the battle in Dyfed last year?"

Brorda nodded. "Eli of Elfæl. He calls himself Protector of South Powys but the territory he claims is unlikely."

"Get rid of him and his warband of West Saxon scum. They're unpredictable in the front line and I don't want them at my back. They change sides as hares change sex."

At your back? Sweet Savior, Offa couldn't fight a battle tomorrow. Brorda sighed, in no way consoled by Egfrith's flicker of amusement.

"They are mounted," the younger king of Mercia reminded. "Light cavalry, which we lack. They could be useful."

Offa picked up his crown and turned it in his hands. He thought slowly and thoroughly, then stooped with an eagle's plunge to the prey. "What dœs he want?"

"Nothing we want. Powys," said Egfrith mildly. It was not quite a reproach for Offa's determination to give Cadell a lesson he had already learned.

"Call him. And call Cenwulf." Offa dismissed the physician and his assistant, the guards, the priest, the servants. He coughed blood, cursed it and wadded the linen in his fist. He shoved his crown onto his lank hair. Sick or not, he pursued his greatest entertainment — throwing conspirators into each other's arms.

Cenwulf stooped under the tent flap and kneeled to Offa. As usual he contrived not to notice Egfrith. At Offa's gesture he stood, smoothing his well-trimmed beard with a ringed hand. A fastidious man. Then the Powys noble came in, doing his best to treat his two armed guards as chance-met companions. Egfrith sent them out.

Offa nodded amicably at his guests. Cenwulf and Eli eyed each other indifferently, yielding no overt recognition. How many times had they met to hammer out their plots? Or had their romance cooled? Cenwulf had attacked fiercely enough in Dyfed. Brorda had never seen Eli near at hand. Neither had Egfrith, by his bemused expression. Egfrith knew all the pœts' work and all the annals; here was a British noble from the old sagas, not in defeat but in all his insufferable arrogance. His yellow hair flowed halfway down his back over fine mail and at his neck was a great gold collar whose termini were two snarling boars. Brorda looked more closely. He knew that collar. A half-pound of worked gold, missing from Tamworth treasury. The last Briton to wear it was another Mercian ally, Cynddylan. Now seemingly it was a betrothal gift between conspirators.

"Tell me," suggested Offa, folding his hands on his chest like a benevolent host, "what brings Cadell's kinsman with a force of *Wealas* and West Saxons to Mercia's aid."

"Not friendship, lord king. The Saxons took shelter with me from Dyfed's anger after Egbert left Britain. Now they can earn their mead by helping to settle this trouble." Eli was a good speaker, gentle with an air of contained passion.

First move to Elfæl, Brorda decided. Offa was amused.

"Not friendship?" Offa urged benignly.

"Powys has fallen to dangerous and incompetent men. Someone will have to gather the fragments when it falls. Not a handful of regional lords, not one king in the north and another king in the south. One man."

"And you will help bring about the fall of Powys? In the interest of Powys?" Offa spoke kindly, inviting trust.

Eli smoothly sidestepped the trap. "Powys defeat grieves me deeply, but I serve my country as I can."

"Cenwulf, your advice?" The elder king twisted in his chair. Sweat stood out on his forehead like fat on a tallow candle, but he was smiling wickedly.

"Who can turn down fighting men now and good administration later? But these West Saxon rebels . . . " Cenwulf hesitated, dropping his smoky blue gaze thoughtfully. He knew Offa's hatred for Egbert. "They may be suitable in reserve."

Still courting, thought Brorda. *We must make quite certain these two never share their wedding feast.*

Offa's smile slowly broadened. On his parched and sweating face it was a terrible expression, a rictus. "You may go."

The traitors separated like oil and water outside the tent. Inside Offa asked his quiet son, "Well? What do you counsel?"

"Have nothing to do with Eli."

"And Cenwulf?"

Egfrith got to his feet and stood a moment looking down at his father, his hoarse and haggard teacher of blood politics. "You of all men know that."

Offa frowned, worrying that the lesson was lost, as his son walked out of the tent. *Enough,* Brorda thought. But it wasn't yet enough.

Offa fainted twice during the dull hot evening and threatened the physician with torture when he brought leeches. Egfrith looked to the battle plans. Cenwulf came with smiling sympathy which lifted Brorda's hackles. Offa raged at his own weakness and struggled up on an elbow to hurl orders already quietly carried out. Long after it was too dark to read, Brorda sat beside his old friend's camp bed with the Horatian odes forgotten in his hand, wondering what makes a man loyal beyond all reason.

In the cool dark, Offa got up to walk with Egfrith around the camp on Hiraddug hill. His Mercian nobles followed the kings, but a small group held themselves apart with Cenwulf. Or was that Brorda's imagination? The Anglian and Saxon sub-kings trailed after, making no attempt to conceal their animosity.

At the fires and watch posts, the landowners and their levies cheered the kings. Offa was his own luck amulet, wrapped in forty years' victory unshadowed by defeat. *Except against Powys*. Brorda kept that thought to himself. If Caradog were still angry they might be able to squeeze Powys between west and east, as Offa thought, then toss Engelfeld to Gwynedd afterward. If Powys and Gwynedd had made their peace . . . It was a chilling thought. The British were on their own territory, backed to a wall and dangerously provoked. That was Cenwulf's doing. Earlier he had been passionately advising Offa to make a drive west and throw the *Wealas* into the sea.

Offa had smiled ominously. Cenwulf wouldn't be throwing anyone into the sea unless he threw himself in. That notion somewhat lightened Brorda's mood.

Offa seemed stronger now. He dismissed his retinue, all but his son and Brorda, and turned his back on the camp. Egfrith put an arm around his father's shoulders, a rare gesture of affection that made Offa glare suspiciously, and took himself off to patiently sort the last problems.

Guards, sub-kings and the anxious physician fell behind as Offa and Brorda walked together to the old stronghold's crumbling western earthwork. Dry grass rustled under their feet, giving off an aromatic scent of summer. Some of the evening's heaviness was lifting as the night cleared; a crescent moon sailed up over the distant lowlands of Mercia at their backs. Brorda shook his head. *What are we doing here? People flee from us, even those who spoke English at their mothers' knees. This is hostile territory in an alien country.*

Upstream beyond two miles of broken woodland, the British camp was only a reddish glow of many fires against the sky. Two miles due west lay the nearest ford and the highest navigable point on River Clwyd, now showing its rusty sand bars at summer's low water. At dawn they would be there, at the red riverbank, crossing west through Rhuddlan ford.

"Counsel Egfrith after I die," said Offa abruptly. "And make sure Cenwulf dœsn't get his chance. He's too much like me. He will try."

Brorda turned in surprise at this talk of death but found only the usual expression of keyed energy and impatience on Offa's sharp features. When Offa's time came he would snarl refusal at the death angel and demand to rule forever. *Would that you could, dear friend.* In the meantime he would strengthen the guard on Offa's tent. Cenwulf could try now as well as later, given an opportunity, and Offa's fever would conceal the evidence of poison.

"Agreed?" pressed Offa.

Brorda thought of saying, Find another watchdog for Egfrith, I'll take vows at Saint Peter's Woking, or perhaps take Leoba to Rome and live in sanctified sin. Instead he smiled ruefully at forty years' habit and said, "Agreed."

Offa tore out a cough as his restless gaze roved west and south. "I have not been easy to serve." *A challenge.*

"Not particularly." Brorda's reach for humor rang hollow. Egfrith was easier. But Egfrith was not Offa. In a hundred years people would probably say, wonderingly, that Offa's border had been dug by a giant. In one sense it would be true.

Offa snorted, his own nearest brush with humor at these times. "All to what purpose?"

Brorda remembered another time he had heard that question from Offa. *Killing a tyrant is easy enough, but then what?* Offa had demanded. *All to what purpose?* They had been two young men on leave from the king's bodyguard, leaning on their scythes in a Hwicce farm field with wheat and cornflowers laid waste around them, talking a new Mercia into existence. Offa was in a fey mood tonight. Battles usually made him pace and prowl, not indulge in the rhetoric of unanswerable questions.

"You know the purpose," Brorda told him as patiently as he had forty years ago.

"Laws forged from superstition. Diplomacy with Frankish kings before they knew the word. It was you who shaped Charles, just as you shaped Brochfael—"

"You think so? I suppose you think bloody Elisedd shaped me."

Who else? Warlike Powys had tutored young Offa in survival, and he had learned well. Brorda resumed, "Steady trade. Just taxes. The first working coinage in Britain since the Romans. Church reform. English unity, to the extent that's possible. Fair dealing with the British."

Offa shook his head. "I hear Elisedd's ghost laughing."

"What in God's name will you do with Engelfeld? Let alone Powys?"

"Nothing." Offa laughed with a sound of tearing parchment and began to cough. "We will make a strategic retreat. Rule *Wealas*? Who can? Not even other *Wealas.* Wreocansæte is still a running sore after a hundred years. I would gladly summon their damned Cynddylan from hell to take it back. So tomorrow we will slap them down, take hostages and tribute, and withdraw east."

"To the dyke?"

"You want me to hand over Chester too? Are you working for idiot Cadell?" Offa demanded, still pursuing his black humor.

No more or less than Cadell's pœt was working for Offa. The wise man loves peace above nations, though Brorda, looking south toward the camp glow. "Send an envoy to make peace. Tonight."

"Don't be a fool. Let East Anglia and Kent see a *Wealh* refuse tribute?" Offa's voice softened as much as it could. "I thought of it nonetheless. So did Egfrith. Cenwulf has prevented that now."

Much later they drank strong British mead over the drafts board in Offa's tent. Candlelight yellowed the king's white hair again, gently filled out his drawn face with a healthy bloom and unnervingly swept away the years. An amber glare lit the chests and bed and carpets but left the tent corners in brown shadow. Luxury. Brorda remembered days of civil war, when they slept turnabout watch in rainy wastelands and argued to stay awake on endless night rides. Comfort now was no repayment for friends consumed by carrion birds or for all the blood they had shed. Never enough. There was no repayment, no redemption. Offa thought he would see eternal peace, despite his grim doubts about the priests' promises. He would hate it; hell flames would suit him better. And soon he would be leading a rebellion against heaven's realm. *Sacrilege on top of treason — tonight I'm too old to provoke either confessor or executioner.*

Offa turned over fallen gamesmen one by one as though he could find answers underneath. Frowning. Still pursuing his strange uncertainty. "But will others know the purpose?"

"Soon." It was tempting *wyrd* to say that. Brorda crossed himself. "Laws, diplomacy, they'll question it all. But truth stands for now and all time."

"New pœt?" asked Offa dryly. "Or has your ambitious young friend from the lakehead sung a spell on you? I hear he finally won his crown."

"You accuse me of collusion with an enemy?" Brorda smiled. *Friend? A strange idea. Not too strange.* "No. I have never heard him sing."

"The Romans ruled all Britain from the chalk cliffs to Pictland," Offa was back on the track of his idea. "Now we have all these little kingdoms. Can one man hold it again?"

"Did one man ever?" Brorda shrugged and began to stack the draftsmen. "But we had better find a way. Otherwise Britain will become a Frankish backwater or a haven for northern pirates."

"*Cymry* and *Saeson.*" Offa's voice was a dry rustle. Brorda watched him closely; he almost never used the British language. "I could make their damned alliance work, as I have made a single people of the southern English. Almost."

This was the dream they had harvested with wheat and wildflowers that sunny day forty years ago. There was no point now in saying that Kent was in rebellion, the West Saxons were biding their time, Wreocansæte was seething, even the other Anglians hated Mercian supremacy. And the British would fight as long as they had pœts to make songs.

"Strategic retreat," Brorda told his king. "Then we'll make better treaties."

Offa nodded shortly, collected the counters and folded the empty gameboard.

Not long before dawn, Egfrith and the Spanish physician came to tell Brorda that Offa was dead.

26 July 796 + Rhuddlan

At Rhuddlan ford, copper sunlight poured over the Tegeingl hills under a shallow arch of green sky. First light whetted the spears above the dark mass of the British host and lit the banners of nobles and kings. Above all the rest floated Gwynedd's rearing crimson dragon and the golden stag of Powys. Cadell had the center. Gwynedd made up the right wing. Penllyn's bodyguard and foot levies made up the left wing with Tegeingl and Meirionydd. The Armorican archers kneeled before Cadell's line and behind them stood Merfyn's Manaw warriors.

No one was talking much. Mostly Brys heard the creak of saddle leather, horses impatiently rattling their bits, small sounds of mail and weapons. Under the hooves, the bruised river meadow breathed scents of meadowsweet and dog rose. *Green summer, high summer.* Brys sat Carnlas between Cadwr and Elgan under the Penllyn raven banner. Nearby Addonwy was arguing with one of the Penllyn men about something they would all forget within an hour. Brys tested his grip on the resined spear shaft. Another smear of resin on his forehead held his diadem in place. *If you want me, here I am.*

East across River Clwyd, as the scouts had warned, the first English foot warriors crested the hill in a dark ragged wave. Brys watched the English walk steadily down the long slope to Rhuddlan. *Too many.* They halted a spear cast east of the ford. Soon a handful of men rode down with standard bearers, the sub-kings of East Anglia, Kent and the South Saxons. Under Mercia's black eagle standard Brys saw only one pale crowned head. Offa must be ill, as they said; he had always fought his own battles.

Dawn glowed from amber to blue and glittered on the mail of the Mercian bodyguard at Egfrith's center. Brys narrowed his eyes at the bright eastern sky, searching for Cenwulf. Overhead, birds layered the air above the sandy red bank and the ford shallows in their own battle order. A single eagle pivoted highest on a great sweep of pinions and a few kites wheeled below her. Floating over the bright river reflection, always first to descend, were the crows and ravens.

Two Mercians walked down to the ford. One of them was a big white-haired man; the other wore rich robes and carried green branches. Brorda and Offa's archbishop were coming in truce. Cadell sent out Brys and the bishop of Llanelwy. The old churchman strode toward Mercia with his white hair floating from his tonsure and his homespun robe pulled up through his belt like one of the warrior saints. Brys held Carnlas to a walk beside him until they reached the west bank.

"In the name of Our Lord and with the blessing of Archbishop Hygebert of Mercia and the Britons," Brorda called out in his archaic accent. "Are there terms of peace?"

Brys leaned across his saddlebow to the Llanelwy bishop. "Do you recognize Hygebert of Lichfield as your overlord?"

"My son, no man can serve two masters." The old man's wit was less ravaged than his face. "I serve God, not Offa."

Brys flung a hard voice back across the river, all the way to Egfrith. "Peace is yours — when you give hostages and tribute to Cadell Powys, and when Lichfield's priest kneels to his mother church of Llanelwy."

Brorda and Hygebert turned away abruptly. Brys, searching the dark ranks of Mercians on Egfrith's left wing, at last saw a gold-on-red eagle standard.

"Cenwulf!" Brys flung up an arm at the ravens creaking overhead. "They have come for you. Feed them well."

"You invited them. You feed them," the faint English words floated back.

Brys and the bishop returned to the British host. The old man walked straight through the lines to the rear, where his monks raised a soaring harmony of alleluia. Cadell's battle line shifted restlessly.

Across the river the English swept into motion with a roar, thunder in the east. About half of the force moved down, foot levies and landowners' men and the East Anglian royal bodyguard. The Mercian bodyguard and nobles stayed back. Egfrith's strategy; Offa would have plunged straight in. Pol yelled orders, and war horns boomed on both sides of River Clwyd. Brys regained his place and shouldered his shield.

Cadell nodded. Pol lifted a hand as the English waded out of the ford and onto the west bank. A brazen trumpet call. On the right wing, Gwynedd surged forward in a curve toward the river; to Brys on the left it looked dead slow. When the English were in range the Armoricans loosed their arrows, shafts ticking on each other in midair before they seared into the English line. A few men stumbled and went down. Another flight was in the air before the first arrows fell. It slowed the advance, but at a run the English companies soon crashed into the center. Cadell's bodyguard boiled into action.

Brys gave Elgan his command. *Now.* Penllyn and Meirionydd and the Powys lords' bodyguards on the left jolted into motion. Brys picked up Carnlas from trot to hand canter. The marshy ground gave underfoot and made slow travel but at least it kept the English from bracing their spears under their feet to gut the horses. That was his last clear thought for a while.

Impact. Speed and shock drove them deep among untrained English levies, who scrambled to give ground instead of going for the horses' bellies and hamstrings. Brys speared above enemy shields, seeking the life and finding it, as they pushed seaward along the river. They thrust through the levies, onto the shield wall of the East Anglian household guard. That was harder work. Brys saw a few Penllyn men unseated and lost under the hooves. *Cadwr? Still at my right.* Pushing forward through a stubborn English tide, they broke out into clear ground. If they slowed they would be engulfed by seasoned foot fighters. Brys heeled Carnlas ahead into the thick of it, lashing at English skulls with deadly forehooves. Clearing a space. And another. Onward.

At last they won through the struggle into open river meadow. Brys's spear was gone, and his sword was bloody. When Elgan shouted them together, they cantered back behind the embroiled battle line to the center. Mostly intact. Cadwr was still with him. Cian tore past with a knot of his brothers, throwing themselves into Powys's battle for some reason of their own. Brys craned to see across the river. Cenwulf and his two brothers waited there with the bulk of Egfrith's bodyguard. *Come over, fight our battle. How can we tempt you?*

Cadell yelled. Brys rode to him and found the king shouting in panic about scouts and West Saxon cavalry. That had to be Eli. About time.

"Where?"

"South. Upstream." At the British rear, a few frightened green levies threw down their weapons and ran. Cadell's center sagged back. Any more desertion and the English would roll over them like a runaway cart.

"Forget them." Brys twisted in the saddle, looking around for Cyngen. What he saw shocked him cold. Elgan had already seen. And they could do nothing.

Cenwulf had been tempted. Already midstream in River Clwyd, he led the second Mercian assault in a gleaming mailed wall. In Cenwulf's path, still intent on harrying the scattered first wave at the river bank, were Gwyddien's wing and Cyngen.

Brys hurled his voice like a square-headed spear, both threat and offer. "Cenwulf!"

The English noble paused in the brackish ford water to yell something back, unheard with the noise and distance. But Brys watched with a catch in his throat that could be laughter as Cyngen turned to see the Mercian attack. Cadell's heir took his only option. As the first English spears hissed onto the west bank, he broke away and rode for the right wing with his squadrons. Straight south toward Eli's force. If they met—

Knee to knee with Cadell, Brys shouted, "I have to take Penllyn out. South."

"But Egfrith." Cadell stared at him in white-eyed shock. Without Penllyn the left wing would break; without the left wing the center would break.

No time to argue. Brys reined away.

Cadell shouted after him, his voice lost under the battle noise. Brys didn't need to hear the words. *Brys. Don't do it. Don't go to Eli.*

Brys wheeled back to his Penllyn force, already forming up on Cadell's left again, and yelled them out after him. No time to explain. Elgan didn't question it. As they streamed south between the fleeing foot fighters and the supply wagons, Cenwulf's bodyguard struck hard and Egfrith led the iron wall of his own guard down into the ford waters.

Cyngen and Gwyddien had come around in an upstream river meadow. Brys, riding low on the grey horse's neck, raced south on the main track. One glimpse of Cyngen's face. A grin, then doubt, then shock, then iron determination and a raised sword. *You think I've changed sides and come to attack. Elgan thinks I've gone mad, begins to wonder at something worse. This is only the start.* Brys veered wide of the bodyguard wing and pounded south past them, yelling for Cyngen to wait. Did he hear? Where in hell was Eli? At the ford downstream from River Clwyd's confluence with River Elwy, at the woodland margin he saw Elfæl's boar banner floating on the wind.

Brys reined hard, plunging Carnlas to a halt. Elgan nearly rode over him, and Cadwr came up at white heat, shouting, demanding to know why they'd been pulled out of the battle. *Don't worry, my dear, you'll have your fill.* Brys reached and caught Elgan's arm.

"Take Penllyn back in if I don't return. Forget Egfrith. Kill Cenwulf at any cost." Not waiting for an answer, he heeled forward and cantered to Eli. Elgan and Cadwr followed but stopped short.

Eli sat his white horse beside another man, a West Saxon mercenary captain whom Brys had last seen at an Aachen banquet table with Egbert. A well-bred murderer, Heilyn had said in his usual running commentary. Eli was sleek and pleased with himself. *See, Penllyn comes begging to me.*

"Cousin Cynfarch. Why have you come? My scouts say the battle is not yet—"

"Come now. Not later."

"Our plan, if you remember, was a messenger at the right time." His elegant voice had a slight edge. He touched his gold torc nervously. *Yes, it's still there.*

Brys drew his sword. The West Saxon's hand moved to his hilt but stopped there. A prudent man. "Our plan has changed. We'll do this my way."

"Your way?"

"*Braint.* You are a traitor, as my father was a traitor. Come to Cadell's aid now and you'll be a hero. Remember I'm at your back. One false move and you die—I'll tell the king you were riding to join Cenwulf."

Eli gave him a long calculating look. *You still think you can talk your way through it, a family trait.* "And if I don't?"

"You die here." Brys lifted the sword point. "As you die, pray for your daughter Gwladus—your death is her face price."

Eli swallowed hard and turned to gaze over his gathered squadrons. He looked harder at the Penllyn force at Brys's back. A sudden commotion there, the movement of many horses. Brys risked a glance. Cyngen and Gwyddien's wing had come to swell the Penllyn ranks. *Merciful god, the risk.* At last Eli looked at Brys with naked hatred. Then, unbelievably, he gave the order. A mutter of anger or confusion, but the Elfæl bodyguard and the West Saxons moved forward slowly at first, then broke into a canter. Brys circled to ride close behind them, herding them northward like a cattle dog, and Elgan fell in beside him with the Penllyn guard and Gwyddien's wing.

"Do you understand?" Brys asked. Someone else had to know, and if necessary, tell Cadell.

Elgan looked sick. "I heard."

Brys dug his heels into Carnlas's ribs and surged forward. They covered the mile to Rhuddlan in minutes. When they drove in northward on the river margin, Egfrith and the weight of the English army were locked in close fighting with the Mathrafal guard.

Cyngen went in first, yelling like the wild hunt, against Offa's merciless veterans who wrote their reputation in blood. Eli led in his mixed force and Brys hurled Penllyn in at their backs, blocking the southerners from leaving the field.

The lines clashed together. English warriors angled their spears under their boots wherever they had solid ground to meet the charge, and unwary British horses plunged onto the long blades. A few bold men crouched to disembowel and died under the hooves. A slaughterhouse reek rose as horses and men sank screaming into blood and stinking offal. *We'll never get out of this alive.* He couldn't see Cadell. Anyone. He saw only contorted faces falling under his blade and spears licking toward him like eager tongues. One blade ripped a jagged path up his right thigh. Brys yelled in pain and rage and swung down hard on the spearman. He felt the grit of neck bone as his sword came free. Everything darkened and slowed. All spinning to a narrower vision. And clear.

Elgan yelled for them to dismount. Brys slung his shield behind him to slide down, suddenly washed in cold sweat, and his leg buckled under him. Addonwy caught him as he staggered. Torn down the muscle, not across it. He could walk if he kept moving and didn't let it stiffen. *Good enough for now. Now is forever.* Brys shook the mist out of his head.

Midday. The sun stood high above red Rhuddlan in a cloudless July sky. Carrion birds in the river willows lifted their wings and spoke of gratitude. River Clwyd's waters were churned pale red.

"Egfrith," Brys croaked. He had left his voice upstream. "And Cenwulf."

Addonwy grinned and pointed east across River Clwyd. "They're retreating to Hiraddug."

Mercia in retreat? More likely regrouping on higher ground. But if we pursue quickly enough . . . Cyngen led Gwyddien's wing toward the ford, and after him streamed the British reserves and untrained foot levies.

Dry through a month of rainless days, the meadows drank blood, and a flat death smell now overhung the morning's bruised scent of flowers. The English fell back in good order, making their enemies buy each foot of ground. For a while the loudest sound was the shatter of bodies hitting the shallow ford waters as the fight moved east. Far behind the British host a great many-voiced alleluia rose again.

In the river meadow the wounded shielded themselves as well as they could from the battle grinding over them. Everywhere the dead, those who sold their lives for the mention of honor, sprawled in the soaked grass. Among them the Armoricans kneeled to recover their arrows for another flight, a grisly task. Brys saw two girls ride through the meadow among the reserves, one with white-blonde hair flying loose and the other with hair like flowing heather honey.

At the river margin Brys stumbled near a body lying half in the stained water. Brassy yellow hair brown at the roots, blue eyes full of blue sky, a fine mail shirt and a great gold boar-headed collar: Eli had paid his debt late but in full. Brys kneeled stiffly to pull the torc from his cousin's throat and pushed it down the front of his mail shirt. *Cynddylan's torc will not be battlefield plunder twice, not while I live.*

Stepping down into River Clwyd's slow current among his guard, Brys saw the mailed rampart of Mercian forces holding the slope opposite, buying time for the king to move east. Then Cyngen led the strengthened center into the river crossing under Powys's stag banner; the British host followed. Gwynedd men with twelve-foot spears waded River Clwyd beside Merfyn's flame-haired Irish cousins, Rendil Osmodson's fair kindred and the men of South Powys. Gwydron crossed the red stream at Caradog's side singing like the morning's first lark.

The quiet of midday dropped between bursts of fighting. Rising in green Powys hills, scattering summer light across its shallows, flooding the salt estuary, the river swelled its voice to a deep subterranean roar. Thigh-deep in the ford waters, Brys saw his own blood eddy toward the sea, an offering.

The Mercian nobles and the Tamworth bodyguard held the east road between the ford paving stones and the alders. Ravens clattered and shifted in their green branches, watching dead men drift in the reedbeds. Brys called Penllyn to him on the east bank; the silk ravens on his green banner floated under their living kin as they climbed toward the English. The Mercians were ragged from losses and weary from two river crossings but now they held the high ground. Someone sounded a bronze British war horn. Powys and Gwynedd surged up the slope, a dark flood tide, churning more water out of the ford and slipping on the muddy track. The lines ground and clashed. Caradog went straight through the shields roaring like a bull. Cyngen struck and twisted at the heart of the fight like a deadly flame. Brys stabbed and slashed, barely able to move in the crush, trying to stay upright on his stiffening leg as blows hammered on his shield.

The red bank beside the road was crumbling and littered, the undergrowth torn and trampled. There Brorda and his captain fought with shields lapped. Brys searched the banners and faces. Saxon nobles, East Anglians. Leave them. At last he saw what he wanted. His mouth tasted of cold metal, of revenge, as he drove toward three fair brothers near the trees under a gold and red banner. The tallest wore a helmet with a nose flange. Cenwulf.

Brys stepped across the body of a Penllyn cousin to face his enemy. *No priest to protect you from sorcery? No captive girl on display?* The river rush faded behind so that he heard clearly the harsh pull of each breath. Hesitation would kill him. He threw himself toward Cenwulf.

Cenwulf stepped back quickly and raised his sword. His first stroke split a long wedge from Brys's shield, cutting through the iron shield rim. Brys twisted and trapped the blade long enough to stab for the throat above his mail. But Cenwulf deflected the sword stroke.

Shield to shield, they watched for the next move in each others' eyes. Brys saw that Cenwulf equalled him in fear and need to kill, not in rage. *I am your death.* He worked at Brys's shield again, a woodcutter. His size and strength would prevail soon. Brys tried the unexpected. When the shield split, he hurled the forward half at Cenwulf's face. *Buy time. A second blade for the throat.* But Cenwulf lashed out with a serpent reflex as Brys drew his knife. The sword blurred down toward his head. At the last instant someone shoved him hard sideways, and the blow struck his unshielded right shoulder. Bone splintered. A blinding shock of pain. Brys yelled and rammed his sword blade bloodily along Cenwulf's arm. Then Addonwy leaped forward from his right as a second blow descended, robbing him of another chance. Cenwulf stepped aside and was gone.

Another Mercian shield rim sliced his forehead. Brys staggered back against one of his men and went down with his eyes full of blood.

Every time Brys opened his eyes and looked out over Rhuddlan ford, the sun was lower in the west. *A long time, no time, inconstant and changeable time. Green leaves hushing overhead, the river murmuring not far away.* He lay under a tree, head pillowed on someone's cloak. Once he tried to sit. Bad idea. If he lay still, he could watch the leaves and listen to the river. If he moved much, blackness swallowed him again.

One time he saw that the battle had moved east but he knew there was still fighting by the distant shouts and screams. Occasionally a horse or man stumbled west across River Clwyd to safety. *Powys. We held our own.* Finer points of victory and defeat seemed abstract just now. Someone lying near him asked for water. Brys decided to bring water from the muddy river, but nothing in his body obeyed. Now the other lay still under a thick smell of blood and ordure. Gutted, intestines trailing. *British or English, dœs it matter? One or the other.*

Another time Heledd sat by his feet with the sunset slanting across her golden eyes and her tawny hair blowing free. She reminded him of the saint's winged golden cat, a wild creature about to take flight. Blood stained her cheek as though she had brushed her hair back with a smeared hand. Later she sang to herself and braided her honey hair. *You waited by another Powys ford long ago, watching the battle at River Tren.* Slowly Brys explored the wreckage of his body one-handed. Someone had strapped up his right arm with his sword belt. Linen was wadded inside the mail shirt, blood-soaked now. His diadem was still on his brow. Cynddylan's great gold torc circled his neck. Who put it there? Only Heledd had that right. *The land gives us life, the land claims our bone and blood, the land absolves us.*

A horse was tied to the tree but it was brown and the harness was wrong. No red leather, no silver bells. *I left her in Amwythig,* Heledd explained. *Cenwulf would have known I planned to run. You wanted to kill him too. It seems we both have to wait.* Brys told Heledd about her *englynion*. She listened gravely, watching him from her hawk eyes, then told him to stop talking and rest. *Just for a while, cousin.* Heledd leaned to kiss him on the forehead before she left. In the late sun it became the kiss of the diadem on his brow, burning gold.

The last time he stirred, the sun was bleeding across the Gwynedd horizon, and everything was quiet. A raven sat on the gutted man's chest. *Brân. Wait, little brother.* Brys squinted into the sunset and saw himself below, riding through the ford on Carnlas. Today he had waded through on foot. Was he going to see Brorda a month ago? But he was bloodstained and grimy, riding slowly, looking at the ground. Coming this way. *What happens when I meet myself? A rare opportunity for study.* Then the raven took flight almost under the stallion's nose. Carnlas reared and Cadwr dismounted. Now I'll never know, Brys tried to explain. But I'm glad you're here. Take the diadem. You'll make a better lord anyway.

Shut your mouth, Cadwr said. *You've taken a blow to the head, you're making less sense than ever.* The neck of a leather bottle. Strong mead slopped across his face and into his mouth.

Fully awake. So was the searing, immobilizing pain. Whatever Gwladus had done to stop the bleeding, she could do nothing for splintered bone. Full of broken glass, grinding every time he stirred. Cadwr's hands moved over him lightly, finding the damage. More of the drink, mercifully, numbed his senses.

Cadwr kneeled to wash his face carefully. Dirt and tears and blood. "Do you remember the last time I had to clean you up?"

"Never."

"Don't talk dull," Cadwr told him mildly. "You decided to see what would happen if you kicked a wasp's nest."

"I didn't kick this one. Blame Cadell. But he learned his lesson. I did too."

Cadwr grinned. "That's more like it."

Somehow he was swaying on his feet in Cadwr's grasp. *Fair hand of god.* "Where are Cadell and Cyngen?"

"They're meeting with Egfrith, working out a peace."

"Cenwulf?"

"Offa's kinsman? I don't know. Can you ride?"

"Yes. My collarbone is broken. I'll be all right." *For an hour. Bleeding again. All I need is an hour. Uncertain Cadell, inexperienced Cyngen, boastful Caradog, Egfrith the dreamer. Cenwulf is too strong. Someone needs to control him. Kill him, better idea. Maybe not today.*

A fallen alder made a mounting block, thankfully. Brys got into the saddle, and Cadwr swung up behind.

"Christ in glory. Where did you get that thing?" Cadwr had just noticed Cynddylan's torc. "Get rid of it. Now. Throw it into the river."

“I need it. Not as good as ravens but it will have to do. Where’s the parley?”

“At the tavern downstream. You’re not going to any parley, my dear.”

“Cadell needs me. Promise. Otherwise God knows what he will say.”

“God knows what you’ll say after a knock on the head.”

“God knows what I’d say anyway.”

Cadwr laughed. He’d always had a good laugh, warm and honest. Maybe that was why Meirwen liked his awful jokes . . . *Meirwen.* Brys leaned back on his brother, content to drift with the river.

Cadwr, torn between common sense and Cadell’s need, turned the stallion downstream. Brys was quiet until they got to the tavern gate, where Cadell’s one-armed Armorican commander passed them inside without question. Once they got down Cadwr kept an arm around Brys, though he seemed steadier.

In the warm July evening the kings were meeting behind the deserted tavern at tables pulled into the orchard. Candle lanterns swung from the trees. Cadwr found it sad and senseless; they could as easily have gathered in this pleasant garden to celebrate a wedding or a good harvest. Instead, there were bloodstained bandages, tired faces and voices ground down by a day’s grim work.

Cadell Powys and Egfrith of Mercia, talking quietly through their priests, seemed to share an understanding. Egfrith seemed a quiet and bookish man but he had his wits about him. Now Cadell listened patiently to the bitter objection of a light-haired Mercian noble with a bandaged arm. When Cadell saw Brys his face lit with startling warmth. An English victory in Mercian territory, the English noble was saying. When he turned Cadwr recognized Cenwulf. Flanking him were two brothers, judging by their resemblance; they all had eyes like wolves. Cenwulf stared when he saw Cynfarch Penllyn take a place at the table. His look was so lethal that Cadwr dropped a hand on Brys’s left shoulder, sending a message. *Harm my brother and you answer to me.*

Then Cenwulf saw Cynddylan’s torc around Brys’s neck. He paled, then flushed, eyes fixed on the heavy gold collar as though he’d seen his own ghost. Then he took great pains to look anywhere but at Brys. So that was the point of all this, getting at Cenwulf. At least it shut his mouth.

The two kings got on with negotiating their peace. Redhaired Merfyn, blood still speckling his skin like darker freckles, stood near Caradog Rhos, who had his left arm in a sling. Cyngen, his grey eyes cold in an impassive face, maintained a chilling watch on the English. Standing behind his brother, Cadwr began to realize by the way they spoke that the great and terrible Offa was dead.

Brys made sense after all. “Tegeingl is neither Mercian hidage nor Powys cantref. It stays with Gwynedd. We’ve all had enough of movable territories.” Was that a promise, or a warning, that Penllyn wasn’t movable? Idris Meirionydd smiled at the sanded table top.

Caradog rumbled his approval. Cenwulf angrily began to speak, but Egfrith agreed before his noble could make trouble again. Owain Tegeingl looked from king to king and wisely decided to hold his tongue. Cadell thought about it, demanded and received full shipping rights from Caradog and sullen Owain, and agreed. Clever. Powys would no longer be burdened with dyke construction and any further border war in the north, a sure trouble spot. Let Caradog have what he wanted, both the territory and the war.

A warm breeze breathed in from the river as they signed documents. A few men stood, stretched, walked around to ease stiffness. Brys braced to stand but thought better of it. Or couldn't stand, Cadwr feared. It was time to get him away. But then King Egfrith came to sit beside him on the bench; surely Offa would never have done that? Brys asked him something in English.

The Mercian king nodded and said in British, "Brorda is well. He is keeping a vigil with my father's body."

Cadwr was momentarily surprised that they seemed on friendly terms, then realized that as far as Brys was concerned he was beyond surprise.

"Tell Brorda he has my prayers. I mourn your father, lord king," Brys said. "He was a great man. Not a friend of Powys, but we could have done far worse for an enemy. He was honorable and just."

"He also spoke well of you, Cynfarch," Egfrith said.

Cadwr heard a flicker of dry humor behind the words, some reference that Brys understood. What had he been playing at — merciful God — with Offa of Mercia?

Brys glanced at Cenwulf, who was deep in talk with his brothers near the orchard wall, and said quietly, "Egfrith, take warning. Cenwulf was poised to attack you from the rear once you were in the river. Eli was waiting to attack Cadell."

Egfrith looked at Brys for a long time, considering and discarding several answers. "What happened?"

"Eli was persuaded to join Cadell. Cenwulf could not attack you alone."

"Persuaded?"

Brys said only, "Cenwulf will try again."

"He will not be given an opportunity." The English king's mild voice made the death sentence all the more chilling.

"We could have settled this whole matter yesterday, Egfrith. At this table. Saved scores of lives." Cadwr heard the sharpening edge of pain on his brother's voice.

"I said the same thing." Egfrith levered himself wearily onto his feet. He looked more closely at Brys. "Shall I send for my physician?"

Brys shook his head. "Thank you. Tell Brorda."

The lanterns swung in the trees under the small green apples, dancing their light and shadow up into the branches. Cadell's priest scratched with his quill, sanded and scratched again. Cadell and Egfrith signed, then the sub-kings, cantref lords and witnesses. Cyngen put down the quill and straightened. He was frowning in Brys's direction, about to speak. What was wrong? When Brys leaned more heavily, Cadwr looked down. On the bench he saw blood pool briefly and soak into the weathered wood, then pool again. *I'll be all right, you said. Liar. Bleeding yourself white.* Enough. Brys had had his say, signed his treaty, frightened the English noble with his cursed torc. Cadwr got him on his feet, out through the orchard and onto the horse. By the time they reached the track he was unconscious again. Cadwr fought down the knot in his throat. *You never did know when to stop.*

A quarter mile south Cadwr slowed for the ford but still took it at a plunging canter. Half a mile west was the farm where they were taking the wounded. Losing that much blood, it could be too late. Stupid. Too intent on his performance with that gold trinket. Cadwr knew what it was well enough; it was in all the old songs. Someone passed him on a white horse at a flat gallop. When Cadwr reined among the torchlit farm buildings Cyngen mab Cadell Powys was there ahead of him, yelling for a surgeon.

Cadwr staggered under his brother's weight but got him through the door and onto a table. A girl with white-blonde hair was washing the last man's blood off it. Brys sprawled loosely, and Cadwr rolled him onto his side to unlace the mail shirt. If he stayed unconscious, if he survived the loss of blood, maybe he wouldn't die of shock and wound poison.

The surgeon had the look of a monk, though his white hair was untonsured. He washed his hands and looked over torn flesh and misshapen bone with a bleak expression Cadwr had hoped not to see. A dark woman brought him the small deadly weapons of surgery: lancet, spatula, probes and knife. The whitehaired man moved between her and Brys's body on the table, blocking her view.

"Go, my dear. There's a time to run."

"Not now," she said, and under the smeared blood Cadwr recognized Meirwen.

After that they were too busy to talk, though the surgeon asked him not to go far.

When Cadwr walked out into the summer dark toward the river, Cyngen followed. On the trampled riverbank he showed Cadell's heir the gold boar-headed collar.

Cyngen thoughtfully turned Cynddylan's torc around in his hands, examining the precious object with reverent care. It was slightly bent from true now, a little more bloodied and battered. Then he handed it back to Cadwr with an unspoken question.

Cadwr sketched a cross over it, grasped it firmly and flung it out into the deepest midstream of River Clwyd below Rhuddlan ford. An offering.

21 august 796 + llandegla yn iâl

A small sound, a dimple on the black surface, rings glimmering silently outward toward the grassy margins of the pool, and it was done. The bent pin tumbled end over end, quickly disappearing. Meirwen got up and brushed the grass from her knees.

"Dœs it really matter what I offer?"

"Do you think it matters?" Mæn Pedr sat crosslegged under the hazel tree in the twilight.

"The prayer matters." *At least it staves off terror and futility.* But to say that to Mæn invited questions she couldn't answer.

"Good. Remember that another person might think the pin important—how large, how sharply bent, whether thrown or dropped, in which direction, at what hour."

"And whether a raven or a wren flew overhead at the time?" She went to sit beside him. The grass still retained its afternoon warmth.

Mæn was smiling, by the sound of his voice. "You're not indulging in cynicism?"

"No. I'm talking to fill the silence." Having said that, Meirwen had no wish to talk for a while. She lay back on her folded hands, looking up at deep blue sky encircled by venerable trees. The brightest stars were already out, faintly reflected in the still pool. The evening was almost calm; only restless birch and alder stirred their leaves. Within the circle of sky the Swan soared up toward the rooftree of heaven and onward to the unseen western sea.

For the first week Meirwen had avoided the sanctuary grove with its lofty trees and bleak votive images surrounding the pool near the talkative River Alyn. Their shadows made her watchful even by daylight. Then Mæn had brought her after dark to sit silently until the small creatures resumed their night activities. Offerings chimed on the branches on windy nights, making grove and spring a sounding board, raising music for the stars' slow dance through the seasons. Now she found it safe and peaceful.

A lantern swung through the trees beyond the gate, accompanied by the quiet voices of monks coming from compline. Meirwen got to her feet and found Mæn Pedr already on his way to the gate. They took this quiet time every evening. The monks welcomed Pedr whenever he joined them, but no one here expected healers to abandon the sick to sing the offices. They walked past the unlit sanctuary shrine, used mostly for solitary meditation now, and out through the open gate into the monastery compound. The old healing-cells within the enclosure had been dismantled and rebuilt near church and refectory. It was more efficient this way, and there was still the old shrine for those who wanted a tranquil convalescence or death.

Meirwen entered the cell nearest the gate. The novice who had been sitting on watch rose silently to leave. The clean room smelled of honey, partly because its wooden bench and table and shutters were waxed regularly, partly because of the beeswax candles. She went to the table and lit two tapers from the guttering oil lamp. This luxury had shocked her at first, burning wax candles when rushlights or tallow would do, but Cadwr had said the abbot at Llanfor had sent them to be used freely, not hoarded. She carried one of the candles to the sleeping shelf, where Mæn was already kneeling to take a pulse.

Brys looked asleep, but when he felt Mæn's touch at his throat he opened his eyes. The dark shadows under his eyes and cheekbones, his gauntness, still unnerved her. Mæn folded back the linen sheet. The thigh wound was healing well and they had pulled the sutures cleanly from his brow; his mangled right shoulder was the worry. Mæn lifted the compress and briefly rested the back of his hand on the raw scab, causing a wince which Brys tried to suppress. The poppy syrup helped, but Mæn grew more sparing of it as the vial dwindled. The bone was knitting, miraculously, but the skin would not heal and fever persisted. The surrounding flesh was red, swollen and hot to the touch. It had been that way since Mæn had brought him south from Rendil's farm, then from Llanelwy abbey, two weeks ago. Meirwen sat on the edge of the sleeping shelf and took his left hand, earning a smile. He didn't remember the journey here, which was just as well. Sometimes he thought he was at Rhiwædog, sometimes at Mathrafal. Sometimes he thought he was a prisoner of the English, sometimes a monk at Llandegla.

The priest came in a few minutes later to hear his confession. Meirwen went out to stand beyond the doorway spill of candlelight until the priest called her in to take the wafer and wine with Brys. In a while Mæn returned with the Llandegla surgeon, a whitehaired man with a burn scar between his brows in the old way. By then the priest was making his final prayer.

"My hand will be steady tomorrow, my dear, don't worry," the surgeon said.

Meirwen knew this, having assisted him three times in the last fortnight. It didn't help. He stepped inside when the priest left, confirmed their assessment and went to finish his rounds with Mæn. Soon after that someone arrived at the outer monastery gate. More lanterns traveled through the night, and a novice scurried with messages. Soon Cadwr came along with his saddlebags over his shoulder and kissed her cheek before he went in to Brys. When Mæn returned they could take a late meal, Meirwen told herself, or she could go to the refectory now and get something—

Nausea caught her first. Meirwen stepped around the corner of the whitewashed cell and threw up neatly between two rue plants. She had put off eating for too long again. When she turned back wiping her mouth, she nearly collided with Cadwr.

"Is he asleep?" she asked.

"No." Cadwr looked at her too carefully. "How many months?"

Meirwen walked around him. *Let it be.*

But Cadwr caught her wrist. "Is there something you've forgotten to tell Brys?"

"Nothing he needs to know."

"Are you mad? You're as bad as he is. 'Don't tell Meirwen, she'll worry.'"

It was meant as a joke, she knew that, but the tears sprang anyway. Cadwr pulled her into his arms to comfort her. No taller than Brys but more solid. She was ready to be comforted. The tears started in earnest. Mair mother of God, she would be weeping and snuffling for another six months. It was worse than morning sickness.

"All right, all right." Cadwr was patting her back. "Do you want me to come in with you?"

Meirwen bit her lip. "Is this a good idea?"

Cadwr lifted her chin, drawing her eyes. "What are his chances tomorrow?"

"Good if it's a bone splinter." But she knew quite well why Mæn Pedr had called for confession and last rites, and why he had called Cadwr north from Penllyn again. "If the infection is in the bone or too deep in the flesh—" She was going to cry again.

"It's a good idea," Cadwr said gently. Then he handed her a piece of traveler's bread.

Brys was drifting when she sat on the edge of the sleeping shelf. He opened his eyes at her touch, took in her tearstained face and Cadwr standing at her shoulder. Frowned. He was frugal with words these days; words took strength. Meirwen fortunately needed no words. As she had done once in an Aberffraw inn, she placed his hand on her belly, not that there was anything to notice yet. Realization took him a moment, as it had three years ago. Brys smiled and closed his eyes. *Now you know. A good idea.* She gathered herself to go, but he had kept her hand and she hadn't the heart to break his grip.

So they were still sitting when Cadwr came back with the priest, Mæn Pedr, the old surgeon and a handful of sleepy monks. The youngest novice, the one who sang as he helped the surgeon, brought Meirwen a hastily twisted crown of flowers and greenery from the monastery herb garden: sage, yarrow, vervain, rosemary, flowering thyme. Cadwr produced a folded parchment which Brys had carried for three years against the day she would change her mind.

Mæn Pedr spoke for Meirwen, who was without family. Brys demanded to sit up, leaning on Cadwr, and promised Meirwen his lands and goods, his hand to protect her and her children, and his love. Meirwen swallowed her last refusal and made her own promises. The priest blessed their union, swallowing any doubts about its longevity, and went to his bed. The wedding guests congratulated each other, witnessed the marriage contract and left them with the usual bawdy suggestions, unlikely to be carried out tonight.

After the third hour, when the morning sun was bright without heat, they carried Brys outside to a trestle table under a canvas fly. Mæn gave him as much henbane and poppy syrup as he dared, and the Llandegla surgeon reopened the wound to remove bone splinters and infected tissue, liberally applying the monastery's astringent wine. Cleanliness, prayer and honey salve would have to do the rest. By evening the fever, redness and heat were lessening; the swelling lasted another two days. In ten days Brys could walk unaided. A week after that the lady Onnen sent a cart to bring them home.

8 september 796 + penllyn

West of Cynlas the track passed into drowsy afternoon shadow as the sun slid below the shoulder of Mœl y Llan. Brys was amused at being carted home like a sack of flour but he lacked the strength to stay on a horse for long anyway.

They travelled slowly, since the taciturn carter let his oxen find their own lazy pace, and other traffic passed them steadily. Farmers were hauling barley sheaves from their valley fields up to their hill farms, honey in the comb and cheese wheels to Rhiwædog, apples and fresh bread and buttermilk to Llanfor abbey. Elgan and the three men on escort rode ahead or behind most of the time, to vary their pace. They were mainly an honor guard; Cadell and Egfrith were strictly enforcing their new peace.

A barefoot monk on his way home to Llanfor recognized Brys and strolled alongside chatting for a while. He offered the most interesting gossip on his large and quarrelsome family at Llangywair, then blessed them and hiked off whistling.

"Do you know him?" Meirwen asked, swinging her feet idly over the wagon's tailgate.

Brys had a lock of her loose hair curled around his hand to admire its copper lights. "I know his cousins better. Troublesome, it's true, but they all sing like nightingales."

"Are people always so offhand with their lord in Penllyn?"

Brys laughed. "Why not? We're a small cantref, not a rich one. People know each other and they're plainspoken. Wait until you see them take me to task when I'm hearing law cases. This isn't Mathrafal or Aberffraw."

"So I don't need to wear this after all." Meirwen turned it glittering between her hands.

The narrow gold diadem Onnen had sent was the object of their afternoon's debate. Brys privately thought it was Onnen's own diadem, now relinquished, but he kept the thought to himself. It would distress Meirwen.

"Wear it on high feasts or in hall. People like to see us keep custom. Or wear it all the time as I do." He liked the small weight of it on his brow, a reminder.

"You were born to it."

"You married it." Brys took it from her hands, knowing she would never put it on herself, and rested it on her auburn hair and freckled forehead. "You see? Lady Meirwen, the one who captured Cynfarch Penllyn. Or do you like Cynfarch bardd Cadell better? I promised to be in Mathrafal for Cadell's Michælmas feast. You'd better come and show off your belly to chase the girls away."

"Shameless." But she smoothed her hands over her belly where the fullness was still mostly imaginary. When she had stopped wearing a belt last week Brys had vexed her by offering a pillow to make things more obvious. "I see you're back to normal."

"About time." Brys kissed her and told her some things he proposed to do with her tonight, if not sooner, now that he was back to normal. It was getting harder all the time to make her blush, though easier to provoke her laughter.

In the oakwood beside River Meloch they passed a woman walking slowly, carrying a bundle. A last refugee from Tregeiriog, or maybe she was a British Mercian coming home to Powys. Brys had the carter stop so he could hand her down a gold ring and the basket of monastery food remaining from their meal. He would have no beggars in Penllyn.

"Do good, my fair son." She looked up in his direction, but her eyes were clouded white. Whatever she saw, it was not Brys. *Another man, another country, another life.*

Heledd was never far from his thoughts. After the fall of Pengwern she must have fled into the hills from cantref Tren. She would have found her way west — where else could the last of Cynddylan's house flee? — to the monasteries and courts of Iâl, Cæreinion, maybe Penllyn.

Somewhere Heledd had found sanctuary. Maybe in Mathrafal, more likely in Iâl, but Brys chose to believe she found safety in Penllyn where she shared a bond of blood. Some would say she wandered here still. An hour's talk with Heledd would answer a year's worth of his questions. He considered what she might say — his captor, his bright spirit, his desolate wanderer. It took no effort to find out. When he closed his eyes the murmur of east-flowing Dyfrdwy carried her voice. *Do good as the chance comes to you — otherwise we inherit desolation.* Her voice braided into wind in the oak leaves, the creaking cart wheels, the hush of the distant river.

At Llanfor, where the track flanked the wooded hillside toward the timber church, Meirwen awakened him. A noisy foot-race had engulfed them. Children swarmed around the cart laughing and shouting. When Elgan rode forward to herd them off, they called out that the cart was their finish line. The winner, a skinny brown girl with her dress pulled up through her belt, jogged panting to Meirwen's perch on the tailgate and handed up a garland of wildflowers. Meirwen put it on smiling and took an armful more from the other children. One for Brys, one for Elgan who grinned and hung it at his saddlebow instead, one for Addonwy who tipped it rakishly back on his red hair. They rolled forward again, scattering blossoms, with a gaggle of children whooping and cavorting ahead of them. They had planned a quiet arrival at Rhiwædog, but the talkative monk from Llangywair, Brys guessed, had seen to it that it should be otherwise.

River Dyfrdwy was low in its banks, diminished by a dry summer and flowing quietly. The cart rolled down into the ford and out across the tawny river meadows, turning south. Rhiwædog lay out of sight beyond an eastward shoulder gilded with sunlight and harvest. Their escort of children skirled ahead as they climbed through clustered farms to the ford on River Hirnant. Brys saw that the three smallest children were tiring and falling behind. He slid down to lift each of them squirming into the cart, not an easy task with one arm in a sling. Meirwen got down, too, and they walked on hand in hand.

At Hirnant a sturdy figure heaved out of the stream waters with his kilted robe dripping at the hem and a fishing pole in his fist. The abbot from Llanfor offered them a fine salmon from his string of seven, then neatly turned a blessing on the image of loaves and fishes, to feed the multitude.

"I'll be content to feed Penllyn, father," Brys laid the fish carefully on the wagon bed. Years ago the abbot, with more enthusiasm than he taught catechism, had taught him how to tickle trout. He was mildly Pelagian, good soul, and cheerfully unconcerned that this was certainly heresy. "Do you still preach on Jesus the fisherman?"

"Sunday, if you would like. Welcome home, my dear."

They waded Hirnant as the cart jounced through with its freight of giggling children. Spray flew from the spinning cartwheels in a rainbow shimmer, and sunlight touched the spokes in a blur of light and shadow, flickering gold and leaden grey, silver and green, until the cart lurched out onto the steep east bank. Brys and Meirwen came out of the water laughing as his garland started to ravel and shed petals onto the swift current.

People lined the track winding up to Rhiwædog, silent at first and then calling out good wishes. Among them Brys saw their young monk grinning in satisfaction;

two farmers who had passed them earlier; Gwladus shining in a plain novice's robe: servants from Rhiwædog hall and laborers from its fields; a few cousins.

Onnen came forward to kiss Meirwen on each cheek, and Angharad brought Olwen's two boys down to claim their aunt. Cadwr embraced Brys, careful to explain it was only dust in his eyes. Brys, not deceived, smiled over his brother's shoulder at Meirwen and wondered if the abbot could spare another fish or two to feed this multitude.

Someone had given Meirwen a small sheaf of barley and a handful of apples; with her unbelted dress and loose garlanded hair she looked like the lady of fertile meadows and bountiful streams. Brys took her hand again as they walked up through the gathering crowd. He saw people smiling at their garlands and their twined fingers. *Good.* By tomorrow the first enterprising pœts would be singing in his hall about the new lord who defended them and the lady who sustained them, fields in golden harvest, bees in the hive, fish in weirs, a fruitful garden. Now to make it true.

PART IV

Anno Domini 796

Gwnae ny wna da ae dyuyd.

Sorrow not to do good as it comes.

– *Canu Heledd*

Once they crossed the border, rain slashed horizontally out of the grey western hills into their faces. The wind that drove it slapped back their hoods and had them clutching to close their cloaks. The horses labored through deepening mud and sudden rivers that scoured the track.

Brorda and his Tamworth escort were soaked through three or four layers of wool by the time they reached Llangollen at mid-morning. The Penllyn bodyguard men also complained of the cold, Brorda gathered, struggling to follow their dialect.

As they rode, Cynfarch pointed out an ancient monastery church, a waterfall, a grove of leafless birches standing white against a black hillside. Brorda admired and asked courteous questions, but the unspoken observations were louder: farms with fields gone to thistle and burdock, houses standing charred and empty. But God willing their wars were behind them, now, in the first blossoming of Egfrith's peace. Mercia's most ruinous wars had always been with Powys; Egfrith was especially committed to peace with Cadell. Without the peace, Brorda would not be entering Powys on a mission as pleasant as collecting a long-promised Irish hound pup.

"I have my eye on one for you. She's not the biggest or boldest but she is the smartest," Cynfarch was telling him now. His hood was pushed back so his hair streamed rivulets onto his shoulders, but he seemed improbably cheerful. "Still, you must choose for yourself."

"I trust your judgment," Brorda said. *On dogs. On statecraft. On this investigation into friendship.*

All the same it was unnerving to be entering this country with only a handful of lightly armed men, half of them British. Brorda had been here before, as Cynfarch would know, on Offa's first unlucky campaign to crush Elisedd's power. Then Brorda had warned Offa that not even the terrible Edwin of Northumbria had defeated a Powys force on Powys soil, though he caused rivers of blood to flow through it. Offa had to find out for himself. Maybe that was why Brorda's neck prickled now in the track's darker reaches, where years ago they had marched into ambush after ambush. The *Wealas* had struck hard and faded into mist, disappeared into folds in the rock, Brorda had sworn — sank into the matter of this land for which they seemed insanely determined to die.

West of Llangollen, River Dyfrdwy looped north around a rock outcrop. Nearby was the southernmost reach of cantref Iâl, Cadell's own home territory. Elisedd's grave mound lay just out of sight on a small tributary, Cynfarch said. Better for everyone if that savage king lay forgotten in an unmarked grave, Brorda thought, and left them all in peace. Cadell's son had shouted the name as a battle cry at Rhuddlan.

Soon afterward Cynfarch said they were in Edeirnion, the eastern region of Penllyn. The sun came out past Corfæn, where the track bore southwest to skirt the dark mountains, and steam rose in clouds from their sodden clothes. Light transformed the sullen landscape, striking brilliant cloud reflections in the flooded river meadows and raising a handful of rainbows above the leafless oakwood on the north bank. Cattle and horses drifted about the higher pastures, their flanks glossed with pale golden sunlight. As they passed river farms and several churches, steam rose as a silver mist from their dark thatch. Prosperous countryside, lovely in its wild way.

Brorda also noted, from long habit, that this was thoroughly defensible terrain. Steep slopes overlooked the tracks north and south of Dyfrdwy, and the wooded heights offered good lookouts. Some larger farms had gated earthen walls or timber stockades much stronger than livestock alone required. More than one of these fortified farms on the north bank commanded the river valley, upstream and down, from strong positions. A massive timber palisade was under construction at one place. His bodyguard captain and escort men were also taking stock, perhaps uneasily. His captain had discreetly tried to dissuade him from this visit; the *ealdorman* might have his throat cut by night in this den of hill bandits. Peace was difficult to trust again after this summer's costly battle.

Common folk, out fencing or ditching or driving their milking herds home, greeted Cynfarch with more affection than deference; he in turn asked about their families and harvests. Once he stopped to examine a sick heifer, advising the farmer on fodder and getting a heated debate for his trouble. He rode on laughing. Brorda smiled, better understanding their affection.

Like his cantref, Cynfarch was fairer in sunlight than in shadow. His black hair had dried in tangled curls; he took off his gold circlet to comb it into order lefthanded. He still had his habit of pushing one hand through his belt, even when he was riding. Cynfarch pointed out fishing weirs and his own outlying wheatfields. By the time they rode through fragrant evening cooksmoke from the river farms, they were at the gate of Rhiwædog.

Penllyn's cantref court lay in a shallow trough between gentle slopes, with only drystone walls and thorn hedges enclosing its home pastures and orchards. It looked like any large prosperous farm in Elfed with its scattering of plain timber outbuildings and sheds, a barnyard with mud flooding over the paving stones, a kitchen garden with a few fruit trees, a modest hall. People were working around the barn, and children and dogs were underfoot everywhere.

A freckled young woman wearing a gold circlet like Cynfarch's brought out a worn silver guest cup set with rock crystal and emeralds. She was late in pregnancy; two small freckled boys skirmished around her skirts. Brorda drank the wassail cautiously, knowing the power of British mead, and passed it to Cynfarch, who introduced his wife. Meirwen took the cup back gravely and had a frank look at Brorda. When she was satisfied she smiled and welcomed him in English with a strong Tamworth accent. Formalities done, Cynfarch took his time kissing his wife. A love match, Brorda decided. Conflicting reports had Cynfarch variously keeping a mistress in Mathrafal, betrothed to Cadell's daughter, or recently married. Brorda had expected to meet the daughter of another powerful cantref lord — if that was what Cynfarch Penllyn was calling himself these days — a pretty, demure young girl, a flawless ornament to an ambitious young man. Brorda was better pleased to discover a tall young woman with steady eyes, callused hands and freckled children.

Inside the plain buildings, Rhiwædog's age and affluence became more apparent. Beams were carved or inlaid with silver interlace, walls were painted and hung in fine needlework, benches were deeply cushioned, some windows held glass panes, tableware was finely crafted in silver and imported glass. The book cellar was well stocked. The guest house linens were clean, herb-scented and riotous with embroidery. In the chapel, the altar ware was gold. Everything was well crafted, in good repair, polished and clean. In Elmesæte a few great halls that Edwin had not burned were like this, ancient and rich. Brorda, enjoying an extraordinarily good meal, watched his captain suspiciously revise his estimate of hill bandits. *Never underestimate your enemy,* he would have cautioned once. Now perhaps he would say equally, *Always understand your friend.*

Cynfarch's hall was noisy with people coming and going. Some were clearly family. The big grey woman had charge of the food and the steady flow of ale and mead. A girl with honey-blonde hair, strikingly beautiful even in a novice's homespun robe, brought a toy for the children, who ran about the hall until their nursemaid caught up with them. Cynfarch's black-haired brother Cadwr was acting as steward, and his pregnant wife kept Meirwen company on the dais. A succession of singers and musicians came to entertain as they ate. After the tables were cleared and stacked away, two young men competed in extemporizing the three-line stanzas they called *englynion.* Cynfarch gave a silver ring to the winner and explained carefully to the loser where his sound-pattern had failed. Both youths seemed to be his students.

As the evening went on, as Brorda half expected, someone called on him for a song. He excused himself as unfamiliar with their harps but offered a favorite riddle that he kept on hand. He saw puzzled stares and heads leaning together. Perhaps it didn't make sense in the British tongue? Then a redhaired girl, also big with child, leaped to her feet shouting, "An ox!" and won the bracelet Brorda offered. Cynfarch watched his people try this diversion with unconcealed pleasure. One arm had found its way around his wife's waist.

Demands flew for another riddle. Fortunately Brorda had another two in reserve; after that he could beg off gracefully. And then he could ask what had piqued his curiosity for years. "Cynfarch, will you sing?"

A moment's silence. At first Brorda thought he had violated courtesy in some unknown way. The dark brother stepped forward protectively. But Cynfarch nodded to his bodyguard captain, the big man who looked like a murderer but spoke mildly. From a pillar he lifted down a harp strung in metal and carved with the head of a snarling wild cat. Cynfarch instructed one of the young *englynion* pœts to try the tuning. Another lesson.

It was only when he put the harp to his left shoulder and played that Brorda understood his error. The string song was cleverly constructed. He might never have noticed, but for Cadwr's reflex, that treble and bass never sounded together. Cynfarch's right hand rested on the sound box while his left hand flew over all of the strings, short silver and long bronze. Brorda needed no explanation of Cynfarch's deception. A lord must be strong and capable, demonstrably so, for his land's good fortune.

Then Cynfarch sang. He had a fine speaking voice but his singing voice was quite beautiful. Brorda leaned for the words. This was nothing like the stiffly stylized pœtry he had heard Brochfael's old *pencerdd* sing, but plain words beautifully flown together. *Our best songs about Mercia don't translate well,* Cynfarch had said once, taunting Offa's minister; this one was certainly about a Powys war with Mercia. But to Brorda's ear it was about a great deal more. Remarkably, the pœm spoke of a young woman, bereaved and solitary, wandering in madness through her own devastated country. This country. This cantref. Brorda recognized the names of places they had ridden through today.

When Cynfarch let the last string song die in his bronze and silver wire — letting the sound shimmer to a haunting echo but also unable to damp the strings — tears furrowed some faces. Many others were thoughtful. When he tipped the harp forward his captain quickly took it again. Everyone here treated Cynfarch as though he were a precious book rescued from a burning hall. It wasn't far off the truth, maybe, since rumor said he had nearly died after Rhuddlan. Now he was in his element, lord of his small realm.

Brorda pondered, not for the first time today, on his own unlikely acceptance of an improbable invitation. Cynfarch had probably expected him to decline — as he had almost done. Why had he come? Not to witness a dangerous enemy building power in his own territory. Not to observe a minor British king dispensing wealth and earning renown in his own court like something from the legends — though Egfrith would be as fascinated by this as he had been unnerved by the Elfæl traitor, Eli. Brorda was still wrestling with the idea of simple friendship, against all odds, in this generation.

The torches at the door were guttering in their brackets when they left the hall. Meirwen wrapped her shawl closer and crossed the courtyard shivering and laughing with her sister-in-law. Cynfarch put a hand on Brorda's shoulder and steered him toward the kennel. The hounds were asleep in the straw under a candle lantern, mother and pups tumbled in a snoring heap with the boy who tended the kennel. They were handsome dogs, large and well shaped, though Cynfarch said their sire was his cousin's deerhound and not the dam's Irish mate.

"You can choose tomorrow," Cynfarch said. "The boy needs his sleep."

Brorda smiled to himself as they closed the door again silently. Another man might have been more concerned for the dogs. *Why do I resist? A year ago friendship would have been treason. Now it's only good sense.* Apart from Egfrith, who increasingly chose his own ministers and advisers, he had enjoyed no real friendship since Offa died. *If I'm not careful I'll become a lonely old malcontent, suspicious of all that's new. Since when am I so miserly with the word* friend*?*

He pinched out the candle in the guest chamber and fell into a dreamless sleep.

In the morning Brys brought all seven pups and the bitch out into a pasture to let them romp. They were about twelve weeks old, big enough to leave their dam. He and Brorda watched them all together, and while the dog-boy held the others in leash, watched them again separately.

It was a crisp sunny day with a small breeze lifting off the lake. Brys breathed in the winter pasture scents of earth and fallen oak leaves and cow dung. Another two months, three months, until spring in Penllyn. Meirwen's baby would be born. Fields, forests and streams would break into new life. Everything would start fresh. Brys had much to do in Penllyn, although he had already strengthened their defences and increased training, and he had more to do in Powys. Peace would make more pleasant things possible. Most of all he wanted to row Meirwen around the lake, take her climbing to his hidden spring above Rhiwædog, oversee the calving, sow the spring wheat, make songs, take students, help the seasons turn. In peace.

"Don't tell me which one you marked," Brorda commanded, clearly enjoying himself. "Let's see if we think alike."

"A wager?" Brys suggested. "You offer another three riddles in hall tonight if you guess wrong. If you guess right, it's my turn."

"Done." Brorda laughed and offered his hand to shake like a Frisian wine trader, then dropped it abruptly.

"I wondered if you noticed last night," Brys said easily to spare him. Brorda was perplexed enough already, uncertain whether he was wise to come here, without being embarrassed as well.

"A good performance in every way," Brorda said dryly.

Brys laughed. The strength in his right arm was steadily improving, even if it would never be normal. Mæn had instructed him to strengthen the muscles every day by lifting his arm in circles with a stone in his fist. A servant, seeing this last week, had asked nervously if he were casting a spell. By reassuring her Brys had missed an opportunity to spread a new rumor. The old ones were wearing thin. It was time for another visit to Mathrafal.

The pups were all full of life, affectionate, eager for adventures among the tumbled rocks and hare forms at the top of the pasture, and as well behaved as any pup can be for two minutes together. Brys saw Brorda labor over his choice. In some strange English way, obviously, he was choosing more than a dog. Choosing how much to let his guard down, choosing how much to trust his host. *Fretting over nothing. Be wary as you wish. Trust as you wish.*

Finally Brorda chose the female pup with the light patch on her left ear; not the leader, not the boldest, not the biggest, but the smartest.

"Why?" Brys asked, taking her leash from the boy and handing it to Brorda.

"Her sense of humor," Brorda said. "Look at her. She's telling the others she won."

"So did you." He was pleased that Brorda had seen the same quality. "She'll keep you on your tœs. Maybe she likes riddles too."

They walked the dog down to River Hirnant, deep in spate after last week's rain, across the stepping-stones and over to the reedy marsh that was the lower end of Llyn Tegid. From there River Dyfrdwy flowed all the way down into Mercia. Brys dropped a twig onto the river, as he had dropped a thousand since he was breeched, and wondered how far it would go. Mercia had always been a mysterious land, too dangerous to travel, a source of invading armies and unlikely tales. Now perhaps he could see cantref Tren without a spear in his back, maybe even lost cantref Elfed.

In hall that night, Brys made a tale of his bet with Brorda and offered a gentle satire of an endlessly convoluted English riddle. People laughed at the waywardness of it, especially Brorda, but they were annoyed when in the end Brys pretended to forget the answer. His joke came back at him, since he had to scramble to make up something. It was all quite foolish. But like Brorda with his teasing pup, they all needed to laugh sometimes.

"Will you stay for Christ's mass?" Brys asked diffidently afterward. Surely Brorda had travelled too far to stay only a day or two, but maybe it was enough that he had come at all.

"Egfrith is in London for a church dedication but he returns in a few days." *Maybe, in other words. No commitment.*

Tonight they stood near the tree margin on the south height, the one that gave Rhiwædog its name of the bloody slope. A battle took place there long ago, people said, but no one now remembered the year or the combatants or the cause. More than once, when the court was threatened with attack, the slope had also provided a route for women and children and servants to escape to the hills by night. Across dark Hirnant, someone was out walking with a horn lantern swinging on the end of a staff. Was it the cattle thief again? He might have to set an extra watch. But the lantern bobbed off toward Llanfor, leaving a trail of distant plainchant. It must be one of the Llanfor monks keeping up his night courage with a song.

"How is Egfrith managing Cenwulf?" Brys asked, as he had to sooner or later.

"There's only one way to manage Cenwulf," Brorda said at last. "I need not say more."

"No."

"For a distant royal cousin, Cenwulf has great popular support. Egfrith talks of exiling him."

"Merciful god, Brorda, that will only deepen his resolve. He'll go straight to Frankia and put his head down with Egbert while Charles encourages their romance. Either that or they'll kill each other."

"One could hope." Brorda laughed from the belly. "And sometimes exiles have accidents."

Brys was quiet for a moment, caught by sudden grief for Heilyn. "Surely cutting down all his rivals was Offa's great error. We all pay for it in the end."

"Yet somehow we must secure Mercia. We can only do that by weeding the garden, as Charles calls it, or by ignoring the weeds and letting them flourish. And I fear that would bring anarchy on the Northumbrian scale. What would you do, Cynfarch?"

Both the question and the trust startled Brys. "I'm the wrong man to ask about Cenwulf. I would kill him, quickly, making sure that he understood why. Not exile him and certainly not let him know he faced exile."

"Or he would surely kill first."

Brys shook his head slowly. "How is it, Brorda, that we can coldly discuss murder? What dœs it say about our *daioni*?"

"'Goodness and mercy shall follow me all my days. . . . Maybe that innocence is only possible to cloistered churchmen. Good men — and women, I know—have an obligation to curb the evildœrs. For our families, for our kingdoms, we must survive."

"Must we kill to survive? Surely that makes us no better than Cenwulf, who kills for pleasure," Brys said as they started down the slope. A last sliver of moon was rising over Edeirnion, silvering the turbulent ribbon of distant Hirnant.

Brorda clasped his shoulder for a few paces. "Keep asking those questions, my friend."

As they crossed the home pasture, they heard a rider on a winded horse halt at the gate. The guard, no longer a sleepy boy but four of Elgan's veterans, challenged him. Discussion. Confusion. Brys walked over, while Brorda courteously held back, and heard the exhausted rider struggling to explain his errand. He urgently wanted Brorda.

Brys led his guest and the messenger to his book cellar, lit a sconce and turned to leave. Brorda, already tilting the parchment to the candlelight, motioned him to stay. When he finished reading, the Mercian nobleman sat heavily on the nearest bench and put his face in his hands. Brys glanced over his head at the mud-spattered messenger. He looked stunned with disbelief. Or with terror, more than a long ride alone into British territory would explain. Brorda wiped his face with a shaking hand and handed the letter to Brys.

Brys read the four scrawled lines of Anglian script. They were a blow to the heart, but simple shock quickly gave way to cold fear and a full realization of Brorda's despair.

Egfrith was dead, having fallen suddenly ill with stomach pains and convulsions in London. He had ruled for only a hundred and forty-one days. His wife and son had vanished. After only a day or two of insurrection, the *witan* council had agreed on a new king of Mercia and the southern English, a royal kinsman who had often counselled Offa to crush rebellious Kent and the British kingdoms: Cenwulf.

Brys went outside to send for Elgan. Full readiness, he ordered quietly, and a messenger to Mathrafal. All of their other plans were in place, the strategic plans they had hoped never to need again. He sent the messenger off to get food and a bed. After that there was nothing left to do.

Alone with Brorda, he scarcely knew what to say, could scarcely comprehend the depth of the man's loss and desolation. Brys sat on the bench and put an arm around Brorda, who made no move to shrug it off.

"You'll be safer here for the time being," Brys said after a pause. He laid his diadem on the table, suddenly too great a weight to bear, then deliberately put it back on.

"Safer consorting with an enemy?" Brorda salvaged a fragment of his wit. "Let's not give Cenwulf an excuse to rescue me. Neither one of us would survive his protection."

In the morning, Brorda made his gracious farewells and rode eastward to the English border. The hound pup loped ahead, happily unaware that there was no turning back.

Glossary

Armorica	now Brittany, the western promontory of France
awen	inspiration, the breath of perception
braint	moral right, law-right, the right to hold power
British	Celtic-speaking Britons who held all Britain before the English arrived; in AD 793 various kingdoms controlled the areas now called Wales, Cornwall and Scotland
cantref	a British province or territory
Cerne	a god, lord of beasts, leader of the wild hunt; once called Cernunnos
Cernyw	a British kingdom, now Cornwall
Cymry	fellow-countrymen, British, now called Welsh
English	all the Germanic peoples who came into Britain from the third century AD on, especially Anglians (including the Mercians), Saxons, Jutes and Frisians
Gwynedd	a British kingdom northwest of Powys, roughly covering the modern county of Gwynedd; ruled by King Caradog; variously enemy or ally of Powys
hual	fetter; a heavy chain of gold or silver signifying kingship
Lleu	a god, lord of light, lord of all skills; once called Lugus
Madron	a mother goddess, once called Matrona among many other names
Meirionydd	a cantref on the Irish Sea, sometimes part of Powys and sometimes of Gwynedd
Mercia	an English (Anglian) kingdom bordering on Powys
pencerdd	a king's court poet, harper, historian, sometimes envoy

Penllyn — "lakehead," the area around Llyn Tegid or Lake Bala; sometimes a cantref of Powys, sometimes a cantref of Gwynedd, perhaps sometimes an independent kingdom

Powys — a British kingdom bordering on Mercia

torc — a heavy neck ring, usually of gold, signifying kingship; by AD 793 it was archaic

Wealas — foreigners; English word for the British (*Wealh* is singular)

Wessex — an English (Saxon) kingdom of the southwest, under Mercian rule

Wrekin — a steep hill rising sharply out of level land southeast of Shrewsbury

wyrd — English word for fate, destiny

PRONUNCIATION OF WELSH WORDS

Welsh vowels generally have a clear sound. Pronunciations of vowels and diphthongs vary between North Wales and South Wales. In North Wales U, Y and EI in particular are sounded more toward the back of the mouth and in the throat.

A — as in *tad* (father), pronounced as in English *dad.*
E — short as in *fel (like),* pronounced as in English *tell;* long (usually with circumflex) as in *pêl* (ball) pronounced as in English *rail.*
I — soft as in *dim* (nothing), pronounced as in English *pin*; long as in *mil* (thousand), pronounced as in English *keen.*
O — short as in *ton* (a wave), pronounced as in English *cot;* long (usually with circumflex) as in *môr,* pronounced as in English *more.*
U — short as in *pump* (five), pronounced as in English *pimp*; long as in English *keen.*
W — short as in *cwm* (valley), pronounced as in English *tomb;* long as *in ffwl* (fool), pronounced as in English *fool.*
Y — short as in *bryn* (hill), pronounced as in English *limb;* long as in *dyn* (man), pronounced as in English *dean;* obscure as in *yn* (in), pronounced as in English *udder.*

Diphthongs generally have a hard clear sound:

AE, Al, AU, EI, EU — pronounced as in English *eye.*
AW — *ah-oo,* a little like English *fowl.*
EW — *eh-oo,* a little like *eh-you,* without consonants; no real English equivalent.
IW, YW — *ee-oo,* as in English *yew.*
WY — oo-ee, as in English *gooey.*
OE, OI, OU — as in English *oil.*

Welsh is a rich, throaty, even guttural, language. To Welsh ears, English sounds constricted at the front of the mouth. Most Welsh consonants are pronounced as in English. A few are different:

C — always hard as in English *cat.*
CH — guttural, as in Scots *loch.*
DD — soft TH sound as in English *soothe.*
F — as English V.
FF — as English F.
G — always hard as in English *get.*
I — as a consonant, pronounced as English Y.
LL — the "hissing L," pronounced with tongue against upper teeth at side of mouth.
NG — nasal, as in English *hang.*
R — rolled slightly; not a common Welsh consonant.
RH — rolled strongly.

SI — pronounced SH as in English *show.*
TH — hard TH sound as in English *theatre.*

For detailed information on Welsh pronunciations, see a Welsh dictionary or language text such as *Living Welsh* from Teach Yourself Books, the source of some of these simplified examples.

ACC-ent usually falls on the penultimate (second to last) syllable. Some examples of names and terms from *Awen*, with approximate pronunciation for English speakers showing the stressed syllable:

Brochfael — BROCH-vile (CH as in loch)
Brys — BREES (roll the R, rhymes with peace)
Cian — KEE-an
Cynddylan — Kun-THUHlan
Cynfarch — KUN-varch (CH as in loch)
Cyngen — KUNG-en
Eli — EL-ee
Elisedd — El-EEseth (soft TH)
Gellan — GELL-an (hard G, hissing L)
Heilyn — HAY-lin
Heledd — HEL-eth (soft TH)
hual — HEE-al
Llywarch — LLUH-warch (hissing L, CH as in loch)
Meirwen — MAREwen
Merfyn — MER-vin
pencerdd — PEN-kayrth (soft TH)
Taliesin — Tal-YESS-in
Tegwy — TEGwee

old english (anglian and saxon) names and terms

Old English is much more robust and guttural than modern English, and sounds a little like modern German. Every C is hard; for example, Cenwulf is pronounced "KEN-wolf." The AE diphthong produces a long "ah" sound in Anglian dialect and a shorter "eh" sound in Saxon dialect. This is sometimes reflected in how the names are written, for example, Athelbert (Anglian) and Ethelbert (Saxon). SC is pronounced SH; for example, *scop* (poet) is pronounced *shoap.*

For a good idea of how Old English sounds, ask your public library for a recorded recitation of the great English poem *Beowulf,* possibly composed in the eighth century.

Awen: The Historical and Literary Background

The spirit of Powys still captures the imagination. To this day the ancient landscape is mostly high moorland and forest broken by pasture and grain fields, netted in lovely streams, dotted with towns grown like crystals between the folded hills. Powys, throughout its few centuries of existence, displayed a characteristic high-handed flamboyance. As a border state under relentless military and cultural assault for generations, it was warlike, hardy, illuminated by uncounted native saints, hospitable to poets, jealous of its rights and honors, prone to changeable alliances and hostilities, sometimes treacherous. Poetry is the one lasting gift Powys left us, and the heart of Powys is the poetry cycle *Canu Heledd.*

Heledd's name is not found in the annals. Her story might be lost altogether but for the poetry that makes her the emblem and the speaker for her tormented country. Only an extraordinary work of literature can speak across the centuries, as *Canu Heledd* does, in images and ideas that have meaning for our wholly different lives today. Heledd, as narrator of the poetry, speaks of the consequences of war, the fragility of peace, personal responsibility and ethics, and war's particular costs to women. It stands out sharply from other poetry of the era, most of it male-dominated heroic elegy and eulogy lauding a warrior society.

Heledd appears in genealogies of the Cyndrwynyn, the royal house of eastern lowland Powys that apparently ended with the defeat and death of her brother Cynddylan; at least one genealogy gives her name not as Heledd but as Elen. A few late folk rhymes are attributed to her and to other family members. Several place names of Llanheledd (Heledd's Church) indicate a later belief that Heledd founded churches either as benefactress or as a holy woman. All of these could be later embroideries, possibly inspired by a popular story or poem.

Heledd means "place of salt" or "salt pit" in Welsh; in Old English, with a slightly altered pronunciation, it means "warrior." This name seems surprisingly appropriate—resonating with connotations of sorrow, preciousness, payment, blood, perhaps Lot's wife turning to a pillar of salt—for a heroic tragic figure from the past. Is it perhaps too appropriate? *Canu Heledd is* considered unhistoric, since it describes events that are otherwise unrecorded. It would not be unreasonable to suggest that *Canu Heledd* may be a deliberate creation, an early work of historical fiction which the poet deployed for a specific purpose, probably political but now unknown.

Long after the passions and events that gave rise to the cycle were forgotten, long after the poet's name was forgotten, the cycle's other timeless themes led copyists to preserve *Canu Heledd* through the centuries.

The poet's name has not survived, but his surviving stanzas hint at his background and experience. He spoke of diverse matters: war, territory laid waste, farming, herding, natural history, the rich life of the court, the poverty of a homeless wanderer, and a ruler's privilege and obligation. His scant knowledge of lost eastern Powys was perhaps gleaned from tradition or travellers' tales. He balanced his praise of the warrior caste's heroic ethos with demonstration of its cost to the larger society. Remarkably, he portrayed a woman as a thinking and feeling person whose actions could destroy but instead could have preserved peace. His attitudes to women were shaped and limited by his cultural perceptions, however; for this reason among others, this poet was almost certainly a man and not a woman. He displayed a surprisingly modern view of the relationship between guilt and madness. "My tongue did it," Heledd cries, "How can I stay sane?" and, "Alas, not to do good as the opportunity comes."

The few Christian traces in the poetry suggest Pelagian views on ethical conduct rather than accepted church doctrine. (Interestingly, Powys copyists may have distributed heretical Pelagian documents as late as the mid-eighth century, suggests David Dumville.) All in all, the poet had an unusual, even radical, vision for his time.

Canu Heledd's metre, diction, consonance and imagery are masterful and effective in the surviving stanzas. At several points in the cycle the poet uses disciplined understatement; elsewhere he applies a relentless layering of remorse and grief. The images are so neatly turned and are contained in so few words that they are difficult to translate briefly. Yet the cycle's topics and viewpoints are inconsistent, suggesting a fragmentary nature and later revision. The first poem praises Cynddylan for a fairly standard catalog of virtues including courage, ferocity and generosity. Later, less cohesive poems follow Heledd's aimless wandering through a devastated landscape. An unknown number of stanzas are lost; an original ending may be among them. Welsh triads represent Heledd and two other homeless wanderers as finding sanctuary at last in a royal court; this may be the substance of a lost *Canu Heledd* ending. This poet was too deliberate, too deft, to have let his cycle trail off into incoherence as it does now.

Highly skilled in the Welsh poetic tradition, seemingly capable of references to classical and biblical literature, fond of contrast and irony, a keen observer, widely experienced, compassionate, acknowledging women within his cultural limits, without overt animosity toward the Mercian enemy, a man who loved Powys: who and what was the poet? An educated man of his era was almost certainly a trained bard, a churchman or a member of the ruling elite. Given the absence of decisively Christian themes, he was probably not a churchman. It may be that the *Canu Heledd* poet was of privileged rank, associated with a royal house of Powys in the ninth century and formally trained as a professional poet. In truth we can say little more about his identity, having at our disposal too few ninth-century personal names and histories.

One name we do know because it was carved in enduring stone, not entrusted to copyists and parchment, though today it is too badly weathered to read. A man who was literate but not Xuent in Latin wrote the text for Elise's Pillar "at the command of my king Cyngen." Elise's Pillar stands near the ruined Valle Crucis Abbey north of Llangollen. In the ninth century, this site lay near the boundaries of the Powys cantrefs of Penllyn and Iâl, the original home of the Cadelling kings such as Cyngen. The writer used striking phrases evocative of contemporary Powys poetry. He knew Powys history and genealogy. He was probably educated in at least two languages and may have held a privileged position in Cyngen's court. His clear and shapely lettering, was drawn carefully for the stonemason's chisel to incise. His text is extremely long for a stone inscription and conveys considerable feeling for his territory of Powys and its ruler. The writer, apparently a man of importance in Powys, added his own name to the inscription. It was a famous name from history and legend, the name of a king of Rheged in the "old north" two centuries earlier; Cynfarch Oer, the father of Urien Rheged, had given his name to the Cynferchin line. The name also appeared in the genealogies of Penllyn, whose ruling family may have claimed a bond of blood with Heledd's Cyndrwynyn house. Cyngen's man wrote his name as Conmarch; today we write it as Cynfarch.

Cynfarch's concerns, which were necessarily his king Cyngen's concerns, were intensely political, though their significance is now unclear. The historical and genealogical claims he made for Cyngen appear to have refuted the *Historia Brittonum,* a volume of history and folklore compiled around mid-ninth century in the neighboring kingdom of Gwynedd. They may also have challenged the territorial ambitions of the Gwynedd king Merfyn or his son Rhodri. By the mid-ninth century, Gwynedd, not Mercia, was emerging as the great threat, indeed the final threat, to an independent Powys. It may be that the weapons deployed in the last battle for a sovereign Powys included Elise's Pillar and the poetry cycle *Canu Heledd*.

Nothing else is known historically of this Cynfarch, yet the apparent date, as well as his expertise, position and passions, seem to parallel those of the *Canu Heledd* poet. It is not wholly impossible that the Cynfarch who wrote the text of Elise's Pillar also composed *Canu Heledd.*

Elise's Pillar, originally erected as a four-meter standing cross, must have been an impressive monument. Inscribed crosses of its kind are rare in Wales but well documented as a Mercian design. When the cross was raised sometime after 823 A.D., Mercia was in decline and Powys may have been stronger economically, culturally and militarily. It may be that the construction of Offa's Dyke Finally made possible peace, or at least impasse.

War was more usual. From the mid-eighth century reign of Elisedd through Cyngen's reign, British Powys and Anglian Mercia were certainly enemies and sometimes actively at war. Several major battles recorded for this region between 760 and 823 presumably involved Mercia and Powys. An invasion in 784—its final battle is called Maes Derwen or Akenfeld in *Awen*—may have proved most damaging to Mercian interests. Within three years Offa took several important steps to strengthen his power. In 786 he welcomed legates from Pope Hadrian, one of whom also visited "parts of Britain" which likely included Powys. In 786 Hadrian approved an archbishopric at Lichfield, in the heart of Mercian territory and Mercian control. In 787 Offa had his son Egfrith anointed king and co-ruler, a decision that may reflect Offa's fears for his own survival.

Also around this time, Offa undertook the huge earthwork project that still carries his name. The ditch and wall of Offa's Dyke indelibly marked a border "from sea to sea" between the English and Welsh kingdoms, most notably between Mercia and Powys. The westward-looking placement of the dyke through hilly country that generally slopes eastward makes it clear that this border, as later historians claimed, was built by OVa to protect Mercians from Welsh attack. OVa's Dyke is more imposing and more complete along the old Mercia-Powys border than in other stretches to the south, where perhaps it was less needed. The border may have been negotiated by both countries or unilaterally imposed by Mercia; either way, it eVectively separated the two peoples and may have created relative peace on the troubled borderland. West of the border it may also have created awareness of shared British identity; British nations that had warred incessantly for centuries began to forge diplomatic marriages and alliances.

If the Canu Heledd poet lived through the wars between Powys and Mercia, his experience would inevitably shape his view of Powys political realities. It would be natural, when he created a poetry cycle about a long-ago Powys disaster, to set it against a familiar backdrop of border war in which the faceless, implacable enemy lay eastward in Mercia.

Heledd, Cynddylan and the seventh-century loss of lowland Powys clearly had special significance for the *Canu Heledd* poet. In *Awen* I suggest that he gradually built the Heledd poetry out of personal obsession with an abducted kinswoman and an old Powys tragedy. Historians disagree about the relative violence of Mercia's seventh-century acquisition of lowland Powys, with theories ranging from peaceful absorption to cataclysmic war. The poet portrayed the event as a brutal invasion with devastating consequences: a dear country laid waste, territory forever lost, the royal household slaughtered, the sole survivor Heledd wandering homeless and deranged by grief.

The poet may have regarded Heledd, consciously or otherwise, as personifying the sovereignty of Powys, according to the foremost modern *Canu Heledd* scholar. Jenny Rowland demonstrates that in several stanzas the poet characterizes landscape features as women. It may be that he saw both Heledd and her country as raped and left for dead.

We can only guess at a date for *Canu Heledd,* its companion cycle *Canu Llywarch Hên* and a possible lost cycle about the hero Llemenig. Scholars have proposed mid-ninth to late tenth century dates on linguistic grounds, but the linguistic evidence is ambiguous. The poetry makes no reference to the Danish and later Norman invasions which threatened Powys from the mid-ninth century onward. Instead the threat is identified as Mercian military aggression, although it was absorption by Gwynedd that ended Powys independence in 855.

The poet may have avoided openly identifying the real threat. A blunt warning about Gwynedd might have been dismissed by his audience, possibly including his king. Cyngen's brother-in-law was the energetic, aspiring king of Gwynedd called Merfyn Camwri (the Oppression) or Merfyn Frych (the Speckled). Merfyn's equally ambitious son Rhodri was Cyngen's nephew. Perhaps the poet chose instead to guide Cyngen or his nobles to see a parallel between perilous inattention to military threat and perilous inattention to dynastic threat. In the late 820s Mercia's violent invasions of Powys would be fresh in mind, though Gwynedd's growing strength would soon loom larger on the horizon. This is only speculation, naturally. A relationship evidently exists between *Canu Heledd* and political events of the late eighth and early ninth centuries, but today we can only guess at its nature.

Why the poet chose to address his own Powys through Heledd's bleak story—whether it was his own creation, a storyteller's creation, or half-remembered history—is a more difficult question. Others have supposed that the poetry's desolate quality must derive from a time of great despair in Powys. Looking back across more recent wars and devastations, I question this. True, our dreadful warfare and genocides have produced bitter and viciously ironic poetry, but some of our most despairing poetry in many languages was written in times of peace, prosperity, and optimism. Much was written to warn of dangerous times ahead. The *Canu Heledd* poet likewise may have intended to warn of coming disaster brought about by arrogance, selfishness, lack of political foresight, all the sins that Heledd confesses of her heedless early life. Destruction will come not from enemies massed on a carelessly defended eastern border, the poet may have been saying, but from ambitious men awaiting their opportunity in the west; the real danger lies in Powys's internal fragmentation, fratricide and who knows what other failures and misfortunes, and in Powys's repulsion of potential allies through Cyngen's apparent military aggression. Whatever specific meaning it conveyed to his fellow countrymen, the poet's artistry would ensure that his audiences paid full attention to Heledd's story.

A reader deserves to know the proportion of history to fiction in any work such as *Awen.* I have never knowingly altered the facts; but I build fictional bridges to span the historical chasms that bedevil students of early medieval history. *Awen* represents my best attempt to reconstruct events and circumstances, but it inevitably crosses more void than solid ground. There is a great deal we will never know. Did Heledd and Cynddylan live or were they a poet's creation? What conflict led to the battle at Rhuddlan in 796 A.D.? Who fought it and who won? What was the cause of Egfrith's death? We may never have answers, least of all generally accepted answers. Even when history is carved in immutable stone like the Elise's Pillar text, endless debate tests its veracity and significance. I have drawn on the *Canu Heledd* englynion to shape this story as much as possible. Many of the images and events of *Awen* spring from these stanzas and from other early poetry.

Most of my premises are based on current literary studies, historical analyses and archaeological findings. I have read with a deeply sceptical eye for bias and propaganda; when possible I consulted the original sources in Welsh, Latin and Old English. Nonetheless, medieval scholarship is a running wave. Antiquarian historical theories of the last century are now mere curiosities, however seminal they were once; as time passes, new theories will doubtless render *Awen* and many other books less historical and more Fictional.

In *Awen I* question statements and beliefs that some writers have taken at face value. Both the historian Bede and Charles the Great's teacher Alcuin, for example, are justly revered for their wisdom and learning. Yet both men wrote with ignorance and hatred of British affairs. Their accounts of British events, persons and customs must therefore be considered in light of their bigotry. Similarly, our record of the shift from indigenous religion to Christianity in Britain comes entirely from Christian writers with a personal interest in exaggerating the universality of conversion and the extinction of earlier beliefs. Increasingly, our keener investigation of early literature, folk survivals and archaeology gives us a broader and more complex view.

Searching for the places and people mentioned in Awen can be arduous. Few landmarks survive. Mathrafal, which may have been a Powys court as early as the eighth century, is a grassy hummock today. Aberffraw lies beneath streets and houses. Rhiwaedog is still a working farm, well-known in Penllyn as a former seat of power, but its oldest building dates from centuries after the time of Cyngen Powys. Our oldest manuscript containing *Canu Heledd* dates from the fourteenth century. The lettering which Cynfarch drew for Elisedd's memorial cross has all but worn away.

On the whole, little but the landscape itself remains visible that would have been familiar to the people portrayed in *Awen*. Once again, eighth-century Powys and its people belong to the geography of the imagination.

Further Reading on Early Medieval Britain

Stephen Allott, *Alcuin of York: his life and letters.* William Sessions Ltd.: York, 1974.

P. C. Bartrum, *Early Welsh Genealogical Tracts.* University of Wales Press: Cardiff, 1966.

Rachel Bromwich, *Trioedd Ynys Prydein.* University of Wales Press: Cardiff, 1978.

H. M. Chadwick, et al., *Studies in Early British History.* Cambridge University Press: Cambridge, 1959.

Nora Chadwick, *The Celts.* Penguin Books: Harmondsworth, 1970.

Nora K. Chadwick, et al., *Studies in the Early British Church.* Archon Books: Hamden, Connecticut, 1973.

K. R. Dark, *Civitas to Kingdom.* Leicester University Press: Leicester, 1994.

Wendy Davies, *Wales in the Early Middle Ages.* Leicester University Press: Leicester, 1982.

—*Patterns of Power in Early Wales.* Oxford University Press: Oxford, 1990.

Ann Dornier, ed., *Mercian Studies.* University of Leicester Press: Leicester, 1977.

Nancy Edwards and Alan Lane, eds., *The Early Church in Wales and the West.* Oxbow Books: Oxford, 1992.

Peter Berresford Ellis, *The Druids.* Constable: London, 1994.

—*Celt and Saxon.* Constable: London, 1995.

John Ferguson, *Pelagius: a historical and theological study.* AMS Press, Inc.: New York, 1978.

Patrick Ford, *The Mabinogi.* University of California Press: Berkeley, 1977.

—*The Poetry of Llywarch Hen.* University of California Press: Berkeley, 1974.

Sir Cyril Fox, *Offa's Dyke.* Oxford University Press: London, 1955.

G. N. Garmonsway, *The Anglo-Saxon Chronicle.* J. M. Dent and Sons Ltd.: London, 1977.

R. C. Hoare, *Giraldus Cambrensis, The Itinerary Through Wales* and *A Description of Wales.* Dent: London, 1976.

David Hill, *An Atlas of Anglo-Saxon England* . University of Toronto Press: Toronto, 1981.

Emyr Humphreys, *The Taliesin Tradition.* Seren Books: Bridgend, 1989.

Kenneth Jackson, *The Gododdin.* Edinburgh University Press: Edinburgh, 1969.

Dafydd Jenkins, trans. and ed., *The Law of Hywel Dda.* Gomer Press: Llandysul, Dyfed, 1990.

D. P. Kirby, *The Earliest English Kings.* Routledge: London, 1992.

The Making of Early England. Schocken Books: New York, 1967.

Lloyd Laing, *The Archaeology of Late Celtic Britain and Ireland c.400-1200 AD.* Methuen & Co. Ltd., London, 1975.

—*Celtic Britain.* Granada: London, 1981.

J. E. Lloyd, *A History of Wales.* 2 vols., Longmans Green and Co. Ltd.: London, 1967.

Guido Majno, *The Healing Hand.* Harvard University Press: Cambridge, Massachusetts, 1977.

Jan Morris, *The Matter of Wales.* Penguin Books, Harmondsworth, 1986.

—*Wales: in the First Place.* Clarkson N. Polbter, Inc.: New York, 1982.

John Morris, ed. and trans., *Nennius, British History and The Welsh Annals.* Phillimore: London, 1980.

Stuart Piggott, *The Druids.* Penguin Books: Harmondsworth, 1968.

Alwyn and Brinley Rees, *Celtic Heritage.* Thames and Hudson: London, 1976.

Melville Richards, *Early Welsh Territorial Units.* University of Wales Press: Cardiff, 1969.

Anne Ross, *Pagan Celtic Britain.* Cardinal: London, 1974.

—*The Pagan Celts.* B. T. Ballsford Ltd.: London, 1986.

Jenny Rowland, *Early Welsh Saga Poetry. D. S.* Brewer: Cambridge, 1990.

Anne Savage, *The Anglo-Saxon Chronicles.* Guild Publishing: London, 1988.

F. M. Stenton, *Anglo-Saxon England* . Oxford University Press: London, 1975.

F. M. Stenton, *Prepara frory to Anglo-Saxon England* . Oxford University Press: Eondoll, 1970.

W. H. Stevenson, ed., *Early Scholastic Colloquies.* Oxford University Press: London, 1929.

Lewis Thorpe, trans., *Einhard and Notker the Stammerer: Two Lives of Charlemagne.* Penguin Books: Harmondsworth, 1969.

V. E. Watts, trans., *Boethius: The Consolation of Philosophy.* Penguin Books: Harmondsworth, 1987.

Sir Ifor Williams, *The Beginnings of Welsh Poetry.* University of Wales Press: Cardiff, 1972.

—*Canu Aneirin.* Gwasg Prifysgol Cymru: Caerdydd, 1978.

—*Canu Llywarch Hên.* Gwasg Ptifysgol Cymru: Caerdydd, 1978.

—*The Poems of Taliesin.* English Version by J. E. Caerwyn Williams. The Dublin Institute for Advances Studies: Dublin, 1975.

Machlou Sant
ARMORICA
Bro Celien
Carnac
Morbihan
Gwened
Aquitania
SPAIN
Cordoba